Lilian Harry

LOVE & LAUGHTER
THREE LITTLE SHIPS

Lilian Harry grew up close to Portsmouth Harbour, where her earliest memories are of nights spent in an air-raid shelter listening to the drone of enemy aircraft and the thunder of exploding bombs. But her memories are also those of a warm family life shared with two brothers and a sister in a tiny backstreet house where hard work, love and laughter went hand in hand. Lilian Harry now lives on the edge of Dartmoor where she has two ginger cats to love and laugh at. She has a son and daughter and two grand-children and, as well as gardening, country dancing, amateur dramatics and church bellringing, she loves to walk on the moors and – whenever possible – to go skiing in the mountains of Europe. She has written a number of books under other names, including historical novels and contemporary romances. Visit her website at www.lilianharry.co.uk.

Lilian Harry

LOVE & LAUGHTER
THREE LITTLE SHIPS

Love & Laughter
First published in Great Britain by Orion in 1998

Three Little Ships
First published in Great Britain by Orion in 2005

This omnibus edition published in 2011
by Orion Books Ltd
Orion House, 5 Upper St Martin's Lane
London WC2H 9EA

An Hachette UK Company

A CIP catalogue record for this book is available
from the British Library.

ISBN 9781407234298

Printed and bound in Great Britain by Clays Ltd, St Ives plc

www.orionbooks.co.uk

LOVE & LAUGHTER

To Lesley, with love

Chapter One

Geoff Pengelly burst in from the street, his red hair standing on end, school tie little more than a knot of coloured string around his neck, blue eyes ablaze. He tore into the narrow hallway, almost colliding with a guest on his way out, skidded on the multi-coloured rug his grandmother had spent so many evenings making out of old rags, and hurled himself through the kitchen door to where the rest of the family was finishing breakfast.

'It's *over*! The war's really over! They've given in – just like that – the Japs've *given in*!' He skidded to a halt by the kitchen table, almost knocking his mother over as she started to her feet. 'Mum, it's over, we've *won* – Dad'll be able to come home.'

Lucy Pengelly stared at her son. 'Where d'you hear that?'

Geoff jigged impatiently from one foot to the other. 'Everyone's talking about it. People are coming back from work already – they've all got two days off. We'd have heard it ourselves if we'd got the wireless on.'

'Us'd have had it on too, if you'd got that accumulator charged yesterday like I told you,' his grandmother said from the end of the table. 'Always putting things off till tomorrow, that's your trouble. Why, when I was a liddle maid—'

'Never mind that now, Mum.' Lucy sat down as suddenly as she'd jumped up. 'If it's true that the Japs have given in . . .' She looked at her son again. 'Why? I thought they'd never surrender. Said they couldn't lose face. What happened?'

1

'I dunno. It's those big bombs the Yanks dropped, I think. Couldn't take it.' Geoffrey spoke with a touch of scorn. 'They should see what it's like in Plymouth. We had *thousands* of bombs and we never gave in.'

'These were atom bombs, though, weren't they?' Arthur Pengelly said. 'They were bigger than anything that's ever been used before. Just one of 'em could do more damage than all the bombs we had during the whole of the Blitz.'

Lucy had a brief vision of a Japanese city, laid waste in a few minutes by just one huge bomb, as Plymouth and Portsmouth and other cities had been in weeks or months by thousands. She tried to visualise the kind of explosion it must have been, to wreak even more terrible damage than had happened during those flame-filled weeks of the blitz in 1941 and all the others that had followed. In one night . . . But her sudden, unexpected flash of compassion for the innocents who had burned in the Japanese pyre was swiftly overtaken by the realisation of what it meant to her, to the family, to the whole of Britain, to the world . . . The war was over. *Over*.

And Wilmot would be coming home.

It would be a curious celebration.

In a way, it had all been done already, when the news of Victory in Europe had come at the beginning of May. Then, there'd been some warning and everyone had known in those last few days that the announcement would surely come. Mr Churchill, whose rousing speeches had kept their hearts up through the darkest days of the Battle of Britain, Dunkirk and the Blitz, and who had brought them the great news of D-Day, seemed reluctant to speak too soon of victory. But at last at three o'clock in the afternoon, he had made his historic broadcast and then everyone had gone mad, waving flags, blowing whistles, climbing lamp-posts and dancing all down the streets. Every ship in Devonport and the Sound had let off their hooters, and every church that was still standing and had bells to ring chimed in to join the general cacophony. And Lucy's mother had written to tell her that it was just the same back in Pompey. Every ship in the harbour, every church bell, every whistle and every wooden rattle, every drum. And for those who had no instrument, every pair of saucepan lids.

The rejoicings seemed to have been going on ever since. Dancing in the streets had extended to organised street parties, and for every ship that came home there was a new parade with bands playing and crowds to greet the returning heroes. And heroes they were, Arthur Pengelly said, every one of them. He'd served in the Great War – the one they were now calling the First World War – and he knew.

However, for all the gladness, there were still some hearts that ached: for the men who would not come home, and for those who were still caught up in the conflict. The war in the Far East had not yet ended and there was still the fear that many would die in action. And still many thousands held prisoner, in conditions that Lucy hardly dared think about.

'He says they're being treated well,' she'd said to her mother-in-law in the early days, holding the scrap of paper that was all Wilmot could send. 'He *says* so.'

'And what else could he say?' Maud Pengelly demanded, mopping her eyes. 'They're not going to let anyone tell the truth, are they? If it's all true what people say about the way they're torturing our boys and making them slave—'

'Mum, don't,' Lucy begged. 'It doesn't help to torment ourselves. We don't know that it's true. And it might not be all the camps, anyway – just one or two.' She looked again at the scrap of paper, at Wilmot's name scrawled at the bottom of the few lines. Did it look shaky, as if written with a trembling hand, the hand of a man tortured and sick? 'We've got to keep going,' she said desperately. 'We've got

3

to look after the children and ourselves and make sure Wilmot's got a home to come back to.'

She'd known even then that she was fooling herself, trying desperately to keep up a pretence because she could not bear to think of Wilmot, her darling, cheeky-faced sailor husband, being tortured and beaten but, as the time dragged by, she'd had to face it. The stories were too many to be discounted; and she came to understand that it would be wrong to go on pretending. If only I could share it with him, she'd thought then, if only I could help him bear it . . .

Now, however, on this dull and drizzly August morning, it was over at last, and soon, surely, Wilmot would be coming back. To a home that wouldn't be just as he remembered it, but a home nevertheless. And even though the house had been damaged – and again she turned her memory away from the thought of that night – it still stood, and they'd even been able to keep the business running. It was still a hotel – or more properly a guest house – of sorts. And already she'd begun to make plans to rebuild, to improve, to look forward.

With Wilmot home again, the plans would leap ahead. For Wilmot would surely come out of the Navy now, and settle down at last in civvy street. He would be at home all the time, a husband who shared her bed every night instead of occasionally, a father who could help bring up his children. And he would be filled with enthusiasm for this new life, full of plans for the future. The war would be behind them and, as the songs all said, there would be love and laughter, and peace ever after.

Tomorrow – when the world was free.

Lucy had been just eighteen when she first met Wilmot Pengelly. It had always been on the cards, of course, that she would marry a sailor. There were so many of them in Portsmouth, stationed on HMS *Vernon*, or over at Gosport

4

on the submarine base, HMS *Dolphin*, or serving aboard the many ships that were based in 'Pompey'. All the same, the Travers family weren't best pleased that it looked like being a Plymouth chap.

'I can't see why she had to pick a Devon boy,' Emily Travers said to her husband when Lucy went out to the front door to say goodnight to Wilmot, the first time she brought him home. 'Aren't there good enough ones in Portsmouth? I don't want her moving down to Devonshire.'

'You're being a bit previous, aren't you, girl? She's only known the bloke a week. Anyway, he'll be off back to sea before they can get too serious about each other, and his ship probably won't come to Pompey again.'

Lucy, too, dismissed her mother's fears. 'Don't be daft, Mum. You won't lose track of me. Even if I did move to Devon – and I'm not saying I ever would, mind – I'd still come back and see you. And it's a smashing place for a holiday.'

Emily sniffed. She and Joe hadn't had a holiday since they'd been on their honeymoon, back in 1908, and that had just been a weekend spent with her mother's cousin in London. Holidays were for people who could afford such luxuries, not for the likes of the Travers family. 'Plain, ordinary folk, that's what we are,' she said. 'It's all we can do to keep a home for you youngsters, with food on the table and clothes on your backs, never mind gallivanting round the countryside on holidays. But I suppose that chap knows all about such things, what with his mum and dad running a hotel in Plymouth.'

'I don't think it's a very big place,' Lucy said. 'Nothing really grand. It's just a sort of guest house, for commercial travellers and people wanting a bit of a holiday.'

However, any sort of hotel seemed grand to Emily. 'Don't you let it go to your head, that's all. I don't want you getting serious about a chap you're hardly ever going to see.'

5

'Serious!' Lucy said, and laughed. 'Wilmot's not the serious sort. He's always laughing and joking – that's what I like about him.'

'That doesn't mean he can't be serious about a girl,' Emily said, and she repeated her fears to Joe later on, as they got ready for bed. The rest of the family were all asleep – Lucy and her sisters in the back bedroom, the two boys in the front room downstairs. 'There was a look in his eye – he's proper sweet on her, you can tell he is. It's not that I don't like him, Joe – if you want the truth, I think he's the best of all the boys she's brought home yet – I just wish he was a Pompey chap.'

'Well, he'll be going off to sea soon.' Joe had been working on Wilmot's ship, doing repairs as it lay moored against the jetty in the dockyard, and he knew that the job would be over in a few days. 'I daresay they'll forget about each other in a couple of weeks. You know what our Lucy's like. She likes a bit of life – she's not the sort to stay indoors mooning after a chap.'

Wilmot did go away soon. His ship continued on its journey to Scotland and Scandinavia, and Lucy continued her life as before, setting out each morning to work at the naval outfitters where she was an apprentice, and going to the pictures with her sisters or out to walk along Southsea front with her friends. She didn't seem bothered about getting a new boyfriend, so when Emily opened the door one evening to find Wilmot standing on the step, a battered kitbag beside him, she wasn't altogether surprised.

'Wilmot! What on earth are you doing here?'

His cheeky face, ruddy from weeks at sea, looked anxious. 'I came to see Lucy, Mrs Travers. Is it all right? Is she in?'

'But where've you come from? I thought your ship was on its way to Scotland.'

'It is. I mean, it's there now, but I got a leave pass.' His eyes went past her, trying to see into the narrow passage-

6

way. 'I've only got tonight – it took me two days to hitch-hike here and I'm due back on Monday morning.'

'Well, you'd better come in.' Emily felt disturbed but knew better than to try to resist the inevitable. She looked at his kitbag. 'I don't know that we can offer you a bed.'

'Oh, that's all right, Mrs Travers. I wouldn't ask you. I can stop at Aggie Weston's or somewhere. If I can just put it in the passage –' He lifted the bag and humped it into the house, following her through to the back room. 'Is Lucy in? I didn't have a chance to let her know –'

Only Lucy's father and brothers were in the room when Wilmot entered it. Joe was sitting in his armchair by the fire, and Vic and Kenny were at the dining-table doing their homework. They looked up, bright eyed, and Joe laid his newspaper on his knees.

'Well, you're a surprise.'

'I just came to see Lucy,' Wilmot repeated, as if he'd walked round from the next street.

'Oh, she's not here,' Vic said immediately, nudging his brother. 'She's out with her new chap. Got a smashing car, he has – they're out in it all the time, aren't they, Ken? Something high up in the Navy, isn't he?'

'Admiral,' Kenny confirmed. He was eleven, only a year younger than his brother and almost as like him as a twin, with the same curly, reddish hair and freckles. Wilmot had found it difficult to tell them apart until he noticed that one of Vic's front teeth was chipped. It had happened in a fight, Lucy had told him. You'd never get Kenny in a fight, he took everything as a big joke.

'It's true,' Vic nodded, grinning at Wilmot's dismayed glance at Emily. 'Getting married in the cathedral, they are – Kenny and me're going to be bridesmaids!'

'Get off with you,' Emily told them severely. 'Don't you take any notice of them, Wilmot, they're just being silly like boys their age always are.' She turned as they heard footsteps coming down the stairs and Kitty appeared at the

7

door. She had just washed her hair and it was screwed into paper curlers, only a few strands of dark auburn showing. All the Travers family had inherited their colouring from their mother, from the blazing carrot of Vic and Kenny's tousled curls to the rich auburn waves that shone and rippled like a winter sunset around Lucy's head. Kitty's and Alice's came somewhere in between – golden red for Kitty, and the fawny ginger of a biscuit for Alice.

'Go and tell your sister Wilmot's here. They're upstairs, the girls are, doing a bit of sewing. There's not room down here with the boys' homework spread out all over the table. As for you two –' she addressed her sons again – 'you can pack that lot away and go and help your dad out in the garden. There's plenty of potatoes to pick up, so he told me.'

'Dad's not out in the garden. He's here reading the paper—' but Emily gave Joe such a glance that he rose immediately and laid his paper on the arm of his chair, and all three went out, the boys giving Wilmot a wink as they departed.

'Here she is,' Emily said as they heard a light patter of footsteps on the stairs, and in the next moment Lucy stood at the door, her face flushed, violet eyes brilliant. She took a step towards him.

'*Wilmot* –'

Emily slipped through the door to the kitchen and closed it behind her. Wilmot and Lucy stared at each other for a moment, and then with a swift, stumbling movement were in each other's arms. Wilmot held her close and she felt the rough blue serge of his tunic against her cheek before she lifted her face for his kiss.

'Wilmot – oh, *Wilmot* – I've missed you so much.'

'I've missed you too, Lucy. I've hated being away from you.'

'It's been like having a huge hole inside me – part of me's been taken away.'

8

'I know. I know. It's like that for me too.'

They stood for a few minutes wrapped in each other's arms, breathing in each other's warmth. In the tiny kitchen on the other side of the door, they could hear Emily filling the kettle and getting out cups and saucers. They couldn't keep the family out for long. In a few moments the door would open again. Alice and Kitty would be wanting to come downstairs, Joe and the boys back in from the garden.

'We'll go for a walk,' Lucy said. 'As soon as you've had some tea. You must be starving.'

'I don't know. I don't care. I just wanted to see you again – I wanted to make sure –'

'Make sure of what? Didn't you get my letters? I've told you, over and over again.'

'I know,' he said, kissing her. 'I just wanted to make sure I wasn't imagining it all. I wanted to make sure you were real.'

They didn't get engaged that weekend – not officially, anyway. Joe would never have allowed it. But before Wilmot set out on the long journey back to Scotland, they had promised to stay faithful to each other and considered themselves as engaged as if Lucy wore a ring on her finger. And to mark their promise, Wilmot bought her a tiny brooch which formed his own initial.

'You don't need to wear it so everyone can see it,' he said. 'Just so long as you've got it, that's all I want.'

'Oh, I'll wear it.' She pinned it on her blouse. 'I don't mind people knowing that you're my boy. I *want* them to know.'

Wilmot went back to sea. After that, the Travers family became accustomed to finding him on their doorstep, sometimes expected, often unannounced, his kitbag beside him. It became quite apparent that it was only a matter of time before the engagement was made official, and Lucy was just twenty-one when, with Wilmot's tiny diamond sparkling on her finger, she walked up the aisle of St Mary's church, Portsea, to join him at the altar.

'It's a shame there aren't more people on the groom's side,' Emily murmured to her husband when he stepped back from giving the bride away. There was quite a crowd behind them – Vic and Kenny now growing youths of fourteen and fifteen, and all Joe and Emily's own brothers and sisters and their families from all over Portsmouth and even 'over the water' in Gosport. On Wilmot's side, however, there were only his parents, Arthur and Maud Pengelly, and an uncle and aunt from Torpoint – a place nobody else had ever heard of. 'He's an only child and there's nothing to be done about that, but I'm surprised there aren't any other relatives. Mr Pengelly's got another brother, from what I remember.'

'It's a long way to come from Devon for a wedding,' Joe muttered back. 'And they couldn't close the hotel – had to leave someone in charge of things.'

Wilmot was wearing his naval uniform, the square collar pressed till there wasn't even the tiniest of creases, and his lanyards shining white. His brown hair, usually tousled and hard to keep tidy, was brushed flat and shone with hair cream, and his fresh, ruddy complexion looked as if it had been polished as hard as the black shoes that gleamed on his feet. He laid his round, white-topped cap down on the seat as he stepped forward to wait for his bride, and when he turned to watch her walk up the aisle nobody could doubt the love that shone from his face. His blue eyes glittered brightly and he looked, Emily thought with sudden tenderness, almost ready to cry.

Lucy stood beside her bridegroom, tall and slender in the billowing white wedding dress she'd made herself. Her hair rippled down her back like a lion's mane, glowing through the white lace of her veil. She had wanted to draw it up at the back of her neck and pile it on top of her head in a mass of curls, but it had made her look taller than ever and when she'd tried on her head-dress the little white diamante coronet had been almost lost amongst the rich auburn, and the veil had hung awkwardly. So she had brushed it out instead and it added a splash of warm, shimmering colour to the cool white of her bridal gown.

Alice and Kitty waited behind her, each in robin's egg blue. It had seemed to Joe and the boys sometimes that the whole house had been a froth of shimmering fabrics, spreading everywhere so that there was barely room to have a bit of dinner, let alone sit down and read the paper or for Vic and Kenny to do a bit of Meccano. And then there'd been the wedding presents, arriving daily: saucepans, cups and saucers, tablecloths, bedlinen – you name it, those two seemed to be getting it. More than he and Emily had ever got at their wedding, Joe was sure. But it took a lot to set up home, and even though they were starting off in two nice furnished rooms down in Plymouth they needed some of their own stuff.

Still, it would seem empty after they'd gone. For the last few months the whole household had revolved around this wedding, and in a few hours they'd be gone and it would be all over bar the shouting, as the saying went. He listened to Lucy's voice, soft but firm as she made her vows, and was surprised to feel a sudden ache in his throat and a sting of moisture in his eye. He rubbed it surreptitiously with his finger and hoped nobody had noticed.

The neighbours had turned out to see Lucy leave the house, and they were there again when she came back on the arm of her new husband, followed by the guests.

As well as needlework there had been cooking and cleaning going on for the past week, and the two downstairs rooms had been made ready for the reception, with a table borrowed from next door and chairs all around the walls. Even then, it would have been a squash if the weather hadn't been fine and most of the guests able to spill out on to the pavement or in the back garden.

11

They were still there when Lucy and Wilmot left to catch their train to Plymouth, and it looked as if they were settled in for the evening when probably someone would drag a piano out into the street and everyone, neighbours and all, join in the party. Wilmot's parents and his uncle and aunt were catching the same train at the town station. Lucy giggled, feeling slightly embarrassed, as Wilmot hustled her into an empty compartment, making sure it was a no-corridor carriage. It seemed rude to be so pointedly making it clear they wanted to be on their own, but Wilmot ignored her protests, tossed his cap on to the seat and kissed her soundly.

'I've been waiting for this moment. Just getting you to myself – that's the trouble with weddings, there's too many people about. I shan't have another one.'

Lucy gave a little squeal. 'I should hope not! What a thing to say to your wife on her wedding day.'

'It's my wedding day as well.' He tilted his head back to look at her more seriously. 'Well, Mrs Pengelly, how does it feel to be a married woman?'

'How does it feel to be a married man?' she parried, and he gave her a wicked wink.

'Tell you that later. Or maybe –' He glanced out of the window. They were trundling along beside the top of the harbour, with the shimmering expanse of water on their left and Portsdown Hill on their right. 'I was thinking we might have time to do something about it now.' He cuddled her close against him and nuzzled her neck.

Lucy gave a little cry of alarm. 'Wilmot! Don't be so daft – we'll be in Fareham any minute. And someone might get in.'

'They won't dare. I'll do my famous imitation of Frankenstein's monster.' He pulled a terrifying face and then laughed. 'It's all right, maid – I can wait. I've waited long enough already. I want it to be special, tonight. As special as I can make it.'

12

Lucy blushed. Such things weren't a topic of conversation in the Travers household, but Wilmot had a breezily frank approach. It came of being a sailor, he told her, and it was why all the nice girls loved them.

'Go on. I'm the only nice girl you know.'

'You're the nicest, I'll say that.' But she knew that he was as innocent as she. Whatever his mates got up to when they were in port, Wilmot had saved himself for her. She had no fear at all that he would ever be unfaithful, any more than she would.

Feeling inexplicably and rather pleasantly older, secure in the knowledge of their love, she settled back into her husband's arms and gazed contentedly out of the window. This was the start of their new life together, and it was going to be good.

The sun beamed down from an almost cloudless sky, but as the train rumbled on into the west, a tiny cloud appeared as if from nowhere. It travelled slowly across the sky, small and dark, with no more than a rim of white. And when it passed across the sun, it cast a chill shadow on Lucy's face.

But, by that time, suddenly exhausted by the excitement of the day, she was sound asleep in the arms of the man she had vowed to love, honour and obey until parted by death.

Chapter Two

Lucy settled in quickly enough to being a sailor's wife. She liked Plymouth, though it seemed odd not to be able to see the ships in the harbour, like you could at Portsmouth; you felt more a part of things there, she thought. But she liked going up on the Hoe and looking out at Plymouth Sound. You could see the ships coming in and out, and it was lovely on the wide expanse where Drake had played bowls and even today people walked and played games and had picnics.

Below, the cliff fell away in terraces of white rock, and there were little bathing pools cut into the stone, and diving boards perched over the sea. There was a big swimming-pool, too, that had only just been built, and it was full of people at weekends and during the holidays. Lucy and Wilmot went down there quite a lot in the first few weeks of their marriage. Lucy had always enjoyed swimming and the whole family had spent a lot of time on the beach at Southsea, going there every fine Sunday during the summer. She was surprised to find that Wilmot wasn't so keen, but with her encouragement his awkward splashing turned into a passable crawl and they raced each other across the semicircular pool.

'I thought all sailors'd be able to swim,' she said as they climbed out and sat drying themselves in the sun. 'What would you do if the ship sank?'

'Since we'd probably be about a thousand miles from land, I don't think being able to swim would be much help,' he said. 'Anyway, why should we sink?'

'They said that about the *Titanic*,' said Lucy, who had

14

been two years old when that disaster had happened, so couldn't remember it but had heard enough about it since. 'I'd feel funny, going to sea if I couldn't swim.'

'Well, I can now,' Wilmot said, getting bored with the subject. 'So if ever the ship does go down, you'll know it's because of you that I don't drown.' Lucy shuddered and begged him not to talk like that.

Their carefree days didn't last for long, however. Very soon after that, Lucy began to feel sick in the mornings and it wasn't long before her doctor confirmed that she was expecting a baby. Geoffrey Edward was born exactly eleven months after their wedding, weighing eight and half pounds despite the fact that Lucy had been sick almost continuously throughout the pregnancy. Wilmot wasn't there to welcome his son into the world, though: his ship went to sea the day before Geoffrey was born, and didn't come back for a year.

They had better luck with the second baby, Patricia Ann. This time, Wilmot's ship was in refit in Devonport for the last three months of the pregnancy and he didn't go away until Patsy was three months old. This time, he could wonder with Lucy at the tiny fingernails and the first smile, but he missed the first tooth and the day when she began to crawl. However, he was back again for her first birthday and he was there two months later when she let go of the armchair she was standing beside and took her first unsteady steps across the room. By this time, Geoffrey was just over two years old and starting to put sentences together, and when Wilmot went back to sea he told Lucy it had never been so hard to leave.

'They're both so interesting now,' he said. 'I mean, you can almost hold a conversation with Geoff, and Patsy's not going to be so long before she's chattering away like a magpie. By the time I come home again they're going to be different all over again.'

'I know.' Lucy leant her head on his shoulder. 'Sometimes, I wish you could come out of the Navy, Wilmot. I

15

know I went into it with my eyes open – I knew you'd be away a lot – but I didn't realise just how bad it would be and how lonely I'd feel without you. And it does seem so hard, the little ones growing up without you. They need their daddy.'

'Well, I've signed on till I'm thirty. There's nothing I can do about that. I reckon we'll think about it then, eh? I know Mum and Dad have always hoped I'd go into the hotel with them. It's only another five years.'

Five years. That made it 1940. It seemed a lifetime. Geoffrey would be eight and Patsy six. But it was something to look forward to.

'Would you mind coming out? You love the Navy, and going to sea.'

'I did when I was single. I don't love it so much now, I can tell you.' He grinned wryly. 'I reckon that's why they make us sign on, because they know blokes will all want to come out the minute they get wed.' He gave her a kiss. 'Anyway, maid, it's not so bad this time – I'll be back in six months' time. We'll have Christmas together.'

They had agreed they would like to have three or four children. Wilmot envied Lucy her family life and said he didn't want his nippers to be 'only' children, as he had been. It was all right in some ways, but children needed company.

'We'll just give ourselves this break,' Lucy said, 'and then we'll have another one. It won't be too far behind the others, and if it is, we'll just have to have two, for company.'

'Twins'd be nice, if you could arrange it,' Wilmot said.

But it wasn't twins. Instead, when Patsy was three and Geoffrey just starting at infants' school, Zannah came along.

They didn't call her Zannah at first. Susannah was her name, too long by half, Maud Pengelly said critically, and if they were going to shorten it to Susie or Sue, why not call her Susan in the first place? But Lucy stood firm. She liked the name Susannah and the child could shorten it herself when she got old enough, if she wanted to. None of them had thought of 'Zannah' – that was the baby's own idea, when she first began to speak and try to say her name. 'Zannah,' she said firmly, splaying a starfish hand over her chest. 'I Zannah.' And so Zannah she became.

'It's pretty,' Lucy said. 'And unusual too. But then you're a pretty and unusual little girl, aren't you, my love?'

Zannah enchanted everyone. She was like a miniature version of her mother, with the same deep red-gold hair and porcelain skin, and eyes of an even deeper hue of violet, almost purple, fringed by long, thick lashes. Her soft lips were always curved in a smile that lit her whole face, and she had a fascination for names. As well as her own, she would adapt and alter other people's in order to be able to say them, and the names had a magic of their own, so that people enjoyed hearing them and often others began to use them too.

'Grammy,' she said, climbing on Maud's knee, and 'Grampy,' when playing with her grandfather's fingers and bending her head sideways to listen to the ticking of his watch. And Grammy and Grampy they became, even to Patsy and Geoff.

As she grew, she was full of questions, listening gravely to the answers. Family relationships interested her deeply and she spent hours trying to work out what an uncle was, or a cousin. Going to Portsmouth was like a voyage of discovery with all the family there – uncles who turned out to be her mother's brothers yet not her father's, one auntie who was married to an uncle who for some reason wasn't Mummy's brother, another auntie who didn't have an 'uncle' of her own . . . It was all very confusing and needed constant explanation.

'She's a real little livewire, that one,' Lucy's father said when Lucy had put her to bed one night and sunk exhausted into a chair. 'Keeps you on your toes, doesn't she?'

'Oh, I know. And it's no good telling her she'll understand when she grows up – she wants to understand *now*. We've learnt to be very careful what we say in front of her, otherwise there's a real inquisition.'

'Kiddies that age are all the same,' Emily said. 'She's a sweetheart.'

There was a short pause. Then Lucy said, 'What do you think about all this talk of Hitler, Dad?'

Adolf Hitler had been coming into the news more and more. He'd started by getting into the German government, even though he was really an Austrian, and he'd seemed like a good thing for Germany, which was suffering deeply in the Depression that had overtaken the whole world. He'd got the country back on its feet and he'd organised the youth into an enthusiastic movement, dedicated to keeping fit and turning Germany into a nation of pure Aryans. Lucy had seen him at the pictures, on the Pathé Pictorial newsreels, and you could tell the people thought the world of him. He'd opened the Olympic Games in Berlin and then he'd held a big rally in Nuremberg, with thousands of people crowding to hear him and cheering their heads off as they lifted their arms in his special salute.

Joe shook his head. 'I don't take to the feller meself. All that shouting and waving his arms – not like our statesmen. There's no dignity in it. And he don't look like a proper leader, neither – he just looks commonplace, with that silly moustache and all.'

'He frightens me,' Emily said. 'The way he yells – I get the feeling people are scared to cross him. And he seems to want to take over other countries. I mean, Germany's joined up with Austria and now he's talking about Czechoslovakia. Suppose they don't want to be part of Germany? I don't know that it's a good thing to let Germany get too big anyway – look what happened before.'

'The war to end all wars,' Joe said. 'I don't believe it.

There'll always be wars, and it's people like this Hitler who cause them.'

Lucy went back to Plymouth feeling disturbed. Wilmot was on a new ship now, HMS *Exeter*, a big cruiser with eight-inch guns. She was suddenly aware that it was a fighting ship and Wilmot was part of a fighting Service. Until now, she'd thought of the Navy merely as a part of the ordinary structure of life, a job for men who liked ships. But those guns were meant for shooting. For killing.

'I don't want to think of you having to go to sea in a war,' she said. 'I'm glad you'll be coming out soon.'

Wilmot looked at her gravely. 'Don't bank on it, maid. They won't be letting men come out if there's a war. They'll be getting more in – conscripting them.'

She stared at him. 'But if you've served your time—'

'That doesn't count. Not if there's a war.'

She was relieved when Mr Chamberlain went to Munich and came back waving his 'piece of paper' and declaring that this meant there would be 'peace in our time'. Peace. She felt as if she had been holding her breath for months and could only now let it go in a great sigh of thankfulness. She cuddled her three children close, feeling the hot tears in her eyes as she realised how anxious she had been.

'Why are you crying, Mummy?' Zannah asked, twisting her head sideways to look up into Lucy's face.

'Because I'm happy, sweetheart. Because I'm very, very happy.'

'*I* don't cry when I happy.'

'That,' Lucy said, 'is because you've never been as happy as I am at this very moment.' And she held Zannah extra tightly, knowing now that she had been carrying within her a deep fear for these children, a fear that she hadn't realised until now. I'd fight to the last breath for them, she thought, but thank God I won't have to.

The relief was short lived, however, and all too soon the

19

talk of war began again. Politicians turned against Mr Chamberlain, saying that his policy had been one of appeasement, and that Hitler wouldn't be stopped in his drive to take over all of Europe. Already he had broken his agreement to leave Czechoslovakia alone, and now he was turning his attention to Poland. If he marched upon Poland, Britain and France would be united in declaring war upon him. The fears began again, looming all the blacker because of the relief that had been felt, and the government began to take positive precautions.

'It's been nothing but leaflets coming through the door,' Emily said on Lucy's next visit to Portsmouth. 'Rationing this, that and the other – we're all going to have to have books full of little squares and the grocer'll have to cut them off every time we buy something. Can't you just see the time it'll take? And the queues of people, all getting more and more fed up waiting while he does it. I mean, it's never going to work, people won't put up with it. And then there's the blackout.' She gestured at the pile of coarse black cotton material draped over Joe's armchair. 'Curtains I've got to make with that lot, and Joe's got to put them all on frames so we can fix them up to the windows every night and lift 'em down in the morning. It's either that or have the horrible stuff hanging there all the time like a funeral parlour. Well, half the people just aren't going to bother, are they? It stands to reason they won't.'

'They'll be in trouble if they don't,' Joe said, coming in. He was carrying a basket of soft fruit, grown on the allotment. 'There's going to be wardens going round all night to see if there's a light showing. It'll be a punishable offence.'

'You mean they'll put people in prison? Old women who can't manage it for themselves and got no one to help them?' Emily drew down the corners of her mouth and sniffed. 'If it's going to be like that living in a free country, we might as well let Hitler invade and get it over with.'

20

'Mum! Don't say that.' Lucy looked at the heap of black fabric. 'It's horrible, I know, but they say the Germans will send planes over to bomb the cities, and they can see even the smallest glimmer from up there. You wouldn't want to be responsible for Pompey getting bombed.'

Emily sighed and shook her head. ''Course I wouldn't. Sorry, love. It's just getting me on edge, that's all. We're getting the air-raid shelters next week, did I tell you that? Andersons, they're called – like little tiny Nissen huts, only half buried in the ground. Your dad's got to dig a great big hole in the garden, just as if he didn't have enough to do. And then they'll sound a kind of siren to tell us when the planes are coming, night or day, and we've all got to go and crouch down like rabbits in a burrow. I don't know what the world's coming to, I'm sure I don't.'

'And what about the boys?' Lucy asked quietly. 'Will they have to go in the Forces?'

Emily turned sharply away, and Lucy knew that this was the cause of her ill temper. Vic was twenty-four years old now, and Kenny twenty-three. They'd both served apprenticeships and had good jobs: Vic worked as a mechanic in a big garage, and Kenny was a Post Office engineer out at Telephone House, in Southsea. Vic had a steady girlfriend, Eileen Foster, and they were planning to get engaged soon and then married in a couple more years, but the talk of war could change all that.

'All young chaps will get called up,' Joe said heavily, 'unless they're in a reserved occupation or got some other reason why they shouldn't go. Our Vic and Kenny are just the sort they'll be looking for.' He moved across to his wife and patted her awkwardly on the shoulder. 'It's not necessarily going to come to it, love. There's still a chance—'

'A *chance*!' Emily rounded on him. She had always had the quick temper that went with red hair, although it was generally over almost as soon as it had begun. 'I thought we had a chance last October when Mr Chamberlain came back waving that piece of paper, and look where we are now. Peace in our time! Barely nine months ago, that was, and here we are digging holes in the garden and making blackout curtains. There's going to be a war, you can't tell me otherwise, and our boys are going to get caught up in the thick of it. You were in the last lot, Joe. You know what it's going to be like. And they say it'll be worse this time.'

Joe sat down on the blackout curtains, ignoring his wife's bitten-off cry of exasperation. Lucy, watching them both, thought that her father looked suddenly old. Tired and worried, as if he'd seen enough and didn't want any more. He was nearly sixty, he'd been through a world war and survived it – survived too the flu epidemic that had followed it, killing both his parents and his brother Jim's son Fred. Apart from when he was in the Army, he'd worked hard all his life in the dockyard and brought up a family of five children, and it was time he had a rest. He shouldn't be worrying about a war.

Nor should her mother. And nor should I, Lucy thought with a sudden pang of terror for her own husband and children.

'What about you?' Emily asked her. 'I suppose they're doing all the same things in Plymouth – building shelters and all that. You'll be evacuated, won't you? You won't want to stop there in the front line.'

Lucy stared at her. 'Evacuated?'

'Yes, of course.' Her mother was impatient again. 'They haven't talked of nothing else here, when they haven't been going on about ration books and blackout and Andersons. All the kids have practised at school. They'll be took off by train the minute it starts and we won't know where they've gone till they've got there, and they'll just live with strangers till it's all over. But it'll be all right for you, you'll be able to go with them being as Zannah's still little and your hubby's in the Services and away all the time.'

Away fighting in the war, Lucy thought. She shook her head. 'They haven't said anything about evacuation in Plymouth.'

'What d'you mean, not said anything about it? They must have.'

'No. Plymouth's a neutral evacuation zone. They don't think we'll be in any danger.'

Her mother stared at her, 'Not in any *danger*? But that's daft. Of course Plymouth'll be in danger, same as Pompey will be. It's a naval base, isn't it? There's a big dockyard there. What makes them think the Germans won't bomb it?'

Lucy shrugged. 'How do I know? I just hope they're right.'

'I can't see the reason.' Emily turned to her husband. 'Can you, Joe? Can you see the reason? I mean, Plymouth's as important as Pompey, far as the Navy goes. It don't make any sense.'

'Your mother's right. You didn't ought to stay in Plymouth if there's a war. It's not safe for the kiddies.'

Lucy felt trapped. 'Well, what else can I do? I can't come back here. And if there's no evacuation programme I can't go anywhere else. I'd have to pay it all, and how can I do that and keep a home going in Plymouth for Wilmot to come back to? No, I reckon I'll just have to face it out.'

'Well, you've got to get a decent shelter, then. Has that hotel got a cellar? You'll have to get down there if anything happens. I don't reckon it's any good getting under the stairs, like they say – if a bomb hits your house, a few wooden stairs aren't going to stop it. You get down in that cellar.'

'But the hotel's two streets away.'

'You'd better go and live there, then.' Emily wasn't going to be put off. 'Got plenty of bedrooms, hasn't it? And there won't be many people going to Devonshire on their holidays, I can tell you that now.' She glanced at

23

the clock. 'You'd better be going if you're taking the children over to Gosport to see your Uncle Percy and Auntie Daph. You know what she's like, tea'll be on the table at five o'clock sharp and woe betide anyone who's late.'

Lucy lined the three children up and inspected their hair and faces and hands. Geoff had managed to lose a garter as usual, so that one grey sock had concertina'd round his ankle, and his dark red hair stood up in a tuft that no amount of smoothing would force to lie down. She found a bit of elastic and put a couple of quick stitches in it to make a new garter and gave up on his hair. Zannah was, as always, as clean as if she'd just stepped out of the bath, her clothes tidy and her golden-red hair shining like fireglow around her face. Patsy, although tidy enough, still managed somehow to look as if she needed a good brushing, but there was never anything to be done about that.

They went out and walked through to Commercial Road. The Guildhall lions lay watching over the big square and Lucy led the children past the memorial to the soldiers who had died in the Great War, and into the park. They always enjoyed walking this way down to the ferry which would take them across the harbour to Gosport, but today Lucy looked at the figure of the soldier, crouching over his machine-gun, and felt a sick shiver of fear.

The harbour seemed different too. There were a lot of ships in, a lot of coming and going. The masts and rigging of HMS *Victory*, Nelson's flagship, loomed behind the semaphore tower and she heard the thin notes of a bosun's whistle, sounded as a ship slowly passed, in recognition of Britain's most famous admiral.

The ferry-boat was small and stubby. It took about seven minutes to cross the harbour, and in that time Lucy looked about her at the scene she had known so well all through her life, and tried to imagine the city of

Portsmouth and the town of Gosport laid waste by enemy bombs.

And Plymouth too, for surely her mother was right. Surely the Germans wouldn't ignore one of the most important naval bases in the country. Surely there wouldn't, in the end, be anywhere at all they would ignore.

The shiver that had taken her as she passed the bronze replica of the soldier gripped her again, and her teeth chattered as wave after wave of cold shudders shook her body.

Mum's right, she thought. They wouldn't be making all these preparations if they didn't know it was going to happen. It's not a question of *if* – it's *when*.

And by all appearances, it's going to be soon . . .

Back in Plymouth, she looked around for signs of preparation. Just as in Portsmouth, Anderson shelters were being delivered and gas masks issued. It looked just as serious, but there was still no talk of evacuation.

'Our boys'll get the Germans long before they get this far,' Arthur Pengelly said staunchly. 'Look at it this way, my handsome. They've got to come all the way down the Channel. Coming *past* Portsmouth on their way. They're not going to bother coming down here, putting their own lives at risk – never mind the extra fuel, those planes use up a lot of petrol, it's not like taking the family jalopy out for a Sunday afternoon run – not when they could bomb Portsmouth to bits.'

Lucy had to admit it made sense, though the idea of her beloved Portsmouth being 'bombed to bits' sent a chill through her body. All the same, there was a niggling sense that it didn't really ring true. If that really was what would happen, wouldn't the Navy send its ships to Plymouth, where they'd be safe? And wouldn't the Germans follow them?

'Your mum's right, maid,' Maud said suddenly. 'You belong here with us. Down in the cellar of a night – if there are any raids at all. You and the little 'uns could have those attic rooms to sleep in. You'm round here half the time as it is, helping out.'

Lucy smiled. It was true that she spent a lot of time at the hotel, helping her mother-in-law make beds or sweep the rooms, and helping Arthur with the books. Even though she had her hands full with the three children, it was still nice to share her days with the family and she enjoyed meeting the guests. Life as a naval wife could be very lonely.

'Thanks, Mum,' she said. 'I'll stop where I am for the time being, though. After all, we still don't know that there's definitely going to be a war, and I want to keep the home going for Wilmot to come back to. I don't want to give up the house if I can help it.'

Wilmot was away again. The *Exeter* had gone down to the South Atlantic, cruising round the Falkland Islands and South America. At least he'll be out of it, she thought, if there is a war. It'll never get that far. The thought of Wilmot being involved in a war at sea made her shiver. She remembered their laughing talk when she'd taught him to swim properly. '*If the ship goes down, I'll probably be a thousand miles away from land . . .*' No, she couldn't think about that.

But it was not long before Lucy discovered, as so many thousands of others were to discover, that when war came, you had to think the unthinkable.

Like the rest of the country, she listened with dread and horror to Mr Chamberlain's announcement on the radio on Sunday, 3 September. '*I have to tell you that no such undertaking has been received and that consequently this country is at war with Germany . . .*' Lucy, sitting at the kitchen table with Maud and Arthur, found that she had one hand covering her mouth while the other reached out blindly for

26

comfort. '*You can imagine what a bitter blow this has been . . .*' Their hands met in the middle of the table, hers and Maud's and Arthur's, fingers clasping tightly. '*May God bless you all . . . I am certain that right will prevail . . .*'

'Let's hope he'm right,' Arthur said at last into the long silence that followed. 'Let's just hope he'm right.'

'Oh, Arthur,' Maud said, her voice shaking. 'Arthur, what be going to happen to us? And what about our Wilmot, out there at sea? What be going to happen to Wilmot?'

'He's all right,' Lucy said fiercely, as if saying so would make it true. 'He's nowhere near Germany. He'll be safe down there in the South Atlantic. The war won't get that far. Why should it?'

Arthur glanced at her as if about to say something, and then changed his mind. She knew what it was, though. He was going to ask her why she thought they'd let big, modern ships like the *Exeter* and the two other ships down there on patrol – the *Ajax* and the *Achilles* – stay there when they'd so obviously be needed somewhere else. But it would take them weeks to get back, she thought desperately, weeks, and by then it might all be over. Wasn't that what people were saying? All over by Christmas, that's what a lot of folk reckoned.

Lucy went home that afternoon, glancing anxiously up at the sky, wondering when the first raids would come. She knew that people had already started to leave some of the big cities. Children had been pouring out of Portsmouth and London, making for the country. There had still been no evacuation plans made for Plymouth, so she supposed that the authorities must think that there was no danger. She hoped they were right. She hoped, too, that she was right about Wilmot. He *must* be safe, down there in the South Atlantic.

To everyone's surprise, however, it was the South Atlantic and Wilmot's ship the *Exeter* which made some of the first news of the war.

Chapter Three

After the tension of the months before the war began, and the dread of that sad announcement that brought an end to 'peace in our time', nothing much seemed to happen.

People said that in some places the air-raid warnings had sounded as soon as Mr Chamberlain had finished speaking, as if the German planes had waited until that moment to make their appearance overhead. But there had been no enemy aircraft, no bombs, and for a long time, it seemed as if nobody knew quite what to do first. It was as if two boxers had come out of their corners at the sound of the bell and then stood facing each other, uncertain as to who was supposed to throw the first punch.

'People are already starting to come back from the country,' Emily wrote from Portsmouth. 'They reckon there's no need to be out there. And the way some of the kiddies are being treated, you wouldn't credit . . . Not all of them of course, it's just a big holiday to a lot of them, what with only having to go to school half days and all. But nobody seems to think it's going to be as bad as all that, after all.'

'They'm living in fool's paradise, then,' Arthur said when Lucy read the letter out. 'The Germans aren't playing party games. They'm just getting themselves ready. They'll hit us with all they've got, you see. And maybe if people didn't spend all their time staring at the sky they might see what's happening in other parts of the world.'

Lucy looked at him with a sudden rush of fear. 'What other parts of the world?'

Arthur screwed up the corners of his lips, as if annoyed with himself. 'Don't think about it, maid. I shouldn't have said nothing.'

'What, Dad?' Lucy's back tensed. 'What are you thinking of?'

'It's no good backing out of it now, Arthur,' Maud said. 'You'd better tell her what's on your mind.'

Arthur sighed. 'Well, you'll see it for yourself soon enough. It's this *Admiral Graf Spee*,' he said to Lucy. 'Pocket battleship, they call her. Been chasing our merchant ships all over the oceans, picking 'em off then zig-zagging off so no one can tell where her'll be next. Well, stands to reason us can't let 'em go on like that, so the whole of the Atlantic Fleet's been after her. And now—'

'The Atlantic Fleet?' Lucy repeated. Her voice sounded small, almost tiny. How, she wondered, could she have missed knowing all this? 'But – she's not gone south. She's not –'

'Her's gone all over the place,' Arthur said. 'It hasn't made all that much news yet and I was hoping – me and Maud was hoping – it'd all go quiet. But now they reckon her's going right down the South Atlantic, and those three ships are the ones that are there, and there's going to be –' He caught his wife's eye and chewed his lips again. 'Look at it this way, my pretty,' he said at last. 'There'll be a bit of a fight over it all. Bound to be.'

A bit of a fight. Before many days had passed, the *Graf Spee* was all you heard about on the wireless, all you saw in the papers. The Battle of the River Plate, they called it, and after it the *Graf Spee* had been forced into the port of Montevideo for repairs and sanctuary. While there, she was safe, but the moment she came outside the three-mile limit of neutrality, the ships awaiting her would pounce.

By this time, Lucy and the Pengellys were, like the rest of Plymouth, following the news avidly. Despair hit them when a false signal came through saying that the *Exeter* had been sunk with all hands, and until the rumour was scotched Lucy knew what it was to be a widow. Even when, just before Christmas, the *Graf Spee* was finally caught and scuttled, she could not be sure that Wilmot was safe. Sixty-one men aboard *Exeter* were reported dead, and there was no way of knowing if Wilmot were one of them. At last the *Evening Herald* published a list of all those killed, and she had to read it a dozen times before she could be convinced that Wilmot's name wasn't there.

'It might still be a mistake,' she said, almost as if she were unwilling to believe that he might be alive. 'They might have left his name off . . . Mum, I can't bear to think it's all right and then find out it's not.' She thought for a moment of those dark, cold nights when she'd believed herself a widow. 'I don't think I will be able to believe it till I see him walk in that door again.'

'I know, maid,' Maud said, 'but us've just got to put our trust in God and have faith, like the bishop says down St Andrew's. 'Tis all us can do.'

Lucy thought of all the men who had already been killed. No doubt many of them, and their wives and mothers too, had put their faith in God as well. And they were dead all the same. Her memories of the days and nights when she had thought herself bereaved were dark and cold, and she knew that only the warmth of Wilmot's arms about her would banish them.

She had to wait until February for that reassurance, but at last the *Exeter* and *Ajax* came home together, steaming up the Sound beneath bruised clouds still full of snow, with the Hoe crowded by people who had gathered to cheer their arrival. Lucy was tempted to take the children down to St Levan's Gate to meet Wilmot at the very first possible moment, but Arthur and Maud dissuaded her.

'You don't know what time he'll come ashore, and you don't even know he'll be coming out of St Levan's. You belong to be at home, with a fire lit and the kettle on. That's what he'll appreciate most.'

Reluctantly, Lucy agreed. She knew they were right, it was just that she had waited so long for Wilmot to come home that she felt she couldn't bear to wait a moment longer than necessary. And the time it took him to get from the dockyard to home was time they could be spending together, even if it was just on a tram . . .

She made fresh cutrounds and got hold of some clotted cream and put out a pot of home-made blackcurrant jam and the best teacups. She put clean sheets on the bed, washed the children and herself, brushed their hair a dozen times, brought in a bucket of coal so that no one would need to go outside again for the rest of the evening. She sat down with her knitting, got up again and peered out of the window. The afternoon was closing in already but there wasn't a light to be seen; people had already put up their blackout curtains and the streetlamps hadn't been lit for months.

Lucy hesitated. She didn't want to put up the blackout, it seemed so unwelcoming, but she couldn't see any more to knit and she couldn't make the children sit in the dark. Besides, even the firelight would send out a glow that would bring the warden knocking on the door. She sighed and let the curtain drop. Wilmot would have to come home in the dark after all.

A movement on the corner of the street caught her eye and she lifted the curtain again, her heart suddenly in her throat. Yes. There was someone there. Someone coming this way. Someone who strode with a free, slightly rolling gait; someone who carried a kitbag; someone who—

'Wilmot!'

Not caring that the light from the fire would spill into the street, Lucy flung open the front door and rushed outside. He caught her in his arms just as she tripped on a loose paving-stone, and held her there, hard against him.

31

Laughing and crying all at once, she clung to his blue-clad arms and burrowed her face against his rough serge chest.

'Oh, Wilmot – Wilmot . . . I thought you'd never come home again . . . I thought you were *dead*.'

'Dead?' he said, and the sound of his voice brought a fresh flood of tears. 'Dead? It'll take more than a few Germans to kill me, Lucy. Now, let's get inside out of the cold and I'll tell you about the penguins.'

They were the only ones who wore evening dress, he said. He sat beside the fire, built halfway up the chimney to welcome him home, and demolished half a dozen of Lucy's cutrounds, spread lavishly with blackcurrant jam and topped with cream. They were the funniest birds you ever saw, waddling along on their hind legs – well, he knew they were the only legs penguins had, but it *looked* as if they were up on hind legs, like a performing dog – and coming up to you so trusting. And the way they stood about in groups, like little old men having a natter, it was a proper comical sight.

'We had to stop down there in the Falklands quite a while to get all the repairs done. Good job they're British, those islands. Mind you, the South Americans are mostly neutral, they'd have taken on any job, but it would've been a queer thing to have been in one of their harbours alongside a German ship. But the islands being ours, they looked after us like heroes.'

'And so you were,' Lucy said. The family was clustered about him, as tightly as they could get, everyone wanting to be close. Geoff and Patsy were on the floor, each with an arm wound around their father's legs, and he had Zannah on his lap. Lucy sat opposite in her own armchair, but she'd pulled it closer so that she could touch him still, and she knew she'd get her chance to be closer later on. 'The papers have all been full of you, and you've been on the wireless and everything.'

'There's talk of us going to London,' Wilmot said, half shyly. 'Going to see the Lord Mayor. And there'll be a reception here in Plymouth too, with Lord and Lady Astor.'

Lucy's eyes sparkled. The Astors almost ran Plymouth between them. Lord Astor was Lord Mayor, and his wife – even though she was born an American – had become the first woman to sit in Parliament. Seeing them both at once was as good as seeing the Lord Mayor of London any day.

'Well, you deserve it,' she said. 'You deserve medals, all of you.' Her face grew sad. 'But what about all those men who were killed, Wilmot, and their poor families? They can't be feeling very happy now, with the ship back and their men never coming home again. I feel ever so sorry for them.'

'I know.' Wilmot's face twisted then hardened. 'And I've promised to go and see one or two of the wives, Luce. Tell 'em a bit about it – not much.' His eyes seemed to see something she would never see, never even know about. 'Couple of my oppos copped it – we always said we'd look out for each other, do anything we could. Well, there's nothing left to do now, and I don't suppose they really want to know what happened. I don't want to go into it all anyway, but it don't seem right to just not bother. I mean, I've got to go and pay my respects.'

'Yes, of course. I'm sure it's the right thing to do.' Lucy thought back to those moments when she had thought herself a widow. 'I'd have wanted someone to come and see me.' She remembered the names of men Wilmot had said were his best mates. 'Teddy Endacombe, or Knocker White. I'd have liked it if they'd come.'

'Well, they won't be coming anyway,' he said quietly. 'It's Teddy Endacombe and Knocker White's missuses I've got to go and see.'

The leave passed all too quickly. Most of the time they spent at home or going round to see Maud and Arthur.

33

Once or twice they left the children at the guest house and spent an afternoon at the pictures. They saw Laurence Olivier and Vivien Leigh in *Wuthering Heights* and took Geoff and Patsy to see Judy Garland in *The Wizard of Oz*. Generally in the evenings they put up the blackout curtains to shut out the weather and played cards or listened to programmes like *ITMA* or *Band Waggon* on the wireless. After the nine o'clock news they would listen to Lord Haw-Haw and jeer at his sneering, plummy voice and futile efforts to scare them.

As Wilmot had said, there were receptions held for the crews of the ships both in Plymouth and in London. He came home bemused. 'We marched all through London with a band in front of us, and people waved flags and cheered like we were royalty. And then we had our dinner – lunch, they called it, but it was a proper dinner really – at the Guildhall. You've never seen anything like it, Luce. It's like a huge church. And there was all long tables and china plates that I swear had gold on them, and cut glasses to drink out of. I tell you what, the ratings' Mess is going to seem a bit of a comedown after that.'

'You wouldn't like to live like it all the time, though,' Lucy said, half afraid that their small terraced house and few bits of china would also seem a comedown. 'I mean, it's not like real life, is it?'

Wilmot grinned and pulled her close. 'Don't worry, maid. I wouldn't swop our home for all the Lord Mayors' palaces and parlours in the country. I reckon I've got all I want here, with you and our little tackers. And once this war's over I'll be content to stop here.'

'You mean you really will come out of the Navy? As soon as you can?'

'As soon as I can,' Wilmot promised her. 'And it can't be too soon for me.'

It didn't look as if the war would soon be over after all.

Christmas had come and gone, and the Battle of the River Plate brought it home to everyone that a war really was being waged. The merchant ships that had been so much at the mercy of the enemy were now protected by convoys of naval ships, but that didn't stop the battles. It seemed as if the Navy was going to be at the forefront of this war, rather than the Army or the Air Force.

'Mind you, the weather's got a lot to do with it,' Arthur said. 'Look at it this way: it's been a rough old winter and the Germans aren't any keener to fly their planes than we are. That'll change, come the better weather, you see if it don't. I reckon things'll start happening come spring.'

He was right. The war seemed to be happening everywhere but in Britain. It seemed, during those cold months when rationing had bitten deeper and all kinds of rules and regulations been imposed, that Hitler had forgotten his threats to invade. Instead, he was concentrating on Scandinavia and troops were being sent there. Denmark had already fallen and the situation in Norway didn't look much better.

And so far there hadn't been a single bomb dropped.

'Not that we want them,' Emily said when Lucy went to spend Easter in Portsmouth. 'And there's more people than ever come back from the evacuation. Your dad reckons it's just a lull. They're getting themselves ready, that's what he says.'

'That's what Wilmot's dad says too,' Lucy said. She looked up at the sky, glittering with barrage balloons. 'D'you think those'll really keep the planes away?'

'Well, they're not going to want to fly into them, are they? And if they come in below them our lads'll shoot them down straight away.'

Vic and Kenny had both been called up. Vic, who had got married a month before war was declared, had gone into the Army, into the local regiment, and had already done his training – six weeks' square bashing and peeling potatoes, he said when he came home for his first leave. It had changed him, Eileen said. He ironed his own trousers and he'd learnt to be tidy. 'If being tidy's going to win the war, he'll do it all on his own. We can't leave anything lying about but what he picks it up and polishes it.'

Kenny was in the RAF. They didn't seem to be so bothered about tidiness. He wore a white scarf carelessly round his neck and talked about training as a mechanic, maybe even a pilot. He took Geoff up to Hilsea and they watched planes coming in to the small airport at Airspeed.

'Uncle Kenny's going to fly a Spitfire,' Geoff said, and spread his arms wide, making zooming noises as he ran round the room. 'I hope there's still a war when I'm old enough to fly Spitfires.'

'Geoff!' The edge in Lucy's voice betrayed the fear she still felt for Wilmot, now back at sea again. 'Don't you dare say such wicked things!' But it was all a game to nine-year-old boys, and she didn't even want him to understand the reality of it all.

Even her sisters were preparing to do their bit. Alice was married too, and her husband Ted was in the same regiment that Vic had joined. They were expecting to go to France soon. They had no children and Alice had decided to go back to her job as a nurse. There would be plenty needed soon enough, she said grimly.

Kitty, who was only just twenty, was talking about going into one of the Women's Services. They'd started the WRNS up again after disbanding them after the Great War. Emily was horrified at the idea and Joe inclined to put his foot down, but what could you say? The girl would be twenty-one in less than a year and the Government was talking about conscripting women anyway.

'I don't know what the world's coming to,' Emily said, as she did a hundred times a week now. 'To think of women fighting!'

'I keep telling you, Mum, we won't be fighting.' Nobody

36

looked less like fighting than Kitty, standing on tiptoe to look in the mirror and curl her glossy dark red hair. She wrapped a scrap of fur round her neck like a scarf and looked like a tiny, bright-eyed fox. 'We just do the shore jobs and that means more men can go to sea.'

'I'd rather you didn't bother,' Lucy said. 'I wouldn't mind a scrap if my Wilmot didn't have to go to sea.' But she knew that nobody was going to get release in this war. It was going to be all hands to the pumps and get it over with.

The Allied Forces withdrew from Norway after only a couple of weeks' fighting. Mr Chamberlain resigned as Prime Minister and Winston Churchill took his place. A week later, the Germans started their air attack on the Low Countries, and the word *blitzkrieg* entered the language.

'I told you, my pretty,' Arthur Pengelly said when Lucy was back in Plymouth. 'I told you what it'd be like. They'm softening 'em up with dive-bombers and then sending in the tanks. And nobody seems able to stop 'em.'

'They can't do that here,' Maud said. 'They can't get tanks across the Channel.' But she spoke without conviction and nobody argued with her. They all knew, in their sinking hearts, that the Germans could.

'Our boys will stop them,' she said. 'There's plenty of troops over in France now, and we've got the finest Navy in the world. And the RAF . . .'

'The RAF haven't been proved,' Arthur told her. 'They only just got going in the last war. Nobody knows how they'd manage, not really.'

They were soon to find out. In less than a month, British troops came back from Dunkirk, white faced, bandaged, exhausted – and those were the lucky ones. There were many others left dead on the beaches and in the fields of Normandy. Amongst them was Lucy's brother Vic.

There was no doubt now that the war was real.

The summer brought the Battle of Britain, and now nobody could say the RAF was untried. Another flock of young men was killed, like doves in the air, and the family had a new worry. Kenny had achieved his ambition to be a pilot and was based near Chichester. He flew Spitfires, just as he had promised Geoff he would, and when he came home his talk was peppered with 'flaps' and 'prangs' and 'ditches'. He seemed to lead a charmed life, always returning from operations, always with a grin on his face, though to Lucy, when she saw him, the grin seemed fixed, and behind the merry eyes lurked a soul that was filled with dread.

So far, the Germans had aimed all their attacks at the British airfields, determined to kill the only power that could really prevent their invasion, but as the Battle of Britain drew to a triumphant close and the people began to draw breath, they changed their tactics. And in September 1940, the bombing began in earnest.

Many of those who had returned from evacuation during the 'phony' war now hurried back again to new billets. The authorities still considered Plymouth to be safe, and at first it seemed that they were right. The first raids were over London: as night fell on 7 September the docklands were already ablaze, the fires caused by hundreds of tons of bombs falling like rain throughout the day. This time, the RAF seemed powerless to stop them. Even the Thames was set on fire as blazing stocks of rum, sugar and paint were scattered from the ruined warehouses to float on the water. And when a river was on fire, one fireman remarked grimly, you really knew you were in trouble.

All through September it continued. In October, Londoners began to forsake the street shelters for the safety of the deep Tube stations. Photographs appeared in the newspapers and film on Pathé Pictorial, of shattered streets, destroyed buildings. And it wasn't just London. Other cities were getting their share too: Liverpool, Bristol, Southampton, Coventry . . .

38

Before the bombing started, Lucy had been thinking of going back to Portsmouth for Christmas. Vic's widow Eileen had had his baby now, a little girl with really red hair, she wrote to Lucy, and she was going to call her Victoria after the daddy she'd never know. Lucy badly wanted to see the new baby, but now she hesitated and decided against it.

When she heard about the huge bomb that had been dropped on Portsmouth on Christmas Eve, demolishing an entire street, she was glad she'd stayed in Plymouth, and when the blitz hit Pompey on 10 January she was frantic.

'How do we find out what's been happening? How can they let us know?' The guest house was on the phone, but the Travers' little terraced house in Portsmouth wasn't, and phone lines were down anyway. Emily couldn't even have got through from a phone box. 'They could all be dead.'

'No news is good news.' Maud was staunch as usual, but they both knew that these days no news could just as well be bad news. They both waited anxiously, listening for the phone to ring, looking out of the windows for the telegraph boy on his red bike.

It came at last, a buff envelope that Lucy opened with shaking fingers. 'They're all right,' she said, her face twisting in a grimace of a smile that turned quickly to a sob. Her legs trembled suddenly and she sat down. 'Oh Mum, they're all right.'

After the first of Portsmouth's blitzes there was a mass burial in Kingston Cemetery. Everyone hoped this would be all they were to suffer, but there was another blistering attack on 10 March. Once again, Lucy was beside herself with fear until the telegram came to tell her the family had survived.

And still there had been no major raids on Plymouth. True, there had been a few bombs dropped, apparently by planes that had passed over on their way to Bristol and flown off-course, but the danger still didn't seem especially great, and there was no mention of evacuation.

'They'm right after all,' Maud said. 'Plymouth's not going to get it. They can't get right down here, see, they'm just concentrating on the places that are easy to get to.'

Coventry? Lucy thought. Liverpool? Surely Plymouth wasn't any harder to reach than these cities, and look what had happened to them. And why should Bristol be bombed and not Plymouth? She was conscious of dread every night when she went to bed, dread every morning when she woke.

Only ten days later, on the very day when King George VI and Queen Elizabeth came to visit Plymouth and take tea on the Hoe with Lady Astor just as if it were peacetime, her dread was fulfilled. The Germans came at last, that night and the next, and began systematically to flatten Plymouth. Lucy had never missed Wilmot so much. She could only be thankful that she had by her side another man who had come to be, not only her friend, but a friend to the whole family, David. David Tremaine, who had suffered his own terrible loss and knew all too well what a German bombing raid could do.

Chapter Four

David Tremaine was born in Cornwall in the summer of 1903, seven years before Lucy. His father, Pascoe Tremaine, editor of a local newspaper had gone to war in 1914 and was killed at Passchendaele. His mother, Kathleen, a London girl, had stayed long enough to bring David up in the village where he was born, and then gone back to look after her ageing parents.

David took after his father. As a boy, he had spent many hours in the newspaper office, helping to produce the paper. He had even been entrusted with one or two small reporting jobs – going to the local flower show and listing the winners, writing a story about a ship that was wrecked in a nearby cove. It wasn't a big ship and nobody was killed, or he wouldn't have been given the story, but it was a thrill for him to see his words in print all the same.

When he was old enough, he got a job on the same newspaper, under the editor who had taken over when David's father joined the Army, and after he had served his apprenticeship and achieved some independence he began to work his way up, first joining the staff of the *Western Morning News* and then going to London, where he lived for a time with his mother and grandmother, his grandfather having by then died. By the time the Second World War started, he was married with a twelve-month-old baby son.

For some time during the late 'thirties, David had been working for a specialist Government publication and had become an expert on naval matters. Not much of his work

41

appeared in newspapers these days: he spent his time gathering information to be published in Government reports, or in advising those civil servants who would in turn advise their ministers. His work involved travelling between the main naval ports of Portsmouth, Plymouth and Chatham, and for some time he had been in the habit of staying at Pengelly's. He found it homely and comfortable, he said, nicer than the big, impersonal hotels, and after a while he was as much a friend as a paying guest.

'He's a nice sort of a man, that David Tremaine,' Maud remarked. He had been on his way out just as Lucy came in with Geoff after school, and immediately offered to take the two older children up on the Hoe. It was long before talk of war had seriously begun, and the newspapers were full of talk of Edward VIII and Wallis Simpson. Zannah was still a baby, still called Susannah, and she was red faced and crying that afternoon with teething problems. Lucy thanked him gratefully and watched him walk away up Lockyer Street, tall and loose limbed between the two children, Patsy holding his hand and skipping, and Geoff talking away nineteen to the dozen about what he had done at school that day.

'He's bringing his fiancée down to stay soon,' Lucy said, soothing Zannah with a bottle of cool water. 'There, there, lovey, that's better, isn't it? You've got yourself all hot and bothered . . . They're getting married at Christmas. Heather, she's called. He showed me her photograph.'

'I hope they'm wanting separate rooms,' Maud said a little sharply. 'I'll have no goings-on in my house. Mind, he doesn't seem that sort of a chap, I'll say that for him. Decent, like.'

David brought Heather down a few weeks later. Maud gave them not only separate rooms, but she put them on different floors, too: David on the top floor, where the rooms were really attics, and Heather on the first floor in one of the best rooms.

'Tell us all the best places to go,' David said to Lucy. 'I want to take Heather down to Cornwall to meet my auntie there and see where I grew up, but she wants to see Devon as well. We're going to hire a car for a day or two and then go on by train.'

'You need to ask Wilmot really. He's the one who was born here.'

'You've lived here for quite a while though, haven't you?' Heather asked. She was a pretty girl, with soft brown, naturally curly hair and wide hazel eyes. She obviously adored David and it was clear he thought the world of her. They held hands all the time and Lucy had inadvertently caught them kissing on the landing, just outside Heather's room.

Wilmot was in port just then, and at David's suggestion the four of them spent Saturday afternoon and evening together. While Maud looked after the children, they all squeezed into the Baby Austin David had hired and set off for Dartmoor. They roamed about the wide, empty spaces and picnicked beside the bubbling East Dart before returning to spend the evening in Tavistock, calling in at the Royal Oak in Meavy for a last drink on the way back.

'That was lovely,' Lucy sighed, leaning her head on Wilmot's shoulder as they sped back across Roborough Down. 'We hardly ever get out like that, all on our own. It was as good as being on holiday.'

David and Heather left next day, taking the train down into Cornwall over the Brunel Bridge that spanned the broad reaches of the Tamar.

When they got married, Lucy sent them a telegram (rejecting Wilmot's suggestion of a rude one and settling for 'Best wishes for your new life together'), and the next time David came to stay at Pengelly's he was a happily married man with a baby on the way.

David never talked about his work. He came to Plymouth

about once in eight weeks, and she knew that he went to Portsmouth and Chatham with about the same frequency. Wherever else he went and what he did in between, he never said and she never asked. You didn't ask anyone anything these days; there were too many posters up exhorting you to 'be like Dad, keep Mum', or telling you that walls had ears. She knew, however, that an attack of TB had left him unable to join the services.

In that first winter of the war, when he came to Plymouth he walked down Lockyer Street of an evening and sat with Lucy in the small back room. He played with Geoff and Patsy and sat Zannah on his lap and told them about his own baby son, little Stevie. Lucy was busy knitting balaclava helmets and socks, but with a few scraps of wool she made little pom-pom balls for him to take back to Stevie. She asked if Heather and the baby were going to go into the country, but David shook his head.

'I want her to come to Cornwall and stay with Auntie Meg, but she won't hear of it. Says she wants to keep our home going. And then there are the mums, of course.' His own mother was getting on and still living with the ancient grandmother, and Heather's mother was also still alive and in poor health. 'She doesn't feel she can leave them.'

'It's not easy,' Lucy said, and told him how her mother had thought she ought to get out of Plymouth. 'She can't believe it's any safer than Portsmouth.'

'She may be right,' he said soberly. 'Isn't there anywhere you could go?'

'Not really. We don't know anyone outside Plymouth, and if they're not evacuating it means you have to pay.'

'Mm.' He thought for a minute or two, then fished a piece of paper out of his pocket. 'Look, I'll give you my aunt's address down in Cornwall. I'm sure she'd know somewhere you could go, if you do want to leave the city. I'm still trying to persuade Heather to go down there – she might agree if she thought you were going to be there too.'

44

Lucy thanked him, but she knew she wouldn't use the address. Her home was here in Plymouth now, and she couldn't leave Maud and Arthur. Arthur hadn't been at all well lately, he always suffered with his chest in winter and just lately he'd been getting pains when he climbed the stairs or walked up to the Hoe.

Lucy thought of the three children as David gave her the address of his aunt in Cornwall. She still shared her mother's anxieties about the safety of Plymouth. It would be better for them out in the country, and there couldn't be anywhere much safer than Cornwall, but just at present she couldn't see any justification for leaving.

'I'll remember it, if they do look like bombing us,' she said, and smiled at him. 'Now, before you go I'll make us a cup of cocoa.'

They sat together before the fire, companionably drinking cocoa. The children were all in bed now, and it was nearly time for the nine o'clock news. David didn't seem inclined to move, and Lucy didn't feel like reminding him. It was nice, the two of them sitting here together, nice company, and she got little enough of that, when all was said and done.

'What d'you think's going to happen?' she asked after a few moments' silence. 'It wasn't over by Christmas, was it? Will it be over by next Christmas? They say the fighting's awful in Denmark and Norway now. It's as if he wants to take over everything.'

'I think he does. And he's got a lot of power. We can't just sit by and let him walk all over the world. If he was a good man it would be different – except that a truly good man wouldn't even want that sort of power. But he's not good. He's not even bad. He's evil, Lucy, and we've got to fight evil.'

Lucy looked at him. She had never heard David speak in such a serious tone before, and he knew what he was talking about. 'David, that sounds awful.'

45

'It is awful,' he said soberly. 'It's a bad business altogether, Lucy, and I'm very much afraid it's going to get a lot worse before it gets better.'

They sat silent for a few minutes, looking into the fire. Lucy tried to fight down the dread that was rising in her. She had already been through it once, when Wilmot was involved in the Battle of the River Plate, and after that triumphant return she'd thought her own battle over. Now she knew that as long as the war lasted, it would never be over.

'I don't know how I'll manage if anything happens to Wilmot,' she said in a trembling voice. 'I try not to think about it. I try not to think about the danger and the fighting and people getting killed. But we can't push it away and pretend it's not happening, can we? Some people *are* going to get killed – men and women and children. Some people are going to feel like I feel now, trying not to think about it, and they're going to have to face it. So we've all got to. We've all got to face it together.'

'I'm afraid we have.' He turned his head and looked at her. 'And that's what will help us win, Lucy. The feeling that we're all in it together – that if we pull together and help each other, we'll get through it. It isn't just what happens in the fighting, you see – it's what happens behind all that.'

'At home,' she said. 'All the way down from the Government to little back rooms like this. D'you really believe that, David? D'you really believe that people like me, just staying behind with the kids and keeping a home together, can have a real effect on the war? It sounds daft, put like that.'

'Not daft at all,' he said, and there was a new, strange note of tenderness in his voice. 'No, Lucy, it doesn't sound daft at all . . .'

They stared at each other. Lucy noticed for the first time how very dark his eyes were, almost black with a narrow rim of deep blue. She saw the tiny movement of a muscle in his jaw, and felt a tremor deep inside.

'David –'

'Lucy,' he said, and moved slowly closer. 'Lucy –'

The kiss was brief, a quick, hard touching of lips before they both drew back, startled and confused. Lucy turned away, her hands over her face.

David muttered something she couldn't hear and then said swiftly, 'Lucy, I'm sorry. That shouldn't have happened. Look, I'd better go.'

'No.' She turned back. 'It's all right, David. It doesn't matter. It – it was just one of those things.' She lifted her hands away from her face. 'It was talking about Wilmot and the war and everything. I was upset and you wanted to comfort me – that's all it was.'

'Yes,' he said slowly, 'that's all it was.'

'Let's listen to the news,' she said, and switched on the wireless. 'And I reckon you could do with another cup of cocoa before you go back. It's bitter out there. You'd never think we were nearly halfway through April.'

David hesitated, then sat back. The usual burbles and whistles filled the room as the wireless warmed up, then they heard the measured tones of the BBC announcer start to read the news, and they looked at each other in dismay.

Denmark had surrendered. Hitler had won another country.

David continued to stay at Pengelly's during the summer and autumn of 1940. The kiss was never repeated, nor even referred to, but he and Lucy drew closer as friends. Sometimes, guiltily, she thought of that moment by the fireside and knew that if circumstances had been different, there could have been a different relationship between herself and David. If there had been no Wilmot, no Heather . . . But she turned such thoughts away as soon as they arose. Entertaining even for a second the idea of never having known Wilmot – of there never *being* a Wilmot – was wicked. And if there had been no Wilmot, there would never have been a Geoff, or a Patsy. Or Zannah.

No. David was not, nor ever could be, more than a friend. Nor did either of them want to be more than friends to each other.

He was in Plymouth when battle-scarred ships returned from Dunkirk, bringing the shattered remnants of the BEF. He was there again when the Battle of Britain was at its height. Walking on the Hoe together, with Geoff and Patsy running ahead and Zannah stumping between her mother and David, a chunky fist clasped by each, he and Lucy looked up at the hot blue sky and imagined the fighting going on over other parts of the country. Lucy thought of her brother Kenny, up there in his Spitfire, and she wept again for her other brother Vic, who was lying dead somewhere in France and would never see his baby.

David disengaged his hand from Zannah's and reached across to her. 'I know,' he said quietly, and she thought that he did know, that he needed no explanation.

The bombing raids had begun now. The first had been on 6 July, only a month after Dunkirk; Plymouth had heard its first air-raid siren a week before but there had been no bombs then. Now, a lone aircraft flying high came in almost unnoticed and from a clear blue sky brought sudden destruction to a row of houses in Devonport and killed three people, one of them just a boy.

'So they can get this far after all,' Maud said to her husband, but the words were scarcely out of her mouth when the second raid came, less than twenty-four hours later, and this time five people were killed, and Home Sweet Home Terrace, which bore the brunt of the attack, became suddenly a place of horror and fear. After the worst of the daylight attacks towards the end of September, when more

48

than a dozen people were killed at Stonehouse, Lucy made up her mind and moved the family into Lockyer Street.

David's baby son Stevie was a two-year-old now, and Heather had given David a snap of his birthday party to show Lucy the next time he came to Plymouth. He looked fat and jolly, a big grin on his face and chocolate smeared round his mouth. Heather had made a cake and there were two candles on it – ordinary white household candles, but Stevie didn't seem to care. David was in the picture too, looking proud and happy.

'I wish he could bring her and the baby down some time,' Maud said when Lucy showed her the picture. 'I liked her, she's a real nice young woman.'

'I like her too.' Lucy and Heather had started writing to each other, mostly talking about the children, but Heather had said how difficult it was for her to get out at all now, what with the baby and three old ladies to look after. David helped as much as he could, but you couldn't put too much on to a man in wartime, and he was often away anyway. She wrote cheerfully, without grumbling about this – indeed, she often said how lucky she was to have her mother still alive, and for Stevie to have two grannies and a great-grandma – but Lucy could tell she was tired sometimes, and David confirmed this.

'She looks worn out. I do all I can to help when I'm there, but the lion's share falls on her shoulders. It might be a bit easier if they were all under one roof, but my mother refuses to budge out of her own home, so Heather's backwards and forwards all the time.'

'Won't your mum go down to Cornwall? She used to live there, after all.'

'I've suggested it, but she wants to be near Stevie. He's her only grandchild – so far.' He gave Lucy a funny, rather shy little smile and she looked at him with sudden excitement.

'What do you mean – so far? Is Heather expecting again?'

'Well – yes, we think so.' He couldn't stop his smile from spreading now. 'Only it's early days – not even two months – so don't say anything yet. Just in case it's a false alarm.'

'No, of course not. But you don't really think it is, do you?'

'No,' he said, looking inordinately pleased. 'We're pretty sure.'

'Oh, that's lovely. Well, you haven't hung about, have you? What will Stevie be when it's born?' She began to count on her fingers. 'Let's see, it's September now – another seven months you think, so it'll be born some time in April – and he'll be just two and a half. Goodness, Heather's hands are going to be fuller than ever.'

'I know. I'm a bit worried about that myself, but she hasn't turned a hair. Says the mums can help out, it'll keep them occupied.' He grinned again. 'They'll probably be fighting over the pair of them.'

'Well, I think it's lovely.' Lucy looked a little wistfully at Zannah, who was on the floor playing with a set of coloured wooden bricks that Geoffrey had had when he was two years old. 'I'd like to have had another one. Just one more, a year or two younger than her. But what with the war and Wilmot being away all the time . . .'

'He's bound to come home soon,' David said, but she shook her head.

'It doesn't seem the right time now. It doesn't seem right to bring children into the world when things are so awful. It's different for you, you've only got the one kiddie and you've got to get your family together, but we've got three and I think we'll have to be satisfied with that.' She leant forward and gathered Zannah into her arms. 'And this one's such a little pet – I can't believe God would give us another treasure like her.'

David went back to London on the night train. When Lucy woke next morning, it was to the news that London had been bombed yet again.

'Why doesn't he *make* her go down to Cornwall?' Lucy fretted. 'He's got an auntie there with a big house and nice garden, he's told me all about it, he ought to tell Heather she's *got* to go.'

'You ought to know why,' her mother-in-law said. 'You wouldn't go if it was you, and you had Wilmot coming home.'

Lucy had to admit she was right, and it seemed almost as if people were, in a strange way, getting used to the bombing. In her letters, Heather described how young girls were shrugging off the danger and going out with their boyfriends just the same, to the pictures or dancing. They'd got fed up with letting Hitler rule their lives, she wrote.

By Christmas, there was no more doubt that the whole of Europe and beyond were gripped in the fiercest war the world had ever known, surpassing even the horrors of the Great War of 1914-18. The cities which had not yet been hit waited, and in January Lucy began to suffer the nightly torments of not knowing what was happening to her family in Portsmouth. On the same day that she received her first telegram, telling her that they had survived the worst night of bombing yet, she also received a letter from David.

'I'm so thankful to be able to tell you that Heather's agreed at last to go down to Cornwall,' he wrote. 'All the mums are going with her, so the whole family will be safe. I'll be bringing them down next week, after I've been to Portsmouth, and we want to break our journey in Plymouth for a night on the way. Book us three rooms at Pengelly's for next Wednesday!'

'Oh, I'm so glad,' Lucy exclaimed, and wrote back immediately, telling David that the best rooms in the house would be ready for them, and enclosing a note for Heather, to say how much they were all looking forward to seeing her, and that Zannah was already getting excited at the thought of seeing Stevie.

However, Zannah was to be disappointed. While David

51

was in Portsmouth, while he was actually visiting Lucy's family and sitting in Emily and Joe's back room, eating cottage pie and going with them down to the shelter as the siren sounded yet again, there was another raid on London. The house he and Heather were buying, where Heather and her mother and baby son were living, received a direct hit, and all three were killed outright.

Chapter Five

It was on 20 March that David came back to Plymouth for the first time since the death of Heather and his baby son.

As usual he said nothing about his reason for being there but Lucy knew that it was something to do with the visit of the King and Queen. They had come, as they were doing to so many other cities, to see the destruction, and they didn't just go to the smartest parts of Plymouth, they went to shabby backstreets that had been made more squalid still by the bombs that had torn the mean little houses apart. They looked about them, their faces sad and stricken, and talked to the people who were struggling to repair damaged homes or rescue their few possessions; they talked to them just as if they were personal friends.

'They've been bombed themselves,' Maud said. 'Buckingham Palace itself has been hit. They know what it's like.' But Lucy didn't think they did. They hadn't seen their entire home smashed to pieces, and had to go to some refuge post and queue up for hours and ask for ten shillings to buy clothes for the family. They hadn't had to wonder where they would lay their heads that night, or the next, and know that they'd never see their possessions again, that all they'd worked and striven and scraped for had gone for ever, or, worse still, that they'd never see loved members of their family again.

But that wasn't really their fault, and Lucy supposed they were doing their best, so with Maud and Arthur and the two girls she went up to the Hoe and cheered the King and Queen as they walked about with Lord and Lady Astor.

Geoff was there with the school, all looking very smart with their hair brushed until it shone and their socks held up smooth and unwrinkled by new garters. They had each been given a small paper Union Jack to wave, and the bright flags fluttered bravely in the March breeze, the red stripes echoed by the broad red bands on the Smeaton Tower.

David was there too, mixing unobtrusively with the press reporters and photographers. A visit by the King and Queen would be reported in all the local newspapers, to boost morale. They had already toured the city, through streets lined with cheering people. Lucy managed to get quite close, gazing with admiration at the shy, pleasant face of the King and the bright cornflower-blue eyes of the Queen.

David came to the guest house later that evening. He dropped his suitcase in the hall and came straight into the kitchen, looking tired. Lucy, who was slicing onions for supper, turned and went over to him, holding out her arms.

'David. Oh, David –'

He looked at her and his face was full of anguish. It was only a few weeks, she thought, and the shock probably hadn't even started to hit him until then. But somehow, seeing her, with onion tears on her cheeks and real sorrow in her eyes, broke down all the defences he had built up in those few weeks. He stumbled towards her and as she folded her arms about him he laid his head on her shoulder and began to weep.

His tears weren't the sort she would have expected. Not quiet, not restrained, but loud and noisy, with gulps and snorts, the sort of tears a child sheds, and his body shook and shuddered in her arms. He put his own arms around her and clung to her, and amidst his sobs there were words, words she could only just make out; pleas for his wife and baby to be returned to him, a tormented outpouring of sorrow.

Lucy stood quite still, only her hands moving as she

patted his shoulders and stroked his heaving back. She murmured to him as she would to a child, but her voice was thick and shaking with her own grief. She was aware of someone coming into the kitchen but only knew who it was when she felt her mother-in-law's arms around them both and heard Maud's voice in her ear.

'There, there. The poor lamb. The poor, poor lamb.' Nobody knew, perhaps not even Maud herself, whether the 'lamb' were David himself, the baby Stevie or Heather. Or even the old woman who had died. 'Let it out, then. Let it all out. You'll feel better when you've let it out.'

'All at once,' he said in a choked voice when at last he could speak. 'All at once. I saw the house when I went back . . . There was nothing left, nothing.' He lifted his head and looked into Lucy's eyes. 'Nothing.'

'Oh, David. It's terrible. It's awful.' At no other moment, even when she had thought herself a widow, even when she had waited in terror to hear if her own family had been killed, had the reality of the war been brought home to her quite so savagely as at this. Heather, the laughing bride; Stevie, the fat, jolly two-year-old – and the new baby, the unborn child growing in Heather's womb. All gone. Nothing left. The tears that ran down her face now had nothing to do with onions.

'I wanted to go in,' he said. 'They wouldn't let me. They said it was too dangerous. I could see there was nothing left – it caught fire, you see, it was burnt out, there were only a few roof-timbers all blackened and scorched, and great slabs of crumbling plaster hanging off the walls. It stank of burning . . . I knew there couldn't be anything to find, but I wanted to go in just the same. I wanted to be there – just to be *there*.'

'Of course you did. Of course.'

He looked at her. 'You understand that? They all thought I was crazy. Perhaps I was, for a while. I fought with them . . . I was a bit of a nuisance, I'm afraid.'

'It was your home,' Lucy said. 'Of course you wanted to go in. You wanted to be there with them.' You wanted to say goodbye, she thought, but didn't say it. Of course David hadn't actually wanted to say goodbye – he hadn't wanted to lose his family at all, he'd wanted it not to have happened – but he'd wanted, for just a while, to stand where they had died, to try to share it with them.

Maud had been busy with the kettle. Now she laid her hands on David's shoulders and pressed him gently into a chair at the kitchen table. 'Here's a cup of tea,' she said. 'I've put in a drop of Arthur's whisky. He doesn't drink it really, we just keep it for medicinal purposes, but he likes a drop in his cup of tea at bedtime sometimes.'

David's tormented face twitched with a faint smile. He rubbed one hand over his face and looked with surprise at his wet palm. Maud handed him one of Arthur's handkerchieves which had been airing on the rack that hung above them.

'Mop yourself up. And don't bother to say you're sorry. It does us all good to shed tears at times like this, and goodness knows you've got more cause than plenty of others.'

'And no more than many,' he said, his voice still shaking. 'You don't know what it's like up there.'

'We've heard,' Lucy said. 'We've seen pictures. And in Portsmouth.'

'I know. I'm sorry. I've seen it there too. The Guildhall gutted, shops destroyed, whole streets flattened. Liverpool as well. And Coventry – Coventry's a nightmare.' He shook his head. 'The worst of it was she'd just agreed to go down to Cornwall. I was going to bring them all, just a few days later. They'd have been safe . . .' His voice shook and thickened again and he bowed his head, covering his face with the big khaki handkerchief.

'Oh, David.' Lucy could think of nothing to say. There were no words for this kind of occasion. She put out her hand and laid it on his head, feeling the crispness of the thick, curling hair beneath her fingers. I'm so glad we never let that kiss go any further, she thought. I'm so glad he doesn't have anything to feel guilty about.

Clearly, though, he did feel guilty, horribly guilty that he hadn't argued more, insisted that Heather leave London. It didn't have to be Cornwall, it didn't have to be so far away, she could have gone to Hampshire or Berkshire or into the Cotswolds, anywhere she wanted to go. She didn't have to be evacuated, to go to whatever billet was chosen for her, he would have paid, paid willingly, for a cottage they could rent, a house big enough for them all. He should have kept on at her, worn her down as in the end he had done, but he should have done it sooner.

It all poured out as he drank Maud's tea without noticing it. All his guilt and grief and anger, flooding out in the kitchen of the guest house as he hadn't been able to let it loose anywhere else. 'She would have been all right,' he said hopelessly, over and over again. 'They would all have been all right.'

It was useless for Lucy to say that Heather had made her own choice, that she was a strong-minded woman, that it wasn't just her, the old ladies had refused to leave as well and that she'd felt obliged to stay to look after them. David listened politely but it was obvious that he either didn't hear her or just didn't believe it. He should have insisted, and he hadn't.

'But you did. You told me you did.'

'Not enough,' he said with a curious obstinacy. 'I didn't do it enough.'

By the time she took the children up to bed, Lucy was exhausted. Her own sorrow had come to the surface again and, with it, all her old anxieties about Wilmot and the family in Portsmouth. But there was no comfort for her while David was in such distress and she felt a desperate sadness that she could not be more comfort to him.

David went out, saying he wanted to walk up to the Hoe again now that it was quiet after the royal visit, and she felt a guilty relief as he closed the door. The children were fractious after the excitement of the day and she washed them quickly and bundled them into their pyjamas.

'Now, say your prayers.' She knelt beside them and added a special prayer for Uncle David. 'And for Auntie Heather and baby Stevie up in heaven.'

'Why do we need to say prayers for them?' Zannah enquired. 'Doesn't God know they're in heaven?'

'Don't be a twerp,' Geoff said scornfully. 'There's millions of people in heaven. He can't know them all.'

'He can,' Patsy argued. 'It says in the Bible, he knows even the sparrows, they told us that at Sunday School. If he knows sparrows, he's bound to know all the people.'

'I bet he doesn't. I bet he doesn't know all the people who've gone up in the past year,' Geoffrey said, making it sound as if going to heaven was like moving up a class in school. 'There's millions of people getting killed in the war. He can't know them all at once.'

'Yes, but they're not all going to heaven. The Germans won't be going to heaven. They'll be going to—'

'That's enough!' Lucy interrupted sharply. 'You don't have to talk like that, either of you. Just say "God bless Auntie Heather and Stevie, and their grannies," and then get into bed and let's hear no more chatter till tomorrow.'

'Can I say God bless the Queen as well?' Patsy asked. 'I thought she was ever so pretty.'

'Yes, you can say God bless the Queen.'

'And the King,' Geoffrey said.

'*And* the King.'

'And Princess Elizabeth and Princess Margaret Rose.'

'Yes, and that's all. Just say "and everyone else I know".' Lucy was desperate to see them asleep in bed. It seemed dreadful to feel cross with them over prayers, dreadful to want their chatter to stop when little Stevie and others like him would never chatter again, but her nerves felt stretched almost to breaking-point. David's anguished tears had upset her more than she'd realised at the time, when she was trying to give him comfort. Now, all she wanted to do was sit down by herself and pour out all her own feelings, first on paper to Wilmot and then, at last, to herself in her own tears.

'And everyone else I know,' the children said obediently into their steepled hands, and then scrambled into bed. Lucy bent and kissed them tenderly and they wound their arms around her neck.

'I'm sorry baby Stevie's dead,' Zannah whispered.

'Yes. So am I.'

'I don't see why babies have to get dead. It's not their fault there's a war.'

'I know.'

'Stevie wouldn't have wanted to be a soldier even when he was grown up, so why should he get dead?'

'I don't know, Zannah. I just don't know.' She looked down at the little girl. 'How do you know he wouldn't have wanted to be a soldier?'

'His face isn't like a soldier's face,' Zannah said, already half asleep. 'He's too kind. He wouldn't ever have wanted to hurt people.' She rolled her head away and her eyes closed. Lucy saw their movement under the thin skin of her eyelids and pulled the bedclothes up around the small, still-chubby body. What a little oddity Zannah was. She often came out with these remarks about people – and so often, Lucy reflected, she was right. Would she have been right about Stevie?

No one would ever know now.

Lucy kissed the older children goodnight and went downstairs. Maud and Arthur had left the kitchen to sit in the living-room. She could hear the *Band Waggon* tune being played on the wireless and the sounds of the comedians' voices. Richard Murdoch and Arthur Askey – normally she enjoyed their jokes as much as anyone else but tonight she just didn't feel like laughing.

Now, at last, she had time to herself, time to release her own suppressed feelings, yet now that she was alone, she did not know quite what to do after all.

When the first drone of enemy aircraft came, she was still sitting idle in her chair, her letter to Wilmot unwritten, her tears unshed. By the time the planes departed she had news of a different sort to impart. And her tears were the most bitter yet.

The wail of the siren wasn't any different that night from all the other times it had sounded. Many times already it had brought death and destruction to some part of the city, but never on the scale of that night of 20 March 1941. There was nothing to tell the people who ran to their shelters, or those who shrugged and didn't bother, that tonight was going to be so different.

'Quick. Down to the cellar.' Arthur was halfway downstairs, dragging his trousers on over his pyjamas, his braces dangling. 'Get the little 'uns up.'

'Oh, I'm so *sick* of this.'

Lucy brushed past him on her way up. They had evolved a routine. Maud made for the kitchen where she put on kettles and made flasks of cocoa and tea. Arthur gathered together a bundle of blankets and pillows which were kept ready on the landing. Lucy got the children up and dressed and, together with any guests who were staying, they all made their way down the steps to the dank, cavernous cellar which had only ever been used for storing things that nobody really knew what to do with.

The children had been deeply asleep after their exciting day and were hard to rouse. Patsy, at six, was of an age to be afraid of the snarling drone of the bombers as they approached, and the harsh rattle of the ack-ack gunfire.

She trembled as Lucy pulled her, still barely awake, from the bed, and whimpered.

Geoff was awake in an instant, making ack-ack noises back. He made for the window to look out and Lucy dragged him back sharply. 'Don't be so stupid! You know we mustn't show a light. Do you want them to see us and drop bombs right on top of the house?'

'I was only going to look for a second,' he grumbled. 'It's not fair, you never let me see. I shan't have anything to tell my grandchildren.'

'You won't have any grandchildren to tell if we don't get down to the cellar quickly. Now get dressed and go downstairs to Grampy.' She turned her attention to Zannah, who was snuggling back under the bedclothes. 'Wake up, sweetheart, we've got to go downstairs. Come on, lovey.' She drew the warm body into her arms, feeling a moment of hatred for the enemy who were threatening her children's lives. 'Let's just wrap this blanket round you.'

Zannah yawned and stretched, her heavy eyelids quivering with sleep. Lucy lifted her into her arms and Zannah let her head droop on her mother's shoulder. Pausing now only to snatch up the blanket, Lucy scurried out of the bedroom and down the stairs.

The drone had increased to a roar, drowning out all other sound. As the family and guests crowded down the cellar steps, it throbbed about them, reverberating in the stone walls, shaking the earthen floor, vibrating in the lath and plaster ceilings, in the floorboards, in the joists and in the deepest, most fundamental framework of the whole house. It wouldn't stand it, Lucy thought, the noise itself will shake it to bits, shake us all to bits. And she clamped her hands to her ears and then thought how much worse it must be for the children. She looked at Geoffrey's face, alive with excitement and fear; at Patsy's, white and quivering; and at Zannah's, the colour of ashes, her mouth wide and stretched in a scream of terror that nobody could hear.

61

'Zannah! Oh, Zannah, my baby, my poor, poor baby.' She clasped the little girl against her and reached out for Patsy and Geoffrey, pulling them close. The roar was all about them and even though it seemed to fill the air so that no more sound could possibly find room to be heard, even though it was so loud that you felt you could reach out and touch it, the thuds and crashes of exploding bombs made it seem no more than a whisper, and the family cringed and cowered together beneath the black and heavy weight of it.

It went on for hours. It had been just half past eight in the evening when it had started, and by the time the all-clear sounded and they raised their heads and stared shakily into the gloom of the cellar, it was almost dawn.

'Whatever's happened out there?' Lucy whispered. 'What are we going to find?'

Nobody answered. Maud was huddled on a blanket with Arthur, their hands so tightly clasped that the skin was white and stretched. The two or three guests – a sailor whose ship had put into Devonport for repairs and whose wife had come down from Scotland to spend a few days with him, and an old man who had been bombed out of his home in London – were also crouching on the cold, damp floor against the wall. David was close to Lucy. His arms had been around her and the children all night, but now he moved away slightly and she saw that his face was taut and streaked with tears and dust.

'At least they're out of it now,' she said quietly, touching the arm that had held her so strongly throughout the tumult. 'At least you know they don't have to suffer any more.'

He turned and looked at her as if she were a stranger. Then his face cleared a little, and he nodded. 'Yes. I know they're not afraid and suffering. But – oh, Lucy –'

'I know.' Painfully, she disengaged cramped arms from around the children and stretched stiffened legs. The others were moving too, slowly as if they had forgotten how. One by one, they stood up, moving uncertainly, looking at each other, nobody wanting to be first to go up the cellar steps and see what lay above.

'Come on,' David said, taking hold of himself. 'We can't stay here for ever. I'll go first. We'll need to be careful . . .'

Nobody asked why care was needed. Even little Zannah knew that there might be no house above them now, that nothing but wreckage might await them, that they might not even be able to open the cellar door. We might be buried alive here, Lucy thought with a sudden sick fear.

David and the sailor went up the cellar steps together and when they pushed gently on the door it swung open, and they saw to their relief that everything seemed just as usual above.

'Oh, thank God,' Maud kept saying as they moved through the rooms. 'Oh, thank God, thank God . . .'

The rooms were heavily curtained. No light filtered through, yet they seemed faintly lit by a dim redness, a glow that was perhaps a particularly fiery sunrise. And in the silence, that had seemed so absolute after the planes had gone at last and the explosions ceased and the rattle of ack-ack stopped, could be heard a growing hum, a more subdued kind of roar, like the voice of a giant beast woken from slumber and still half-snoring.

'I think it's light enough to open the blackouts,' David said quietly, and Lucy turned out the lights while he pulled back the curtains and then lifted the wooden frame away from the living-room window.

There was a moment of silence. The red, flickering glow flooded into the room. There was daylight in it, though not much yet, but the daylight was lost in the ferocity of the crimson and orange and black of the flames that burned over Plymouth after the destruction of that night.

'Spooners has gone,' Arthur said later. He and David had gone out, picking their way through the debris, trying to

63

make sense of this new, flattened Plymouth. 'Spooner's, and the Royal Hotel, and God knows what else. Derry's Clock's still there, but you can't make out where you are, half the time. There's bits of buildings – you can recognise some, but then there's others that don't look like anything at all. And some have just gone, nothing but rubble left. You couldn't even say there was *streets*, let alone buildings. And there's still fires burning and firemen trying to put 'em out, and miles and miles of hosepipes. We gave up and come home, there wasn't no use trying to get through it all.'

'We were just in the way,' David said. He looked exhausted, Lucy thought, and she knew that his own grief was very close to the surface. He had seen what London had been like, what his own home had suffered, and the pictures of Heather and Stevie, and Heather's mother and grand-mother, were still vivid in his mind. She laid her hand over his and wondered if he had noticed. 'I should have helped . . . I ought to have been able to do something.'

He had come back because he was worried about Arthur. The older man had looked ill and grey, the skin around his mouth a bluish white. He looked better now he was back, with a cup of tea in front of him, but his breathing was still ragged. He ought to see the doctor, Lucy thought, but what doctor would be holding surgeries this morning?

David got up suddenly. 'I'll go and see if there's anything I can do. I can't sit here.'

'But what can you do? What can anyone do?' Maud was in tears again. She had started crying when David had first opened the curtains to reveal the glow of flames as the city burned. 'It's all up – they've beaten us. We can't –' She sat upright in her chair, her body quivering, tears running down her face.

Lucy spoke sharply. 'Don't talk like that, Mum. We're not beaten. London, Pompey, Coventry, Liverpool – they've all been through this, and so've a lot more places, and *they're* not whining about being beaten. So don't let's hear any more talk like that, if you don't mind.' She looked at David, knowing he had to go. 'You'll be careful, won't you?'

He nodded wearily and she felt a sharp stab of pity for him. He had lost so much. 'We're still here for you,' she said quietly. 'You matter a lot to us, David.'

He looked at her, and still she wasn't sure that he really saw her. 'There may be people,' he said. 'People buried . . . I must go and help.'

They heard him stumble along the passage and out of the front door. It closed behind him, leaving only the sounds of Arthur's ragged breathing, and Maud's quiet sobs.

Chapter Six

David spent the day in the devastated streets, scrabbling under piles of rubble for the bodies of survivors. In many places, the fires were still burning, defeating the firefighters' efforts to put them out, and no one could get near. Too often, the bodies he did find were of those who had not survived, and he came home that evening white and shaking from what he had seen.

They spent the second night, as they had spent the first, crouching in the cellar beneath the house, listening to the holocaust as it burst above them.

'How long can we go on like this?' Lucy whispered. 'All our cities destroyed – they're tearing the heart out of Britain. We'll never be able to get back to normal.'

'Don't let's say "never",' he murmured, and she knew what it must cost him to say that, when he had lost so much already. 'We've got to get through it somehow. Nothing will ever be the same again – but we've got to survive, or there's no point in any of it.'

They came out next morning, fear gripping their hearts as they took down the blackout. There was hardly a window left with glass in it. The splinters were buried in the fabric of the curtains, shards that were too grimed with smoke and dust even to glitter. Amidst the flames that still burned were billowing clouds of black, oily smoke that blotted out the orange glow. And as the daylight grew stronger and the sun's rays managed to penetrate the gloom, they could see that a thick pall of dust hung over the entire city.

Lucy left the children with Maud and Arthur and went

with David to see the damage. Little as she desired to look at the destruction, something in her wanted desperately to understand it, to share the horror of the experience with those who had lost everything they possessed. It was the same desire that she had felt after the blitz on Portsmouth, a need to share it with her family. But she hadn't been able to go then, and she'd had to rely on her mother's letters, the newspapers and the BBC news for information. Now, she could see it for herself, and knew that all the terrible stories she had heard were merely the tip of an horrific iceberg.

Together, with others who had come out to stare in stupefaction, they wandered aimlessly through streets that had once been familiar and were now the stuff of nightmare.

Many of the buildings had simply been blown apart by the bombs and great craters pocked the ground while bricks and blocks of concrete and girders of wood and steel lay strewn around them. In some places, it was impossible to see where the road had been and where the buildings had stood. Of the walls that remained standing, most were crumbling and broken, their roofs smashed and caving in. A few bits of furniture hung at crazy angles and possessions lay mixed together, some broken beyond any hope of repair, others inexplicably untouched.

Other buildings had been set on fire, and in many of them the flames still raged. As before, the streets were a tangle of hosepipes and the firemen, white with exhaustion beneath the grime, were battling grimly to contain flames that had been out of control for hours and would never be contained but must, in the end, be left to burn themselves out.

'Plymouth's gone,' Lucy said, staring at the inferno. 'Plymouth has gone for ever.'

But Plymouth had not gone.

Much of it had been destroyed. The centre, the tangle of streets, the great shops – Spooner's, Dingle's, Jay's the furniture store, and many others – were smashed to pieces. Drake's Circus had been completely burned out. Old Town Street, Cornwall Street, George Street, Union Street and the Octagon – all had been devastated. Charles Church and St Andrew's Church – the cathedral of the city – were gutted shells.

It was said that the fire had been so intense that gold in a jeweller's shop window had melted and run away down the gutters.

But some buildings still stood, inexplicably untouched amongst the ruins. Derry's Clock still ticked defiantly on its tower, a landmark for those bewildered by the desecration of the city. Leicester Harmsworth House, where the newspapers were produced, still stood in Frankfort Street, surrounded by wreckage. And in those shops and offices which remained, people still went to work, picking their way through rubble to get there.

For a fortnight they were left in peace to collect themselves. Help came from all over the country: firemen already worn out with the bitter experiences of fighting the raids in their own cities, arrived to help Plymouth in her hour of need. Bulldozers came to help clear the streets, and builders and roadworkers to make the damaged buildings safe. Burst water pipes and gas mains were repaired, electricity restored. It all took time and people were forced to struggle on without for days that looked like stretching into weeks or even longer. Nevertheless once their initial shock was over, the Plymouthians bounced back, refusing to be beaten. Like those others in similarly hit cities in other parts of the country, they thumbed their noses at Hitler.

David went back to London. Before he left he hugged everyone in the family, promising to come back soon, making them promise to take care of themselves. 'Go down to the cellar every night,' he said. 'Never mind whether there's a warning or not. Just go.'

They did, for the first few nights, but the cellar was cold

and damp, and as the warning siren remained silent night after night, they began to hope that the enemy had abandoned Plymouth. There wasn't much left to bomb, after all.

'If we could only leave a few mattresses down there it wouldn't be so bad,' Maud complained, 'but they'd be covered in mould in a week. And it isn't doing Arthur's chest no good, having to spend all night in that damp atmosphere.'

'I still think David's right,' Lucy said. 'We just don't know when they'll come back.'

Inevitably there came a night when Arthur refused to go. He had a bad cold, and he blamed the nights in the cellar for it. 'It'll be pneumonia if I goes down there tonight, and it'll be the death of me. I'd rather die in me own bed.'

Maud wouldn't leave him, so Lucy took the children down by herself. There were no guests in the hotel now. They dragged a mattress down the stairs and lay there alone in a corner of the dank little dungeon, watching the flickering light of the hurricane lamp on the green-patched walls.

'I don't like it,' Patsy whimpered. 'I don't like it down here by ourselves.'

'I don't see why we have to come,' Geoff said grumpily. 'Grampy and Grammy have stayed in bed. Why can't we?'

'You know what Uncle David said.' Lucy would rather have been upstairs in bed herself. 'There might be another raid, and you know how bad they've been.'

'There hasn't been for ages. Not for *weeks*.' He poked with his finger at the skin forming on his cup of cocoa. 'Why can't we go out to Dartmoor, then, if it's so dangerous here? Lots of people do. Billy Madge's mum and dad do, they go out every night and take their tent. Billy says it's smashing, just like real camping. There's lots of people go.'

'We haven't got a tent.' Lucy knew about the thousands of people who trekked out of the city each night. They slept where they could, with or without tents. She'd thought about it, thought about going out to Yelverton or Tavistock, or perhaps to Ivybridge. Or just getting on a train and getting off at some tiny station – Clearbrook or Whitchurch, perhaps – and finding shelter where she could. But it wasn't as easy as that. You had to get everything together, you had to make your way back next morning – it took half the day, just going and coming back. And she didn't like the idea of sheltering in some barn or under a hedge in all the cold of night and the bad weather, with all sorts of people about.

'This cellar's safe enough. As long as we're down here we're all—'

The wail of the siren interrupted her and she gasped and grabbed for the children's hands. They clutched each other, even Geoff's bravado gone as they listened to the familiar snarl of the approaching planes.

'Oh no,' Lucy whispered, and gathered Zannah close against her heart. 'Oh, not again. Not again, not again . . .'

It was several minutes before she thought of Arthur and Maud.

'Grammy and Grampy,' she gasped. 'They're still upstairs. Why haven't they come down?'

'Perhaps the house has been bombed,' Geoff suggested, and she was so terrified that he might be right that she cuffed him sharply.

'Don't say such things!' Gently, she shifted Zannah from her lap on to the mattress. 'I'll go and fetch them. They mustn't stay up there.'

'Don't go and leave us alone!' Patsy was obviously terrified. 'Mummy, please –'

'I've got to fetch them. I can't leave them.'

'*Mummy* –'

'I'll only be a minute.' She tried to unpick Patsy's fingers. Zannah was clinging too. 'Let go – let *go* –'

'I'm coming too –'

'*I'm* coming –'

'*No!* Stay here – I'll be back before you know I'm gone. Geoff, look after them. Patsy, do as Geoff tells you – look after your sister.'

'*Mummy!*'

The crash of a bomb almost immediately overhead obliterated Lucy's voice and the voices of the three children. Almost without knowing it, she was up the cellar steps, only half aware that the children were close behind her. The bomb did not seem to have fallen on the house, but the walls were crumbling, sheets of plaster dropping away as she ran panic-stricken up the main stairs towards the bedrooms, and she could hear the roar of fire from somewhere outside, and the crash of breaking glass.

'Mum, Dad – where are you? Why haven't you come down?' She was aware suddenly of someone behind her, of the light from a torch throwing her shadow on the walls, and she jerked round. 'Whatever are you—*David!*'

He stood a step or two below her, lowering the torch so that the beam did not shine in her face. 'I came in on the last train. The raid hadn't started – Lucy, why aren't you in the cellar? What are you all doing up here?'

She looked past him at the children, crowding past to clutch at her skirt. 'I told you to stay downstairs. I *told* you.' She looked helplessly at David. 'I came to fetch Mum and Dad. They wouldn't come down. I don't know why they haven't come out of their room.' Half fearfully, she looked back up towards the bedroom door. 'I can't leave them there.'

'Go down. Take the children down.' He pushed past them. 'I'll bring them. They're probably still asleep.'

'In *this*?' But Lucy knew that the two older people had managed to sleep through a number of the raids, and that Arthur had started to use earplugs. It was quite possible

71

that both were lying there, their ears stuffed with cottonwool, oblivious of the uproar in the skies.

'Go on. Go downstairs. Get the children out of this.' He gave her a push. There was another explosion, closer than before, and the house shook. Lucy heard a crash from one of the rooms, as if something heavy – a wardrobe or a dresser – had toppled over. She felt a scream rise in her throat and stumbled down the stairs, dragging the children with her.

'Quick. Back in the cellar.' They were at the foot of the stairs now, only yards from the cellar door. It stood open, the darkness of the steps yawning below. And as Lucy blundered towards it, it seemed to lift away from its hinges and hang trembling in air that had become suddenly visible, a shimmering curtain of darkness shot with blinding white light. The stairs themselves lifted away and hovered for a moment before falling slowly back into place. The walls became fluid, billowing outwards with the flimsiness of net curtains blowing in a fierce wind, and the wallpaper fluttered and was shredded to a million tiny flakes. The house was filled with a sharp, hot wind that brought with it a flash of light, like a bright, gleaming sword, and screamed a banshee scream before it fled away into the night. In an instant of clarity Lucy felt she understood everything: the secret of the world, of the universe, of life itself, and she knew that she had seen what men since time began had seen, and what they had described as the Angel of Death.

The explosion came last of all. But Lucy did not hear its sound.

The house was not completely gutted. Enough rooms were left habitable for the family to live in, and the experts said that rebuilding would be possible. Nobody knew when it would be possible – there was already far too much rebuilding needed in the city for anyone to give a date or make any promises – but the walls could be shored up and the torn roof patched, and the doors and windows replaced so that what was left could be made secure.

Arthur and Maud had both been saved. They had woken shortly before the bomb had fallen and had been struggling into their clothes even as David and Lucy met on the stairs. Arthur's hand had been on the doorknob when the explosion had shaken the house and the blast flung him across the room, landing mercifully on the bed. Maud, sitting down to put on her shoes, had been narrowly missed by a shard of glass as big as a spear, which had impaled the pillow where, only ten minutes earlier, her head had been resting.

David had saved Geoffrey's life, and Patsy's too. Seeing that Arthur and Maud were all right, he had turned his attention to the children. The blast had scattered their bodies over the passageway but Geoff was already staggering to his feet, blinking and holding his head. He looked up at David and his eyes filled with tears.

'I didn't mean it to happen. I didn't mean it.'

'Of course you didn't, old chap. It's not your fault.'

'I should have done what Mum said. I should have stayed in the cellar.'

'It doesn't matter.' David's eyes were on the ceiling above Geoffrey's head. He spoke quietly. 'Just go over by the front door, old son, will you? Just go and wait for me there.'

'I want Mum.'

'By the door, Geoff.' David's voice was tight. He came slowly down the stairs and moved towards the two girls, lying huddled by their mother's body. 'Go on now, there's a good chap.' The ceiling above the stairwell was shaking, the walls buckling slowly outwards. Off the stairs now, he quickened his steps, moving swiftly down the hall to the three huddled bodies. *'Geoffrey!'*

The boy was beside him, catching his sleeve. David felt his panic and bit back the anger that was born of his own

73

fear. The boy was only eight or nine years old . . . He bent and touched the three faces, feeling their warmth. Please God they were still alive. He could hear the creaking, tearing sounds of wood being pulled apart. The stairs. The walls. The ceiling. He flung a glance of dread and apprehension upwards, caught a glimpse of Arthur and Maud stumbling down, yelled at them to get out, away from the stairs that were about to give way, away from the walls and the ceiling that were about to come crashing down. He grasped Lucy's shoulder and dragged her along the floor, brought her to the front door just as Arthur wrenched it open, ran back for the girls. Geoff was in his way and he thrust him out, then bent towards the two crumpled bodies, lifting both in his arms, turning to stagger back along the passage, towards the open door, towards the red and flickering heat that was pouring in from the street.

The walls buckled and the ceiling drooped, slowly, like a bellying hammock slung between the rafters. The stairs folded inwards and crashed. A beam dropped from somewhere high in the roof. It fell across David's path and caught him a stunning blow across the shoulders. It knocked the two girls from his arms and he fell across their bodies, pinned to them by the long and heavy slab of wood.

When Lucy was well enough to hear what had happened, they told her that David had a broken shoulder and had lost his left arm. Her daughter Patsy was in another part of the hospital. Her back had been injured and it was unlikely that she would ever be able to walk again.

Zannah – her baby Zannah – had been killed outright.

Chapter Seven

When Lucy looked back at that time, after the war had ended and before Wilmot returned, she thought of it as the lowest point of her entire life. Nothing, she thought, could be any worse than that moment when they told her that Patsy was crippled and Zannah, her lovely Zannah, killed.

It was as if darkness had descended on the world, a great engulfing blanket of solid blackness that swallowed everything it touched. She moved in an enshrouding fog which barely parted to let her through, and there was no light, not even the tiniest flickering pinpoint of light, to show her the way. The fog dulled sound as well, so that she couldn't properly hear what was said to her, couldn't make sense of the noises she heard, and her ears were offended by laughter and music so that she shut them out and ignored them. Her only interest, as she slowly and reluctantly awoke to life around her, was in the war news, and she listened avidly to reports of air-raids and battles at sea, and followed on a map the advances of the German forces in Europe, stabbing little black-headed pins in to show where the Front was at its most active.

'I don't like it,' Maud said to Arthur. 'It's not healthy. It's morbid.'

'I don't know what we can do about it,' he said. 'I've tried. I told her, it's the living you ought to be bothering yourself about now, maid, not the dead. They're safe enough. It's that little Patsy who needs her mum, and young Geoff. But she just looked at me as if she didn't know what I was talking about.'

Maud shook her head. 'It's the worst thing that can happen to a woman, losing a child. And Zannah was like a little princess. We all miss her.'

''Course we do. 'Course we miss her. But Patsy and Geoff are the ones that need their mum now – specially Patsy, poor little toad.'

Patsy had been brought home from hospital. There was nothing more that could be done for her, the doctors said, and she lay propped in a bed brought down into the living-room, staring out of the window during the day and reading or listening to the wireless in the evenings. Geoff played games with her when he was home from school, but Patsy tired quickly. She suffered from headaches and asked for the curtains to be drawn because the light hurt her eyes. At eight o'clock she was carried into the small room next door that had been used as a store-room and was now converted to a bedroom for her to use, and when there was an air-raid warning she was carried down the cellar steps.

The main stairs had been replaced. The blast had done no more than rip them from their roots and bring down a ceiling with them, leaving most of the rooms intact. By the time Lucy came home from hospital, the house had been patched up a bit, and when Patsy returned it was taking guests again. There were still people coming to Plymouth, needing accommodation, and the few rooms that Maud and Arthur kept open were nearly always full. But the work of just these few rooms kept them as busy as if the whole building were packed night after night, and they looked to Lucy to help.

'It's not the bed-making and washing, that's the same as ever it was,' Maud said. 'It's the shopping. Getting their ration books and standing in queues hour after hour and trying to get stuff to make a decent dinner of an evening and a breakfast to send them out with. And we couldn't even do that at first, what with all the gas being cut off all over the city.' She sighed and rubbed her face wearily. 'And you can't get a girl to come in and work now, they're all off doing war work, joining the Forces or going into munitions or driving buses – there's no end to it all. They're even talking of putting them in the dockyard.'

'I can't help it, Mum. I'm just so tired all the time. And Patsy takes up a lot of my time, you know that.'

Maud did know. Patsy wanted a lot of attention these days, and you couldn't blame her. It was terrible for a kiddy to have to spend her days in a bed, looking out of the window at the others, or in what was no better than a pram. And knowing she'd never be any different, that was the worst of it. Nothing but a lifetime of just sitting and being wheeled about.

'All the same, there's a war on,' she said. 'I know it seems awful, Lucy, but we've all got to pick ourselves up somehow and carry on.'

David said the same when he came to see them. He spent less time in hospital than they'd expected, considering he'd lost an arm, but it was a while before he came back to Plymouth. He'd gone down to Cornwall to stay with his auntie, taking his mother with him, and he came up in the train one day. It was in the middle of May, not long after Mr Churchill had come to Plymouth. Churchill had driven through the streets in an open car, perched up on the back of it so that everyone would get a good view, and he'd waved his cigar and made the V-sign. Arthur was still talking about it.

'Didn't know he was coming till half an hour before,' he told David. 'The police went round in a van, telling folk. Well, a lot of 'em were on their way out for the night – getting on for four o'clock, it was – so there weren't that many crowds, but those of us that did stop got a proper sight of him. And he got a proper sight of us too, and of Plymouth. You could see he was upset. Tears in his eyes, they said he had. "God bless you all," he said. I heard him with my own ears. "God bless you all."'

77

'His wife looked proper smart,' Maud said. 'I was surprised – I mean, he's no oil-painting, is he? You can see why they call him the British bulldog. But she's lovely, and she was dressed lovely too, a spotted fur coat – snow leopard, it said in the paper – and a scarf over her head with bits of his speeches printed on it. I thought that was handsome.'

'Mind you, not everyone was pleased – got a bit superstitious about it, some did. Thought there'd be a raid that night, like when the King and Queen came. But there wasn't. I don't reckon Hitler's got the nerve to bomb old Winnie!'

'And how's Lucy?' David asked when their reminiscences had run dry. There'd been no sign of her since he had arrived, and he was afraid that she didn't want to see him. He hadn't heard from her since the raid, and had been torturing himself by thinking that perhaps she blamed him for Patsy's injury and, worse still, for Zannah's death.

Maud and Arthur exchanged glances.

'Well, she's well enough in herself,' Maud said. 'I mean, she had a bit of a knock on the head and a few bruises here and there, nothing much to make a song and dance about, and they're all healed up. But she's taken it bad, there's no saying otherwise, and she don't seem able to pull herself out of it somehow. I've told her, there's many have had to suffer as bad and worse, and we can't all sit about crying all the time – not that she does, it might be better if she did have a good cry and let it all out, but she—' Maud stopped abruptly and flushed scarlet. 'Oh, I'm *sorry*. I forgot you'd lost your little one just the same. And Heather too. Oh, what must you be thinking of me!'

David shrugged and made a wry grimace. 'Don't worry, Maud. You're right. There are a lot of us going through the same thing. That's why I wanted to see Lucy. It sometimes helps to be with someone who – well, who's been through it too.'

Maud nodded. She rested her eyes on his empty sleeve, pinned up on his shoulder. 'And how are you keeping yourself? It's a bad job, that.'

'Bad enough,' he agreed, 'But at least it's not my right arm. I've still got the useful one! Mind, you don't realise just how much you use an arm till it's not there any more – not to mention the fingers and thumb. I've had to learn a lot of new tricks.'

The door opened and Lucy came in. She stopped when she saw David and hesitated for a moment. Her face whitened and then the colour came flooding back and tears sprang to her eyes. She ran the last few steps and flung herself into his one-armed embrace, weeping against his chest.

'David! Oh, *David*.'

'It's all right,' he said softly, holding her firmly against him. 'It's all right, Lucy. I'm here. I'm here. Just cry it out, now, just cry it out. It'll make you feel better. You will feel better.'

'I'll never feel better,' she sobbed. 'David, didn't they tell you? Zannah—'

'I know. I know about Zannah.'

'And Patsy – she'll never be able to walk again. Oh, David, it's not fair, it's not fair.'

'I know. War isn't fair to anyone. *Life* isn't fair. But we all expect it to be. That's why it comes as such a shock when we find out the truth.'

'Why Zannah?' Lucy whispered. 'Why did it have to be her? She was such a lovely little girl, David.'

He said nothing, just kept stroking her shoulders with his one hand. Maud and Arthur got up and quietly left the room. David drew Lucy down into a chair and pulled another close. He placed his arm around her shoulders again and she leant her head on his shoulder.

'I don't think I can bear it, David, I don't think I can go on living.'

'Of course you can,' he said firmly. 'Of course you'll go on living. You've got Patsy and Geoff depending on you. And Wilmot. What do you think he's going to say if he comes home and you're not here? If you haven't waited for him.'

'I want to. I want to be here, but – it's so hard. It hurts so much. I don't think –'

'Listen,' he said, and cupped his hand under her chin, making her look into his face. 'Listen to me, Lucy. I *know* how much it hurts. I *know*. And I've gone on living. Don't you think there have been times when I've felt like this too? When I've felt the pain was just too much to bear? And do you know what I tell myself when it gets too bad?' She shook her head. 'Shall I tell you?' He waited for her answer.

'Yes, please, David,' she whispered at last.

'I think of the people who will be even more hurt if I stop living. My mother. My aunt. *You*. Your children, Arthur, Maud, even Wilmot who's away fighting, risking his life for us. And others, people you don't know, friends and family who are less important to me, but who would all be affected in some way, however small. And who am I to say how small the effect would be?' He looked at her for a moment and then said quietly, 'My pain would be ended, but theirs – well, whatever pain they already have, I would just be adding to it. Spreading mine around all of them, all of *you*. I don't think I have any right to do that, Lucy. I think it's my job to keep that particular pain to myself.'

Lucy was silent. Then she said, 'And it's my job to keep mine.'

'Do you think so?' David asked. 'I'm not saying I'm right, Lucy. It's just what I believe.'

'I know. But Zannah – I'm not the only one, David. There's Wilmot, and all the rest of the family. And Patsy, she's like a ghost. And even Geoff – he's not the same. It's hurting them too.'

'And will it hurt them any the less if they lose you as well?' he asked, and she bowed her head.

They sat quietly for a while, then Lucy said, 'I'm a selfish pig, David. You went through all this and you lost your wife as well as your baby. And I haven't even asked about your arm.'

'My arm?' he said lightly, shrugging so that the stump, reaching halfway to where the elbow ought to have been, moved. 'Oh, I haven't seen it for a few weeks now. Ask about the rest of my body.'

Lucy laughed, and the unexpected sound seemed to warm the air. She lifted her head and looked at him, then gave him a crumpled grin and rubbed the back of her hand across her nose. 'I really have been a selfish pig, haven't I?'

'No,' he said. 'No, you haven't. Not at all. You've been an ordinary young woman who's gone through a terrible time.'

'But there are so many people going through just the same. Worse.'

'And they all hurt just as much as you. We all suffer the same, Lucy. We just have to get through it as best we can, and nobody has any right to tell us how we should do it.'

'All the same,' she said, 'this is war. We can't give way. We've got to carry on, like you said. We can't let Hitler beat us.'

David smiled and took her hand. 'That's the stuff.'

'I shan't let him beat me,' she said seriously. 'For a while, I thought he had. But I'm not going to let him do it. None of us is going to let him do it. We won't give in to him, David. We won't.' For a few minutes, she was silent again, as if summoning all her strength to fight this new and so much harder battle. And then she looked at him again and smiled. 'Well, come on, then, David. Tell me about the rest of your body . . .'

Slowly, Lucy dragged herself out of the despondent slough into which she had fallen immediately after

Zannah's death. There really was too much to do, she told herself, to give in. And it was up to everyone to make it clear, in whatever way they could, that they were *not* giving in. That was the answer, she thought. Show people. Show Hitler. Show them all.

That was why someone had gone down to St Andrew's church the day after it had been bombed. The roof had been blasted away, although the walls still stood, and the bells hung undamaged in the tower. And over the main door someone had hung a plank of wood with the single word '*Resurgam*' carved roughly on it.

Rise again, Lucy thought. That's what that person had been saying. We'll rise again, all of us. We won't give in.

'Come on,' she said, going into Patsy's bedroom on 1 June. 'We're going out. We're going up on the Hoe, dressed up in all our best clothes, and we're going to show everyone that we're not beaten.'

Patsy turned from the window and stared at her. 'On the Hoe? In our best clothes? But why?'

'I told you. We're going to show Hitler we won't be beaten.'

'But he won't see us. It's only people round here who'll see us.'

'I know. And they're the ones who matter.' Lucy knelt beside her daughter's bed. 'You see, if we look miserable we make other people miserable. But if we smile and look bright and cheerful – why, that helps them to feel better. And it spreads, like ripples when you throw a stone into a pool of water. And if we start it off this morning – and other people do it as well – well, it could spread as far as Hitler himself in the end. And that's how we can show him we won't be beaten. Just think, if everyone did it—'

'The war would stop,' Patsy said. 'It would just stop.'

She held up her arms for Lucy to remove her nightie and wash her. Lucy dressed her in a summer frock she hadn't worn since last year, a favourite that had been just a little bit

82

too big and now fitted perfectly. For a moment, she felt a lump in her throat, thinking of Patsy as she had been when she last wore that frock, running along the grassy Hoe, laughing and playing tag with Geoff and Zannah. The tears stung her eyes and she brushed them away impatiently.

She didn't think the war would come to an end just because she and Patsy went walking on the Hoe, but who knew what great effects stemmed from small beginnings? And it had to be better than looking miserable.

It was all she could do, after all. All she could do, and the least she could do.

Chapter Eight

The worst of the blitz was over. As May passed into June, and June into July, and the blazing days of summer softened to the mellowness of autumn and then the first sharp frosts of winter, the raids grew more sporadic and less intense. There was still damage done, still people injured and killed, but there were no more nights of terror spent listening to the incessant, unbearable barrage of explosions, and no more dawns of fire.

'Us mustn't sit back and think it's all over, all the same,' Arthur said. 'There's still a war going on, and the Germans won't leave us in peace till it's finished with.'

Peace! It was a word from an age gone by, a word from fairytale. Lucy could scarcely believe that there had once been a time when she and Wilmot had strolled arm in arm on the Hoe and gone swimming in the little rockpools. She looked down at the big semicircular pool that had been opened soon after she'd first come to Plymouth, and thought of how she'd taught Wilmot to swim, how he'd raced her and won. How they'd taken Geoff and Patsy across the Cremyll ferry to Cawsand and played with them on the beach. How they'd caught the train out to Yelverton, even as far as Princetown once, and walked on the moor and picnicked in the heather.

She hadn't liked Princetown much. It was a gloomy place, its houses all grey and uniform – prison officers' houses, Wilmot said – and she hated the huge stone prison itself, a great barracks of a place with hundreds of windows. There must be prisoners behind each of those windows, thieves and murderers, and she loathed the idea that they were there, looking out at her and the children.

She wondered now what it was like to be in prison during a war.

She wrote to Wilmot every day, even if it was no more than a line or two before she said goodnight. Letters came sporadically from him. He couldn't say much but she guessed he was in the Mediterranean, and then, after Pearl Harbor, in the Far East.

By the middle of April 1942, a year after the bombing that had killed Zannah and left Patsy in her wheelchair, the news was all of a new battle – the Battle of the Java Sea. The *Exeter*, it seemed, was fated to be involved in these great sea encounters. This time, however it seemed the *Exeter* was fated altogether.

Lucy was in Portsmouth when the news came through. She sat white faced in her mother's back room and listened to the wireless. Patsy was lying in her grandfather's big armchair, her legs propped on a little wooden stool he had made for her. Geoff, now ten years old, was playing with some old Meccano that had once belonged to Vic.

'*Exeter*'s gone down,' she whispered through lips that suddenly refused to move properly. 'Mum, did you hear that? They've sunk the *Exeter*.'

'It could be just a rumour,' Emily said. There had been rumours like that before. But they both knew it wasn't. The BBC was very careful about the news it broadcast and never told you anything that wasn't true. 'And the men could have been saved. There were other ships about as well.'

Despite her words, Emily was as frightened as Lucy. They sat close together, their arms about each other, listening. Geoff, sensing something wrong, looked up and opened his mouth to speak, but Lucy shushed him with a quick flap of her hand.

There had been three ships lost, they heard then and later, as more news filtered through. HMS *Encounter* had gone, and an American ship, the USS *Pope*. It had been a tremendous battle, and *Exeter* had already been hit and damaged when she was caught between four enemy cruisers. She had no power left, and no chance against such force.

'But what about the men?' Lucy asked desperately. She asked the question again the next day, and the next, but there was no answer. Nobody knew what had become of the sailors aboard her.

'They think a lot survived,' Joe said, reading the *Daily Express*. 'They think they managed to get ashore. They were probably taken prisoner. We'll hear soon.' But no word came, and Lucy went back to Plymouth not knowing, once again, whether she were widow or wife.

'I can't bear to think about it,' she said to David. 'And I can't *stop* thinking about it. I think of him going down on the ship, swallowed up in the water.' She shuddered. 'There'd be sharks, wouldn't there? And then I think about him trying to swim about, trying to stay afloat . . .' She remembered his words to her before the war, when she'd discovered he couldn't swim. *If the ship went down, I'd probably be a thousand miles from land anyway* . . . 'And even if he did get ashore – what happened then? Did they just wander about in the jungle?' She had only a vague idea of what the jungle might be like, and pictured tigers stalking through dense, tropical undergrowth, and snakes rearing broad, vicious heads and spitting venom from hissing mouths. 'Or did they get caught? And if they were caught, why hasn't anyone let us know? They're supposed to let people know, isn't that one of the rules?'

'The Japanese don't follow the rules,' David said grimly. Nobody had wanted to believe this to start with, but it had been growing increasingly clear. Some of their prisoners had been allowed to write home, more as a sop to international demands than anything else, but the cards and letters had been little more than brief scrawls, all saying much the same thing – that the prisoners were being treated well. And this was something that fewer and fewer people now believed.

'You hear such awful stories,' Lucy said. 'We don't know what they might be doing to them, David. I can't bear to think of Wilmot being – being *tortured*.'

It was a year before they heard from Wilmot, a year during which Lucy lived with a gnawing anxiety that couldn't be ignored or forgotten. Outwardly, she continued as normal, hiding her fear with a ready smile and keeping a joke always on her lips. She had never forgotten David's remarks about pain; that if you didn't keep it to yourself, it would be passed on to everyone else, and would multiply as they in turn passed it to others. She came to see her own anguish as something to be kept imprisoned in her own heart. Like the men in Princetown, it must be incarcerated where it could do least harm.

When the telegram finally arrived, she could not believe it. She stood with the buff envelope in her hand, staring at the scrappy piece of paper with its uneven lettering, shaking her head, the tears running down her face. After a moment, she felt the weakness in her legs and sat down on a kitchen chair.

'He's safe. He's alive. He's a prisoner. He's *alive*.'

Arthur had yelled up the stairs for Maud as soon as he saw the telegraph boy's red bike propped against the kerb. She came running down and they both stared at Lucy, who was still clutching the sheet of paper. Arthur reached over and took it out of her fingers.

'She's right. He's alive. Our Wilmot – he's a prisoner. He'll be coming home. Once this lot's over, *he'll be coming home*.'

'I knew it,' Maud breathed. 'I knew my boy couldn't be dead.'

They hugged each other, she and Arthur who scarcely ever touched each other in public, then Arthur went over to the cupboard where they kept the medicines, and the half bottle of whisky.

'I reckon this calls for a bit of a celebration.'

None of them particularly liked whisky, unless it was in one of Maud's hot toddies, made for colds and coughs, but they sipped at the thimblefuls he poured into sherry glasses, and choked a bit and wiped their eyes and laughed. It relieved the tension. Lucy even held out her glass for more, and Arthur gave her a reproving look.

'Now then, maid. No need to turn to the bottle now.' But he poured a drop more, just enough to wet the bottom of the glass, and she tipped it into her mouth. 'Where are the children? We ought to tell them their dad's safe.'

There was no need to ask where Patsy was. She was in her room, reading one of Lucy's old storybooks, *The Phoenix and the Carpet*. Patsy had taken to reading a lot, and her appetite for books was voracious. Her present book was about a family of children who had found a magical creature and a magic carpet to go with it. It was as if she had discovered the joys of travelling by imagination, now that she could no longer do so physically.

Geoffrey was a different matter. Now eleven years old, he was seldom indoors. With other boys, he roamed the ruined streets, clambering on heaps of rubble, making dens in bombed-out houses. It was useless to warn him of the dangers, useless to forbid or punish. He was a growing boy, hungry for adventure, and the streets of Plymouth, ripped apart by war, were an adventure playground.

The only person who had any influence with him was David. David had saved his life that night when the house had been bombed and Zannah killed. He had dragged him clear just as the heavy beam came crashing down, had taken the blow himself and lost his own arm. David was a hero, with the hero's badge of an empty sleeve, and Geoff worshipped him.

David's visits were infrequent, however. He was kept

busy in London mostly and came to Plymouth about once a month, usually staying no more than a night or two, taking the opportunity whenever he could to go on down to Cornwall to see his mother and aunt.

'Where is that boy?' Arthur demanded impatiently now. He was still holding the telegram in his hand. 'He ought to be here. Here's his dad in a prison camp and *he's* out running the streets. You ought to keep a firmer hand on him, Lucy.'

'He's a boy. He's got to have his freedom.' But neither of them had the heart for this well-chewed bone of contention. The whisky was warming them, along with the knowledge that Wilmot had survived the sinking of the *Exeter*.

Next day, it was all over the papers. Pictures of the ship, sailing from Plymouth, the story of the hunting of the *Graf Spee* all over the South Atlantic until she was trapped in Montevideo harbour and scuttled by her captain. The story of the *Exeter* sinking a year ago in the fearsome battle of the Java Sea, and the long silence before news came of the miraculous survival of her crew.

There was plenty of cause for celebration. The men hadn't, after all, been eaten alive by sharks. They hadn't been machine-gunned in the water, nor run down by Japanese ships. They hadn't struggled desperately until the waves closed over their heads and they were drowned.

'It's a miracle,' Lucy said, the relief flooding through her in great sweeping waves. 'Oh Dad, it's a real miracle.'

'You're right, maid.' He lifted his glass. 'You're right.'

They smiled at each other and touched their glasses together, and Maud began to sing 'Pack up your troubles in your old kit bag – and smile, smile, smile.'

None of them, just at that moment, gave much thought to the reports of what was happening to the men in those Japanese prisoner-of-war camps.

Chapter Nine

By the time the news about the *Exeter* survivors had been received, the war had progressed on several different fronts.

Japan had rolled over the Far East like a mighty tank. Singapore had already fallen. Now Hong Kong had been taken, and in Parliament members listened appalled to the stories told them by Anthony Eden of the terrible atrocities the Japanese had committed there. Soldiers bound hand and foot before being bayoneted to death, nurses raped and tortured, civilians butchered . . . The stories went on, each one more sickening than the last. It was almost impossible to believe the evil that had been unleashed upon the world, and impossible to believe that it would ever end.

'Once this sort of thing's started, how is it ever going to be stopped?' Lucy asked in despair. 'It's everywhere. It's like a horrible plague, all over the world, and every country's being infected. I don't see how it can ever be stopped.'

David was with her. They had taken the children up to the Hoe, and stood there on the broad, grassy expanse, staring at the grey waters of the Sound. Somewhere out there, thousands of miles beyond the horizon, was Wilmot. What was he suffering under the rule of these barbaric people?

Geoffrey had other problems. Sweets had been put on ration last summer and they hadn't been allowed to have any icing on the Christmas cake. He was fed up with having only one pot of jam with his name on, to last a whole month. He'd almost forgotten what bananas looked like, and the only time oranges had been in the shops was just before Christmas; even then, there had only been one each. He kicked his feet moodily on the grass and looked up at the sky.

'We used to be able to fly kites. We're not even allowed to do that now.'

'You know why,' Lucy said.

'Doesn't stop them flying huge great barrage balloons, does it? I don't see what harm a tiny little kite would do amongst all that lot.' He glared at the huge grey balloons, floating like a herd of elephants above them. 'I'd fed up with the war. It's just spoiling everything.'

Lucy sighed. She couldn't argue with that. It had spoilt years of her marriage, years of the family life she and Wilmot ought to have been sharing. It had spoilt years of Wilmot's life, and God knew what he was enduring now.

'Mum, I can see Janet and Betty over there,' Patsy said. 'Can I go over and talk to them?'

'Take her over there, Geoff, there's a good boy,' Lucy said, and Geoff pushed the wheelchair away. He wouldn't have done that if David hadn't been here, she thought, he would have argued and sulked at having to go and talk to a crowd of girls. He was being specially difficult about Patsy just at present. It was natural for a boy of his age, of course, not to want to play with girls, but surely he could show her a bit of kindness. He could run off at any time, after all, and climb and jump just as he'd always been able to do. Sometimes, she thought that was why he stayed out so much, so that he wouldn't have to help with Patsy.

'We've got to keep believing we'll win,' David said. 'I know it's hard, but it's the only way.'

They leant on the railing and looked down at the little rockpools. The sea washed in and out of them, the water clear and silky. Nobody was swimming there. Even though it was still only early spring, a day like this would have had some of the bigger boys out with their trunks and ragged towels, leaping off the rocks into the waves, yelling with the excitement of it. But now a lot of those youths were already

91

training for the Armed Forces, and many of those who had been here when she and Wilmot came to swim a few years ago were dead.

She wondered if an afternoon diving off rocks would ever seem exciting again to those who survived, who had seen action at sea, in the air or on land in all those many countries now fighting out the biggest and worst war the world had ever known. Perhaps by then even boys would have had enough excitement.

'It's been going on for nearly four years,' she said. 'Four *years*! I'd never have believed it.' She paused. 'Zannah would have been six now.'

'I know. And Stevie would have been five.'

'Oh, David. Will we ever get over it?' She looked at him, standing beside her. He was looking out to sea, his profile sharp against the sweep of the waterway, his fair hair beginning to shade to grey. He looked tired and worn. Whatever work he did, it was exacting, and although he'd adjusted to having only one arm, she knew that it couldn't be easy. There were all the things you did that really needed two: carrying things, getting dressed of a morning, buttering a slice of bread (when you could get the butter). All the little things that people did all the time without even thinking of them, but which must add to the burden of his days. 'You must miss Heather terribly,' she said, thinking of how much Heather would have helped him.

'I do. I miss her all the time.' He turned his head and looked down into her eyes. 'But it helps a lot, having you.'

Lucy felt a small shock and remembered, without warning, that kiss they'd once shared, the kiss that had told her that there could be so much more between her and David, so much that was forbidden. She stared back at him speechlessly.

'I can't tell you how much it means to me, coming to Plymouth,' he went on. 'There's nowhere else that means home to me now, only Pengelly's. And you and Maud and

Arthur and the children – you're my family to me now.' He glanced away to where Geoff and Patsy were the centre of a group of children, boys and girls. They were all laughing, and one of the girls broke away to do a series of cartwheels across the grass. 'Geoff especially. I feel sometimes as if I was given the chance to save him to make up – a bit – for not being there for Stevie.'

Lucy stared at him. She felt enormously touched. She put out her hand and laid it on his empty sleeve. 'But you lost your arm –'

'I'd rather lose both my arms than have lost Geoff, or you or Patsy that night,' he said, almost savagely. 'I wish I *had* lost them both, if it could have kept Zannah alive. Listen,' he went on his voice low. 'Listen, Lucy. I know I shouldn't be saying this. Wilmot's alive and in prison and God knows what conditions he's living under. And I'd never do a thing to hurt either of you, you know that. But while this war's on – well, I want you to know that you are the most important person in the world to me. I love you, Lucy. I love you as deeply as a man can love a woman. And I don't think that's ever going to change.' He stared at her and she saw the truth deep in his eyes, and beside it the misery of its hopelessness. 'I know it can never go anywhere. I know you'll never be able to love me, but – I want you to know. And to know that if you ever need me – *ever* – I'll be there.'

Lucy tried to speak but her throat had closed up and her lips were like stiff bands across her frozen face. She shook her head a little and felt the hard ache of tears in her throat find release in her eyes. The salty water scalded her cheeks. She reached out a hand that shook and laid it again on his sleeve, but there was an arm in this sleeve, a warm, living arm in which tiny muscles jumped at her touch.

'Don't say anything,' he begged. 'I shouldn't have. I never meant to tell you. Don't let it make any difference.'

'But of course it makes a difference.'

93

He looked away, his mouth tightened. 'You won't want me to come again. I've spoilt everything.'

'No. *No*. It – just takes me a little while to get used to, that's all.' She laughed a little, breathlessly. 'David, I thought we were just friends.'

'We are. We *should* be. We will be. That's if – if you don't tell me to go away.'

'I'm not going to tell you to go away,' she said quietly. 'I'll never tell you to go away. I couldn't bear it if you weren't coming to see us whenever you can.' She lifted her eyes and looked him full in the face. 'I want you to go on thinking of us as your family, David. We *are* your family. Geoff – wouldn't be here if it weren't for you. And besides that – I love you too.'

The silence seemed to encompass the entire Hoe. It was as if everyone walking there, all the children playing, had stopped and turned to stare. Lucy gave a quick look round, unnerved, but it was her imagination, nobody had stopped, they were all continuing as before, the children were screaming and laughing, the adults strolling, just as if nothing had happened. She looked back at David.

'It won't come between me and Wilmot,' she said. 'It's a different sort of love. I won't ever be unfaithful to him, or anything like that. But after him and the children, you're the one who means most to me, David. And I don't think *that's* ever going to change.'

'I don't want us not to be friends,' he said a little unsteadily. 'I don't want it to spoil that.'

'Neither do I. And it won't.'

He put out his hand and she took it in both of hers. They smiled at each other and, as they stood there, Geoff came running up and tugged at their linked arms to gain attention.

'Mum! *Mum!* Terry Leeming's got a football. A real one. He got it from his uncle in Birmingham. He says I can be in his team if I go for practice now. I said I would, I can, can't

I? Can't I, Uncle David? You'll tell her I can, won't you, she'll let me if you say so, you will say so, won't you, *won't* you?' He was hopping from foot to foot with excitement and David and Lucy both laughed.

'All right, I'll say so,' David said, and Lucy nodded, her face suddenly alight as it had not been alight since Wilmot had last been at home. 'But what about Patsy? Bring her back over here first.'

'I can't. I haven't got time. I've got to go now, or I can't be in the team –' Geoff was already racing away across the grass. 'Janet's bringing her back, she'll be all right. See you at teatime, Mum.' He was gone, disappearing into a motley gang of twelve-year-old boys yelling football slogans as they disappeared across the Hoe.

'Boys!' Lucy exclaimed, and remembered her wonderings of a few moments earlier. 'Well, it's good to know that they're still boys after all. I was beginning to wonder.'

'Boys,' David said as if uttering a great truth that no one had ever perceived before, 'will *always* be boys.' And he set off across the grass to retrieve Patsy in her wheelchair.

There were raids throughout 1943, less frequent but always destructive. However, the defences were better now and enemy aircraft were met by a determined barrage of anti-aircraft fire and rockets. The searchlights lanced the night sky with a vivid web of long white spears and sometimes you could actually see the plane caught in the beam before it was shot down. One crashed at Stoke and its crew died in the flames. During the same raid, a huge bomb landed on the police headquarters, bringing down half the roof and coming to rest, unexploded and menacing, on the landing just outside the courtroom.

There were now thousands of houses in Plymouth waiting to be repaired. Some could still be lived in, their roofs patched up with tarpaulin and their windows boarded over. Others were smashed beyond repair and stood with gaunt jagged walls over craters that had once been cellars or foundations. Gardens that had once been lovingly tended were now tangled jungles of weeds. It never seemed to be the useful or pretty plants that ran riot, Lucy observed. You never saw cabbages or roses taking over and flourishing like dandelions and thistles did.

'They say the Germans are making coffee from dandelions,' Maud said. 'Or is it acorns? I don't fancy it anyway. Mind, I don't say no to a nice drink of dandelion and burdock, but I don't know how you make it.'

'People ate rats in the siege of Paris,' Patsy said. She couldn't go to school; most of those that hadn't been bombed had by now evacuated their children to the countryside, and the one or two still functioning were too far away, and in any case they couldn't take a child in a wheelchair. But Lucy was doing her best to see that Patsy's education didn't slip. Every week she walked through the ruined streets to the temporary library and got out as many books as she could, using the whole family's library tickets. She brought home books about history and geography, and read them herself so that she could talk about them with Patsy. Geoff brought home his own homework and Patsy did it too, and Arthur suggested she could help with the accounts for the hotel.

'It's only adding up. She could manage that. And look at it this way: it'd be a sight more useful than working out how long it takes to fill a bath when some daft fool's left the plug out, like that homework young Geoff had last week.'

Plymouth was full of Americans now. They came on ships that were larger and somehow more warlike than British ships, but when they came ashore they were ready for a drink just like the British tars. They filled the pubs in Union Street and washed like a tide through the city, scattering chewing-gum, chocolate and dollars amongst the children who soon learnt to follow them, chanting 'Got any gum, chum?' When Geoff came home the first time, displaying his prizes, Lucy was furious.

'It's no better than begging. You're not to do it.'

'But they chuck it at us anyway.' He spoke in an injured tone. 'And I brought the chocolate home for you and Patsy and Grammy. I thought you'd *like* it.'

Lucy sighed. What could she say, when he was giving his sister a bar of chocolate such as never came her way these days? She knew that a lot of people welcomed the Americans, and why not? They were like a breath of fresh air, bringing with them an air of freedom from the constant sense of dread that had become part of the British way of life. The Americans hadn't been bombed, they hadn't suffered from food shortages or rationing, they knew their folks at home were safe, they were young and energetic, well fed, strong and healthy. It was like a glimpse of another life to see them swinging through the streets and hear their talk. Nearly as good as being at the pictures.

All the same, it worried her a bit to see them flashing their money about and throwing sweets and things at the children. And it wasn't just the children. They were interested in the girls – it was only to be expected, they were young men with lots of energy – and they'd brought things to entice them as well. More chocolate, and things like scent and pretty underwear and stockings made of nylon, that were as sheer as silk and had real seams down the back.

Lucy began to hear the phrase that was to become so commonly used amongst young British men, bitterly jealous of their American rivals: 'Overpaid, oversexed and over here.' You couldn't blame them, she thought, but you couldn't blame the Americans either. They were all human beings.

The last raid came at the end of April 1944. Nobody knew then that it was the last, as the cloud of aircraft came snarling in over the Sound to drop its bombs over Oreston and the waterfront, burning out the Western National bus depot. Nobody even dreamed that it could be the last, for immediately afterwards the coasts and rivers of Devon and Cornwall became a hive of naval and military activity, with ships massing in the Channel and tanks and lorries filling the roads and lanes.

'We'll be a bigger target than ever,' Arthur said. 'It's handing it to them on a plate. The Jerries'll be over and bomb the lot.'

But they didn't come. The tanks went on arriving, the ships gathered, and suddenly, one morning in June, vanished as if they had never been. And on the wireless came the news of the invasion of Normandy. D-Day.

'Let's hope it won't be like Dieppe,' Maud said, listening anxiously, but it wasn't like Dieppe. This time, the Germans had been caught unaware and the Army forged into France. At last, the tide seemed to be on the turn.

'I can really dare to start thinking we might win after all,' Lucy said to David. 'It really does seem as if it might all be over.'

'It does,' he said. 'Not by Christmas, perhaps, but – maybe not too long after.'

Geoff was disappointed by D-Day. It was exciting that the Army had invaded Normandy, he conceded that, and he took a lot of interest in keeping track of their movements, sticking pins in the big map Arthur had put on the wall to show where the different forces had got to. But the streets that had been so full of vitality as the Americans roved about, scattering largesse, were now empty again. The colour had gone, leaving them no more than the grey ruins they had been before. And the chocolate and chewing-gum had gone with them.

He wasn't the only one disappointed. There were a lot of young girls in Plymouth, Lucy thought, who were also going to miss the fun and excitement, although in their case, a good many of them had something else to remember their new, big-talking boyfriends by.

'He said we'd get married,' was the cry now. 'He said he'd take me to *Hollywood*.'

Well, Lucy thought again, they were all human beings. And war was a lonely time for the girls they left behind.

Nineteen-forty-five. The sixth winter of the war. Lucy could barely remember what peace had been like. The carefree, youthful days at home in Portsmouth, when she had spent her days working at the naval outfitters, and her life with her friends, her family and Wilmot, seemed like a distant dream. Had they ever really happened?

The fighting continued, and now it was the Allies who were pushing home their offensive. The Russians were marching into Europe; they drove a spearhead through Poland, the country that had been at the heart of the war, and took Warsaw, the city which had suffered more than any other under the Germans. By the end of January they were just a hundred miles from Berlin and it really began to look as if the war might be coming to an end.

'But not in Japan,' Lucy said. 'And that's where Wilmot is.'

Her own family were caught up in it all. Alice had lost her husband Ted at Tripoli. She had stayed in her nursing job at the Royal Hospital in Portsmouth, and she'd been on duty the night it was bombed. All through the barrage she'd rescued patients from the damaged wards and afterwards she'd been awarded a medal. Once the worst of the blitz seemed to be over she'd volunteered as a nurse in the WAAFs, and when D-Day came she flew to France in Dakotas, bringing home the wounded.

Kitty was doing well in the Wrens. She went across the Gosport ferry every day to work at HMS *Dolphin*, the submarine base. Later on, she was posted to Portland and she managed to 'wangle' a few trips down to Plymouth to see Lucy. She was as pretty as ever, like a bright-eyed little furry animal with her curly red hair, and she seemed to be thoroughly enjoying the war.

'The main thing is to have as much fun as you can,' she said. 'Life's too short to be miserable. Keep smiling through, that's what they say, and that's what I do. Anyway, it's our patriotic duty to keep the boys happy when they're at home.'

Lucy wondered how many boys she'd kept happy, and what her mother and father thought about it, but Kitty laughed at her fears.

'I shan't get caught. You don't have to, these days. And I don't go with them for money or anything. I mean, some girls will do anything for a pair of nylons or a bottle of scent. I'm not like that.'

'I bet you don't say no, all the same,' Lucy said, unable to keep a tinge of disapproval from her voice.

Kitty gave her a sharp look. 'Listen to me, our Lucy. I don't go with just any bloke that comes along. I've been with a few, yes, because I like them and they're lonely and might go off and be killed next day – but I don't do it for what they can give me. I enjoy it too, you know. And it isn't serious. It's just fun.'

Lucy couldn't look at it like that. To her, making love with a man was a very serious thing indeed. Something she'd only ever done – only ever would do – with her husband.

'Don't tell me you've never fancied anyone else,' Kitty said, watching her and seeming to read her mind. 'Not all this long time, with Wilmot away for years.'

'Well, I haven't, then,' Lucy said indignantly, and then stopped and bit her lip. There wasn't much point in looking down on Kitty if she couldn't tell the truth herself. And there had been someone else. She had never made love with him, never done more than kiss – just once – but she'd told him she loved him, and meant it.

David.

'Well? You see?' Kitty's voice was triumphant. 'Who was he, then? One of the Yanks?'

'No! It wasn't like that at all.' Lucy was scarlet, and as angry with herself as with her sister. 'It – it's completely different.'

'Oh yeah?' This was an expression Kitty, with many others, had picked up from the Americans. 'How different?'

'It's not the same as what you're doing, not the same at all. We – we love each other.'

'Lucy!' This time, to Lucy's surprise, the disapproval was in Kitty's voice. 'Oh, Lucy, how can you? With Wilmot in a Japanese POW camp. Oh, I think that's dreadful. At least I make sure my boys aren't married.'

'*No!*' There was nothing for it, Lucy saw, but to tell her the truth. 'I told you, it isn't like that. We've never – we've never done anything about it. We never will. And I haven't stopped loving Wilmot, it doesn't make any difference to Wilmot and me. It's just happened, that's all. We love each other, but we'll never do anything about it, never.' She paused, unable to take the final step of speaking David's name. 'He's Wilmot's friend as well,' she said at last in a low tone. 'He'd never do anything to hurt him.'

Kitty stared at her, and Lucy saw the light dawn on her face.

'It's David, isn't it?' she said slowly. She knew David well; he always came to visit the family when he was in Portsmouth. 'It's David. David and you.'

'Not David and me. I told you, we've never—'

'It's all right. I believe you.' She added, almost from habit, 'Thousands wouldn't.' Her eyes softened and she reached out her small, strong hand and covered Lucy's. 'Oh, Luce. You poor thing.'

The tears sprang to Lucy's eyes. She felt their heat with some astonishment. She had never wept for herself and David, never seen their story as a sad one. There had been too many other things to weep for, and the affection between

101

them had been a source of strength to them both. But now she saw it with Kitty's eyes – a loss, a deprivation, a bud that could never flower, a flower that could never fruit.

'It's all right,' she said a little harshly. 'There's plenty of worse things happen at sea.' And the truth of that phrase, so commonly used, hit her afresh; and she thought of Wilmot, struggling in a sea of flames, and the suffering he might be enduring even now.

Beside that, an unfulfilled love seemed little to weep about.

Lucy's brother, Kenny, piloted a Lancaster. He flew on sorties over Germany, and one night he went to Dresden and came back with death in his eyes. He had looked down, he said, and seen a firestorm below him; a holocaust of flame which surely nobody could have survived. The bombing had been so intense that their blast and the fires they had started had created their own wind, fanning the flames into an inferno. It was like looking into the jaws of hell.

'Well, they done it to us,' people said. 'Serve 'em right, don't it?'

But Kenny shook his head. For the first time, he had realised that there were people down there, not just 'Germans', the mythical storybook trolls of imagination, black and evil hobgoblins, but children still at school, babies in prams, girls and boys just growing up, pregnant women and elderly people. People who hadn't asked for war, who had thought themselves safe in a city that was known only for its beauty and had nothing to do with the conflict.

'It's supposed to bring the end of the war closer,' he said, 'but that's not much comfort to them, is it?'

After a while, he was taken off bombers and given a desk job. They said it was for health reasons, and indeed Kenny was never quite the same again. The ready smile had vanished, the jokes disappeared, and when he went for a walk he walked alone.

Lucy felt as if she had lost both her brothers.

All the talk now was of the end of the war. The blackout was taken down, some of the streetlamps lit. Church bells rang out wherever there were bells to ring and ringers to ring them. The Allies crossed the Rhine and the Russians marched steadily nearer to Berlin. Hitler was said to be in hiding, and his mistress, Eva Braun, with him. And then, at the beginning of May, came the news of his suicide.

'It's all over. It must be all over now.'

David found Lucy up on the Hoe where they had walked so many times during the past six years. They stood silently together, looking out over the waters, looking towards Drake's Island and the breakwater and the tiny pencil shape of the Eddystone Lighthouse far beyond.

'I know what you must be feeling,' he said after a while. 'It may be over in Europe, but it's not ended in Japan. The war still goes on there.'

'I sometimes wonder,' she said, 'if I'll ever see Wilmot again.'

The desolation in her voice struck him to the heart. He put his arm round her shoulders and held her firmly against him. 'You will. You must. He's survived all this time.'

Lucy had received infrequent and scrappy letters from Wilmot. The Japanese allowed their prisoners only the minimum of communication, and nobody believed those who said they were well treated. Lucy could barely guess at what was happening to Wilmot.

'We can't be sure of anything,' she said to David. 'You know that. We may think terrible things can't happen, but they do. They've happened to us already. Why should they stop?'

'Well,' he said, 'at least if the war's over in Europe we'll be able to concentrate on the Far East. It won't go on much longer, Lucy. The end really is coming.'

It came – for Europe – only a few days later.

*

VE Day.

The streets of Plymouth rejoiced. A grand parade of all the Services, the Home Guard, ARP wardens, nurses and everyone else who had a uniform to wear, marched through the city from St Jude's to Stonehouse, with a Royal Marine band at its head. People strung bunting from their houses, pianos were dragged out into the streets and dancing went on into the early hours. They looked up at the skies which for six long years had brought death and destruction, and they cheered to see the stars above. Those same stars had looked down impassively, uncaring, when the bombs had fallen, blotted out by the searing flames. Now, however, the skies were clear and brought no threat, and once again they could be loved.

Lucy joined in the celebrations. You couldn't not join in – you had to be glad. There were many others like her, she knew, who smiled through stiffened lips, who felt the hollow ache for loved ones who were still away, still imprisoned or fighting. How did they feel, knowing that it was over for so many while they still toiled on in peril of their lives? But you had to be glad. You had to join in.

And then it was all talk of rebuilding. Plans for the new Plymouth city centre. Plans for houses – the new prefabricated houses, more like shoeboxes than something you'd want to live in, but welcomed with enthusiasm by their new occupants. Lucy went to see one and couldn't help being impressed. It all looked so new, so clean, and they even had bathrooms. Bathrooms, for people who had always been accustomed to a tin bath hanging on a nail outside and brought indoors on Saturday nights! And refrigerators, too. Those who hadn't been bombed out were quite jealous: there was little chance of bathrooms and fridges for them.

So many buildings were still in ruins. The shells of St Andrew's church and the stately Guildhall, both gutted, towered over the still-flattened streets. They had gone on holding services in the church ever since the bombing, and the word *Resurgam* was still in place over the church door. Inside the roofless building they had planted flowerbeds which glowed with the colour missing now from the smashed windows, so that despite the damage it was an inspiration to go inside and hear the familiar prayers and the voices of the choir lifted in the well-known hymns.

But life still wasn't easy. Big stores like Spooner's and Dingle's had had to move their premises, just as the smaller shops had done. You couldn't shop easily any more, going from one to the other; they were all miles apart. With the incessant queueing, which hadn't improved even though the war was over, it made every shopping trip a major expedition.

After the first euphoria had died down, the realisation slowly dawned that things weren't going to improve overnight. There would still be rationing – in fact, even more foods were to be rationed now, including bread, which had never been short before. There would still be power cuts and shortages of coal. You still wouldn't be able to get decent furniture, or pretty crockery, only 'utility'; nor lace tablecloths, nor nice paint and wallpaper to do up rooms that hadn't been touched for six long years.

Still, at least you could go to bed knowing that you weren't going to be woken by the wail of the air-raid warning, though. At least you knew your men were safe and would be coming home for good.

Except, of course, for those still in the Far East.

In the end, it was only eight weeks that the world had to wait. A long, slow eight weeks, and a terrible end, when all was known. But at last, when Lucy had almost given up, came the August morning when her son Geoff came racing in from the streets, his hair standing on end, shrieking the news.

'It's over! It's finished! The war's *over*!'

Chapter Ten

It was January 1946 before Wilmot finally came home.

First of all, the prisoner-of-war camps throughout the Far East had to be located and the prisoners freed. There was some urgency in this, for there were fears that the Japanese would execute their captives. However the terrible wrath of the Western world, evinced in the atom bombs dropped on Hiroshima and Nagasaki, had had its effect and the occupying troops were in the main able to march in and take over without resistance. Emperor Hirohito had declared surrender, and that was enough for his defeated people.

Wilmot's first letter didn't seem so very different from those he had sent from the camp. It was scribbled and uninformative, but Lucy knew that he was going to hospital and would stay there until they were sure he was fit to travel home.

'What does that mean? What have they been doing to him?'

Other prisoners began to return. The stories of what had gone on in the camps began to circulate, horrifying accounts of brutality. If you didn't bow your head as the camp commander passed by, it was likely to be chopped off. If you were lucky enough not to be killed, you risked a punishment so cruel that you might well wish you had been. The food was very nearly at starvation level, and the diseases of malnourishment were rife. Boils, sores, digestive disturbance became commonplace, and this led to other diseases. Everyone suffered from dysentery, and every day someone died.

Lucy wrote long letters to Wilmot, telling him how much she was looking forward to seeing him again, telling him about the family and the hotel, but even that wasn't easy. She couldn't tell him about the children without referring to Patsy's wheelchair, and she was acutely conscious of the fact that she wasn't mentioning Zannah. It didn't seem right to be talking about two of their children when they'd had three – but what could she say about Zannah? When Wilmot had gone away, she'd been a chubby toddler, all smiles and cuddles. Now – she just wasn't there any more. He knew this, of course, had known it for years, but somehow now it seemed to be happening all over again, and the pain was just as sharp as ever.

As Wilmot's return grew nearer, Lucy found her initial excitement gradually replaced by apprehension. He had been gone for five years. It was longer than they'd enjoyed married life, when you counted all the times he'd been away before the war. They'd both been through so much in that time; they must have changed, both of them. She went to the mirror and looked at her reflection. Six years of war had tired and aged her; she was no longer the bright-faced bride or the happy young mother he would remember. She was thirty-five years old and there were lines at the corners of her eyes. The deep violet was still there, and the burnished red-gold of her hair, but there were a few white hairs amongst it now, and she dared not pull them out for fear that seven more would appear in place of each one.

Suppose he was disappointed with her. Suppose he didn't love her any more.

Suppose she didn't love him.

Lucy pushed the thought away, angry with herself for even letting it touch her mind. Of course she still loved him. And of course he wouldn't have changed. Nothing could change the Wilmot she remembered, the fresh-faced sailor full of jokes and cheeky remarks. There might be a few adjustments to make, but there would be too much to

107

do to let silly fears spoil things. A home to find, for a start. And a job for Wilmot, for surely he'd be coming out of the Navy now. If it hadn't been for the war, he'd have come out years ago.

'I'm sorry now I let the house go,' she said to her mother-in-law. 'It's been good of you to let me and the kids stop here all this time, but we ought to have our own place. And you'll want the rooms now, to get the guest house on its feet again.'

'Don't talk so daft. This is your home for as long as you want it. And I don't think you'll find it so easy to get a place of your own anyway. There's more people looking for homes than there are places for them to live, you know that. And you'd never get a prefab, not while you can go on living here.'

Lucy knew this was true. She sighed. It would have been so much better to start off with Wilmot on their own together. Good as Maud and Arthur had been, a couple needed to be private, especially when they'd been separated as long as she and Wilmot had been.

'Besides,' Maud went on, 'I'm a bit worried about Arthur. He's not looking right to me. I don't like the idea of him trying to do all the work here on his own when you've gone.'

'Oh, I wouldn't let him do that,' Lucy said at once. 'I'd still call in every day and lend a hand with things, same as always. After all, when Wilmot's at work—'

'And what work,' Maud asked, 'do you think a man who's spent the past four years in a prisoner-of-war camp is going to get?'

Lucy stared at her.

'You know what they say about those places,' Maud went on. 'Torture camps, that's what they call them. Wilmot's not going to be the man he was, don't you expect it. And he'll be thankful to have some work to do here, without going out tramping the streets to look for it.'

'But he's got a trade.'

'Which he's not touched for four years.'

'Mum, how can you talk like that?'

'Because we've got to face it.' Maud folded her lips tightly together. 'Don't think I *like* it, Lucy. It's my own son we're talking about, I haven't forgotten that. But you've seen what's happening already. Men coming home in their demob suits, all full of what they're going to do to get the country on its feet again – and then, a few weeks later, what are they doing? Knocking on the door asking you to buy brushes, that's what. And they're the lucky ones! Look, I've seen it before, after the first war – men coming home to jobs that weren't there any more, men who'd been good enough to fight for their country and now weren't wanted any more. Chucked on the rubbish heap.'

Lucy was silent. She felt a sick horror descend on her like a grey, slimy sponge, wrapping itself about her face and head. Putting up her hands as if to brush it away, she cried, 'But Wilmot won't be like that! He's clever, he'll get something—'

'My friend Mrs Endacott's George is clever,' Maud said. 'He couldn't even get a job selling brushes.'

Lucy's apprehension grew. Wilmot was supposed to be coming out of the Navy. Suppose he decided to stay in. They would never have a proper life together. Suppose the Navy didn't want him anyway – how would he feel? Suppose Maud was right and he couldn't get a job. It would be so cruel, after all he had suffered, to find that his country didn't want him.

Perhaps the hotel was the answer after all.

Lucy thought about it. Pengelly's had never been more than a guest house, taking in a few visitors at a time. It had brought in enough income to keep Maud and Arthur, and Wilmot when he was a boy. There had been just enough guests through the war to keep it going, and Lucy's naval allowance had helped, but there wasn't enough to keep two families if Wilmot left the Navy, especially with some of the rooms needed for her and Wilmot and the children. And the whole house needed refurbishing. It hadn't been redecorated in over six years. The outside looked shabby, the once white walls grubby and peeling, and blackened by smoke from the fires of the blitz. The window-frames were in poor condition and some of the sashes were broken. And inside, when you came to look at it properly – for you got used to it when you lived there all the time – was downright scruffy. Skirting-boards knocked and chipped by Geoff's bike and Patsy's wheelchair; wallpaper discoloured and starting to come away; ceilings yellowed by tobacco smoke; paintwork scraped and carpets threadbare. The whole place needed gutting and then starting again, she thought.

It would have been too, if it had been bombed properly. And she almost laughed at herself for wishing that the Germans had made what Arthur would have called 'a proper job' of it.

Well, there'd be plenty to keep Wilmot occupied, getting the place up to scratch. And plenty for her to do as well. New curtains to make, bedlinen to sort out – all it needed was the money. Just a minor problem, really.

They had hoped that Wilmot would be home for Christmas, but as the winter drew on and November came, they knew that there would be no chance of this. Ships from the Far East took a good eight weeks to get home, and Wilmot hadn't even been given a date for leaving. And then, suddenly, came the news that he was on board an aircraft-carrier, together with a crowd of other ex-POWs, and leaving Singapore next day. He would be home some time in January.

'January!' Lucy gasped.

'We'll have our proper Christmas then,' Maud said. Tears were running down her cheeks and Lucy had to remind herself that Wilmot was as precious to her as he was to Lucy herself. Her only son, her only child . . . She thought of Zannah and the grief that was always in the back of her mind, and thought of how it would have been if she hadn't had Geoff and Patsy as well. The whole world gone at once. She hugged Maud with sudden understanding and made up her mind that she wouldn't be possessive, she'd let Wilmot's mother have her share of him. And at the same time, she wished again that they had their own home. It wasn't going to be easy.

Upstairs in her bedroom, she looked again in the mirror. Her eyes went past her own reflection to the bed. She'd slept on her own now for over four years, and pretty well most of the time before that. It was going to seem queer having someone else in bed with her. *Someone else?* she thought with a tiny flicker of hysteria. It was Wilmot she was going to share with, for heaven's sake! Wilmot, her husband. And they wouldn't just be sleeping, either . . .

They'd be making love. That was something else neither of them had done in all those years. She looked back at her reflection, seeing the doubt in the wide violet eyes, wondering if she would be able to remember what to do, how to do it. She'd thought of it often enough at first, and then tried not to think about it, pushing it away, successfully for the most part, except when she lay bitterly lonely in the middle of the night, and when she dreamed about it. She'd remembered how it felt then, all right.

Suppose it didn't work. There had been the odd occasion even quite early in their marriage when Wilmot just hadn't been able to do it and no amount of cuddling or stroking had made any difference. Usually it was because he was tired or had a cold or perhaps had drunk a beer too many in the Mess, and they'd just laughed it off. It didn't matter because they could cuddle and kiss anyway, and there was always the next night. But what would four years such as he had just endured have done to him?

I'll just have to play it all by ear, she decided. I'll have to let him set the pace. Work his way back into life the best way he knows, and I'll help him all I can. There's going to be so much for him to learn again, and he's the one who's been through the worst time. It's my job to help him and make him strong again.

The thought seemed to bring her the comfort she needed. The thought of drawing on her own reserves, her own strengths, to help the husband she loved so much and had missed so badly. And I *am* strong, she thought with sudden surprise. I've grown strong during all these years – I've had to. Bringing up the children on my own, helping Wilmot's mum and dad, practically running the guest house at times . . . even losing Zannah and having Patsy crippled, and learning to get on with things just the same. It's all made me strong.

She looked with some wonder at the reflection in the mirror. Her eyes had darkened to the deep purple of pansies, and the white hairs amongst the burnished gold didn't seem to matter quite so much after all. It was her strength that mattered, her strength and her love, and that was what Wilmot was coming home to and what she would offer him.

They had Christmas, of course, the first post-war Christmas, with a thin layer of icing on the cake, roughed up with a fork to look like snow, and a Father Christmas made by Patsy out of brown paper with a scrap of red paint to stand on top of it. There was a Rupert book for Patsy, who had followed the little bear's adventures in the *Daily Express* right through the war, and a *Hotspur* annual for Geoff. There were sweets and chocolates from the whole family's ration, saved up for weeks, and there was a bowl of oranges on the sideboard, a chicken and a proper pudding for dinner, and a tin of peaches and clotted cream for Christmas Day tea.

'It's almost as good as pre-war,' Maud said, looking at the laden table. What with sandwiches and a dish of tinned pilchards and some salad, the feast looked good enough to compete with any pre-war memories. David, who had come to spend Christmas with them, raised his eyebrows and laughed.

'It looks as if you're expecting an army!'

'It's a practice run,' Lucy said with a smile. 'We're going to do it all again when Wilmot comes home.'

'Of course. And when d'you think that'll be?' He slid Patsy's chair up to the table and made sure she could reach her knife and fork. 'Some time in January, isn't it?'

'About the middle, we think.' Lucy felt her heart skip. It did that a lot these days. 'You'll come, won't you, David? For the party?'

'Oh.' He looked a little nonplussed. 'I don't know – do you think Wilmot will want me here? I mean, he'll just want his family.'

'You *are* family. You know that. You've been here all through.' She glanced at Geoff. She didn't need to add, *You saved his life*.

David was less certain. He didn't think Wilmot would necessarily see him as part of the family. He would want Lucy to himself, without another man hovering in the background. They'd been friends four or five years ago, and before the war, but that didn't mean he had a place here now. Wilmot was hardly likely to have spent the last four years aching to see another man.

'I think it'd probably be best if I don't come down to see you all until after Wilmot's had a chance to settle in,' he said, passing Geoff the sardine and tomato sandwiches.

Lucy stared at him, surprised by her own dismay. Somehow, without really thinking about it, she had assumed that David would be here. He'd been here through all the most important parts of the war, good and bad, and although they'd agreed that they could never let their friendship deepen, he was special to her. More special than she'd realised; more necessary.

113

'But –' she said, and then caught his eye and stopped. There was a tiny warning in it, and a flicker towards Maud and Arthur. Lucy bit her lip and glanced at her mother-in-law. To her relief, Maud wasn't even looking at her but was concentrating on cutting into the Victoria sponge, but she knew what David's look had meant.

'Things will be different from now on,' he said to her later as they said goodnight outside her room. 'They have to be. We can't be the same sort of friends as we have been. It wouldn't be right.'

'But there was nothing wrong. We never—'

'That's not the point. I'm glad, very glad, that we never let anything happen.' He sighed a little. 'It could have done, so easily . . . but things have been very different during the war, Lucy, and now they've got to change again. You do see that, don't you.'

Reluctantly, she nodded. She did see it, really, she had just never thought of it until now. There had been too much else on her mind and somehow she'd just taken it for granted that David would always be there, just as he always had been.

'We'll all have to go back to where we were before,' she said and heard him sigh again.

'Do you think that's possible? I think we're going to have to find new ways. It isn't going to be easy, Lucy, for any of us.' He paused for a moment. He was very close and she could feel his breath on her cheek, could even, she thought, feel the beating of his heart. For one moment she wanted to forget everything, to throw all this caution and sensibleness to the winds and take him into her bedroom and make love together, just this once, just this last chance . . . but it wasn't possible. It wasn't possible for either of them.

She reached up and touched his cheek, feeling a deep sadness that something was slipping away from her, something she needed and would now never have.

'Goodnight, David.'

114

His eyes turned upon her in the dim light. He bent his head and brushed her lips with his, very gently, very tenderly, and she gasped with the shock of it and knew that he felt it too. The moment came again, more powerfully than ever; and once again, they let it pass.

'Goodnight, Lucy. Goodnight.'

January came. Lucy was restless, unable to settle. She roamed about the house with a sheet of paper in her hand and a pencil, trying to make notes about what needed doing. The amount of wallpaper would run into acres, she thought, and what wallpaper was there to be had anyway? None of that sort of thing had come into the shops yet. It took time, she supposed, to get organised again. Factories had been taken over for other things, for munitions and uniforms and utility furniture. Army blankets had been made on looms previously used for carpets. It would take time to get them into production again. And paint, they'd need gallons and gallons of it. Nothing wrong with a nice drop of distemper, Arthur said when she mentioned her worries, do a nice pale green or blue everywhere, that was all that was needed to freshen things up.

'I'd just like a bit of real colour,' Lucy said wistfully. 'And some nice patterns. It's years since we've had that sort of thing. It would make us all feel so much better.'

'Why do you want to feel better?' Arthur asked. 'Isn't winning the war enough for you, my beauty?'

It ought to be. It ought to be enough for anyone. And to begin with, of course it had been. But once the singing and dancing in the streets had stopped, once the bunting had come down and the Union Jacks been put away again, once winter had come with its rain and its greyness, it didn't seem to be quite enough any more. There were no more raids, no more fighting, no more killing and being killed, it was true. There were no barrage balloons like herds of elephants in the sky, no searchlights at night, no banshee

115

siren, no rattle of ack-ack. You could see your way at night in lit streets, you could use a torch, you didn't have to worry about the blackout. It ought to have been enough. And yet . . .

If it had been summer, it might have been better, Lucy thought, picking her way through streets that were still heaped at the sides with rubble, still pocked by craters. A bit of sunshine would have helped, but the greyness seeped into everything, into the jagged ruins of once fine buildings, into the mud of tangled gardens, into the weary grind of having to put it all right again. A scruffy guest house, a ruined street, a wrecked church, a gutted Guildhall. Everywhere you looked, there was damage to be repaired, and the task seemed too enormous even to contemplate.

And in the midst of it all, she had this terrible, gnawing feeling of excitement mixed with dread. I ought to be happy, she thought. I ought to be over the moon. Wilmot's coming home. He's coming home. And sometimes I feel so scared I almost wish he'd stay away . . .

No. That was an *evil* thought. She hated herself for letting it into her mind. She wanted him home, she was looking forward to it, it was all she'd dreamed of all these years, and to prove it she tossed aside her plans for the guest house and threw herself into a frenzy of preparation.

'I don't see why *I* have to help scrub the stairs,' Geoffrey objected. 'Patsy doesn't have to do anything.'

'Daddy's coming home, Geoff. Don't you want him to see our home looking as nice as possible? Don't you want him to feel happy to be here?'

'I bet he'd be happy even if we didn't do all this washing and stuff. Men don't bother about all that.'

'Sailors do,' Lucy retorted. 'They keep their ships spick and span all the time. Now stop arguing, Geoff, and when you've done that you can clean the front windows.'

She knew she was overdoing it. She knew that Geoff resented the extra work, and she knew that he was right, that Wilmot probably wouldn't even notice, but she was driven by something deep inside, a sense of something that wasn't just excitement, something she was afraid to examine. And it made something to do while she waited.

The middle of January. The ship was thought to be coming into Southampton, but nobody really knew. It could be Portsmouth or Portland or even Plymouth itself. Nothing seemed certain, these days. All you could do was wait. Every morning, Lucy woke with a fluttering heart, wondering if this would be the day. Every ring on the doorbell brought her to her feet. Every time she went out, she returned with her heart in her mouth, wondering if he'd arrived in her absence and was even now sitting in the kitchen, his hands wrapped around a mug of tea, talking and laughing with his mum and dad, the old Wilmot, fresh faced and cheeky, with a joke always on his lips.

When she'd hurried along the pavement and up the steps to the front door, down the narrow hallway and into the kitchen, to find that he wasn't there at all, she never quite knew whether she was disappointed or relieved.

'He'll let us know when he's coming,' Maud said. 'Soon as the ship docks, he'll send a telegram. We'll get warning.'

Other men were coming home too. There was hardly a day went by without some street being decked with bunting and Union Jacks, and houses with 'Welcome Home' banners strung from their windows. You couldn't go down the street without passing some chap in a greatcoat, carrying a kitbag and looking tired and excited all at once. The street parties were over, but there was always the sound of singing and piano-playing coming from some-where, and children going to school boasting of 'my dad' who had come back from the war with medals all over his chest and a coconut in his kitbag.

And there were the men who had come back earlier, the ones Maud had talked about, who trudged the streets with a different sort of bag: a cardboard suitcase filled with brushes or books to sell, men whose faces were weary and disillusioned, who wondered what it had all been for and why they had ended up like this.

The front door opened and closed. Lucy, alone in the kitchen, didn't even bother to lift her head. It would be Maud back from her friend Mrs Endacott, or Arthur home from the pub where he sometimes called in for a pint. Or Geoff, back from the game of football he'd at last been released to play.

The kitchen door opened before she had time to register that the footsteps in the passage were none of these. The figure in the doorway cast an unfamiliar shadow. There was a bulky look about it that she didn't, at first, recognise. It was only when she saw the two kitbags and the dark blue greatcoat that she began to understand.

'Aren't you going to say hallo to me, Lucy?' the man in the doorway asked. 'Aren't you going to give your husband a kiss after all these years?'

Chapter Eleven

'*Wilmot!*'

He stood there in the doorway. Wilmot. In that first, dazed and blinding moment, she caught a glimpse of the changes – the weathered, yellowish skin, the folds around the eyes, the narrow lines running from his nose to the corners of his mouth – but she wasn't looking for changes: she was looking for things she had known before, remembered, dreamed about.

It was all that she had ever dared hope for.

She was on her feet, her chair thrust back so sharply that it toppled, and he moved towards her at the same moment. They met in a hug so fierce she thought she wouldn't survive it, a clasping of arms about bodies that strove to forget, to obliterate the years that had stood between them; and a kiss that almost drowned and swallowed them both.

'You didn't let me know –'

'I couldn't. I wanted to surprise you –'

'Wilmot, I've missed you so much – it's been so awful.'

'Lucy. Lucy. *Lucy*.'

They kissed again and again. Their tears mingled, salty on lips and tongue. She felt his warmth, his solidity, and marvelled. It was really Wilmot, Wilmot himself here in her arms, no longer a dream, no longer a fantasy. She touched his hair and felt almost sick with the enormity of it all. He was here. After so much had happened, he was here at last.

'Wilmot, your hair –'

'What? What about it?' He was kissing her face, burying his nose in her neck.

'It's grey. Some of it's quite grey.'

He stood back abruptly and she looked up into his face, catching her breath. She had never seen that look before, that sudden withdrawal, that stoniness.

'Well? It's hair, isn't it?'

'Wilmot, don't look like that. It doesn't matter – of course it doesn't matter. We're older, we're both older.' She was panic-stricken, thinking she had spoilt it already. 'I've got grey hairs myself, look, lots of them.' She would not have believed, a few days ago as she stared into the mirror and wondered whether to pull them out and risk the seven more, that she would have actually pointed them out to him. 'Just think, I'm thirty-five, that's middle-aged!' She laughed, trying to make him laugh too.

'And I'm thirty-eight.' There was a twist to his mouth and she wished she hadn't mentioned ages. Thirty-eight was only two years off forty, and didn't they say something about being too old at forty? But he doesn't deserve it, she thought, he was only thirty-two when all this started, he doesn't deserve to have the best years of his life taken away from him like that.

'Oh, Wilmot,' she said, reaching up to kiss him again, 'it's *so* lovely to have you back.'

He caught her against him and covered her mouth once more with his. To her relief, the moment seemed to have passed and once more they were caught up in their joy at being together again. And all too soon, their privacy was invaded. The front door opened again and they heard the tramp of feet as they were wiped on the doormat, the sound of voices. The usual murmuring as Patsy's wheelchair was manoeuvred into the passage, the sound of Geoff's voice as he recounted the highlights of the afternoon's football game. And then they were in the kitchen, all of them, filling it with noise and movement which stopped abruptly as they saw who was there. And Wilmot was buried beneath a rush of bodies as everyone – everyone except Patsy – rushed to embrace him.

'Wilmot! Oh, my boy, my boy.'

'Wilmot –'

'Dad! *Dad!*'

And from the wheelchair, left pathetically out of it all, 'Daddy, Daddy.'

They broke away at last. Lucy touched her husband's arm – it took her a second to overcome the immensity of being able actually to touch his arm – and glanced towards Patsy. Wilmot, still in the midst of hearing Geoff's excited and largely incoherent account of the football game, looked across the kitchen table towards his daughter.

There was a tiny silence.

Patsy was now nearly twelve. Sitting there with her legs covered by a blanket, it was difficult to believe that there was anything wrong with her. She looked like a normal little girl, with hair tied back in pigtails, her slim figure just beginning to develop. She looked as if she was just sitting there, could jump up and walk and run at any moment like any other twelve-year-old girl, but they'd been told this would never happen. She would never do any of these things again. The family were used to it now, but how would Wilmot feel?

'Patsy?' he said quietly, almost wonderingly, and he went across to her and knelt beside her chair, putting his arms around her. She wound her own arms around his neck and he laid his face against hers, and Lucy saw that he was crying. 'Oh, my little Patsy.'

Geoff, cut off abruptly in his chatter, looked downcast. Lucy flicked her fingers towards him.

'Now, you don't need to look like that, our Geoff. There'll be plenty of time for us all to talk to Daddy and tell him all we've been doing. But what he wants now is a cup of tea, so put the kettle on for me, there's a good boy, and then take those kitbags up to my – *our* – bedroom. Show Daddy how strong you are. He's a real man now,' she said to Wilmot, conscious that she was talking too quickly, her voice running on with aimless chatter. 'He looks after us all.' There wasn't a scrap of truth in it. Geoff was an ordinary thirteen-year-old, more interested in football and getting out with his mates than in being the 'man of the house'. And in any case, Arthur was that.

Wilmot turned. 'No, don't take them both. Leave that one down here.' He grinned. 'It's got some presents in.'

'Presents!'

Geoffrey was alight again at once. He dragged the kitbag into the kitchen, forgetting his mother's instructions, and began to unpick the cords around its neck.

Wilmot laughed. 'Don't get too excited, old son. There's no toys, I'm afraid. Just a few tins of fruit I managed to get hold of in Singapore. They told us you didn't get much of it at home so we all brought as much as we could carry.'

'Tins of fruit!' Lucy stared as the cans of peaches and apricots came out of the bag, and then began to laugh. Her laughter was high pitched and uncontrollable, and after a few minutes Maud pushed her into a chair where she leant her head on her hand and laughed herself into a weak silence.

Wilmot stared. 'What's so funny?'

'It's the tins of fruit,' his mother told him. 'We didn't think you'd have had much of that kind of food all these years, either. So when they were in the shops just before Christmas, Lucy got some specially. Queued up for hours, she did. We had one at Christmas and then we saved the other two for when you came home. They're in the cupboard now.' She nodded her head and Geoffrey opened the cupboard door and took the two cans out, one in each hand. 'You see? Peaches and apricots . . .'

The first few weeks were a mixture of joy and dismay.

They would have been better in their own place. A married couple needed time and space and privacy to feel their way back after years of separation. Years in which each had suffered misery unknown to the other, misery they would never be able to convey because there was just too much of it and anyway the memories were too sharp, too painful to recount. And yet they needed to know. How else, Lucy thought, could they ever understand?

'We heard such awful stories,' she said to Wilmot. 'Men being beaten and tortured. I worried about you all the time.'

'And don't you think I worried about you?' he demanded, as if she had criticised him. 'You're not the only one who worries about other people. You don't know what it was like out there.'

'I know. I know. Don't take it like that,' she begged. 'I didn't mean it that way. I just wanted you to know – I love you so much, Wilmot, I was frantic.'

He stared at her, then he reached out and pulled her towards him. 'I love you too, Lucy. I'm an ungrateful sod. It's just that – well, you don't know, you'll never be able to picture it. I can't tell you –'

'Try. Try. I'll never be able to understand if you don't try. I'll never be able to share it with you.'

'*Share* it!' He gave a harsh bark of laughter. 'Lucy, you don't know what you're saying. You can't *share* it. How can you? It's over – thank God – and I don't want to have to go through it all again. It was bad enough the first time. I just want to forget it now, that's all, forget all about it, forget it ever happened, *forget* it, can't you understand that?'

'Yes, yes, of course I understand. I'm sorry, Wilmot. We won't talk about it again.'

But he couldn't leave it alone. Nothing that had been suffered in Plymouth, nor anywhere else, was as bad as being in a Japanese POW camp. As he walked the ruined streets and stared at the shattered buildings, his lips curled a little. Why hadn't anything been done? Why was it still in such a state? Bombing? He and his mates had been bombed at sea, bombed by aircraft and fired on by other ships. 'And *we* didn't have shelters to go to. We just had to take it.' The big shops smashed, the churches left as gutted shells? 'Yes, but you still *had* shops, didn't you? Spooner's and Dingle's and all those, they just moved somewhere else, didn't they? They still kept going, you could still buy things. And they kept on having services at St Andrew's just the same, never mind that the roof was gone.' Rationing? 'Look, don't talk to me about rationing, everything's rationed on a ship at sea, everything, all the time. Didn't you ever realise that?'

And he was right, Lucy thought sadly. Everything they had suffered, Wilmot had suffered too. And more, so much more. More than she would ever know.

She had clues to it, though. They came without Wilmot knowing it, in his behaviour during the day and even more so at night, when she lay awake, listening to his fevered mutterings, or woke to his screams.

'No! *No!* You can't do that – oh my God . . . Let me out of here, let me out, *let me out* – oh, *Christ* . . .'

She woke him as soon as she could, only seconds after he had woken her with his cries, and he would stare at her with wild unrecognising eyes, eyes that had fear in them, and pain, and murder. There were moments when she almost feared that he would turn on her, as if she were one of his tormentors, as if he truly believed himself back in that nightmare world.

'Wilmot. Wilmot, it's me, Lucy, your wife. Oh Wilmot, my poor darling, my sweetheart.'

And suddenly he was awake, trembling and soaked with sweat, quivering in her arms, sobbing like a baby, muttering incoherent words that might perhaps have told her everything, had she only been able to understand.

He might indeed have told her at those times, deep in the night, but she soothed and shushed him, unable to bear his pain, wanting only to smooth away the terrors and give him the comfort he so desperately needed.

'It's all right, darling. You're here with me. You're home again. It's all right. They've gone now. Nobody's going to hurt you. Nobody's ever going to hurt you again.'

It was as if she had another child, she thought when his sobs had quietened at last and he had drifted back to sleep, still cradled in her arms. Another child to tend and care for, to give her strength to and to shield from the world.

But what of her own need for comfort and strength?

Wilmot had been home for three weeks when David came again. He was sitting in the kitchen reading the paper, a mug of tea at his side, and he turned his head slightly sideways and frowned as the other man walked in.

David stopped in the doorway, then moved quickly forwards, holding out his hand. 'Wilmot. It's good to see you again. How are you?'

Wilmot rose slowly. He didn't take the hand David was offering. His eyes went to the empty sleeve but he made no comment. Instead, he said rather coldly, 'I didn't know the guests were allowed in the kitchen.'

David let his hand fall. 'I'm sorry. I don't suppose you remember me. David. Tremaine. I used to come here before – before the war. We spent quite a bit of time together.'

'Oh, I remember you,' Wilmot said, but not as if he had only just recognised David. Clearly, he had known him the moment he opened the door. 'I remember you all right. Even if I didn't, they all talk about you all the time.'

David flushed a little. 'Oh, I'm sure they don't,' he said uncomfortably. 'Not all the time! They must be much too pleased to have you back to bother with me.'

'Yes, you'd reckon so, wouldn't you?' Wilmot agreed without pleasantness. 'You'd think they'd be glad to have me back. The returning hero. The long-lost son and husband and father. You'd *think* they'd be pleased.'

David looked at him. 'Look, perhaps it would be better if I went . . .'

'Do what you like,' Wilmot said indifferently. 'Mind you, you'll have to pay for your room even if you don't stay here. That's only fair, isn't it? 'Tisn't easy running a hotel, can't have guests ratting on their bookings, we'd be bankrupt in no time if everyone did that.'

'Wilmot. What's the matter? We used to be friends.'

'Yes, that's what I thought.' Wilmot's voice was cold, and bitter. 'And you've been friends with Lucy too, haven't you? All through the war, all the time I've been away.'

'For God's sake, Wilmot. You're not suggesting there's been anything wrong between me and Lucy? There never has been. There never would be. You can't believe we'd—'

'Listen,' Wilmot said. 'I can believe anything of anyone. I've *seen* what people can do to each other. I've seen worse things than you can imagine. Anything's easy for me to believe.'

David sighed. 'But that's different.'

'Is it? How is it different?'

'Lucy's your wife. And she's – well, she's Lucy. She would never betray you. She's absolutely loyal.'

'Be your age,' Wilmot said. 'I've only been home three weeks but I can see it. Blokes who've come home and found their wives living with other men. Found they've got more kids than they thought. Found their homes empty and the missus disappeared to God knows where. And how about the ones who've buggered off to America, eh? Couldn't even stay in the same country. That's how loyal women are.'

'But that's not Lucy. She hasn't done any of those things. She's still here. She loves you.'

'So she says,' Wilmot said gloomily. 'So she says.'

He sat down again and leant both elbows on the table,

126

burying his face in his hands. 'Oh my God. I'm sorry, David, I don't know what I'm saying. I don't know what gets into me. When something unexpected happens, someone walks in and takes me back to those days, it seems like something happens in my mind. It's like a click. I can't explain it. I'm *sorry*.'

David moved swiftly round the table and laid his hand on Wilmot's shoulder. 'It's all right. It's all right.' He felt the bones beneath his fingers. Wilmot didn't look as thin as he'd feared. They'd built him up in hospital, nursed him back to health. He'd been down to six stone when he came out of the camp, Lucy had told David when she wrote, though it was difficult to believe. He must have looked like a skeleton. Now he was up to ten stone, and although that was still light for his build, it wasn't more than just ordinarily thin. David reminded himself that Wilmot had suffered more than anyone could dream, and that his real recovery would need more than just feeding up.

'You don't have to worry,' he said, pulling out a chair and sitting down. 'It'll get better in time. It will.'

Wilmot lifted his face and David saw with pity that it was wet with tears. 'Will it? And how would you know?'

His truculence was returning. Lucy had hinted at something like this. It's been so bad for Wilmot, he can't take in the fact that anyone else has had a bad time, she'd said. It isn't his fault.

David disliked referring to his own suffering, but now he shrugged his shoulder, lifting his empty sleeve. 'I've had my ups and downs.'

Wilmot stared for a minute, then nodded. 'Oh, yeah. You lost that in the blitz, didn't you? And what did they do? Take you to hospital, did they? Made it all neat and tidy, sprinkled you with Dettol, bandaged you up, sent you home to Mum. Made sure no nasty germs got into it . . . Shall I tell you what happened to a bloke in our camp who lost his

127

arm? Shall I? It just got left, that's what. I don't know why he didn't bleed to death. We bandaged it with what we could, we gave bits of our own shirts and wrapped them round his stump, and there was no anaesthetic for him, nothing to put him off to sleep, not even a drink. It didn't stop him bleeding, either. The blood kept on coming through the rags. You could always tell where he was after that from the flies.' He paused and lifted his mug, took a long draught of tea. 'It went bad, of course. Bound to, wasn't it? Stank to high heaven – God, I never smelt such a pong.'

'What happened to him?' David asked after a pause, and Wilmot threw him a contemptuous glance.

'Well, what d'you think happened? Went mad, of course, and died. It didn't take all that long, but I reckon it was too long for him.'

There was a silence. David felt sickened by the story and all that it implied. He felt a deep pity for Wilmot and all the men who were tortured by such memories.

'You lost that the night Patsy copped her lot, didn't you?' Wilmot said suddenly. 'And Zannah. You lost your arm. Patsy lost both her legs, and Zannah – we lost Zannah.'

David wished he had not referred, even obliquely, to his own losses. He knew that if he tried to identify with Wilmot, if he mentioned Stevie and Heather, it would only add to the other man's bitterness. And Wilmot was right, after all. In the context of Patsy and Zannah, his arm was little enough to lose. He thought suddenly of the saying one quoted at times. *I'd give my right arm* . . . He hadn't even done that. He'd only given his left arm.

'I'd have given both my arms to have saved them,' he said quietly. 'I'd have given my life.'

'Yeah,' Wilmot said, too wearily even to mock, 'yeah.'

It was with deep relief that David heard the front door open and Lucy's footsteps coming along the passage. She opened the door and came in, already chattering about the shops, the queues, what she had managed to buy at the butcher's. She stopped abruptly just inside the kitchen.

'David! You're early – I didn't expect you till this afternoon.'

He smiled and stood up. Normally he would have gone to her, given her a light kiss. This time, he didn't move, simply held out his hand and, with a flicker of a glance towards Wilmot, she shook it gravely.

'How are you, David?'

'I'm well. And you?' Their eyes met and their feelings communicated with the ease they had grown used to: half sadness at having to suppress their normal easy, friendly delight in each other's company, half amusement. It seemed so farcical, Lucy thought, and wondered what had happened between David and Wilmot.

'Your room's ready for you,' she said, and then decided that this was ridiculous, they couldn't go on like this, 'but you'll have a cup of tea first. I'll put the kettle on. And you'll have your supper with us as usual. I know Wilmot will want to talk to you.'

The faces of both men told her, in different ways, that she knew no such thing, but she ignored them and went to the sink to fill the kettle. She lit the gas, keeping her back to them, and heard with relief the sound of David moving his chair slightly to sit down again. When she turned back, Wilmot was finishing his tea.

'So how's it going, then?' he asked David in perfectly normal tones. 'Still in the same job, are you?'

Patsy had been out with her grandparents. They didn't often take her out these days because the wheelchair was too heavy for them to push up hills, but it was a bright afternoon and Maud said it seemed a shame for the child to sit indoors all day. They could get her up the slope of Lockyer Street and on to the Hoe if they both gave a hand to it, and Geoff could walk that far with them and help too, even if he did want to go off with his friends straight after. So that was what they'd done, and they came back full of news.

'The Promenade Pier's being all cleaned up and the rubble taken away. I wonder if they're going to rebuild it.'

'No, they'll do the houses first. They're just making it safe.'

'I reckon they'll get the big swimming-pool going, though. Look at it this way, people will want it, in the summer.'

'David!' Maud was first into the kitchen, pulling off her woolly gloves and unwinding her scarf. 'Oh, you're early.'

'Is Uncle David here?' Patsy manoeuvred her chair through the doorway. 'You haven't been to see us for ages,' she accused him. 'There's all sorts of things I want to tell you. And I've read that book you lent me, have you brought the next one?' Patsy was working her way steadily through the stories of Arthur Ransome. 'I've read *The Wouldbegoods* as well, Mum got it from the library. Have you read that? I like Oswald Bastable best, he's so clever. It isn't magic though, like *Five Children and It* and *The Phoenix and the Carpet*, it's just about an ordinary family.'

David laughed and pulled her wheelchair towards him. 'And what's wrong with ordinary families?'

'Well, they're just ordinary, aren't they? I wish I had a magic carpet and could go anywhere I wanted.'

'You wouldn't like it when you got there,' Wilmot said. He had been watching his daughter, his eyes veiled behind half-closed eyelids. 'And what about your dad, don't I get a kiss?'

'Oh yes.' But there was a tinge of doubt in Patsy's voice. Wilmot didn't normally ask for a kiss every time she came in. 'But you're here all the time now, aren't you, and we only see Uncle David now and then.'

There was nothing anyone could say in response to this. David's 'now and then' was seldom more than six weeks between visits, whereas Wilmot had been away for years, but nobody missed the innocent implication of Patsy's words.

'Well, is there any tea in that pot?' Maud asked, a shade loudly. 'Or have you drunk it all?'

'It's not long made.' Lucy refilled the kettle and got out more cups. Suddenly, everyone moved and became busy, Arthur pulling off his cap and unwrapping his muffler, Maud helping Patsy out of her coat and Lucy putting away the shopping she had queued for. The kettle whistled and she dropped another spoonful of tea into the pot and poured boiling water on top. Maud filled a jug with milk and set the little bottle of saccharin tablets on the table.

'I'll just get the sugar out for David.'

'Oh, David has sugar, does he?' Wilmot's voice, like Maud's, was a trifle over-loud. 'Why's that, then, David? Saccharin not good enough for you, is that it? Rather use our sugar, would you?'

'David doesn't use our sugar,' Lucy said quietly. 'He brings his own.'

'You're giving him our bowl.'

'Which was filled with David's sugar the last time he came.' Lucy set the bowl down and put a spoonful of sugar into David's cup. She gave her husband a look as she did so, a look that dared him to question her further. Wilmot's eyes narrowed and the skin around his mouth whitened and looked taut.

David said quickly, 'It doesn't matter, Lucy. I'd just as soon have saccharin.'

'Why? You don't like it. It's your sugar and you can choose how you have it. You leave more here than you use, anyway.'

'It doesn't matter,' he said again, and Lucy sat down, biting her lip. Maud gave her a quick glance and poured tea for everyone. The rest of them passed the saccharin bottle around in silence.

'They say there's been snow up north,' Arthur remarked,

131

apparently oblivious of the atmosphere. 'Had any up London way, David?'

Lucy laughed a rather brittle laugh. 'London's not exactly "up north", Dad.'

'Well, it's more north than Plymouth is,' Arthur said with irrefutable logic. 'They could have had snow. Mind you, we don't want it, do we, not now the football's getting going again. I've been telling our Wilmot, he ought to come and see Argyle play, but he don't seem interested.'

'I've been up to the ground,' Wilmot said. 'It's a shambles.'

'Well, it was bombed, wasn't it? Same as everything else round here. It don't mean the team doesn't play, it don't mean we can't go and support them.' Arthur sucked at his tea. 'We've all been through it. We've all got to carry on.'

Lucy looked at him. Arthur was sixty-seven years old and showing it. He ought to have retired years ago, ought to be able to take life a bit easier, but instead he'd been forced to carry on, struggling to run a small hotel all through the war, seeing the houses all around him bombed and blazing, seeing his own house damaged. He probably wanted nothing more than just to sit in his armchair and smoke his pipe and listen to the football and the boxing on the wireless, and stroll down to the pub and have a yarn with his mates. But instead, he had to carry on.

And Maud too, although she'd always been a big woman, she looked worn and tired, as if she'd had enough. They've both had enough, Lucy thought, and it's up to me and Wilmot to take it off their shoulders.

She talked to Wilmot about it later that evening, as they got ready for bed. It was the only time they could be private together, in this half-hour before sleeping, but that didn't mean Wilmot was always ready to take advantage of it. Already, Lucy had learned that she was wise to choose her moment for raising a difficult subject.

'Your dad looks a bit run down,' she remarked, pulling off her jumper. 'I think it's getting a bit too much for him, running this place.'

'Well, he doesn't do all that much, does he?' Wilmot was already in his pyjamas. He took off his clothes in two movements – vest, shirt and jumper in one go, trousers, pants and socks in the second – and left them heaped on the floor. He used to be so tidy, she thought. All sailors were – you had to be, on a ship. Now, he didn't seem to care any more. 'You do the books and all the paperwork.'

'I know, but he still does quite a bit around the place. And your mum, she's run off her feet with the beds and cooking. I do as much shopping as I can to take it off her, but it's still a lot of work. And there ought to be more, now that we'll be getting more guests.'

'God knows why.' He was in bed now, dragging out the sheets and blankets that Lucy had tucked in that morning, punching his pillows into a crumpled ball. 'I can't see why anyone would want to come to this godforsaken hole.'

'Wilmot! It's your *home*.'

'It's a godforsaken hole,' he repeated. 'Plymouth *and* this so-called hotel. I mean, look at it, Lucy. Think what it used to be like – a place you could ask people to. It's a dump now.'

She wasn't clear whether he meant the city or the house now, but his words could be fairly applied to either. 'Well, it's up to us to get it back again, isn't it?'

'How d'you mean?'

He didn't really want an answer to that, she thought. His tone was truculent again, daring criticism or even the mildest suggestions which could be construed as criticism, but she went doggedly on.

'Well, we could start by keeping it clean and tidy.' She couldn't help the acidness in her voice as she glanced at his heap of clothes. 'We could do a bit of decorating. Freshen up the guest rooms. There's some new curtain material at the Co-op, I thought I might get some. It'd be so nice to have pretty curtains after all that blackout.' She bit her lip. Blackout was something that was likely to start Wilmot off again. *You were lucky to have lights to hide*. 'And we ought to get some new crockery. I know it's only utility, but at least we could have cups and saucers and plates that matched. It would look much nicer in the dining-room.'

Wilmot whistled. 'You've got big ideas, haven't you? New curtains, tea sets – you'll be wanting to carpet the place from top to bottom next.'

'Well, it wouldn't hurt to do that either. Carpet makes a lot of difference to a place. And we've never replaced the carpet that was ruined when we had the bomb.'

'And where's all the money coming from?'

'We'll have to earn it,' Lucy said quietly.

Wilmot's demob papers had come through. He was no longer in the Navy. Lucy had wondered how he would take this, but he just looked them over and then pushed them aside as if they were of no interest and went back to reading the strip cartoons in the *Daily Mirror*. *Jane* was his favourite, of course, but he liked the lantern-jawed *Ruggles* as well. He seemed far more interested in their careers than in his own.

'What do you mean, earn it?' he demanded now, firing up at once. 'Are you telling me I'm lazy? Workshy, is that it?'

'No, of course not.'

'I'd have thought I'd done my bit for a while,' Wilmot said, as if addressing a third party, a whole crowd of third parties massed somehow in a corner of the bedroom. 'I'd have thought four years in a Jap prisoner-of-war camp – not to mention two years at sea before that, fighting enemy ships, living in fear of bombs and torpedoes – I'd have thought that was enough for a while. I'd have thought I was entitled to a bit of time off. Not a holiday, I wouldn't ask for anything as much as that, but just a bit of peace and quiet to get over it all. I'd have thought that was the least I could ask.'

'Wilmot, don't,' Lucy begged. 'I didn't mean that, you know I didn't. Of course you're entitled to some time to yourself. I just meant – well, someone's got to do the work, and your mum and dad are getting on, it's not fair to expect them to . . . I'm not saying *you're* not being fair,' she added hastily, seeing his face, 'just that we've got to sort things out. *Think* about it. That's all.'

'Well, that's not what it sounded like to me,' he muttered, watching her pull her nightdress over her head. 'It sounded to me as if you expected me to come up with something. All this talk about carpets and curtains and so on. *You've* had the use of the money all this time, Lucy. I didn't spend it, stuck there in POW camp.'

'I know.' She slipped into bed and put her arms around him. 'I didn't mean anything like that, Wilmot. I shouldn't have brought the subject up. I'm sorry.' She tried to draw him close but she could feel the resistance in him and her despair grew. 'Cuddle me close, love, like you used to do,' she whispered. 'Cuddle me close and forget all that. Let's just be us for a little while, shall we?'

Slowly, the resistance melted and he became soft in her arms. And then his body hardened in a different way and she gave a small sigh of relief and uttered a soundless prayer of thanks as she welcomed him and surrounded him with her own softness and her strength. And afterwards, as he fell asleep still wrapped in her arms, she prayed again that this night, at least, he would sleep without dreams.

For herself, however, the nightmare seemed scarcely begun, and as she lay awake, staring into the darkness, she felt more lonely than ever she had felt during those years of separation and fear. During that time, she had always been able to believe that the Wilmot she had known and loved still existed, and now she knew that he did not. Somewhere out in the Far East, at some time during those terrible years, the Wilmot she had known and loved so much had died and gone for ever.

Chapter Twelve

There were other times when Lucy was almost able to believe that Wilmot was recovering from his experiences. Times when he seemed no different after all from the Wilmot she had known, the cheeky sailor she had fallen in love with and married. He would wake from a good night's sleep, clear eyed and refreshed, reaching for her in the big bed. Their loving then was good, leaving her warmed and comforted. It was just a matter of time, she told herself. You couldn't expect him to get back to normal overnight. Look how long it had taken her to get over losing Zannah. Well, she still hadn't got over it, she never would, you couldn't ever really get over losing a child. And it was the same for Wilmot. He had to learn to live with his memories, just as everyone else did, and he *was* learning. He just had to take his own time.

'Let's take the kids over to Cawsand,' he said one morning just after Easter. 'It's time young Geoff learnt to swim.'

'Geoff can swim,' Lucy said, surprised that Wilmot didn't know this, then bit her lip. Of course he didn't know. There were a thousand things he still didn't know. 'David taught him.'

'Oh? That can't have been easy, with only one arm.' She wondered whether he was jealous, but there didn't seem to be any hidden meaning in Wilmot's tone. 'Well, I daresay he won't mind too much swimming with his dad, will he?'

'Of course he won't. He'll love it. They'll both like a day

out. So will I.' She snuggled up to him. 'It's nice of you to think of it.'

'Why shouldn't I think of it? I can still remember what it's like to be a father, you know.' He took in a breath and then said, 'I'm sorry, Lucy. I shouldn't have said that. I just get riled at times.'

'It was my fault.'

'No, it was mine. Let's forget it and start again. How about taking the kids to Cawsand today? We could go swimming.'

'They'd like that,' she said, smiling at him in relief. 'You can give Geoff a race. He's quite a good swimmer already.'

They got up and told the family their plans over breakfast. Patsy's face lit up, but Geoff scowled.

'I said I'd go up Central Park and play football.'

'You can do that any time,' Lucy said, 'but it's a lovely day and Daddy and I want to have a day out together.'

'We could do *that* any time.'

'But I want to do it today,' Wilmot said. 'You can run round and tell your mates you won't be coming. Tell 'em you'll play football tomorrow.'

'They might not play tomorrow. They might want to go fishing.'

'Then you can go fishing with them.'

'But I wanted to play football—'

'For heaven's sake,' Lucy said in exasperation, 'stop arguing, Geoff. You spent the whole war wishing Daddy was home, and now he is, you can't be bothered to spend a day out with him. Now, go and tell them you won't be playing football today and then come back here as fast as you can. It's much too nice a day to spend hanging about waiting for you.'

Geoff pushed out his bottom lip but said no more, and when he came back he looked more cheerful. Some of the other boys were spending the day with their families as

137

well, and the idea of a day on the beach was evidently more appealing.

'Don't make things difficult, Geoff,' Lucy said to the children in a low voice, as they waited in the passageway for Wilmot to come downstairs. 'We have to be very careful with Daddy. He's had a terrible time and it's affected him. It's almost like an illness.'

'You mean he's gone barmy,' Geoff said bluntly. 'That's what happened to everyone who was out there.'

'Geoff!' Lucy stared at him, shocked. 'That's a terrible thing to say.'

'Well, it's what everyone else says. The men who've come back from Japan just aren't the same any more. They've all come back funny in the head.'

'I don't care what people say. *You're* not to say such things. Daddy's not – not *any* of those things. He's just had a horrible time, worse than anything you can even think of, and he's got to have time to get over it all. And we've got to help him.'

The bedroom door opened and closed above them. Wilmot came down the stairs. He had found a pair of grey flannel trousers and a sports jacket that Lucy remembered from before the war. He had no tie on and his shirt was unbuttoned at the neck. He looked an ordinary father, ready to take his family out for the day, and when he gave them all his old cheerful grin Lucy's heart contracted with love.

'Right, then. Let's go, shall we?' He picked up the basket Lucy had packed with sandwiches, a Thermos flask and a bottle of water. Arthur appeared with an old deflated car inner-tube and dumped it in Geoff's arms. Lucy piled the towels and swimming costumes on to Patsy's lap.

'Aren't you useful,' she said, smiling at her daughter.

'Just a pack-mule, that's me,' Patsy said. 'A trolley. I sometimes wonder if there's any room for me in this wheelchair, when you've finished piling stuff into it.'

'Oh, we always put you in first, just to make sure,' Lucy

assured her. 'What I'm saving up for now is a chair with an engine and a trailer, so that we can all get in as well and save on bus fares.'

They manoeuvred the chair out of the front door and down the steps to the pavement. They were to take the ferry to Cawsand, and getting Patsy's wheelchair on to the boat was something of a problem. But the ferryman was helpful and soon she was installed between the seats, waiting eagerly for the short voyage across the Hamoaze.

Lucy sat with Wilmot, her hand on his arm. The sun was warm on her face and there was just the lightest of breezes. Gulls swooped around the boat and filled the air with mewing cries. The Hamoaze was busy with craft, much of it taking holidaymakers on trips up the river or across to Cornwall. Men and boys were fishing from Devil's Point, and the beaches at Bovisand and along Tinside were already thronged with people.

'They *are* starting to come back,' she said. 'Visitors. I know the centre's still in ruins, but the beaches are here still, and all the pools, and the lovely scenery. People need holidays, Wilmot, and they're starting to take them. It'll be even busier in the summer.'

'I suppose it will,' he said, and she tugged a little on his sleeve.

'Don't you see what it means? The hotel business will get better. It'll be worth making those improvements, Wilmot. It's worth thinking about expanding.'

He turned his head and stared at her. '*Expanding?*'

'Yes.' She hesitated. This was meant to be a holiday, but Wilmot seemed to have recovered his good mood and she had to take her chances when they arose. 'I was thinking – next door was much more badly damaged than our house was. I don't think the people are ever going to live there again. We could buy it – extend the hotel. It would be one way of making it pay while we all lived there. There just aren't enough rooms otherwise. It makes sense, Wilmot,' she went on eagerly. 'I've been thinking about it a lot and—'

'You've been *thinking* about it?' he interrupted. 'Without mentioning it to me? Shouldn't we be talking it over together? Just remember, *I'm* home now. I know you've done all the work for the past few years but I can take over from now on. You just concentrate on your own job – running the house and looking after us all.'

He turned away again and Lucy sat silent, watching the green heights of Mount Edgcombe come closer. She felt confused and uncertain.

Wilmot was right, she told herself. He was the man of the house and it was for him to decide what course their future took. She ought to be pleased that he was taking an interest, that he wanted to take on the responsibility. And yet, she was the one who had been at home, who had helped run the hotel, who knew its problems. Surely her voice counted for something.

And she wasn't at all sure that Wilmot was yet ready to take over the reins of the household, let alone a business. He was still suffering, she knew that. She hardly dared to guess at what was going on in his mind sometimes, when he sat staring into space, his face white under the yellowish tinge he still bore, his eyes cloudy with pain. What visions did he see then, she wondered, what agony did he relive?

He needed her help desperately. But sometimes she felt that she was losing her way and did not know how to give it.

Going to Cawsand was like going abroad, to some foreign fishing village on a Greek island, perhaps, or a tiny Italian harbour. The village was like a haven after the turmoil of Plymouth, untouched by bombing, the little stone cottages all set higgledy-piggledy in the twisting streets. The beach was a perfect horseshoe, with bright, clear water shimmering over the golden stones, bordered by low cliffs and thick, green woods.

Wilmot carried the basket with their lunch in while Lucy pushed the wheelchair and Geoff raced ahead with his towel still tightly rolled under his arm. A few other people were making their way to the cove, but there was plenty of room for everyone to find a space and soon Geoff had stripped off his clothes and was running into the sea.

Lucy spread a towel over Patsy's lap and started to get her clothes off. Wilmot stared in surprise.

'You're not putting her in the water?'

'Yes, why not? She loves it, don't you, Patsy?'

'But will she be all right? I mean, she can't walk . . .'

'That doesn't matter. We can carry her down the beach. Once she's in the water, she can float on the tyre. Blow it up now.'

'But people might stare at her.' He sounded really upset.

Patsy looked up at him. 'It's all right, Dad. I don't mind. I'm not ashamed of my legs – why should I be? Anyway, who cares if they want to spend their day looking at me instead of having fun?' He still looked doubtful and she added, 'I've been in the water before, Dad. I like it. My legs feel all right then – they feel like they used to. I can float and I can even swim a bit, using my arms.'

'Well, so long as you're sure,' Wilmot said. 'I don't want people staring at you, that's all.'

Lucy went on getting Patsy ready. When she was decent in the costume Lucy had made for her, she lifted her out and took her down to the edge of the water. She sat her down with her legs in the shallow, softly bubbling foam, and then came back to Wilmot. He had started to blow up the big inner-tube with a bicycle pump.

'You're not ashamed of her, are you, Wilmot?'

'Of course I'm not! She's no different from any other kiddie, she's just been hurt, that's all. Just like a soldier or a sailor who got wounded in the service of his country. I just don't like the idea of people looking at her.'

'Look,' Lucy said. 'Patsy's going to be like this for the

rest of her life. Another sixty or seventy years, probably. She's going to want to do things just the same as any other person, and she's going to have to get used to people staring. It's only the rude, ignorant ones who'll stare anyway.'

'That's all very well, but—'

'But what?' Lucy asked when he fell silent, glowering down the beach at Patsy, who was taking her weight on her hands, letting the waves lift her body as they came in. 'But what, Wilmot?'

'I just don't like to see it,' he burst out. 'My daughter, with her legs like that. I don't like people looking at her and knowing—' He stared at her, and to her dismay she saw tears in his eyes. 'I'm not ashamed of her. I'm *proud* of her. Maybe it's myself I'm ashamed of – that I wasn't here to look after her, to look after Zannah, *all* of you . . . Look –' he began to fumble with his clothes, his fingers shaking – 'I'll go in the water with her now. I'll do anything. Anything you want – for all of you.' His voice was trembling as if he were on the brink of weeping. He pulled off his shirt and dragged his trousers down. Like the rest of them, he had come out already attired in his swimming costume, navy woollen trunks. He stood up and picked his way down the beach.

'Oh, Wilmot—' Lucy felt a great pity well up in her and her own tears rise. She mustn't give way to them, mustn't let Wilmot's changes of mood upset her. Only a few months ago he'd still been in a Japanese POW camp, watching his friends suffer and die, not knowing when it would be his turn. It wasn't surprising he was having problems settling down.

She slipped out of her sundress (cut down from an old frock) and went down to join her family. Wilmot had lifted Patsy in his arms and was taking her out into deeper water. He let her float on her back and when Lucy joined them Patsy was laughing, relaxed, her useless legs drifting like a mermaid's tail. She was suddenly struck by a resemblance between Patsy and her father. All the children had inherited Lucy's red hair although none had quite the depth of violet-mauve of her eyes – except Zannah, she thought with a pang – but there was something in the shape of Patsy's face, in the curve of her lips, that was taken directly from Wilmot. The same cheeky smile . . .

It struck Lucy then how seldom Wilmot smiled like that now. The cheekiness had gone. Even when he tried, there was a difference, a touch of bitterness, a hardness that hadn't been there before. It was only in Patsy's laughing face that she could discover the Wilmot she had known and loved.

'Come on,' Wilmot said. 'Show me how you can swim.' He turned her over gently in the water, keeping one hand beneath her chin, the other under her stomach. Patsy moved her arms in the breast stroke. Wilmot moved along with her and they progressed through the water together with Lucy watching. A small wave broke over Patsy's face and she spluttered, then turned her head to laugh at them. Lucy and Wilmot caught each other's eye and smiled, and Lucy felt the warmth of her love once again in her heart.

Geoffrey had been swimming with some other boys, their bodies plunging and splashing in the water like porpoises. He came dashing up to his father.

'Race me, Dad! Race me to that rock.'

He was off before Wilmot had a chance to respond, his wiry body flashing through the waves. Wilmot, startled, took his eyes off Patsy and hesitated, then swam more slowly after his son. He didn't look at home in the water, Lucy thought. He probably hadn't been swimming since the beginning of the war – except when the *Exeter* had been sunk and he'd been left floundering in the Java Sea.

If the ship ever does sink I'll probably be a thousand miles from land anyway.

Geoff had reached the rock and was hanging on to it, watching his father's approach. Even at this distance Lucy could see the surprise in his eyes. Clearly, he'd expected to be overtaken and beaten in the race. He'd *wanted* to be beaten. He'd probably told the other boys all about his father, boasted to them.

Suddenly, Lucy knew she couldn't bear to see the contempt in his eyes. She steadied Patsy and called out.

'Time for lunch! Come on, Geoff, you've been in the water long enough now. I'm taking Patsy in and we'll have our sandwiches.'

Geoff stared at her. 'But we've only just got here –'

'I know, but we're all hungry. We'll have our picnic now.' She was walking into the shallows, Patsy drifting lightly beside her. 'Don't argue, Geoff. You'll be able to go in again later.'

'Not for an hour,' he grumbled. 'You never let me go in for an hour after I've eaten anything. Can't I stop in a bit longer, Mum? I'm not that hungry, honest.'

'I said, don't argue.' They were on the beach now, and she had to carry Patsy up to her wheelchair. The stones hurt her feet and she half staggered, then felt Wilmot beside her.

'I'll take her. Don't want you falling down, the pair of you.'

'Thanks.' She smiled at him and he took Patsy from her arms, as gently as if she were a baby.

Geoff came grumbling up the beach but cheered up when given a marmite sandwich and a whole boiled egg to himself. This was one of the great treats of the day, boiled eggs all round, and later came the second when Lucy gave Geoff a sixpence and told him to go and buy ice-creams for himself and Patsy. Ice-cream was one of those things you just hadn't been able to get during the war, and it was still a novelty. Even now, you couldn't get cornets, only thin slices off a block, sandwiched between two wafers, but it

144

was ice-cream and already dripping as Geoff came back along the beach.

They waited for an hour and then Wilmot took Patsy into the water again and let her 'swim' for as long as she liked, while Lucy and Geoff raced to the rock several times, reaching it neck and neck. Lucy touched it first twice and Geoff twice. The fifth time, she said, would be the decider, and she slowed up just enough to let him get there first, knowing that although he'd wanted his father to beat him he wouldn't want to come second to his mum.

They came up the beach together, laughing. The tide had come right in since they'd arrived and was now half out again. Wilmot and Patsy were back on the beach, surrounded by the debris of the picnic, but there were a few biscuits left and Lucy nibbled one, suddenly hungry. She sat on the blanket and leaned against Wilmot.

'It's been a lovely day. I hope you've enjoyed it, Wilmot.' She looked anxiously up into his face.

He grinned down at her. 'It's been a smashing day. You know, I've never been all that much of a one for beaches – not till I knew you, anyway. Couldn't ever see the pleasure in it, somehow.'

She wondered at that, knowing that he had grown up in Plymouth, within a few hundred yards of the Hoe and all those bathing pools, within easy reach of such beaches as this. But in Portsmouth, even in Southsea, she'd known people who weren't fond of the water and never went swimming. You didn't have to be a fish just because you lived beside the sea.

'Well, now you know what fun it can be we'll have to come again. And the children have enjoyed it. It's so nice to be all together again and to come out like this for picnics.' She began to pack up the bags and roll up the damp towels and bathing costumes. 'Let's have another day out before Geoff goes back to school. We could get the train and go out on the moor.' She paused suddenly, folding the blanket.

Geoff had already started to push Patsy's wheelchair up to the road. 'Wilmot – let's have another baby.' The words were out before she could stop them and she heard them with astonishment. She hadn't even known she was going to say them, hadn't known she was thinking about it.

He turned and stared at her. '*What?*'

Lucy flushed a little. 'I was thinking – when I said we were all together again – we're not, are we? We haven't got Zannah. And we never will have, and I know another baby would never take her place, nobody could . . . But I would like another one, Wilmot, I really would. Perhaps even two. We always said we'd have three or four, didn't we? You always wanted a big family. And now the war's over –'

To her dismay, Wilmot's face clouded over. More than clouded – it was like thunder. She gazed at him, feeling suddenly frightened. What had she done?

'My God!' he burst out. 'Don't you think I've got enough on my plate? No job – no proper home of my own – a family to support already – and you want *more*? You want us to start all over again, with a bawling kid keeping us awake at night, needing new clothes and nappies and all the gubbins . . .? Lucy, there's been times since I came home when I've thought I was going mad, but now I wonder if it was me at all. It's you. You're off your rocker.'

'Wilmot—'

He had turned away, was already taking his first stride up the beach. Lucy started after him and the blanket unfolded in her arms, came loose all around her like a flopping skirt and almost tripped her up. 'Wilmot – don't, please. I'm sorry. I shouldn't have said it. It was just – I don't know, I just suddenly felt . . . oh, *Wilmot.*'

At the pleading note in her voice, he turned. He was standing slightly above her on the beach and looked taller and somehow, she thought in her distress, stronger. He looked down at her and she reached out her hand, trying to sort out the blanket with the other.

'I'm sorry,' she said again, helplessly.

He grunted again. The anger had faded from his face. 'Well, all right.' He watched her struggle with the blanket. 'But don't let's hear any more about it, all right? It's not the right time, Lucy. Okay?'

She blinked rapidly, hoping he would not see her tears. The blanket was tightly folded again and she came level with him and took his arm. 'I do love you, Wilmot.'

He nodded. 'Come on. We'll have to hurry if we want to catch the next ferry.'

Lucy didn't think there was any need to hurry. If they didn't catch the ferry, there would be another one, and there weren't many nicer places than Cawsand to while away the time in the sunshine. But she said nothing and they walked up the beach together to where Geoff and Patsy were waiting, and then they walked back through the narrow streets like any other happy family after a day at the seaside.

Chapter Thirteen

Gradually Plymouth, like the rest of the country, dragged itself up out of the slough and began to construct a new life. For Plymouth, perhaps more than for any other city save Coventry, this meant an entirely new centre.

'We have an opportunity now to make a new Plymouth,' the City Council said. 'The old Plymouth which we loved has gone for ever. Now we must make the most of our opportunity to build a modern city, a city that will go forward proudly into the second half of the twentieth century.'

The local papers were full of the plan for the rebuilding of the great shops, the theatres and hotels which had been destroyed. Paton Watson, the city engineer, and Sir Patrick Abercrombie had designed it back in 1943 after the blitz had reduced so much of the city to rubble, but the work did not begin until March 1947, almost two years after the war had ended.

The winter of 1947 was the most bitter of a series of cold winters. The snow started in January and kept on falling. Lucy's mother wrote from Portsmouth to say that the King and Queen and the two Princesses had come to Portsmouth at the end of the month to set sail on HMS *Vanguard* for their visit to South Africa. The platform at the Harbour Railway Station had had to be swept clear of snow so that the red carpet could be laid. They were coming back in May and it would be nice if Lucy and Wilmot and the children could come for a visit then and see the Royal Family.

'They're saying that Princess Elizabeth might get

engaged then,' Lucy said, reading the letter at breakfast time. 'She's fond of that young Prince Philip of Greece. The King's said that if they still feel the same about each other when she comes back from this trip he'll let them get married.'

'I don't know how "they" know so much about it,' Arthur grunted. 'I wouldn't be telling the world and his wife if it was my girl getting sweet on a sailor. Mind, he's wise to take her out of the way for a bit, stands to reason a young girl like that isn't going to know her own mind.'

'Arthur!' Maud protested. 'What a way to talk, when your own son went into the Navy and brought home a nice young wife.'

Lucy smiled, pleased with the compliment. She and Maud hadn't always seen eye to eye, you couldn't expect it with two women sharing a house, especially a kitchen, but they'd got on well enough. 'I'd like to go to Pompey in May,' she said. 'It would be nice to see the King and Queen and the Princesses. Geoff won't be able to, of course.' Geoffrey had left school now and started work in the dockyard as an apprentice. 'But you and me could go, Wilmot, and take Patsy.'

'Well, we'll have to see about that, won't we?' Wilmot said. 'Depends how busy we are.'

Wilmot had more or less settled down, though he still suffered from the terrible nightmares which made him cry out at night and tore his temper to shreds for days afterwards, but Lucy had learnt to cope with his moods. She tried never to reproach him, knowing that he suffered deep remorse whenever he had been unfair to her or one of the children, telling herself that it wasn't really the true Wilmot who shouted and swore and stamped about the house, or who sat sullen and silent for hours on end. It was the man the Japanese had made of him. Somewhere deep inside, the real Wilmot still lived and, if she were only patient enough, one day he would come back to her.

149

Wilmot's main comfort at this time was Patsy. From the moment he had first seen her in her wheelchair, unable to jump up to greet him, he had shown her a tenderness that not even Lucy received from him. Irritable, even surly, for so much of the time, he rarely failed to find a smile for his daughter, and he would take her up on the Hoe and for long walks through the ruined Plymouth streets, pushing her wheelchair tirelessly, the two of them chatting endlessly, or sometimes companionably silent.

Lucy was thankful that he could find such comfort, and glad to see it strengthened after the day on the beach. If she could not reach him herself these days, at least their child could touch his heart, and anything that could save him from the torment of his memories was to be welcomed. It was a shame he couldn't find a similar bond with his son, she thought sadly, but Wilmot and Geoff seemed to be drifting further and further apart and it was as much Geoffrey's fault as his father's. Or perhaps it was nobody's fault, but just another sad result of the war and the separations it had forced upon families. And perhaps Wilmot's return had been just at the wrong time for Geoff, who had been for so many years without his father and had perhaps built him into a hero in his boyish mind.

Nobody could describe Wilmot now as a hero. When he wasn't with Patsy, he resorted to his only other comfort – the rum bottle.

He had grown used to his daily 'tot' when in the Navy: from the age of eighteen onwards all sailors were given the traditional issue of strong, dark rum. They were supposed to drink it at once but some of them saved it so that they could have a 'bender' at the end of the week. Nobody had been given rum in the POW camps, of course, but it had been one of the things they all longed for and Wilmot seemed intent on making up for lost time.

'Just because Lord Nelson was pickled, it doesn't mean you've got to be too,' Lucy said once, acidly, referring to the story that Nelson's body had been brought back from war preserved in strong brandy, but she didn't have the heart to nag him. He'd had little enough pleasure from life in the past few years.

She had said no more about another child, and put the longing away from her. She knew that Wilmot would not be able to cope with the added responsibility, nor to the division of her own attention. How could she give a baby the devotion it needed, when Wilmot was as likely to wake crying in the night, and demand more? It wouldn't be fair to any of them, least of all the baby. But despite all her resolve, there were times when she could hardly bear to look into a pram or to see the joy on a young mother's face.

After a few desultory attempts to find a job Wilmot had agreed that it was best to take over the running of the hotel, and Arthur and Maud were now officially retired, although they still helped out here and there. It was the only way a living could be made: wages to staff of any kind would have eaten up any profit. Once again, Lucy had suggested expanding.

'I've told you before, you're talking daft,' Wilmot said. 'We can't afford to buy property. Especially ruins that have got to be rebuilt. We've always managed to make a living out of this place before.'

'That was before the war,' Lucy said, 'and you had more rooms to let then. Wilmot, it just isn't feasible to run this place as it is at present. Look at the figures.'

Wilmot shrugged the figures away and grew annoyed when Lucy persisted. He was in charge now, he told her, and she'd be better off looking after her own side of things than interfering with his. And couldn't he smell burning coming from the kitchen?

Lucy went back and took the potatoes off the heat. They'd boiled dry while she was talking to Wilmot in the little office, but they'd only just caught. He must have a nose like a bloodhound's. She poured some more water into the pan and it hissed fiercely, in much the same way as Lucy would have liked to do at her husband. There were times, she thought, when it was hard to keep a still tongue.

For most of the war, Lucy had helped both Maud and Arthur with the running of the hotel. She had done every job there was to do, from making the beds and cleaning the lavatories to cooking breakfasts. In the last few years, she'd more or less taken over the accounts and done all the ordering, the paying and the tax returns. She knew those accounts as well as she knew her own purse.

At the same time, she had encouraged Wilmot to take over. She'd wanted him to feel he was worth something, to know that he could do a proper job. He'd been lucky to have a business to walk into, but he'd needed all the encouragement and support Lucy could give him, and she'd given it willingly. She'd shown him how to work out all the figures, how to order food and the various materials needed for cleaning and maintenance, how to cope with all the official forms which seemed to multiply daily. He listened and looked and nodded, and said he understood, but it was probably better for Lucy to go on doing the work as a sort of secretary. She continued, maintaining the fiction that he was now in charge, but it came as a shock now to realise that he actually believed it, and that her work was virtually discounted.

It was the same for many women, she knew. Women who had taken on men's work during the war and now found themselves pushed aside. Naturally, the men wanted their jobs back. They'd been torn away from them and made to go and fight when they didn't want to, gone through all sorts of hell, and now they wanted to come back and resume their lives. However, that didn't make it easy for the women who had driven buses and worked in offices or on farms, and even done dangerous war work, like driving ambulances or joining the Services. They'd tasted freedom and independence. They'd lived their own lives, made their own decisions, not had to answer to anyone. And now, suddenly, they were back in the kitchen, treated like skivvies. Like some sort of lower order.

'We've got brains and we've learnt to use them,' Kitty said to Lucy when she came down to Plymouth for a few days' holiday. 'We aren't going to say yes sir, no sir, three bags full sir any more.'

That was all very well when you weren't married, Lucy thought, but a husband needed to be looked up to. He needed to feel he was master in his own house.

And yet she knew that she was right over the hotel. Unless they let more rooms, they wouldn't be able to make a living, and the only other road led to bankruptcy.

The winter brought a halt to most of the plans to rebuild Britain. For months, snow lay like a frozen blanket over the country. The frost went down to twenty degrees, the coldest since records had begun in 1890. Power cuts were imposed to save fuel, and police patrolled the streets warning shopkeepers against using lights or any other electrical appliances during the prohibited hours. From nine in the morning until four in the afternoon, except for the dinner-hour, the power was cut to every home. Street-lights went out again and it was as bad as it had been during the blackout itself. What traffic dared to take to the streets, creeping slowly along the icy roads, was brought to a halt more than once, unable to negotiate the hills, and people who were on their way home from a long, cold day at work, had to get off the buses and walk for miles. And at home, as often as not, they found only a meagre fire, for coal was rationed and hardly ever available.

People died of cold.

The city transport department did its best. Men came out with water tenders and sprayed the roads with saltwater, which was supposed to melt the thick icy covering. Instead, it too froze, adding a new layer to the solid crust. Along the edge of the beaches the sea itself froze, forming a foamy ridge of crystalline billows. Out on Dartmoor, ponies and sheep perished in their hundreds.

'We'll have a hot summer after this,' one man said to Lucy as he shovelled away the latest fall of snow from the pavement in front of his house. 'You see if we don't.'

So we might, she thought, but it wasn't much comfort just now, with the country as cold as Siberia.

The thaw came in March, though they said that on Dartmoor it would be June before all the snow, frozen in hollows, would melt. It came only slowly, though, and was followed by more bad weather. In April, a gale swept the city and left a trail of destruction, sweeping away newly built walls and hoardings. The task of rebuilding, which had barely begun, had to be started all over again.

In May, Lucy took Patsy to Portsmouth. Geoff wasn't interested in seeing the King and Queen anyway, and Wilmot grumbled that there was too much work to do in the hotel for him to be able to leave. Lucy, knowing that he wanted her to feel guilty about going away, took no notice. It was time she went to see her own mum and dad, she said; they were getting on the same as Arthur and Maud were, and didn't see much of her and the children.

Wilmot came to the station with her and they got Patsy's wheelchair into the guard's van and lifted Patsy into a seat in the nearest carriage. Kenny was coming to meet her at the other end, Lucy said, and she put her arms round Wilmot's neck and kissed him.

'I'll miss you.'

Guiltily, she realised that she always felt fondest of Wilmot when they were about to be parted. She could see him then as he had been, not as he had become, knowing that tonight she would not be disturbed by his nightmares nor saddened by his lovemaking. It didn't happen so often now – he found failure in that area even harder to bear than his other failures – but he still turned to her from time to time, at first loving and gentle, and then gradually despairing, berating her for not exciting him, complaining that it was her fault, she wasn't ready quickly enough, he'd been all right a few minutes ago and now it was too late . . . He beat at the pillows with his fists in frustration and Lucy lay beneath him, helpless. If she moved it was wrong, if she didn't move it was wrong, she must caress him, yet she must not touch him *there*, or in *that* way, or at all. It was her fault, her fault, her fault . . .

There was only one way out of the awful state he was in. Lucy tried everything she could think of, loathing herself all the while, and eventually she would succeed. By then, she was usually in tears, and perhaps it was her tears that helped him, for he smiled then as he raised himself above her, smiled as he looked down into her sobbing face. And afterwards he collapsed on her body, almost unconscious with exhaustion and she wrapped her arms around him, sobbing still, but whether for herself or for him she scarcely knew any longer.

For a few nights now, away in Portsmouth, she would at least be able to sleep undisturbed.

The train steamed along the coast, up the estuary towards Exeter, along the cliff at Dawlish, through the tunnels in the red rock at the edge of the shore. Patsy sat with her face pressed to the window. She was thirteen now. Her face had lost its childishness and acquired an attractive thoughtfulness. Her vivid eyes sparkled with life. If she weren't in a wheelchair, Lucy thought sadly, she'd have the boys after her any time now.

But what boy would want a girl who couldn't even walk?

It was several hours before the train finally pulled in at Portsmouth Town station. Patsy had wanted to go on to the harbour, only another five minutes; she enjoyed the sensation of being almost at sea, with the water visible below the boards of the steps and platforms and the big Isle of Wight paddle steamers waiting at the end. But the town station was nearer for Kenny to come, and Lucy was at the window waiting as the carriage came to a halt on the bridge overlooking the Guildhall Square.

'We'll have to be quick. We've only got a few minutes to get the wheelchair off and you into it.'

'Well, if you get left on the platform you'll have to come and meet me at the harbour anyway,' Patsy said with a grin. 'At least it can't go any further than that without dropping into the sea.'

It might have been a good idea to have done that after all, Lucy thought. She was always anxious about getting Patsy, the chair and all their luggage off in time, before the guard blew his whistle. People were usually helpful and there was generally a porter to help, but you never knew . . . And suppose Kenny wasn't there, suppose for some reason he hadn't made it? She leant out of the window, ignoring the warnings not to do so, and stared down the platform, looking for her brother's red head.

There was no sign of him.

Oh, Kenny, she thought in exasperation, where are you? It was almost impossible for her to manage everything by herself. If he didn't come, she'd have to get a porter to help her out of the station and find a taxi, if there were such a thing to find, and goodness knows what that would cost. She turned her head as the train came to a halt, looking for red hair. He might have a hat on of course, but Kenny seldom wore anything on his head. And then she heard her name being called.

'Lucy. *Lucy*.'

It wasn't Kenny's voice. Unbelievingly, she turned her head again, and watched as a tall figure came down the platform towards her. She stared into his eyes and then, as he lifted his hand and opened the door, she stepped down and found herself held against his chest.

'Lucy,' he said, folding his one arm about her and burying his face in her hair. 'Lucy. It's so good to see you.'

'David,' she said, and felt the tears sting her eyes.

David had withdrawn from their lives during the last few months. His work in Plymouth had ended with the war and although he still came down to Cornwall to see his mother, he seldom broke his journey to visit the Pengellys. His presence in Portsmouth came as a complete surprise to Lucy.

'David! I never thought you'd be here.'

'I'm writing a piece on their trip to South Africa.' David had returned to ordinary journalism after the end of the war. 'I couldn't come to Pompey without seeing your parents and when they told me you were coming – well, I'm afraid I couldn't resist the temptation to come and meet you.'

'I'm glad. I've missed you.'

They looked at each other, standing on the station platform surrounded by Patsy's wheelchair and their luggage, the feeling between them acknowledged without words – the feeling that had grown early in the war, perhaps even before that, perhaps had been there since their very first meeting. The feeling that had grown and deepened to love, and would never alter.

David wasn't staying with the Travers: he had a room in a small seafront hotel at Southsea, about fifteen minutes' walk away. The next morning he came down after breakfast and spent the day with Lucy and Patsy, and at Emily's insistence stayed for supper.

'I can't eat your rations,' he objected. 'I had to give my book to Mrs Watson at the Seahorse, I ought to eat there.'

'Go on, we can squeeze in an extra one,' Emily said, giving him a push. 'Anyway, didn't you bring us that lovely tin of ham and those eggs? I reckon we can spare you a few veg out of the garden to go with them.'

The *Vanguard*, carrying the King and Queen and the young Princesses, steamed back into Portsmouth Harbour on Sunday evening. Lucy and David pushed Patsy's wheelchair to the Sallyport and carried her up to the top of the walkway. From here, they could see straight across the narrow entrance to the harbour and across to Gosport on the other side. The tall tower of Holy Trinity church stood out behind the buildings of HMS *Dolphin*, the submarine base, and all along the seawall at Haslar as well as on Gosport Hard itself, people could be seen waiting to see the ship bringing Their Majesties home.

'You'd never think this little entrance was big enough to let big ships through,' Lucy said, looking at the neck of the harbour. 'And there's all that huge space hidden away behind.'

'That's what's made Portsmouth so important.' David gazed out towards the Isle of Wight. 'It's sheltered, too. Look, Patsy, there she comes.'

The smooth grey ship slid through the water towards them, surrounded by the tugs and yachts which had gone out to meet her. *Vanguard* was a warship, but she was used by the King whenever he needed to go to sea. He was a sailor himself and had served in the Royal Navy in the days when he'd never dreamed he would one day be King. Now *Vanguard* was dressed overall, flags of all colours flying from her masts to her bow and stern, and her decks were lined with sailors, their white cap-covers gleaming in the evening sunshine.

'It's lucky they've come back after May the first,' Patsy observed. 'It wouldn't have looked nearly so nice with the sailors still in black caps.'

The ship passed so close that they could clearly see the King and Queen, with the two Princesses, standing on the bridge. Patsy waved and cheered with the rest of the crowd and Lucy felt a lump come into her throat. The King and Queen had stayed with their country all through the war, refusing to leave for the safety of Canada, refusing even to leave London. It was said that the Queen had even said she was glad when Buckingham Palace had been bombed because now she could 'look the East End in the face'. Only now, when their country was safe at last, had they left to visit another part of their empire.

'I wonder if they'll let Princess Elizabeth get engaged to Prince Philip now,' she said as the ship proceeded up the harbour. Faintly, on the still air, they could hear the thin, high whistle of the bosun's pipes as *Vanguard* passed the Semaphore Tower and the masts of HMS *Victory*, lying in dry dock in the dockyard. All ships entering Portsmouth Harbour made this mark of respect to *Victory* and her admiral, Lord Nelson. 'It would be nice to have a royal wedding.'

'I bet they will,' Patsy said as they made their way back down the steps and began to walk through the streets of Old Portsmouth. 'I bet she'll have twelve bridesmaids, too. Can we go and see them again tomorrow, Mum? They're going to drive all along the road from the dockyard to the Guildhall Square and the Lord Mayor's going to have a big reception for them there, and then they're going to catch the train to London. We can go, can't we? Grandma was showing me the route in the *Evening News*.'

Lucy laughed. 'Of course we can. So long as you don't mind the crowds. You might not be able to see much, you know.'

'Well, it's worth a try,' Patsy declared. 'And I certainly won't see anything if I stop at home. You don't mind helping to push me, do you, Uncle David?'

He smiled at her. 'I don't mind at all.'

They walked on through the streets, so many of them still showing the damage of war. There had been very little rebuilding here yet, and the craters and ruined houses had become overgrown with dandelions, thistles, grasses and the arching bushes of buddleia. For a few moments nobody spoke, and Lucy glanced sideways at David.

She was still rather shaken by the surge of joy she had felt upon seeing him again. It was several months since they had met, and she had received only two letters from him, both addressed to Wilmot as well as herself. She had tried to hide from herself just how much she had missed him during that time, knowing that he was right to distance himself. Wilmot had made it more and more clear that he did not welcome David's position in his family. 'Getting his feet under the table' had been one of his kinder references. It was in vain that Lucy tried to convince him that there was nothing more than friendship between them, and even though she did not think that Wilmot genuinely believed she had been unfaithful to him, there was a tiny core of honesty in her that would not let her forget the kiss they had shared, nor the longings that had torn at her heart. Perhaps Wilmot sensed it; perhaps although he wanted to believe in her, some subconscious knowledge fed his jealousy.

The crowds who had come to see *Vanguard* return to Portsmouth were dispersing, many of them wandering along the seafront past Clarence Pier towards Southsea. Lucy pushed Patsy's wheelchair, feeling more content than she remembered feeling for a long time. It's as if we were a family, she thought. And yet she had walked like this with Wilmot and Patsy and Geoffrey often enough, along the Hoe, the four of them a real family, and not felt so content.

She glanced again at the man walking by her side. He was tall and rather thin, his empty sleeve pinned tidily against his jacket as always. He was forty-four years old now and his hair was beginning to grey at the temples. He looked faintly tired, his eyes shadowed, but she knew the shadow was not of weariness but of grief. He still mourned the family he had lost in the blitz; he would mourn them always.

Sadly, Lucy wished that she could give him comfort, but that was forbidden them.

The next morning dawned rather dull, with a light drizzle damping the air. It seemed that everyone in Portsmouth was intent on seeing the King and Queen and their daughters drive through the city. The streets were decked with flags, and every schoolchild was lined up along the route, each clutching a Union Jack. David came early to collect the family, and he, Emily and Lucy made their way to the Hard, taking turns to push Patsy's chair.

'It's a shame your father didn't feel up to coming,' Emily said. 'He thinks a lot of the King and Queen.'

'Wilmot's dad was always one for the Duke of Windsor,' Lucy remarked. 'While he was Prince of Wales, anyway. He doesn't think so much of him now.'

'Well, nobody does. Spent the war nicely out of the way, didn't he? And they say he was a Hitler sympathiser anyway. Still, we don't want to talk about that today. Here's a good spot.'

They settled themselves at the edge of the pavement to wait. It seemed as if the whole of Portsmouth and Gosport was there that morning, waiting to see their King and Queen. Lucy remembered the day they had come to Plymouth and walked on the Hoe, six years ago. She had gone up to see them, with Maud and Arthur and her two daughters. Patsy had run in front of her, she remembered, her pigtails flapping. Zannah had been so excited at the thought of seeing the King and Queen, and so comically disappointed that they hadn't worn their crowns.

The crowd began suddenly to cheer and the sound swelled about her like the roar of waves on a stormy shore. The car containing the King and Queen and the two

Princesses was coming out of the dockyard gates and along the thronged road. Lucy turned her head again and watched, and saw their smiling faces and their gently waving hands.

They're just people, she thought in some surprise, and then laughed at herself. What had she thought they were? Creatures from a fairytale? She remembered Zannah's disappointment that they were not wearing crowns, but she was glad of it. They were people, like herself and David.

Almost too late, she began to join in the waving and cheering, and to her great delight, the Queen's head turned at that moment and the china-blue eyes met hers. Just for a moment, Lucy felt that the Queen – the Queen of England herself – knew of the existence of Lucy Pengelly.

Chapter Fourteen

As had been expected, Princess Elizabeth became engaged to Prince Philip of Greece soon after her return from South Africa, and the wedding was announced for November. It was the lift the country had been waiting for. Suddenly, everyone was in a turmoil of excitement.

'They say she's getting presents from all over the world.'

'I wonder how many toast-racks they'll have!'

'They'll probably have to be gold-plated or they won't let them on the table.'

'Never mind nattering on about toast-racks, I just want to see her wedding dress.'

Predictably, most of the men professed boredom with the whole affair, but it was men who were doing most of the organising, Lucy pointed out, and men who wrote the newspaper reports and read out the news on the wireless. And it was a man's wedding too, as well as a woman's!

'You'd never think it was,' Wilmot grunted. 'I haven't seen any of the papers wondering what *he's* going to wear to get married in.'

'He'll wear his naval uniform, of course, same as you did.' Not that Prince Philip's uniform would be anything like Wilmot's – he was an officer, with lots of scrambled egg on his cap and gold rings on his sleeves, whereas Wilmot had been in the matelot's square rig. Still, it was the uniform of His Majesty's Royal Navy, and something to be proud of.

Prince Philip would look really handsome in his uniform, she thought. Half the women in the country were in love with him now, and envied the pretty young Princess her luck.

Wilmot was doing his best to forget the years he had spent in the 'Andrew'. He still called Plymouth 'Guz' and talked about his friends as 'oppos' and rum as 'grog' but the time at sea and in the POW camp were something he preferred to push out of his mind. Mostly, with the help of his daily 'tot', he managed it, but he couldn't control the dreams he still had at night.

Lucy didn't know what to do. When he'd had too much to drink, Wilmot was surly and unapproachable, and when he was sober it seemed a shame to upset him by bringing the subject up. Anyway, she would rather use those times to talk to him about the business.

'The place next door is up for sale,' she told him, coming back after another interminable morning spent queueing for this and that. 'The people are never coming back. They've moved out to Tavistock to be near their daughter. It's our chance, Wilmot.'

'Our chance? Our chance to do what – chuck our money down the drain?'

'Our chance to expand. Wilmot, we'd be daft not to. That place is going to go for a song. And next-door-but-one could go the same way. We could stretch right along three buildings. These houses would knock into one easily. Pengelly's could be a real hotel.'

'I thought it already was a real hotel. Why do we keep making all those beds if it's not a hotel? Why do all those people keep coming to stay?'

'Not enough beds,' Lucy said, refusing to rise to his sarcasm. 'Not enough guests. We've been into all this before.'

'And I said no before.' He was beginning to get angry, as he always did when he felt himself to be losing an argument. 'You say we'd be daft not to do it – I say we'd be daft even to think about it. Do you have any idea what it would cost?

We haven't got money like that. Where's it going to come from? Tell me that.'

'The bank,' Lucy said calmly, although her heart was thumping. 'The bank will lend it to us.'

'In a pig's ear!' Wilmot said scornfully.

'They will,' she said quietly. 'I've asked them.'

Wilmot stared at her. 'You've *asked* them? You mean you've been to the bank, without even discussing it with me, and you've *asked for money*?'

Lucy nodded. She kept her eyes fixed on his, as if this would help her keep control. She saw the dawning of real anger.

Wilmot came slowly to his feet. His face was suffused with a dark, angry red, his eyes were bloodshot and small between narrowed lids.

'You went to the bank without me? You didn't even mention it?'

'I've mentioned it often enough. I went to see if there was a chance, that's all. I haven't *done* anything, Wilmot.'

'Haven't *done* anything?' he repeated on an angry laugh. 'I should say you've done quite a lot. Taken matters into your own hands, made me look a fool – I should say you've done a bloody sight too much.'

'I haven't made you look a fool. I just went to ask, that's all. I haven't made any arrangements or signed anything.'

'I should hope not! I should hope they'd have more sense than to let you.'

Lucy controlled her anger. 'I managed to look after things pretty well while you were away, Wilmot.'

'That's right,' he said, 'chuck that at me. It always comes back to that, doesn't it? The brave little woman at home, keeping the world turning while her good-for-nothing husband goes off to play soldiers. Or sailors. It doesn't matter which, we're all tarred with the same brush, aren't we? It's all our fault there are wars in the first place, so why shouldn't we—'

165

'Wilmot, stop it! I've never said any of those things. Of course I don't think that.'

'Oh, pull the other one, it's got bells on,' he said wearily. 'Look, Lucy, I'm not a fool. I know what you think of me. I can see it in your face. A drunk and a fool who'll never be good for anything. Run a hotel? Provide for a family? Don't make me laugh!'

'Wilmot, that's *enough*.' Lucy realised that she'd been clutching her bag of shopping all this time. She put it on the table. Why had she started this now, of all times? She'd meant to wait until this evening, get them both settled down with a good supper inside them and get round to the subject gradually. Blurting it all out the minute she came in was bound to be a disaster.

However, it was done now. She unbuttoned her coat and went to put the kettle on. A cup of tea would do them both good and perhaps bring the temperature down a bit. And the matter had to be discussed some time. The talk she'd had with the bank manager had brought that home to her.

'Life isn't going to be easy for any of us,' he'd told her, 'but for some, there are opportunities and it's just a matter of recognising and taking them. I think you may be right – this is just such an opportunity for you.'

Lucy had felt a quiver of excitement. 'You mean you think we'd be right to expand the hotel?'

'It's certainly worth thinking about,' he said. 'We'd have to go into all the figures, of course, but you're in a very good position where you are, and if there are adjacent buildings becoming available . . .'

Lucy had come out almost dizzy with excitement. The bank manager had spoken cautiously, but she knew that even the slightest encouragement would not have been given if he hadn't felt there was a worthwhile chance. She would talk to Wilmot about it first, she'd thought, and then they could put their plans to Maud and Arthur . . .

And now it was all in ruins, before she'd even got her coat off.

She made the tea. Wilmot was sitting at the table, watching her. She could feel his eyes on her as she moved around the room, getting a bottle of milk out of the safe outside the back door, taking cups off their hooks, warming the teapot just before the kettle came to the boil, then dropping in a spoonful of tea and pouring the water on. She put the knitted teacosy over the pot and put sugar in Wilmot's cup before pouring out.

'Well, you might give it time to draw,' Wilmot said sullenly.

'It had three minutes.' She put the cup in front of him and then sat down opposite. 'Look, I'm sorry I let it out like that, I didn't mean to.'

'No, you meant to keep it a secret till you'd got it all worked out, I suppose.'

Lucy sighed. 'I didn't mean that either. I meant to wait till later so that we could talk about it properly. I've done some sums. I can show you the figures.'

Wilmot said something very rude about the figures, and Lucy felt her temper rise again. 'It's our living I'm talking about, Wilmot. Or maybe you're not interested? Perhaps I should have just handed you the bottle of rum instead of making tea?'

'And what's that supposed to mean? You're saying I'm a drunk now, is that it?' His eyes glared at her. They looked smaller than ever, like a pig's. She felt a wave of revulsion.

'Well,' she said, 'aren't you?'

The silence dropped between them like a stone into water. Lucy heard her words echo in the room. Appalled, she jumped up and ran round the table, putting her arms around his neck and cradling his head against her breast.

'I'm sorry! I'm sorry, Wilmot. I didn't mean to say that, I didn't mean it. I don't think that about you. I love you. I want us to work together. Wilmot . . .'

He drew away from her. She could feel the stiffness in his shoulders and neck. Desperately, she caressed his face, his hair, she bent over him and kissed him, pleading as she did so.

'Don't look like that, Wilmot. Don't hold yourself away from me. Please. *Please*. I love you, I didn't mean any of it, you know I'd never do anything without talking to you first.'

'But you did,' he said, 'didn't you?'

'*No!* I just went and asked, that's all.'

'Without talking to me first. Without even *mentioning* it to me. How can I believe you, Lucy? How can I trust you? When you go behind my back like that? You talk about us working together, but you don't do it, do you? How do you think that makes me feel? It makes me feel that *you* don't trust *me*. You don't think I'm enough of a man to work for my own family.' His voice had changed as he spoke, from sullen indignation to reproachful sadness. He tilted his head to one side and looked at her, and she saw a shadow of the old Wilmot and felt her tears begin.

'Of course I trust you. I'm sorry, Wilmot. I'm sorry.'

'There's no point in any of it, is there, if we can't trust each other? If we can't talk things over together, we can't work together. I suppose it never occurred to you that *I* might be making plans as well? Plans for our future.'

'Plans?' she said. 'You've been making plans?'

'Well, why not?' He stared at her. 'You're not the only one round here with a brain, Lucy.'

Lucy flushed. 'I didn't mean –'

'That's just it, isn't it?' he said. 'You say a lot of things you don't mean.'

Lucy was silent. She stood with her hands still on his shoulders, aware that if she moved away he would take that as a sign of offence, and be offended in his turn. She closed her eyes, feeling slightly sick.

Wilmot put up his hands and removed hers from his

shoulders. He stood up and turned to face her, then laid his hands on her shoulders. He looked down into her eyes and she knew exactly what he was going to suggest. It was what he always suggested, whenever they had had a disagreement, whenever she had begun to appease him; whenever he sensed that the balance of power between them had shifted his way. It was as if he knew that only then could he successfully make love to her.

'Let's go upstairs,' he murmured. 'Everyone's out. Never mind the shopping – or the tea. Let's go upstairs, and then we can talk about these plans we've both been making.'

There was nothing Lucy wanted to do less, but she knew that if she refused, Wilmot would revert immediately to his surly bad temper, and there would be no chance of further discussion for days, if not weeks. And there was always the chance – she told herself this every time – that this time he would be happy again, become the old Wilmot, the one she had fallen in love with.

She followed him up the stairs.

Wilmot's plans, it turned out, were not so very different from Lucy's. A cynic might have suggested that he had had none of his own at all, but Lucy was determined not to be cynical. She was simply thankful that he was prepared to discuss them.

'Of course, I thought of buying next door myself, ages ago,' he said as Lucy brought him a cup of tea in bed half an hour later. 'I suppose you didn't think to lace this tea a bit? It makes it taste much better . . . never mind. Yes, I remember mentioning it at the time. I suppose that's why you thought of it now, you remembered what I said.'

Lucy looked at her cup. She knew he was watching her, waiting for a reaction, but she was determined not to make one.

'It's getting the money that's the problem, but since

you've been into the bank and enquired it looks a bit more hopeful.'

'They'd want to talk it over with you, of course,' she said quickly. 'With both of us.'

'Oh, you won't need to be there,' he said off-handedly. 'I'll take over now.'

Lucy didn't speak for a moment, then, very carefully, she said, 'I think I ought to come too. I can explain the figures.'

'I think,' Wilmot said dangerously, 'that I can understand your little sums, Lucy.'

Lucy took in a breath. She got out of bed and pulled her dressing-gown around her. It was the one she'd made for her trousseau, a warm camel-coloured wool, and it had seen her through sleepless nights with the children, through the even more sleepless nights of the blitz. Without either speaking to or looking at Wilmot, she went out of the room and along the landing to the lavatory. She shut herself in and then stood there, leaning her head against the wall.

It doesn't matter, she told herself. As long as we just *do* it. As long as he's happy and feels he's in charge. As long as we can make a living, none of it matters.

She looked at the chain hanging from the cistern. Wilmot had told her very little about the camp, but he'd said once that men were whipped with chains like that. She reached out and drew it towards her, looking at the links, feeling them against her palm, imagining the pain. I mustn't get angry with him, she thought. I don't know what he suffered out there.

She went back to the bedroom and started to get dressed. Wilmot was still in bed, cradling his cup in his hands. Lucy smiled at him, but she knew that the smile was stiff and unreal.

'All right,' he said, in one of those tones most calculated to annoy women, 'what have I done this time?'

'Did I say you'd done something?'

'You don't have to say. It's written all over you. The way you stormed out –'

'I didn't storm out. I walked out quietly.' It would be better not to answer him at all, yet if she kept silent he would go on needling until she did. Lucy felt the frustration rise in her again, the helplessness.

'You were muttering to yourself!'

'I was not.'

'Well, anyway, I can see you're working yourself up to something,' Wilmot said. 'Another quarrel, I suppose. My God, why is it women can't talk about anything without turning it into a quarrel? Doesn't matter what it is, it's always got to be an argument. The next thing is, you'll start crying, and then I'll be supposed to feel guilty and tell you it's all right, don't upset yourself, we'll do whatever it is you want. Oh, I know the whole thing word for word, we've been through it all before, times without number, we—'

'*Shut up!*'

Lucy's voice cut across Wilmot's like a chopper cutting into a tree. He stopped abruptly, his mouth still half open, staring at her.

'Lucy –'

'I said, shut up.' She stood in her blouse and petticoat, her skirt in her hands, glowering at him, all her resolve gone. 'I've heard enough. You do this every time, Wilmot. You do your level best to make me feel in the wrong, to make me feel guilty – and it doesn't matter what we've been talking about, we always end up like this. We never ever talk properly because *you* turn it into an argument. Not me – you. And we don't even argue about whatever it is we're talking about. It's always a list of your complaints, all the things I do wrong, until I'd do anything to stop it, just to keep the peace. And I've had just about enough of it.'

Wilmot raised his eyebrows. 'Now who's complaining? Now who's making a list?'

'Oh no,' Lucy said. 'You don't get round it that way. You

don't make me feel guilty this time, Wilmot. I told you, I've had enough.'

'So what are you going to do about it? Put a gag on me?' He giggled suddenly. 'Or wear one yourself. That'd be a better idea.'

Lucy gave him a withering look. 'I'm not doing either. I'm going to go downstairs and unpack the shopping. Then I'll get dinner ready. Then I'm going to go into the office and spend the afternoon working on the figures I talked about with the bank manager, and when I've done that—'

'Yes? When you've done that?' He was sneering, but in his eyes was a gleam of something that looked like fear.

'I'll talk them over with your father,' Lucy said deliberately. 'The hotel does belong to him still, unless I'm very much mistaken. And neither of us can do anything without his agreement, in case you've forgotten.'

She pulled her skirt over her head and fastened it about her waist. Then, without another glance at her husband, she went out of the room and down the stairs.

Wilmot lay back on the pillows. His heart was beating jaggedly and he could feel the heat on his skin. He reached under the bed and dragged out a bottle, half full of strong brown rum, and he poured a generous measure into his teacup and drank it down.

'Women!' he said on a swaggering note, and then, bitterly, 'Bitch! *Bitch!*'

It was Patsy who brought him round in the end. She listened as her parents and grandparents discussed the plans at mealtimes, and watched her father's face, sulky and glowering. Later, she asked him to take her out for a walk and he pushed her chair up to the Hoe where he could sit on a bench and they could gaze at their favourite view.

'I don't think I'll ever get tired of coming up here,' Patsy said. 'It's always different – all blue and shining on fine days

172

and then grey and stormy like this afternoon. I never know which I like best.'

Wilmot glanced at her in surprise. He hadn't really wanted to come out this afternoon, he'd wanted to stay at home and pick another argument with Lucy, but he found it difficult to refuse Patsy. She was so dependent. She couldn't just walk out and bang the door behind her when she wanted a bit of fresh air, she had to ask someone to take her. And she was the only one who seemed able to soothe these moods of terrible frustration that gripped him, when he felt almost as powerless as he had in the Japanese camp. That's what it is, he thought, staring out at the grey, choppy waters of the Sound. I feel just like I did back then, trapped in a world I can't control, and it scares me. It's daft. I know I'm not going to be hurt or tortured like we were there, yet I feel just as scared. No wonder I want to hit out and scream and bash the nearest person. I just wish it wasn't Lucy I wanted to bash. It's not fair on her. It's not fair on anyone.

'I'd have thought you'd like the fine days best,' he said to Patsy, but she shook her head.

'I like it whatever it's like. The fine days are lovely, but the stormy days are exciting. Look at it now. Look at the way the wind's blowing the tops off the waves and making them break. You can see why they're called white horses, they look just like horses' manes, galloping across the water. And look at the sky. The clouds are really racing each other – and that one's crying, see? You can see the rain, like a black curtain. It'll blot out all Rame Head and Mount Edgcombe in a minute, just as if they weren't there at all. It's gorgeous.'

Wilmot looked. He had seen storms at sea, the waves forty feet high and the bow of the ship ploughing through them, rearing until the vessel stood almost on its stern before dropping into the trough beyond, and then lifting again, up and up, endlessly through the roaring ocean.

Sometimes it seemed like fun. More often, it was something to be endured, something that could be dangerous and frightening and, at best, deeply uncomfortable. He supposed there had been a wild sort of beauty in it too, but he hadn't appreciated it at the time and didn't think he would now, if he were out there.

'You're a funny kid,' he said to Patsy, seeing for the first time the light in her eyes, eyes as changeable as the sea itself, sometimes a soft blue, sometimes – as today – a strange, greenish grey. Her red-gold curls were whipping round her face, stinging it with colour, and she turned to him and laughed.

'I'm not. I'm ordinary – I just can't walk.' A restlessness flickered across her face. 'Maybe that's why I love the sea so much, and the stormy weather. I feel sometimes as if the wind could blow me away, as if I could just fly with the clouds, up there in the wild sky.' She stared upwards for a moment or two, then added, 'It's why I love swimming, because in the water I'm not trapped any more.'

Trapped. That word again. And she feels it too, Wilmot thought, watching the exhilaration in his daughter's face. That's what we've got in common, why we understand each other. We're both trapped, she in her wheelchair, me in my memories.

Patsy turned to him suddenly, fixing her eyes on his. 'You will agree to what Mum wants to do with the hotel, won't you?' she said, and the unexpectedness of her question took him by surprise, so that he answered without thinking, and heard his words with astonishment.

'Yes. Yes, I suppose I will. It makes sense really, I know that. It's just that –' He shrugged helplessly. 'I don't know what it is, I just want to argue with whatever she suggests. It's daft, I know.'

'It's not,' Patsy said quietly. 'It's because for years you weren't allowed to argue at all.'

And maybe she was right, he thought, wheeling her back

down Lockyer Street. Maybe that's all it was. But Lucy wasn't a Japanese guard. She was his wife, who loved him, who'd worked hard and endured her own suffering all these years, and didn't deserve to be treated so badly.

I'll do better from now on, he resolved. I'll change. I'll beat these trapped feelings and sulks and tempers. I'll forget about the camp and all the things that went on there.

I'll be the man I used to be, and I'll start to pull my weight.

Changes, however, weren't so easy to bring about, and it was not long before Wilmot was floundering again. The trouble was, he thought, he didn't even know it was happening, and how could you change what you didn't even know you were doing? And the feelings of frustration, of fear, of being trapped, were too powerful for Wilmot to fight. They swept over him and overwhelmed him, like those forty-foot waves he had known at sea, and his only defences were to swagger, to boast and, in the end, to drink.

Lucy was cautiously pleased when he told her that he was willing to look into the idea of expanding the hotel. She made an appointment with the bank manager, who looked at the figures again and talked them over with Arthur and Wilmot. Lucy stayed at home, thinking that three would be a crowd in the manager's office, and when the men returned she looked at them anxiously.

'What did he say?'

Wilmot gave her a cocky look. 'Ate out of our hands, just like I said he would. Didn't he, Dad? He says my idea of buying up next door and the place next door to that when it comes up is a good one, but he says we ought to make an offer now for next-door-but-one – make sure we get it before anyone else steps in. Then we can do the whole conversion at once.'

Lucy stared at him. She let pass the implication that the plans had been all Wilmot's – she had already resigned herself to the fact that she would never be given credit for all her hard work. But she hadn't dared believe that the bank manager would be prepared to loan them enough for the whole job at once.

'You mean he'll let us have all the money? Straight away?'

'Well, not straight away,' Arthur said. 'We've got to get the work done, see, and then the bank'll pick up the bills as they come in. Then we don't take out a big loan. I wouldn't have thought of that myself, but he had it all worked out.'

'Well, you're not a businessman, you see, Dad,' Wilmot said. 'I mean, you've never had to worry yourself about that sort of thing. But me and Mr Dyson, we get along just like that.' He made a circle with his thumb and forefinger. 'Pengelly's will be all right now, you wait and see. We'll be as big as the Duke of Cornwall before we've finished!'

Lucy sighed. The Duke of Cornwall was the biggest and best hotel in Plymouth. It had been specially built as a grand hotel and took up a whole corner all to itself. Three houses knocked together in Lockyer Street were never going to be able to compare with that.

'Don't let's get carried away,' she said. 'There's a long way to go before we can even begin to compete with the Duke. There's getting the money organised, getting plans drawn up, working it all out . . .'

'Yes, well, I might have expected you'd throw cold water on it,' Wilmot said. 'It's always the same with women. Got to stick their five eggs into any discussion, and when you let them it's all cold water and wet blankets.' He glared at Geoff who had begun to giggle. 'And you can keep your nose out too. I don't know what you find so funny about the idea of trying to build up a business.'

'It's not that, Dad,' Geoff said. 'It's cold water and wet blankets.' He snorted with laughter again.

Wilmot glowered at him. 'You've had too much of your

176

own way. Not enough discipline. You'll get a shock when you're called up for National Service, Geoff.'

'I'm looking forward to it,' Geoff said. 'It'll be a chance to get away from this place.'

'Geoff!' Lucy exclaimed and he shrugged and gave her a half-shamefaced, half-sullen look.

'Well, wouldn't you? I mean, I've never been anywhere but Plymouth, and half my life I've spent hiding from bombs. And look what a dump it all is. It's going to be years and years before it's all rebuilt. I'm fed up with it. I want to see a bit of life.'

'And just where do you think you'll see that?' Wilmot asked scornfully. 'Every town and city in the country's been bombed, and most of the rest of the world as well. It's the same everywhere. You won't see any different sort of life anywhere else.'

Geoff shrugged. 'I reckon it was better in the war. There was a bit of excitement then. It's just dull now, dull and dreary.'

Lucy looked at him. He was fifteen years old now, growing fast and filling out. She had wanted him to stay at school and do School Certificate, but he'd refused and got his apprenticeship instead, abetted by Arthur, who said there was nothing like an apprenticeship to set a young chap up in a trade. Now he went off to Devonport dockyard early every morning in working clothes, with his lunchbox under his arm, and didn't come back till nearly six.

'You don't know when you're well off,' Wilmot said to him. 'You don't know you're born.'

'Oh, you can't say that,' Lucy said. 'He works hard, and he only gets Saturday afternoons and Sundays off. It doesn't give him much time to have any pleasure. He's still a boy, Wilmot.'

'When I was that age, I was already in the Andrew. I was away at HMS *Ganges* and they didn't give us much rest there, I can tell you. There was no one to make my bed for me either, and we only got a bit of pocket money.'

Lucy said nothing. Geoff made his own bed, but he didn't do much else to help around the hotel. Why should he, when he worked long hours and handed over his pay packet unopened of a Friday night, regular as clockwork? Lucy took what she wanted for his keep and gave him the rest back to spend as he liked, hoping he would save some.

'Leave him alone, Wilmot,' she said. 'It was different when you were a boy. And you had some good times in the Navy before the war, you can't deny that.'

'That's not the point. The point is that the boy's always moaning. He ought to be thankful for what he's got.'

'Like you are, I suppose,' Geoff said.

Wilmot started to rise from his chair and Lucy reached out swiftly and grabbed his arm. '*No*, Wilmot! Geoff, apologise at once for being cheeky.'

'Why should I? It's true. He's always griping on about something. I get fed up listening to it.'

'You don't have to sit in the same room as me if you don't want to,' Wilmot began, and then, as Geoff started to get up, '*Sit down!* I'm talking to you.'

'Well, make up your mind,' Geoff said, and Wilmot's face flushed a dark red.

Lucy recognised the signs and groaned inwardly. There had been more and more of these quarrels between father and son lately and Geoff was growing less willing to accept Wilmot's authority. It was understandable in a way: he had hardly seen his father until he was thirteen years old, and the Wilmot who had returned after the war was a stranger to him. Whatever Geoff had expected of his father, Wilmot had been a disappointment to him, and whatever Wilmot had expected of his son, he hadn't found it in Geoffrey.

David and Geoff were more like father and son than Wilmot and Geoff were, she thought sadly. Wilmot had evidently thought so too, and had made no bones about his resentment: 'It's easy enough to be a hero when you've got a comfortable bed to lie in at night.'

'David's had a hard war too,' she had pointed out. 'He lost his wife and his baby in the blitz. And he lost his arm saving Geoff's life. It's no wonder he takes a lot of interest in him.'

'Well, it's time he stopped taking an interest,' Wilmot said. 'There's nothing to stop him getting married again and having a son of his own.'

David hardly ever came to Plymouth to see them now, but it hadn't made any difference to Geoff. He wrote regularly and talked about going to London during his holidays. Or down to Cornwall, where David's aunt still lived.

Lucy sometimes felt as if she spent her days trying to keep the peace between Wilmot and his son. Patsy was all right, she was the apple of her father's eye and could do no wrong. And at least there was no problem with her staying out late at night or having unsuitable boyfriends. But Geoff just seemed to set out to aggravate – deliberately making remarks that would inflame Wilmot's temper, and then being cheeky and making it all worse.

'Stop it, the pair of you,' she said sharply. 'I'm fed up with all this squabbling. We used to be such a happy family.'

'When I wasn't here, you mean,' Wilmot said.

Before Lucy could deny it, Geoff muttered, 'You said it.'

There was a dead silence. Lucy closed both eyes. If he doesn't hit him now, she thought, he never will, and there isn't a thing I can do about it.

Nothing happened. She opened her eyes again. It was as if the whole world had come to a standstill. Nothing had happened, nobody had moved. Geoff and his father faced each other across the kitchen table. Wilmot's eyes were bulging and Geoff looked half challenging, half scared.

Patsy, in her wheelchair at the other end of the table, was gazing from one to the other, terrified.

Slowly, Wilmot began to rise to his feet. Both fists were clenched. He leant across towards Geoff.

Geoff scraped his chair back. Big though he might be for his age, he didn't have Wilmot's bulk. He glanced sideways at his mother and she recognised the panic in his eyes, the realisation that he had gone too far, and jumped up.

'All right,' she said, raising her voice to just below a shout. 'All *right*. That's enough. Stop it now, both of you. *Stop* it, Wilmot. Sit down and listen to me.'

For a moment, she thought it wasn't going to work. She didn't have the authority after all. But then, perhaps because they both wanted to stop but wanted to be told to do it, the two relaxed. Wilmot unclenched his fists and laid his hands flat instead on the table. Geoff sat back in his chair. And then, slowly, Wilmot sat down too.

'That's better,' Lucy said. She stayed on her feet, looking from one to the other. 'Now listen to me, both of you. I told you, I've had enough of all this bickering. This used to be a happy home, and I mean when we were all here together. Now, we've all had a hard time, but so has everyone else. There's nothing different about the Pengelly family. And some people have had a lot worse. There's always someone worse off than yourself, remember that. What we've got to do now is pull together and make things better again. They're better already. Two years ago, we were looking forward to being like we are now. We were still at war. You were still in camp, Wilmot. We were looking forward to what we've got now, thinking it would be paradise.'

'Some paradise,' Geoff muttered.

'I said *stop* it!' She had rarely spoken to him so sharply, and she saw the hurt on his face. 'Now look. Your father's trying to look to the future. He wants to build up Pengelly's to a really good, big hotel – not as big as the Duke of Cornwall, perhaps, but one of the best in Plymouth. And I

180

want to help him. And that means a lot of hard work for us, and a lot of help from you. *And no more arguing*. Do you understand? We'll never get anywhere at all if we're always arguing and squabbling.'

She paused. Wilmot was looking pleased, Geoff sullen. She felt a pang of remorse, as if she had let him down. It wasn't his fault, after all, if he'd found it difficult to accept his father after so long. And Wilmot had never really been fair or understanding of Geoff's problems. He'd expected to be hero-worshipped, and indeed Geoff had been quite ready to do that at first, but he'd been rejected and criticised from the very first. You couldn't expect a boy to put up with that.

I'm sorry, Geoff, she said silently to his bent head, I'm sorry, but I've got to keep your father happy. It's the only way.

She could only take one step at a time, and at least Wilmot was now willing to work at building up their future. That was the biggest step they had taken yet.

Chapter Fifteen

By the time Princess Elizabeth and Prince Philip were married, in November, the plans for the conversion of the hotel were well under way. The house next door had been bought, and although the owners of the next one hadn't yet decided whether or not to sell, Lucy was hopeful and had got the architect to draw up plans that could include the extra building if and when it became available. She stopped outside whenever she came back from the shops, gazing along the façade, hardly able to believe that they had already achieved so much.

Maud and Arthur were leaving most of the work to her and Wilmot now. In their late sixties, and having lived through two world wars, they were both tired out and wanted nothing more than a few years' peaceful retirement, but they still owned the hotel and nothing could be done without their approval. And that was just as well, Lucy thought, for if Wilmot had had the freedom to do as he pleased, there was no knowing what would have happened. During the past few months, he had veered wildly from proposing extravagant schemes they would never be able to carry out, to moods of deep gloom in which he prophesied ruin for them all.

'Look at all this money we're borrowing. We'll be paying it back for the rest of our lives. We'll *never* be able to pay it back. I don't know why I let you talk me into this.'

'I thought it was your idea, Wilmot.'

'That's right, blame me! It's always *my* fault, isn't it? *My* fault we're on the verge of going bankrupt, *my* fault we'll all end up in the gutter.'

'We won't. Look, it's all right, everything's going to plan.'

'*Your* plan. I should never have listened to you.' And he disappeared upstairs where, as Lucy knew very well, he would pour himself a glass of rum and sit gazing sullenly out of the window as he drank.

She had grown used to his moods. The best course, she had discovered, was to carry on as if nothing had happened. Eventually, he would come downstairs, stumbling and slurring his words, either truculent or restored to a good humour which brought him to her side, pinching her bottom and kissing her neck with slack lips. Either way, the rest of the day would be a tightrope for the whole family to walk, and the end of it would come in bed that night, with Wilmot's increasingly desperate efforts to make love to her and Lucy's equally desperate efforts to help him.

'It's your fault. You're frigid. How can a man make love to a woman who's frigid?'

Perhaps I am, Lucy thought miserably, but I never used to be. And she would hug and caress him, striving to bring him the release he longed for. Just let him do it and get it over with, she prayed.

Even when he was successful, she sometimes wondered if he actually enjoyed it. She could feel no passion in him, no tenderness. I could be a doll lying here, she thought, and when it was finished at last she would turn over and lie staring into the darkness, conscious of a sensation of having been dirtied all through her body, and her tears would creep silently down on to the pillow.

The Royal Wedding occupied the newspapers for weeks and everyone brought out their bunting and celebrated just as they had at the end of the war. Lucy, Maud and Patsy listened to it on the wireless. The commentator talked

183

about the people who were gathered in Westminster Abbey, mentioning them by name – foreign kings and queens, dukes, duchesses, prime ministers, lords and ladies – and describing the women's clothes. He seemed to know them all. When the Princess herself came into the Abbey on the arm of her father, the three women leant forward, eager to picture the wedding dress as he described it.

'Oh, I *wish* we could see it all,' Patsy lamented.

'You will tomorrow. There'll be photos in all the papers. And we'll go to the pictures next week and see it on the newsreel.'

'It won't be in colour, though. I'd like to see it in colour.'

Lucy made up her mind to get Patsy a book of the Royal Wedding, just as soon as one was published. She had books of the Coronation of George VI in 1937, with beautiful colour pictures of the King and Queen in their robes, and of their crowns and the orb and sceptre. A book of the wedding would be a lovely present for Christmas, if it came out in time.

Lucy had done a good job with Patsy's schooling, even Wilmot had to admit that. Nobody else had bothered much, and even after the war was over the schools didn't want wheelchairs – even if you could have got one up the steps and through the narrow corridors that they all seemed to have. However, Lucy's own education had stopped at fourteen and there didn't seem to be much more she could teach Patsy now. She still brought home books from the library, but the girl was bored and restless, wanting something more to do.

'I reckon that girl could help with the accounts,' Wilmot said one day soon after the Royal wedding. 'She's as bright as a button with figures.'

'She's just a child still,' Lucy said, but he shook his head.

'There's plenty her age out at work. She's coming up to fourteen. And she's always got her head in a book, she could add up our sums standing on her head, couldn't you, my pretty?' he added as Patsy herself wheeled her chair through the door.

'It's about the only thing I can stand on, then,' she said with a grin. 'What sums d'you want added up?'

'The hotel sums,' Lucy said. 'Your dad thinks you could do the accounts.'

Patsy's face brightened. 'What, me? Do the books and the ledgers? Oh yes! And I could be a receptionist as well. Sit in the front hall behind a desk and give the guests their keys and answer the phone, and all that. I don't need to be able to walk to do those things. Oh, Mum, please say yes! I'd be doing a proper job, just like our Geoff. Say yes, *please*.'

Lucy looked at her. Patsy's eyes were sparkling, her face shining with eagerness. Wilmot too looked pleased and excited, and it was that more than anything that made up her mind.

'All right. You can try it, anyway. We'll give you a month, just like any other girl. But you'll have to treat it as a proper job, mind, you'll have to work the right hours and everything.'

'I will! Oh, I *will*.' Patsy hugged her father's arm. 'I'll be the best receptionist you've ever had.'

'That won't be hard,' Wilmot said with a flash of his old humour. 'You'll be the *only* receptionist we've ever had.'

There was a lot of accounting to do, and a lot of costing. The new parts of the hotel would need complete rebuilding and refurbishing. As well as new carpets, curtains and furniture throughout – none of them easy to come by in these days of austerity – that meant washbasins in every room and a bathroom and lavatory on every floor. All the floorspace had to be calculated, and materials chosen. Every smallest item had to be costed before the bank would give them the money.

The work of rebuilding made life harder than ever. It seemed that everywhere you went, there were builders, creating rubble and dust wherever they moved. Windows were taken out and either boarded up or covered with tarpaulin, which flapped in the wind and kept everyone awake at night. Lucy had hoped that next door could be rebuilt first, leaving the original Pengelly's to be run as normal until the last minute. For a while, this seemed to work well enough, but there came a day when the builder in charge told them they'd have to break through.

'That means we won't be able to take guests,' Wilmot said. He stared accusingly at Lucy. 'We won't be able to make any money at all.'

'I know. We knew that would happen.'

'But what are we going to live on? The bank's not going to pay our grocery bill.'

'It's all been costed in,' she explained. 'It's all right, Wilmot. It's all been taken into account.'

He stared at her and she could see his mind working. He'd known it was all taken into account, of course, but he'd forgotten it. Then he'd panicked and now he was feeling a fool. She felt sorry for him.

'I'd forgotten it myself,' she said, telling a white lie. 'It was only when I looked at the figures . . . There's so much going on, nobody can keep it all in their head.'

'No,' Wilmot said, relaxing a little, 'they can't. Of course, I remembered as soon as I started to think about it properly. It just took me by surprise, that's all.'

'Me too,' she agreed, and gave a small sigh of relief that the moment had passed safely.

The few guests who had booked in were passed on to another guest house in the next road. Lucy promised to send them details of the new Pengelly's when it was open again and hoped they'd all come back, if only out of curiosity. Once they'd got through the doors, she was sure they would stay.

'We've got to make the foyer really attractive. Nice and bright, with carpets and chandeliers.'

'*Chandeliers?*' Wilmot gasped. 'Blimey, what's this going to be, Buckingham Palace?'

'Well, just one, hanging from the middle. Not a real chandelier – more a sort of cluster of separate lamps.' The narrow passageway was being done away with and the two front rooms turned into a wide hallway. Lucy had spent hours ensconced with the architect, discussing plans and ideas, keeping some, discarding others. Wilmot had been there too, at first, but he'd found the whole process irritating and eventually declared that it was 'women's work'. Now, she thought resignedly, he seemed to have taken on the task of vetoing all that had been decided.

He'd stopped coming to the bank too, leaving everything in Lucy's hands. She spent hours in the manager's office, going through the figures and making sure that nothing had been forgotten, as well as keeping a strict eye on the spending. She had no intention of putting them into any more debt than was absolutely necessary. She knew Mr Dyson well now and trusted him, and she thought he trusted her too.

'I'll leave it to you to explain that to your husband, Mrs Pengelly. You've got a very good understanding of it all.'

'We're not doing anything we can't afford,' she said to Wilmot now, 'but we're never going to get a chance like this again. We've got to make the best use of every penny.'

'And chandeliers are the best use, are they?'

Lucy wished she hadn't used that word. 'I told you, it's not really a chandelier, just a hanging lamp. It's not really expensive, Wilmot.'

'It's the only thing that's not, then. What with enough carpet to cover Argyle football ground, curtain material to stretch from here to Tavistock and enough light bulbs to keep St Andrew's church going for a twelvemonth, I'm beginning to wonder if we're not paying for the whole of Plymouth to be rebuilt. I tell you, Lucy, it frightens me, it really does. How long is it going to take to get ourselves out of this debt? I wish we'd never gone in for it, I do really. We should have been content with running a decent little guest house, like I wanted to in the first place.'

So now it's my fault again, Lucy thought. She said, 'We went through all that, Wilmot. We couldn't make enough to keep us all.'

'Well, I could have got a job.' He stared at her, daring her to tell him he couldn't or hadn't wanted to. 'That would have been better than shackling ourselves to a millstone like this.'

'*Do* you shackle yourself to a millstone, Dad?' Geoff inquired, coming through the door in time to hear the last words. 'I thought you tied it round your neck.'

'And you needn't be so cheeky, clever-clogs!'

'Sorry. I was only joking—'

Wilmot swung round furiously. 'Joking!' he exclaimed. '*Joking!* Yes, that's what's wrong with this house. There's too much joking going on. Too much bloody silly *joking*.'

'Oh, for Christ's sake,' Geoff said disgustedly, 'a bloke can't say a word in this house these days without getting his head bitten off—'

'And you can stop that swearing. You know your mother doesn't like it.'

'She has to put up with it from you, though, doesn't she,' Geoff said rudely. 'But then, you're the boss around here, aren't you. Head of the household, the brains of the business and all that. I *don't* think!'

Wilmot stood quite still, glaring at him. Lucy saw his fists clench at his sides, saw the ugly colour flood his skin. She stepped forward, holding out one hand, knowing that if he lost control of himself there would be nothing she could do about it.

'Wilmot –'

He flung her a glance of furious exasperation and turned angrily away. 'Oh, don't worry, Lucy. I'm not going to touch your precious boy. I wouldn't soil my hands. But you'd better do something about that tongue of his, or I warn you, I'll hurt him one of these days, hurt him badly. I won't be able to help myself.'

He pushed past the wheelchair and Lucy heard his feet stamping up the stairs. She looked at Geoff and her eyes filled with tears.

'Oh, Geoff. If only you'd stop goading him so much. To hear him say a thing like that . . .' She shook her head in a wave of sadness. 'There used to be nobody who liked a joke better than your father. Nobody I ever knew . . .'

The rebuilding of the hotel took up most of Lucy's attention. The worst part was over and their living accommodation was more or less back to normal. Instead of the old family kitchen there was a new, bigger kitchen with proper big cookers and two sinks. It wasn't homely, but Lucy didn't intend that the family should use it; they were to have their own place, where they could make tea or their own meals if they wanted, but mostly, she thought, they'd eat what was being cooked in the main kitchen.

'I can just as easily make the family's dinner while I'm cooking for the guests. Your mum will help too, and the girl, of course.'

'Girl? What girl? It's the first I've heard about a girl.'

Lucy sighed. They had been through it all before, but Wilmot greeted each stage of the development as if it had been sprung on him entirely unawares.

'We'll need a bit of help around the place. Your mum and I can't do it all. You know that, Wilmot. We discussed it. We thought we'd advertise a bit nearer the time. There must be plenty of young girls around here who'll be pleased to have a job.'

Wilmot grunted. Apart from intermittent bursts of enthusiasm, he now took little interest in the new plans. He spent the mornings getting in the builders' way and then went out, saying he had appointments, but really,

Lucy knew, to go to the pub. She let him go without comment. He was better out of the way. In fact, she dreaded his occasional interference, which invariably led to problems and had twice brought the builders to the point of walking out.

Wilmot was drinking continuously now. In a way, he seemed better for it. He was seldom drunk, at least not noisily or belligerently. In the mornings, he was slow and grumpy, and usually had a headache which he attributed to 'nerves', and liable to be quarrelsome, but once dinner time was approaching and he could go out for his 'appointments' he became more cheerful. He returned at one o'clock, then spent the afternoon either snoring in a chair or up on the Hoe, where he sat for hours staring out at the ships in the Sound. By teatime he had already started on his bottle of rum – his 'daily issue', he called it – and this kept him placid during the evening.

Lucy tried to make sure he had no more than two glasses each evening. If he just stuck to that amount and it kept him happy, she thought, there couldn't be much harm in it, but sometimes she thought the bottle was going down quicker than that.

The decorators had arrived now and all the walls were being painted. Lucy had suggested that Wilmot should help with this, but after seeing his first attempts she steered him towards the family rooms. Geoff helped too, at the weekends, and even Patsy could paint the dados from her wheelchair.

'I'm not a bad hand with a brush meself,' Arthur said, and took on the decorating of his and Maud's room.

'I don't think much of the colours,' Wilmot said, finding fault as usual. 'Couldn't you get something a bit brighter?'

'We're lucky to be able to get the paint at all,' Lucy told him. 'You'd think it was against the law. Well, so it was for quite a long time. Remember that, Dad, when all we could get was brown? I quite like this nice green and cream myself, it looks fresh.'

When the painting and decorating had been done, the linoleum arrived, and the carpet squares Lucy had bought to go over it. She walked from room to room and along the new corridors, marvelling. You wouldn't think it had been two houses once. Wilmot was right – it really was almost as good as the Duke of Cornwall!

She had leaflets printed and sent them out to all their old guests. When she came to David's name she hesitated, then made up her mind and wrote a letter to go with it.

'Why not be our first guest?' she suggested. 'It's such a long time since we saw you, and Geoff and Patsy would love it if you came. You ought to be here, if anyone should.'

Wilmot might not like it, she thought, sealing the envelope and sticking a penny stamp on it, but just this once she wasn't going to worry about what Wilmot thought. She didn't know what they would have done without David all through the war, and it wouldn't be right to leave him out now. And she wanted to see him herself.

For the first time for months, Lucy admitted to herself just how much she wanted to see him.

Pengelly's Hotel reopened for business on 2 May 1949, a Monday. As usual, in all naval ports – everywhere there was a sailor, in fact – the first had been marked by the sudden blossoming of white cap-covers. The world seemed suddenly a brighter, sunnier place.

'It's going to be all right now,' Lucy said, hugging Wilmot's arm as they stood in the new 'foyer' – a grand name for what had once been two rooms and a passage. 'We'll make it work, you'll see.' She was feeling extra excited because David was coming today. Wilmot hadn't seemed to mind after all, perhaps because they'd also invited the bank manager, Mr Dyson, to lunch in the new dining-room, with the architect and the lawyer who had guided them all through the intricacies of planning. Wilmot was dressed in a new suit for the occasion and looked proud and, she thought, rather distinguished. She touched the greying hair at his temples with her fingertips. 'Pengelly's is going to do very well for itself.'

'Well, so it ought to,' he said. 'We've worked hard enough on it.'

Lucy bit her lips together and tightened her forehead to keep her eyebrows from shooting up into her hairline.

'And you've done your share,' he conceded generously. 'You've turned your hand to a lot of things you've never thought you'd have to do. I appreciate that, Lucy. You've been a good wife to me.'

She smiled at him. Perhaps from now on things would be better after all. Perhaps he'd get his confidence back, start at last to forget those dreadful things that had happened to him in Japan, perhaps he'd stop having nightmares and stop drinking quite so much and be able to make love again properly. Perhaps the old Wilmot would come back at last.

'I love you, Wilmot,' she said, hugging his arm close against her. 'I really do, you know. I love you.'

The new front door swung open. They both looked towards it. And Lucy gasped and felt her knees begin to tremble as David Tremaine walked towards her.

'You've done a marvellous job, Lucy.'

The day was almost over and she and David had walked up to the Hoe to watch the sun set. Wilmot had disappeared, probably to the pub, and Patsy, tired out by all the excitement, stayed at home reading and listening to the wireless. Geoff, who had come home from the dockyard only when it was all over, was still eating his own supper and said he might walk up to meet them later on.

'It's been hard work,' she admitted, 'but I've enjoyed it – most of it.' She gave him a wry grin, thinking of all the frustrations they had suffered, when materials didn't arrive or the wrong carpet was delivered or the builders had complained about Wilmot. 'It's wonderful to see it all finished. I just hope we can make a success of it now.'

'You will. You must be the first hotel in Plymouth to have really pulled things together and started fresh. The first small one, anyway. Most of the others still seem to be struggling along just as they were.'

'It seemed to be an opportunity. We were able to get help from the city planners as well as the bank. That's not likely to happen again. And being able to buy next door so cheaply . . .'

'It took courage, all the same. And that's why I know you'll make a success of it now. Someone like you is bound to be successful, Lucy. You're strong.'

'Am I?' She turned and looked up into his face. 'I don't always feel strong, David.'

'I doubt if anyone does. It's keeping going through those times that shows who's strong and who isn't. Hanging on when you feel most like giving up. There must have been times like that.'

Lucy leant on the railing and looked down at the rockpools and the big semicircular bathing-pool where she had taught Wilmot to swim.

'Yes, there were. I wondered if we were doing the right thing. Maud and Arthur never said anything, but they must have wondered too. And Wilmot –'

'Wilmot did say so.'

'Yes. Over and over again.' She gave him a rueful smile. 'Everything that went wrong was my fault, my idea. And quite honestly, most of it was, so I couldn't argue with him. I used to pray that it would all turn out right in the end so that I wouldn't have let them all down.'

'It's not what he's saying now,' David observed, looking out across the Sound at the golden pathway made on the sea by the setting sun. 'He's like a dog with two tails, and taking all the credit.'

'It's nice to see him so happy. He's been through a terrible time, David.'

'And does that give him the right to make you miserable as well? He *has* made you miserable, hasn't he?'

Lucy said nothing for a few moments, then she said slowly, 'It's not about rights. Life isn't like that. We can't talk about *rights*, as if we were born with a contract made with the rest of the world. We don't have any rights over the way other people behave or treat us.'

'Don't you think so? Don't we have a right not to be hit over the head as we walk down the street, or robbed, or our houses set on fire? Don't we have a right to live in peace?'

'We haven't for the past ten years,' Lucy said. 'Those sorts of rights are made by law, and when the law wants to take them away it just does. We didn't have those sorts of rights in the blitz, did we?'

'Things are different in wartime.'

'Things are different whenever the big high-ups want them to be,' Lucy said with a touch of bitterness. 'But that's not the sort of rights we were talking about, David. We were talking about ordinary people living together. I don't have any right to expect Wilmot to be different from what he is. Especially after all he's been through. He didn't ask to be sunk at sea or spend years in a POW camp being tortured and beaten and seeing his friends die. What happened to his rights then, David? And doesn't he have a right to expect me to understand and help him? I'm his wife. It's what I promised to do.'

'So Wilmot has rights, even though you don't,' he said after a moment.

'He has the rights I give him,' she said. 'Those are the only rights we have, the ones other people give us freely and willingly. There aren't any others, and expecting them only brings trouble.'

A small silence fell. They stood close together, leaning on the rail, their fingertips almost touching. At last David said quietly, 'It's a harsh philosophy, Lucy. Hard on yourself.'

'I can't help that,' she said. 'It's the way I feel. Maybe if we were all harder on ourselves it would turn out to be quite easy after all.'

He pursed his lips slightly and tilted his head, as if half acknowledging the truth of such a paradox. 'And where does it leave us?'

'Us?' Lucy said.

'You know how things are with us,' David said softly. 'We both know. It hasn't changed, has it – the feeling we have for each other?'

Lucy shifted her glance away from the golden pathway. She turned her head and met his gaze. The violet in her eyes had deepened to the purple of the encroaching dusk. Her face was pale.

'No. Nothing's changed.'

'And nothing is going to, is it?'

'How can it?' she asked with sudden passion. 'You can see how my life is. How can I walk away from all that? How can I walk away from *them*? It isn't just Wilmot.'

'I know.'

'They have the *right*,' she said, using the word deliberately, 'they have the right to expect me to be there. To keep faith. I have to keep faith, David.'

'Because of them?' he asked. 'Because of their needs?'

Lucy looked away. He saw the torment in her face, the struggle to face her own truth.

'No,' she said at last, 'because of mine.'

David stayed for a week. He was writing a book about the rebuilding of the three major naval ports, Plymouth, Portsmouth and Chatham. As he had always done, he ate his meals with the family, talking easily with Maud and Arthur, having long conversations with Patsy and setting off in the evenings for walks with Geoff. They took the ferry to Torpoint or to Saltash and strolled along the foreshore of the rivers that fed into the Hamoaze, and one evening they took the train to Yelverton and walked back across the moor, coming home by moonlight.

What they talked about on these jaunts, Lucy never knew, but she could see the contentment in Geoff's face when they returned, the pleasure he had felt in the company of the man who had been like a father to him.

Wilmot said nothing. He behaved as if David were not there. Now that the hotel was open he had undertaken certain duties – mostly those of welcoming new guests, supervising in the dining-room, keeping an eye on Patsy as she did the daily accounts. He dressed smartly every morning and stood at the new front door, proud to be seen as the proprietor of Pengelly's. But by eleven o'clock he had begun to look at his watch, and at twelve he disappeared, returning at one for his dinner – the family still ate their main meal of the day then, leaving Lucy free to cook for the guests in the evening – and spending the afternoon either on the Hoe or dozing in an armchair.

Lucy never said that she thought the hotel would run just as well if Wilmot were not there. She didn't even allow herself to think it. She told herself that he would find his own level, that he was a support to her and the rest of the family just by being there, that the place would fall apart without his presence in the background.

There were times, quite long periods in fact, when she almost believed it.

She said goodbye to David at the end of the week, knowing that he would leave an emptiness behind him. They said goodbye in the foyer, with other guests leaving at the same time, and no chance for a private moment.

'It's been so lovely to see you again,' Lucy said, giving him her hand. 'Don't leave it so long next time. Come and see us again.'

'I will.' His eyes looked into hers. 'Lucy –'

196

'We'll always be friends,' she said quickly. 'Nothing is ever going to change that.'

'I know.' He hesitated, then smiled at her. 'It's all right. I won't say anything to embarrass you. I just want you to know – you have a *right* to my friendship, Lucy. A lifelong right.'

She smiled, remembering their conversation on the Hoe. Rights could only be given, not claimed. 'And you have a right to mine.'

A final look, a final moment of silence and a brief, firm handclasp, and then he was turning away, was gone through the new front door. And Lucy stood there, feeling bereft, unable for a moment or two to move. The hotel seemed suddenly empty.

Chapter Sixteen

Now that the hard work of getting the hotel refurbished was over and guests had begun to arrive, Wilmot began to try to mend his relationship with Geoffrey. He had been very hurt by Geoff's sarcastic remarks, and ashamed of his own behaviour. It's time we both grew up, he thought. Geoff's not a nipper any more and maybe it would be better if I treated him like a man.

As always, he went to the other extreme and when Geoffrey's eighteenth birthday came around he took him off shopping and, without a word to Lucy, bought him a motorcycle. When they brought it home, Wilmot driving it rather uncertainly with Geoffrey wobbling on the pillion, Lucy was horrified.

'Oh, Wilmot. I don't like motorbikes. They're dangerous. What did you want to give him that for?'

Wilmot shrugged. 'He's a man now. Eighteen years old. I was serving on ships at that age. Anyway, you can see how pleased he is with it.'

Lucy could. For once, Wilmot had done the right thing as far as Geoff was concerned. He was like a dog with two tails, propping his new toy up on its stand outside the hotel and polishing it almost every time he came back from a ride.

'You've got to admit, Mum, it's a real smasher. It's a single carburettor Triumph TR5 Trophy. It's a competition bike – been made for scrambling or trials – but it's just as good on the road. I'm thinking of joining a club.'

'What do you mean, competitions? What are scrambles and trials? You're not going racing on it!'

198

'Well, scrambles are sort of races. Only on rough ground, not on race–tracks. It's fun, Mum. And trials are where you do sections like hills or streams and bits of rocky track, anything rough where you can get a bike through. You've got to be able to ride really well. You can come and watch, you'll enjoy it.'

Lucy didn't think she would enjoy it at all. She looked at her son, standing tall and broad, his red hair glinting in the sun, and realised suddenly that Wilmot was right. He was a young man now, no longer a boy. He was growing up, away from her, and the motorbike would take him away even faster.

Geoff took out his handkerchief and polished away a minute speck of dust. He had other ideas about the bike, ideas he wasn't going to tell his mother. Girls liked a chap who could take them about without having to use buses, and a motorbike was glamorous and exciting.

He couldn't do anything about that, however, until he had passed his test. As a learner driver, he could only ride alone or with a qualified rider on the pillion. Wilmot had got his licence years ago, so the two of them went off together several times a week, heading out towards Dartmoor or along the coast into Cornwall or eastwards to the South Hams. They went to Newton Ferrers and Noss Mayo, where Maud and Arthur had spent their honeymoon, and parked the bike on the cliffs, looking down at the blue lake of the estuary.

'It's smashing being able to get out of Plymouth,' Geoff said as they unpacked the sandwiches Lucy had given them. 'That bike's the best present I ever had.'

Wilmot felt a glow of pleasure. For once, he'd done the right thing. He saw himself and Geoff going off on long jaunts together, maybe taking a tent and staying away for several days. It would be like being young again. It would be his second chance to be a proper father, teaching his boy about camping and lighting fires and cooking in the outdoors. Perhaps they could even run to a small boat later on and go sailing or fishing.

'I can't wait to go to scrambles with it,' Geoff went on dreamily. 'I reckon it'll go really well. I might even be a racer, like Geoff Duke. He won the Manx Grand Prix, only of course he was riding a Norton. Did you know, Dad, Nortons made bikes for the Army during the war . . .'

His voice chattered on and Wilmot adjusted his dreams. Well, he supposed they could go to scrambles together, and even to races, though he didn't think Lucy was going to approve of Geoff's ambition to take part in either of them. Trials weren't so bad, they were all about skill and there wasn't much danger involved, but maybe that wouldn't suit Geoff. Boys liked the spice of danger, he thought ruefully, as long as they didn't know what it really meant.

It didn't matter anyway. It didn't matter what he and Geoff did, so long as they did something together, so long as they could be a proper father and son, and it looked as if the bike had succeeded where all the other things he had tried had failed.

Geoff put in for his test at once, and passed straight away. Wilmot banged him on the back and took him down to the pub for a drink. To his dismay, however, Geoff went off on his own next day, without inviting his father to come with him.

'What did you expect?' Lucy asked. She still didn't like Geoff having a motorbike, and now he'd passed his test it stood to reason he was going to be off on his own. 'Next time we see him, he'll have a girl on the pillion.'

'I thought we'd go on having rides out together,' Wilmot said aggrievedly. 'I thought he'd been enjoying it.'

'I daresay he did.' Lucy felt sorry for him. He'd tried so hard, and now he looked like a woebegone little boy, deserted by his friends. 'But he's eighteen years old, Wilmot. He's not going to want his dad along with him. Did you want Arthur with you when you were that age?'

200

'I was in the Navy when I was that age,' Wilmot said, but he had to admit she was right. He'd been after the girls, like his mates, flaunting their sailors' uniforms and snogging in the back row of the pictures, wondering how far they could go. And some of those girls had been ready to go quite a way, too, the trollops.

He thought of Geoff, picking up some flighty piece of goods and taking her out on the back of his bike. Down to Newton Ferrers, or out on Dartmoor. I ought to have given him some advice, he thought, I ought to have told him what's what. Now, it seemed suddenly too late and he found a new anxiety to add to his disappointment at being left behind.

'I thought the bike'd bring us together a bit,' he said. 'You said we ought to find something, and I reckoned that was it.'

'Well, so it was. But he's growing up. You can't expect much different.' Lucy laid her hand on his arm, feeling a glow of affection. He really had tried, and it was a shame he was disappointed. 'But he won't forget it was you who gave him the bike, Wilmot. He'll always remember that.'

Geoff quickly acquired a string of girlfriends who were eager to ride pillion. Jilly became one of them very soon after arriving at the hotel.

Jilly was the maid at Pengelly's. She had been there for two years now, mostly helping Lucy with the cooking. Soon, she would take full charge, leaving Lucy free to concentrate on the management, and there would be another maid, perhaps two, as well as the daily cleaning woman who had been coming in for the past year, for Pengelly's was expanding again. The third house in the row had been bought at last and the conversion to turn it into part of the hotel was almost complete. Even Wilmot had not been able to complain that the venture had been anything but a success.

Jilly had come to Pengelly's from Cornwall, where her

mother had been looking after David's aunt ever since she first began to be ill. Her illness was one of those creeping diseases of old age, creeping slowly in the case of David's aunt, but everyone knew that she would gradually become more and more helpless. Mrs Penfold had done housework for her ever since she first moved to Cornwall, and they had become friends. Now Mrs Penfold had let her own small cottage and moved in, so that she could be a permanent nurse and companion, and David had suggested that Jilly might be just the sort of girl Lucy wanted for the hotel.

'She needs a live-in job and she wants to come to Plymouth – see a bit of life, she says.' He grinned. 'But she's a nice, decent sort of girl – you won't have any trouble with her.'

'Send her to see me,' Lucy had said, and Jilly had arrived with one small suitcase and an old carpet-bag given her by David's aunt. She was small and dark, with sooty-lashed blue eyes and a soft, burring voice, and she seemed willing enough to turn her hand to anything she might be asked to do.

'She'd make a good waitress,' Lucy said. 'Or a receptionist. She's bright enough, and she's very pretty.' But Patsy was receptionist. They had made her a little office behind a tiny counter in the entrance hall, and she sat there all day, her wheelchair barely visible, welcoming new guests, giving them their bills as they left, and doing the accounts. It was a cook that they really needed, and Jilly loved cooking.

By now, Lucy had got used to the bike and the girlfriends and she didn't take much notice. Geoff was young and enjoying life, and she was too busy to wonder what her maid was doing during her time off. She didn't realise that as soon as the evening meal had been served and as soon as Geoff had come in from work and finished his own supper, Jilly's apron was hung on the hook behind the door and the two of them were off on the motorbike. By then Lucy was in the family living-room, thankful for the chance to put her feet up after a long day's work.

Running a proper hotel was very different from looking after the simple guest house Pengelly's had been before the war, she reflected. The country was at last getting back on its feet. Most of the rationing was coming to an end, and things were coming into the shops – new things, well made, not utility any more. People were earning better money and starting to go on holidays again, and Devon was, as always, a favourite destination. A lot of people came to Plymouth, even though there was still so much rebuilding still to be done. The new Royal Parade had been opened by the King in 1947 and shops were being built all along one side. There were going to be a new Dingle's, a big Spooner's and John Yeo's, and a new Co-op. A lot of the shops were still trading from the row of Nissen huts that had been put up all along George Street, and when they were gone at last the new Civic Centre would be built in their place, and there was even talk of a new Theatre Royal. Plymouth was going to rise again, like a phoenix, from the ashes.

All this work brought people to Plymouth – people from other cities, wanting to see what was being done, men from the ministries in London, architects and businessmen who were all interested in the new Britain. And they all wanted good accommodation.

'It's solid value for money we've got to give,' Lucy said. 'Comfortable rooms with good beds, and decent food for their bellies. None of your fancy French cooking – what men want is a proper meal. Roast beef and Yorkshire, and good bread-and-butter pudding or a nice apple pie with clotted cream. The sort of food they've longed for all through the war.'

Clotted cream was the most popular item on the menu. They had it on scones, on toast and jam, and on breakfast cornflakes, as well as on their apple pies. They had to be shown how to eat it, on top of the jam rather than underneath it, and without butter, but to a man they loved it and asked for it again and again. Lucy started to serve afternoon teas as well as lunch and dinner, and non-residents came in especially for her Devonshire scones.

'We'll be able to fill the new rooms three times over,' she said, doing the accounts with Patsy. 'It's just a pity we can't buy up any more of the houses in the row!'

'For God's sake,' Wilmot said, coming into the office, 'give it a rest. Champagne tastes on lemonade money, that's your trouble, Lucy. Let's be satisfied with what we've got.'

'Being satisfied with what we'd got didn't get us where we are today,' Lucy said tartly. 'The old guest house wouldn't have been able to survive as it was. If you'd had your way, we'd be out on the streets now, and how satisfied would you have been with that?'

'If I'd had my way?' Wilmot glanced around him at the newly painted walls, the real chandelier that had replaced Lucy's 'cluster', the dark red patterned carpet that covered the floor where they had put linoleum a few years before. 'I thought I *had* had my way. Wasn't it all supposed to have been my idea in the first place?'

Lucy gave him a withering look and turned back to the accounts. She had little patience with Wilmot these days. At some point since the evening when the new hotel had first opened and she had stood on the Hoe with David and talked about rights, she had hardened towards her husband. She knew he was drinking more than was good for him, but all her efforts to help him stop had been in vain and she had finally shrugged her shoulders and left him to it. Sometimes, she was aware that she had shrugged her shoulders of him altogether.

However, there was never time to think about that now. Always, there were other things to claim her attention. New furnishings for the hotel, as more and better products came back on the market. New menus, as more ingredients became available, and new suppliers as local businesses got back on their feet.

'I want to support local farmers as much as possible,' she said. 'It's good for them as well as for our guests. Strawberries from Bere Alston, that sort of thing. The produce is good and it's fresher than buying from London, but it's got to be the right price.' She drove a hard bargain, but she generally got what she wanted.

Arthur and Maud had never bought from London, never even thought of it. They had bought locally all their lives. Lucy seemed to be moving in different circles these days, and they couldn't keep up with her.

'Best if you retire properly,' she said to them. 'You've worked hard all your lives, you deserve a rest. Put your feet up, go to the pictures of an afternoon or up on the Hoe and sit in the sun. Leave it all to me now. You don't have to worry any more.'

Arthur was glad of a rest, but he found it hard to give up entirely. After breakfast he went out into the front hall – he'd never got his tongue around the word 'foyer' – and sat on the little green chaise-longue, keeping Patsy company and having a chat with the guests as they paid their bills or went out for the day. But once the early morning bustle was over and the hotel quiet, he drifted into the back room with Maud. On fine days, he went out and sat up on the Hoe as Lucy had suggested, hobnobbing with his cronies there, or he walked round the new streets, watching the rebuilding. To her relief, he found this a fascinating new hobby and came back every day with something to grumble about.

'I told you, it's just like a kid's building blocks. All square. No character to it.'

'It'll be convenient, though.' They went through all the old arguments about wet feet and roofing over the lot, with Arthur and Wilmot like a Greek chorus, chiming in with each other as if they'd rehearsed for hours. Sometimes,

Lucy wanted to scream at them, but she held her tongue. So long as it kept them happy . . .

Happy? When she had a rare moment away from thoughts of the hotel, she caught up the word and wondered about it. What was 'happy'? She'd thought she knew, back in the early days when she had first known Wilmot. Happiness then had been the excitement of waiting for him to arrive on the doorstep, grinning that cheeky grin, his kitbag dumped beside him. Happiness had been strolling along the front at Southsea, her arm in his. Happiness had been getting married, those first nights of loving, the days of sunshine when she'd taught him to swim in the big new swimming-pool. Happiness had been when he'd come home when Geoff was a year old, and when Patsy had been born, and Zannah . . .

Had there ever been any happiness since then?

It was useless to think about it. Since then, there had been fear and dread and terror, and a constant, gnawing anxiety. During those dark days, what she had now would have seemed like paradise. It *was* paradise, in comparison. You had to admit that. You had to be satisfied with what you'd got.

This is where I came in, she thought, as she remembered her own reply when Wilmot himself had told her that. Being satisfied with what you'd got didn't get you anywhere else.

I don't know where we would all be if I'd been satisfied, if I'd just sat back and waited for other people to get on with life. Mum and Dad both getting older, and tired after all they'd been through, Wilmot a bag of nerves after all *he'd* been through, Patsy in her wheelchair . . . Only Geoff could have been any help at all, and he'd been no more than a boy when the war ended, with a boy's interests, and when he'd got old enough to leave school he'd wanted his own life, and it wasn't in the hotel. And why should it be?

The responsibility had rested squarely on Lucy's

shoulders. For all she'd pretended to defer to Wilmot, for all she'd let him take credit, the responsibility had been hers. The bank manager had known that, and if he hadn't believed she could do it – she, not Wilmot – they would never have got that loan.

She went to the bathroom and looked in the mirror. She'd hardly had time lately to examine her own face, but she did so now. There were lines appearing round her eyes and the crease of a frown in her forehead. But her skin was still pale and fine, and her eyes as deep a violet as ever. And although there were a few white hairs appearing on her head, they were sparse amongst the thick, springing waves of auburn, only slightly faded from when she was a girl.

Happiness was whatever you chose to make it, she thought. Twenty-five years ago, it would have been a kiss from a good-looking young sailor. Twenty years ago, the birth of her first baby. Ten years, just to have her family safe around her.

And today? In ten years' time, would she look back and see that happiness had been hers now all the time?

Perhaps happiness was, after all, just being satisfied with what you'd got.

The first time Geoff took Jilly out on his motorbike was in the spring of 1951. He took her for a ride on the moor and when they came to the town of Tavistock he parked the motorbike in the square and they walked down the road to the bridge. They leant over the parapet and looked down into the river.

'You can see quite big fish here sometimes. Salmon. They jump up over the weir. Those steps at the side were made for them to jump up when the water's too low for the weir.'

'It's pretty.' People were walking along the broad stone pathway beside the river. 'Where does that go?'

'To the Meadows. It's the local park. It's nice.' They left

the bridge and walked down the steps to the pathway. It ran high above the tumbling, rock-strewn river. The old walls of the Abbey ran alongside, and there was an arch to go through before they reached the Meadows. The opposite bank was thick with trees and bushes, and ducks swam in the rushing water or preened their feathers on the rocks.

The Meadows was a broad open stretch of grassland, with large oak and beech trees shading its walks. It reached right down to Drake's statue, at the corner of Plymouth Road, and across to the narrow canal which ran the four miles from Tavistock to the mining village of Morwellham, on the banks of the Tamar. There was a children's paddling pool and a sandpit, and in another part there were a few swings and an old steamroller that someone had left there for them to clamber over. Between the canal and the road there were rose gardens, tennis courts and a bowling green.

'It's lovely,' Jilly said as they wandered hand in hand along the canal banks. 'It's my favourite place in the whole world.'

Geoff grinned. 'And how much of the whole world have you seen? You've never even been as far as Exeter.'

She turned wide blue eyes on him. Her hair gleamed in the sun with the iridescence of a starling's wing. 'I've seen pictures.'

'It's not the same as going there.' Geoff swished the water with a stick he'd picked up. 'I want to go all over the world. I want to see everything.'

'You ought to join the Navy then, like your dad.' But she spoke wistfully, hoping that he'd say he didn't want to do that.

To her surprise, he did. 'I'm not joining the Navy! All they ever do is go to sea. I don't want to spend months just staring at the water. No, when I get my call-up I'll go in the Army. They get sent all over the world.'

'I thought most of them went to Germany.'

'Well, that'd be a start. And some go to Cyprus or Israel – there's plenty of other places. Anyway, I don't care where it is, so long as it's somewhere. I'm fed up with Plymouth, Jilly. I've never been anywhere else either. Well, I've been further than you.' He grinned. 'I've been to London.'

'Have you? Have you really? What's it like?'

'Well, it's still a bit of a mess, but they're getting a lot of it rebuilt. Of course, they're getting the Festival of Britain all ready now. That's going to be worth seeing. I'm going in the summer, when I get my holiday. Here –' he looked at her, his eyes bright – 'why don't you come with me?'

'Me? Come to London with you?' She stared at him. 'How could I do that?'

'Easy. We'd just get on a train and go.' He laughed at her. 'You just buy a ticket at the station.'

'Oh, you – I don't mean that. I mean – well – you and me, going to London together. What would people say?'

'They'd wish they were coming too. You ought to come, Jilly. You ought to see London. And this Festival, it's going to be smashing. Everyone will want to go.'

'I know, but . . . It would take more than a day, wouldn't it? I mean, we couldn't go and come back on the same day.'

'Good Lord, no. We'd need nearly a week. There's going to be all sorts there – the Dome of Discovery, the Skylon, the fair at Battersea Gardens. And I could show you all the other things too. The Tower, and St Paul's, and Westminster, where Princess Elizabeth got married, and Madame Tussaud's – oh, everywhere.' He looked at her. 'We could stay with Uncle David.'

'Uncle David? You mean Mr Tremaine?'

'Yes. Your mum lives with his auntie, doesn't she? He's got a house in London, he could put us up. I stayed with him last time. He's got plenty of room.'

'I don't know – I mean, my mum just did cleaning and that sort of thing.'

'So what? She looks after his auntie now, she's a sort of

209

companion. Anyway, what difference does that make? It's you I'm asking, not your mum.'

'Yes, but I'm just a hotel assistant.'

'And I'm just a dockyard apprentice.' Geoff shook his head. 'I don't know what you're worrying about. Uncle David will be pleased to see us.'

'Well, he's always been very nice to me,' Jilly admitted. 'But going to stay with him – I'm not sure.'

'Well, *I'm* sure. I'm sure I want you to come and I'm sure he won't mind a bit. He won't even make you share a room with me.' He grinned at her blush. 'It'll be much better fun than going about on my own.'

'Go on, you'll find another girl to go with you. You've got loads of girls wanting to go out with you.'

'Maybe I have,' he said, suddenly serious, 'but I'm not sure I want anyone else. I think I just want you.'

They walked on, suddenly silent. They had walked the length of the Meadows beside the river and then back along the canal. They went out into Plymouth Road and met the children coming out of the primary school on the opposite side. The bus station was crowded with green double-decker Western National buses, coming from and going back to Plymouth, Okehampton, even Exeter and Bude.

Tavistock was like the hub of a wheel. As well as the bus station there were two railway lines, one the main line between Plymouth and Exeter and the other the branch line between Plymouth and Launceston. It must always have been busy, Geoff said. It was one of the stannary towns, where metals had been brought for weighing in the mining days. He took her back to the big square, surrounded by the handsome buildings of the Town Hall, the big church and the old Abbey gateway, and showed her the plaque that told you all about it.

They went into the pannier market behind the Town Hall where people were selling produce – crusty, yellow cream in big bowls, mounds of vegetables and fruit, cheeses and bacon. Someone had a stall where they were selling garments they'd knitted or sewn, someone else had things made of wood. It was like an Aladdin's cave where you could buy anything you wanted.

'I'd like to live here,' Jilly said, fingering a handknitted cardigan. 'I'd like to do all my shopping here.'

'Well, maybe you will one day.' Geoff took her out again, and through an archway into the main street. 'I'll tell you where you can get the best doughnuts in Devon, shall I?'

They walked up the hill and almost at the top found a small bakery. It smelt richly of new-baked bread and cakes, and there was a queue right out on to the pavement. They joined the queue and bought hot pasties and a bag of doughnuts, rosy with jam squeezing out through their sides, then carried them down a steep flight of steps and went back through the Meadows to sit beneath the big oak and beech trees by the river, eating their lunch.

'You will come to London with me, won't you?' Geoff said presently.

Jilly sat quiet for a while, looking at the river. She knew quite well that she was in love with Geoff, and she was pretty sure she wasn't the only one. She'd seen those other girls on the back of his motorbike before he'd asked her out. What she didn't know was whether he was in love with her. It didn't seem likely, with all those other girls hanging about. How many of them had he already asked?

'I don't know,' she said. 'I don't want to decide straight away.' She turned her head and looked at him with her sooty-lashed eyes. 'Let's wait a while, shall we?'

Geoff looked as if he was about to argue, then thought better of it. He laid his hand on hers. 'I'd really like you to come.'

I'd really like to go too, she thought. And he did look as if he meant it. His face was open and his eyes looked straight at hers, darker than usual with just a blue rim round the wide black pupil. And he hadn't made any passes at her, not like some of the boys she'd been out with at home.

'I'll think about it,' she said a little breathlessly. 'I'd like to – but I'll think about it.'

'Think yes,' he said, and his eyes were intent. 'Think yes – yes – *yes*.'

They went in August. By then, Lucy had got used to their friendship and as long as they stayed with David she knew they wouldn't come to any harm. She didn't think there was anything serious in it – Geoff was much too young for that, and Jilly was even younger, only seventeen – and she'd rather he was in London with a girl than wandering about on his own. You never knew what might happen to a young lad in the big city.

'Mum thinks I'll get snatched away and sold as a white slave,' Geoffrey said with a grin as they settled into their seats on the train. 'Good thing I've got you to look after me.'

'What's a white slave?' Jilly asked. 'I didn't think there were any slaves now, anyway.'

'Well, they're –' He glanced at her and decided not to go into it. 'I don't know, really. It's just a sort of saying. I like going on this line, don't you? All along the beach, in and out of the cliffs – it's like something out of an Enid Blyton story. I used to read her books when I was a tacker.'

'I bet she'd been down to Devon and Cornwall,' Jilly said. 'A lot of the places she wrote about are just like the little coves and villages round here.'

They spent the journey gazing out of the window, giving themselves marks for spotting church towers or spires (one for a tower, two for a spire) and doing the crossword puzzle in the paper Geoff had bought at the station. Jilly had made some sandwiches and brought a bottle of lemonade, and they had these at about twelve o'clock, and soon after that the train pulled into Paddington station.

'It's enormous,' Jilly said in an awed whisper. 'Look at the roof, Geoff, it's like those pictures of the Crystal Palace. You'd never think it had been built just for railway trains.'

'Wait till you see the Underground.' Geoff was already striding away towards the exit, a suitcase in each hand. Jilly hurried after him with her old carpet-bag and followed him down the steps. She wrinkled up her nose.

'It's a bit smelly. D'you really mean to say people came down to places like this to shelter during the air-raids? It must have been horrible.' She waited while Geoff bought tickets, and then followed him to the top of the escalator. 'Oh, we haven't really got to go on that, have we?'

'It's all right. It's just a moving staircase.' He hefted one suitcase under his arm and took her hand. 'Just step on and stand still. You don't have to walk down if you don't want to.'

Jilly stood rigid, her hand resting tentatively on the moving banister. As they approached the bottom she gave him a nervous look, and he grinned and held her hand tightly.

'Now just step off. That's right. It's a good job you've got me to look after you. Now we have to look on that map and see how to get to Chalk Farm station.'

They emerged at last on the corner of a busy road. Jilly took a deep breath.

'Well, it's not what you'd call good fresh air, but at least it's air. I don't know what that stuff down there's called.' She looked at the shops and the traffic and giggled. 'Not much like a farm, is it?'

David lived in a side street a few hundred yards up the hill from the station. The street was quite different from the main road, which was lined with small shops and, like most streets in London, still pocked with occasional bomb sites. David's street was built of tall houses with steps going up to their front doors and more steps going down to basements. There were tall poplar trees shading the hot pavements, and in some of the small front yards there were babies in prams or plants growing in pots.

'It looks ever so posh,' Jilly said.

Geoff led the way up a flight of steps and rang a bell. There were several bells, Jilly noticed, each with a different name on. She remembered that Mr Tremaine had told her mother that he had divided his house into flats. He had just kept the ground floor and the basement for himself, and there were two floors above that. It sounded sensible, though she wondered why he hadn't just sold the house if it was too big and moved somewhere smaller.

She glanced up and down the road, feeling nervous again. It was all so different from the village in Cornwall, even from Plymouth. She had never realised how big London was, so big that you could get on a train and travel for half an hour or more and still be in the city, with not so much as a bit of lawn to remind you of the country. She wondered what Mr Tremaine was going to be like. She knew him of course, she'd known him for quite a long time, but that was down in Cornwall where people were different – slower, more relaxed. Here, they all seemed to be anxious and in a hurry, pushing past you in the Underground, frowning, grey faced. Would Mr Tremaine be different too?

Then the door opened and he was there, dressed a little differently in rather smart trousers and a white shirt rather than the grey flannel bags and old Fair Isle jumper he wore in Cornwall, but otherwise looking just the same with his friendly smile and crinkly grey hair. He held out his hand in welcome and as Jilly rather shyly gave him hers, he pulled her gently towards him and kissed her cheek.

'Welcome to London, my dear. Welcome.'

The Festival was all Geoff had promised it would be. They went twice to the main Exhibition, wandering for hours amongst the stands and demonstrations. It was to be a celebration of Britain's recovery from the war, the King had said when he first suggested the idea, a resurgence of the Great Exhibition of 1851 when the Crystal Palace had been built and all the world had come to show its wares. It was like that now, a gathering of countries that less than ten years ago had been at war, a symbol of peace.

Geoff's favourite was the Dome of Discovery, a huge, steely saucer-like structure that looked as if it came straight from a science-fiction film and had displays of what the future would be like that left them gasping and incredulous. Just outside this was the tall, slender Skylon, a graceful ellipse that pointed skywards like a sign of hope.

But best of all were the evenings, when they went to Battersea Park. The fair was the biggest and the best ever seen in England, and Geoff and Jilly became children again, riding on the scenic train, tiptoeing along the swaying bridges of the Treetops Walk to look down through the fairy-lights at the heads of people beneath; laughing themselves helpless in the hall of mirrors or on the cakewalk. They went on switchback rides, roundabouts and ghost trains, and it was late at night when they finally made their way back to Chalk Farm on the last bus, sitting in the front seat at the top and holding hands as they gazed dreamily at the lights of London swaying past.

'It's been a gorgeous holiday,' Jilly said on the last evening. 'I've never had such a lovely time in my whole life.'

'Nor have I.' Geoff took her hand in his and stroked the fingers gently. 'I didn't know it was possible to be so happy. I don't really want to go back, do you?'

'I don't know. I wouldn't want to live in London, not all the time.'

'Nor would I, but – going back seems so ordinary. Going back to the dockyard, the same as usual, only seeing you in the evenings.' He hesitated and she glanced at him and saw the colour came into his face. Suddenly, her heart began to beat a little faster. 'Jilly,' he said, speaking quickly now so that his words almost tumbled over themselves. 'Jilly, I love you. I want us to get engaged. Will you? Will you marry me, when we've got enough money? Please, Jilly – say you will. Say yes.'

'Geoff –'

'I know we can't get married for ages,' he went on desperately, 'but if we could just be engaged – you see, I'll have to go away before long, I'm bound to be called up and I might have to go anywhere.' The idea of seeing the world seemed suddenly to lose its appeal. 'If we were engaged before I went – well, I'd feel better. I'd know you were waiting for me. Oh Jilly, I do love you. Say you love me. Say you will.'

'Oh, Geoff,' she said tremulously, 'of course I love you. Of *course* I'll marry you.'

Chapter Seventeen

Geoff's call-up papers came just before Christmas. To everyone's surprise, he had chosen to go into the Army rather than the Navy or the Air Force. Lucy, recalling his early ambitions to fly a Spitfire, was relieved by this – a motorbike was bad enough. Wilmot was slightly put out that his son didn't want to follow him into the Navy, but he didn't argue. It seemed that he was learning at last that Geoff was a man now and would make his own decisions.

By the middle of January, he would be gone. Geoff and Jilly decided that they could not wait another two years or more to be together. They wanted to be married now.

'Now?' Lucy said blankly when they told her. 'Get married? But you're not even engaged.'

Jilly blushed. 'We were thinking of getting engaged at Christmas. I've been looking at rings.'

'Have you asked Mrs Penfold?' Lucy asked her son, ignoring the idea of rings. 'Have you asked her if Jilly can get engaged? She's not even eighteen. I don't know how you can be thinking of such a thing.'

'I knew it was daft, letting them go jaunting off to London together,' Wilmot said. 'Bound to lead to trouble. Here –' his brows came together in a frown – 'you're not in trouble, are you? Geoff?'

'No. *No*. Of course not.' Geoff's face was scarlet, Jilly's a bright pink. 'I've never – we've never –'

'All right, all right,' Lucy said hastily. 'So long as that's all right. Now look, you must see you can't get married. You're both much too young. And with Geoff going away

217

straight after, what sort of a marriage would it be?' She was painfully conscious that her own marriage had begun in a very similar way. 'You both need to grow up a bit more,' she went on quickly. 'You'll be separated a long time – suppose you meet someone else? It can happen, you know. I know you don't think so now, but it's true. It won't hurt you to wait a couple of years till Geoff's out of the Army, and then if you're in the same mind—'

'We will be. We know we will be.'

'You *think* you will be,' she said, but she remembered the certainty of youth, the knowledge that nobody else, *nobody* – with the exception perhaps of Romeo and Juliet – had ever felt like this, had ever loved so intensely. She looked at them helplessly, and silently thanked God for a law which prevented youngsters like this from making dreadful mistakes, at least until they were twenty-one.

'Just get engaged at Christmas,' she said. 'Geoff's not going off to war. You'll have plenty of chances to see each other. By the time he comes out again you'll be that much older and more sure. It's the best way.'

'Two years!' Geoff said when they were alone again. '*Two years!* It's a lifetime. I can't wait that long, Jilly.'

'I don't know what else we can do,' she said miserably. 'If they won't give you permission . . . And even if they did, I don't think my mum would. She doesn't approve of young marriages either.'

It was David who came in for the most censure. They had stayed with him in London, and for some reason everyone had got the impression that if it hadn't been for that holiday Geoff and Jilly would never have fallen in love. There were plenty of girls in Plymouth just as pretty and just as keen on Geoff, Lucy said, and plenty of boys who would be pleased to take Jilly out. It was bound to lead to trouble, letting them go off for a whole week on their own. What had David been thinking of? Hadn't he kept an eye on them?

'I didn't do anything,' he protested when Lucy rang him up to tell him what had happened. 'They went off on their own every day to the Festival, or to see the sights. They slept in separate rooms—'

'I'm not saying they didn't. I hope I can trust my own son.'

'Well, what are you complaining about?' he asked reasonably. 'If they'd stayed in Plymouth instead of coming to London, they could have gone off all day just the same, out to Dartmoor or down to Cornwall. They would still have felt the same about each other. What's the difference?'

There was a difference, but Lucy couldn't explain it. She put down the telephone receiver feeling dissatisfied and unhappy. It was the nearest she and David had ever come to a quarrel and she lay awake that night, tears she couldn't explain drifting softly on to her pillow. I wish I hadn't gone on at him, she thought sadly. I never see him these days, and I have to ring him up and grumble at him, and he's right, it's not his fault.

She wasn't the only one. David's aunt complained to him as well. Mrs Penfold was very upset, she said, and half inclined to tell her daughter to come home straight away. No doubt Geoff was a nice enough boy, but she didn't want Jilly tied down so soon. Twenty-one was quite early enough. She didn't even approve of their getting engaged.

'I suppose I can't stop that though,' she said to Lucy when she came to Plymouth to talk over the situation. 'I can't stop her wearing a ring or saying they're getting married one day. I just wish they'd not got serious so quickly.'

'So do I,' Lucy said. 'Mind, I've nothing against your Jilly, she's a nice girl and a lovely little cook, and I daresay she'll make a good wife some day. Same as my Geoff will make a good husband. It's just too soon.'

The two women nodded at each other. They got on well

and Mrs Penfold stayed a day or two longer, seeing the sights of Plymouth and admiring the new shops before she returned to Cornwall.

Geoff and Jilly went shopping for an engagement ring and on Christmas morning Geoff put it on Jilly's finger. She gazed at it, turning her finger so that the light flashed on the three tiny diamonds, and her eyes sparkled as brightly with tears as she looked up at him.

'It's lovely, Geoff. It makes it seem so real.'

'I wish it was a plain gold one, without any stones,' he said, and she nodded.

'So do I. But it'll come. Now we're engaged – they won't really make us wait all that time, Geoff.'

'It's having to go away makes it so much worse,' he said. 'They're sending chaps out to Korea now. They only get a few weeks' basic training and then they're gone. I might be away the whole two years.'

'You'd think your mum and dad would understand,' Jilly said. 'Them having been separated all that time.'

However, that was just why Lucy understood, just why she didn't want them tied to each other too soon. Wilmot had been a fresh-faced, laughing young husband when he'd gone to war – and he'd come back a changed, bitter man. She couldn't believe such a thing would happen to Geoff, but suppose it did? And even if that didn't happen, there was the chance that Jilly might not stay faithful. It was all too easy for a young, attractive girl to fall in love with someone else.

Just as she had fallen in love with David.

For a long time now, Lucy had suppressed her feelings for David and her deep sadness that they could never be together. She had used the hotel as a means of escape from them, immersing herself in the work of the conversion, of the development of the hotel, building up the business to the success it now was. All the time she had told herself and Wilmot that it was essential as a means of making a living

220

for the family, she had known that there was more to it than that. It was a means of survival without the man she loved.

Now, with Geoff and Jilly's story unfolding before her, she could not blind herself any longer to the deep love and the deep wretchedness that still smouldered inside her body, her mind, her heart.

During the day, by keeping busy, she could keep the thoughts at bay; but at night, exhausted though she might be in body and mind, she could not hide any longer from her heart. Her feelings flooded in and she would lie beside Wilmot for hour upon hour, torn by the misery, the loneliness, the thought of the wasted years.

I can't let it happen to those two children, she thought. If they're meant to be together, if they really love each other, two years will not be too long to wait. And if they can't wait – well, I may have saved them both from this.

But it was not something she could tell them. There was nobody she could talk to, except for David. And for the first time in her life, and over this very matter, she had quarrelled with him.

Geoff went for his basic training in January. He was away six weeks and then came home for a brief leave. It was only a month since the King had died, and the whole country was saddened, but in Geoffrey's face Jilly saw more than that. She touched his cheek and felt the ache already in her heart.

'You're going away.'

He nodded. 'Korea.'

Jilly sat down on the settee and he sat beside her, holding both her hands. She turned her face against his shoulder and he put both arms round her and held her tightly, feeling the dampness of her tears on his shirt.

'It's not fair. It's not *fair*.'

'I know.'

'If only we'd been able to get married. We could have

been married at Christmas. What difference would it have made to anyone else? I'd be your *wife*.'

'Oh, Jilly.'

'It's all I want,' she said passionately. 'Just to be your wife. It's going to be so horrible, knowing you're all that way away, on the other side of the world, and us not married. Why couldn't they let us, Geoff, why?'

'I suppose they meant it for the best—' he said helplessly, but she broke in angrily.

'The best? How could it be for the best? It's just old people being mean to young ones, that's all. Just because they've got the power to stop us! It's not right, Geoff. We're not children, we're adults, we're grown up, we work for our living. Why shouldn't we be able to decide for ourselves?' She stared at him, her face white. 'Look at you. You're a soldier, you can go off and fight for your country, even for someone else's country, but you can't get married. It's stupid. It's *cruel*.'

'Oh, Jilly – Jilly, don't upset yourself. There's nothing we can do about it. Don't let's spoil the last few days we've got together.' He held her against him again and for a few minutes she submitted, weeping against his shoulder. Eventually she gave a long shudder and pulled away. Her wet face was set, her eyes narrowed with determination.

'I tell you what, Geoff. They're not going to stop us being married. Oh, maybe not in a church, we can't do that – but we can be married as far as *we're* concerned. I feel as though we are already anyway. I'm your wife, Geoff, even if some bloke in a frock hasn't said a lot of words over our heads. And this weekend is going to be our honeymoon.'

He stared at her. 'Jilly, what are you saying?'

'I'm saying we're going to go away together.' She lifted her chin. 'We'll tell your mum we're going down to Cornwall to stay with my mum for a couple of days. We'll find ourselves some nice little place to stay – a bed and breakfast or something, in Torquay – and we'll be married,

222

just for a few days.' She looked at him and grasped his hands. 'It's all we've got, Geoff,' she said urgently. 'It's all we're going to have for maybe two years. But at least we'll have that, and they won't be able to take it away from us.'

Lucy wasn't best pleased to hear that Geoff and Jilly were going down to Cornwall for most of his leave. She didn't mind giving the girl her time off, she said to Wilmot, but she didn't see why they couldn't spend it in Plymouth. Didn't they realise Lucy was the boy's mother and would want to see as much of him as possible before he went away?

'They're being selfish,' Wilmot agreed. 'All youngsters are selfish. But there's nothing you can do about it. You can't lock Geoff in his room.'

They went on the motorbike. It wasn't particularly good weather for motorcycling, but they couldn't afford the train, they needed all their money for their accommodation, and besides, Lucy might have wanted to come and see them off and she would have known they weren't getting on the train for Penzance. Going on the motorbike, nobody knew which way they were heading.

The motorbike puttered through Plympton and along the road to Ivybridge and through Buckfast, past the big abbey that the monks were building. The road twisted between high banks, not much more than a country lane in places. They came to Newton Abbot and then Totnes. The earth was very red around here, and the banks were starred with huge yellow primroses, their faces as big as half-crowns. The hills rolled gently on either side, the grass already lush. When they came within sight of Torbay, Geoff stopped the bike and they sat and gazed for a few minutes.

'It's lovely,' Jilly said softly. The bay curved in a great horseshoe, bounded by the long, high cliffs of Berry Head on one side and the arm of Babbacombe on the other. Torquay lay at the heart of the bay, with the town of Paignton close beside it, like a sister. The sun was out and the whole scene was bright with the green of fields and woods, the glowing auburn of the earth and the stretching, glittering blue of sea and sky.

'We'll come here for our proper honeymoon,' Geoff said, and she squeezed his arm.

'This is our proper honeymoon. Only, nobody will ever know it but us. It'll be our secret all our lives.'

'If it's our honeymoon,' Geoff said, 'we ought to be married, and you ought to be wearing a ring.' He felt in his pocket and brought out a small box. Inside was a plain golden ring. Jilly took it out and held it reverently, her eyes sparkling with tears.

'It's a proper wedding ring. Oh, *Geoff*.'

'Well, what did you expect?' he asked. 'A curtain ring from Woolworth's? This is our proper wedding, Jilly.' He took the ring back and held her hand in his. Then, looking into her eyes, he said, 'I, Geoff, take thee, Jilly, to be my wedded wife. To have and to hold, from this day forward, in sickness and in health, for richer for poorer, for better for worse, so long as we both shall live.' He grinned a little and said, 'I hope I got it in the right order, but it doesn't matter, so long as it's all there. I love you, Jilly.'

'I love you too,' she whispered, and in a husky voice she repeated the vows. The tears were pouring down her cheeks as he slipped the ring on her finger. 'No, let me take the engagement one off first, or they'll be the wrong way round. There.'

They stared at the gold band on her finger. Jilly's heart was beating fast. She looked at Geoff and saw in his face the same awe that trembled through her body. The wind in the trees was like a choir, and when she heard a blackbird call it was like a peal of bells.

'We're married now,' she whispered. 'We're married.' And then, with a flash of mischief, 'You may kiss the bride!'

They went on into Torquay. The road ran right along the seafront, where palm trees grew along the pavement, just as if they were abroad. The pier jutted out into the sea and there were two harbours, an outer harbour and a small inner one, filled with little boats that were all heeled over on the mud because it was low tide. The shops were clustered around the harbour and the main road ran up the hill.

Geoff drove on to Babbacombe and they stopped on the cliff road and looked again at the broad sweep of the bay and the red escarpment of Berry Head on the far side. The sea met the sky with only a thin, dark rim of horizon to separate them, and sailing boats danced with white horses on the glittering blue.

'Let's find somewhere to stay here,' Jilly said.

It was still only the beginning of March and the holiday season hadn't begun yet, but there were a few small guest houses and some private houses advertising bed and breakfast. They looked at them and finally chose a small guest house with green window-frames and daffodils growing in the garden. It stood high up on the cliff, with the same view out right across the bay to Berry Head. The woman who answered the door looked at them a little doubtfully.

'I don't know. I've only got one room vacant.' She glanced at Jilly's left hand and Jilly lifted it proudly.

'We are married. This is our honeymoon. My – my husband's a soldier, he's going away next week. We don't have much time.'

The woman's face softened. She looked about sixty, small and plump, motherly looking. 'You poor things. It was like that for me and my first hubby. Married just after the war started and then he went away. We had two days together, and that was all.'

'Was he away a long time?' Jilly asked as they followed her into the house and up the stairs.

'Oh, he never came back, maid. Killed at sea, he was. No, that two days was all I had of married life. Then I met my

Harold and we've been married thirty-five years come next August, but I still think of my poor Bill, you know.'

Thirty-five years! It was the first war she was talking about, the 1914-18 war. The little chill that had touched Jilly's heart faded. It was all so long ago, it was like history.

'This is the room.' The woman stood back to let them see. It was small, almost filled by the double bed, and there was a narrow utility wardrobe in one corner and a dressing-table in front of the window. The bed was covered by a brown satin bedspread and looked fat and bulky, as if there were a thick eiderdown underneath.

'It's lovely,' Jilly said. 'Isn't it, Geoff?'

'And that's the bathroom door, opposite. I usually charge a shilling for a bath, but you can have one for nothing.' She had obviously taken a fancy to them, or perhaps she had some fellow-feeling even though her own short-lived marriage had been so long ago. 'If you want to bring your things in and get settled, I'll have a cup of tea ready for you in the lounge.'

Mrs Turner, her name was, and she was kindness itself. The only trouble was that she had taken such a fancy to Geoff and Jilly that she didn't want to let them go. She kept them talking in her overstuffed front room with its fat, billowing sofa and armchairs smothered with satin cushions and lace antimacassars and plied them with tea and bisuits until they began to despair of ever being alone. Then, quite suddenly, she got up and said briskly, 'You'll be wanting to go out for a walk now. Get some of our good fresh sea air into your lungs. I do high tea at six, so you've got an hour. My Harold will be home then, he'll be pleased to meet you.'

They found themselves out on the pavement. Geoff had brought the motorbike into the little front garden and they left it there, not daring to take it out. They'd been told to go for a walk, so go for a walk they would have to. Side by side, they set off on the route Mrs Turner had pointed out, which took them towards the cliffs.

226

'I thought we'd never get away,' Jilly said, giggling. 'She's ever so nice, but she can't half talk!'

'I wonder what time she'll let us go to bed,' Geoff said. They were on a cliff path now, high above the sea. 'I know she means to be kind but we've only got these two days. I don't want to spend them listening to her, I want to be with you.'

'You will be with me. We've got all night and all tomorrow night.' She blushed a little and held his hand tightly. 'And we can be out all day tomorrow. We're going to have a lovely time.'

To their relief, Mrs Turner seemed to have exhausted her fund of chatter. She welcomed them back an hour later and served them a high tea of steamed plaice with tinned peas and new potatoes and bread and butter, and sponge cake. Then she told them they could sit in the lounge until ten o'clock if they wanted to, and retreated to the back room where they could hear her talking to her husband. They sat on the sofa for a while, wishing they dared to go upstairs, and then went out for another walk. It was dark now, though, and a chilly wind had sprung up, so they went back. They hesitated in the hallway, and then Mrs Turner popped her head out.

'I'm just making a cup of tea. I'll get Mr Turner to bring it in to you.'

'He wants to have a look at us too,' Geoff whispered to Jilly, and she giggled. 'After this I reckon we can go upstairs.' They sat down again on the sofa. The cushions were glossy and elaborately stitched, not the sort of cushions you could ever really lean against. Over the mantelpiece there was a mirror cut out in a fancy design, and the light was shaded by a lampshade made of shapes of glass. On one wall there were three plaster ducks in flight.

At last they were able to go upstairs. They took turns in the bathroom, washing and cleaning their teeth. Neither wanted a bath now. The day seemed to have dragged interminably towards this moment and they didn't want to put it off any longer. All the same, while Geoff was in the bathroom and Jilly took the opportunity to scramble hastily into her nightdress, she wished suddenly that she could prolong it after all. Her heart was skipping unevenly in her breast and she felt shaky and almost sick. She got into bed and sat up, her arms round her knees, listening anxiously to the sound of Geoff letting water out of the washbasin.

He came in wearing his pyjamas. They looked at each other and smiled nervously.

'I feel a bit scared,' she said with a little laugh. 'It's silly – I feel as if we hardly know each other.'

'I know. I feel like that too. But it's just us. We're just the same people really.' He came closer and sat on the bed. 'It seems so funny, doesn't it? Getting into bed together. I mean, it isn't really anything to do with loving each other. It's just a bed. We could love each other anywhere. In a field. Behind a haystack.'

She giggled. 'Not so comfortable, though.'

'No.' He put his arms round her and she leant against him. 'I really do love you, Jilly. I love you all the time. I always will. If – if you don't want to do this – well, you don't have to. I don't want to do anything you don't want.'

'I know. I love you too, Geoff.' She took in a deep breath. 'And I want us to love each other properly. We – we're married, remember?' She freed her left hand and lifted it so that he could see. 'Proof!'

They laughed, and suddenly it was all right and they held each other close and began to kiss. Geoff's arms tightened, like iron bands around her trembling body, and he kissed her lips and then her cheeks and eyes and ears. He buried his face in her neck and his hands moved over her body, stroking her back and shoulders and then her waist and breasts. Jilly caught her breath. His fingers splayed out across her breasts, his palms cupping their fullness. He pushed aside the open neck of her nightdress and touched

228

the skin, and he pushed her gently back on the pillows and laid his body alongside hers.

'Jilly. *Jilly*.'

'Take off your jacket,' she whispered. 'I want to feel your skin.' With shaking fingers, she unbuttoned his pyjamas and pushed the cotton back, spreading her hands over his chest. He had no hair on his chest, it was smooth and lean and young, but there was muscle there, shifting beneath the skin, and there were muscles in his arms too, quivering with power. She felt weak.

Geoff undid the rest of the buttons on her nightdress and she moved so that she could pull it up over her body. He had never seen her in anything less than a bathing suit. She sat up and pulled the nightdress over her head lifting her arms in a motion that was unconsciously graceful, like a statue he had seen once in a museum, or like an old painting. Her breasts were smooth, lifting with the movement of her arms, and he put out his hand and touched one of them, as tenderly as if he were touching a baby's cheek. She laid the garment aside and looked at him, shy and proud.

Geoff stroked her body, very gently. He was aware that there would never be another time like this, never another first time. He wanted to savour it, to make it last. He trailed his fingertips tenderly over her shoulders, down the valley between her breasts, circling in the crease underneath, outlining their curves. He lifted one slightly towards him and bent to lay his lips upon the swelling flesh, folding them about the stiff, hard nipple. He slipped his other arm around her shoulders and held her firmly, letting his hand slide down her body, exploring the slight curve of her belly, the indentation of her waist, the swell of her hips.

Jilly put her arms around him and lay back, her body arched towards him. He could feel the rapid beating of her heart, like a bird in his hand. He slid his hand down again, touching her thigh, marvelling at its silkiness, and very

229

gently, with the tips of his fingers, touched between her thighs.

Jilly gave a shuddering sigh and he felt his heart leap. His fingers were moist. He stroked more firmly and felt her move beneath him. Suddenly, his pyjama trousers were an encumbrance and he dragged them off. A powerful urgency invaded him and he forgot about making it last. He forgot about everything except the desperate rapture of the moment. He flung himself down against her, on top of her, and thrust himself hard against her.

Jilly cried out and tried to move him. 'No. Not there.' She wriggled beneath him and the movement inflamed him further. He thrust again. 'Geoff. *Wait*.'

'I can't –'

'Yes, you can.' Her voice was soothing, though it still trembled. She put her hands under his hips and lifted him slightly, shifting her body beneath him, and then she took him in her hand, the touch of her fingertips an almost exquisite torture, and gently guided him. 'There.'

It didn't feel any different to Geoff. There was still a resistance. He pushed cautiously, aware now that he might be hurting her, and he heard her gasp a little. A wave of despair broke over him. He wasn't doing it right, it wasn't going to work . . . And then, quite suddenly, the resistance gave way as if something tore, something thin and fibrous like a piece of silky fabric, and although Jilly cried out again she also gripped him firmly with her arms and pulled him tighter against her. And he was conscious of being in a different place, as if he had slipped with his whole body into a warmth, a comfort, that he had never imagined existed, and he gave a shudder of his own, a long rippling quiver of delight.

'*Jilly*.'

'Geoff, I love you.'

'I love you.'

Their bodies moved together, gently and slowly, skin

sliding on skin like silk on silk, the warmth and excitement flowing between them as if they were truly one person, one body. Jilly put her hands on his head, one each side, and brought it down to hers and they kissed, a long, slow kiss that seemed to complete the union of their bodies. But it was more than bodies. It was as if their souls too had met and flowed each into the other.

It could not last long, that first time, however much they wanted it to. The excitement was too much for them. All too soon, they were lost again in the swoop of passion, drawing them up and on, all else forgotten. It was like climbing a mountain, a shimmering glass and crystal mountain. And then they were at the peak, poised briefly before that final lift into space, into a place where none could follow and they clung to each other, shaken and dizzy, and then fell slowly, slowly, back to earth and awareness.

'I never thought,' Geoff whispered in her ear when they could speak again at last, 'I never *dreamt* it would be like that.'

'We're truly married now,' she murmured back. 'We're truly, truly married . . .'

Chapter Eighteen

The Korean war was at its bloodiest that winter. To those at home, it was difficult to comprehend. The unfamiliar names – Osan, Kumyangjang, Suwon and Seoul – came uneasily to British tongues. The concept of the battle against Chinese Communism, coming so soon after the six-year war against Hitler's Nazism was almost too much to grapple with. And as those at home always did, Lucy and her family focused their attention on the one thought that meant the most to them: the thought that Geoff was out there, that he might at any moment be fighting, wounded, killed.

'It's just too much,' Lucy said to Wilmot. 'We've been through it all before. Why does he have to be taken away from us, just when we were getting ourselves together again?'

Wilmot grunted and she gave him a despairing look. Since Geoff had gone he had become more uncommunicative than ever, and she was sure he was drinking more. The bottle of rum he kept openly on the shelf and opened immediately after their evening meal wasn't going down so fast, but she had discovered another one, half full, under the bed and a third hidden in the coal-bunker. How many more bottles were secreted about the house, and how often did he drink from them?

'Is it like Japan?' she asked, her voice trembling a little. 'I mean, if he's taken prisoner, will they –'

'How the *hell* do I know?' Wilmot came to his feet and swept his hand across the kitchen table, sending a bottle of sauce flying. His face, always unhealthily sallow these days, was flooded with dark colour, so that he looked bruised all over. 'How the hell do I know what those little yellow bastards will do? I've been trying to forget it all these years – d'you think I want it all brought back to me? D'you think I want to think of my own son, caught in the same bloody trap I was in? I tell you, Lucy, if you had my memories –' He closed his bloodshot eyes, squeezing them tightly as if to shut out the unbearable pictures.

Lucy sometimes thought she had. She had lived through so many of his nightmares that it was almost as if she had shared the experiences themselves. Normally she would not have dreamed of bringing them back to him, but now Geoff was out there, and she tortured herself with her imaginings.

'Anyway, he's not been taken prisoner and probably won't be,' Wilmot growled, sitting down again. He was looking really ill, she thought, blotchy faced and red eyed. She had thought several times lately of asking him to see a doctor. Yet what would a doctor do but tell him to stop drinking? 'He's just a National Service squaddy, he won't get sent into battle.'

Lucy didn't know whether to believe that or not. If the National Servicemen weren't going into battle, why had they been sent there? She listened to the news and read the papers, and if she went to the cinema she watched the scenes shown on Pathé Pictorial and her fears returned. Geoff, she thought, Geoff. He's just a baby still.

She thought again of the last few days before Geoff had departed. He'd spent all the time he could with Jilly and, seeing them together, Lucy had wondered if she'd been right to forbid their marriage. They were so obviously in love, and they seemed well suited. If only they'd been a few years older, she would have been happy to give them her blessing – but she could not believe that two youngsters not yet out of their teens were ready to pledge their whole lives.

They needed the protection that she and Mrs Penfold, aided by the law, could give them.

'I know it hurts,' she had said to Jilly, coming on her crying in the kitchen. 'I know you feel the world's come to an end, but it hasn't, you know. Geoff will be back almost before you know it, and if you're of the same mind then—'

To her astonishment, Jilly whirled on her. 'You *know*? How can you possibly know? You've never been in my position! You don't know anything about it at all.'

Lucy shook her head. 'I may not have been in exactly the same position, but I do know what it's like to see my man go off to war.'

'But he was your husband, wasn't he?' Jilly said. 'You'd been married for years. You had children. At least if he didn't come back, you would have had all that just the same.'

'It still hurt just as much to see him go. More, probably. And then we had all those years of waiting. I want to save you from that, Jilly.'

'Save me?' the girl said bitterly. 'How can you save me from that? I'm having to wait just the same. And just how is stopping us getting married going to save me from a broken heart? Do you realise, if anything happens to Geoff they won't even let me know? It'll be you they tell – not me.'

'But I'm his mother—'

'And *I* ought to be his wife. That's what he wanted me to be.' Jilly stared at her and Lucy was shocked by the expression in the girl's eyes. 'And you stopped us from getting married. *You*.'

'It wasn't just me,' Lucy protested weakly. 'Geoff's father didn't want it either – nor did your own mother. We all—'

'They'd have agreed if you had. You could have persuaded them. They'd have listened to you.'

Lucy tried to deny this, but she knew in her heart it was true. She could have persuaded Mrs Penfold, overridden

Wilmot. She gazed helplessly at Jilly, seeing how thin and pale the girl looked, her cheeks pinched, her vivacity dimmed. But I *was* right, she thought, I *was*. This will pass. Everything passes.

'Please believe me, Jilly,' she said gently. 'The time will go and I'm sure Geoff will be all right. And if you both still love each other when he comes back, then we'll arrange the biggest wedding you want, with the most beautiful dress in Plymouth and a reception here in the hotel, everything you could ask for.'

Jilly looked at her, then she reached behind her back and untied the strings of her white apron. She took it off and laid it on the kitchen table.

'I don't want a big wedding, or a white dress,' she said coldly. 'I don't want a reception in the hotel. Don't you understand? I just want to be married to Geoff and I want to be married to him *now*.'

She turned and walked out of the kitchen, leaving Lucy staring after her, feeling at a loss, and as if she were the young girl and Jilly the woman, with a woman's wisdom.

That was ridiculous. What Jilly was feeling now was nothing more than calf-love, the first stirrings of desire as felt by any young girl. Intense enough, to be sure, and easy for such a young girl to mistake for the real thing. And it might well turn out, as time went on, to be the real thing. Young love had developed into maturity before now. But more often, it didn't, and that was why there was a law to protect such young lovers, to protect them from themselves.

I *was* right, she told herself. I *was*.

Whether she had been right or not, there was nothing to be done about it now, and Lucy's attention was soon distracted by a telephone call from her sister Alice, in Portsmouth. Her father had had a heart attack and was in hospital. Could she come at once and see him?

'Oh dear. Oh, how awful. Poor Mum.' Lucy's brain raced, trying to think of ways and means to leave the hotel. It wasn't a busy time for guests, but they had decorators in, and refurbishments going on, work being done on the new part . . .

'Of course you've got to go,' Patsy said, seeing her mother's indecision. 'I can look after everything, and Jilly will help me. Pompey Gran and Grandad need you now.'

Lucy set off next day from Plymouth North Road station, still with misgivings in her heart. Since her confrontation with Jilly, there had been an atmosphere of strain in the hotel and she felt as if a grey shadow hung over her life. It was almost like a premonition, she thought, staring out at the sea lapping the red cliffs as the train ran along the shore. As if something awful is going to happen, changing all our lives.

Well, so there probably was. Her father was ill, wasn't he, and perhaps going to die. Wasn't that enough to have premonitions about? Wasn't that enough to cast a shadow over her spirit?

And yet . . . Somehow, Lucy felt that there was something more than that, and her thoughts turned, inevitably, to her son.

Geoff had written that he was going on a few days' leave soon. The news had given her hope. Things couldn't be too serious, if they were being sent on leave, although the news hadn't cheered either Jilly or Wilmot.

'Have you seen where they're sending him?' Wilmot demanded, as if it were a personal insult. 'Japan! *Japan!* He'll be spending his leave with a lot of little yellow buggers who don't know the meaning of humanity, and what sort of a leave is that going to be, eh? You tell me that. Why, he'll be afraid to go to bed at night for fear one of 'em'll creep in and murder him while he sleeps.'

'Wilmot, don't talk like that. We're at peace now.'

'Peace!' Wilmot echoed. '*Peace!* Those swine will never be at peace.'

Lucy hoped he was wrong. Surely the H-Bomb had cowed the Japanese for ever; they would never rise above the threat of such damage again. The papers still talked about it from time to time – the aftermath of the huge bomb, the radiation sickness, the cancers . . . It was a terrible thing that had been done, more terrible than anyone could have imagined, but it would surely prevent anything worse.

'It hasn't stopped wars though, has it?' Wilmot had said. 'It hasn't stopped boys like our Geoff from being sent out there to fight all over again.'

Lucy bit her lip and stared out of the train window. She'd thought that once the war was over and Wilmot home again for good, all their troubles would be over, but that wasn't what life was like, was it? Somehow, as soon as one trouble was over a new one came to take its place.

While Lucy was away in Portsmouth, Jilly did her best to help about the hotel. She had taken over all the cooking and now oversaw the work of the two girls who came in each day to make beds and clean rooms – not that there was much to do at present, with the hotel taking so few guests. She helped Patsy too, for independent as Patsy had become in her wheelchair there were still a few things she could not manage.

'You're as good as a sister to me,' Patsy remarked as Jilly helped her to take her bath. 'There's not many people I'd let help me like this. I'd sooner go dirty than let some near me!'

'Well, if Geoff and me had had our way, that's what I'd be.' Jilly hung up the towel. 'And you'd be—' She stopped suddenly and Patsy looked at her curiously.

'I'd be what? Here, was that a letter you had from our Geoff this morning? I thought you looked a bit upset afterwards.'

'Yes.' Jilly glanced away and when she looked back Patsy was dismayed to see her eyes full of tears. 'Oh, Patsy, it all seems so awful – you just can't imagine. Here–' she fished it out of her apron pocket – 'I'll tell you some of what he says. I just don't know how he can bear it.'

'Bear what? I thought he was on leave.'

'Yes, in Japan, and he doesn't like it much, I can tell you. He says it reminds him too much of what his dad went through out there. He doesn't like the people at all, although I suppose you can't blame him for that. But that's not the worst of it.' She glanced at the letter.

'So what is? What's the matter with him?'

'It's what they've been doing in Korea. Listen, Patsy.

I would never have thought I could do things like we're expected to do out here, Jilly love. Killing people. Not just soldiers, that would be fair fighting – but ordinary people, people who've done nothing to hurt me nor ever would. Last week my mate Billy Watkins shot two old people who were just working in their paddy-fields, for nothing. All they did was come out of their house to work – an old man and an old woman, like Grammy and Grampy. And he shot them dead. And I tell you what, Jilly, if he hadn't done it I would probably have done it myself. That's what they've done to us, you see. That's what they've turned us into out here – brutes. Savages. And cowards too, because we know that if we didn't do it the sergeant would shoot us.

I don't know what's going to happen when our leave ends. A lot of the blokes are saying they won't go back. Billy Watkins is almost going mad with thinking about it all. And some of the others – Jilly, I've seen things I don't want to tell anybody about ever, people torn to bits, bits of people that were still alive, begging to be killed and put out of their misery like you'd put an animal out of its misery, men screaming and crying and asking for their mothers . . . Sometimes I think I've died and gone to hell, and I know that hell can't be any worse than this. And you're all I've got to hold on to, you and the memory of our—'

Jilly stopped abruptly and folded the letter up as if Patsy's eyes could read through the paper to the words he had written.

'I thought we'd finished with all that,' Patsy said, her voice shaken. 'I thought the war was over and this was supposed to be peacetime. People like Geoff and you – you were supposed to be able to look forward to living a normal life.'

'Normal!' Jilly said bitterly. 'Does anybody know what normal is any more? Maybe we've all got so used to war that we think *that's* normal.'

'But it was supposed to be so good. Love and laughter –'

'And peace ever after,' Jilly finished. 'Well, we can stop thinking that, I reckon. There's boys like Geoff getting killed out there, and even if they do come back, what are they going to be like? Look at your dad. He was supposed to have been like Geoff once, all full of jokes, and look what happened to him.'

Nobody looked less full of jokes than Wilmot these days. He had given up all pretence that he wasn't drinking heavily, and took his first drink of rum when other people were having morning coffee. The strange thing was that he didn't really seem drunk a lot of the time. Or perhaps it was so long since anyone had seen him truly sober that his slightly slurred speech and unsteady gait had just become a part of his everyday being and simply went unnoticed. And if he was depressed and surly most of the time, that was how he'd been ever since he came back from Japan, and it was excusable in view of what was happening to Geoff. He knew what it was like out there, he told anyone who would listen, he knew what those boys were going through.

'I blame myself,' he said, sitting at the kitchen table with his head supported in shaking hands. 'I should have stopped him. I should have made him go into the Navy. I put him off that. It's all my fault.'

'Don't talk daft,' his mother said sharply. 'Geoff made up his own mind, it was nothing to do with you.'

'Nothing to do with me? I'm the boy's father, aren't I? How can it be nothing to do with me? A boy looks up to his dad, takes notice of him. I shot my mouth off too much about what it was like below decks and that's what turned him off the Navy. But for me he'd have been sitting pretty on a messdeck now, seeing a bit of the world. Instead of that he's going through bloody hell out in Korea and chances are we'll never see him again.'

'Wilmot!' Maud glanced at Jilly, sitting white faced at the end of the table. 'Watch your words, for goodness' sake.'

'Why? She knows. He's written enough to her, for God's sake. Told her more than he's told the rest of us, I'll be bound. Well, hasn't he?' he demanded belligerently, looking at Jilly.

Jilly bit her lips. 'What Wilmot writes to me is private between us, Mr Pengelly.'

'Oh, I'm sure it is. All that lovey-dovey stuff. I know, I used to do a bit of that meself. And much good it did me, too.' He glowered around the table, as if daring anyone to challenge him.

Nobody did. Maud got up and started to clear the table and Jilly helped her. She wondered whether she should tell them the truth about herself and Geoff, but she could not bear the look on Wilmot's face if she did. She carried dishes to the sink, feeling his eyes on her. Since Geoff had gone, she had felt this more and more – Wilmot's stare, cold and inimical. As if really, deep down, he blamed her for Geoff's departure, however much he might claim to blame himself.

240

'I suppose you blame me too,' he said suddenly. 'You think it's all my fault he's gone, and my fault you didn't get married before he went.'

Jilly glanced at Maud. The older woman sighed and frowned slightly, shaking her head.

Wilmot sneered. 'All right, I know what you're thinking. Don't rise to the bait. That's it, isn't it? You think if you don't say anything I'll shut up, and it won't matter what I say or what I think. Nothing matters so long as it isn't said, that's the way of it, isn't it? Keep it all bottled up inside, keep it to yourself, don't bother other people . . .' There was an edge of raw pain in his voice and Jilly turned quickly, responding to the pain, wanting to soothe and comfort it, but he sensed her reaction and warded her off with an upraised hand. 'Well, and maybe that's right after all. Because you can't do anything about it, nobody can, it's there inside me for ever and nothing can help, *nothing*. D'you hear me? I've got to live with it burning me inside, eating me away, and there's *nothing anyone can do about it, ever.*'

'Wilmot –'

'Mr Pengelly –'

Maud and Jilly spoke together, both moving towards him, but Wilmot was on his feet, his hands held out before him, shaking his head from side to side.

'Don't come near me. I don't want you near me. I don't want anyone.' His pain was almost too much to bear. 'I told you, it's all my fault Geoff's gone, my fault, and if anything happens to him it'll do for me too. And maybe that'd be the best thing all round, for I'm no use to man nor beast here, I know that.'

'Wilmot, don't talk so stupid.'

'Stupid? Stupid? And what's so stupid about facing up to the truth, eh? Tell me it's not true, tell me what good I've been these last four years or so, and then tell me who's talking stupid.'

'Wilmot, you're not well.'

'I haven't been well,' he said, 'since a little yellow bastard with slit eyes took a bayonet to my backside and chucked me into a chicken-coop for a fortnight.'

'Oh, Mr Pengelly,' Jilly said, her eyes filled with tears, 'you had a terrible time. We all know that.'

'And I'm still having it,' he said. 'I go through it all over again, night after night, just as if it was happening to me same as before. And during the day I think about it.' He picked up the half-empty bottle of rum which had been standing on the table. 'And you wonder why I drink. This is the only friend I've got.'

'If only we could help –'

'You,' he said to Jilly, 'you could help. And shall I tell you how? By getting out. By going away from here and never coming back. Every time I look at you, I think of my boy, out there where I've been, living in hell. Every time I look at you I think of him, taken prisoner, killed, tortured like I was, like I've seen other blokes tortured. Every time I look at you, you make it all worse.'

'Wilmot! You can't talk to poor Jilly like that!'

'I can. I have. And if she really wanted to help me, she'd go.'

Maud turned to Jilly. 'Take no notice of him. He's not responsible for what he says.'

'But it's what he feels,' Jilly said quietly, her face ashen. 'He can't help what he feels.' She looked at Maud. 'I can't stay here if I make it so much worse for him. I can't do it.'

Maud stared at her. 'You're not seriously thinking of going?'

'I don't see what else I can do.' Jilly turned her eyes on Wilmot. He had sunk back into his chair and lain his head on his arms and now he was sobbing, his shoulders heaving. 'Look at him. He's suffering such a lot. Perhaps I'd better go, just until Mrs Pengelly gets back – but maybe she won't want me either. Not if it hurts him so much.'

She walked quietly out of the kitchen.

Maud stared after her, one hand lifted as if to prevent her going, then she let her hand drop to her side and moved instead to give what comfort she could to her son. Like Lucy, sitting now by her father's bed as she watched his life ebb away, she was beginning to wonder what it was all about, and why life seemed to be crumbling just when they had all thought it would be so good.

Chapter Nineteen

Joe died a week later. He regained only a confused consciousness, occasionally aware of where he was, opening his eyes to stare around him with a kind of bemused dismay, clutching at the hand of whoever sat beside him. His legs had swollen with dropsy and the nurses said he shouldn't be given too much fluid, but his mouth was dry and he begged constantly for water, for a drink. Lucy dipped her finger in the glass and wet his lips, but he shook his head painfully. 'A *drink*. A proper drink.'

'It's cruel,' Kitty said. She had got special leave and spent as much time as she was allowed beside his bed, sitting there as smart in her Wrens uniform as if she was going on parade. She was an officer now and full of cool authority, but even she was daunted by the nurses. Lucy could see that she longed to pick up the glass and hold it to her father's mouth, let him drink his fill, but she didn't quite dare.

'What would it matter? He's dying anyway. Why shouldn't he have a drink to make him feel better?'

'Kitty! Don't talk like that.'

'Why not? You know it's true. So do they. They told us. It's terrible to refuse him a drink. He's *thirsty*.'

They had moved away from the bed while the nurses sponged Joe's flaccid body, and were talking in whispers, but Lucy glanced anxiously towards the bed. 'He might hear you.'

'He can't hear anything. Lucy, you know he's only got a few days. Perhaps no more than hours. We're going to have to face it.'

'Yes. I do know.' The nurses had finished and the two women moved back beside the bed. Lucy reached out and touched her father's cheek with one hand, smoothing the skin gently. He was sleeping now, relieved for a while of his misery. She wished he would just slip away like that, without knowing any more.

Lucy started to speak, but the words would not come, Instead, she began to cry, silently, her head bowed, the tears dripping on to her laced fingers. One of the nurses, tending a patient on the other side of the ward, noticed and hurried over, looking with professional anxiety at Joe, but Kitty waved her away.

'It's all right. It's not Dad. My sister's rather upset.'

The nurse nodded and went back to her other patient. Kitty slipped her arm around Lucy's shoulders and held her close. 'What is it, Lucy? Is it Wilmot? Or Geoff?'

Lucy started to speak again and lifted both hands instead, holding them up for a moment or two before letting them drop in a gesture of despair that told Kitty more clearly than any words. It was both. It was everything.

'You're tired out,' Kitty said quietly. 'You're just tired out. And you need David.'

Lucy lifted her head and stared at her. 'How do you –?'

'I'm not blind,' Kitty said. 'I know how you feel about him, and how he feels about you. Oh, it's all right – nobody else knows, or if they do they're keeping quiet about it. And nobody would blame you, anyway. Not with Wilmot the way he is.'

'We've never –'

'I don't suppose you have,' Kitty said with the ghost of a smile. 'Not that I'd blame you if you did. Quite honestly, I think you're mad not to. I would, like a shot, but then I'm not married, and never likely to be.'

'We don't even see each other.'

'I know. It's all right, Lucy. You don't have to explain to me. I know you'd never do anything wrong – not like me.'

245

Kitty grinned cheerfully. 'I'm the black sheep in this family! All the same, it's David you need, isn't it? That's why you're so unhappy – because the one man you really want, the man who could take all those burdens off your shoulders and make life worth living, is the man you can't have.' She shook her head compassionately. 'No wonder you say life isn't fair.'

'It's not just that. It's all the other things. Much worse things. It's much worse for other people.'

'So it may be. But that doesn't make our own pain any the less,' Kitty said. 'And it doesn't mean we have to be ashamed of feeling it.'

They sat quietly for a few minutes. Joe was still asleep, his breathing quieter than it had been for some hours. Kitty reached out and smoothed back his thin grey hair.

Lucy opened her mouth to speak, but before she could utter a sound there was a strange rattling from their father's throat. They both turned swiftly, reaching out to help him, but Joe was beyond their help. He lay rigid, his eyes suddenly wide open, hands reaching up like stretching claws.

'Dad –'

'Nurse! Nurse! Come quickly –'

The nurse was at the bedside, leaning over him. She took him by the shoulders, raised his body from the pillows, held him for a moment. And then Lucy and Kitty, watching in frozen dismay, saw the final shudder convulse his body, heard the last breath sough from his body.

There was a moment of silence. The nurse laid him back gently on his pillows and closed the staring eyes. She looked at the two sisters. 'He's gone. I'm sorry.'

They nodded, unable to speak, then Lucy leant over and kissed her father's still-warm cheek. Kitty pressed the heels of her hands against her eyes for a minute or two and then did the same.

'We'll have to go and tell Mum.' She looked at the nurse.

'Can he stay here for a while? So that she can come in and see him?'

They left the ward slowly, their arms around each other's waists.

The family gathered for the funeral a week later. Vic's widow Eileen, who had married again, came with her new husband, Bob, and twelve-year-old Vicky. Alice, who was living at Cosham, came with her husband John and son Michael. Kenny, who hadn't married and still lived at home but had a string of girlfriends, brought none of them. He was beginning to look older, Lucy thought, seeing the lines of tiredness on his face and wishing he would settle down. Other, more distant, relatives came as well; aunts and uncles and cousins from Portsmouth and Gosport and further afield than that.

Neighbours and friends came. People who lived in the streets where Joe and Emily had spent their marriage, mates who had known Joe at work in the dockyard, men who said they had been at school with him years ago. The throng grew and grew as they poured into St Mary's church, and Lucy felt a lump in her throat as she gazed around her. She would never have believed that her father had known so many people, made so many friends.

Wilmot had travelled alone on the train from Plymouth. Lucy had gone to the town station to meet him, watching anxiously as he descended a trifle unsteadily from the carriage. Don't get drunk, she prayed, don't make a show of us. Not now . . . She went forward to greet him and smelt the rum on his breath. If you let me down now, she told him with her eyes, it'll be all over between us. I warn you.

Wilmot saw and understood the warning. He glowered and said, 'You needn't look like that. Stroll on, a bloke's got to have a drop to sustain him on these godawful trains. Even your dad wouldn't have begrudged me that.'

Lucy ignored the 'even'. She wondered if she had been

wise to ask him to come, whether she shouldn't have told him to stay at home, but people would have wondered. 'Just keep off it now you're here,' she said, and reached up to kiss him. 'It's good to see you, Wilmot.' And just for a moment, it was. She had been lonely here by herself, she realised, with no one to turn to for her own comfort. She rested her head against his shoulder.

Wilmot grunted and put his arm round her shoulders, but the moment passed quickly. He turned to get his luggage from the train and, stumbling, dropped a shopping bag on the platform. Lucy heard the clink of bottles and then the sound of breaking glass. Her husband swore.

'Bloody hell. We'll have to go to an off-licence on the way to your mum's.'

'I said, keep *off* it,' Lucy snapped. 'It's my dad's funeral tomorrow. Do you want to turn up drunk?'

'Do you want me to turn up at all?' he demanded, and the brief rapport was gone. He threw the broken bottle into a litter-bin and marched ahead of her, indignation keeping his gait steady, and she followed, her heart sinking, and heard him give his instructions to the taxi-driver. 'And stop by that place at the end of Arundel Street. Got to buy a couple of presents.'

Presents! she thought bitterly. The best present you could give me would be *not* to stop there. However, she said nothing, only sat silent in the back of the taxi and waited as Wilmot went into the off-licence and came out with a couple of wrapped bottles. He heaved himself in beside her and gave her a look that dared her to say a word.

I can't bear it, she thought, and knew that he would not be in the church tomorrow, and that she would never forgive him for it.

David came. Lucy did not know who had let him know – probably Kitty, or perhaps Alice – but he was there at the church when she arrived with her mother and sisters, and he came forward and took Emily's hand in his for a moment and then walked into the church beside them. Nobody said anything. Kenny was the only man of the immediate family present, and he kept his mother's arm in his, so David fell in quite naturally beside Lucy.

She felt him looking down at her and lifted her eyes to meet his. The last time they had spoken was when she had berated him on the telephone over Geoff and Jilly. She tried to put her feelings into her eyes, and he smiled a little and gave the minutest of nods, and she felt comforted.

'Where's Wilmot?' he murmured, and she grimaced.

'At home. At Mum's. He – wasn't fit to come.' She glanced away. There was no need to hide anything from David, but she felt a great wash of shame. Wilmot had spent the previous evening drinking, and been difficult to wake this morning. If the funeral had been in the afternoon, he might have been able to attend. Perhaps, she thought, recalling how he could be the day after a bender, it was as well that he couldn't. At least he couldn't make an exhibition of himself in the church, or at the graveside. The thought of him doing so made her shudder.

She felt David slip his hand beneath her elbow. It felt strong and warm, the grip solid and reassuring. Oh David, she thought, it feels so right to have you here with me, walking beside me, giving me your comfort and your strength. I know it ought to be Wilmot, but it feels so much better that it's you. It ought always to have been you . . .

Shocked by the thought, she tried to concentrate her mind on the service. The family had followed the coffin as it was borne up the aisle by six undertaker's men, solemn in their black suits. It stood now before them on the bier, closed and silent.

She glanced sideways towards her mother. Emily was standing like a poker, rigidly still, her face like stone. She would not cry, Lucy thought, not here in front of all these people. Emily belonged to the school who saw tears as an imposition on others, grief as something private. She would cry when she was alone, and not even in front of her own family.

Lucy wished that she could be as disciplined, but she knew that the tears were close; she could feel their heat behind her eyelids, the ache of them in her throat. David had dropped his hand from her arm in order to hold his prayer-book, but she felt for it now, slipping her left hand into the crook of his arm and gripping it tightly. She felt his arm tighten in response, holding her hand firmly against his side, and the words of the prayers misted before her eyes. Dad, she thought. Dad. And she looked again at the coffin. Was it all worth it? Was it a good life, in spite of all the hard times?

Wilmot joined them at the graveside.

Thank God, Lucy thought when she saw him coming, that it was all over, the last prayers said, the earth sprinkled on the coffin, the first shovelful heaped on top. Even at a distance, she could see that his steps were wavering and unsteady. He'd either started on his bottle almost as soon as he got out of bed, or he'd been in the pub already. She drew a deep breath, wishing him anywhere but here, and went forward quickly, determined to avoid a scene.

'Wilmot! You've come – are you feeling better, then?' The fiction was that he had arrived from Plymouth the worse for flu. 'You oughtn't to have come out in this cold wind,' she scolded him gently, taking his arm. 'You'll be getting your bronchitis again.'

He stared at her. He certainly looked ill, she thought, with his flushed face and bleary eyes, but would anyone really mistake the signs of drunkenness for influenza? Just don't speak, she begged him silently, just don't draw attention to yourself.

'What are you all coming out for?' he demanded. 'Don't tell me it's all over.'

'Of course it is. Ten o'clock, you remember?' She kept her voice bright. 'You seemed so tired this morning, I didn't have the heart to wake you. And you know you're not well.'

'Not well?' His voice rose to a belligerent shout. 'Whaddoyoumean, not well? I'm as well as I've ever been. I shoulda been here. I shoulda been at the funeral. As senior shon-in –' he stumbled over the words – 'shenior *son-in-law* – I shoulda been *here*.'

Lucy thought so too, but not in his present condition. She glanced around her. People were moving away, gathering around Emily, looking her way and murmuring together. She felt her face burn with shame.

'Wilmot, you shouldn't have come. We'd better go home straight away.'

'*Shouldn't have come?*' His voice rose again. 'Whaddoyoumean, shouldn't have come? I was his shon-in-law, wasn't I? His *only* shon son in-law.'

'No, John and Bob were his sons-in-law as well.'

Wilmot sneered. 'John and Bob! They'm newcomers. Been in the family five minutes and think they can take over.' He struck himself on the chest. '*I* was the first. Been in the family since – since – when was it, nineteen-thirty, thirty-one?'

'Thirty-one. Wilmot, let's go home.'

'Nineteen-thirty-one,' he declaimed. 'That's over twenty years, that is. That's seniority.'

'Yes, but –' Lucy was beginning to feel desperate. People were staring and she knew that she could not pass this off as flu. And Wilmot was starting to lower his head angrily. If he lost his temper . . .

David was beside them. He took Wilmot's arm in his hand. 'Hallo, Wilmot, old chap. Good to see you again. Look, why don't we make our way home and get the place opened up and ready. I daresay Emily wants the family and a few of the friends to come back for a drink and a sandwich. She'd be glad of your help – as senior son-in-law.'

Wilmot paused and stared at him suspiciously. 'Are you trying to get rid of me? Because if you are—'

'No,' Lucy broke in hurriedly. 'Of course David's not trying to get rid of you. But he's right. Mum needs someone to get home ahead of the rest, and it's our place to do that. And you ought to be out of this cold wind.' What they would do with Wilmot when they got him home, she didn't dare think, but she had to get him away from here, away from the churchyard and all these people. 'Come on. Let's go home and get the kettle on.'

'Kettle? I'd have thought you'd be offering a proper drink.'

'We are. Sherry. And beer for those who want it. But some of the ladies will want a cup of tea, and maybe some of the men as well.' He was allowing her to steer him along the path now, towards the gates that led out on to the road. David, on his other side, kept his hand discreetly under Wilmot's arm and between them they guided him past the crowd and on to the pavement. Lucy paused, feeling suddenly helpless. They couldn't take Wilmot on a bus in this state.

'It's all right.' David seemed able to read every thought in her mind. 'The taxis are waiting. We'll take one of them. Come on, Wilmot, old chap. You'll feel better once you get home. Maybe a lie-down, eh? Before the rest arrive . . .' They got the suddenly heavy body into a taxi and directed it back to the house. Wilmot slumped against them in the back. He muttered something, but Lucy could not catch what it was, and she didn't much care. All she wanted to do, all she longed to do, was get him home and out of sight before the rest arrived.

And that was what they did. It was a struggle, and by the time they'd accomplished it Lucy was hot, breathless and dishevelled. When her mother returned, accompanied by

Kenny and Kitty, with Alice and Eileen and the rest following behind, Wilmot was safe in bed upstairs and already snoring. Heaven knew how much he'd had to drink that morning, Lucy thought, and just at present she didn't care. She was able to tidy her hair, puff a bit of powder on her face and stand in the front room, passing round glasses of sherry or pouring cups of tea, and keep up the pretence that he had flu, and that was all she cared about. Her father's funeral had not been spoiled after all.

But only just, she thought grimly, and not through any efforts on Wilmot's part. She remembered the thought that had gone through her mind when she met him at the station. *If you let me down now, it'll be all over between us.*

He had let her down, and she knew, with ice-cold certainty, that it was all over between them.

Chapter Twenty

After everyone had gone and the clearing-up had been done, Lucy and David slipped out for a walk together. They cut through the streets to Southsea and strolled along the front towards Clarence Pier.

'What will your mother do now, d'you think?' David asked as they looked out over the Solent towards the Isle of Wight. The sky had hazed over with fine cloud and shimmered like a vast dome of mother-of-pearl above their heads. The sea was flat calm, as pale and smooth as grey watered silk. The island seemed to float on the horizon, its silhouette knobbly with trees, the spire of Ryde church tower like a spear pointing to heaven.

'I suppose she'll stay where she is. Kenny's still living there and Kitty comes home when she can. As long as she's got them to look after, she'll be all right. She'll miss Dad, though. They've been together for over forty-five years, David.'

He nodded. 'It's a long time. It must seem as though half of her has been torn away.' His voice was sad and Lucy knew he was thinking of Heather. They had been married for only a few years, yet he still grieved for her. How much worse was it going to be for Emily?

'And what about you?' he asked. 'How are you going to be?'

'Oh, I'll be all right. It's not as if I saw all that much of Dad, after all. I only—'

'I didn't mean that,' he said quietly, and she stopped and looked up at him.

'No. I don't know, David. I don't know how I'm going to be now.'

They walked on. Clarence Pier had been damaged in the war and they struck inland to avoid it, then made their way through Old Portsmouth to the Sallyport, where they had taken Patsy in her wheelchair to see the *Vanguard* come in with the King and Queen and Princesses aboard. How hopeful I was then, Lucy thought, gazing across the narrow neck of the harbour entrance towards Gosport. Wilmot was home and although he was obviously still suffering the after-effects of the war, I really believed he would get better and be the old Wilmot. I really believed we would have a good life together. And now . . .

'I don't know if I can stay any longer with Wilmot,' she said abruptly. 'He's been getting worse and worse, and now . . . Behaving like that at Dad's funeral. I don't think I can ever forgive him that.'

'He was very fond of your father,' David said gently.

'So why get drunk? Why come along late and make a show of himself? Why couldn't he keep off the bottle, just for a few hours, and behave like a decent human being?' Her voice shook. 'It was all I asked of him, David. It's not a lot. If he was going to do that, he ought to have stayed at home in Plymouth. He didn't have to come all this way, just to make an exhibition of himself and show me up and humiliate me.'

'I think Wilmot takes a drink whenever he finds life a bit too difficult to handle,' David said. 'Whenever things get too much for him. It's his way of getting through it. Obviously, he was upset that your father had died, and he needed a drink to help him cope with that. And then the funeral . . . I'm not condoning it, Lucy, I'm just trying to understand it.'

'Well, I can't understand it and I don't want to,' she said bitterly. 'The rest of us didn't have to get drunk. The trouble with Wilmot is that he doesn't remember what it's like to feel sober, and if he doesn't have a drink for a while he thinks he's ill. He doesn't give himself a chance. He's weak, David, that's his trouble, just plain weak.'

'Don't you think he has some justification? After all he's been through?'

Lucy turned and faced him. 'David, he wasn't the only man in a Japanese camp. There were hundreds of them, thousands. Are they all drunks now? I know they had a terrible time, I know they'll never forget it – but they haven't all given way to it. A lot of them are building their lives again. They've put it behind them. Wilmot's just never left. In his mind, he's still there. It's as if he doesn't *want* to leave.'

'That's crazy—' David began, but she interrupted him.

'It's not. It sounds crazy, I know, and it's a crazy thing to want to do, but it's as if he wants to hang on to the – the *sympathy* it got him when he came home. He was fêted. The returning hero. All that. We all made a big fuss of him, we made allowances for him, and he liked it. Mind, I don't blame him for that. After what he'd been through, it would be surprising if he didn't enjoy a bit of pampering, and I was glad to give it to him. We all were. But you can't live like that for ever. That's his trouble – he can't let it go and just be ordinary Wilmot Pengelly again, doing a job of work. So he's using it, trading on it, and because he won't let it go, he still suffers, he dreams about it night after night. And he drinks. And he'll go on drinking until he does let it go.' She paused and added quietly, 'And I don't think he ever will.'

They stood in silence for a while. The sun had begun to sink behind the island. It cast a diffused apricot light through the feathery clouds and touched the small, springing waves with gold. Gulls wheeled and screamed overhead, and one of the Isle of Wight paddle steamers, the *Whippingham*, the one that had been to Dunkirk, churned its way past them into the harbour, making for the railway station jetty.

'So where does that leave you?' David asked. 'Lucy, I hate to think of you living your life like this. You've had almost six years of it now, and I've watched you getting paler and thinner every time I see you. Not that I've seen much of you in all that time,' he added in a lower tone.

'I know. And I've missed you, David.' She hesitated and then said, 'I don't know where it leaves me. I feel I've had almost as much as I can take. I looked at him when he arrived yesterday, and I knew what was going to happen, and I thought – I thought, if you do this to me, Wilmot, it's all over between us. And he has done it.'

'And is it all over?'

She nodded, her eyes on the tall, thin tower of Gosport's Holy Trinity church. 'Yes. I think it is.'

The silence fell again. David's hand felt for hers and he held it in his strong grip. 'What will you do?'

She closed her eyes and leant against his shoulder. 'I don't know. I haven't thought about it. Or maybe I've thought too much.' Her shoulders lifted and dropped again. 'I just don't know what I'll do.'

'The hotel –'

'That's the worst of it,' she said. 'The hotel – Maud and Arthur. They're getting old, it's their home, I can't just abandon them. And then there's Patsy. She could run the place, but she needs help. I can't leave her. It's like a web, David, a web I'm trapped in. Wherever I turn, there's another strand, pulling me back to the centre. And he's in the middle of it all, like a spider.'

'Lucy –'

'I shouldn't have said that,' she said rapidly. 'It sounds awful. He isn't like a spider at all. He's just Wilmot, poor, pathetic Wilmot, who's had a horrible time and can't get over it. And he needs help like the rest of them. I know that. I'm just tired of giving it.' She grimaced. 'The truth is, I'm just not a very good wife.'

'Oh now, you can't say that. You've done all you could.'

'Perhaps,' she said, 'but I'm not doing it any more. Oh, David.' She leant her head against him again and gripped his lapels in her hands. 'All I want to do is come to you,' she said shakily. 'All I want is to walk away from it all – just walk away, without ever looking back – and come to you and stay with you, for the rest of my life.'

He stared down at her bent head, and then he put his arm around her shoulders and held her tightly against him. The sun had dipped below the Island now and the light had turned to a soft, violet dusk. The few people who had been strolling near by had disappeared. David and Lucy were alone.

'You know,' he said quietly into her hair, 'you know that if ever you want to come to me, you must just come. I'll be there. I've always been there for you.'

'I want to come,' she said in a muffled voice. 'I want to come now.'

'Oh, Lucy,' he said, and his voice trembled in his throat. 'Lucy, Lucy, Lucy . . .'

'I know it's wrong. Nobody will want to know us. All our friends . . . But I can't help that. I've had enough, David, I've had enough of it all. I want to come back with you now,' she said rapidly. 'I want to come back to London with you. I don't want to go back to Plymouth with Wilmot – I *won't* go back. I feel – I feel that if I go back now, I'll never get away. Something will happen – something will prevent me. I couldn't bear that, David.' She lifted her head and stared up into his face, her eyes purple in the gathering dusk. 'If I go back now, I'll be caught all over again in the web.'

'Lucy, you're upset, you're overwrought. You're worn out by the last few days – you spent nearly a week sitting with your father, looking after your mother. And now the funeral. And Wilmot. You're in no fit state to make decisions.'

'I'm fitter than I've ever been. I haven't just begun to feel

258

like this, David. I've loved you for years – you know that. Even during the war – even when Heather was still alive. And you love me too. You always did.'

'Yes,' he said, 'I always did. But we both knew it couldn't happen.'

'And now it can,' she said. 'We can make it happen.'

'But not like this. It can't be like this, Lucy, you must see that. You've said it yourself, you can't just abandon Maud and Arthur. And what about Patsy? How could you live with me – with yourself – knowing you'd just walked out on them all?'

'But I've told you,' she said desperately, 'if I go back now, something will happen, something terrible, and I'll have to stay. I know it will. And then I'll never get away.'

By the time they returned to the house, they had talked in the same circle a dozen times, and still nothing had been decided. David urged her a dozen times to take time to think about it, to consider all the consequences before taking an irrevocable step. And a dozen times Lucy repeated that she dared not, that she had a premonition, that if she set foot again through the swing doors of Pengelly's Hotel, she would never be free . . . As they walked slowly back through the darkened streets to the house where she had grown up, she was beginning to tire, though. Her arguments had lost their febrile passion, and David could only hope that a night's sleep would complete the work.

'You know I love you,' he said as they came within sight of the house. 'You know there's nothing I want more than to be with you, but we can't do it at such cost to others. We would never be able to live in peace with ourselves.'

'David, I can't bear it.'

'You can,' he said, holding both her hands in his. 'You can. You're strong, Lucy. That's why you've come so far and done so much. And we *will* be together, I promise you that. We just have to wait a little longer.'

'I think we've waited too long already,' she said sadly, and turned away from him to go indoors.

She had to go back, of course. She knew that already, and knew that her moment of rebellion had been just that: a moment, no more. Going back to London with David, leaving Wilmot to return alone to Plymouth, knowing that Patsy was expecting her to come home, not to mention Maud and Arthur – no, it was impossible. A dream to play with.

'I shall come, all the same,' she said to him as they said goodbye at the railway station. 'As soon as I can make proper arrangements. I know I can't just abandon them all, but this is my life and I've lived it long enough for others.'

'I wonder if we ever have,' he said. 'I wonder if we even know . . . Goodbye Lucy, my dearest dear. Take care of yourself.'

They gazed at each other. The engine humphed impatiently at the end of the platform and a cloud of steam billowed out.

Wilmot had boarded the train first with the luggage and now his face appeared through the swirling mist. He stared at them suspiciously. 'How long are you going to be, Lucy? The train's just about to go.'

'I know. I'm coming.' She did not take her eyes away from David's. She hardly cared what Wilmot thought. He'd know the whole truth before long, anyway. 'Go back and wait for me –'

'I'd have thought you'd had plenty of time to hobnob together, the two of you.' His voice was jealous and he leant out and gripped Lucy's arm. 'Come on. Get aboard.'

'Wilmot, let go –' The whistle blew and the engine let out a trumpeting fanfare. Lucy gave David a despairing glance. 'David –'

'Go on, Lucy.' She was as close as she could come to

refusing to go, and he knew it. He gave her a gentle push. 'I'll see you again soon.'

'Yes. Yes. Soon.' Reluctantly, she climbed aboard and stood looking out through the open window. *'David –'*

'Goodbye, Lucy. Goodbye.' He stood still on the platform, looking at her, his hand thrust into his pocket. He tried to convey his feelings with his eyes. For two pins, he thought, he would have wrenched the door open and dragged her out again.

I love you. He saw her mouth shape the words and nodded them back to her. The wheels began to rattle, the pistons to scrape, and the train slid past the platform. Lucy was receding from him, her eyes wide and desperate. He closed his own eyes and shook his head, and when he opened them again she was almost gone, her face no more than a blur.

'David. I love you . . .' He must have imagined it. He could not possibly have heard her voice over the noise of the engine, but he carried the sound with him as he turned away and walked along the platform to catch his own train, and it rang in his ears all the way back to London.

'I don't like that fellow,' Wilmot said as soon as they were settled on the train. They had a compartment to themselves, and as there was no corridor, there was no fear of interruption until at least Eastleigh. Lucy looked at him in alarm. As far as she knew, he had had nothing to drink that morning, but he had been carrying a bag when they arrived at the station and she knew he had been to the off-licence on the way.

'Don't be silly. David's been a good friend. We've known him for years.'

'You've known him for years. Always in and out of the hotel. Don't think I don't know what's been going on.'

'I've told you before,' Lucy said, her heart beginning to

261

thump, 'nothing's been going on. David and I have never—'

'So you've said, so you've said.' He sounded offensively bored, as if hearing a lie for the hundredth time that he had never believed in the first place. 'Look, Lucy, I'm not a fool. I can see the way you look at each other. Does it really make any difference whether you've been to bed together or not? You'd like to, that's what matters. And one day, you will.'

Lucy was silent, shocked by his perception. She could not deny the truth of his words. She bit her lip and stared out of the window, knowing that Wilmot was watching her.

'You see?' he said, and he sounded tired and depressed. 'You see?'

Lucy turned swiftly. 'Wilmot –'

'Why don't you stop pretending?' he asked. 'Why don't you stop making out you're the good, loyal little wife – when all the time you're thinking about *him*, wanting to be with him? Why don't you stop being such a hypocrite?'

That stung her. 'Hypocrite? What do you mean? I'm not a hypocrite!'

'You are. Look at you. Lucy Pengelly, the little white saint. Butter wouldn't melt in her mouth. And look what she's got to put up with, saddled with that drunken sot of a husband, never does a hand's turn, no more good to her than a sore arse. That's what people say about you, isn't it? That's what you want them to say.'

'No, of course it isn't! I've never complained –'

'Well, of course you haven't,' he said. 'You're a saint, aren't you, and saints never complain. It's part of being saintly.'

'You're talking a lot of rubbish,' Lucy said coldly.

'I'm not. Just for once, I'm not.' He looked at her, curling his lip in a sneer. 'Saint Lucy. Except that we know different, don't we?'

'I've told you, I've never done anything wrong. I've never been unfaithful to you.'

'Listen,' Wilmot said, 'I may be a drunk but I'm not a fool. I saw the way you looked at him. I've seen the two of you these past few days, slipping away together whenever you've got the chance. I've seen your heads together, plotting and planning. You're going to leave me and go to him, aren't you? Well – aren't you?'

Lucy gasped. It was almost as if he had read her mind. She stared at him, feeling her face whiten as the blood drained away. Her head spun and she felt sick. 'I –'

'Don't try to make excuses,' he said. 'Don't try to cook up some sort of explanation. Just say yes.'

'Wilmot –'

'Just say yes,' he repeated, almost as if it was what he wanted to hear.

Lucy found her voice. It was no more than a husky whisper. 'What – what would you do if I did say yes?'

Wilmot looked at her and she saw his expression shift and knew that it wasn't what he'd wanted to hear. Despite his words, he had wanted her to say no. He wanted her to tell him that she had no intention of leaving.

His eyes dulled, and she knew that it was too late now, too late to do anything about it.

'What would I do?' he repeated flatly. 'I don't know. Chuck myself off a cliff, I should think.'

For the rest of the journey, they hardly spoke. Soon after that, the train had pulled into Eastleigh and several other people had climbed into their compartment. From then on, they were not alone again until they arrived at Plymouth. Somewhere between Dorchester and Bridport Lucy had produced a packet of sandwiches and a Thermos flask of tea, and offered them to Wilmot. He accepted a couple of sandwiches but refused the tea and took a bottle of beer from his own bag. She watched uneasily, hoping that he would not start heavy drinking, but it seemed he had only the one bottle with him.

Lucy nibbled her own sandwich. It was like dust. She stared out of the window, taking no joy in the passing scenery, thinking of Wilmot's words. It wasn't the first time he had threatened suicide, and she had on several occasions been frightened enough to take sharp knives out of the kitchen drawers and conceal them. But gradually she had come to believe that his threats were empty, designed only to draw attention to himself, and there was no real meaning in them. For a long time now, he had said nothing about killing himself.

Now, however, he had started again, and this time she was afraid that he meant it. There was a flatness in his tone that was quite different from the dramatic threats he had made before. It was as if he really didn't care whether he lived or not.

He can't feel like that about me leaving, she thought, feeling cold. He doesn't love me, any more than I love him. He doesn't really want me. Why would he talk like that? He'd be glad to get rid of me, glad to have the place to himself.

Or would he? Without her there, what would happen to Pengelly's? Maud and Arthur wouldn't be able to cope with running it. And she wouldn't dream of leaving Patsy as well – Patsy would come to London with her, she and David had agreed upon that. There would be nobody left who knew how to run the place. Wilmot would have to pull himself together and take charge.

She knew that he wouldn't do that. She knew that he couldn't.

It would be too much for him. If Lucy left Pengelly's the whole place would collapse. The responsibility of the hotel, of his own ageing parents, would crush Wilmot like a rock. He would not be able to bear it, and whatever happened it would be her fault.

By the time the train arrived panting at North Road station and they were gathering their bags together to disembark, Lucy knew that she was still trapped, as surely and as tightly as ever she had been, and there was no escape. She would not be able to leave Pengelly's and go to David.

I knew it would never happen, she thought as she scrambled down from the train and stood dejectedly upon the platform. I knew that if I didn't go from Portsmouth I wouldn't go at all.

And David had known it too. She had seen it in his eyes as he stood on the platform and watched her slide away from him, and as she cried her last words of love into the billowing steam.

Chapter Twenty-one

She couldn't give up that easily.

The hotel wrapped itself around her again like an octopus, its many and various demands like clinging tentacles, so that as fast as she disposed of one, another half-dozen were fastening themselves to her mind. The decorators, the builders, the plumbers, the carpet-fitters . . . The family – Maud, Arthur, Patsy . . . and Wilmot, hitting the bottle harder than ever, all pretence cast aside.

'I just wants a word about the west wall, that damp patch'll have to be seen to . . .'

'Look, the carpet you wanted ain't in yet, but we got another pattern you might like, it's a sort of bright orange with black bits in . . .'

'That new bathroom, it won't do the way you want it, the runout's too level, see, the water won't run away, take half a day to empty. Us'll have to raise the bath, and that means . . .'

'Lucy, have you noticed Arthur's colour lately? I don't like it. He looks proper grey round the gills sometimes, but he won't go to the doctor, I wondered if you'd have a word . . .'

'Why does everything depend on me?' Lucy asked in desperation. She was in the office with Patsy, working on the latest estimate for the redecorating. 'Can't anyone make a decision for themselves? How did they all manage while I was in Portsmouth?'

'They waited till you came back.' Patsy was eighteen

now, and would have been a tall young woman. She took care of herself and kept her long, dark red hair as glossy as a Christmas bell. Her skin had the faint translucency of fine bone china and her eyes were the deep, velvety purple of summer pansies. She was a beautiful girl, Lucy realised suddenly, and wondered why she had never noticed it before. What a shame she was confined to a wheelchair. What man was ever going to want to marry a girl who couldn't walk?

'Well, I'm tired of coping with it all. It's time your father pulled his weight.'

Patsy glanced sideways at her. 'You ought to know by now. Dad's never going to be any help.'

'Patsy! You shouldn't talk like that about your father –'

'Oh, face facts, Mum.' There was no bitterness in the girl's voice, just sadness. 'Dad's just been getting worse and worse, and he's not going to get any better. Not the way things are. He's drinking all the time.' She paused. 'I had to tell him to go away yesterday. He was getting himself in a state – people were looking at him. It's bad for the hotel, I know, but it's worse for him –'

'What do you mean, in a state?' Lucy interrupted. 'What was he doing?'

'Oh, nothing much. Just talking, really. Talking to everyone. Nobody could put their head round the door without him starting on them. It was only the workmen, but what are guests going to think if he does it to them? And he feels so awful afterwards, I know he does.'

Lucy gazed at her. 'Was he drunk?'

'Well, more or less. I mean, he always is, to some extent. He must be, he drinks so much, it's just that he's got used to it so it doesn't show like it would in another person.' Patsy looked at her mother. Her eyes were glimmering with tears. 'Mum, something's got to be done to help him. I can't bear seeing him like that.'

Lucy sighed and ran her fingers through her hair. Kitty

had persuaded her to have it cut short while she was in Portsmouth and it clustered in fiery curls around her face, with only a few silver hairs gleaming among the rich auburn. 'I'll take away all his bottles. He won't be *able* to drink.'

'I don't think that'll stop him. I expect he's got them hidden all over the house.'

'I'll find them. I'll find them all.'

Patsy shook her head. 'He'll just get more, Mum. You can't lock him up. Look –' she shuffled amongst the papers on her desk and produced a sheet of newspaper – 'I was reading this. It's about something called Alcoholics Anonymous. It's a sort of association for people who can't stop drinking.'

'For heaven's sake!' Lucy exclaimed. 'We don't want him joining a *club*!'

'It's not like that. It's to help them stop. It was started in America before the war. People go to meetings every week and they help each other. They have to stop drinking absolutely. Never touch another drop.'

'I can't think of anything better,' Lucy said. 'Or anything more unlikely. Your father's never going to agree to that. He likes his drink. It's just about all he lives for.'

'But it's not doing him any good. I've been reading about it, Mum. It's not just about getting drunk – it'll make him really ill. He already *is* ill. It says here, it's an illness, this not being able to stop drinking. And these people can help. They look after each other.' She laid the paper down and looked at Lucy. 'At least we could *try*. Try to get him to join. If he went to just one meeting – just to *see* . . .'

Lucy twisted her lips together in doubt. 'I can't believe he'll agree, Patsy. But all right, we'll try.' And it just might work, she added to herself, and if he really did give up drinking, perhaps he'd take over the hotel and look after his parents, and then I could go . . . Oh, David, David . . .

*

268

Wilmot stared at her. He wouldn't even look at the sheet of newspaper at first, and when he did he ripped it into pieces and threw them to the floor. Lucy's heart sank. She hadn't really expected anything different, but now her last shred of hope was destroyed.

'If only you'd just think about it, Wilmot –'

'Think about it? *Think* about it? There's nothing to think about. You're saying I'm a drunk, that's it, isn't it? You've been chucking out hints for months and now you're saying so outright. Just because I like a drop of winter warmer. Look, we had a rum issue every day in the Navy, every bloke over eighteen got it, a proper tot of good Navy rum – stronger than any of this watered-down stuff you get ashore. Would they have issued us that if it had been bad for us? Would they?'

'I don't know why they issued it,' Lucy said. She was half afraid of Wilmot's fury. His temper had grown worse than ever and she dreaded the day when he lost control completely. 'Someone told me it was to kill the germs in bad food when they were at sea for long periods on the old sailing-ships. Or to keep the men under control . . . I don't know. But it can't be good for young boys to be given strong drink, day after day, week in, week out. Of *course* they get used to it, of *course* they can't give it up. And they end up wanting more and more. It stands to reason.'

'Well, we didn't get it, did we? Not us poor buggers who ended up in Japanese prison camp. Not the blokes that slaved and died on the Burma railway. Not the poor sods who spent months in solitary confinement, surviving on a bowl of mouldy rice a day. None of us got rum issue then. We went without for years.'

'Well, you're certainly making up for it now,' Lucy snapped.

Wilmot looked at her. His eyes were red rimmed and bleary, his skin grey, his chin rough and unshaven. She felt disgust, mingled with pity. I shouldn't have said that, she thought. He's right. And he has to have allowance made for the suffering he endured.

'So that's what you think,' he said. 'Never mind what we did, going to sea and fighting for our country. It's all forgotten now, isn't it? Chasing the *Graf Spee* all over the Atlantic till we got her to her knees. We lost men then, if you remember. We were damaged then. But we didn't give up. Off out to the Med, sinking German ships – out to the Far East. Have you got any idea what it was like out there, fighting those Japs? Don't you think *you'd* want to forget it all, Luce?' he said more quietly. 'Don't you think *you'd* want a drink now and then?'

Lucy gazed at him. Pity was uppermost again, disgust merely lingering at the edges. 'Yes,' she said, 'I expect I would. But, Wilmot, don't you think you're drinking too much now? Don't you think it's got the better of you? It's making you ill, you see, and when you can't stop you need help. You'd be so much better if—'

'Can't stop? Who says I can't stop? I can stop any time I want to. *Any* time. Drink's not a problem to me, Luce. It's you that's got the problem.'

'Wilmot, how can you say that? It's not me who can't get up in the morning, who starts on the bottle at breakfast-time, it's not me who can't walk straight by lunchtime or talk without slurring the words. And just as well too, because if we were all like you this hotel wouldn't be where it is now and we'd all be in the gutter.'

'That's right, chuck that at me. It always comes to that, doesn't it? You're the one we all depend on, the one we've all got to thank. And have we got to thank you! On our bended knees, three times a day and facing Mecca. Nothing else will do, will it?' He snorted his derision. 'Oh, stroll on. Saint Lucy! Saint *bloody* Lucy.'

Lucy sighed. It didn't matter how she tried to approach the situation, it always ended like this. And she knew just what would happen next. Wilmot would slam out of the room and go straight upstairs to one of his hidden caches and drink. It was an act of defiance against her. An act, she was beginning to fear, of sheer hatred.

Since returning from Portsmouth, they had been sleeping in separate rooms. Nothing had been said. Lucy had simply removed her belongings from the bedroom and moved into Geoff's room. It was smaller but at least she had it to herself and didn't have to step over the pile of clothes Wilmot scattered around the floor, or sleep with the stink of stale rum and beer in her nostrils.

Nor did she have to endure his sexual attentions, doomed for months now to messy and painful failure.

She bent to pick up the tattered shreds of newspaper he had scattered on the floor. So much for Alcoholics Anonymous. Perhaps they would work for some people, but surely only if you really wanted them to work. There was no point at all in forcing someone to attend who wouldn't even admit they had a problem.

I could walk away from it all, she thought. I could leave him to drink himself to death. He's going to do it anyway, whether I'm here or not. I could tell his mum and dad that we've got to sell the hotel – they could retire on the proceeds and buy themselves a nice bungalow in Newton Ferrers, like they've always wanted – and Patsy and me could go to London. To David. It's what I ought to have done the minute we came back from Pompey.

She couldn't give up that easily.

Now that the idea of selling the hotel had entered her mind, Lucy found herself considering it more and more seriously, convinced that it was the answer for them all.

In the few years since the war, she had almost singlehandedly built it up from a small, inexpensive guest house to a smart hotel, patronised by businessmen who wanted somewhere of class to stay but didn't want to pay Duke of Cornwall prices. Pengelly's, standing a little nearer to the Hoe, met their expectations. Newly refurbished, extended and with a good dining-room where they could entertain their business friends, it quickly acquired a reputation and was now amongst the best-recommended of all Plymouth hotels.

At the same time, it had not lost its family atmosphere. The entrance hall, enlarged and carpeted, had kept a fireplace in which Lucy made sure logs were always burning in winter, or kept bright with a large display of flowers in summer. Two or three small tables with armchairs and a sofa arranged around them invited guests to make themselves comfortable while they waited. And Patsy's bright smile welcomed them as soon as they walked through the swing doors.

Pengelly's would be a good buy. And now that the country was picking up and Plymouth's rebuilding progressing more quickly, people would be looking towards the city for business opportunities. It surely wouldn't be hard to sell.

She began to take more notice of Maud's worries over Arthur.

'What does the doctor say?'

'Tells him he's got to take care of himself. His heart's not strong.'

Lucy looked at her. 'What do you think he ought to do?'

'Do? What can he do? It's age, that's all there is to it.'

'Well, you could think about retiring,' Lucy ventured.

Her mother-in-law stared at her. 'Retire? I thought we already had retired. All I do these days is give you a bit of a hand with the vegetables and that, and Arthur does nothing. Polishes a bit of brass now and then. Nothing more. If that's not being retired, I dunno what is.'

'No, I mean move somewhere more convenient for you. Somewhere without a lot of stairs. A nice little bungalow of your own. Newton Ferrers way, perhaps – you know you've always liked it there.'

'A bungalow? Newton Ferrers? *Are* there any bungalows in Newton Ferrers?'

'I've no idea,' Lucy said, startled. 'It was just that you've always talked about it . . . we could find out. If you think you'd like it. It doesn't have to be there, of course, you could stay in Plymouth. Or Plympton, it's nice there. You can choose what you like. But it could be better for you than being here. It would be quieter.'

'Not be in the hotel any more?' Maud said. Lucy could not tell whether the idea pleased or dismayed her. 'Not be here with the rest of you?'

'Well . . .' It wasn't perhaps the moment to say that she herself was thinking of leaving, leaving both the hotel and Wilmot. Certainly not to say that she wanted to sell the hotel to provide the money for this new bungalow, for Maud and Arthur's retirement and a home of some sort for Wilmot. 'It's just a suggestion,' she said. 'Just something to think about.'

'Well, I don't know,' Maud said, and it was still impossible to say whether she liked the proposal or not. Perhaps she wasn't sure herself. 'I don't know. I'll have to talk to Arthur about it. What does Wilmot say?'

'I haven't actually mentioned it to him,' Lucy confessed. 'I thought it was best for you to think about it before we go any further.'

'Yes, probably just as well,' Maud said, to her relief. 'Well, I'll turn it over in me mind. I suppose it'd help the hotel a bit. Give you a bit more room for guests.'

'Yes, I suppose so.' Lucy hadn't thought of that. She had been looking on it simply as a first step to selling. 'But that's not why – I mean, don't think I'm trying to get rid of you, Mum.'

'No,' Maud said, and smiled at her. 'I don't think that.'

She went out and Lucy sat back in her chair. She felt a little guilty. She had always got on well with her mother-in-law, and they had lived through some difficult times

273

together. They had shared so much. She felt ashamed of her planning now and wished she could have taken Maud into her confidence, but that was impossible. You just did not sit down with your elderly mother-in-law and tell her you were planning not only to break up the family home but to leave her son as well.

The door opened again and Jilly came in. She gave Lucy an uncertain glance.

'Could I talk to you for a minute?'

Lucy hesitated. She hadn't seen much of Jilly since she had come back, hadn't given her much thought. The girl looked peaky, she thought, and rather miserable. Pining for Geoff, probably. Well, there was nothing to be done about that, and she'd have been just as lonely if they'd been allowed to get married before he went away.

'Is it important, Jilly? I've got rather a lot on my mind at the moment.'

'It's about Geoff's dad. He doesn't want me here.' Jilly's eyes filled with tears. 'While you were away – he told me then, he said he couldn't stand me about the place. He said I reminded him too much of – of Geoff – and that made him think about the camp. He said he'd be better if I left – he said you'd all be better . . . Well, I just wanted to know if he'd told you, and what you thought about it, that's all.' The blue eyes were huge. 'Because I think maybe he's right and it would be better if I went away.'

Lucy stared at her. 'Went away? *Wilmot* told you to go away?'

Jilly lifted her shoulders. 'Ask old Mrs Pengelly. She was here when he said it.'

Lucy leant her elbows on the table and lifted her hands to her face. She closed her eyes. I'll walk out now, she said to herself. I'll get up from this table and walk out of this kitchen and out of this hotel and go straight to North Road station and get on a train for London. Just as I am. I won't even bother to put a coat on. I'll telephone David from

274

Paddington and he can come and fetch me and we'll go back to his house and that's where I'll live from then on. I'll never come back again, never, and they can just get on as best they can without me.

'Well,' she said, 'he hasn't said anything to me. He's probably forgotten all about it by now. I wouldn't worry about it any more, if I were you.'

'No, all right.' Jilly half rose and then stood hesitant once more. 'There – there was just one more thing. I think I ought to tell you – I mean, I'm not actually sure, but I think I may be—' She was interrupted by a call from the front hall. She stopped abruptly and they stared at each other. 'That sounded like Patsy!'

'It did.' Lucy was on her feet. 'Oh my God, what's happened now? Don't say Arthur's been taken ill. Or Maud –' She pushed past Jilly and they ran together down the short corridor to the front hall. 'Patsy, what is it? What's happened?'

'Mum,' Patsy said faintly. 'Oh, *Mum* –'

Lucy stopped short. The years reeled away as she took in the scene before her. The boy in his dark blue uniform, the brown sack over his shoulder, the buff envelope in her daughter's hand. The scrap of paper with its letters stuck unevenly across it.

'A telegram,' she said, and wondered at the sudden flood of dread. It wasn't such an uncommon occurrence, after all. Guests frequently sent telegrams to the hotel. Patsy's face, however, bone white, told her that this was no ordinary telegram, and behind her she heard Jilly's gasp and knew that her dread was shared. 'What is it? Patsy, *what is it?*'

'It's Geoff,' Patsy said dully. 'Mum – Jilly – Geoff's missing.' She stared at the telegram again, her lips moving as if she were reading the words silently to herself, as if by reading them once more she could make them say something different. 'Missing in action . . . presumed *dead* . . .'

Chapter Twenty-two

Wilmot took the news worse than anyone else. Predictably, his response was to turn to his only friend in the world: his bottle.

'For heaven's sake,' Lucy said. She was beyond patience with him now. 'Don't you have any willpower at all? Don't you have any self-respect? Don't you think the rest of us are just as upset? *We're* not taking to the bottle, are we? *We're* not drinking ourselves stupid night after night.'

'It's different for you. I'm his father.'

'And I'm his mother. And Patsy's his sister, and your mum and dad are his grandparents, and Jilly –' It was difficult to say what Jilly was. 'Jilly's his fiancée. Or was.'

'A son's special to a man,' Wilmot blustered. 'Ask anyone.' He lifted his bottle and went to pour another glass of rum.

Lucy snatched it away. 'No more special than he is to his mother. Wilmot, I am sick and tired of you taking everything that happens as if it only happens to you. This is mine as well. I brought Geoff up all those years when you were away, I knew him a thousand times better than you did, he was my companion, my right hand –'

'Oh, that's right. Bring it back to that again. I wasn't out in Japan on a bloody picnic, you know. I just happened to be fighting for my country. For you. Or perhaps you'd forgotten that.'

'Of course I haven't forgotten it. I'll never forget it. But it isn't what we're talking about now. It's Geoff we're talking about, Geoff. And he's missing – presumed dead. Wilmot,

Geoff is almost certainly, *dead*.' Her voice rose in a cry for help, for comfort and understanding.

Wilmot turned aside and away from her, and when he replied his tone was filled with his own angry pain. 'I know. I *know*. You don't have to keep on about it. For God's sake – anyone would think you enjoyed repeating it, over and over again. Geoff's dead,' he mimicked her. 'Geoff's dead. Anyone would think you had to keep on saying it just to believe it.'

'I do. I do. I can't believe it if I don't hear the words. I can't take them in. Wilmot,' she raised her tear-stained face towards him, 'we shouldn't be rowing over it. We should be helping each other. Holding each other. Hold me now, Wilmot, please. Just put your arms round me like you used to and hold me close for a few minutes. For God's sake, I just want some comfort, can't you see?'

He stared at her, then, very deliberately, he reached across the table and took back the bottle she had snatched from his grasp. He poured the drink she had denied him and lifted it to his lips in a long swallow.

'That's my comfort, Lucy. The only comfort you can trust.' He put the glass down and looked at it, and his lip curled a little. 'And there's precious little comfort even there now,' he added quietly. 'Precious little comfort to be had anywhere now.' He lifted his eyes towards her. 'It's all my fault. Everything that goes wrong in this family is my fault.'

'Wilmot, don't be silly.'

'Silly. Yes, that's what I am, that's all you think of me, isn't it? Silly. Silly to join the Navy in the first place, silly to go off to war, silly to get sunk and caught by the Japs, silly to come home, silly to let Geoff join the Army – silly, silly, *silly*.' He laughed suddenly and Lucy tried to close her ears against the ugliness of the sound. 'Silly to be born at all.'

'Wilmot –'

'Well, isn't it true?' His voice was truculent. 'Wouldn't it have been better for everyone if I'd never been born?'

Lucy sat very still, then she raised her head and looked at him. She felt bitterly sorry for him, but over-riding her pity was anger, and a sour, gritty disgust.

'You're pathetic,' she said at last. 'That's what you are. It doesn't matter what happens, you've got to take it for yourself, as if you're the only one with a right to feel bad about it. It's got to be you, you, you, all the time. Never mind me, never mind Patsy or your mum and dad, or poor Jilly. You've got to be the centre of attention. And do you know something? I've had enough of it. *Enough*.'

He stood up suddenly, scraping his chair back, and stumbled towards the door. Lucy watched dully. She had done her best. She had tried to give him comfort even when she needed it most herself, she had asked for his help, and nothing had penetrated the barriers he had created about himself. There was nothing left for them now.

Arthur was completely broken. It was as if he had reached the point where he could not have stood any kind of bad news, and this was the worst imaginable. He made no fuss, demanded no attention, simply retreated into himself and seemed to fade away before their eyes.

He didn't even want to listen to the wireless, even when his favourite programmes were on – *Music While You Work* or *Workers' Playtime* during the day, *Ray's A Laugh* or *Take It From Here* in the evenings. The only programme he asked for, plaintively each evening, was *Dick Barton – Special Agent*, and Maud and Lucy had to explain to him over and over again that it wasn't on any more, the new farming serial *The Archers* had taken its place.

'Why did they do that, then?' he asked, his moustache trembling. 'I liked Dick Barton, and Jock and Snowy. They had some good stories. This farming stuff won't last, people aren't interested in that kind of thing.'

'I quite like it myself,' Maud said. 'Dan and Doris and their kids – that young Phil's a caution – and all the village people. It's nice family stories.'

'Bit of action, that's what people want,' Arthur grumbled. '*Geoff* liked Dick Barton.'

Nobody answered. They all knew that Geoff had liked Dick Barton, making sure he was in at a quarter to seven each evening to hear the exciting, galloping music that began it, or listening to the omnibus edition on Saturday mornings while he worked on his motorbike.

Maud, at seventy, was as stalwart as ever. She had been through so much in her lifetime, Lucy thought, that she had either grown hardened to grief or had developed huge inner resources. She made no secret of her distress, but she didn't let it weaken her either. She just got on with living and with looking after them all. She was like a rock in the centre of a sea of grief, letting them all wash up against her and cling for a while. Dimly, Lucy realised how much she had depended on her mother-in-law all these years.

'You've always been here. I don't know what we'd have done without you.'

'Don't talk so silly,' Maud said. 'We just do whatever we've got to do. You've kept us all going. Look what you've done for Pengelly's. We'd never have got the place going like you did after the war. It would still be a little guest house, or we'd have gone bankrupt. You know what things were like.'

'And maybe Geoff would still be alive,' Lucy said, but Maud shook her head.

'That would have happened just the same. You've got to remember God's will. If he wanted Geoff—'

'But *why* should he want him?' Lucy struck the table with her hand. 'Why does it have to be the people *I* love that God wants? Why can't he wait for them to get old, why can't he let them have their lives first? Little Zannah, and now Geoff – and he can't even let Patsy have a proper life, she's got to be hurt. And Wilmot. He says he'd be better off dead and sometimes I think he's right. What sort of a life has he got, for heaven's sake? Why doesn't God take *him*?'

'*Lucy!*'

'I can't help it. I'm fed up with God taking everything that means anything to me. I'm fed up with it!'

She heard a sound behind her and turned in her chair to meet her husband's eyes. They stared at each other and she knew he had heard her words.

'Wilmot –'

'It's all right,' he said. 'It's all right. I know now. I know what you really think.'

'Wilmot, come and sit down. I didn't mean—'

'It's all right,' he repeated, and turned away. Lucy jumped out of her chair and ran to catch him by the arm. 'Let me go.' His voice was dull and flat. 'Let me go.'

'No! You've got to come and sit down. Let me explain.'

'I heard what you said. I know what you meant.' He dragged his arm loose. 'It doesn't matter. Nothing matters any more. Just let me go.'

Lucy fell back, staring at him. He gave her a look of bottomless despair, his eyes like pits, and turned away. They heard his footsteps going down the passage and out of the back door.

'Oh, Mum . . . What do you think he's going to do?'

'Nothing silly,' Maud said, but she sounded shaken and uncertain. 'He wouldn't have the energy. Don't worry, Lucy.'

'He heard what I said. He heard me say why didn't God take him?' She sat down and buried her face in her hands. 'If he does anything, it'll be my fault.'

'He won't do anything. He'll just drink a bit more and forget about it. You know that's what he'll do. It's what he always does.' Maud reached over to touch her hand. 'Lucy, we've got to hold on, we've got to get through this together. We've got to help each other. We can't give up now.'

We can't give up now. Lucy took her hands away from her face and stared at her mother-in-law. She thought of her plans, her idea of selling the hotel, establishing Maud and Arthur in a nice little bungalow, giving Wilmot enough money for a place of his own, and then taking Patsy and herself to London to be with David. And she saw them for what they were.

Dreams. Golden, insubstantial dreams.

She could never do it.

Jilly was inconsolable.

'If only we'd got married before he went,' she sobbed. 'We wanted to be married and you wouldn't let us. I should have been his *wife* . . .'

'It wouldn't have made any difference,' Lucy began helplessly, but Jilly turned on her in a fury.

'Of course it would have made a difference. It would have made a difference to *me*. It would have made a difference to *him*. How can you say it wouldn't have made any difference?'

'I only meant, it wouldn't have made any difference to – to what happened.'

'I know that,' Jilly said with bitter scorn. 'I'm not a *fool*, Mrs Pengelly. But it would have made all the difference in the world to us.'

Lucy was silent. It was difficult for her to accept Jilly's words, for they presented Geoff to her as if in a different world. Not her son any longer, but a grown man, married, with a life of his own. Perhaps that's why I didn't want them to be married, she thought. Because I didn't want him to take that step away from me, the last step a child does take away from its parents. After they're married, you have to take a back seat. They don't have to wait to be twenty-one then, to be independent.

But that's why they *do* have to wait till they're twenty-one. Under that age, they're just too young to take

281

responsibility for their own lives. Until then, parents have to do it for them, it's what parents are for . . .

'It's not fair,' Jilly said bitterly, just as Lucy herself had said years ago. 'Old enough to go to war, old enough to fight for his country – or someone else's country – but not old enough to live his own life. It's not *fair*.'

'Life isn't fair,' Lucy said, as she had herself so painfully learned. 'It's no use expecting it.'

'But you could have made it a bit *more* fair. You could have let us get married.'

Lucy sighed. She felt sorry for the girl, very sorry – but they'd been all through this before. And seeing Jilly's grief wasn't helping her to get over her own. She said, rather tersely, 'Yes, maybe I could, but I didn't, and nothing can change that. We can't turn the clock back and do things differently. And it doesn't help to keep going on and on about it, it really doesn't. We've got to look forward now, Jilly, we've got to start building our lives up again. And you're young. You'll get over it. You'll find someone else—'

'*Oh!*' It was like a shriek. Jilly stared at her, wild eyed. 'You don't understand, do you? You just don't understand. You never will. Oh, what am I going to do, what am I going to *do*?' She lifted her fists to her forehead and clutched at her hair.

Lucy watched her. 'You're hysterical, Jilly. You'd better take yourself out for a walk, or find something to do. It isn't a bit of use giving way like this.'

'Isn't it? Isn't it? Then perhaps you could tell me what would be any use. Oh, it's no use asking. You won't help me. You wouldn't before and you won't now. Oh, Geoff, *Geoff* . . .' She broke into sobs.

Lucy bit her lip. It wasn't helping any of them to let the girl go on like this. Perhaps she'd be better off away from the hotel, away from them all. Out of Plymouth, removed from the house where she had lived so close to Geoff, from

282

the places they'd visited together, she might begin to recover. And she wouldn't be there to remind the rest of them of what might have been.

'Look,' she said gently when Jilly's sobs had subsided a little, 'why don't you go home for a while? A break would do you good. Your mother would be pleased to see you, I'm sure. It would help you to forget.'

'I'll never forget,' Jilly said. 'I don't want to forget.' She wiped her eyes and looked thoughtful. 'Do you want me to go? Do you want to get rid of me? Would you like me to leave altogether?'

'Jilly, it's not that –' Lucy began, and then stopped. Perhaps it would be best, after all, if Jilly left them and found herself another job. Better for Jilly herself. 'I just think we could all do with a break,' she said. 'Go home for a few weeks, Jilly, and then we'll see how we feel.' She touched the girl's arm gently. 'That's all I'm suggesting. Let's give ourselves time to think.'

Jilly looked at her. There was something in the girl's eyes, Lucy thought, a hesitation, as if she had something else to say, but the moment passed and Jilly shrugged and moved away from Lucy's touch.

'All right. If that's what you want.' She sounded tired, defeated. 'I'll send Mum a telegram and I'll go tomorrow.'

Lucy nodded, and turned away. There was work to be done, and enough time had been spent in talking and grieving. In a week, the hotel was to be fully open again, and if Jilly were not to be here a new cook must be found, and more help employed in the kitchen and bedrooms. Life must go on. And at some point, she must find time to write to David and tell him she wasn't coming to London after all.

The thought was like a knife slicing into her heart. This time, she thought, it really must be all over. I just can't bear the pain of seeing him again, talking to him, knowing what we so nearly had, knowing that it will never, never be possible . . .

283

From today, she must cut David out of her life as surely and irrevocably as Geoff had been cut out. As if he too were dead.

Jilly had left the hotel the day after her talk with Lucy, and the Pengellys didn't expect to see her again. She seemed to have recovered from her hysterics and her face was pale and set as she humped her suitcases downstairs. The family were waiting in the front hall and Patsy had called a taxi which was already parked outside.

'You will come back, won't you?' she said as Jilly came round the desk to hug her. 'You're only going for a holiday.'

'I don't know. It depends on your mum.'

'She'll want you to come back. I know she will.'

Jilly shook her head doubtfully and gave Patsy a kiss. 'I wish you could come and stay with me in Cornwall.'

'I will. I'll come in the summer. But you'll be back here by then.'

'I might be. But if not –'

'I'll see you in the summer,' Patsy promised. 'One way or another, I'll see you then. And I'll come and stay when you have your holidays as well.'

Jilly smiled. 'You've been a good friend, Patsy. I wish we could have been sisters.'

'We are,' Patsy said, suddenly serious. 'We're proper sisters.'

'The taxi's waiting,' Lucy said, and Jilly turned away and went out through the swing doors. At the foot of the steps, she paused and looked back, waiting as Patsy wheeled her chair down the ramp.

Geoff's bedroom window was high above her, an attic window looking out over the rooftops towards the Sound. Lucy slept there now, but to Jilly it was Geoff's room and always would be. She stared up at it, almost imagining that she could see his face there, peeping down, and his hand waving.

Geoff . . .

She turned abruptly and got into the taxi.

The family stood hesitant on the pavement. Arthur glanced from Lucy to Wilmot. 'Well, isn't anyone going to go with the maid? Give her a hand with her bits and bobs?' His moustache quivered. 'A fine send-off, this is, I'll be bound. Pengelly's can do a bit better than this.' He pulled open the door of the car and started to climb in.

'Dad!' Lucy protested. 'You can't –'

'I can. I'm doing it.' He glowered out at her and glared at his son. 'I'm ashamed of you, Wilmot, I'm ashamed of the pair of you. Letting a little maid go off all by herself. Well, her's always been a proper helpful and kindly maid to me, and I'll not let her go like this. *I'll* give her a hand, and I'll see her on her way proper. The rest of you had better get back about your own business. I daresay you've all got jobs to do.'

He slammed the door shut and the taxi started up. Lucy made one more effort to stop him, but she was too late. The car was drawing away from the kerb.

Nobody spoke. Lucy glanced at them, feeling her colour heighten. 'Well, what are you all staring at? I suppose you think I should have gone with her?'

Wilmot shrugged and turned away. He had already lost interest. Maud and Patsy gave each other a swift look. Maud said, ''Tis up to you, maid. 'Tis not for me to say what you should do.'

'Well, I don't mind saying,' Patsy declared. 'Yes, Mum, I do think you should have gone with her. Why not? What quarrel do we have with poor Jilly? All she's done is love our Geoff, and he loved her too. Would he have wanted you to send her away with nobody but Grampy to help her with her bags? Would he have wanted her to be sent away at all?'

'I didn't send her away. It was her own wish.' But Lucy remembered with discomfort that conversation with Jilly. It *had* been Lucy's suggestion. 'It was the best thing for her,' she said pleadingly. 'She needed to get away, to start to forget. She can't live her life grieving for Geoff. She's young –'

'She needed someone to help her,' Patsy said bluntly. 'She needed someone to love her, and not to feel she was being thrown out.' She paused for a moment and said, 'You know she'll never come back, don't you?'

'And if she doesn't, that will be her own decision. She knows there's a job here for her at any time.'

'A job!' Patsy said bitterly. 'When she ought to have been one of the family.'

She turned her chair round and wheeled it back up the ramp. Lucy hurried forwards and pushed from behind. She felt disconcerted and upset. And, uncomfortably, that Patsy was right and she had treated Jilly shabbily.

Writing to David was the hardest thing she had ever done.

We've spent half our lives doing this, she thought, sitting at her desk with a sheet of paper in front of her. Half our lives trying not to love each other, half trying to find a way to be together . . . we were always going to hurt someone. Wilmot, Maud, Arthur, the children . . . All we've ended up doing is hurting ourselves.

Once again, however, there didn't seem to be any choice. She could not leave Wilmot now, with his anxiety over Geoff smothering him in a black cloud of depression. She could not leave Arthur, whose burst of energy when Jilly left had evaporated once more, leaving him like a grey shadow haunting the recesses of the hotel. She could not leave Maud, who had stood by her and offered comfort when she herself had most needed it.

And she knew that even if *she* had done so, Patsy would not leave them. And she could not leave Patsy.

Oh David, David,
I love you so much, and I have to let you go. Since

Geoff went away, everything has been so impossible. I feel I am all that is keeping this family together and if I leave them now, they'll fall apart. I can't do it to them. I can't do it to poor old Arthur, who won't even understand, or Maud who will be so disappointed, or Wilmot who will just drink himself to death. And Patsy – I don't know what Patsy thinks of me these days, but I know that if I walk out now, she'll think even less of me. And she won't come too. She'll stay behind and take on this burden. I can't do that to her, and I can't bear to think of losing her.

She stopped writing. Her eyes were too full of tears and the page was blurred and dissolving under her gaze. She lifted her head, trying to draw the tears back into herself, not wanting to let them fall, but they ran out of her eyes and flowed like a burning river down her icy cheeks.

'I love you so much,' she wrote again, 'but we have to say goodbye. Don't write back to me, David. Don't ever write to me again. I won't have the strength . . .'

She folded the page quickly, before she could change her mind, pushed it into an envelope and addressed it to his home in London. She found a stamp and stuck it on and then got up and walked out of the hotel and down the street to the postbox. The red pillarbox swallowed her letter as if it had not eaten for a week. She stood in front of it, staring at the wide black mouth, desperation welling up inside her. The letter was there, only a foot away from her, and yet it had gone. It was as far away from her as if she had sent it to the moon, and until David received it nobody would know what was inside it.

There was no way in which she could prevent him getting it and opening it and knowing what she had written. By next morning, he would know. By next morning, it would be all over.

Lucy turned and walked back up the street. She passed

287

Pengelly's without a glance and walked on up to the Hoe. For an hour she paced there on the wide, green expanse overlooking the Sound, where Drake had once played bowls. She leant on the railings and gazed down at the little bathing-pools in the rocks and the big semicircular swimming-pool where she had taught Wilmot to swim so long ago, and she lifted her eyes and looked out across the glittering sea past Drake's Island and the breakwater, to the thin, pencil shape of the Eddystone Lighthouse, sharp as an exclamation mark on the far horizon.

When she came back to the hotel she had, with some determination, put all her previous life behind her, and was ready to start again.

Chapter Twenty-three

Jilly finished the washing-up and dried her hands. She left the dishes piled on the wooden draining-board to dry, and wandered out through the back door into the garden. It was a perfect May morning, with a few late narcissi flowering beneath the gnarled branches of the old apple trees and a flurry of small birds dashing to and fro with beaks filled with tiny, struggling worms and insects. She sank into a battered deckchair and closed her eyes.

Her mother was still indoors, looking after old Mrs Tremaine. David's aunt was over ninety now, almost blind and very frail, though she still had, as the villagers observed, all her marbles. It irritated her profoundly that she could no longer see to read, and one of Jilly's jobs was to spend half an hour or so, at intervals during the day, reading her latest library book aloud. At present, they were working through Dickens, all of whose books old Mrs Tremaine had read years ago but wanted to revisit, and when they'd finished those they were going to start on Anthony Trollope. In between, she liked something lighter, a Regency novel by Georgette Heyer perhaps, or one of Elizabeth Goudge's family stories.

'You read very nicely, dear,' she said as Jilly fell silent. 'Now let's be quiet for a bit. Tell me what you can see, and I'll be able to imagine everything.'

So Jilly would describe the garden; the last lingering flowers of spring, the primroses in the bank, the violets scattering their purple freckles in the grass, the snowy blossom on the apple trees. She talked about the blackbird's nest in the hedge and the scurrying bluetits who were already feeding their first brood in the hole in the stone-filled Cornish bank. She painted a word picture of the pale blue sky, feathered with high white clouds, and when Blackie, the cat, came stalking through the grass she lifted him on to her knee and guided Mrs Tremaine's hand to his furry back.

After that, they sat quietly together and just listened to the sounds: Blackie's purring, the twittering of the bluetits, the alarmed shriek of the blackbird when it noticed the cat, the rustling of the breeze amongst the leaves. Sometimes it was so quiet that Jilly fancied she could hear the whisper of the clouds flying high overhead, and the murmuring of the violets at her feet.

It seemed a very long way here from the horrors of war. Jilly remembered her childhood. She had grown up in the village, only five years old when the war began, but it seemed to have made little difference down here in deepest Cornwall. They had had no air raids, no sirens, no bombs. The blackout hadn't made much difference to villages that had never had streetlights anyway. Even later, when American soldiers had been stationed near by, it hadn't seemed like war, more like a big, cheerful party that went on for months, until suddenly, mysteriously, they all disappeared and the wireless and newspapers had been full of something called D-Day. After that, although the war still dragged on and rationing got worse even here, where people grew their own eggs and vegetables, everyone seemed much more optimistic and it hadn't come as a surprise at all to know that the whole thing was over and the country could look forward to peace again.

Peace. Love and laughter. Buried softly here in this little Eden, Jilly knew that they could have known nothing of the reality of war. Even though some of the young men had gone, never to return, their names now carved on the little stone cross that had been placed outside the church, the village had not really understood what it was like. *She* had not understood; not until she went to Plymouth and saw the destruction there, and looked into the greyness of the people's faces and felt the miasma of weariness and depression that hung over them like an old, encrusted cobweb. They were getting themselves together, the determination that had got them through the war was pushing them on, but she could feel their tiredness, their growing hopelessness as things got worse instead of better, as rationing increased, as they faced the enormous and daunting task of rebuilding the city, their homes, their lives.

It seemed that no sooner had they begun this, than Korea happened, and it all started again. Not the bombing, not the air-raids, but the grinding misery of seeing their young men go off to fight just when they'd been expecting to start living their own lives. The anguish of knowing that some of them would not come back.

Geoff had not come back. Jilly could hardly believe now that he would ever come back. And his name would not appear on any stone cross. He would be forgotten.

David found her there in the old deckchair, her eyes closed, listening as his old aunt liked to listen, to the birds singing and the sighing of the breeze. There was another chair beside her and he dropped into it and stayed quiet, waiting for her to realise he was there. After a bit, she stirred and opened her eyes, and then turned her head.

'Mr Tremaine.' She sat up straight. 'I didn't know you were there.'

'I've been very quiet. I thought you might be asleep.'

'I might have been. I don't know.' She closed her eyes again momentarily. 'Sometimes I think I'd just like to go to sleep and stay asleep for ever.'

'Jilly –'

'It's all right. I don't mean it that way. Just that it's so peaceful, being asleep.' She hesitated. 'And there's always the chance that I might dream about Geoff.'

He gazed at her and reached out his hand.

'It's almost as good as being with him again,' she said. 'It *is* as good, while I'm dreaming it. Dreams are so real, aren't they? And afterwards I've got another memory to think about. To treasure. Even if it's not real, it still seems real to me, and dreams are all I've got now.'

He said, 'It takes a long time before it starts to get better. But it does, you know, in the end.'

'I know. But I haven't got a long time.' Her cornflower eyes looked into his. 'I've got to get better quickly. You see, I'm going to have a baby.'

David leant back in his chair. He didn't let go of Jilly's hand, although it twitched a little in his grasp, as though it wanted to escape. He kept a firm hold of it while he considered her words. It was an important moment, and he didn't want to risk mishandling it.

'Does anyone else know?' he asked at last, and she shook her head.

'I'll have to tell Mum soon. I'm four months gone. She'll notice.' She glanced down at her body, blushing. David realised now that she had changed already, that her breasts had become fuller. Perhaps her waist had begun to thicken too. Changes that wouldn't be noticed if you weren't looking for them, but would now become swiftly more apparent. She had left it late enough to tell anyone, he thought.

'Are you all right? Have you seen a doctor?'

She shook her head. 'I know what's the matter. I'm not *ill*. I haven't even had morning sickness. That's why I didn't think I was expecting at first. I mean, there was just nothing. Except –' She blushed again. 'Well. You know. And I thought that was just because I was upset, with Geoff going away, and – and us not being able to get married.' She glanced away. 'We pretended we were,' she said in a low

292

voice. 'We went away on the bike – we called it our honeymoon. Geoff gave me a ring. We *felt* married.'

'Oh, Jilly,' David said, his voice filled with pity.

'I suppose you're disgusted. You think I'm a slut.'

'I don't. I don't think that at all.'

'No better than I should be. That's what people will say about me.' She laughed without mirth. 'I've never understood that saying. I mean, why should anyone be better than they should be? It don't make sense.'

'Jilly, no one's going to say that about you.'

'Oh, they will,' she said with quiet certainty. 'A lot of them will.'

'Then they're not worth bothering about.'

'They are,' she said. 'People are always worth bothering about. Even the nasty ones.'

David was silent. He felt suddenly that this young girl, who had been deemed not old enough to marry, was possessed of some wisdom. He wondered what advice he could give her, what help. He wondered how he could have the temerity to suppose that he could advise her at all, only minutes after hearing the news, when she had known and lived with it for weeks.

'Have you made any plans?' he asked.

Jilly shrugged. 'What plans can I make? What does a girl like me do? There's homes for unmarried mothers. You go there and have your baby, and then someone comes along and adopts it. That's one thing you can do. Or you can stop at home – if your family don't chuck you out – and have the baby there and keep it. And it grows up with everyone knowing about it. But I don't know about *plans*. It depends on other people, doesn't it? A girl like me can't do much on her own.'

'What do you want to do?'

'Well, I'm not giving it away,' she said in an almost savage tone. 'It's my baby, mine and Geoff's, and nobody else is having it.'

'Well, that's one thing, then. And do you want to stay at home?'

She glanced at him sideways. 'I don't know where is home,' she said simply. 'If Geoff and me had got married, I suppose we'd have stayed in Plymouth. Got ourselves a couple of rooms somewhere or maybe stayed at the hotel. I could have gone on working in the kitchen . . . But they won't want me now, and this is your auntie's house.'

David stared at her. It had not occurred to him that she had, literally, no home. Her mother still owned a small cottage in the village, but it was let to a man who worked on a nearby farm and had a family of four. There was no question of turning him out. He thought of saying that of course this was her home, she must stay here, but it wasn't for him to say any such thing. It was, as Jilly had pointed out, his aunt's house, and an old woman in her nineties might not be at all pleased to find herself sharing her home with a baby.

He felt helpless. But that was nothing, he told himself, to what Jilly must be feeling. Having to absorb this new development, so quickly after losing Geoff . . . The baby was like a time-bomb, ticking away inside her, and although there were another five months before it was actually born, she would have to make her decisions and organise her life well before then. She had hardly any time at all. And the decisions were momentous, affecting not just her and her mother and even his aunt, but her baby too – her baby most of all, he realised suddenly. A new person who wouldn't stay a baby long but would become a toddler, a child, an adult.

He thought of Lucy. She was the child's grandmother. She would help. She had never backed out of a responsibility yet, in all the years he had known her. She had suffered blow after blow and always come back, if not smiling, at least determined not to be beaten.

'You'll tell Mrs Pengelly, of course,' he said, thinking aloud, and was surprised when Jilly drew back, almost snatching her hand away.

'*No!* No, I won't – I can't –' Her voice was edged sharply with distress. 'You mustn't either. Promise me you won't. *Promise.*'

'But why not?' He didn't tell her that he couldn't. Nobody else knew about Lucy's letter. He had carried it around with him for three days and kept reading it, and still he couldn't quite believe what it said.

'Jilly,' he said, 'she ought to know. She has a right to know. It's Geoff's baby.'

'And you know what she'll have to say about *that*,' Jilly said bitterly.

David sighed. She was probably right. Young girls who found themselves 'in trouble' didn't have many friends. Some mothers and fathers supported their daughters, but many turned their backs on them. The picture of the shawl-wrapped figure trudging through the snow with her bundle of shame wasn't so very far from the truth.

'But your mother won't turn you out,' he said. 'She'll help you, I'm sure. And so will I. We'll all sit down together round the table and have a talk about it. You can't manage on your own. You've got to have support.'

Jilly's eyes filled with tears. 'Oh, Mr Tremaine. I don't know what to do –' Her lips trembled and her voice wobbled away into a sob. She put her face in her hands and began to cry.

David laid his hand on her shoulder. It quivered and shook under his palm. He felt deeply sorry for the girl. A few months ago, she had had so much: a young man who loved her, the joy of looking forward to a life together, to a family. Now the young man was missing, probably dead, and she faced the world alone, worse than alone. She had to face the censure of a society that had little compassion for girls in her position, that would stigmatise her and her baby. And the stigma would extend to her mother too, and even as far as Plymouth to the Pengellys.

He wondered if she was right about Lucy. Would she reject the girl her son had loved? There was only one way to find out, but it was a way he of all people could not take.

'Tell your mother,' he said quietly. 'Tell her soon.' He hesitated. 'Unless you'd like me to tell her? I will if you want me to.'

'Oh no,' Jilly said. 'No, I'll do it. I'll do it this evening, after your auntie's gone to bed.' She fumbled in her pocket for a handkerchief, blew her nose and gave a wry smile. 'You'll probably find me packing to go tomorrow.'

'Jilly, don't say that. I'm sure your mother will help you. Look, I'll go in and have a chat with my aunt now, and then I've got to go. I promised to go and see the builder about those repairs to the roof. I'd like to see them done before I go back to London.'

He leant his head back again and closed his eyes, listening to the birdsong and wondering why he had to go back at all. Every time he came down to Cornwall, he felt more reluctant to leave again. Perhaps it was time to think about a permanent move. There was nothing in London for him now, only his job, and he sometimes felt he'd had enough of that. At forty-nine, he was too young to be thinking of retirement, but he could surely find a job in the West. On the *Western Morning News*, perhaps. Or the paper where he'd begun his career, the one his father had edited back before the First World War.

If Lucy had come to him, of course, things would have been very different. He would have had her to work for. A purpose in life. Now, it all seemed rather empty.

He went indoors, where his aunt was now downstairs, having had her morning wash and breakfast in bed, and was sitting in the small sunroom with Blackie on her lap. The sunroom was not too warm at this time of day but sheltered from the breeze, and the air was scented with the flowers

Jilly's mother grew there. His aunt looked as fragrant as the flowers, tiny and dainty in her clean cotton dress with a snowy-white apron, edged with lace, in case she spilled anything, her curly hair like a halo of soft white clouds about her face.

'Is that David?'

'Yes. I'm just going to see the builder about the roof.'

'Little Tommy Pascoe.' David's aunt knew everyone in the village, had known most of them all their lives. Because she had been unable to see them for several years, each had assumed a point at which she remembered them best, mostly as children. 'Are you sure he'll be able to manage it? I wouldn't like him to fall off and hurt himself.'

David smiled. 'Tommy's a good worker. He won't fall.' Pascoe & Son were the biggest building firm in the area and had started to build a new council estate away over near Redruth. 'I'll tell him to look in and say hallo before he starts work.'

'That would be nice. I'd like to have a chat with Tommy again. He used to come here to collect conkers, you know, from the horse-chestnut trees in the drive.' The old lady's faded eyes turned towards him and he felt his usual little spasm of surprise that they couldn't see him. She didn't look blind at all. 'Have you been talking to little Jilly?'

'Yes. She's in the garden, under the apple trees.' He hesitated. 'She looks tired. And it really doesn't seem as if he's coming back.'

'She's had such a sad time,' Margaret Tremaine said. 'So much in love . . . It's the worst time to lose someone. The worst of times and the best of times, as Dickens might have said.'

'How do you mean?' David was always fascinated to hear the workings of his aunt's mind. 'How can it be both?'

'For the same reason. Because they hadn't had time for the first flush of rapture to diminish. The worst of times, because she hadn't had time to discover his faults, and the best because she'll always remember their love as being perfect. She'll never have any regrets to sour the memories.'

David said nothing. He thought Jilly was going to have plenty of regrets. Life was not going to be easy for her. It never was for the girl who was left, literally, holding the baby.

'I think she's going to need quite a lot of help and support,' he said carefully. 'She really did love Geoff, and they badly wanted to be married. She'll always regret that.'

'Oh, I know. And so, I think, will other people. Especially those who prevented it.' The soft eyes were reflective. 'Poor Jean Penfold is already tormenting herself with it. And perhaps Geoffrey's mother is too. Or maybe she hasn't begun to think about that yet. She has her own grief to contend with.'

'Yes, she does.' David thought again of the letter in his pocket. He wanted nothing so badly as to be with Lucy again, helping her bear her sorrow, but she had turned away from him, and he knew that she could not be persuaded to turn back. Their last chance had come, and slipped them by.

And he too was grieving for Geoffrey for he too thought that Geoff must be dead. Nobody seemed to have thought of his sorrow, but in his heart the pain was as sharp and searing as if the boy had been his own son. And for years, he had been very nearly just that. The boy he'd saved from the blitz, the boy he'd given his arm for. The boy he'd walked with on the Hoe and talked to and taught to swim. Lucy's son. His loss, as well as hers, and nobody seemed to realise it.

So deep in thought was he then that he almost missed his aunt's next words. He just caught them, lingering in his ears, the second before they vanished into the spring air, and he jerked his head up and looked at her in astonishment. '*What* did you say?'

'I said, you know Jilly's pregnant.' The old voice was

298

touched with reproach. 'Really, David, if you can't be bothered to listen to me –'

'I'm sorry. I was listening – I just got distracted for a moment . . . Pregnant?' He echoed the word almost unbelievingly, as if he had no idea that it might be true. 'But how do you know? Did she tell you?'

'David, I'm over ninety years old. I don't have to be told things. I can hear it in her voice.'

'In her *voice*?'

'Of course. When she reads to me. It's a situation that crops up quite frequently in fiction, and whenever Jilly comes to a passage about babies, her voice softens. And if it's a young girl like herself, unmarried but expecting a baby, she has some difficulty in controlling her emotions. It's hardly surprising. Are *you* surprised?'

'That Jilly can't control her voice? Or that she's pregnant?' He shook his head, bemused. 'I don't know . . . She's told me, as it happens. Just now – a few minutes ago. She felt she had to tell someone. She doesn't realise that you know.'

'Well, of course she doesn't. I wouldn't be so foolish as to let her see that I've guessed, not until she was ready to tell me. So it's true . . .' The old lady fell silent for a few minutes. 'Poor child. Poor, *poor* child.'

'I don't think she knows quite what to do,' David said after a moment.

'I don't suppose she does, but at least she'll do nothing silly. Not now she's told someone. That's always the danger period, you see, when a girl hasn't told anyone yet. That's when there's a risk of her doing something foolish.'

'Something foolish' meant either trying to get rid of the baby, by falling downstairs or jumping off a chair, or even by going to some shady backstreet harridan who made a living out of young girls' mistakes; or, worse still, by throwing herself into a river or taking too many aspirins. David shuddered at the thought of either of these measures.

Thank God she had told him, he thought, and hoped his aunt was right that the danger was past.

'I told her she must tell her mother. Then we can have a talk together, the three of us, and decide what's best to be done. She said she'll do it this evening.'

'After I've been safely packed off to bed.' The wrinkled face was amused. 'Do you know, David, one of the most irritating things about getting very old is that you are treated as if you are very young . . . and more often than not, by those who haven't been on this earth more than five minutes! Well, I'll forgive her this time but I'd like to be part of any future discussions. That's if she'll allow it, of course.'

'I don't think she's really in a position to object,' David said with a sigh. 'A young girl like Jilly, in the situation she's in, has very little choice. What can she do if her mother turns her out – if *you* turn her out? She won't be able to find a job, nor a home. A home for unmarried mothers would take her in, but only until after the baby's born. And then she'd have to give it up for adoption. She wouldn't be able to keep it.'

'And does she want to keep it?'

David thought of the intensity of Jilly's voice as she'd said, 'It's my baby. Mine and Geoff's. And nobody else is having it.'

'Yes,' he said, 'she wants to keep it.'

'Then perhaps,' his aunt said, stroking Blackie, 'the situation isn't so very difficult after all.'

Chapter Twenty-four

Wilmot leant over the railings along the road on Plymouth Hoe and stared out over the Sound. It was a fine, sunny morning and the sea reflected the blue of the sky. The waves moved in endless small ripples, as though someone had hammered it all over very gently, and the tiny waves were frosted with white. Across the Hamoaze, the green hills and woods of Mount Edgcombe seemed to float like an island seen in a dream.

He had dreamt of this during all the years he had spent in the Japanese camp. Sometimes the dreams had been waking ones, the vision conjured up deliberately. He had lain on his bed of filthy straw, listening to the whine of mosquitoes and the hums and buzzes of countless other unidentified insects, and tried to transport himself through space and time, to his own country, to the place where he had grown up.

He had pictured the Sound – oddly enough, he'd as often conjured up a memory of it on cold, windy days, with the sea like pewter, as on days like this – and thought of days spent here as a small boy, clambering like a monkey on the rocky cliffs, leaping in and out of the pools, running down to the Barbican early in the morning to cadge some fish from the boats that had just come in . . .

All these ideas and many more had drifted through Wilmot's mind as he had lain in the camp so far away, or gone about the work he and his fellow prisoners were forced to do. If he had not had them to cling to, he would not have survived. And sometimes they had come into his night-time dreams as well, the real dreams over which he had no control, and he would believe himself back at home, walking in through the door to find his family complete – Lucy, Geoff, Patsy, Zannah, his mother and father – and just sitting down to their tea. There was a place laid for him too, and they would all leap up and throw their arms about him, and he would take his place, surrounded by the warmth of their love, and know that from now on everything would be all right . . .

The dreams had been so vivid that he could not believe, when he woke, that they hadn't been true. And as he had lain looking at the bamboo walls of his hut and listening to the shouts of the Japanese guards and the groans and grumbles of the other men, his body and heart flooded with disappointment so bitter that he had not known how to bear it.

He had tried not to dream that dream, but it was no good. Every few weeks it came back to torment him, and even in the dream he began to be aware of the disappointment to come, and he would turn to Lucy as he sat down at the table and say, 'It *is* real this time, isn't it? I really am home . . .' And then he would wake and know the bitter truth and the cruel disappointment yet again.

The years in camp had seemed endless. He did not know how he and the other men had endured them. It could only have been the determination of the body to go on living, the seed of life in mind and heart that was intent on keeping itself alive. Otherwise there were times for all of them when they could have just lain down and died. But dying wasn't as easy as that, even when you were suffering the most dreadful privations. Unless you were ill or weakened or beaten to death, you just kept going, even when you knew you didn't want to, even when you were ready to beg to be put out of this grinding misery.

Nobody begged the Japanese, however. The contempt and loathing they felt for their captors would not allow them to give that satisfaction. They kept their pride, even when it was in tatters like the rags they wrapped around their bodies, even when it seemed shredded beyond repair. They never discarded it utterly and it was probably that which saved many of them in the end.

Wilmot straightened up from the railings and walked slowly down towards the Barbican. All things come to an end, and so the war had ended and with it their incarceration. Those prisoners who survived were sent first to Singapore, where they were fed and treated for their various illnesses, and made fit to go home again. And then the dream had come true at last and he had walked along the ruined street and in through the front door and down the passage to the kitchen.

At the door, he had paused for a second, afraid that it was going to be the same thing all over again – the family sitting round the table, the joyful reunion, the vivid reality of it all that caused him to ask for reassurance that this time it really was true, this time it wasn't a dream, and then the slow, cruel awakening . . . He thought of the day the camp had been liberated, the grinning American soldiers, the medical examinations, the journey to Singapore for more examinations and treatment and learning to eat good food again, the long voyage home . . . You couldn't have all those memories in a dream. It had to be real.

All the same, he had felt sick with apprehension as he pushed the door open and saw Lucy there, alone. And then she jumped up and rushed at him, and after that the reunion was all that he had desired, and this time he did not wake up.

So what had gone wrong?

Wilmot was down by Mayflower Steps now, the jetty from which the *Mayflower* was supposed to have set sail for America with the Pilgrim Fathers. The fishing-boats were all about him, tied to bollards and stanchions, their nets draped over the decks and masts to dry, and their crews putting a few more knots in here and there where something had torn a bigger hole. Lobster pots stood about as well, but the fish had all gone, brought in early that morning and sold on the quays. Lucy herself came down here some mornings to buy fish for the dining-room, and at first Wilmot had come with her to carry the baskets. He'd enjoyed the bustle and the noise, but it was a long time now since he'd come. A long time since he'd had anything much to do with the running of the hotel.

He stopped and sat down on a bollard. Nobody took any notice of him. He rubbed his hand over his face, trying to work out what had happened to the joy of coming home, the happiness he'd looked forward to so much, the love, the laughter that had been so much a part of life before the war had torn them all apart.

There was no doubt it was his fault. He had survived the war but he hadn't been able to survive the peace. He'd lived through the tortures of the camp, but he hadn't been able to live with the memories. Until he came home, he hadn't realised the effect they had had on him. It was like losing your voice with a bad cold; you didn't know it was gone until you tried to talk to someone.

Wilmot had not known that his personality had gone. He had not known that the years had brought about a terrible change.

It hadn't taken long to find out. He had been as surprised as Lucy when he had snapped at her over his grey hair, during those first few moments of their reunion. He'd been as disconcerted over his reaction to her mention of age, but maybe it wasn't so surprising. He'd wanted to come home and find everything just as it had been when he'd gone away, before the war. He'd dreamed of it all being the same. The children, all three of them, grown a bit of course, but essentially the same. Lucy, the girl he had left behind, vibrant with energy, her hair vivid with no trace of white. And it hadn't been the same at all. She'd actually drawn his attention to her grey hairs. She'd stressed that they were both older – reminding him at once of the lost years. And then there'd been the children . . .

Geoff, a fourteen-year-old youth, with a voice that was breaking and gravelly. And Patsy in her wheelchair, bringing tears to his eyes. And no Zannah.

He'd known all this, of course, but it had not seemed real to him until that moment, when his dream was shattered. Not as cruelly as in the camp when he'd woken to that other terrible reality, but cruelly enough, for now he had to face what had been happening to others and what was happening now, and his own situation, which had occupied his mind with such concentration for the past four years, was supposed to take second place.

'I know you've had a dreadful time,' Lucy had said to him, 'but it's over now. You're home again. We've just got to get on with living.'

She'd helped him as much as she could. She'd held him and comforted him in the night, when he woke from his new dreams, the nightmares that took him back to camp as vividly and as cruelly as those camp dreams had brought him home. She'd asked him about the camp, had said she wished she could share the misery so that he could be relieved of some of it. And he'd turned on her then, telling her she couldn't share it, wouldn't want to if she could know only a tenth of what it was like . . . He'd told her he wanted to forget it and she'd said they would never talk about it again, but even that hadn't been right for him. He couldn't leave it alone. He had to keep bringing it up, comparing life at home with life in camp, shrugging their wartime experiences aside because his own had been so much worse.

It was as if the torment would never stop. It went on and on, reaching out to him from the Far East, clawing him back into that endless hell, and nothing would blur the memories, nothing except the bottle.

It was a joy, at first, to taste rum again, to take a long drink of beer. A simple joy, nothing more, which brought a warmth and comfort that he could find nowhere else. Seeking that comfort, he drank more. And more. He was not dependent on it, he told himself, he wasn't what Lucy had started to call an alcoholic. He was just taking the only comfort he could find, and why should he not? Wasn't he entitled to it?

By the time it stopped bringing him comfort, it was too late. He could not manage without it. He tried going without, and felt ill and shaky and disoriented. As soon as he took a sip, he felt better. His body needed it. It was as simple as that, and he was angry when Lucy refused to accept this.

She despised him now. He knew that. The love she had once felt for him had turned first to pity and then to disgust. She looked at him now with loathing and if he tried to touch her she flinched away, as if she felt soiled. Deep in the mists of his fuddled mind, he thought that she blamed him for everything – for Patsy's injury, for Zannah's death, for the war itself. If he hadn't brought her to Plymouth, she could have been evacuated somewhere safe; if he hadn't been in the Navy they could have moved out of the city. If, if, if . . .

It was another form of torture.

And this time, it was a torture that wouldn't end. There was no release from this pain, no going home at the end of it – unless you looked on death as home. Sleep would be enough, Wilmot thought, the chance of a long sleep without dreams . . . but how could you know that was what it would be like? Suppose death was filled with dreams, with nightmares you couldn't wake from? He shuddered and drew back from the thought. Having to dream for eternity of that camp, of the hideous things that went on in it, never able to wake again . . .

He got up abruptly, walking quickly onwards. There was

no escape in the end, he knew that, but it was like being in the camp: you had to keep trying. That spark of life inside you, however tiny, however defeated, would always strive to keep afire. Until in the end it was dowsed for ever.

He turned and walked back along the fish-quays past the fishing-boats and the lobster pots. The pubs were opening now and he thought of going into one. It was a long time since he'd had a drink, but the rum he had taken soon after breakfast had tasted sour, and his stomach had heaved against it. He thought of this new development with fresh despair. It had happened several times lately, and with the comfort of the bottle taken from him, what would he have left?

Nothing, he thought, sinking down on to the bollard he had chosen before. He stared down into the narrow channel of black, scummy water between the quay and the nearest fishing-boat. There would be nothing left at all.

Wilmot sank his head into his hands. He felt the tears seep down through his fingers, hot and stinging. The weight of the world's despair settled like an old man of the sea upon his shoulders, and he knew that he would never be rid of it.

If he could only destroy it now. If he could only take it, this huge growth of misery, and cast it into the bottomless pit where he himself was falling, perhaps then he could rid the rest of the world of its clinging fingers, its grey, slimy tentacles. If it were indeed all his fault, perhaps he could after all mend things. Put right the evil that had come about. If he could take this burden with him into nightmare, perhaps the nightmare itself would be easier to endure.

He stood up. He walked to the edge of the quay. The fishermen had all gone into the pubs to have their midday bite – Cornish pasties, a tankard of beer. There was nobody to see what Wilmot did.

He stepped down on to one of the fishing boats and

crossed its deck to the boat that was moored alongside. He crossed three in this way and finally stood on the far deck, looking down into deep, black water.

It looked almost welcoming, almost comfortable, like a satiny cushion that wrapped itself around the hulls of the gently rocking boats. It seemed to beckon him to come, and he knew that there would be no dreams after all, no nightmares, just endless rest; the oblivion of eternal sleep.

He let himself quite gently down into the water. Years ago, Lucy had taught him to swim, and he had told her that if ever his ship sank he would be thousands of miles from land, so swimming wouldn't be much use. In the end, he was close enough to be able to swim to shore quite easily. But he didn't bother.

Chapter Twenty-five

Nobody blamed Lucy for Wilmot's suicide, but she blamed herself.

'I knew how unhappy he was. I knew he was depressed. I could have done more to help.'

'Look at it this way,' Arthur said. 'He was drinking himself to death anyway. This was just quicker.'

His moustache wobbled. His eyes were red-rimmed, but although Maud had always seemed the stronger of the two until now, it seemed that he was the one who had comfort to give. Pragmatic as ever, he gave Lucy a direct glance from beneath sparse eyebrows and said, 'He wasn't ever going to be happy again, no matter what anyone did. The Japs took all that away from him. He tried, and God knows *you* tried – we all did – but he was broken in that camp and if you ask me, we ought to be thankful he'm at peace at last.'

'But to be so unhappy, to take his own life –'

'And would you rather he'd gone on feeling like that for the rest of his natural span?' Arthur asked with a logic that could not be refuted.

'It wasn't all unhappy,' Lucy said. 'There were times when he was like the old Wilmot. That day when we went to Cawsand. He was happy then, laughing, helping Patsy to swim, racing Geoff . . .' Her voice choked a little. 'And he and Patsy had happy times together.' She turned to her daughter, sitting quietly in her wheelchair. 'You did, didn't you? He did have happy times, with you?'

Patsy reached out a hand and laid it on her mother's. 'Yes, of course he did. And with you too. But he did find life very hard, and I think hearing Geoff was missing was just the last straw. He couldn't bear it any more. He felt so guilty over it. He was sure Geoff was dead – or being tortured. He knew what it was like and he couldn't stop thinking about it. It was just too much.' Gently, she squeezed Lucy's hand. 'It was nothing to do with you.'

'And now,' Arthur said, squaring his thin shoulders, 'we just got to get on with things. Same as we've always done.'

Never had Lucy longed so desperately for David. Never had she so badly needed to feel his arm about her, his quiet strength supporting her. But she had written to David months ago and told him that it was all over between them, and even though she was now technically free, she knew that Wilmot's shadow lay between them still. She could not abandon her grief and go to another man.

She was haunted by memories of him as a young sailor, fresh faced and laughing, ringing the doorbell of her parents' house in Portsmouth, leaning his kitbag on the doorstep. He'd hitch-hiked miles to see her, sometimes only able to stay a few hours before he had to set off back to his ship. She heard his cheeky voice teasing her mother, cracking jokes with her brothers. She heard him speaking in a different tone when they were alone together, telling her he loved her.

I don't think I can bear it, she thought. What went wrong? What happened to him? But she knew the answer to that, and it was a bitter knowledge.

Other memories crowded in. Their wedding day, and Wilmot's face as he turned to watch her walk up the aisle towards him. The train journey down to Devon. Their first night in their own home – only a couple of rented rooms, but theirs, with no one to tell them what to do. The pain of their first parting and the joy of his first homecoming.

A sailor's life is all honeymoons, she'd been told. It was true that the reunions were lovely, but that didn't make up for not having Wilmot there all the time. As time went on, she'd known that she would be happy to give up that special joy just to have him home all the time, to be a proper family. Especially when the children were born.

He'd been going to come out of the Navy, she thought. Another year or two, and if it hadn't been for the war he would have been back in civvy street, and he wouldn't have changed, he'd have been the same happy Wilmot, and he'd still be alive today . . .

At other times, she was angry. How could he have done this to her? How *dared* he just take the easy way out, and leave her with this pain? He was nothing but a coward, she raged. He hadn't been able to take it himself so he'd dropped out, and left his pain to be borne by the people he was supposed to love best. Her anger didn't last long, however. Always, she came back to the torture and the hardships he had endured in the camp, and she knew that she had no right to rebuke him, she had no experience of his pain and could not understand its depths and its immensity.

She could only close her eyes and let her own sorrow wash over her, her sorrow and her regret and her sadness at the waste of yet another life through war.

Patsy was the mainstay of the family now. She felt her own sorrow and grief, but she did not share her mother's guilt. She stayed at her desk and welcomed the guests with her usual smile, and looked only a little paler than usual, with her eyes just a little more shadowed.

'Are you going to let David know?' she asked Lucy, just before Wilmot's funeral. 'And Jilly?'

Lucy looked at her. The emotion drained from her face, leaving it stony. 'Why? I don't expect to see either of them again.'

Patsy was aghast. 'But why not? David was Daddy's friend. He's *your* friend. And Jilly –' Nothing had been said about Jilly returning to the hotel. It just hadn't happened. Patsy missed her sadly and wanted her back.

311

'Jilly told me that your father took against her in the last few weeks,' Lucy said. 'He didn't want her about. I suppose she reminded him too much of Geoff. So I don't think—'

'But she ought to *know*,' Patsy said. 'We ought to tell her. And David too. He's been part of the family for so long . . . Shall *I* write to them? Would you like me to do that?'

'Oh, do as you like,' Lucy said, turning away. She heard the coldness in her own voice and hated herself for it, but the thought of those two brought fresh pain and she couldn't stand any more pain. 'I don't want to write to them,' she said tightly. 'I don't even want to think about them. But if you want to, you can.'

Patsy did. She wrote to them both, and received letters back. She wondered at David's not writing to her mother, but her surprise was overshadowed by the news that came in Jilly's letter.

She waited until after her father's funeral to impart it to Lucy, when she decided it could wait no longer, and one evening when she and Lucy were alone together she told her about Jilly's baby.

'It's due in November. It must have happened just before Geoff went away.'

Lucy stared at her. Her face was paper white, her eyes huge and almost black. 'A *baby*? Jilly Penfold says she's expecting our Geoff's *baby*?'

'Well, she's not expecting a tortoise,' Patsy said, and apologised at once. 'I'm sorry, Mum, but you look as if – well, as if it's just not possible.'

'It's not,' Lucy said flatly. 'It's not possible. Our Geoff would never have done such a thing. She must have had another boy, she's blaming it on him. The slut!'

'Mum, don't say such things. Of course she's not putting the blame on him. She never had anyone else, she was crazy about Geoff, you know she was. They wanted to get married.'

'Yes, and she blamed me because they didn't. This is her

312

way of getting back at me. She wants to shame me.' Lucy was beyond reason. The blood had rushed back into her face and she was scarlet now with fury. 'She wants to shame us all, she's just being vindictive. The slut. The hussy. The *trollop*.'

Patsy didn't know what to do. 'Mum, don't talk like that. Jilly's a nice girl, you know she is. She really loved Geoff, and he loved her. They – they were so upset they couldn't get properly married.' She hesitated. 'I think they considered that they *were* married. That time they went off on the bike – I think they took it as their honeymoon.'

'Then they'd no right to. I never heard anything like it. Going off together, pretending they were married. Where did they stay? Tell me that. Nowhere decent, you can take that for granted, no respectable place would have taken in two bits of kids like that and let them share a room. Why, it's disgusting. Disgusting!'

Patsy said nothing. She had never seen her mother so wrought up. It was as if all the sorrow of the past year, all the stress of the years before, had built up like lava in a volcano and was now erupting. She could almost feel the heat of her mother's anger. She knew there was nothing she could do to stem the flow; it would have to burn itself out. If, indeed, it could.

'Anyway, I still don't believe it,' Lucy was saying. 'Geoffrey was properly brought up, he knew right from wrong even if she didn't. He would never have done such a thing, never. I never had any doubts about him, not for a minute.'

'They were in love, Mum,' Patsy said. 'They wanted to be married. And Geoff was going away, they knew they wouldn't see each other again for months, maybe not for two years. They just wanted something to remember.'

'Well, she's certainly got that! But I don't believe it's Geoff's, all the same.'

'Why should she say it is, if it isn't? If it was another boy,

313

she could marry him and give the baby a name. There'd be no point in her saying it was Geoff.'

'Oh, who knows what's going on in that girl's mind?' Lucy said irritably. 'She's in a mess and she's looking for someone to get her out of it, that's all. Obviously the real father won't own up. Perhaps he's already married. She's looking to us to give her a home, that's what she's doing, away from the village so that her friends don't know about her shame. What's she going to do with it, does she say? Give it away for adoption, I suppose. That's how much it matters to her. That's how much Geoff matters.'

'She says she wants to keep it. It's part of her and Geoff.' Patsy held out the letter. 'Read it, Mum. I'm sure she's telling the truth.'

Lucy brushed the letter away. 'Easy to say that now. It'll be a different story when it's born.' Clearly, she was determined to see the worst of the situation and there was nothing that Patsy could say that would change her mind. 'Oh, take it away, do. I've got too many things on my mind to be bothered with a brazen little hussy like that Jilly Penfold.'

Patsy opened her mouth and then closed it again. She turned her wheelchair and took herself out of the living-room, down the passage and into her own bedroom. She sat there for a while, smoothing the letter out on her lap and looking at it, trying to imagine what Jilly must be feeling.

David knew about it, apparently, and so did his aunt and Jilly's mother. They were all standing by her. They hadn't tried to persuade her to give the baby up, and David's aunt had told her there was a home for her in her house for as long as Jilly needed it.

So it wasn't true that she was just looking for somewhere to go, another home, and Patsy felt convinced that she wouldn't change her mind about keeping the baby. Why should she? I wouldn't, Patsy thought, I couldn't ever give up my own baby, and I don't believe Jilly will either.

It'll be my niece, she thought, or my nephew. The only one I'll ever have. She wondered if her mother had thought of it like that, although she knew that Lucy wasn't thinking clearly at all. Too much had happened to her in the past year or so. Too much to be able to take it all in.

Patsy felt as sorry for her mother as she felt for Jilly.

Nothing more was said about Jilly's baby. Maud and Arthur were not told.

'They should know about it,' Patsy said. 'It's Geoff's baby it's their great-grandchild.'

Lucy turned on her. 'Don't call it that! You know I don't believe it. And I told you I didn't want to hear it mentioned in this house again. All this trouble, and you want to bring more. Can't you understand, Patsy, how I feel about it?'

'Yes, I can, but you've got to understand how other people feel too.' Patsy faced her mother bravely. 'It's not just you, you know. It's Jilly as well. She's *having* the baby. And it *is* Geoff's – you know that. How would you have felt if it had happened to you and Dad, if you'd been expecting our Geoff, and Grammy and Grampy had said they didn't want anything to do with you? If Dad had died then? How would you have felt?'

'It didn't happen to me. We didn't give way. We waited. We got decently engaged and then married and we never touched each other that way till our wedding night. And if Jilly had done the same, she wouldn't be in this pickle now.'

'And she and Geoff would never have known what it was like to love each other properly,' Patsy said quietly. 'Geoff would never have known what it was like. He'd have gone to Korea – perhaps to death without ever having made love.'

'*Patsy!* That's *filthy* talk!'

'It's not. It's true. Do you really wish he'd died without ever knowing what it was like?'

'He's not dead! We don't *know* he's dead,' Lucy said

fiercely. 'I don't even *think* about that sort of thing. Neither should you. Why, you're only eighteen years old. And in your position –'

'You mean because I'm never going to know either. Because nobody is ever going to want to marry me, because I'm a cripple.'

'Oh, Patsy –'

'It's what you meant, isn't it?' Patsy said, ignoring her mother's outstretched hands. 'I'm stuck in this wheelchair, so no one is ever going to be interested in me. No one will ever love me or marry me and *I won't ever have any children*.'

Lucy gazed at her. Once again, she reached out, but Patsy shrugged away her hands.

'Have you thought what that means? Do you think that because I'm shackled to this chair for the rest of my life, it means that I'm happy about that? Doesn't it ever occur to you that I might want to be loved? That I might want to be married and have my own children? Hasn't it ever occurred to you to think what it must be like for me? It's like being in a prison. Dad was in a prison, and look what it did to him. And *he* got out! I shall never get out.'

'Oh, Patsy. I'm so sorry.'

'Sorry doesn't help,' Patsy told her brutally. 'You've obviously never thought of it, but I've had a lot of time to think about it. I think about what it would be like to have someone who loved me, someone who put me first before anyone else. And I think about the children.' She raised her eyes and looked full into her mother's face. 'I'm never, ever, going to have children, am I? *Am* I?' And, without waiting for the shock to die from Lucy's face, 'That baby Jilly's going to have is Geoff's. You know it is. It's part of our family. It will be my nephew or niece. The only nephew or niece I'll ever have. *And you won't have anything to do with it*.'

She gripped the wheels of her chair and jerked it

restlessly back and forth. 'What right do you have to decide we're not going to have this baby in the family, Mum? What right do you have to make that decision for Grammy and me, and Pompey Grandma and all the rest? What about Geoff? Suppose he comes back and finds out what you've done? And the baby itself. Don't you think the baby has rights as well?' She stared at her mother with eyes that were huge, as black as ebony in her taut white face. 'And how many people have you got left to love that you can throw away this chance?'

In August of that year the Olympic Games were held in Helsinki. The world was once again playing together, although even the Games could not hide the conflict that still raged so bitterly in Korea, nor the threat of the Mau-Mau terror in Kenya, nor the advance of French troops into Vietnam. All over the world there were still clouds, some no bigger than a man's fist, some already grown to looming shadows. Peace had come, and yet it still seemed as far away as ever.

Lucy threw herself into the work of the hotel. This summer was the busiest yet, and all her vision and hard work was paying off in the number of guests coming through the swing doors. She spent all her waking hours in the office with Patsy, or in the kitchen with the new cook, or simply overseeing the work of the rest of the staff. There were five chambermaids now, several waiters in the dining-room, a porter and two girls helping in the kitchen. There was no machine for washing dishes, nor for washing clothes – sheets, pillowcases and towels went to the laundry, as staff was cheaper and more readily available than machinery – but Lucy had invested in two new vacuum cleaners which were used daily on the new fitted carpets.

Pengelly's had earned its reputation in Plymouth. The dining-room was open to non-residents, at lunchtime as well as in the evening, and local businessmen came here with clients, as well as couples who wanted an evening out. Plymouth was coming back to life and needed somewhere sophisticated. Lucy was aiming high.

Maud and Arthur had decided to retire properly at last. The hotel had changed too much for them; it was no longer their home, and it held too many sad memories. Tired, and wanting a rest in different surroundings, they found a tiny cottage in Newton Ferrers, overlooking the river, and moved into it with their own familiar furniture. The cottage had no garden, but there was a tiny paved courtyard at the front and they filled it with old sinks and chamber-pots full of bright flowers, and hung baskets from the low roof, and Arthur made window-boxes for the wide stone sills. There was just room amongst all this riot of colour for the two deckchairs that Lucy gave them for a housewarming present, and they sat there for hours, watching the life of the river and passing the time of day with their new neighbours.

They seemed to be happy at last, Lucy thought with some wonder, away from the city where they had lived all their lives through all the turmoil of two world wars. She wrote to her own mother in Portsmouth and told her about their new contentment, and Emily wrote back to say she was going to live with Alice. 'I'll be better there,' she said. 'I'm fed up with being on my own. Family's what you want round you when you're getting on.'

Family. But my family's dwindling all the time, Lucy thought, and although she still couldn't bear to believe that Geoffrey was dead, somehow his face refused to come to her mind and she could not imagine him ever being at home again. I've only got Patsy left now, she thought sadly.

Patsy said no more about the baby. She knew that it was useless to keep going over the same ground; if the seeds had been sown, they would either sprout or die. She hoped they would sprout, and in the meantime she kept writing to Jilly and looked forward to the baby's birth.

'I'm coming down to see you then,' she wrote. 'I deserve a holiday and I've saved my wages for the fare. I can manage on the train, so long as someone comes to meet me. I want to see you and I want to see the baby!'

'I'm looking forward to seeing you here,' Jilly wrote back. 'Mum and Mrs Tremaine and Mr Tremaine all say you'll be welcome as the flowers in May. There's a lovely little bedroom here, it's going to be the baby's later on and we're painting it yellow, like sunshine, but you'll sleep in it when you come. It looks out over the orchard and the birds sing so loud in the morning it nearly bursts your eardrums. And there are lambs in the fields now, and next-door donkey's had a foal. Come soon, so I can show you it all.'

Patsy read the letter over and over again, imagining the old house set amongst the fields and woods in that mild, leafy part of Cornwall. She thought of the baby lying in its pram beneath the apple trees, the pattern of leaves against a blue sky making a canopy above its head, the music of the birds and the lambs . . . It would be five or six months old before that could happen, of course, because it was due in November, but what pleasure a six-month-old baby would take in watching the hurrying birds and the dancing lambs. I'll go then, she decided, but I'll go sooner anyway. I'll go when it's born, whatever Mum says.

Jilly's baby might not bear the family name, but Patsy, for one, was determined that it would be a true Pengelly.

Chapter Twenty-six

How many people have you got to love that you can throw away this chance?

The question haunted Lucy day and night. To all outward appearances she was her normal efficient self, perhaps rather more brusque than usual, less glad to suffer fools. Who could blame her for that, though, her friends said to each other, when you thought of all she'd been through? The Plymouth community, the businessmen and women, the city council, the bank, looked on her with growing respect and never dreamed of the torment that kept her awake at night.

The only nephew or niece I'll ever have . . . The only grandchild I'll ever have, Lucy thought. Because Patsy was right, she was never going to have children. There would be no more young Pengellys.

This one would not be a Pengelly either, but it would have been if it hadn't been for me, Lucy told herself. If I'd only listened to those two youngsters, so young but so much in love, if I'd only let them get married, we'd be looking forward now to the next generation. I'd be looking forward to being a grandmother.

Doesn't the baby have any rights? Doesn't it have a right to its own family? Suppose Geoff came back and found out what you'd done?

Patsy's voice had been terse and uncompromising. She'd laid it out in black and white, refusing to accept shades of grey. Lucy had seen it in black and white too, but as if in a photographic negative – where Patsy had seen white, she had seen black. And Patsy had seen things Lucy had not even thought of. She had seen the baby as a person, growing up, a person who had not asked to be born in this way, who had done nothing wrong; a person who needed a family, who needed love. The love that Lucy was denying it.

She felt crushed by the weight of her guilt, and began to understand a little of what Wilmot had been feeling in those last few weeks. Guilt, she thought, was a terrible thing. Especially when you could do nothing to put it right. When you must carry it to your grave.

How many people have you got to love that you can throw away this chance?

Chance. The word, echoing in Lucy's mind for the thousandth time, caught for a moment like a cobweb on a nail and hung there, whispering over and over again. *Chance, chance, chance* . . . Had it been thrown away? Or was it still there, drifting in the breeze, waiting to be caught and held . . .

Did she really have to carry this guilt for the rest of her life?

The baby was not yet born. There was time yet. Surely – *surely* there was time.

Patsy had been down to see Jilly in the summer. She said that the girl was blooming, her skin a smooth golden brown, her hair shining. Pregnancy suited her. She hadn't had a moment's sickness, she had no backache or heartburn, and she carried her burden lightly before her. She seemed to live in two cotton smocks, one bright blue, the other as green as beech-leaves, which she alternated, and she wore scuffed sandals on her feet. As far as Patsy could see, she possessed no other clothes.

'She says she doesn't need them. She'll be back to normal in a few months.'

Lucy said nothing. She hadn't been ready then to comment, but she thought of sending Jilly another smock, or perhaps a dress. She could make her a maternity dress in no time. Although her angry pride was slowly dissolving, some of it still lingered in her heart, however, making it impossible to yield completely.

She couldn't forget it, though. She couldn't forget the baby that was coming, the baby that was a part of Geoff, might even look like Geoff. She could remember Geoff so clearly as a baby, his round head almost bald but shaded with a ginger fuzz. The red hair that had come down through the whole family from her own mother. Would this new little member of the family have it too?

Her thoughts brought her up short. *This new member of the family* . . . I've changed, she thought in wonder, touching the words delicately in her mind. I've never thought of it like that before, but it's right. It feels right.

By October, the anger had all gone, leaving only a huge yearning to see her grandchild and to make friends again with the girl her son had loved. Patsy was right, she thought. This was her grandchild, the only grandchild she was ever going to have. There had never been any real doubt of that in her heart, she had just rejected the idea of Geoff and Jilly making love before they were married. But it was natural, wasn't it? Of course he had wanted to love Jilly properly before leaving her for two long years. That was why they'd wanted to be married.

You couldn't stop young love, nor hot blood. It had happened to plenty of young people during the war. Lucy had known some of them, boys and girls she had been at school with, who had 'anticipated marriage' as it was called, and had found themselves 'in trouble'. Some had been lucky enough to get married but others, like Jilly, had found themselves with a baby that had no father. Some of those fathers hadn't even been British. They'd been Polish or Canadian or American. Some had been black.

She thought of Patsy's question: did she really want Geoff to die without ever knowing the pleasure of making love? And she looked into her heart, honestly, without prejudice, and knew that the answer was no. I hope they were happy, she thought. I hope they felt really married, and close. I hope it was good for them, the little that they had.

It was as she thought this, that Lucy knew she must go to Cornwall and see Jilly, the mother of the only grandchild she would ever have.

Bodmin Moor was bleak and treeless, but as the train ran into the lusher part of the county Lucy saw trees that were clothed in gold and brown, glowing like amber against the robin's-egg blue of the sky. From some parts of the track you could see both north and south coasts – the broad sweep of Widemouth Bay, with Bude at its heart to the north, leading down to the rocky inlets of Perranporth and Polzeath; the craggy coves of Mevagissey and the steep cliffs of Minack to the south. The Cornish peninsula narrowed the further west you went, and its character seemed to change with every turn of the track, yet in the centre it could be curiously dull and without feature other than the brown moors and the gaunt fingers of disused mine-workings.

It took two changes on to tiny branch lines before Lucy was able to alight finally at the nearest station to old Mrs Tremaine's house. For the first time, as she stood on the platform holding her small suitcase, she wondered what she would do if David himself were there. It had not occurred to her until this moment that he might be. She felt suddenly nervous. I should have let them know I was coming, she thought. I should have telegraphed ahead. But she hadn't wanted to do that, nor to telephone. She'd wanted to arrive unannounced, so that she could see for herself Jilly's reaction to her, and know what her own was.

The house was about a mile from the station, along a lane bordered on one side by a high, Cornish bank with a hedge on top, and on the other dropping away into a steep, tree-filled valley. Somewhere far below Lucy could hear the rippling of a stream. Some of the trees had begun to turn colour, the sprawling, hand-like leaves of the horse chest-nuts now tawny, the oaks a soft brown, the copper beeches a dramatic splash of deep purple and the common beeches spattered with green and rusty gold like a treasure trove long buried and now come to light. The leaves that had already fallen formed an amber carpet on the floor of the valley, lit by the dappling sunshine that flickered down through the gently shimmering leaves.

It was a warm afternoon. There was only the slightest whisper of a breeze amongst the branches. A few birds flew silently amongst the branches and a squirrel startled Lucy by suddenly running across the lane in front of her and straight up the grey, elephant-leg trunk of the nearest beech where it sat on a branch chattering furiously. It was as auburn as the leaves that sheltered it, with tufts of red hair on the tips of its ears, and Lucy gazed at it enchanted.

The road had begun to descend now and soon she came to a small stone bridge under which ran the little river that had carved this steep, narrow valley. Lucy paused for a moment, resting her case on the low parapet, and looked down into the clear water. A few small fish darted amongst the weeds and she saw a small, long-tailed bird, yellow as a canary, flirting its wings on a rock in the middle of the stream, and then caught her breath as a kingfisher darted away from her, a jewelled flash of red and blue, brilliant as a diamond in the sun.

Slowly, Lucy walked on. No vehicle had passed her since she had left the little railway station, no person had walked along the road. The peace of the narrow lane, the deep woods, the glittering stream, was having a strange effect on her heart. It was as if a tight knot, tied years ago, perhaps as long ago as the beginning of the war when Wilmot had first gone away, was beginning to loosen. I didn't even know it was there, she thought in some surprise, and even laid her hand on her breast as if to feel it.

The stream now ran beside the road, tumbling in a deep, narrow cutting. In spring, there would be primroses along its banks and bluebells carpeting the woods like a glimpse of the distant sea. And the starry snowflake flowers of wild garlic, and the royal glow of purple violets.

I've lived in cities all my life, she thought, and wondered why. Perhaps it was time to make a change. A small hotel somewhere in the country, surrounded by woods and meadows, where people could come to ease the pain in their heart . . . The changing colours of the leaves, the soft rustle of the breeze, the singing of the birds . . .

It wouldn't always be like that, of course. There would be days of rain and wind, cold, dismal days when nobody wanted to set foot outside; days when she would light fires indoors, big log fires with comfortable chairs set around them and lamps on low tables casting a warm, cosy glow . . .

She had arrived at a house. A long, low-roofed house, washed with white, standing back from the road with a garden of flowers before it and a little gate set in the hedge. She stopped, gazing at it a little uncertainly, and then caught a glimpse of the orchard that lay to one side. Hardly an orchard, really, no more than a few apple trees scattered on a rough lawn, but Lucy was more interested in what stood beneath the trees.

A pram. An old pram, high-wheeled, with its shade up and a bit of old net curtain stretched across to keep off cats and birds.

It can't be, Lucy thought, but she had her hand on the gate and it swung open beneath her touch. Scarcely knowing what she was doing, her heart suddenly thumping in her breast, she took a step or two up the path . . . and then another and another, until she was on the rough grass, under the trees, until she was standing beside the pram, looking down in wonder, gazing at a tiny, still-crumpled face, at a round head, almost bald, but just fuzzed over with hair that was already faintly ginger . . .

Geoff. It was Geoff, all over again.

She did not know how long she stood there before she heard a door open and knew that someone was walking across the grass towards her. She turned, still in a haze of wonder, and felt almost no surprise at all to see that it was David. I'm dreaming, she thought, the whole thing is a dream: the walk from the station, the trees and the squirrel and the kingfisher, and now this, a baby that's Geoffrey all over again – and David. It must be a dream.

She watched him cross the grass. Something had happened to him: his one arm was caught up against his chest in a sling. He was thinner than she remembered and looked gaunt, as if he had been ill. Or was just getting older and sadder. But his smile was as warm as ever, and his eyes as tender.

'Lucy.' His voice held the same sense of wonder. 'Lucy, what are you doing here? How did you know?'

'How did I know? Know what?' She glanced at the pram and remembered suddenly. '*Oh!* It wasn't due till November! I hadn't even thought – David, is everything all right? The baby – Jilly – this *is* Jilly's baby, isn't it?' Of course it is, she thought wildly, no other baby could look so much like Geoff. 'David?'

He was laughing. 'Yes, it's Jilly's baby. Your grandson. Born yesterday. The nurse said it was too soon to bring a baby outside, but Jilly insisted, she said this was too good a day to miss. I rather think she was right.' He looked at Lucy. 'We sent you a telegram this morning,' he said. 'I walked down to the village post office and did it myself, but you couldn't possibly have got here so soon.'

'I left early. I – I wanted to see her before the baby came.' Lucy met his eyes steadily. 'I wanted her to know that I was coming to see *her*. To make it all up. I was ashamed, you see. I've been behaving so badly.' Her eyes filled with tears and she gazed at him helplessly. 'Oh David. I don't know what's been the matter with me . . .'

'Lucy, Lucy.' He couldn't touch her. She wondered how he managed, with no hand or arm to use, and felt a sudden spurt of anxiety, but he was still speaking and she couldn't interrupt him to ask. 'Lucy, you've had a horrible time. It's been so hard for you. All these years – and then so much happening, so suddenly. Nobody can blame you for what you've felt.'

'But I've been so unkind,' she wept. 'So unkind to poor Jilly. She'd lost Geoff too, and they wanted so much to be married, and I wouldn't agree . . . And now this poor baby, this lovely little baby . . .'

'I know. I know.' He made an impatient sound. 'God, I wish I could just *hold* you! Put your arms round me, Lucy. Rest against me. It's all right, you won't hurt me . . . Oh, *Lucy* . . .' His voice softened, a whisper so low and deep that it could have been the sighing of the morning breeze. 'If you knew how I've longed for this.'

'I know. I do know. I've longed for it too.' She raised her head from the warmth of his chest and looked up into his eyes. 'I wanted to write to you, but I couldn't. I couldn't make it happen.'

'Sometimes we have to wait for things to happen in their own time. I wanted to write to you, too, but I knew, somehow, that one day you would come.' He glanced down into the pram. 'And what better day could it have been? We couldn't have arranged this, Lucy.'

They stood quietly together under the apple tree. Beside them, the baby snuffled and whispered in his sleep. Lucy breathed in the scent of David's body, savoured the warmth and the strength of him. But he was thin, she thought, and he'd been hurt . . . 'What happened to your arm?'

He laughed. 'A stupid accident. I fell out of one of the

apple trees. I was going back to London the next day, but I had to stay on. I can't do a lot for myself, you see, and my mother insisted. And Mrs Penfold's been a marvel.' He looked at Lucy. 'Jilly, too. I've got to know her pretty well during the past few months and especially this last fortnight. She's a good girl, Lucy.'

'I know. I know she is.'

'What made you come?' he asked after a moment. 'To make it up with her, I know that. But what changed your mind?'

'Patsy. She talked to me like a Dutch uncle.' Lucy smiled ruefully. 'She pointed a great many things out to me, but two or three things especially stuck in my mind. One was that the baby had its own rights, it was part of the family whether I liked it or not, and it wasn't for me to deny it. And another was that this is the only grandchild I'll ever have.' She looked down into the pram and touched a crumpled cheek with one fingertip. 'I've lost so much, David. Zannah, Geoff, Wilmot. You. I can't lose this little one as well.'

He said nothing for a few minutes. They stood close, looking into the pram. Lucy kept her arm around his waist and he stood firm and solid against her body. Then, at last, he spoke and his voice was deep and quiet and sure.

'There are just two things wrong with that, Lucy. One is that you haven't lost me. You never did. I've always been here, waiting. And the other is that this doesn't have to be the only grandchild you'll ever have. There could be others.'

Lucy stared at him. 'Others? I don't understand. Patsy can never –'

'I don't mean Patsy,' he said. 'But you're not too old to have other children, Lucy. If you wanted them. Are you?'

'I suppose not. I'm forty-two. Women do have babies in their forties, but –' She stared at him and he smiled, and his thin face was alight with love.

'Lucy, I'm asking you to marry me. If you could bring yourself to take on an old crock like me, with only one arm and even that one not much use just at present. But everything else is present and in working order.' He grinned suddenly and for a moment she was reminded of Wilmot, the old Wilmot, with his cheeky grin and wicked jokes. And then the memory faded as abruptly as it had come. This was David. *David* . . . 'We can start life again, together. And there can be a new family, if that's what you would like. A new chance for us all.'

A new chance. A new family. A new life. She let the thoughts drift in her mind, circling together like sunbeams in a gleam of light, cutting through the shadows of the past. And to begin it all, this baby that lay beside them, a tiny bridge between the two lives.

Chapter Twenty-seven

The wedding was planned to take place at Christmas. David's injured arm and shoulder would be mended by then – 'I've got to have *one* arm to hold my wife with,' he said with a grin – and their families would have time to prepare. And not only their families. There was a great deal for Lucy to do as well, and David must go back to London and sell his home there, ready to move down to Plymouth.

Lucy seemed to spend half her time travelling down to Cornwall now, and had bought a small car in which to make the journey. Although it was early November, the weather was still mild and they sat in the orchard for hours, discussing their future and making plans.

'Do you want to take on a hotel as well as a wife?' Lucy asked him, a little diffidently. 'It's hard work. I'm on the go from morning till night.'

David considered. 'I want us to do whatever suits us both,' he said. 'I don't believe in unnecessary sacrifices. I don't know a thing about running hotels, but I can still do my own work. I've been asked to do more books, and they can be written anywhere. If you want to keep it going, I don't see why it shouldn't work. But I don't want you slaving from dawn till dusk, and we don't need the money – I can keep us both. What do you think about it?'

'I'm not sure,' she confessed. 'Sometimes – when I come down here to your aunt's cottage, and it's all so peaceful and tranquil – I think that this is all I could possibly want. Somewhere in the country, surrounded by trees and birdsong. But I wonder if I would get bored, with nothing much to do. I've always had such a busy life, David.'

'And don't you think you'll be busy now?' he said, gently teasing her. 'I intend to be a very demanding husband, you know. And there'll be all those children too . . .'

Children. Lucy's heart gave a tiny lurch. She had never told David about the baby she had wanted so badly after Wilmot had come home. She had never dared raise the subject again after the day at Cawsand, and she'd been thankful later that no baby had been conceived. Now, she thought about starting a fresh family, and wondered if it were really possible.

'David . . . do you really want . . . I mean, I'd love to have your baby – your babies – but I'm forty-two, and you're forty-nine. I've got grown-up children . . .' She caught her breath. 'A grown-up daughter, anyway,' she amended sadly. 'And a grandson.'

'So what lucky children they'll be,' he said. 'And what a shame to deprive any of them of each other.'

Lucy laughed. 'David, you're ridiculous! But would you really like us to have children?' She thought of Stevie and caught at his hand. 'Oh, I'm sorry. Of course you would. And I'd like to give them to you. I *want* to give them to you.'

'And I want to give them to you,' he said quietly. 'A family is something to share. And it would change things for us both. We'd have to think very seriously about the hotel, and even about staying in Plymouth. It's still such a mess – there's so much rebuilding yet to do – and I'd like to bring children up in the country. Somewhere like this place, where they can grow up in peaceful surroundings.' He hesitated, then added, 'Perhaps it's not something we should plan anyway. Suppose we just leave it to chance? Or to God's will if you like to think of it that way.'

'Yes,' she said softly, 'yes I think I do.'

They were sitting quietly, hand in hand, when Jilly came

out of the house. Her slender figure had rounded into maturity since baby William's birth, and her face had a new serenity, though there was still a deep sadness in her cornflower eyes. She had just finished feeding the baby, and she laid him in Lucy's lap, where he gazed up at the drifting leaves, golden and tan against the milky blue sky, and blew small, pearly bubbles.

'He really is like his daddy,' Lucy said, looking down at him with tenderness. She touched his silky, auburn hair with one fingertip, scarcely able to believe that she could ever have refused to acknowledge that he was her grandson. He shifted his gaze from the leaves and looked into her face, and her eyes misted. Geoff, she thought, Geoff, where are you? What happened to you, out there in Korea?

Nothing had ever been heard about him. It was eight months since they had heard he was missing, and the presumption of death meant only that his body had not been found. Sometimes men who had been presumed dead did turn up, usually in a prisoner-of-war camp, but it was very rare. As the months went by, nobody really expected to see Geoff again.

Nobody, that is, except Jilly, who refused to lose hope.

'I wish his daddy could see him,' Jilly said, crouching beside the deckchair. 'I mean, I know he will one day, but I wish he could see him *now*. It's such a shame he's missing so much.'

'His own father missed him as a baby,' Lucy said, remembering Wilmot's first long absence, when Geoffrey had been born. 'But at least I could send photographs. I went to the studios twice and he took some lovely portraits of Geoff lying on a rug, and me holding him. And my uncle Jim took some snaps too. We didn't have a camera of our own, of course, not many people did then.'

Jilly didn't have a camera either, but Geoff had had one and left it with her when he went away. She had taken several films of the baby already, but she had no one to send them to.

'I'm putting them all in an album,' she said. 'Geoff'll want to see them when he comes back.'

Lucy sighed. In a way, it was good to see the girl so certain. You could see she wasn't going to forget Geoff, that she'd truly loved him and still did, that if things had been different she would have been a good wife to him and made him happy. But it was cruel, the heartbreak that she must suffer in the end when she was forced to admit that her baby's father was never coming back. And she'd have to face it eventually, Lucy thought. You couldn't go on living on hope for ever, not when it was false hope.

'That's a good idea,' she said gently. 'You'll value it yourself in later years. I often wish I could have had photos of the children when they were little. Especially Zannah.' She sighed. There was only one picture of Zannah, sitting on Wilmot's knee in a studio portrait of the whole family. It had been taken just before he went away the last time.

'It must have been terrible for you, losing your little girl,' Jilly said. 'I can't imagine anything worse than losing your child.'

'There isn't anything worse. And you never really get over it. You just learn to put the feeling away somewhere in your mind. Like an oyster with a pearl, I suppose, except that it never turns into anything beautiful like a pearl, and it always hurts just as much if you take it out again.'

'Perhaps oysters don't think pearls are beautiful,' Jilly said, and Lucy laughed.

'Perhaps not.' She paused for a moment. 'Jilly, what are you going to do? Will you stay here with your mother?'

'I don't know. I've been thinking about it. I'll need to work, to earn money for us both. I wondered . . . I wondered if I could come back to the hotel.'

'The hotel?' Lucy was startled. 'Back to Plymouth? Would you really want to do that, Jilly?' She thought of the conversation she had had with David, their agreement that children would be better brought up in the country, away from the rubble and turmoil of a slowly recovering Plymouth. 'It would be lovely to have you there,' she added quickly, and looked down at the baby again. Having him there in the hotel, growing up under her eyes, a new life, another Geoff . . . 'But you don't have to come back to work. Just live with us, if that's what you want.'

Jilly shook her head. 'No. That wouldn't be right. I couldn't be a burden on you. We've got to earn our living, pay our way.'

'You wouldn't be a burden. It's the least I can do.' Lucy paused again, surprised by the feeling that had welled up inside her. 'Jilly, if it hadn't been for me you wouldn't have to worry about money, about earning a living, you'd have a pension from the Army, you'd have money for the baby. I owe it to you –'

'No. No, you don't owe it to me. It was our choice that we did what we did, Geoff and me. We wanted to be married so we pretended we were. And now it's my responsibility – until Geoff comes back.' She looked at Lucy, and Lucy saw the fear glimmer in the depths of her eyes, the fear that Geoff never would come back. She's beginning to realise it, Lucy thought, she's beginning to realise it and she's afraid to take it in, she's afraid of the awful grief she'd have to bear.

And in the same moment, she realised that there was more than one way in which she could offer support to the girl. Money was not the only thing she had to give.

'You can come to us any time you like,' she said, gently. 'You can come and work, if that's what you want, or you can just come and live with us. We're your family now, Jilly.' She turned to the man at her side, who had remained silent and watchful during all their conversation. 'David and Patsy and me – and you and William. That's right, isn't it, David?'

He nodded, and she felt an overwhelming gratitude, for they had not discussed this, hadn't taken Jilly's plans into account when making their own, and she knew that they might yet be called upon to make sacrifices. But did that matter, when they had all they wanted anyway? Almost all, she amended, thinking with a pang of her lost son. Even so, they could afford to be generous.

And if Jilly were right, and Geoff did come back . . . well, then there would be nothing more to ask, nothing in the whole of the world.

After that last mild weekend in early November, winter came crashing upon them. Back in London, David wrote that he was having some difficulty in selling the house he had bought. At the same time, he was packing up his belongings – not many, since he had lost almost everything he had owned in the house that had been bombed, and had gathered only a few sticks of furniture since. His arm was still troubling him a little, so progress was slow, but he was determined to be ready for their wedding, a week before Christmas.

Lucy was in the hotel, still trying to decide what to do about Jilly. She wanted to help the girl, and she longed to have her little grandson with her, but she dared not hold out hopes for a future that might never be realised. Suppose she and David decided after all to sell the hotel – what would Jilly do then? And what about Patsy? She couldn't be abandoned. There was so much to consider.

In the end, she asked Patsy for her own opinion and, as usual, Patsy came up with her own brand of pragmatic commonsense.

'I don't know why you worry so much about things, Mum. It's simple. You and David go and live in the country and let me and Jilly run the hotel.'

Lucy stared at her. 'What?'

'We're perfectly capable of it,' Patsy said patiently. 'I do all the accounts as it is, and Jilly knows about the housekeeping side and the cooking. We'd make a good team. And you could go off and live your own life. It's about time you did, after all.'

'But the hotel's been my life,' Lucy said, bemused.

'Then it's time it wasn't. Look, Mum, you've built it up from an ordinary little guest house to what it is now. You've done a wonderful job. But you never really intended to run a hotel, did you – not when you first married Dad?'

'Well, no, not really. I was going to be an ordinary naval wife, bringing up a family – that's all I really wanted. And then when he left the Navy I suppose he'd have found some other job and I'd have gone with him, wherever that was. But the war changed all that, and afterwards the opportunities were there –'

'And you took them. And now you've got another opportunity to live your life whichever way you want. You're getting married again. You can start fresh. A *new* life – not the remains of the old one.' Patsy leaned forwards and gripped Lucy's hand. 'It's a chance for you, Mum – and it's a chance for me too.'

'For *you*?'

'Yes. Don't you see – I don't want to be dependent on you all my life, just because I'm in a wheelchair. If I could walk, I'd be earning my own living, making my own life.' Her voice grew lower. 'I'd be getting married, having my own children. Well, maybe I can't do those things, but I can still earn my living. I'm doing that now, aren't I?'

'Yes. Yes, you are. But –'

'No buts, Mum. I could run this place. All I need is a pair of legs – and that'd be no problem if Jilly could be here. She could run all the practical side with one hand tied behind her back.'

'But she's so young,' Lucy said helplessly. 'And she's got a baby.'

'I don't think anyone's young these days,' Patsy said. 'We

all had to grow up fast during the war. And women grew up faster than anyone else.' She looked at her mother and said seriously, 'Think about it, Mum. I'd love to run this hotel myself, and I'd like Jilly to help me. It's a chance for all of us.'

Put simply, like that, it seemed the obvious solution. Yet Lucy could not quite bring herself to accept it. She thought about it, wrote to David and, when he came to Plymouth again, discussed it with him endlessly.

'Patsy's so keen, I can hardly bear to refuse her, but I just can't believe they could manage. There's such a lot to managing a hotel and Jilly's hardly more than a child. And she's got her own baby to look after. I don't know what to do, David.'

'You don't have to do anything,' he said. 'You can leave things just as they are. Or you can invite Jilly to Plymouth and let her work with you and Patsy. Let them take a lot of the work off your shoulders, and see how they manage. And just wait.'

'Wait? What for?'

'Something will happen,' he said, smiling at her. 'Something always does. Life doesn't stand still, Lucy, my darling. Something will happen, one day, to show you what to do, and I have a feeling it will be something good.'

Lucy looked at him and saw the darkness in his eyes, the love and the tenderness that shone in their depths. A baby, she thought, with a quickening of her heart. Our baby. Yes, that would tell me what to do.

Preparations for the wedding went ahead. The hotel needed some redecoration – with new paints and wallpapers coming on to the market almost daily, Lucy wanted to give the foyer a smart new look. Most of her family were coming from Portsmouth and she wanted to make a good impression.

'I need a good costume as well,' she said to Patsy. 'I

thought perhaps something in blue. It's always been my colour.'

'Yes.' Patsy looked at her mother. Her hair, once the flaming bronze of autumn leaves, had softened to a warm, burnished copper, with just a few silver hairs like streaks of sunshine. Her figure was as slender as ever, and she still bore herself tall and proud. Her skin, translucent as bone china, glowed with her new happiness; she looked as if a lamp had been lit somewhere within.

'You'll look beautiful in blue,' Patsy said. 'A good strong blue, not too light but not dark either. A sort of delphinium colour.'

They went shopping for it together, Lucy pushing Patsy's wheelchair into the big new Dingle's and Spooner's stores, where they could reach every department by lift. They wandered for hours, gazing at the new products that were coming into the shops now, looking at glassware and china as well as clothes, and by the time they emerged Lucy was dazed.

'I can't believe I've spent so much money on myself.'

'It'll be well worth it. You look lovely in that suit.' They had found a costume in exactly the shade of blue that suited Lucy best, a delphinium just as Patsy had suggested. It brought out the deep violet of her eyes, and deepened the auburn tone of her hair. They had found a small confection of a hat that matched it, and Lucy had picked black patent shoes and bag. And Patsy had not been forgotten. For her, there was a warm winter dress in gold and deep brown, with a full skirt that would drape sumptuously across her legs in her chair.

'You'll be my bridesmaid,' Lucy said, pushing the chair back along the newly built Royal Parade, so different from the old streets of Plymouth. 'You'll follow me up the aisle.'

'We'll have to think who's going to push me, then,' Patsy remarked, and then giggled. 'A fine pair David and I are going to look – him with one arm and me with no legs! People will think you're starting a nursing home.'

'Patsy! What a thing to say.' But Lucy laughed too. Then her face grew sad. 'Who do you think I should have to give me away? There's only Grampy, or my brother Kenny. If Geoff had been here . . .'

They moved along the wide pavement in silence, each thinking of Geoff. It was over eight months now since he had been posted *missing, presumed dead*, and there had been no further news. His personal belongings would be returned soon, and they all knew there was little hope of his turning up. Only Jilly clung fiercely to her belief that he was still alive somewhere, and nobody had the heart to try to persuade her otherwise. She would accept it in her own time, and you couldn't hurry such sadness along.

'Patsy, sometimes I feel so guilty,' Lucy said suddenly. 'Being so happy, planning to get married again, when we don't even know what happened to him. It seems so callous, so *cold*.'

'I know.' One of the nice things about Patsy was that she never told you not to be silly, or that you were worrying unnecessarily. 'It's all happened so quickly, hasn't it? Geoff going away, and then the bad news. Jilly and the baby. And then you and David. I'm not surprised it makes you feel strange, it makes me positively dizzy at times. But I don't think you need to feel guilty, Mum. Geoff would have been thrilled about you and David. You know how much he always thought of him.'

'Yes.' He looked on him like a father, Lucy thought, more than he ever looked on Wilmot. Poor Wilmot. How different it would have been for him if there had been no war. He would have grown into a fine man, even-tempered and good-humoured.

'If Geoff does come back,' Patsy went on quietly, 'he'll be glad to see you and David married.'

'I know. I know he would. But – oh, Patsy –' Lucy's

voice broke – 'do you realise, he wouldn't even know his father's dead? We'd have to tell him all that. It's almost too awful to think about.'

A cloud drifted across the sun. The brightness of the day seemed suddenly dimmed, and the clothes they had bought no longer exciting. Lucy pushed Patsy's chair the rest of the way home in silence, glad that her daughter could not see her face. At last they came to Lockyer Street and she paused at the foot of the ramp.

'I am doing the right thing, aren't I, Patsy? It seems so soon after Geoff – and your father . . .'

Patsy turned her head to look up into her mother's face. Her lips were smiling but her voice was grave as she said, 'Of course you're doing the right thing, Mum. You've loved David for a long time. You deserve your happiness. And no one would begrudge you that for an instant.' She paused. 'Life has to go on, you know, and there's no law to say you can't be happy more than once.'

As she spoke, the sun came out again from behind its cloud and shone down on her, illuminating her smile and gleaming on her bright, coppery hair. Lucy gazed at her, wondering why it was that this daughter, who had been so badly treated by life, had so much wisdom in her heart. And then she smiled back.

'Let's go indoors,' she said, 'and try on these gorgeous clothes again.'

Everything was arranged. The repainting and papering was complete, and the hotel looked bright and inviting once more. Lucy's new costume hung in her wardrobe and she opened the door a dozen times a day to gaze at it. She felt like a young bride again, and even more so when David took her into the best jeweller's shop in Plymouth and bought her an engagement ring.

'David! I hadn't even thought about it.'

'I had, though.' He slipped the sparkling diamond on to

her finger and kissed her lips. 'We're only going to do this once,' he said, 'and I want to do it all properly. My darling Lucy.'

'Oh, David.' Her lips trembled under his. It can't be happening like this, she thought, dazed, we're two middle-aged people, we can't be feeling as if we were just eighteen . . . But that was exactly how she did feel. The love and happiness bubbled up inside her, as it had over twenty years ago, and it felt just the same. Perhaps it always did.

They bought a wedding-ring too, but David kept this and she suspected that he looked at it as often as she looked at her diamond. She wished there were something she could give him, and eventually settled on a new watch. He tried it on and she admired it before taking it away again.

'You can have it the day before the wedding, so that you can wear it then.'

The day was close now. All the arrangements were made for the family in Portsmouth to come by train, and Jilly was back at the hotel and taking over the cooking once more. No more had been said about her and Patsy managing the hotel, but Lucy knew that the idea had not gone away, and she found herself considering it more and more seriously.

She took Jilly shopping as well, and they bought a blue dress, a shade or two lighter than Lucy's, which set off her dark hair and exactly matched her cornflower eyes. 'You can walk behind me up the aisle,' she said. 'I want you and Patsy both there. You're a daughter to me now.'

On the last afternoon, she closed the door of the hotel behind her and walked up to the Hoe alone. David was staying in a neighbouring hotel – it was unlucky, Maud had said firmly, for the groom to see the bride on the night before the wedding – and Lucy glanced about her cautiously as she walked up the street, afraid that he too might be walking on the Hoe. But there were few people about on this cold, murky December day, and she pushed her hands deep into her coat pockets and stepped out briskly, feeling the sting of icy air on her cheeks.

How much had happened since she had first come here, she mused, leaning over the rails to look at the little rock pools and the big half-moon swimming-bath. Young and eagerly in love, it had seemed that nothing could mar the happiness she and Wilmot had shared. For a moment, she felt sad again, but then she reminded herself of Patsy's words. Life had to go on – and there was no law to say you couldn't be happy more than once. Whatever Wilmot had suffered, it was over now and he was at peace. Lucy's task was to go on living, to go forward and to enjoy the happiness she had been granted anew.

She gazed down at the pools. The big pool was closed for the winter and empty, ready to receive its annual spring-clean. The others were filled with green sea-water. In summer they were alive with boys and young men, showing off their swimming and diving prowess. Geoff himself had learned to swim down there. Now, they too were deserted.

Lucy felt the tears sting her eyes and for a moment she seemed to see the figures of her husband and son diving into the pools, racing each other, laughing and teasing . . . And then the vision faded and she knew that the cries she heard were those of seagulls, and the figures she saw were nothing but spray. The boy and the man had gone for ever.

Goodbye, Wilmot my dear, she thought, and then she turned away and began to walk back along the wide expanse of the Hoe.

It was fast growing dark. Only a few hurrying figures were visible now in the chilly dusk. She passed them without a glance, and then one in particular caught her eye. There was something familiar about the gait, something about the build and the set of the shoulders that she knew. Something she had always known.

Lucy stopped and stood rigidly still. Her heart felt as if it had ceased to beat.

342

'No,' she whispered. 'No, it can't be . . .' Her mind went back, almost frantically, to the vision she had thought she saw down there on the rocks a moment or two before. The boy and the man, lost and gone for ever. And yet here they were before her, the two merged into one striding figure, one man who approached and then saw her and hesitated, just as she was hesitating, and then came on faster, finally breaking into a run and calling her name.

'Mum! *Mum!*'

'Geoff . . .' Lucy breathed, and her hands fluttered to her throat. 'Oh, *Geoff* . . .'

There was barely time to tell all, and they went to bed at last exhausted by the telling. It was almost too much for Geoffrey to take in. His father dead – his own son born – his mother on the verge of marriage . . . He shook his head, bemused, and didn't know whether to laugh or cry.

They needed to know his story too. How he had been captured and sent to a prisoner of war camp, had escaped almost as soon as he had arrived, and spent months hiding in the bleak Korean countryside before stumbling into a friendly village where he was cared for until he could be handed over to the Americans. He had been repatriated immediately, with no time to let his family know. It was clear that it would take weeks, perhaps months, to tell them, and perhaps they would never know it all.

'The good thing is, I've been invalided out of the Army,' he said, holding Jilly's hands tightly. 'Or will be, soon. I'll be staying at home. So I can take over here, Mum, if you want a rest.'

'Take over?' Lucy blinked. Once again, events were running away with her. She looked at him, suddenly afraid, wondering if he would have the same problems as his father. The pattern was frighteningly similar.

However, when everyone else had gone to bed, she crept into Patsy's room to see if there was anything her daughter

343

needed, and Patsy dispelled her fears. 'It's a wonderful idea, Mum. Geoff knows what it is to run a hotel, and Jilly will be a marvellous help. And I'm happy to carry on doing what I've been doing. It's the answer to everything.'

'Is it? I hope so, Patsy – but I wonder. Your father never got over what happened to him. Suppose Geoff –'

'Geoff's different,' Patsy said firmly. 'He wasn't kept prisoner for years and beaten and tortured. He never lost control of his life – he kept it. He escaped and survived. He came back. And besides –' she grinned wickedly '– he's your son too, don't forget. He's just as bloody obstinate!'

'*Patsy.*' But Lucy was relieved by her daughter's words and she went to bed feeling comforted. Perhaps, after all, everything was turning out for the best. And the main thing was that Geoff was home again, safe and sound, and there would be another wedding in the family, just as soon as it could be arranged.

It was only as she drifted off to sleep that she realised that nobody had told David that Geoff was home.

After the chilly dampness of the day before, it came as a surprise to find the sun shining next morning. The sky was clear, the pale, milky blue of winter, and the air fresh and crisp. Everything seemed to be washed clean, and when Lucy looked out of her window towards Dartmoor she could see the tiny hilltop church of Brentor in the distance, like a finger pointing hopefully towards the sky.

The wedding was to be at eleven. There was good time to serve breakfast to all the family and guests, and then everyone vanished to their rooms to get ready, while the hotel staff rushed to prepare the dining-room so that they too could attend the service.

Flowers weren't easy to come by in December, but there were early daffodils from the Scilly Isles to brighten the dining-room, and hot-house roses for Lucy and the girls to carry. By some miracle, Geoff's uniform had been cleaned and pressed overnight and, when the cars arrived to take them all to church, he took his place beside his mother and they were the last to leave the hotel.

'I'm so glad you arrived when you did,' Lucy said, taking his hand. 'I did so much want you to be here, to give me away . . . Are you sure you don't mind, about me and David?'

'It's been a lot to take in,' he admitted, and she was instantly anxious.

'Should we have waited? Should we have postponed it?'

'*No.*' He squeezed her fingers. 'Don't jump at me, Mum! I was going to say, it's been a lot to take in – hearing about Dad, and seeing William. It'll take me a while to get used to it all. But as for you marrying David – no, that seems absolutely right. After all, he was always part of the family, wasn't he?'

'Yes,' Lucy said. 'Always.'

The taxi drew up outside the church. Inside, they could hear the notes of the organ. They walked into the porch and were met by Jilly, pushing Patsy in her wheelchair, and the priest who came forward smiling.

'Mr Tremaine's here and waiting as anxiously as a young bridegroom,' he murmured, and gave Lucy a broad smile. 'You look very, very nice, Mrs Pengelly.'

Mrs Pengelly. It was the last time she would be called that. When she walked through this door again, she would be Mrs Tremaine, married to the man she loved, and looking forward all over again to a life of new hope.

Geoff stepped beside her and she rested her arm in his and turned to smile at him. David still doesn't know, she thought. He still doesn't know that the boy he treated as a son, the boy whose life he once saved, has been brought back to us. And then the organ began its joyous pealing and they moved forward together, into the body of the church and up the aisle.

David stood before the altar. As the notes of the organ

changed, he turned towards them. He saw Geoff, and Lucy recognised the amazement, the incredulity and, finally, the sheer joy that illuminated his face. And then she could see nothing through her tears except the blaze of heartfelt love in his eyes, as he held out his hand towards her. And she knew that she could, at last, walk with confidence into the world of love and laughter.

THREE LITTLE SHIPS

To all the men and women who were
involved in the great rescue of Dunkirk
and who have given the world a name for the
heights to which human determination and courage can rise.
And to the Association of Dunkirk Little Ships
which, by cherishing these historic vessels,
gives that name tangible form.

Acknowledgements

In researching and writing *Three Little Ships* I am indebted to a number of sources and would like to thank them all equally.

For the original idea: my agent Caroline Sheldon, who listened to a talk I gave about my 'war' books and said that she thought I ought to write one solely about Dunkirk.

For detailed information about the Little Ships, two specific books: *The Ships That Saved An Army* by Russell Plummer (Patrick Stephens Ltd) – a comprehensive record of the 1300 'Little Ships' of Dunkirk – and *The Little Ships of Dunkirk* by Christian Brann (Collectors' Books Ltd) – the stories and pictures of more than 120 vessels which are members of the Association of Little Ships of Dunkirk. These two books helped me to commemorate in my own very small way this brave and wonderful story.

The nine days of Dunkirk were chaotic and it was difficult to disentangle the events of each day to form a cohesive story. I could not have done this without two other books: *Dunkirk* by David Divine DSM (Faber & Faber Ltd) – a careful yet vivid description written by a man who was himself at Dunkirk, commanding the Auxiliary Bermudian yawl *Little Ann* which was lost after running aground on 1 June – and the invaluable Naval Staff History *The Evacuation From Dunkirk* – again telling the story day by day, with the addition of maps, Admiralty signals sent during the time and an analysis of the troops lifted from both beaches and harbour. For more background information and atmosphere, I also referred time and again to *Nine Days' Wonder* by John Masefield (Wm Heinemann Ltd), *The Miracle of Dunkirk* by Walter Lord (The Viking Press,

New York) and *Dunkirk: The Incredible Escape* by Norman Gelb (Michael Joseph).

For information on Army terminology, Naval procedures, how to sail a boat along the south coast, and sundry other bits and pieces, I am fortunate in having a circle of knowledgeable friends who were kind enough to read the relevant chapters and tell me where I had gone wrong. David Farrant MBE, Alan Johnson, Malcolm [name] and Gordon ('Jack') Kemp were all extremely helpful.

However, the burden of my gratitude goes to the Little Ships themselves and to the Association which keeps alive their proud tradition, and to the owners who maintain them with such love and pride. I would like to thank all those who welcomed me aboard their historic vessels during the annual rally at Royal Victoria Dock in May 2004. Raymond Baxter OBE, co-founder and now Hon. Admiral of the Association, and David Knight, the Association's Commodore, were so kind and helpful on that day, and later took on the onerous task of reading the completed manuscript in order to give me their valuable comments.

The museum at Ramsgate is well worth a visit. It has an excellent Dunkirk display, including the Little Ship *Sundowner* which, together with her former owner Charles Lightoller, has a fascinating history. Dover too is rich in Dunkirk exhibits, and a visit to Dover Castle, to see the 'Dynamo' room where the whole operation was masterminded, cannot be missed.

Even with all this help, I can have told only a tiny fraction of the great story that was Dunkirk. With the best will in the world, I feel that I cannot have done full justice to this incredible episode, in which truth was stranger and more dramatic than fiction ever could be. However, I have done my best to recreate some of the atmosphere and the turmoil of those nine days of history with, I hope, as few mistakes as possible, and with all the profound respect due to those who actually took part.

My characters and their three little ships are fictional, but almost all of the other ships mentioned are authentic and, as far as I could ascertain, were in those places on those dates. Many of them can still be seen – the London fireboat *Massey Shaw*, for instance, which continued in honourable service until 1971, appears frequently at public functions and *My Queen* (model for the *Countess Wear*) is still working at Starcross in Devon. The smallest of all, the rowing-boat

Tamzine, is on display at the Imperial War Museum in London. Most others are now in private ownership – some based in quite exotic locations – and the best chance of seeing them is at one of their rallies or at their five-yearly commemorative crossing of the Channel.

May 2005 sees the sixty-fifth anniversary of Dunkirk, and the Little Ships will once again be making their crossing. I hope very much to be there to see them, and to marvel yet again at the miracle of determination and valour that was Dunkirk.

Prologue

May 1940

E ngland was under threat.
Adolf Hitler's army was on the march throughout Europe. Belgium was on the point of capitulation; France was crumbling. The British Army itself had been driven into retreat. Half a million men were crowding into one port; half a million men needed rescue.

From deep within the white cliffs of Dover, the call had gone out for ships – little ships, to take the men off the beaches of France and ferry them to the larger ships waiting offshore. All and any vessels were urgently needed, along with the men to go with them: holiday-steamers, motor yachts and cabin cruisers; stately Thames sailing barges and family dinghies; forty-year-old cutters and brand new cabin cruisers; paddle-steamers and rowing-boats

Eventually, a fleet assembled, such as had never been seen before, and each ship shared a single mission. They were heading across the Channel towards France; towards a single port and its outlying beaches.

Not even Hitler himself could break the spirit of those who took these little ships and sailed them on this most desperate of missions. A spirit that would go down in history and be conjured up for ever by one word; the name of that one French port.

Dunkirk.

Amongst the convoy there were three little ships in particular, each one skippered by a man who hoped to rescue one special soldier and bring him home.

I

Olly Mears, in the London fireboat *Surrey Queen* had promised his wife Effie that he would do his best to bring back their son Joe. Robby Endacott, in charge of the Devon holiday-steamer *Countess Wear*, had promised his mother Hetty that he would try to find his brother Jan. And Charles Stainbank, in the little motor yacht *Wagtail*, had promised his wife Sheila that he would bring her brother Alex home to safety.

Out of half a million men, the possibility of bringing back that one particular man was remote, but Olly, Charles and Robby would keep that promise in mind all through the terror and violence of what was to come; and each would realise the futility of promises made during times of war.

Yet their spirit would endure. And such a spirit – the 'Dunkirk spirit' – can, sometimes, perform miracles . . .

PART ONE

Chapter One

Wednesday, 29 May 1940

LONDON: *Surrey Queen*

'I dunno for sure what it's all about,' Olly Mears said to his wife Effie, in the living room of their terraced house not far from St Paul's Cathedral. 'The bloke what come on board told me a tale about taking kiddies round the coast on evacuation, like we did back last September.' He frowned and shook his grey head. 'I tell you what it seems like to me, though. It seems like they're getting ready for the invasion.'

'Invasion?' Effie was busy at the breadboard, cutting a loaf into thick slices and slapping a wodge of corned beef and a spoonful of pickle between them. She paused, the big breadknife held in one hand and the other clutching the loaf against her bosom, and stared at him. 'You really think so, Oll?'

'Well, summat's up, ain't it? I mean to say, Eff, the news ain't good, is it? Now the Belgians have surrendered, they reckon the Germans are pouring through France. Gawd knows what's happening to our boys over there, but I reckon the Government's at its wits' end with it all. They just dunno what to do next, so they're getting the youngsters out of it, fast as they can.'

Effie put the loaf down on the table. Her face was white. 'But – our Joe. What's going to happen to our Joe, if things over there are as bad as you say?'

She sat down as if her legs had given way under her and Olly came quickly round the table and put his hands on her shoulders. Their eyes went to the framed family photographs on the mantelpiece: the studio portrait they'd had done once, when all the

5

children were little, and then the more recent ones: Dot and Carrie, their daughters, sitting on the railings at Ramsgate and laughing, during that last holiday they'd had just before the war, and Joe, their only son, smiling and looking smart in his Army uniform just before he went away.

Joe Mears had been somewhere in Belgium or France for five months now. He'd joined up almost as soon as the war had started and, apart from a brief leave at Christmas, had been away ever since. Effie, who had lost a brother and a cousin during the Great War of 1914–18, lived every day in terror that he might never come back, and lay awake at night praying that God would send him home safe.

'Joe'll be all right,' Olly said comfortingly, praying in his own heart that it was true. 'I mean, if the worst comes to the worst, they'll bring 'em home, won't they? Don't you worry about our Joe, Eff.'

Effie wiped her eyes with the corner of her pinafore and nodded. Worrying didn't help anyone, especially when there was work to be done. She put her hand up to her husband's and squeezed it for a moment, then got to her feet again and resumed making sandwiches.

'What d'you think'll happen if there is an invasion?' she asked. 'Will they get this far? London's not that near the coast, whichever way you looks at it. They've got to come all the way up from Dover or wherever they land, and they'd never get up the Thames. We've got plenty of soldiers here still, haven't we, and there's the RAF as well. The Jerries'd have a fight on their hands if they tried.' She looked at the breadknife in her hand, as if imagining herself tackling a German soldier with it, and Olly grinned.

'They'd have a fight if they came here, that's for sure! Londoners don't take kindly to being invaded. But you can see why they want to get the youngsters out of the way, all the same.'

'Yes, but that's another thing.' Effie wrapped the sandwiches in greaseproof paper and packed them into his lunch-tin. 'We haven't heard nothing round here about kiddies being evacuated again. There's any amount of them came home at Christmas and stopped here, what with there being no bombs after all. Nobody's said a word to me in the caff about them being sent off again. Drink that tea while it's hot, love.'

Olly lifted the big enamel mug to his lips and sucked the strong brew through his bristly moustache. He was a large man, his thick dark hair greying now that he was past forty-five, but he was still as powerful as he'd been in his twenties. Working on a London fireboat kept you tough, he always said, taking the big boat up and down the river, ready to answer all sorts of 'shouts'. Why, he'd lost count of the times he'd battled with fires raging in dockside warehouses stocked with inflammable materials like sugar, alcohol or paint, ready to explode any minute and send huge fountains of flame into the sky, to descend on everything within range and start a dozen more fires if you weren't careful. But the *Surrey Queen* was equal to jobs like that – they were what she had been built for. You could send sprays of water 100 feet or more from her deck to douse the flames. That meant handling a hose like a giant live snake, ready to turn on you if you didn't keep it under control, and all the time the fire threatened the boat itself as well as the docks. It was no job for namby-pambies, that was for certain.

'Well, we'll just have to follow orders and see. It'll make a bit of a day out for me and the lads, taking a lot of boys and girls for a joyride,' he said with a grin. 'So long as they behaves theirselves. You know what boys are like; holy terrors they are – run riot once they get excited. I don't want no accidents on the boat.'

Effie raised her face for a kiss. 'I reckon it'll be the mess you'll be worrying about. I know what you're like about that boat – keep it more spick and span than I do this house. You'll be on tenterhooks the whole time in case they get the brightwork covered in fingerprints.'

'I'll keep 'em in order, don't fret.' He planted a smacker on her lips. 'I took our Joe out often enough with his mates when they were nippers. I just talks to 'em like a Dutch uncle to start with and they're as good as gold. If they're not, I tells 'em I'll turn the hoses on 'em!'

'You'll be careful, just the same,' she said to Olly as he went to the front door. 'You've made me think, with all this talk about an invasion. I wouldn't be at all surprised if there isn't more to it than meets the eye.'

'Why, what could there be?' Olly asked easily, and swung his canvas knapsack on to his shoulder. 'They're not going to ask us to take 'em to America, are they! Anyway, can't stand here nattering about it. I'll be late for duty at this rate.' He stepped out of the front door, then turned back and gave his wife another kiss. 'Cheerio,

Effie, love,' he said in a voice that was suddenly gruff. 'You take care of yourself, too. And don't you worry about me. We don't even know as this trip's going to be happening. We've only been told to get ourselves ready for it – get in stores and that sort of thing.'

He strode off up the street, leaving Effie staring after him, her strong, square face creased in a puzzled frown. She pushed back her hair, still showing only a few silver hairs amongst the black, and pursed her lips. It hadn't been at all like Olly to go off like that. Usually all she got was one kiss and a cheery 'see you later, love'. It was almost as if he wasn't expecting to be back soon – as if he knew more than he'd let on.

I wonder if it's the King and Queen, she thought suddenly. Olly had come home one day and told her that the two main fireboats, *Massey Shaw* and *Surrey Queen*, had been earmarked to take the Royal Family upriver to Windsor if ever it was necessary. 'What they think, see, is that the roads might be blocked if there's a lot of bombing,' he'd explained. 'They can't block the Thames though, and anyone can see they'd be better off at Windsor Castle than stuck right in the middle of London in Buckingham Palace.'

So far, there had been no bombing and London seemed as safe as anywhere else. It was the coastline, especially around East Anglia and all along the south of England, that seemed more vulnerable just now. Everyone was waiting for Hitler to invade, and although the news from France and Belgium was heavily censored, it sounded very much as if the Germans were getting closer all the time. Every morning now, when Effie woke up, she felt a twinge of dread as she parted the curtains and looked out, half-expecting to see German tanks parked in the street below.

This sudden order for the *Surrey Queen* to take on stores and prepare for passengers seemed ominous. Something big was going to happen, but whether it was a new evacuation of children to the countryside, the movement of the Royal Family to a safer place, or something quite different, she didn't know. Olly didn't know either, or he would have told her – but she could see in his grey eyes that he had the same suspicions as she did. You only got half the story these days.

As she stood there wondering, two figures appeared round the corner; her daughters Dot and Carrie, coming home from work. Carrie, tall and big-boned like her father, worked in a fish shop and

Effie sometimes thought that Bert Hollins, the widowed fishmonger, was sweet on her. She wouldn't have minded that – he was a good *catch*, Olly had said once with a grin at his own wit – but he was at least twenty years older than her. Effie would rather she got herself a boy nearer her own age, but Carrie didn't seem inclined to do that.

Effie felt happier about her other daughter. Small, with a rosy face and dark, curly hair like her mum's, Dot was going steady with Benny Foster from two streets away. There'd even been talk of their getting engaged on Dot's birthday in June, but Benny was over in France now and it didn't look as if he'd be home in time. Dot didn't even know exactly where he was, even though Olly had pinned a big map on the wall of the back room and the family studied it every day, trying to figure out from the news on the wireless where his unit might be. These days, the Authorities told you nothing, that was the trouble.

'What's going on?' Dot asked when she came near enough. 'I saw our Dad marching off up the street as if the wolves were after him. Been called out on a shout, has he?'

'He hasn't, that's the funny thing about it.' They went into the house together, down the dark, narrow passage past the front room to the back room and kitchen where the family spent most of its time. 'He says they've been detailed off to help with this new evacuation. You heard anything about it, either of you?'

'Not a thing. What evacuation?' Carrie shrugged off her cardigan as her mother explained. 'Well, I suppose it's not surprising they've decided it's time all those kids went back to the country. There's a lot of people getting really worried about an invasion.' Her face was solemn and she spoke in a lowered voice. 'You know that Mrs Jennings, from Somers Road? Well, she's talking about gassing herself and the kids, if it happens! And I don't reckon she's the only one, neither.'

Effie stared at her. 'That's awful! It's murder.'

'She says it'd be better for them all to be dead before the Germans gets here, rather than wait for them to come and do it. At least they'd all be together. I don't suppose she'd actually do it, mind.' Carrie balled her hands into fists and screwed up her face. 'I certainly wouldn't. I'd sooner stand up to 'em. I wish old Hitler'd come here himself – I'd give him short shrift.'

Dot laughed. 'I bet you would, too! I reckon we ought to send you

9

over to deal with him. One look at you in one of your paddies and he'd be gone like a shot.'

The kettle came to the boil and Effie put a couple of well-heaped spoons of tea into the brown teapot and poured on the water. 'But why use the fireboats to do the evacuation?' she asked aloud. 'Why not use the trains? Suppose there's a fire in the warehouses along the docks – who'll be there to put it out?' She went outside for the milk, which was kept in the meat-safe in the back yard, and came back holding the bottle. 'I tell you what it seems like to me. It seems like there's something else going on, something that only the Authorities know about and ordinary people like us aren't being told.'

'Perhaps they need the trains for troops,' Dot said doubtfully, sinking into her father's armchair.

Carrie shook her head. 'Nearly all the troops are in France and Belgium, like our Joe and your Benny. I didn't think there were all that many left in England now.'

Effie glanced at her and wondered if her daughters had heard any talk about the situation in France. Perhaps, like most people, they hadn't yet realised what was happening. Perhaps they didn't believe that anything that bad *could* happen to the British Army.

I won't say anything to them yet, she decided. There's no point in upsetting them before we know it's true. But as she stood staring at the crumbs left on the breadboard from Olly's sandwiches, she felt the familiar terror chill her heart at the thought of the danger her son must be facing at this very moment.

Goodness knows, she chided herself, I ought to be used to living with danger, what with Olly being skipper of a Thames fireboat – but she'd never wanted Joe to follow in his footsteps and she'd never in all her days wanted him to be a soldier. He was a clever boy, good at his books, and the master at school had told her he could go far. Shipbuilding, that was what he'd been keen on – not just building them but actually designing them, thinking up new shapes and styles. She and Olly had been pleased as Punch when he'd got that apprenticeship at Tough's Boatyard, and he'd not long finished it when the war started. He could have had a good job there – a real career, old Mr Tough had told him – but the minute Mr Chamberlain made that announcement on Sunday morning, 3 September, telling the country they were at war with Germany, nothing would do but Joe had to enlist. He'd been gone before the week was out, and although he'd managed to get home at Christmas that was the only time they'd seen him since.

Now he was somewhere in France with the British Expeditionary Force, and boys like him were getting killed every day. And then Olly was off on this strange job in the fireboat, taking kiddies round the coast. It didn't make sense. None of it did.

As he marched through the streets to Blackfriars, where the *Surrey Queen* was moored, Olly was almost as bewildered as his wife. The evacuation story didn't ring true at all. The preparations that were being made added up to far more than transporting a few boys and girls down the Thames and maybe up the East Anglian coast. For one thing, the crew had been told they would need a compass.

'A compass!' Olly had repeated, staring at the Naval Petty Officer who had come aboard to deliver their instructions. 'What do we need one o' them for? The only time this ship's ever been to sea was when she come from the boatyard where she was built, on the Isle of Wight. We don't need a compass for the river! And I reckon I can find me way round the coast to Norfolk all right.'

'You'll need one on this trip,' the PO said. He was a man nearing forty, with a weatherbeaten face and eyes narrowed by years at sea, and he spoke in a blunt, abrupt voice as if he wasn't used to people arguing with him. He handed over a sheet of paper. 'That's what you'll need, so anything you haven't got, you'd better stock up on right away. And look nippy about it. You'll need to be ready to go sharpish.'

Olly was still thinking about this as he jumped down to the deck. His mate Chalky White had gone off to the chandler's with a couple of the lads to get the compass and other items from the list. And all those stores – how long were they expected to be away, for God's sake? Did they have to feed the youngsters as well? How many were they expected to carry? He shook his head in mystification and then looked up as another voice hailed him.

'Skipper Mears?'

'That's me.' Olly eyed the man who was standing just above him, hands on hips. He'd seen him about the dock – a short, stocky fellow in his fifties, bald as a coot but with broad shoulders and looking as strong as an ox. 'You're a stevie, aincher? Work on the loading and unloading.'

'That's right. And now I'm working with you.' He jumped down on to the deck. *With* you, Olly noted, not *for* you. 'Me and a few of the other blokes have been detailed to come with you. We've all done boatwork, so you don't need to worry we're a lot of landlubbers. We can work the hoses too. We know what we're doing.'

'That's all very well,' Olly said, still bewildered, 'but we're supposed to be loading up with nippers. What do we need extra hands for? What you going to do, organise games on deck or summat?'

The man laughed. 'Don't tell me you're falling for that tale! Doncher know what's going on? Doncher know what all these boats are being requisitioned for?'

Olly looked at the busy river. For the past day and a half, boats had been coming downriver. Pleasure boats, the sort he and Effie might go on for a Sunday-afternoon jaunt up to Hampton Court. Passenger-steamers that might be used as ferries. He and the other men aboard the fireboat had watched them, wondering what was up, until they'd been told that they too might have to join the convoy, on their trip with the children.

Now, he realised that there were even more boats coming down the Thames, and they weren't just pleasure-steamers either. Headed by Thames tugs, they were a motley crowd of motor yachts, small lifeboats and even dinghies. They were being towed in clusters, and the men in them were looking straight ahead, their jaws set as if they were setting off on some desperate and dangerous mission.

'What in the name of Gawd is all that about?' Olly asked in a low voice. He turned back to the man who had just come aboard his ship. He remembered his name now – Stan Miller. An old Navy man, if Olly remembered right, the sort who knew all the gossip. 'Tell me.'

Stan Miller took him by his arm and ducked behind the canvas dodger that was all the protection the steersman had from the weather. He jerked his head for Olly to bend closer, as if he were afraid of being overheard.

'They're going to France,' he said in a half-whisper. 'You must've heard what's going on there. The Jerries have got our boys trapped. The Navy's brought a load back from Boulogne and Calais but the Jerries have moved in there, so now they're working out of a port further north. Place called Dunkirk. And there just ain't enough

Naval ships to do the job. They needs passenger boats as well to get 'em away. They've requisitioned all these boats, and they're asking for volunteers to take 'em over. And the *Surrey Queen*'s going too.'

'But we're a fireboat,' Olly objected. 'Why should they want us to go?'

Stan crinkled his face. 'Doncher reckon there'll be fires there as well, then? Course there will! Sure as God made little chickens, those bloody Jerries ain't going to sit there and let us take off all our boys without a fight. There'll be ships on fire, docks, and Gawd knows what, apart from bombs dropping and machine-guns going off in all directions. It ain't going to be no picnic, believe me.'

'So *that's* why we need a compass.'

'And extra stores,' Stan nodded. 'And the grey paint and all the rest of it. We might be over there for a while, Skip.' He stuck out a big hand with fingers the size of sausages. 'So here I am. Ready, willing and able, as they say. And there'll be a few other blokes along soon. Reckon you'll be needing all the help you can get.'

Olly nodded and turned to look at the few instruments a London fireboat needed for fighting fires along the banks of the Thames. The steering wheel, the telegraph, to communicate with the engine-room. There was little else – not even a place for the compass they had been instructed to buy.

'Bloody hell!' he exclaimed. 'The compass! *Surrey Queen*'s a steel ship – it'll play merry hell with the settings. It won't be much flaming use to us if it doesn't even show us the right direction!' He glanced anxiously along the quay. There was still no sign of Chalky and Jack Hodge and the other blokes. And now that he knew where they might be heading, a sense of urgency was beginning to grip him.

'France!' he muttered. 'My Joe's over there. He could be waiting now – stuck on one of them beaches, with Jerries and machine-guns on every side.' He paced the deck to the bow of the *Surrey Queen* and stared down the Thames, wishing that he could set off at this very moment. And he thought of Effie, praying every night that her son might come home safe.

Chapter Two

Robby Endacott was on board HMS *Wenlock* in Devonport when he was told to report to the First Lieutenant. Surprised and uneasy, he made his way over the ship, still littered with remnants of the recent repairs, rapped on the open door and waited to be summoned in through the heavy curtain.

The 'Jimmy' was seated behind his desk in the tiny cabin. The bulkhead above the desk was festooned with notices about the running of the ship, interspersed with cartoons cut from newspapers and magazines, and a few discreet pin-ups. Robby was surprised that a man of his age – coming up to thirty-five probably, almost fifteen years older than himself – would still be interested in pin-ups, but then even the Jimmy was a sailor. And looked it too, with his neat beard and moustache, and bright blue eyes beneath bushy eyebrows.

'Able Seaman Endacott?' he said, and Robby nodded. The First Lieutenant looked down at a sheet of paper on his desk. 'I've got a signal here – special job on. Buffer thinks you're the man for it.'

Robby blinked in surprise. Anyone as lowly as himself wouldn't normally be given jobs by the exalted First Lieutenant, the man next in command to the captain. The only sorts of special job he might do would be handed out by the 'Buffer' or a Chief. He said nothing and waited.

The Jimmy looked up and met Robby's eyes. He had a very intense stare but Robby didn't look away. After a moment, the officer nodded. 'I think he's right. Now listen carefully. There's been a signal come through about the men in France. Army men – the BEF.'

'Yes, sir,' Robby said, feeling that some answer was expected yet not knowing what to say. Rumours about the BEF had been circulating for some days now. Everyone knew that they were having a bad time in France, let down by the Belgians and fighting the Germans almost on their own. But apart from last Sunday being called a National Day of Prayer for them and for the war in general, there'd been no real news. He wondered with a sudden lurch of his heart if this might be about his brother Jan, an infantryman in the 7th Cornwalls – but how could it be? The First Lieutenant had said something about a 'special job'.

The officer's voice was now very serious. 'It's a bad situation, Endacott. Holland has gone down, the Belgians have capitulated, the enemy are advancing and the long and the short of it is that the whole of the Army is trapped, more or less on the beaches. They're outnumbered, outflanked and outrun.' He paused. 'It's our job to get them off and bring them back home.'

Robby stared at him. '*Our* job, sir? You mean the Navy?'

'Well, I don't mean just you and me! How else would we get them home, man, other than by sea? And who else is there to do that but us?' His expression changed a little. 'Well, as it happens there *are* others, and this is where you come in.' He jabbed his finger at a chart on his desk. It showed the south coast of England, from Land's End to Dover. 'You're a West Country man, aren't you? Know the area well? Know the waters?'

'Yes, sir. I was born in a village near Totnes, up the river from Dartmouth. I used to do a lot of sailing there and round the coast to Salcombe, that sort of thing. Only dinghy sailing – a friend of mine had an old boat and we used to explore all the creeks. But I don't see—'

The First Lieutenant broke in. 'There are a couple of passenger-steamers there. Not very big. Take people on pleasure trips up and down the river, Totnes to Dartmouth. Know them?'

'Yes, sir. The *Berry Pomeroy* and the *Countess Wear*. I've been on them both plenty of times. My mate worked aboard the *Countess* – I used to help out, when I was on leave from *Vincent*.'

The First Lieutenant nodded as if he knew all this already. 'Right. And that's what we want you to do now. You'll report to

Totnes at nine this evening and make the *Countess Wear* ready for sea. Then you'll take her down the river and along the coast to Dover. The *Berry Pomeroy* will be under command of her own skipper – I dare say you know him too. From Dover, you'll proceed to Dunkirk, and you'll ferry as many men as you can from the beach to the destroyers that will be waiting offshore. *As many men as you can, and for as long as it takes.* Understood?'

Robby stared at him. 'But why, sir? Can't *Wenlock* go? Why do you need little boats like the *Countess*? I don't suppose she's ever even been to sea before. If there'll be destroyers there—'

There was a touch of impatience in the First Lieutenant's voice. 'Because the men will be on the beach, of course. *Think* about it, Endacott. Of course *Wenlock* will be going – half the repairs haven't been done, but we can put to sea and that's the main thing. However, we can't get in close enough for a man to climb aboard. They need boats with a shallow draft, no more than three feet, to get that close to the beaches. And a low gunwhale too. These aren't seamen, Endacott, they're soldiers. They probably can't even swim. And they're weighed down with equipment, if they haven't already lost half of it.'

He pointed to a map of France which looked no more than a page torn from a school atlas. 'See, this is where they're making for now – Dunkirk. They've been pushed through the country and on to the beach, and now they've got nowhere else to go. There are thousands of them there, up to their bloody necks in water.' He turned back to Robby. 'This evacuation started last Sunday. There've been ships going across the Channel for the past three days, but now Calais and Boulogne are both out of action. There's only one port left that we can use, and that's Dunkirk. And Dunkirk's getting hell bombed out of it. The port's almost unusable and the troops are on the beaches. As I said, there are thousands of them – far too many for the ships available. We've got to take all the other craft we can find – boats that can get into the beaches.'

The Jimmy came back to his desk and planted both hands, palm down, on its cluttered surface. When he spoke, his voice was low and intense. 'If we don't get our soldiers back, Endacott, this war will be over before it's even properly begun, and the invasion everyone's so worried about will happen. Hitler will just walk in and take over. Those men are the only Army we've got and we need them, to carry on the fight.' He straightened. 'It's up to us. It's up to the Royal Navy, and that means you and me, and little ships like the *Countess Wear*. Now do you understand?'

Robby swallowed. He tried to imagine the whole of the British Army, including his own brother, massed on a French beach, waiting for rescue while the German army fired on them from the shore. He imagined himself taking the *Countess Wear* – a boat more accustomed to taking holidaymakers on pleasure trips down the safe, beautiful reaches of the River Dart – round the coast and across the Channel to rescue them.

'You'll be under fire,' the officer said quietly. 'And the boat will be under your command. Now do you have any questions?'

There was a challenge in his eyes. Robby knew that he was not expected to question the order at all. It was just that – an order. He was expected to carry it out to the very best of his ability. This was what the Navy had trained him for.

'No sir,' he said. 'No questions.'

Like many sailors, Robby had trained at HMS *St Vincent* in Gosport. He had signed on at fifteen, agreeing to serve for twelve years after he turned eighteen, and made the journey from Totnes to Gosport filled with excitement and trepidation. Devon men were traditionally sailors, but there had been none in his family since his grandfather, who had told many a yarn to the boy as he sat before the cottage door in the sun, or by the fire in the tiny, low-ceilinged kitchen. In his day, the Royal Navy had been entering into the age of steam as well as sail, and the old man liked especially to tell tales of his days aboard HMS *Warrior* – the first ironclad warship, built in 1861, with old Jan Endacott proud to be one of the first boy seamen to climb aboard up her steep sides and stand on the enormous deck. 'Huge, she were,' he'd say, shaking his head reminiscently. 'Huge. You could fit Berry Pomeroy Castle on her deck, and that's no exaggeration.'

Robby, sitting at his feet, would beg him to tell his stories over and over again. 'What was it like to go to sea in her, Grandad? How big were the engines? Did they use the sails as well? Did you have to climb the masts? Did people ever fall overboard?' He had heard the answers time and time again, but there was always the chance that the old man would recall something new, and each time the story was told it would grow a little in the telling.

'Climb the masts!' the old man exclaimed. 'Why, we were up and down the rigging twenty times a day. More, sometimes. And of course we used the sails – you wouldn't waste coal, not when there were a decent wind blowing. Steam were just to get us in and out of harbour, and put on power in battle. Not that the *Warrior* ever did fire a shot in anger,' he added. 'Only in commission twenty year. She were a broadside firer, see – had to turn sideways to let off all her guns, and that were too cumbersome as ships got faster, so she went out of use. But we had a good few years on her, all the same. Beautiful ship, she were. Beautiful.'

He puffed his pipe for a moment or two and when he spoke again, his voice was sober. 'And men fell overboard all the time, specially when they came off the masts. You were supposed to go careful up there, see, walking on the broadarm, but lads that did it every day, they'd get cocky and strut about as if they was down on deck. You only had to put one foot wrong, and you were a goner. Fall on deck and you'd smash like a wooden toy. Fall overboard and you'd smash just the same – it were the height, see – and by the time the ship went about and lowered a boat to row back for you, you'd have gone anyway.' He took the pipe from his mouth and gazed at it. 'I remember one lad fell off the mast just when Cap'n Cochrane – Cocky, we called him between ourselves – were greeting a young officer, come aboard for the first time. He were just at the top of the gangplank when poor Freddy took his tumble, hit the deck head first and spattered his brains all over the young bloke's shoes. I was standing nearby, and believe me or believe me not, neither one of 'em spoke a word for a minute. They just looked at the mess and looked at what was left of Fred, and then the Cap'n saluted and said, "Welcome aboard HMS *Warrior*", calm as you like. You had to be like that, see. Wartime discipline, had to follow it all the time. Same as today.' He gave Robby a straight look. 'Mind you, they sold off all his goods and chattels amongst the crew and sent the money to his mum, and when they asked for volunteers to go to his funeral a third of the ship's company went. Nearly three hundred men! I tell you this, boy, when we sung the hymns the church roof lifted three foot in the air.'

Robby listened, entranced. He knew all about the hardships of life in training as a boy seaman and at sea, but the more he heard the more he longed to follow his grandfather into the Navy. He spent all his spare time on the banks of the River Dart in Totnes, and made friends with a boy called Danny who had an old sailing dinghy. Together, they went off for days at a time, exploring the reaches of the river and camping on its banks. They called at all the villages in their little creeks – Stoke Gabriel, Dittisham, Greenaway – and went as far as Dartmouth, even out to sea. By the time they left school at fourteen, they considered themselves experienced sailors.

'I'm getting a job on the pleasure-steamers,' Danny told him as they walked out of the school gates for the last time. 'I'm going to work on the engines. They'm looking for another boy too – why don't you come?'

Robby shook his head. 'I'm going into the Navy. I'll be fifteen in September – I can join then. I suppose I'll help Dad round the farm for the summer.'

'You could work on the boat.' Danny urged. 'I bet they'd take you on. It's only for a few months, as the boat's laid up in winter. They can get someone else next year.'

It sounded a good idea and Robby agreed. The two boys were allowed a week's holiday, and then they started. By the time he joined *St Vincent*, Robby could handle the *Countess* as well as the grizzled seaman who ran her to Dartmouth and back twice a day, and he marched through the gates of the barracks in Gosport with something of a swagger.

The original *St Vincent* had been a ship moored off the Gosport side of Portsmouth Harbour and the name had been transferred to the old site of the Fortune Hospital when it had ceased to be used as a Marine barracks. It had in its time also been used as a French prisoner-of-war camp, and legends of hauntings and ghosts were used to frighten the new recruits. Robby, who had been brought up on tales of Dartmoor and was determined not to be cowed, however brutal his treatment, shrugged them away. The Ghost of Gunnery Park, he said, was only the Commander's pet donkey which grazed there. He'd heard just the same fearsome braying many times at home, where a pair of donkeys were kept on the farm where his father worked. And it was the night when he'd accepted a dare to creep out and confront the 'ghost' that gained him the respect of the other boys and stopped a lot of the bullying he'd endured until then.

Naval instructors, he had found, didn't take kindly to boy entrants who thought they knew it all. Robby was picked on from the beginning and found himself collecting every punishment going, from being 'cut' with a cane to being struck by the 'stonnicker' – a thick piece of rope with a turk's head knot at one end. With the other boys, he took an icy shower at five-thirty each morning before plunging into an equally icy bath and then, standing with his arms above his head, being inspected by a Boy Instructor who would invariably shout 'Dirty!' and force him to go through the whole thing again. He was made to run naked around the parade ground, scrub the floor of the washroom with his toothbrush and climb the newly-arrived mast in races against other boys to stand at the top by the weathervane, dizzied by the height, until the record of one minute eight seconds was set and couldn't be beaten. He was there when one of his best friends was killed by falling from the mast and then rolling out of the safety-net, and as he stood on the yardarm high above, he was vividly reminded of his grandfather's story. A tremor ran through him, but he thrust his shock away and muttered, 'Welcome to HMS *Warrior*.' Already, he was developing the cool head that the harsh discipline was designed to achieve.

He soon learned his way about the maze of buildings – from Anson, the block to which he had been assigned, to the rifle range and open-air swimming pool, to the main divisional blocks known in Naval fashion as the forecastle, foretop, mantop and quarterdeck, to the Gunnery Park where they raced to assemble the cumbersome field guns, and to the 'Old Ship' which was fitted out to represent a real ship's deck. Twice a week, he was allowed out into the town with the other boys, having been warned not to fraternise with the local girls – a warning that was ignored whenever they thought they could get away with it – and sometimes shared a furtive cigarette in an alleyway with some of the other lads, keeping a wary eye out for the patrols who marched the streets looking for boys who were breaking the rules. You didn't feel much freer outside than you did in, he thought, and with only a shilling pocket-money you couldn't afford to buy a lot anyway. You could get three cigarettes for a penny but there was no point in buying more than you could smoke in an afternoon, as everyone was searched on their return – although if you did manage to smuggle some back, you could sell them at twice what you paid. But Robby wasn't really a keen smoker. He spent most of his cash on going to the pictures at the shabby little Criterion cinema, not far from the *St Vincent* gates. It was ninepence to get in, and that left you a penny for the smokes and tuppence for a few sweets. When that was gone, you just lived for the next Saturday – especially when, against all the rules, you'd found a local girl who was willing to snuggle up in the back seat with you. Maisie Jenkins, from Whitworth Road, had snuggled up with him quite a few times during his last year there.

In those first months Robby, who could already tie most knots, splice ropes, row a boat, sail and use a compass, added to his seaman's skills and learned to read the flag signals and work on larger ships than Dan's little dinghy and the *Countess Wear*. He passed his tests with flying colours – just like the flags themselves, fluttering from the mast when the ship was 'dressed overall' – and went on to train in seamanship, signalling, rifle and cutlass drill, and field and big gun drill. Finally, he went for a six-week cruise in the *Martin*, a 600-ton sailing brig, square-rigged with two masts. It was impossible to stand up between decks and as he hauled on the sails and ran like a monkey in the rigging he thought that this was as near as you could ever get to being in Nelson's Navy. He stood on the yardarm, going with the sway of the ship, thinking of the men who had sailed against Napoleon, of his grandfather on HMS *Warrior* and the boy who had fallen to the deck, and feeling a surge of pride that outweighed all the hardships he had endured. This was the life he had dreamed of and, after three years of hard training and merciless discipline, he was at last ready for it.

Robby thought of all this as he sat on the train bound from Plymouth to Totnes. It was a short journey, yet his mind sped through the memories, shaking them up like a kaleidoscope. He had the feeling that all his training had been directed towards this moment, yet what he was about to do seemed too bizarre to be real. Assuming command of the *Countess Wear* – a little passenger-steamer, used only for pleasure-cruises on the river – and taking her across the Channel to rescue soldiers under fire from the beaches of France: he shook his head, still not quite able to believe it. All the years at *St Vincent* and the subsequent ones aboard ship had been aimed at qualifying him for work on Naval warships, not little pleasure-craft. He almost wondered if it could be a practical joke, but the First Lieutenant wasn't noted for his sense of humour. An initiative test, then? But Robby shook his head again. They had been at war for less than a year, but it was clear that nobody needed artificial initiative tests. Your initiative was being tested all the bloody time, as far as Robby could see.

The train was running between fields of red earth now, with rolling hills beyond and the dark slopes of Dartmoor like a shadow in the distance. He dropped to the platform at Totnes station and hefted his kitbag on to one shoulder. There was just time to call in at home before taking up his new command, and with any luck he could see Molly as well.

Totnes didn't look any different from when he'd left it, the narrow main street running down the hill and under the arch just as it had always done – it was hardly likely to have changed in just a few months, he thought with a grin – and the tall, red sandstone tower of the old church standing out against the blue sky. The river was at the lower end of the town, running between the quays, with the masts of a motley crowd of dinghies, yachts and motor cruisers swaying and bobbing as the tide surged up the river from the mouth of the Dart, ten or a dozen miles away.

Robby didn't go directly down to the river. Instead, he ran the last few yards and jumped aboard a bus that was just leaving for its round of the villages. The driver knew him and shook his head at the fare Robby proffered, glancing over his shoulder to see if anyone had noticed. But no one would have said anything, even if they did. Sailors in uniform, especially local boys, were given lifts and free rides all the time. They were fighting for their country, and any money they did have in their pockets was better spent on the families and sweethearts they had come to see, or on themselves when they had a spot of shore leave.

'Come to see Mother and Feyther then, boy?' the driver asked, pronouncing it 'bye' in his soft, Devon voice, and Robby shrugged.

'Summat like that.' He had never lost his own accent, although it had been sharpened a little by contact with boys from Hampshire and Sussex and other counties while he was at *St Vincent*, and he had learned to keep the broader dialect words and phrases for when he was at home. 'I'll be off again directly, though.' He closed his lips, thinking that perhaps he had already said too much. The Jimmy had told him that the BEF's situation wasn't yet known to the public – nor even to most of the Navy. He found a seat halfway down the bus and sat down quickly, nodding and speaking to everyone else whether he knew them or not. Most of the faces were familiar, but you did that anyway on the Devon buses. Not like those in Gosport or Pompey, where everyone was a stranger and preferred to stay that way.

Robby's parents lived in a farm cottage between Totnes and Stoke Gabriel. It was only two miles from the centre of Totnes and Robby could have walked it easily, but time was short and he was anxious to see them as soon as possible before returning to the quay to pick up his command. Once again, he shook his head in wonder. His command! Only twenty-one years old, a mere able seaman, and he was going to be captain of a ship – a small ship, barely even worthy of the name, but still a ship, going to sea on an important mission, and under *his* command. His heart quickened and he felt a surge of pride and excitement. He wondered if Danny would be on board too. There would have to be a crew – one or two others, to man the engines and maybe take the wheel. It was a long trip round the coast to Dover, even before they set out across the Channel.

Robby knew that he was capable of taking the *Countess* wherever she needed to go. All the same, he felt a tremor of apprehension. I hope to Christ I don't mess it up, he thought. I hope I don't make some stupid mistake and cock the whole thing up.

He didn't have much time for thinking, though. The bus was full of women and a few old men, all coming back from Totnes and wanting to know why he was there, how he was getting on in the Navy, and whether he'd seen any fighting at sea yet. Did he think there was really going to be an invasion? There didn't seem to be all that much going on in the war so far, except at sea and over in Belgium and France, none of the bombing they'd been led to expect. 'Not that we'll get any of that down yere,' remarked a plump woman, resting a basketful of shopping on her broad lap. 'Why, they haven't even evacuated the youngsters out of Plymouth. Stands to reason, they German planes can't get this far.'

There were plenty of evacuees about, all the same. A lot had been brought down to Devon from London – never seen a cow in their lives and refused to drink the milk once they saw where it came from. 'And it's not as if they was clean themselves,' the plump woman told him. 'Dressed in rags, poor little toads, and running

23

with lice. Never slept in a bed, if you can believe it, and didn't know what it was to sit up to table for a proper dinner.'

Robby sat on the bus, looking out at the familiar lanes with their high banks and hedges and listening to the chatter around him. The warm, soft brogue fell comfortingly on his ears and the last of the bluebells were like patches of fallen sky on the new grass. There were still a few primroses here and there, studding the banks with gold, and now and then he spotted a patch of deep purple violets. The pride in his heart was touched with a strange, nostalgic pain and a yearning for the days when, as a boy, he had roamed these lanes and fields, looking for birds' nests and rabbits' burrows. He and Danny had known every inch of it, he thought; where to find a lizard basking on a dry stone wall, where to find a nest of slow worms writhing in a clump of heather, where to see Red Admiral butterflies in a nettle patch or catch sticklebacks and newts in a particular stream or pond.

The realisation hit him like a bludgeon on the back of his head. It was *all* under threat – not just the people but the country itself, the whole way of life. This was England – the part of England that held his heart. He had grown up here, he had expected it to be the same always for him to come back to, as his grandfather had come back. He had never thought as far ahead as his own old age, when he too might sit at a cottage door telling tales of his seafaring days to another wide-eyed youngster, but now he suddenly saw it like a tiny picture in his mind, and he knew that unless the enemy were stopped in their relentless advance across Europe it would never happen. If Germany marched into Britain as they had marched into so many other countries, life would be changed for ever.

Until now, Robby had looked on the Royal Navy as the Senior Service, believing that the others – the Army and the Royal Air Force – were of lesser importance. Now, he saw that each had its own vital part to play. None of them could win this war alone. And they've got our blokes trapped over there, he thought, remembering the First Lieutenant's words. If we don't get them back, we won't have an Army left, and it won't matter what the Navy and the Air Force do, we won't be able to keep the buggers out.

And it wasn't just the BEF itself. It was Jan – Robby's elder brother, named for their grandfather – who had started life as a farrier's apprentice and then, as a member of the voluntary

24

Territorial Army, had been one of the first to go when war was declared. Until now, Robby hadn't given much thought to Jan, assuming that whatever happened he would turn up all right; but now it came home to him that Jan must be one of those waiting to be rescued from the beaches of France. Waiting for Robby and the pleasure-steamer they both knew so well, to come all the way from Totnes to bring him to safety.

My stars, he thought, reverting to one of his mother's favourite sayings, I don't know what I've been thinking of. It's *our Jan* over there. Mum will never forgive me if I don't bring him back safe.

The bus had arrived in Stoke Gabriel and he hurried to get off. The village looked the same as ever, its grey church-tower presiding over the dreaming cottages, the mill pond a wide expanse of still water reflecting the blue of the sky. It was on the river here that Rob and Danny had first learned to row a boat and then to sail, once having to spend hours stuck on a mudbank waiting for the tide and once, when the wind suddenly freshened, finding themselves swept dangerously close to the rugged Mew Stone with its crowds of screaming gulls and gannets. But every experience was a lesson and by the time they left school and started to work on the *Countess*, they were competent sailors, able to read both wind and water, and too respectful of their craft to take foolish risks.

The Endacotts' back door stood open, catching the afternoon sun. In the morning, the sun streamed in through the front of the cottage, where the windows were flung wide to let in the fresh cool scent of the dew on his mother's roses. At noon, it moved round to the back – and Robby's grandfather had always moved with it, to sit on the old wooden bench, whittling at a piece of wood or shelling peas and beans from the garden. He had grown the vegetables himself, his bent figure moving slowly amongst the twiggy branches pruned from the hedges to support them, tying in the straggling tendrils or pinching out the trusses of the tomatoes.

It came as a small shock for Robby not to see him as he rounded the corner. He still hadn't got used to the fact that Grandad had passed away in his sleep, sitting on that very bench, on Easter Monday, one of his last tasks that of planting his broad beans, as he always did, on Good Friday. 'They grow best if they go in on the Easter moon,' he would say, standing back to look with satisfaction at the neatly tended earth. 'They'll be a good crop, you wait and see.'

And so they would, Robby thought, pausing in a moment of homage, but Grandad wouldn't see them. He had planted his last broad bean and now, if all that childhood teaching were to be believed, he was somewhere up above enjoying more celestial food, though how anything could be better than Grandad's home-grown vegetables Robby couldn't imagine.

As he stood there, he heard an exclamation at the door and turned to see his mother come running out. Wiping floury hands on her apron, she flung her arms around him, exclaiming with delight, and he hugged her tightly, aware as he had never been before that their time together was precious.

'Robby! What be you doing home? Us didn't expect to see you.'

'I didn't expect to be coming.' He followed her indoors, ducking his head under the low doorway. 'And I can't stop long – 'tis only a flying visit, like. I've got to be off again by nine.' Already he heard himself slipping back into the local dialect, as he always did when he came home.

'By nine?' She stared at him. 'In the morning?'

He shook his head. 'Nine this evening, mother. There's a big job on.' He stopped, not sure how much he should tell her. But it would be all round the area in a day or two that the little steamer had gone downriver with a young sailor in command, and he was familiar enough in Totnes for everyone to know who that young sailor was. 'The Admiralty's been calling in all boats over thirty feet long,' he said. 'They'm wanted for inshore patrol boats, that sort o' thing.' It was true enough that this had been the first reason for the requisitioning order that had gone out a fortnight or so earlier. 'I'm taking the Countess round the coast. Going to do a bit of work for her living, instead of all these pleasure-trips.'

'The Countess? Well, her's a sturdy old boat, you can't say her's not. But my stars, just fancy them wanting she for war work.' Hetty Endacott shook her head in wonder and went to slide the big kettle on to the range. 'Now, my flower, you'll be wanting a cup of tea and a bite to eat. I made some pasties, fresh this morning, must have known you were coming, and there's some tatties out of the garden and a few early peas.' She was working as she talked, taking teacups down from the dresser shelves and setting out a plate of scones and a

26

pot of home-made strawberry jam. She opened the larder door and brought out an earthenware crock of clotted cream, its yellow crust not yet broken. 'Here's a bite to keep body and soul together till supper,' she said, spooning some into a bowl. 'I dare say your appetite's no worse than it ever was.'

Robby pulled a chair out from the table and plonked himself down in it, already reaching for a scone. It was still faintly warm from the oven, its crust crisply baked and, when he split it, the inside was soft and welcoming to the jam and the thick, rich cream. 'Now I know I'm home,' he said, sinking his teeth into the delicious strawberries, still whole in their glistening, sugary juices. 'We don't get this sort o' tack in the Navy, I can tell you! I'm going to smuggle you aboard ship next time I go to sea, mother, and tell 'em you're my own private cook. The other chaps'll go wild.'

'Get away with you. 'Tis only ordinary cooking. But you can't beat good Devon fare, I'll give you that.' She put two cups of tea on the scrubbed wooden table and sat down opposite him. 'What's this all about then, Robby? This business of the *Countess*?'

He looked across at her. 'I can't tell you no more than that, mother. You know what they say – everything's a secret these days. We don't even know what we'm doing ourselves, most of the time. We just go where we'm sent, and don't ask no questions.' He paused, then said with an attempt at sounding casual, 'Heard from our Jan lately?'

She shook her head. 'No, and I'll be honest with 'ee, Robby, 'tis worrying me something cruel. I mean, the news from over there isn't too good now, is it? That Hitler's getting it all his own way and we don't seem to be doing much to stop un. And like you say, they don't tell us everything, not by a long chalk. Our Jan might be in Belgium, fighting still, or he might be in France. He might even . . .' her voice shook a little ' . . . he might even be a prisoner of war. We just don't *know*.' Her fingers moved nervously on the table, rubbing at a mark that had been there for years.

Robby felt a chill touch his heart. It was only on the bus, coming from Totnes, that he'd given any proper thought to his brother. But as he'd gazed out at the flower-strewn hedges and thought of the tramp of German feet along those narrow, familiar lanes, he had felt a sharp prickle of dread and had a swift vision of Jan, stranded on a French beach while German planes flew overhead. What chance did he, or any of the beleaguered Army, have? And what were the chances of little boats like *Countess* reaching them in time?

'Our Jan'll be all right,' he said to his mother. 'You know what Grandad always said about him – fall into a cesspit and he'd come up smelling of roses. He's the sort who'll always find a way out.'

'Nobody's that sort in wartime,' she said gravely. 'Don't forget, me and your father have been through it all before. He were in the trenches in the Great War, you know, saw a lot o' things he've never talked about. And his brother, your Uncle George that you never knew, he was lost at the Somme. Twenty thousand there was killed, just on the first day. Maybe some of *them* were the sort who always found a way out, too – but there weren't no way out of that.'

Robby stared at her. He had never heard her speak like this before, in that sombre tone, never realised what memories were held in that greying head. For an instant, he understood the depths of her dread for Jan – for both her sons – and shared the cold helplessness of it. Then he drew once again on the training he had been given, sometimes so harshly, and said, 'You don't want to worry, mother. It don't do no good. Me and Jan – us needs to know you'm here, keeping everything the same for when us comes home again. Us needs to know you're smiling for us. There's nobody got a smile like you.'

His mother looked at him for a moment, but as he met her eyes he felt that she was seeing past him, looking at something different, at a terror he couldn't yet imagine. Then the darkness faded and she smiled – a faint, wavering smile, but enough to flood him with relief. He laughed suddenly, not knowing what he was laughing at, and her smile grew until her face seemed once more lit with sunshine.

'You boys!' she said, reaching across to slap his arm. 'You'm full of talk, the pair of 'ee. Charm the birds off the trees, you could. Now, I dare say you'll be wanting to be off to see young Molly, so if you've finished with they scones why don't 'ee run along now and bring her back for supper? She'll never forgive us if we keeps you from her. 'Tis little enough time you've had together these past months.'

Robby looked down at his plate and found to his surprise that he'd wolfed down three scones in a row. And I never even noticed, he thought regretfully, trying to recapture the taste of the home-made jam and cream. Then he snatched up his round, white-topped cap and swung out through the door, bending to give his mother a quick peck on the cheek as he passed.

Already, the moment of dread was beginning to fade and his heart was drumming at the thought of seeing Molly again.

Molly Lovering was in the dairy, churning butter, when Robby reached the farm. The big, north-facing room was cool, yet to Robby it seemed to be warmed and lit by the very sight of his sweetheart, standing by the slate-topped table with her blue frock covered by a big white apron, her sleeves rolled up and her strong arms working the handle of the wooden churn. He stood for a moment in the doorway, taking in the scene. He had always liked the dairy, with its flagstone floor and slate counters, set with big pottery bowls of crusted yellow cream, jugs of fresh milk and the butter itself, with the stamps put ready to decorate each pat as Molly shaped them.

As his shadow darkened the room, she glanced up and her blue eyes widened, her face opening into a smile of delight. 'Robby! What be you doing here?' She didn't stop churning, nor did he expect her to. 'Come and give us a kiss, the butter's nearly there.' She lifted her face and he came swiftly across the room and slipped his arm around her waist, kissing her lips. They were soft and sweet and tasted faintly of strawberries.

Molly wasn't a slip of a thing, like Maisie Jenkins in Gosport, whose waist Robby could span with his two hands. She was short and plump, with arms that swelled with inviting roundness from her rolled-up sleeves and were already brown from working outside. She was strong too – there was muscle in that roundness that came from the work she did, handling and milking cows and, as she was doing now, churning butter. As Robby held her against him, enjoying the feel of her firm yet soft body, she nestled against him and then gave the handle a final swing.

'There! The butter's come.' She turned into his arms and gave herself up to his kiss, and he forgot Maisie Jenkins. 'Now, darlin', tell me why you'm here.'

Robby repeated the story he had told his mother and Molly stared at him in surprise. 'The *Countess*? What do they want with she? And what about the *Berry Pomeroy*, be she going too?'

'Yes – George Ellery's taking her himself. And the *Mew*'s going

29

as well – the old railway ferry, you know, the one that goes from Dartmouth to Kingswear. We'll all be going together on the next tide. I just had time to come and see you, and Mother says you're to come over for supper.' He looked at her, feeling suddenly grave, as if this might be the goodbye they had not yet said. 'You can come, can't you, Moll? I don't know when I'll be home again, see.'

'But if you'm only *delivering* the boat, like?' she said, her smooth brow creased. 'I mean, you'll be back to Devonport then, won't you? You'll be able to come home sometimes.'

'There's a war on, Moll,' he said gently. 'I could go anywhere, any time. I don't know when I'll get the chance to come home again. And *Wenlock*'s nearly ready to sail as well. Soon as this job's done, I'll be back aboard her.'

She bit her lip and lifted one hand to brush back a lock of light brown hair. He saw tears in her eyes. 'It don't seem like there's a war on at all, round here,' she said a little quaveringly. 'Except for the 'vacuees, of course, and a lot of them have gone home now. I was hoping it were all going to come to nothing.'

'It's not going to come to nothing,' he said a little grimly. 'It's going to get worse ... But you don't need to worry about me, Molly. I'll be all right. And all you have to do now is finish that butter and then come home with me for supper, for then I've got to go back to Totnes to pick up the *Countess*.' He grinned at her and gave her another squeeze. 'Seems a bit topsy-turvy, doesn't it – me taking the old *Countess* downriver after all the training I've done on big ships!'

Molly laughed and lifted the lump of butter from the whey with a slatted spoon. Working quickly, with strong brown fingers, she shaped it into small rounds and decorated each with the earthenware stamps – a thistle for one, a sailing ship for another, a cheeky wren for a third. In a few minutes she had finished and covered them with muslin to keep the flies off while they were allowed to dry; then she washed her hands in the deep white sink and dried them on a scrap of towel.

'There – all done. I'll just tell the missus where I'll be to.' She hurried through the door and across the yard to the farmhouse. Robby followed, lifting his face to the sunshine, and heard voices in the farmhouse kitchen. Molly reappeared with Mrs Halford close behind her.

'Robby! What a surprise. And what's this Molly's telling me about the *Countess*?'

Robby repeated his story briefly, hoping that she wouldn't keep him in conversation. She looked at him for a moment and he wondered if she believed him, but she nodded and gave his arm a friendly pat.

'Well, whatever 'tis, I dare say you'll do a proper job. Anyway, you don't want to stand here chattering with me – you'll want Molly to yourself for a while. Off you go now, and don't worry about the butter, Molly, I'll see to it. You don't have to be back till nine.'

Molly gave her a grateful smile and caught Robby's hand. Together they walked quickly out of the farmyard and down the lane leading to the field path to Robby's home.

'Us don't have much time, do us?' she said wistfully, and he looked at her face and gave her hand a squeeze.

'There's always time for a bit of a cuddle, my pretty. We'll go down the woods, shall us? To our special place? Mother won't be expecting us back for another half-hour at least.'

She leaned against him for a moment. 'Robby, is this going to be dangerous? I get a feeling you'm not telling me everything.'

'I can't, maid. You know that. And we got to face it – war *is* dangerous. I can't pretend nothing else.' He stopped just inside the little wood and took her in his arms. 'But it'll help keep me safe if I know you'm thinking of me, and sending me your thoughts. You'll do that, won't you, Moll?'

'Of course I will,' she whispered, burying her face against his white, square-necked shirt. 'I'm always thinking of you, Robby.'

They stood for a moment, close together. Then he took her hand and led her deeper into the trees, to the little clearing they had made their own, where a few silver birches stood on the bank above the river and made a dappled patch of sunlight on the grass.

Chapter Three

Wednesday, 29 May

PORTSMOUTH: *Wagtail*

'I'll do my best,' Charles Stainbank said to the tearful young bride and her indignant parents. 'But breach-of-promise cases aren't easy. You have to have solid proof of intent.'

'And isn't an engagement ring solid proof?' the angry father demanded, thrusting a box containing a ring set with a single large diamond in front of Charles's face. 'Isn't a wedding date proof? A hotel booking for the reception? I can't see what further proof anyone could ask for.'

'The invitations have all been sent out,' the bride's mother added, touching her eyes with a lace handkerchief. 'We've had acceptances from all our friends. The chairman of the Rotary Club – the Lord and Lady Mayoress – it's so *embarrassing* to have to tell them it's been called off.'

'On the other hand,' Charles said, wishing that they had been clients of any other law firm in Portsmouth but his, 'it may be all for the best. If the groom really feels that the wedding would be a mistake—'

'A *mistake*?' The mother stared at him. 'How could it be a mistake? Our daughter's one of the most eligible young women in Portsmouth. And my husband is one of the most well-known men in the city. If anyone was making a mistake, it was us in allowing him to propose to her in the first place. He's simply not good enough for her!'

'Exactly,' Charles said. 'So perhaps it would be better—'

'We don't want him to *marry* her, if that's what you're

32

suggesting,' she said coldly. 'We simply want him to make proper reparation for hurting her feelings. The poor girl's distraught. As any young woman would be.'

'Yes, I see that, but—'

'Listen,' the father said, placing both palms on Charles's desk and leaning over. 'What we want is for this case to be brought to court for proper settlement. I've paid a considerable amount of money for this wedding – dresses, reception expenses, a carriage to take my daughter to the Cathedral – why, it's run into hundreds of pounds. I want that back.'

'It's not just the money, though,' the mother interposed hastily. 'It's our daughter's *feelings*. I really don't know how they can be evaluated in terms of money.'

'But a judge will, my dear.' The big man stood straight again and put his arm round his wife's shoulders. 'That's what a breach-of-promise case is for. So that an experienced man of law can take everything into account and calculate the appropriate sum.' He looked at Charles. 'Are you quite sure you can handle this? I'm sure if your father were here . . .'

'It's perfectly all right,' Charles said coolly. 'I'm quite able to take your instructions. However, it is part of my job to be sure that my clients understand all the implications of an action before taking it too far. Now, I've made quite a lot of notes and I suggest we make another appointment for a week's time, say, when we can discuss the matter further.' He stood up and ushered them towards the door, thankful to bring the interview to an end.

Of all the cases Charles found himself dealing with as a solicitor, breach-of-promise were the ones he disliked most. The idea of taking a young man to court and making him pay for his mistake was distasteful, especially as it nearly always included a strong element of revenge. And having seen this particular bride and her parents, his sympathies were very much with the groom. I'd never have made the promise in the first place if I'd been him, he thought, but they're the ones consulting me so they're the ones I've got to act for.

He considered asking his father if they could decline the instruction but discarded the idea at once. Hubert Stainbank believed in the principle of 'my client, right or wrong'. 'We're not judge and jury,' he would say. 'We only know one side of the story and our job is to put that side before those who are trained to make the right decision.' And his fine, grey eyebrows would draw together over his sharp, pale-blue eyes.

Charles gathered together a few papers and got up from his desk, thankful that the day was over. It all seems so petty these days, he thought – people promising to marry each other and then thinking better of it, old ladies who've got nothing better to do, coming in every day to change their Wills. Don't they know there's a war on? Don't they know we could be invaded at any moment? We'll have more to worry about then than Wills and broken engagements!

Charles was getting more and more frustrated at having to stay in the office when most men of his age were now in the Services. The war news was deteriorating every day, with Hitler's advance through France and Belgium seemingly unstoppable. Soon, the enemy would hold all the main Channel ports. Invasion seemed inevitable.

If nothing were done to stop them . . .

Charles shuddered. Here on the south coast, with Portsmouth one of the major Naval harbours, right in the front line, they were especially vulnerable. And here was he, stuck in an office dealing with the petty grievances of people who didn't even seem to realise what dangers their country was facing, and feeling totally helpless to do anything about it.

I ought to be there, he thought moodily, and slammed out of his office. I ought to be one of them, doing my bit. There must be *something* I could do . . .

Outside, the sun was shining. He had spent odd moments throughout the day glancing out of the window at the small white clouds scudding across the blue sky and wishing he could be on the water. A few deep breaths of good sea air might blow away his jaded feeling. He and Sheila were due to go round to Emsworth this evening to stay overnight with his parents, and he wondered if there might be time for an hour's sail in *Titwillow*. It would be even better, he thought, if they could all pile aboard *Wagtail* and take her out for a picnic, but fuel was restricted now so they only dared use the little cruiser for special occasions, and in any case, you needed a permit to go outside the harbour. And I don't even know why I'm thinking like this, he chided himself. Picnics – pleasure sailing – when we're on the brink of an invasion . . .

Sheila was ready and waiting with the children when he arrived home on his bicycle, and they quickly fitted themselves into the Baby

Austin. Petrol prices had almost doubled only this week, from one shilling and a halfpenny a gallon to one and elevenpence-halfpenny, and the car was used only for essential journeys. A weekly visit to Hubert and Olivia Stainbank was considered essential.

'What's the matter?' Sheila asked quietly when Charles swung the starting-handle and climbed back into the driving seat. 'Has there been any more news?'

He shook his head and stared moodily ahead. 'Oh, nothing new. Just some rather tedious clients.' He turned towards her. 'I just feel I'm wasting my time. Anyone could do what I've been doing this afternoon. And what does it amount to? A couple of silly old women who want to play with their families as if they were counters on a snakes-and-ladders board, changing their Wills every five minutes, and a spoiled Daddy's girl who's had her toy taken away. What good is it all doing? There's so much else to be done – so much that's *really* important.'

Sheila was silent for a moment, then said, 'You can't join up, Charles. You know that.'

'I never said—' He bit the words off and made a wry face. 'Well, maybe you're right. I *do* wish I could join up. I want to be doing something, Sheila – something for my country. And as if it's not bad enough knowing that I can't, I have to put up with my clients sneering at me because I'm sitting safely in a solicitor's office instead of fighting.'

'They don't!'

'Well, they don't come right out with it, no. But those two old ladies who came in today – they can remember the Great War. One of them lost her fiancé – she never did marry. I can see what she's thinking by the way she looks at me. I tell you, I almost expected her to hand me a white feather. I'm sure she would have done too, if she'd had one in her bag.'

Sheila put her hand on his knee. 'Don't let it bother you so much, darling. You're not a coward – you know that, and so does everyone who knows you. *She* isn't aware that you've spent three years in a sanatorium with TB.'

'So what am I supposed to do?' he asked. 'Write it on my forehead? But it's not just them, Sheila – it's me. I want to be part of it – like your brother. I could do something. I'm well enough now.'

'You've still got a weakness in your chest. It wouldn't help anyone if you got ill and had to be brought home. They've got enough to do looking after the wounded. That's what Alex is doing, after all. He's not actually fighting.'

Charles sighed and lapsed into silence. Sheila glanced over her shoulder. In the back seat the twins Nicky and Jonathan, nearly two years old now, had fallen asleep in a huddle of rounded limbs and flushed cheeks while their elder sister Wendy, who had recently learned to read, was deep in one of Enid Blyton's *Sunny Stories*. As far as Sheila was concerned, Charles's tuberculosis, which had been such a worry at the time, had turned out to be a blessing. He was, as he had said, more or less well again, although he'd always have to take care of his health – which meant Sheila taking care of it for him – and because of it, none of the Services was likely to accept him for active service. He could stay in Portsmouth, working in his father's practice – and keeping safe. It was bad enough, Sheila decided, having to worry about her twin brother Alex, who had gone straight into the Royal Medical Corps as soon as war had broken out; she didn't want to suffer the same gnawing anxiety over Charles as well.

Nobody knew how Charles had contracted tuberculosis. For months he had been vaguely ill, catching colds easily and having difficulty in throwing them off. In the end, he seemed to have a permanent cough, a cough which grew worse instead of better. He was losing weight too, weight that with his tall, slender build he could ill afford to lose, and developing a worrying pallor which accentuated the bright flush she sometimes noticed on his cheeks. But Wendy was still a baby then, and not thriving – though you wouldn't think so now, Sheila reflected with another glance at her sturdy, dark-haired daughter – and Sheila herself had taken some time to recover from the birth. She had been appalled and ridden with guilt when her husband had had that first frightening haemorrhage.

It had taken nearly three years for Charles to recover and another before they had felt secure enough to add to their family. Not that they had exactly planned for twins, but as Charles said when he had stood beside her bed, almost bursting with pride, there was nothing like making up for lost time. 'Wonder if we'll be able to pull it off again?' he'd added thoughtfully.

'Only if you're willing to do the whole job yourself!' Sheila had retorted, and he'd laughed and told her he would never be able to do

36

it as well as she could. 'You're an ideal mother, darling. I'd never try to take your place. And I love you very much,' he'd added more seriously. 'I won't ever make you do anything you don't want to do.'

Sheila, who had been brought up a Roman Catholic, had always assumed that they would have a large family, and hoped for at least one more baby. Another little girl, perhaps, so that Wendy could have a sister. If only she didn't have this deeply uneasy feeling that it would be wrong to bring another child into the world, the way things were now . . .

The little car turned east to run along the top of Langstone Harbour and past Hayling Island to Emsworth. Hubert Stainbank had given it to Charles and Sheila when Charles had come out of the sanatorium and they had used it every weekend, to take the children out into the countryside. Now, they saved their motor journeys for visits either to Emsworth or to Sheila's parents in Chichester.

The twins didn't stir until the car had run down the narrow village street, past the Crown Hotel and Maidment's, where Hubert had bought Charles his first bicycle, and turned into the drive of Curlews. As Charles brought it to a halt before the front door, they began to stretch and rub their eyes. Wendy looked up from her *Sunny Stories*.

'I was just getting to the exciting bit.'

'Well, we're not driving round and round just so that you can finish your story,' Sheila said, getting out and tipping her seat forward so as to lift the twins out. 'You can stay in the car if you can't bear to wait till later. Wake up, Nicky. We're at Granny and Grandpa's. Come on, Jonathan, there's a good boy. Look, here's Catcher come to say hello.' The old black retriever had waddled out and stood wagging his tail and sniffing at the twins as they were set down on the path. Nicky laughed and rubbed the dog's wet nose, but Jonathan frowned and stepped behind his mother. Sheila looked exasperated. 'Don't be such a baby, Jon. He's not going to hurt you. He's just a big teddy-bear.'

'Not a teddy-bear,' Jonathan said. 'A *dog*.' He stepped round the animal and went to his grandmother, who was coming through the door. 'Granny!'

'Hello, sweetheart.' Olivia Stainbank swept him up into her arms and smiled at her daughter-in-law. 'He still hasn't forgotten the way Catcher knocked him over. It was an accident, Jon darling. He didn't mean it. He loves you, you know that.' But the little boy hid his face against her shoulder and she led the way back indoors. 'Toby's here, by the way. He's down on the quay with Paddy.'

Wendy put away her book and held out her hand to the other twin. 'Come on, Nicky. Let's go and see Uncle Toby.' They scampered round the corner of the house and disappeared into the garden which ran down to the little private jetty where Hubert kept *Wagtail* and *Titwillow*.

Sheila raised an enquiring eyebrow as she followed her mother-in-law into the house. The square hall smelled of beeswax polish and lavender from the bowl of pot-pourri kept on the hall table. Olivia had been arranging spring flowers in a big yellow jug, and their brightness was like a splash of colour against the darkness of the wood. Olivia, tall and elegant in her pale yellow and grey afternoon dress, looked equally spring-like.

'What's Toby doing home? I thought he was in that new play.'

Olivia made a rueful face. 'It folded, apparently, after only a week. The critics were quite cruel. He came home to lick his wounds. As usual,' she added with a sigh. 'Not that I mind that at all, and I'm glad to have him out of London even though there hasn't been any bombing yet, but I do so wish he could *settle* to something. If only he were more like Charles and could make up his mind to a career. It doesn't have to be law. He's got a good brain, he could do anything if he would only set his mind on it.'

'He's set his mind on acting,' Charles observed, taking Jonathan from his grandmother and giving him a pat on his round, padded bottom before steering him towards the kitchen. 'Go and see what Betty's got for you. I dare say she's been baking cakes and biscuits all morning.' He looked back at Olivia. 'You may as well accept it, Ma. He wants to be a famous actor, and that's it.'

'I know. I don't know where he gets it from. I'm just hoping he won't encourage Paddy to follow him. Not that she doesn't have her own ideas,' she added. 'How I came to have such wilful children, I just do not know!'

Sheila laughed. 'You've said it yourself, Mother. They've got good brains, all of them, and they want to use them. It's just that they have different ideas about how to do it.'

Jonathan emerged from the kitchen carrying a jam tart. He already had jam smeared over his face and was waving the tart

38

dangerously close to the polished panelling. Olivia swooped on him and Charles laughed and took him away. 'I'll take him outside with the others. We'll go and see what Uncle Toby and Paddy are doing, shall we, Jonny? Leave the women to their gossip.'

'You'll probably see the Admiral down there, too,' his mother called after him. 'He's coming over to dinner, since the tide's right. He'll be glad to see you – he was saying only the other day that he hadn't had a talk with you for a while.'

Charles nodded, pleased by the news, and swung out into the garden with his son in his arms. The lawn stretched away to a cluster of small ornamental trees and shrubs that bordered the garden where it met the shoreline. Just past these were the jetty and the boathouse where the dinghy and the new cruiser were kept. Charles could already see his younger brother and sister, helping the children aboard *Wagtail*. He waved and called, and they turned and waved back.

'Hello, Charles!' Paddy jumped ashore and came running to meet him. 'We're waiting for the Admiral. He's sailing round in *Minimus* and he's going to stay the night, so we'll have him for breakfast as well.'

'Instead of bacon and eggs,' Toby added with a grin. He was as unlike Charles as a brother could be, squarely built, with floppy yellow hair and a disarming grin. Physically, he resembled neither of his parents and Paddy, who had inherited their slenderness without the height, said that he was a changeling and had been left by fairies in exchange for the real Toby.

'Oh, you!' she said now, pushing back her fair hair and making a face at him. 'You know what I mean. I wish he'd bring *Moonset*,' she added, referring to the Admiral's motor yacht. 'I wanted to go out on her. But he's being very mysterious about her.'

'Mysterious?' Charles stepped aboard his father's small cruiser. Hubert had had her built by the little boatyard in Emsworth only a year ago, planning to take her on quite long trips, but the war had put paid to that idea for a while. 'What's he being mysterious about?'

'I told you – about *Moonset*. And it's no use asking me any more, because I don't know.' Paddy wrinkled her nose. 'That's the whole point of being mysterious! Perhaps he'll tell you, since you're a *man*.'

39

She rolled her grey eyes. 'Honestly, I love the Admiral but he's *so* old-fashioned!'

'That's because he's old,' Toby said, joining them in the cockpit with a twin under each arm. 'Now, you two sit there and we'll pretend we're at sea in a big storm. I'm the captain and you're the ship's boys, all right?' He stood at the wheel and narrowed his eyes at the horizon. 'Lower the mainsail, you lazy lubbers! Man overboard! Avast there! Splice the mainbrace!'

'Stop it, Toby,' Paddy said, laughing. 'They don't understand – they're too young. Don't take any notice of him,' she told the toddlers, who were huddling together with their mouths and eyes wide open. 'He's just being silly. Ask Wendy to tell you about the three bears.'

The story of *Goldilocks and the Three Bears* was something the twins could understand. They had bears of their own and, because Paddy had golden hair that framed her face in curls, had got the idea that she was the Goldilocks in the story. As Wendy began, Charles turned to his brother.

'You've not got your call-up yet, then?'

'No, and I hope I don't. I'm not a fighting man, Charles. I'd be a liability in the Army.'

'You could go into the Navy. Or the RAF.'

Toby pursed his lips and tilted his head to one side. 'Well, I wouldn't mind the RAF so much. I rather fancy flying a plane, and if I could get stationed on Thorney Island I could still slip home for a bit of Betty's home cooking. But this war's not going to come to anything, is it? I mean, there's been no bombing in spite of all the scare stories, and the Army's knocking hell out of the Germans in France. It'll be all over in a few weeks.'

Charles stared at him. 'What on earth do you mean? It's not going to be over in a few weeks at all. Don't you realise we're in danger of being invaded? Don't you read the papers? Don't you even listen to the wireless?'

'Not much,' Toby confessed with his disarming grin. 'Only the dance music, anyway! Look, half of what they tell us on the news isn't true and the other half happened a fortnight ago. Like when we had all that snow in the winter and it was in the papers two weeks later – just as if we hadn't noticed it! I mean, they're not going to tell us anything the Germans might overhear, are they? All this "Walls

Have Ears" nonsense applies to the BBC as much as to the housewives gossiping on street corners.'

'I suppose that's true to some extent,' Charles allowed. 'All the same, a lot of it must be the truth. And the situation doesn't look good. Surely even you must have heard about the Emergency Powers Act that went through Parliament a few days ago. Don't you understand what that means? Everything – banks, factories, wages, munitions, *everything* – is now under State control. We're all liable to be taken away – from our jobs, our homes, everything – and sent to do whatever the Government wants. We don't have any choice. We're not free any more – and we won't be, until this damned war's over.' He stared at his brother. 'You can't pretend it's not happening, Toby. You ought to know what's going on.'

'Yes, you should,' Paddy broke in. 'In fact, now that the play's folded you ought to volunteer. I would, if I were a man. I'm going to join the Wrens anyway, the minute I turn eighteen. Even if they won't let women go to sea, we can be in the Navy and do useful work. You're just a parasite.'

There was no real bite in her words, though. She and Toby had always been close, leaving Charles to feel the outsider. Sometimes, he thought, he felt more like an uncle than a brother.

'A parasite?' Toby echoed. 'How can you be so cruel?' He placed his hand dramatically on the right side of his chest. 'I can feel my heart breaking – oh no, it's on the other side, isn't it.' He moved his hand quickly. 'Well, it's still breaking, anyway, whichever side it is.'

Paddy ignored him and turned to Charles. 'Do you really think we're going to be invaded? Can't the Army stop it? What's going on over there?'

He lifted his shoulders. 'Nobody really knows, but as far as I can make out, the BEF are having a bad time of it. King Leopold's capitulation was the last straw. I wouldn't be surprised if they were forced to retreat.' He spoke soberly, looking down at the three children, rapt in the story of *The Three Bears*. What would happen to them if Hitler invaded? What had he done, bringing them into such a world?

Paddy stared at him. 'But what about Alex?'

He raised his head. 'Alex?'

'Yes, *Alex*. Your brother-in-law, remember? He's in the BEF, isn't he? He's in France.' She jumped up, making the boat rock. The twins squealed and Wendy caught hold of the cockpit coaming. 'Charles, Alex is over there, in danger!'

'Calm down, Paddy.' Charles wished he hadn't said anything but the situation in France had been on his mind for days now. 'Alex isn't in any more danger than he's been in already. He's a soldier and he's gone to war. You know that.'

'Yes, but – *retreating*.' She shook her head and the bright curls flew about her face. 'It seems so much worse. What will happen to them? There must be thousands. They'll be caught.' Her eyes filled with tears and Charles wished even more that he hadn't voiced his fears. Paddy was altogether too sharp; she caught on swiftly to ideas that passed other people by.

'Look, we don't know that that's what's happening. I've probably got it all wrong.' He glanced round and glimpsed a triangular brown sail blowing towards them. With relief, he said, 'Here comes the Admiral. He'll probably be able to tell you everything's all right.'

'He won't know any more than you do. He's retired.' But she stood up and waved at the figure in the dinghy. There was little heart in her wave now, though, and her body drooped. Charles felt another pang of regret. Things were bad enough without upsetting his young sister. Toby, still feckless at twenty-four, was one thing, but Paddy was only seventeen and deserved to have her innocence preserved for a little longer.

The dinghy was coming up the last stretch of the channel. They could see the Admiral clearly now – upright at the tiller, wearing the dark blue guernsey that he was never seen without and Toby swore had been sewn on to his rangy body, tufts of white hair showing beneath his blue sailing cap. He still wore the Naval 'full-set' of beard and moustache, as bushy as ever but now as snow-white as his hair, and his eyes glittered like chips of blue sapphire above ruddy cheeks. He waved back and brought the dinghy expertly alongside the jetty, where Paddy reached down and caught at the painter.

The Admiral was the family's oldest friend. He had grown up with Hubert and they had never lost their bond. He had been Hubert's best man and stood godfather to each of the three children. He had been especially close to Charles, and had hoped for Charles to follow him into a Naval career, but even as a boy Charles's chest had been weak and although he had applied, the Navy turned him down. When the tuberculosis had struck, the Admiral had been as anxious as the rest of the family, demanding that signals be sent to him at every stage of the treatment. He had paid for Charles to complete his recuperation in Switzerland and was secretly as relieved as Sheila that the young man couldn't be called up for war service.

'Good to see you, boy.' He stepped into *Wagtail*'s cockpit and clapped Charles on the shoulder. 'And you too, you scamps. My heaven, they double in size every time I see them.' He planted a kiss on Paddy's cheek and then bent his glittering gaze on Toby. 'And how about you? Made up your mind what to do yet?'

Toby flushed. He never dared be flippant with the Admiral. 'Not really, sir,' he muttered, looking down, and the old man regarded him for a moment or two, then shrugged and turned away.

'Well, I've made my feelings plain enough,' he said to nobody in particular. 'Country's at war. Up to every able-bodied young man to fight for her. Enjoy a good night at the theatre as much as anyone else, but I can't be doing with a lot of nancy-boys prancing about a stage when they ought to be learning to be men. You'll have to go sometime, anyway.'

'Not if the war ends soon,' Toby replied, lifting his head. 'And if you ask me, it's going to. We haven't had any of the bombing they said we'd get, and Hitler—'

'*Hitler*,' the Admiral said with sudden ferocity, 'will be marching up these very beaches within a fortnight if we don't do something to stop him. And there won't be any acting or lazing or messing about in boats if *that* happens, you mark my words. We'll all be slaves, that's if we're allowed to live at all. Look what's happened in Czechoslovakia. In Poland. In every other country he's stamped on.' He stopped, aware that the children were staring up at him, their mouths open, and bit back his next words. 'Sorry. Speaking out of turn. I'll go and find your father. Got something to tell him.' He glanced at Charles. 'You may as well come along too. We'll leave the kiddies to their games.' He touched Paddy's arm, patted the children's heads, cast a last, scathing glance at Toby and stepped back on to the jetty, marching up the garden path without a backward look. Charles took a deep breath and rolled his eyes at his brother and sister.

'I'd better go with him. It looks as if he's got something on his mind.' He followed the old man, wondering what had caused the unaccustomed curtness in the Admiral's tone.

43

Left on the boat, Paddy and Toby looked at each other.

'Phew!' Paddy said, widening her eyes. 'He was a bit sharp, wasn't he. He's not usually like that.'

'He thinks I'm a coward,' Toby said. 'He's disappointed in me. Charles is all right because he's not fit to serve, but I ought to be out there, killing people. That's what he thinks.' He shuddered. 'But I can't do it, Paddy! I *can't* kill people. I can't even kill a rabbit.'

'I know you can't.' Toby had been taken on rabbiting expeditions when he was a small boy and had returned white-faced, sick and shaking. It hadn't seemed to matter then – he hadn't *had* to kill anything and it didn't seem as if he'd ever have to. But now, with the country at war, killing had become a necessity. And it wasn't just rabbits, she thought. It was people. People like yourself.

'Can't you register as a conscientious objector?' she asked. 'I'm sure I read something about it in the paper. If they pass you, you don't have to go. You can do some other kind of work.'

'But what if they don't pass you? And even if they do, you have to go to prison to start with. Like a *criminal*. And I'm not even sure it's really to do with my conscience. Perhaps the Admiral's right and I'm just a coward. Anyway, I'm sure it'll all be over soon. It's got to be.' He looked up at the still, blue sky, reflected in the expanse of water around them, at the masts of the dinghies and yachts bobbing at their moorings in the harbour. 'I can't believe there are people fighting and killing each other just a few miles away. I can't believe it'll go on and on. Someone will stop it. Mr Churchill will stop it.'

Paddy heard the note of desperation in his voice. She looked at him and saw that he was indeed deeply afraid – not perhaps, of going to war, but of the killing he would have to do. She was the only person in the world, she thought, who really understood just how much Toby hated the idea of killing. But even if she went to the people who dealt with these things and told them, would they believe her? Would it help?

'I wonder what the Admiral wants to talk to Daddy about,' she said, pulling gently on *Minimus*'s painter so that it nudged *Wagtail*'s stern. 'He looked awfully serious. Do you suppose Charles is right and there's something up? Something he knows about? He is an Admiral, after all. They might still tell him things. They might even want him to go back into the Navy.'

Toby shrugged. They sat in silence for a few moments, listening

44

to Wendy's voice as she came to the end of her story. The shore was very quiet, the only sound the soft lapping of the water on the stones. A seabird flew overhead, calling in a raucous voice. As Toby had said, it was almost impossible to believe that there was a war going on less than fifty miles away.

There was something in the quality of the silence, however, that was like a cold finger, touching her mind with fear. There was a war going on. Men were being killed. And it might not end soon, as Toby so desperately hoped it would.

The day might come when Hitler's troops would indeed land on these shores and march through the quiet streets of villages like Emsworth.

Chapter Four

'I t's *Moonset*,' the Admiral said. He was sitting in Hubert's study with Hubert and Charles, and the whisky bottle was on the table between them. 'She's been requisitioned by the Navy.'

'*Moonset* has?' Hubert stared at him in surprise. 'What do they want her for?'

'It's not just her. The order went out over a fortnight ago. You must have heard the broadcast on the BBC. All powered boats between thirty and a hundred feet had to send particulars to the Admiralty within fourteen days. I imagine that's why you didn't put *Wagtail* forward – she's just under the thirty, isn't she?'

'She is, and I couldn't see why they'd want her. I mean, there must be hundreds of craft that size all round the country. What use are all those to the Navy? The smaller ones, anyway?'

'All sorts of uses. They'll take anything – pleasure-steamers, ferries, private yachts and cruisers. They want wooden craft for minesweeping – trawlers and so on, and they need more inshore patrol boats – think how much coastline we've got. That was the original plan, anyway, and I dare say it'll come to it yet. But now there's something else.' He looked at them, his face grave. 'There's a major disaster going on. We're facing catastrophe over in France. Catastrophe. There's no other word for it.'

The other two men were silent for a moment. Hubert rubbed a long, bony hand over his face. He had musician's hands, like Charles, and both were accomplished pianists as well as sailors.

Then he said, 'Disaster? Catastrophe? What are you talking about, Jeremy?'

The Admiral glanced towards the window, as if checking that they were not overheard. Then, very quietly, he spoke one word, and Charles found that he had been holding his breath. He let it out slowly.

'Retreat.'

Hubert's fine silver brows rose almost to his hairline. '*Retreat?*'

'I'm very much afraid so. I've been in touch with Bertie Ramsay – you remember him, we served together years ago, had him to stay a few times. Anyway, he's been on the Retired List for the past two or three years, been pottering about at home with his wife, doing a spot of gardening, messing about with horses and so on – but now he's back in the Service and down in Dover, masterminding the evacuation.'

'The evacuation? What evacuation?'

'From France,' the Admiral said sombrely. 'Look, this hasn't been put out to the public yet, but we're bringing all our men home – or as many as we possibly can. There are thousands of them there, Hubert, making for the beaches, and there's only one way to get them off – by small boats that can get close enough in and ferry 'em to the destroyers offshore. That's what Bertie wants his little ships for now. Forget inshore patrols – we've got the biggest rescue in history on our hands, and if we fall down on this job we may as well give up. We'll have no Army left to fight with. As it is, Churchill doesn't hold out hope for bringing back more than twenty thousand.'

'Is that all?' Hubert said. 'But how many are there?'

The Admiral drew in a short breath and then said in a bleak, quiet voice, 'Around half a million, I believe.'

Charles and Hubert stared at him. In their minds, they were trying to visualise the French beaches, once a holiday paradise with miles of sands and little resorts gay with carousels and deckchairs, now a seething mass of desperate men, waiting for rescue. They both shook their heads, unable to picture it.

'How long have we got?' Charles asked at last.

The Admiral shrugged. 'Who knows? A few days, no more. It's started already: the order went out last Sunday and ships have been going over all this week, bringing 'em back. It's not been made public yet, but I dare say it will be soon – you can't keep that sort of movement quiet for ever. And the Germans aren't going to sit back and let us do this without a struggle. They're bombing the ports continuously. Calais and Boulogne are already out of action.' He slapped the table with his open palm and the glasses trembled and clinked. 'The BEF are sitting ducks over there – sitting ducks! It's an unholy mess, and this damned surrender of King Leopold has made things a hundred times worse.'

'And these boats,' Hubert said, as if trying to make sense of the Admiral's words, 'craft like *Moonset* . . . who's taking them over the Channel? A lot of the owners will never even have been to sea.'

'They're putting a Naval man in command of most of them, and hoping the crews will volunteer. I don't doubt they'll get enough men to take them over.' He lifted his chin and gave them a steady look. 'I shall take *Moonset* myself, of course.'

'*You* will? But—'

'But what? I'm perfectly capable of it and I've been in action before. I'm an Admiral, for God's sake!' His look dared them to object further. 'I'm taking young Peter Murphy with me – good lad, one of the Bosham Sea Scouts – and my handyman and gardener, George Barlow. *Moonset*'s ready – I'm going back to Bosham on the next tide. The minute I get the call, I'll be off.'

'Where do you have to go?' Charles asked. 'Where will the men be waiting?'

'It's a harbour close to the Belgian border,' the Admiral said. 'I dare say most people have never even heard of it.' He paused. 'It's called Dunkirk.'

After dinner, with Betty sent home early, the family gathered in the drawing room. The house was quiet; only Catcher's snores and snuffles disturbed the peace as he lay stretched out in front of the fireplace, fast asleep.

Paddy was the first to speak. Sitting on the floor beside Catcher, her legs curled under her, she looked no more than twelve years old. Hubert and Olivia had been against her being present at all, but Toby had supported her and Charles found himself, for once, in agreement with his brother. He sat beside Sheila, holding her hand tightly and glancing from time to time at her white face. His parents

48

were on the opposite sofa, while the Admiral had been ensconced in the big leather armchair by the fire.

It had been a warm day but the evening was drawing in and the air had turned cool. Charles had lit the fire with some of the wood from an old apple tree, felled last year, and the room was filled with its scent. You could almost, he thought as he glanced round at his family, think we were about to tell stories or play some Christmas party game.

This was no game, however, and he couldn't guess how the story would unfold.

'Tell us what's happening,' Paddy demanded in a tight voice. 'Please. We've got to know.'

'I really think you ought to go and look after the children,' Olivia began, but her daughter interrupted her.

'They're fast asleep. I ought to know, I read them at least three stories. Please, Mummy, don't treat me like a child. I'm seventeen. People only a few months older than me are helping to fight the war.'

Olivia opened her mouth again but Hubert lifted his pale hand. 'Leave her alone, my dear. She's right, it affects us all. We've got to hear what Jeremy has to say.'

They turned their eyes to the Admiral. He was concentrating on filling his pipe, and didn't look up for a moment. When he was certain that it was drawing, he sighed and said, 'It's just as I told Hubert and Charles before dinner. The whole BEF is trapped over in France. The Huns are driving them back to the coast, and we're doing our best to get 'em out. And you know what'll happen if we don't. We'll have precious little Army left. The French coast is just a few miles away. If the Germans hold that, our whole south coast will be left exposed.' He paused, and his face was more solemn than any of them had ever known it. 'They'll invade,' he said gravely.

'So we're going to get them!' Paddy cried. 'We're going to rescue them!' She jumped to her feet. 'We've got to go at once!'

'Patricia!' Olivia's voice was sharp. 'Don't be silly. It's not up to people like us to decide what's to be done.' She looked at the Admiral. 'In any case, I imagine the Navy's doing all it can. Sending ships. They'll bring them back.'

'They're certainly doing all they can.' He took his pipe out of his mouth. 'But even the Royal Navy can't work miracles. Not every time, anyway. And this time, it seems that young Paddy here is right. Up to a point, at any rate. The BEF do need to be brought home, and I'm afraid the Navy can't do it alone.'

'I don't understand—'

'I've just told you,' Paddy interrupted again impatiently. 'He's talking about *Moonset*, aren't you, Admiral? They're going to send little boats to get the soldiers away from France. That's what it's about, isn't it?'

'But that's nonsense!'

'It isn't, Mummy. It really isn't. You see, I heard what they were saying in the study before dinner.' She caught the men's eyes upon her and blushed, but held up her head and met their look defiantly. 'Well, the window was open. I was just outside, I couldn't help hearing. It was lucky I was there, really,' she added. 'There could have been a spy outside, listening.'

They stared at her. Olivia's lips tightened, Charles's twitched and Toby burst out laughing. The Admiral bent over his pipe again, his expression hidden, and Hubert sighed and looked at his daughter as if he wasn't quite sure where she had come from. Sheila was the only one whose expression didn't change, and she was next to speak, in a tight, angry little voice.

'I don't know what you're all finding so funny. None of you seems to realise what this means. If the BEF is trapped, that means Alex is trapped too. He's there now, caught in some horrible hole perhaps, or being taken prisoner. Or – or killed.' Her voice broke and Charles squeezed her hand even more tightly.

'Alex will be all right,' he began, but she turned on him.

'You don't know that! You can't know. Some of them will be killed or taken prisoner – perhaps all of them. Why should Alex be all right?' She turned to her mother-in-law. 'Paddy's right – something's got to be done. Someone's got to go over there and rescue them.'

'Yes, but you heard what the Admiral said. The Navy—'

'He said the Navy can't do it on their own. And the Germans won't let them anyway. They've got ships too, and aeroplanes. Oh, it's awful.' She pulled her hand away from Charles's and covered her face. 'Alex is my twin. He's only thirty. He can't be left to die like a rat in a hole.'

They were all talking at once now. Sheila was crying, Paddy half in tears, Olivia dismayed but clinging to disbelief. Charles was trying to comfort his wife and even Hubert was adding his gentle voice to the hubbub. Only the Admiral and Toby were silent, and after a moment or two the Admiral cleared his throat and the voices gradually quietened.

'Let me give you the facts, as far as I know them. But please remember that I'm in a privileged position. No doubt everyone will know soon, but until it's generally released I must ask you all to keep it to yourselves.' He glanced round ruefully. 'I hadn't intended to tell any of you, except for Hubert and Charles, but I'm afraid young Patricia has rather spiked my guns.'

Paddy coloured but met his eyes steadily. He went on, 'Briefly, as I told you, the BEF is trapped. They – *we* – are withdrawing. "Retreat" isn't a word the British like to use, but withdrawal is a normal military tactic, and it doesn't mean we've lost the war, far from it. It simply means we'll regroup and build up our strength again for a future attack. But it *does* mean that we need to get our Army back to these shores as fast as possible. Paddy and Sheila are right. We can't leave our men there to be butchered.'

Sheila uttered a little cry and he gave her a remorseful glance. Olivia gasped. 'Jeremy!'

'I'm sorry. But you have to realise how serious this is. Otherwise you won't understand why we have to do what is required of us.'

'But *we* can't do anything,' Olivia said. 'It's up to the Navy. They're the ones with the ships.'

He shook his white head. 'No, Olivia. It's not up to the Navy – not entirely. They've got the ships, yes, but ships like destroyers, frigates, even battleships, aren't enough. They're too big, you see. They can't get in close enough to the beaches to get the men off.'

'The beaches? But isn't there a harbour?'

'Yes, but it can't possibly handle the number of men we have to get away. There are thousands, Olivia. *Hundreds* of thousands. And we've only a few days' grace, perhaps not even that. We'll have to use the beaches too. There are miles of beach, but they're shallow. That's why we need smaller boats.'

There was a tiny silence. Olivia stared at him, bewildered. Then Sheila said in a dry, husky voice, 'So what are we going to do?'

'Exactly what young Paddy overheard me saying before dinner.

They're sending little ships. Fishing boats. Thames barges. Pleasure-steamers, lifeboats, motor yachts. Ships like *Moonset*. They'll tow them across if necessary. But if it floats, it's going. A great many have gone already, but now they need more. They're asking for all the boats they can get.'

There was a small silence. Olivia was looking upset and bewildered, Sheila white-faced and shaking, Paddy tense and determined. After a moment or two, Charles said quietly, 'Anything that floats. *Wagtail* floats well enough.' He turned to his father. 'I'd like to take her too, if you don't mind.'

The others stared at him. Olivia began to speak first. 'Don't be ridiculous, Charles,' but her voice was drowned by the others. Hubert said, 'Take *Wagtail*? But she's not even been requisitioned.' Sheila caught his arm and cried, 'Charles, you can't!' Toby gave a nervous laugh, and Paddy leaped to her feet and shouted, 'Yes, yes, you must, and I'll come with you! Toby and I'll *both* come with you – won't we, Toby!'

The Admiral lifted one hand and then waited until the hubbub died down. He drew on his pipe and looked gravely at his godson.

'I'm sorry, Charles. Can't be done.'

Charles stared at him. 'Why not?'

The Admiral sighed. 'A hundred reasons, but let's settle for just a couple. As your father says, *Wagtail* hasn't been requisitioned. There's a good reason for that. Firstly, the minimum length of the craft they've taken is thirty feet – that's what's considered feasible for sailing in whatever waters may be encountered. The Channel's not always like a millpond, you know. Secondly, and I'm sorry about this, Charles, because I know you find it hard to accept, there's the question of your health.'

'My *health*? But I'm perfectly all right – you know I am! There's nothing I can't handle in taking *Wagtail* across the Channel. For heaven's sake, fresh sea air's the best thing for me.'

'But it won't be fresh sea air,' the Admiral said. 'Not on the French coast. It'll be smoke and flame and heaven knows what. And it's not just the air. The evacuation will be done under fire. There'll be bombing. Men will be working at full stretch, possibly for days at a time. This isn't going to be a pleasant day's sailing, Charles. It's action. Naval battle action.' He paused. 'We've already lost several ships – destroyers, motor vessels, even hospital ships, sunk or too

52

badly damaged to proceed further. I can't take the risk of letting you go.'

Sheila still held his arm. 'Listen to what the Admiral says, darling. It'll be too much for you.'

'Too much for me?' he echoed, shaking her hand away. He got up and walked over to the mantelpiece. Paddy, who was still on her feet, slipped back to the floor as he turned and faced them. 'Don't you realise what it's like for me? Don't any of you realise what it means, to be kept out of this war? *Unfit for service* – that's what they call me, as if I were some broken-down old car dumped on a rubbish tip. *Unfit* – to be a soldier, a sailor or an airman or any other bloody – sorry, Ma – thing of use. Unfit for anything better than sitting in a safe little office, with an air-raid shelter in the cellar for if I get frightened, pushing a pen round and doing nobody any good at all, as far as I can see. Just taking sides in their petty little squabbles while the rest of the world fights its way into chaos and *I* can't lift a finger, not even *one little finger*, to help my own country. I can't even defend my own family. And now here's something I could do – something to help, something vital, something that might even help bring back my own brother-in-law – and I'm told it'll be *too much for me*.' He stared bitterly at them. 'I might as well not be here. I might as well give up now.'

They looked back, horrified and embarrassed. Then Sheila said, 'I'm sorry, darling. I didn't mean it to sound like that.' She got up and went to him, laying her hand again on his arm and looking up into his face with tear-filled eyes. 'I just get so frightened. There's Alex in danger, and I'm so afraid for him, but for you to go too – well, I just don't think I could bear it. I could lose both of you. And if it's like the Admiral says it will be, perhaps he's right.' She looked at the old man, sitting by the fireplace with his pipe. 'Couldn't we have a little time to think about it? Does it have to be decided now?'

'It doesn't have to be decided at all,' Hubert said before the Admiral could answer. 'Charles asked if he could take *Wagtail*, and I'm saying no. As far as I can see, that's an end to the matter.'

'No?' Charles took a step towards his father. 'But—'

'I don't think the boat is up to it,' Hubert said. 'She's not built for it. It's too dangerous.'

'I don't accept that!'

'I'm afraid you'll have to. She's my boat.'

'Dad, *please* . . .'

Hubert ignored him. He stood up and looked down at his old friend. 'Thank you for taking us into your confidence, Jeremy. I appreciate it. But if you're going to catch the tide to get home tonight, you'll need to be leaving soon.'

'Yes.' The Admiral stood up too and looked gravely at the family. 'I shall be off now. Want to be ready when Bertie gives me the word.' He put his hand on Olivia's shoulder. 'Don't worry too much. I've spent my life at sea, and I've seen action before. This is just another job, and if it turns out to be my last,' he shrugged, 'well, so be it. I'll do it to the best of my ability.'

There was a short silence, as if no one knew quite what to say. Paddy and Sheila were both in tears, Olivia bewildered, Toby at a loss. Charles was white-faced, his lips pressed together and his jaw tense. At last, Hubert said, 'I'll walk down to the jetty with you.'

'We all will,' Sheila said, still holding Charles's arm tightly. 'We'll come and see you off.'

They moved out through the open French windows. The sun was low in the sky, lighting up the pale, fresh green of new leaves and throwing a golden pathway on the softly rippling waters of the harbour. There was just enough breeze to take the little sailing dinghy home. Paddy caught at the painter and drew the boat close to the jetty and the Admiral paused before stepping aboard.

'I'll telephone you before I go,' he said quietly, and Hubert nodded.

'Yes, please do. And in case we don't see you again before then – good luck.' He held out his hand. 'And let us know the minute you get back.'

The Admiral nodded, and shook his hand. They stood for a moment in silence and then Olivia and Sheila came forward and kissed him. Charles took his hand as well, his face set.

'Good luck, sir.'

'Thank you, Charles.' The Admiral laid one hand briefly on Charles's arm. He gave Toby a curt nod, then kissed Paddy's cheek. 'Look after your mother, now. These are difficult times.' He gave one last, swift glance round at the family and then stepped into the dinghy.

The others stood and looked at each other. Olivia shook her head as if dazed and said, 'I think I'll go to bed. All this has been rather a

54

shock.' She turned and began to drift back up the garden, a silvery ghost in the fading light. Hubert followed her and Charles took his wife's hand.

'Come for a walk.'

They walked slowly along the path beside the creek, watching the dusk creep over the garden and the first stars begin to prick at the sky. Sheila shivered and moved closer, and they stopped and gazed at the little brown sail, disappearing into the glow of the sunset.

Charles spoke again at last, his voice low and quivering with passion. 'How can anyone tell me I can't do this? How can *anyone* stop me going to Dunkirk?'

Paddy sat down on the jetty. Toby stood beside her, smoking a cigarette and staring at the water. He looked sombre, his normal flippant grin absent.

'Are you thinking what I'm thinking?' she asked quietly.

'Perhaps.' He moved his shoulders and turned down the corners of his mouth. 'Actually, I was thinking how nobody even thought for a moment of asking if *I* wanted to help in this. Obviously they all think I'm as unfit as Charles.'

'Or unwilling,' she said. 'But you're not, are you?'

'No, I'm not. I'd like to go, Paddy, but the Admiral doesn't even bother to suggest it – he'd rather take a Sea Scout or a gardener.' He turned to her. 'But I'm as good as any of them in a boat. And I'm not afraid of the danger. It's not being fired at that I object to, it's being the one who does the firing.'

'So why don't you take *Wagtail*?' she asked softly, and when he turned to her, she met his eyes and added, 'Why don't we take her together?'

Toby stared at her. A glimmer of mischief touched his eyes and he grinned. 'We can't. You know we can't.'

'Well, you can't take her on your own,' Paddy pointed out. 'And you know that I'm just as capable as you of handling her.'

He bit his lip, glanced away, then looked back. 'You heard what Dad said. He doesn't think *Wagtail*'s up to the conditions.'

'That was just an excuse,' she said impatiently. 'To stop Charles going. We all know she's up to it – it's what Dad built her for.' She gripped his arm. 'Come on, Toby. We can do it – we can take *Wagtail*, whatever anyone says. All we have to do is go, and it'll be

55

too late to stop us!' She jumped up and gripped both of his hands, gazing up into his face with eyes brilliant with excitement. 'That'll stop them treating you like a coward!'

Charles and Sheila closed the door of the bedroom that had been Charles's when he was a boy, and wasn't much different now except that it contained a double bed, and looked at each other.

'The Admiral's an old man,' Charles said at last, 'but he's going just the same. He can go to sea and risk his life for other people, he can *do* something towards this war, while I . . .' He bit his lip and fell silent.

'While you have to stay at home and be safe.' Sheila finished quietly. She sat beside him in her petticoat and slipped her arm round his shoulders. 'That's what you're thinking, isn't it? But you've got to stop thinking like that, darling. It isn't your fault.'

'I don't care if it's my fault or not! It's the fact that I can't *do* anything! I have to stay at home doing ridiculous things like drawing up Wills and suing unfortunate young men who were silly enough to ask unpleasant young women to marry them, while old men go off and fight my war for me. I have to wait here while the Admiral takes the risks I ought to be taking. While your brother risks his life in the Army. Even Toby will have to join up eventually, and he doesn't even want to. But he could end up a hero, just the same.'

'He could end up a dead hero. So could the Admiral. So could Alex. At least I'll still have you. The children will still have their father.' Sheila's arm tightened about his shoulders. 'I know I shouldn't be saying these things, Charles. I know I'm being selfish and unpatriotic, but I can't help it. I'm glad you don't have to go. I'm glad you can stay safe at home.'

Charles was silent for so long that she was afraid she had gone too far. She looked at him anxiously and then he turned to her swiftly. His eyes were burning with passion.

'I don't want to be killed, Sheila, any more than you do. But you've got to understand – this talk of invasion, it's not just talk. It's a real danger. The Germans are practically at our door. What's happened in Czechoslovakia, in Poland, in Holland and France, could happen here – soon. We'll all be in danger then. It won't be a question of being fit to fight. We'll have no choice. We have no choice now. *I* have no choice.'

She stared at him. 'What are you saying, Charles?'

'I'm saying that I've got to do my bit now. We've got a boat that's capable of crossing the Channel, whatever Father says. It's what he built her for. And I'm capable of taking her. I have to do this, Sheila. I *have* to.'

'But you can't! Not on your own.'

'I won't be on my own. Toby will come with me. Didn't you see his face when we were talking? He feels just the same. He won't be left out of this, Sheila. Just for once, my brother is going to surprise everyone.' He looked at her, his eyes very dark. 'Don't try to talk me out of this, Sheila. Please don't try any more.'

Slowly, gently, he slipped the straps of her petticoat from her shoulders and then quickly removed his own clothes. Naked, they slipped between the sheets and held each other close. For a long time, they lay without speaking, only their hands moving as they caressed each other's bodies. Sheila was quivering and Charles could feel her tears on his shoulders as he held her against him.

'Don't cry, my darling,' he whispered as he kissed her wet eyelids and began tenderly to make love to her. 'I'll be all right. I promise I'll be all right.'

How many other men had made that promise? he wondered. How many other men, stranded in France at this very moment, had made that promise to their wives and sweethearts, their mothers and their sisters? And how many would be able to keep it if others, like himself and the Admiral, didn't do all they could to help them?

Chapter Five

In the end, Robby had told his family the truth about his journey on the *Countess*. Sitting round the kitchen table, with Molly's hand held firmly in his, he had sworn them all to secrecy until the news came out, and they'd listened in silence, save for a little gasp from his mother as she put her hand to her mouth. His father had watched him, his face grave, and Robby was reminded of his mother's words, that for thousands of men in the Great War there had been no way out. For a moment, he wished he'd said nothing, but there had never been secrets between them and he felt a sharp need for their blessing before he left.

'Jan . . .' Hetty said at last. 'Our Jan.' And she turned towards her husband, tears sliding down her cheeks.

'It's a bad do,' Jethro said gruffly, putting his arm round her shoulders. 'But I don't suppose he's in any worse case now than he has been all along. And at least us knows there's chaps like our Robby going over to fetch him back safe.' He looked over to his son. ''Tain't no use telling 'ee to be careful, I know. You'm going to war and you'll have to do whatever's required of you. But us'll be thinking of 'ee and praying for 'ee every minute, till us knows you'm safe again. 'Tis all us can do – wish us could do more.'

'It's all I want,' Robby said quietly. 'It means a lot to me, knowing you're all here keeping things going at home same as usual. 'Tis what we're fighting for, after all.' He squeezed Molly's hand and reached over to lay his other hand on his mother's arm. 'Don't fret, mother. This job's only going to take a few days. And the *Countess*'ll look after me.'

She smiled shakily and then seemed to gather herself together. Looking at the clock, she said, 'It's after eight – there's not much time if you've to be down to the quay by nine. I've made you some fresh pasties, and there's a pound cake in the tin.' She got up briskly, her tears wiped away, and began to clear the table. Molly got up to help and Hetty lifted one hand to stop her. 'You sit there with Robby, maid. He can walk you home on the way to the boat, and we'll fetch 'ee in the morning. We'm coming to see you off,' she told Robby. 'That's right, en't it, Jethro?'

Her husband nodded. 'Wish 'ee Godspeed,' he said. 'And George too, and t'other chaps. Won't do no harm, that, will it? It won't give the game away?'

'No, I don't think so.' Everyone would know soon enough anyway. The whole country would know what was happening in France and at Dunkirk.

Robby looked round the kitchen at his family and tried again to imagine what it would be like – German soldiers coming ashore on English soil, marching through English streets. Here, in Stoke Gabriel, in Totnes. Pushing open the door of this very cottage, thrusting their way in, shouting, stamping, threatening his family – attacking his own mother, his sweetheart Molly . . . He felt sick. It couldn't be allowed to happen. They had to be stopped. But with the best will in the world, unless the Army were brought back, there would be no way of stopping them.

We'll do it, he thought with determination. We'll bring them back because we need them and because we can't leave them there anyway. They're our men – our boys. We've got to get them back, and we will.

And *then* we can show Hitler just what Britain's made of . . .

George Ellery was already aboard the *Berry Pomeroy* when Robby arrived at the Town Quay at sunset. He'd been one of the River Dart Steamboat Company's skippers for years now and knew the river and its tides and peculiarities like the back of his hand. Robby had known him all his life and had worked under his direction during that summer before he'd gone away to *St Vincent*.

George was on deck, supervising the stowing of the last of his stores when Robby appeared. He glanced up, took the old pipe out of his mouth and nodded. 'Heard you was coming, boy. Navy Captain now, be 'ee?'

'Not quite.' Robby jumped on to the deck. 'Are you going all the way?'

'Don't think so. Navy won't trust a poor old Dev'n skipper to go to sea proper. All I got to do is take her to Ramsgate, but whether she'll ever come home again is anybody's guess. Been requisitioned already, see, so I got to come home best way I can.' He looked down at the wooden deck and shrugged. 'Maybe this'll be the last trip I'll ever take in the *Berry*. Seems I've hardly had time to get used to she.'

Robby nodded. *Berry Pomeroy* had only been built two years earlier, in Dartmouth, making his own ship, the twelve-year-old *Countess Wear*, look old-fashioned. He'd have liked to command the newer boat, but whoever had made the decision knew what they were doing. It was on *Countess* that Robby had worked, and he knew her little quirks as well as anyone else on the river, apart from her own skipper and Danny.

'Why isn't Mr Knowles taking *Countess* himself?' he asked. 'If they're happy for you to take the *Berry*, I'd have thought they'd have asked him too.'

'Asked!' George Ellery said with a laugh. 'I don't think 'twas a matter of *asking*. But poor old Sam Knowles is a bit under the weather, didn't no one tell you? Got a growth. Doctor don't hold out much hope for un.'

The sound of hurrying feet caused them both to turn and Robby saw his old friend Danny running down the quay towards them. His round face was crimson beneath the tumble of unruly dark hair and he was breathing hard, but he beamed with pleasure at the sight of Robby in his square-rig matelot's uniform. He skidded to a halt and stuck out his hand.

'Come back to see how it's done then, have you, boy? Us knowed there was a Navy chap coming to take charge, but us never guessed they was that short-handed they'd send 'ee.'

'You mind your tongue when you'm talking to the captain,' Robby grinned back. 'Clap 'ee in irons below decks, I will . . . It's good to see you again, Danny. I thought you might've been called up by now.'

'Not yet, though I've been thinking I might volunteer. Probably will, when this job's done.' He cast a critical eye over the deck. 'All to your satisfaction, is it?'

'Good enough. Got bad news for the brightwork, though – all got to be painted grey. Camouflage, see. That'll give you something to do after, getting the shine back. Any road, we've got a busy night ahead of us. Orders are to take off all the seats and cushions – everything but the life-rafts – and then we're off to Dartmouth at first light to take on stores and enough fuel to get round to Ramsgate. It'll be a long trip for the old girl – couple of hundred miles. And we're picking up another bloke in Dartmouth, so I'm told.'

'Officer?' Danny asked. 'From Dartmouth College?'

Robby shook his head. 'Don't think so. They're only putting one Navy chap on each boat. Got to have three, see, so that one can be getting a rest while the other two handle her. I reckon it'll be one of the company men down there, volunteered for the job.'

By dawn, the preparations were complete and they'd even had time for a few hours' sleep. Rob and Danny dossed down on the seats that served also as life-rafts, and were woken by the *Berry Pomeroy*'s whistle and the sound of voices from the quay. They tumbled up on deck and found a little gathering awaiting them. George's wife and family were there, and behind them were Robby's parents and Molly and, with her, another girl with brown hair twisted into 'earphones' at the side of her head.

Susie! he thought. Jan's girl. Susie Lashbrook. I never thought about her. He felt a moment of guilt that he had forgotten his brother's sweetheart, and wondered who had fetched her along. Someone – his father, most likely – must have gone over the river to Dittisham and brought her back to Stoke.

'Robby!' Molly jumped aboard and caught at his arms. 'I couldn't let you go without saying a proper goodbye.'

'I thought we did that last night,' he said, looking down into her upturned face. 'And it's not goodbye for ever, Moll. I'll be back afore you has time to turn round.'

'I hope so. Oh Robby, I hope so.' She buried her face against his chest. On the quay, his mother and father were looking down at them, but Susie was already on deck, her face taut. She spoke to him quietly, aware that there were others on the quay who hadn't yet been told the real situation.

'You'll find him, won't you, Rob? You'll find Jan and bring him home?'

'I'll try, Susie. But you know there's thousands of men over there. I don't suppose I'll be the one to find him, but someone will. He'll come back all right, don't you fret.'

'I want *you* to find him,' she said, staring intently into his eyes. 'I want you to bring him home on the *Countess*. I want to be here on the quay when you come back with him on deck, looking out for me. Please, Robby.'

He looked at her, wondering how he could tell her what it was like to be at sea and see other ships sink and the men jump screaming into the water, some terribly injured, some even on fire. Robby knew that the chances of finding his own brother were remote, yet in his heart he harboured the same hope as Susie, that he would be the one to bring Jan triumphantly home on board the little ship that they all knew so well. Then reality asserted itself and he shook his head.

'I'll do whatever I can, Susie, I promise you that. The main thing is to get him back, though. It don't matter too much who does it.' He gave her a quick kiss, the first he had ever given to his brother's girl, and then turned back to Molly. 'I've got to say goodbye now. The tide's on the turn – we must be on our way.'

'You'll be careful, won't you,' she said, looking gravely up at him. 'Don't go taking no silly risks, now.'

He smiled wryly, knowing that he'd be taking risks every moment until he was back again – if he came back at all. Then he hopped back on to the quay again to hug his mother and shake his father's hand.

'God go with you, son,' Jethro Endacott said gruffly. 'You'll do your best, I know that, and nobody can ask for more.'

'Bring him back if you can,' Hetty whispered. 'And come back safe yourself. You'm both my boys – I don't want to lose neither of you.' The tears fell despite her efforts, and she wiped them away, first with the back of one hand and then with both palms. Robby, not far from tears himself, hugged her tightly and then jumped back aboard. Molly and Susie were back on the quay and Danny had appeared from the engine-room, ready to cast off.

George Ellery was at the wheel of the *Berry Pomeroy*. He nodded at Robby in the grey light and the two steamers got under way, turning in the narrow reach to head off downriver. Within moments, the little group on the quay were no more than small figures, waving like clockwork dolls, and then they were gone, concealed by the first bend as the river made its way down to the sea.

Danny had gone back below to his engines. Robby was alone in the small wheelhouse. He stood upright, legs braced apart, enjoying the touch of the familiar wooden wheel in his hands once more and feeling a strange amazement that he was there in command of this little ship that he had known so well and heading for an operation of a kind that had never been done before.

He did not know whether it would be a triumphant success or a terrible failure. All he knew was that he had been trained for this moment, that he was trusted and would do his best to ensure its success. It wasn't just up to him; but it *was* up to hundreds of other men like him. He was a small cog in a large wheel, but the wheel depended on every one of those cogs.

We'll do it together, he thought, gripping the little ship's wheel between his hands. You and me, *Countess* – we'll do it together.

Susie, Molly and the Endacotts watched the two little ships out of sight and then turned away. It was almost fully light now, the sun just beginning to come above the horizon. It was going to be a lovely morning, and there was nothing anywhere to show that the country was at war and facing possible invasion.

'You'll come back with us for a bite of breakfast, you maids,' Hetty said, and the girls nodded.

'Thanks, Mrs Endacott, I will,' Susie said. ''Tis no use going back home now. I just need to tidy up a bit afore going to work.' Susie was a maid at Greenway, just across the river from Dittisham. 'I can catch the bus round to Galmpton and walk from there. Madam will understand if I'm a bit late.'

'And I told Mrs Halford I'd be at the farm after breakfast,' Molly said. 'She knows there's summat up.'

They bade goodbye to the Ellerys and began to walk slowly away from the quay to where the farm cart waited, with old Nobby cropping at the grass beside the road. Molly paused a moment to rub his soft velvet nose with one hand, and then climbed up into the cart after the others. They sat on the narrow benches, swaying as the big horse thrust his weight into the shafts.

'It don't seem possible, do it,' Hetty said at last, gazing at the banks still with their freckling of late primroses and misty fringe of bluebells. 'All that fighting going on just over the Channel, and the Germans harrying our boys till they got to send little boats like the *Countess* over to fetch 'em home. It don't seem to make no sort o' sense to me.'

'Nor me,' her husband said. 'But war *don't* make sense, Hetty, whichever way up you look at it. In the last lot we all thought we knew what it was about to start with, but once you been fighting for a while you forgets there was ever a reason for it. You just has to kill as many of the other side as you can and do your best to stay alive. It's for them in charge to decide what 'tis all about, and I'm not all that certain they got the rights and wrongs of it straight in their heads either.'

'So who does know?' Susie asked, her voice trembling. 'Who is it who decides that boys like Robby and Jan have to fight and be killed? Mr Chamberlain said there wasn't going to be no war. Peace in our time, that's what he said.'

'That's right,' Molly agreed. 'Just eighteen months ago, that was, no more, and look at us now. Look at Robby, going off in the *Countess* when he's supposed to be on proper Naval ships. Look at Jan, over there somewhere with God knows what happening. It was lies, that's what it was. Lies.'

'Well, at least Mr Chamberlain's gone now and they've put Mr Churchill in charge,' Hetty said. 'If anyone can put things right again and show Hitler what British boys are made of, he can. We just got to hope it's not too late, that's all.'

'What you've just said is right, Molly,' Jethro said quietly. ''Tis *God* knows what 'tis all about, and He'll be the final judge of it all. We'll say prayers for them all in church, and leave it in His hands.'

The cart clopped and creaked through the lanes to Stoke Gabriel. Across the fields, Molly could see the blue curves of the river, snaking its way to the sea. Somewhere down there were *Berry Pomeroy* and *Countess Wear*, on the first part of their voyage to France.

Robby had told her that there would be hundreds of little ships, many even smaller than these two, going on the same desperate mission. If they failed, the greater part of the Army would be lost and the shores of Britain almost impossible to defend from the invader.

We won't fail, though, she thought, and remembered the speech Mr Churchill had made when he was appointed Prime Minister only a fortnight earlier. *'You ask what is our aim? I can answer in one word: Victory – victory at all costs, victory in spite of all terror, victory however hard and long the road may be: for without victory there is no survival.'* And then, at the end, the ringing exhortation: *'I feel sure that our cause will not be suffered to fail . . . Come, let us go forward together, with our united strength!'*

That's it, she thought. We've got to win, because if we don't we can't survive. And we *will* win, because we've got thousands of men like Robby and Jan, and little ships like *Countess Wear* and *Berry Pomeroy*. That's what he means by united strength – all the little people and the little ships, fighting together.

And the women at home, holding life ready for when the men came home, holding on to the things that matter.

Chapter Six

Thursday, 30 May

In company with the *Mew* and the *Berry Pomeroy*, the *Countess Wear* was in Dartmouth by six. There, jostling together by the Town Quays, their owners bewildered and anxious, they found a small fleet of boats which had been brought round from Lympstone and Exmouth. As the light grew stronger over the wide river mouth so that the green hills were reflected in the still blue water, the Navy bustled about between them, noting their names and capacity, and handing out charts and orders.

George Ellery came over on to the *Countess*'s deck and lit his pipe. Robby, who was overseeing the loading of stores, left his job for a minute or two and came to talk to him.

''Tis a strange old job, this, my handsome,' George said. 'I suppose you don't know no more than the rest of us what it's all about.' He cocked a bright blue eye at Robby, inviting him to share any information he had.

Robby did know more, but it wasn't for him to say. He lifted one shoulder and said, 'Inshore patrol boats, that's what these old girls are going to be. Give 'em a few tales to tell when 'tis all over.'

George drew on his pipe and gave him a narrow glance. 'Ah, mebbe. And all around Dover? Don't 'em want inshore patrols round this part of the coast, then? Mebbe the Germans won't come down this far to invade, is that what 'tis?' He waited a moment, then shrugged. 'Strikes me there's more to this than meets the eye, but I can see you'm not in a position to talk about it. Well, I don't mind a bit of a sea-trip. Make a change from going up and down the river.'

Robby nodded and they turned their attention to the rest of the

66

preparations. The *Countess Wear* was slightly smaller than the *Berry Pomeroy* – a single-deck vessel with an engine-room, a small wheelhouse and just a tiny lavatory or 'heads'. All the same, she could take over 150 passengers and there was plenty of room for the stores. On the way home, Robby thought, they'd need all the space they could get for the men, but by that time they'd have eaten and drunk most of the stores anyway.

The stores were being loaded on by sailors from the college on the hill above the little town – matelots like Robby, not the officers whose training college it was. They brought cases of bread and bacon, tins of condensed milk, cartons of tea and a huge tin of ship's cocoa (known more familiarly as 'kye'). Neither *Berry Pomeroy* nor the *Countess Wear* had been equipped with proper galleys, for the trips they made were never expected to last more than an hour or so, and Robby was relieved to see that a Primus stove, paraffin and matches had been included in the delivery.

'Forty gallons of diesel for you,' the Leading Hand said as two sailors manhandled a large drum from the way to the deck. 'We'll lash it on the stern.'

Robby nodded, his eyes on an officer on his way down the quay with a sheaf of papers in his hand. 'Those our orders, sir?'

'That's right. Make for Dover first, then you'll probably go on to Ramsgate. We've managed to find you a few charts. You should do the journey in about twenty-four hours, maybe a bit more. There'll be plenty of other shipping about but you won't be able to communicate much – you've no wireless transmitter on board and you can't use lights at night, of course. You're on your own as far as navigation's concerned, but you can fly the red ensign and your International Code signal flags to indicate that you're on Admiralty business. Your extra hand will bring them with him.' He gave Robby a sharp look. 'Any questions?'

'Will I be able to refuel if necessary? We're not equipped for long journeys and I'm not sure the extra forty gallons will be enough.'

'You might need to put in somewhere for refuelling – Pompey, probably, or maybe Newhaven – but this'll get you most of the way. With good weather, you should be able to do it – the problem will only come if a storm blows up.' He glanced round as a heavily built man in the square-rig uniform of a matelot, like Robby but with a stoker's badge on his sleeve, came along the quay with the rolling gait of a man who has spent years at sea. 'This is probably your extra hand now.'

'Leading Stoker Bell reporting, sir.' The sailor saluted smartly and hopped nimbly aboard with his bundle of flags. He had grey hair and a grey beard and moustache, clipped short. 'Always thought I'd look for a job on one of these little craft when I left the Andrew – didn't expect it'd come as soon as this.' He spoke with a humorous, Southern Counties twang and Robby, guessing his age to be past forty, thought he'd probably been about to leave the Service when war broke out. He was ideally built to be a stoker, short but powerful, and he looked just the sort of chap you wanted with you on a job like this. 'I'll go down below for a look-see, then I'll get these signals up.' He swung himself down through the hatch to where Danny was already giving the two engines a thorough check.

'Salt of the earth,' the officer remarked, and gave Robby a sharp nod. 'You'll be all right with him, but the ship's your responsibility, understand? Wish you luck.' He then crossed the deck to the *Berry Pomeroy* to talk to George Ellery.

Robby stood in the wheelhouse examining the papers. The charts were old Admiralty ones, yellowing with age, ringed and splashed with tea stains and with fading course lines that must have been drawn years ago. Robby surmised that they were from the College, probably used by officers in training as they sailed the coast, and wondered what history they held, what captains and admirals might have used them at the beginning of their naval career.

The distance from Dartmouth to Dover was exactly 200 nautical miles. He still wasn't clear whether they were to stay there or go on to the main collection point at Ramsgate, but they'd get further orders and be able to refuel there, if they hadn't done so already. He reckoned that by keeping to a speed of eight knots he should be able to make it to Dover without putting in anywhere else, which would save a lot of time. It was a long journey to Dunkirk.

The sun was already climbing over Kingswear as the three little ships slid down the river on the ebbing tide. Once out of the estuary, Robby brought the trio round to an easterly course, leaving the big, lumpy Mew Stone and the smaller Blackstone rocks clear to port. The course angled them away from the rocky cliffs of the south Devon coastline and soon they were abeam of Berry Head and the broad sweep of Torbay.

During the night, Robby had checked the Reeds almanac for the tide times. Knowledge of tides and the way they behaved had been a part of him since he was a small boy, and he knew that in the next twenty-four hours they would get two eastgoing flood tides and two westgoing ebbs. The help given by one would be partially cancelled out by the hindrance of the other but, on the other hand, low water was in about two hours, so they would pick up the benefit of the first Channel flood, which was vital for getting round Portland Bill and, if all went well with the rest of the voyage, it would be daylight again by the time they made Dover. He didn't want to arrive before dawn, not with all the other shipping there was likely to be about by then and none of them carrying lights.

Danny came up from the engine-room and stood by Rob's side, looking at the wide bay. 'Remember coming here for day-trips when we were liddle tackers? My mum and dad used to take me and my sisters a couple of times every summer. And we used to go on church outings and things like that too, remember? Torquay, Paignton, Brixham – it was smashing. I always liked Brixham best, mind. Torquay's a bit too smart for me.'

Robby nodded. 'I liked the sands at Goodrington. Here, look – isn't that the *Lady Cable*, that used to take us on trips round the bay? Reckon she's going too?'

They stared at the motor launch which was heading out of the bay towards them, sending up a froth of spume from its bow wave. The launch was white, with long, lean lines – about forty foot, Robby estimated and had a nice wheelhouse. He'd been aboard her quite a few times on trips round the bay or back along the coast to Dartmouth.

'She've got her flags up,' Danny noted. 'Must be coming along o' we.' He gave the skipper a wave and they watched as the craft turned to set the same course as their own. 'There be quite a few of us now.'

The little fleet continued on its way. The tide had slackened and would soon be in their favour again, pushing them on at about ten knots towards Portland Bill. 'It's about forty miles to the Bill,' Robby said, half to himself, 'and we've got to get there before the tide turns against us again. Otherwise we could take hours plugging away against it – the water comes round that headland like a torrent and it's all rocks.' He consulted the charts again. 'Should make it with an hour to spare if we keep the speed as it is now.'

Jimmy Bell came up with a mug of tea in each hand. 'Thought you'd like a wet, Skip. Yours is down below, Danny.' He settled against the coaming and gazed reflectively at the cliffs, red rocks below fringes of green. 'Pretty, innit? I always liked Devon. Sussex man I am really, but me and the missus reckoned we might stop down this way when I swallow the anchor.' He gave a rueful shrug. 'Dunno when that'll be now.'

The sea was as smooth as glass but the Channel swell, rolling up from the west, lifted the *Countess*'s stern and set her rolling gently as she foamed through the water. Jimmy finished his tea and smacked his lips. 'I'll fry up a few slices of bacon. Did I see some eggs amongst the stores? Better use them before they gets smashed, eh?'

Robby nodded. 'My mother gave me them. They're from our own hens. I live on the Dart, near Totnes – that's why I was given this command, because I know the ship.' He patted the ledge of the wheelhouse. 'Used to work on her in the holidays, that sort of thing.'

'Fresh eggs!' the stoker said with a whistle. 'That's a treat, eh! I'll get started on them now, and afterwards we can set young Danny to trolling for a few mackerel. No sense in wasting good food when it's to be had.'

He was as handy with a Primus stove as he was with an engine, Robby thought when the 'wads' appeared a few minutes later – thick, crusty sandwiches cut from the home-made loaves his mother had given him, filled with crisp bacon and eggs fried soft so that the yolks soaked into the bread. He wolfed them down, realising suddenly just how hungry he was, and nodded approvingly as Danny trailed fishing-lines over the stern for the mackerel abounding in the sea. He started to reel them in almost at once, and soon had a dozen or more in the bucket at his feet. He began to gut them, throwing the entrails overboard and attracting a crowd of herring-gulls that wheeled and screeched around the boat, squabbling furiously over the scraps that tossed in the wake.

'Anybody'd think we were on our flipping holidays,' Rob remarked. They were out of sight of land now and the sun was warm on his face. The *Berry Pomeroy* and *Mew* were not far away, with *Lady Cable* on their port side. To anyone watching, it would look

70

like no more than a small party of pleasure-craft out for a jaunt. 'You can take over for a bit if you like, Danny, and I'll do the fishing.'

Leaving the wheelhouse, he felt a wave of tiredness wash over him. He'd had little sleep last night and they'd been on the move since dawn; he'd been standing at the wheel for over three hours. He sat down abruptly and Jimmy Bell appeared from the engine-room and handed him another mug of tea.

'Get that down you, Skip, and then put your head down for a bit. We've still got a long way to go, and there's a big job ahead of us.' He shook his head and spat over the side. 'God knows what good we can do, little boat like this. Pick up coupla hundred at the most. Drop in the ocean, that's all that'll be.'

'We're to ferry them from the beaches to the big ships offshore,' Robby said. 'Four or five trips and we can save a thousand. That's worth doing, isn't it?'

The stoker regarded him for a moment, then nodded. 'Course it is. If we can dodge the bombs and bullets that long.'

Rob glanced over at Danny. His old friend was still steering a steady course, but his face had paled. 'You don't have to go, Dan,' he said. 'There'll be other volunteers at Ramsgate, and probably more Naval chaps too. You can go home then if you want to.'

'Who said anything about going home, then?' Danny's chin lifted. 'I've already put down me name for the Navy anyway – I might as well see some action now I've got the chance. Anyway, the village has got three other blokes in the BEF as well as your Jan. I'd never be able to hold up me head if I went home without at least trying to get 'em back.'

Robby nodded and said no more. Jimmy dropped below again and Robby went to sit in the bow, staring across the broad bay for the first sight of Portland Bill. The wooden deck trembled gently with the throbbing of the engines and the water creamed against the bows. Maybe we ought to do a bit more painting, he thought, noticing that the brightwork hadn't all been covered with the grey camouflage. He'd do it just as soon as he finished drinking this tea . . .

The feel of cool liquid soaking into his trousers woke him with a jump and he swore as he realised that the last few drops of tea were dripping from the mug tilting in his hand. Shaking his head like a dog, he stared ahead and then rubbed his eyes and looked again.

'There it is! That's the Bill.' A narrow causeway led from the mainland to the swell of the Isle of Portland, with its two lighthouses, the old one and the new, standing on the southern tip. He jumped up and ran back along the deck to the wheelhouse. 'OK, Danny, I'll take her again now. We need to aim for the middle of the Bill itself, see – the tide comes strong round Lyme Bay just there and it'll take us right round the tip. We don't want to be too far off, though. There's an inner passage a cable's length off the rocks. If we miss that we'll be in the middle of Portland Race and it'll chuck us all over the place.'

Danny stood beside him as Rob took the little ship across the sweep of the bay and let the current take them south. The lighthouse reared above them, impossibly close, and he felt Danny stir beside him. 'It's all right, Dan boy,' he said. 'I sailed here a lot when I was on my training – it's just the job for teaching seamanship.' He held the wheel firm in his hands. 'Not that it's a nursery, mind – there've been many a vessel thrown offbeam in this tide. There's five miles of it, see.' He jerked his head at the turbulence just beyond the narrow passage they were using. 'You only know the rocks are there because of all that commotion – but they're there, all right, under the surface.'

'Have you seen boats hit them?' Danny asked.

'Well, it isn't the rocks exactly – you can take quite a big ship over them. It's the way the tide runs, see. The current's so fast, it sort of piles itself up and the waves crash together and throw you all over the shop. They can go right over the top of you, knock you sideways. It can be proper nasty.'

'Ah,' Jimmy Bell said, appearing beside them, 'that's right. Had a couple of narrow escapes myself round here.'

Robby nodded. 'Me too. Thought I wasn't going to come out of it alive, once or twice.' And silently, as he stood at the wheel of a boat built mainly for river cruising, he thanked the men who had trained him so harshly and so well.

Almost caught several times by the ferocity of the current, Robby stood firm, refusing to give way, and suddenly it was over. Followed by the rest of the little fleet, they swept through the narrow passage just off the rocks, borne on a current that was just as fierce below the waves, yet as calm as glass on the surface. He cast a swift glance behind him to make sure the other boats were through as well, and relaxed.

'That's it,' he said thankfully. 'We're all right now. Time for a cuppa to celebrate, eh, Jimmy?'

Jimmy stuck one thumb in the air and dived below again, and Rob felt a thrill of sheer pleasure at having brought his little ship successfully through the tricky passage. Then the *Countess* shuddered and stopped dead, the wheel jinking in his hands. He saw the bow jerk, then the steady note of the engine faltered and began a desperate, guttural choking. For a moment, he thought they had hit a rock; then he glanced behind and saw the small red buoy trailing on the waves and knew instantly what had happened.

'Damn and blast! We've fouled a bloody lobster pot!' He slammed the engine into neutral and shouted for the stoker. '*Jimmy!*'

Jimmy Bell came leaping up from the engine-room. 'What the hell's going on?'

'Lobster-pot buoy,' Robby told him tersely. 'They're everywhere. We've fouled on the line. Get the boathook – see if you can grab the buoy and pull it clear. If it's not wound round too tight . . .' He watched anxiously as the two men reached out with the hook, grabbing the buoy, missed, grabbed again, and finally captured it and dragged it towards the boat. He tried the engine again, but at the first snarl cut back into neutral. 'Oh hell! It's still there.'

'I'll go over the side,' Danny offered, but Robby shook his head.

'We'll go astern, see if that'll clear it.' The engine protested loudly and he went back once more into neutral, afraid of doing real damage. 'Let's try working the gears.' Together, they lifted a section of the wheelhouse floor to reveal the gear-chamber and for a moment it seemed that this might work, but the engine was still unhappy and he knew that the line was still tangled round the shaft. He swore again, furious with himself for allowing this to happen. If they didn't get it clear, they could ruin the engine. He could feel the shame already, not to mention the bitter disappointment of not being able to continue his mission. How many soldiers would die on the beaches of Dunkirk because the *Countess* wasn't there to save them? He tried the gears again, with no success.

'Get the bloody thing onboard. If we can cut the line—' But when they dragged the buoy aboard, it was to find the line shredded and almost broken through. Clearly, the rest of it was still wrapped around the propeller, but at least they weren't anchored to the bottom by the pot itself. Robby tried the engines again, but knew by the sound that the shaft was still fouled. He glowered at the buoy and bit his lip, thinking through the best course to take next.

'Open the inspection hatches, Jimmy. We might be able to get it off through those.'

Jimmy ducked down into the engine-room and opened up the hollow tubes which were let into the hull above the propellers. Unclamping the disc at the top, he withdrew the rod which secured the second disc to the outer end, and peered into the depths. Icy sea-water splashed into his face and he muttered something and reached for the breadknife which he had last used to make egg and bacon wads.

'I dunno if this is going to reach,' he growled, stretching his arm into the depths and sawing away with the knife. 'It don't feel too bad – just a couple of lines wrapped round, that's all . . . Oh, hell! I've lost the flaming knife.' He withdrew his arm and more water sloshed over the top of the tube and into the cabin. 'Sorry, Skip.'

'I'll have to go over,' Danny said again, clattering back on deck and pulling off his rubber boots and heavy jersey and trousers as he spoke. 'I've got my jack-knife – sharp as a razor, it be.'

'Not without a line, you don't.' Robby knew well enough that Danny was a good swimmer, but he wasn't going to take any more risks. 'There are some hellish currents here.' He glanced over the side. They were drifting but not in any danger and now would be as safe a time as any. 'OK, then.'

Quickly, as the boat wallowed, he fastened Danny to a long line and he slipped over the stern. Robby heard his gasp of shock as the cold water hit his almost naked body, and then he disappeared. Robby waited anxiously. He'd seen this done before, but only by experienced seamen and Danny was a river sailor. Moreover, the water was bitterly cold and it was dangerous to stay in for long. I don't know what I'm going to say to his mum and dad if anything happens now, he thought, wishing he'd not agreed to this. I should have thought about the lobster pots. I knew they were there, but I was so bloody pleased with myself for getting through the passage . . .

Danny's head broke surface. 'I've found it, Rob. It's wound round two or three times.' He was already shuddering with cold, but he took a deep breath and disappeared again, while Robby did his best to keep the boat steady. He stared at the water, counting the seconds. A minute went by – too long in this water, it was like ice – and then Danny surfaced, shook his head, took a deep breath and dived once more. I hope to God he don't have to do this too many times, Robby thought. Working underwater was exhausting enough; working under a boat in the cold, murky waters off Portland Bill held all kinds of perils. Even at slack tide, Danny could be swept away from the boat by the current; he might get his own line tangled in the propeller or round some rocks; he might get disoriented, knock his head on the bottom of the rocking boat – the images crowded in on Robby's mind. A fine start to the rescue this would be, he thought bitterly – losing a man before we even get to Dover, and him my best friend and all.

There was a flurry of broken water and Danny's face appeared, water streaming from the black hair plastered to his skull, face as white as bone but split by a broad grin. 'All clear!' He waved a length of line in one hand. 'Jimmy cut one bit and I got the other. And there's no damage done. Pity there's no lobster on the end of it.'

Bell appeared at the hatch, his thumb stuck up. 'OK now, Skip. All battened down again. Start engines, shall we?'

'We'd better get Danny back aboard first,' Robby said, grinning with relief. 'We might need him again.' He sent a small prayer of gratitude winging towards heaven. 'Come on, boy. Up you come.'

Getting Danny back on board the small ship was one of the most difficult things they had had to do yet. You needed something more to hold on to than a couple of hands and arms, Robby thought, stretching down to try to get a purchase on the slippery skin. Twice they thought they had him, only to feel him slither out of their grasp. Robby began to feel anxious again. Danny was shaking with cold; if they didn't get him out soon, he'd be in a bad way. Oh God, let us get him back, he prayed. Don't let us lose him now . . .

'You needs a pair of handles, son,' Jimmy grunted, and managed to get one strong arm hooked under Danny's leg. Together, they dragged him over the stern and landed him like a floundering seal.

'Well done, son,' Jimmy said, handing him a lump of clean cotton waste with which to dry himself. 'Sorry we got no fresh white towels

. . . Get your clothes back on quick and I'll put the kettle on. Nice drop of hot kye, that's what you need.' He ducked below again to start the engine and Robby looked at his old friend and blew out his cheeks.

'That was a bad moment. Thanks, Dan.'

'All part o' the service. Always was master at swimming underwater.' Danny lay on the deck, panting and shivering, then rolled over and sat up. Somewhat shakily, he ran his fingers through his black hair and grinned. 'Reckon I'd better get up in the bow and keep an eye out for more o' they buggers.' Still shivering, he grabbed his clothes and took them with him, dragging them on to his still damp body and scanning the water for more of the little marking flags that swayed above the flock of lobster buoys. Jimmy brought him a mug of thick Navy cocoa and he wrapped his hands around it, sipping the strong brew while Jimmy rubbed his arms and body to bring back the circulation.

A quarter of an hour later they were safely clear, and Robby concentrated on the next obstacle – the Shambles, a shallow bank of shingle just east of the Bill. After that, he would set course for St Albans' Head, where the Purbeck Cliffs dropped a sheer 200 feet into the sea. He could see them clearly, fourteen or fifteen miles ahead. Navigation would be easy for a while now, and their main concern was the tide, once more turning against them.

Jimmy came up from below again, bearing more mugs of cocoa. 'I'll get a bite o' supper together soon. What d'you reckon we should do now, Skip? Go south of the Isle o' Wight or through the Solent? We could pick up some more fuel in Pompey or Gosport.'

'It'd hold us back a bit to do that.' Robby frowned, thinking it through. 'Dip the tank, Danny, see how much we've got.'

Danny disappeared and came back a few moments later, wiping his hands. 'Reckon us've used about two-thirds. Better siphon some out of that reserve drum, eh, Skip?'

Robby grinned at the thought of his old friend calling him 'Skip' but nodded and then gave their course serious thought. 'We did quite a bit of boatwork round these waters when I was at *St Vincent*,' he said at last, 'and I reckon going through the Solent'd hold us up a lot. See, they've got boom defences out round Lymington now – we'd have to get through them first. Then there's bound to be a lot o' shipping about, blacked out and all – and at the far end there's the

76

Spithead forts stuck out in the channel between Southsea and the Island, and there's another boom been put there too, like a ruddy great fence half the way across. I reckon it'd be quicker to go south, past the Needles and St Cat's, and then we can go well below the Owers buoy and won't have to worry about that rocky ledge off Selsey.'

The other two nodded and Danny began the work of siphoning the reserve fuel from the big drum. Jimmy had disappeared again and Robby stood at the helm alone. The little fleet had grown as they proceeded round the coast and he noticed that most of them were taking the same course. George Ellery, who had kept close all the way in *Berry Pomeroy*, gave him a wave and a thumbs-up, and Robby waved back, feeling a sudden surge of contentment.

The sun was just beginning to set as they came south of the island, its glow tingeing the white chalk cliffs with apricot. The sky became an upturned bowl of blue and pink, with streaks of cloud flying like shreds of torn chiffon high above, and Robby glanced astern to see the sun, a ball of deep, flaming orange slipping down the western horizon, turning the broken foam of their wake to a fiery glitter of gold. He caught his breath; bathed in this tranquil peace, it seemed impossible that they were on a serious mission, that there were desperate men waiting to be rescued, that the sea battles he had already been in were any more than a nightmare suffered after too many beers. And then he felt a pang of guilt, thinking of those desperate men, and wished he could drive this little ship faster, to get there the sooner and bring them home.

The smell of frying mackerel touched his nostrils, and he glanced round to see Jimmy Bell appearing with a mug of tea in one hand and a plate of fish and fried bread in the other. Robby grinned his thanks; once again, he had not realised how hungry he was.

'Next few hours'll be the worst, eh?' the older man said after a while, and Robby nodded.

'It'll be dark in half an hour. We'll have to keep a lookout for other ships – none of 'em'll be showing lights. Don't want to get run down.' He drank some tea, grateful for the heat that almost blistered his lips.

'Tell you what,' Jimmy said, 'I reckon it's time you had a bit o' kip. Me and Danny can keep her going. Got eyes like a cat, that boy

77

has, and I done a fair bit o' sailing in these waters meself. You can leave it to us.'

'Right,' Robby nodded, reluctant to hand over but knowing that it made sense. They needed their wits about them for what was to come. 'I'll make a few cheese and pickle wads before I turn in, keep us going through the night.'

'Already done that.' Bell grinned at him in the fading light. 'And there's a pan of kye, ready to be heated up when we needs a sup. You get your head down, Skip. I'll give you a shout if we needs any help.'

Robby handed over the helm and took a last look round before lying down on the deck. He wrapped himself in a blanket and lay looking up at the deepening blue of the sky, pricked now by the first bright stars. For the first time for several hours, he allowed himself to think of his brother.

Where was Jan now? he wondered. Had he made it to the beaches of Dunkirk? Was he staring at this same cloudless sky and waiting to be rescued? Or lying wounded and deserted in some desolate French field, wondering if he would ever see home again?

Or was he already dead, shot down or blown to pieces by an enemy he had never even known?

It doesn't seen real, Robby thought as weariness overtook him and he closed his eyes. It doesn't seem real at all.

Chapter Seven

As Robby was making the first day of his voyage to Dover, the country was at last becoming aware of the danger faced by the BEF in France, and the real threat of invasion. The French had dismissed their military commander, General Gamelin, and appointed General Weygand, a seventy-two year old who had never commanded an army in battle, in his place. The RAF had lost its airfields in France and could now only operate from England, only just able to reach the French coast and back. The news was as bad as it could be.

Carrie Mears was helping out at the café where Effie worked. She had gone to the fish shop that morning as usual, had a row with Bert Hollins and come straight round to tell her mother all about it. Made a pass at her, she said indignantly, and him old enough to be her father! Effie, hiding a smile, told her she might as well stop on. 'We're a bit short this morning anyway, what with Freda being in bed under the doctor, so I'll be glad of a hand. Not that I'll take no lip, mind, and if you chucks in your job here you chucks in the lodgings that go with it, see!'

Carrie grinned and stuck out her tongue. 'Go on, Ma, you'll never sling me out of the house. Who'd bring you a cuppa on Sunday mornings then, eh? Our Dot don't wake up till gone nine and our dad don't even know where the kettle's kept.'

Carrie enjoyed working in the café. She liked the warm, smoky atmosphere and the noise of the customers. They almost all knew each other, for the café served the local street market and both customers and stallholders came in for snacks and meals. Effie opened it at six every morning and began frying sausages, bacon and eggs and making urns of strong tea straight away; the steady flow of custom lasted until four in the afternoon. There was plenty of banter and the occasional argument, and once or twice there had been a real fight, with the local bobby marching in to separate the brawlers, but for the most part the customers behaved themselves and Constable Warner came in himself for the odd cup of tea and corned-beef sandwich.

Things were more difficult now, with the war on and rationing in force, but cafés and restaurants could get extra supplies and it was a marvel, the customers agreed, what a good cook like Effie could still whip up, although they never missed a chance to tease her about some of the dishes she produced.

'Bangers and mash twice for the corner table,' Carrie shouted through the kitchen hatch, 'and beans on toast for the bloke by the door, and him by the stairs wants another cuppa tea, only he says make it look like tea this time, the last lot was like last week's dishwater.'

As Carrie yelled the order through to the kitchen, Effie poked her head round the door, brandishing a dishcloth. 'Who's that, casting nasturtiums at my tea? Don't he know there's a war on? Oh, I might've known it'd be you, Alf Buggins. Well, you knows what you can do if you don't like it, doncher! And if it's *dishwater* you're after . . .' She made to throw her cloth at him and he ducked.

'Hit me with that and I'll have you up for h'assault and battery, Effie Mears.' He winked a bleary eye at her. 'I dunno what a bloke has to do to get a decent cuppa round here. Here, how's that hubby of yours, anyway? Missus told me the fireboats have been took over by the Admiralty. Whass that all about, then?'

Effie came out of the kitchen and stood by his table, her good-humoured face grave. 'To tell you the truth, Alf, we don't really know,' she said quietly. 'There's all sorts of rumours going round but even my Olly didn't know what the real reason was.' She lowered her voice even further. 'There was a bloke in here earlier – that toff what comes in sometimes, you know the one I mean, wears a tie and a bowler hat – and he said how the Army's in a bad way over in France, and the Admiralty's been getting ships together all week to go over and fetch 'em back. He told me there's been boats coming down the Thames for days now, little ones like motor cruisers and such, and they're even taking them over. And I wondered if my Olly could be going too. What d'you reckon about that, then?'

Alf stared at her. 'That's a load of rubbish. Our boys in trouble? We got the finest Army in the world, we all knows that. I tell you what, Effie, you don't want to be repeating talk like that, and you don't want to let that bloke in here again, if you got any sense. Unpatriotic, that's what it is, and I wouldn't mind betting he's one of them Fifth Columnists, put in to spread horrible rumours and upset people. I reckon you oughter go and tell young Bobby Warner about him, get him arrested.'

'Well, I dunno about that but he had a copy of *The Times* with him, and he showed me. Left it behind, he did. See what it says.'

She fetched the newspaper from the kitchen and spread it out on the table, shifting the fresh cup of tea Carrie had brought out for Alf. Moving her finger along the lines, she read parts of the report aloud. 'According to this, the Germans are pushing forwards *"with great violence"* through both Belgium and France, and the Prime Minister of France is talking about his country being in *"great danger"*. I know it don't actually say our boys are in trouble, but you got to read between the lines, aincher?'

He shook his head. 'I still don't reckon things are as bad as all that. I mean, my paper hasn't said nothing about the boys being brought home. Look at this.' He took a folded copy of the *Daily Mirror* from his coat pocket and showed her the headline: *French Drive Nazis Back*. 'That's plain enough, innit? I reckon it's a bit of scaremongering, thass all. Anyway, it don't make sense, sending over a lot of riverboats. I mean, some of them haven't never been to sea. Why, even the *Surrey Queen* herself has never been to sea, not since they first brought her round from where she was built. Come to that, your Olly's only ever worked on the river himself. Not that he ain't *capable* of taking a ship to sea,' he added quickly, as Effie began to bridle, 'but the ship's got to be fit for it as well, ain't she?'

'The *Queen*'s a good boat,' Effie said sharply. 'She's a steel ship – strong as an ox, got to be for the job she does. I don't reckon she'd break up easy. But whatever they want them little boats for, it ain't to take kiddies round the coast.' She shook her head and stared at the two newspapers with their differing points of view. 'I just dunno what to believe. I mean, the *Queen*'s a fireboat – they wouldn't take her out of London if it wasn't for something serious. What happens if a warehouse catches light?'

'There you are, then. It don't make sense, do it?' Alf Buggins folded his newspaper again and finished his tea. 'I'll be off now, Eff, but if you wants my opinion, it's h'invasion they're frightened of, and *that's* what they wants all these boats for. Coastal defences, that's what. They'll be armed, all the lot of 'em, and form a ring of steel round the beaches.' He laid his finger against the side of his nose and nodded. 'A ring of steel – you mark my words.'

Effie stared after him and then went back through the door, looking more worried than ever. Carrie, just dishing up the sausages and mash, glanced at her mother's face. She put the plates down and poured another cup of tea, setting it on the cluttered table in the middle of the kitchen. 'Sit down a minute, Mum, and take the weight off your legs. I'll just go and serve these.' She whisked out into the café and Effie heard some more cheerful banter, then Carrie returned. 'Another two bangers and mash with baked beans. There's some already finished but we'll need to do more spuds soon . . . What did Alf Buggins say? You look as if you've seen a ghost.'

'Carrie, love, I just don't know what to think,' Effie said. 'Me head's going round and round with the worry of it all. The papers all say something different and we haven't been able to listen to the News for days now – I knew we ought to have got the wireless accumulator charged up – and now Alf Buggins reckons they're going to put all them little boats, with the *Queen* and all, round the coast with guns and stuff to fight off the invasion.' She lifted her face and Carrie saw that the dark brown eyes were full of tears. 'I can't bear to think of your dad having to shoot guns and fight German soldiers,' she said tremulously. 'Didn't he do enough last time? And our Joe, what's happening to him? I tell you what, love, I think it must be true – things *are* bad over there in France. They just can't stop the Germans getting across the Channel. They're expecting an invasion any minute, that's what it's all about.'

'Oh, my God.' Carrie sat down on the other chair. 'You mean the Germans are really coming? Here?' She looked around the kitchen, at the clutter of pots and pans, the piles of plates waiting to be washed, the containers of mashed potato, the bottles of HP sauce. 'What are we going to do, Ma? Whatever are we going to do if they come and get us?'

'I dunno,' Effie said, propping her elbows on the table and leaning her head on her hands. 'I tell you, Carrie, I just dunno.'

For a moment, they were both silent. Then Effie took a swallow or two of hot, strong tea – tea that not even Alf Buggins could have described as dishwater – sat up straight, squared her shoulders and looked her daughter in the eye. Her voice still wavered a little, but her words were strong and firm.

'Come on, girl. Sitting here piping our eyes won't do no good, and I'll tell you something else as well – I'm not having no Germans coming here and saying I keep a mucky kitchen. So let's get on with these orders, and then we'll set to and give the place a good clean-up. We don't know that these stories are true, so until we're sure what's what we'll just carry on as usual.' She got up and went over to the stove. 'Them sausages'll be burned to a frazzle if we don't look out, and this stove's thick with grease. I'll make a start on it straight away.'

Carrie's face creased into a wobbly grin. She stood up and put her arm round her mother's shoulders. 'Tell you what, Mum, I reckon even old Hitler himself'd think twice about complaining about the tea if he knew he had you to deal with.'

'Hitler!' Effie snorted contemptuously, lifting four fat sausages from the pan and putting two each on top of the mounds of mashed potato already on the heated plates. 'He's nothing but a strutting little turkey-cock, full of his own importance. It's time someone told him just what they thought of him, and if he came here I'd be pleased to be the one to do it!' She laid down her frying slice suddenly and drew in a deep, quivering breath. 'Oh Carrie, it's all very well to talk but none of us really knows what's going to happen, do we? I mean – look what's happened to all them poor souls in Poland and Norway and Czechoslovakia. Suppose it *did* happen here?'

'I know, Mum.' Carrie picked up the two plates. 'But like you said, there ain't nothing we can do about it, is there? We just got to carry on. I'll take these through and then I'll help you make a start on the stove. You're right – the whole place could do with a turn-out, and we might as well do that as sit around worrying.'

'Yes,' Effie said, staring at the frying-pan and wondering where Olly was now. 'We might just as well do that.'

*

Effie had never gone to the docks to see Olly on board the *Surrey Queen*, but as she and the girls ate their supper that evening she felt restless, impelled by an urge to find out for herself just what was going on. In the end, she put down her knife and fork and looked at her two daughters.

'I'm going down Blackfriars. I want to see what's happening with the fireboats.'

'Why?' Dot too had been picking at her food, her mind filled with thoughts of Benny, somewhere in France. 'There haven't been any shouts, have there?' News of a fire in the docks usually spread quickly and the families of the men on the boats nearly always heard about them.

Effie sighed. 'No, but I can't help thinking it was a bit queer, the way he come home yesterday – as if he was saying goodbye, sort of. I mean, he always says goodbye and gives me a kiss when he goes off to work, but this was different. This was as if he thought he was going to be away a long time. More than the usual overnight duty, I mean. And that story about the kiddies being evacuated by boat – well, I still can't believe that's true. There's that little Lucy next door and her friends been playing two-ball up against the front wall all afternoon. I asked her mum and she hasn't heard a word about evacuation. So what's going on?' She hesitated. 'And then there's all this talk about what's happening in France. And an invasion. Nobody knows whether to believe it or not.'

'Well, that's nothing new,' Carrie remarked. 'Nobody tells us nothing. Half what you read in the papers isn't true. Look at those two we had in the caff today, *The Times* and the *Daily Mirror*, both saying the opposite.' She shrugged and began to pile plates together. 'I suppose we might as well go down to Blackfriars. We might get some idea of what's in the wind.'

'Yes, let's do that,' her sister urged. 'It's a nice evening anyway, and it'd be something to do. We'll get washed up quick and then we'll go – how about that?'

Effie nodded. 'It'll be better than sitting at home wondering. But I don't want your father to think I'm spying on him.'

'He won't think that. He won't even see us, up on the bridge. And we could walk back round by St Paul's. It'll be nice to have a walk together.'

'We'd better not have another cup of tea then,' Effie said, making up her mind. 'I'll only need the lav, and you know there's no conveniences down that way. You two do the washing-up while I goes and makes meself presentable. If your dad does happen to spot us, I don't want him to see me looking as if I hadn't taken no trouble.'

They were ready within twenty minutes and set off together. It was a warm evening and the children who had come back from their evacuation, or never gone in the first place, were playing in the streets. The boys were rolling marbles in the gutter or bowling hoops along the middle of the road and the girls were skipping or playing complicated games of two-ball against the house walls. Dot and Carrie reminisced about how they had played the same game. 'I could do tensy all right,' Dot said, referring to the ordinary swapping of the balls from one hand to another to keep them bouncing in turn against the wall, 'but I couldn't ever get down to threesy, where you've got to bounce one on the ground first and do the other one over-arm.'

'It was twosy I couldn't do,' Carrie said. The more difficult the manoeuvre, the fewer times you were required to do it. 'Funny, 'cause I could manage onesy all right, doing it round your waist, but you weren't allowed to count it if you hadn't done twosy first.'

'Blimey, you're making my head go round with all these numbers,' Effie complained. 'I'm glad we never played that in my day. We used to skip, though. *Salt, pepper, mustard, vinegar*. Double skipping too, with two of you in the rope. And the boys had their hoops just the same,' she added, aiming a cuff at the head of a lad who was bowling his own iron hoop too close to her legs. 'Get out of the way, you little devil.'

The boy stuck out his tongue and called her a rude name before bowling on his way. Dot laughed and Effie shook her head. 'They don't have no manners these days. I didn't even know words like that when I was his age.'

It wasn't far to the river and they were soon walking along the Embankment, staring in astonishment at the scene before their eyes. The river was always busy – they were used to that – but they had never seen this much activity, nor the kind of craft that were there. They stopped on Blackfriars Bridge and gazed down.

'Look at them boats,' Effie said at last. 'It's like a blooming works outing. What's it all about? Where are they going?'

Neither of the girls could answer her. They could only stand and stare, taking in the scene. As they gazed, they began to recognise boats they had seen before but never expected to see in convoy at Blackfriars: Thames pleasure-boats like the *New Windsor Castle*, the *Queen Boadicea*, and the *Princess Freda*; sleek motor yachts and cabin cruisers more often seen on the upper reaches of the river where they would be moored at the bottom of the manicured lawns of expensive houses; even a paddle-steamer with puffs of black smoke billowing from her funnel.

'There's the *Queen*,' Carrie said, pointing. 'And look, the *Massey Shaw*'s there as well.' The *Massey Shaw* was another Thames fireboat, named after the man who had founded the London Fire Brigade fifty years before. 'They're putting any amount of stuff on board.'

'A few stores, your dad told me,' Effie said, staring at the stream of provisions being carried aboard the two ships. 'That's more than a few stores. A couple of dozen kiddies going round to Norfolk aren't going to need all that lot.'

'And what's that bloke doing to the brightwork?' Dot shielded her eyes. 'It looks like he's covering it in grease! Our dad'll go mad. What's that in aid of?'

'There's more in this than meets the eye,' Effie declared. 'I knew it didn't sound right. If you ask me, they're going into action.'

The girls turned and stared at her. 'Into *action*? But she's a Thames fireboat – they both are. They can't go into action!' They were silent for a moment, then Carrie said in a small, fearful voice, 'You don't suppose it *is* the invasion, do you, like Alf Buggins said? They might not be going *into* action at all – the action might be coming here.'

'Here? Right up the Thames to London?' Effie's hand went to her mouth. 'Oh Carrie, it can't be. We'd have been told, surely. If Mr Churchill really thought we were being invaded—'

'Maybe they don't want people to panic,' Dot pointed out. 'But there's got to be some reason why they're covering up the brightwork. And they're painting the hull, see – covering up the red paint with grey. It's camouflage, isn't it? I don't see what else it can be for.'

'I can tell you.' They turned swiftly to see a short, stocky man of about sixty leaning on the bridge beside them. 'I can tell you what

86

it's all about. I heard it meself from a bloke off the *Massey Shaw*.' He paused. 'They're going to France.'

'To *France*?' Effie gasped and covered her mouth with both hands. 'I knew it! Didn't I tell you? Didn't I say so? Oh Dot – Carrie – your poor father!'

'Not into action, they ain't,' the man said. 'Not as such, anyway. They'll be going to fight fires off the French coast. I had it from a bloke in the pub. Our boys are stuck over there, and all them pleasure-steamers and things down there are going to bring 'em back. And they reckon there'll be a fair amount of fire, what with the Germans setting light to anything they can put a match to, so they needs the fireboats as well. That's why they're taking a lot of stores and extra hands.'

'France,' Effie whispered, and the three women stared down again at the activity all across the river. 'So it *is* true. As if he didn't do enough in the last lot. He's not a young man any more.'

'He's tough, though,' Carrie said, trying to sound comforting. 'He's as strong as a twenty year old. He'll be all right, Ma. He'll be doing the job he knows. He won't be in no danger.'

'Won't he?' Effie turned away, as if she were too sick at heart to watch any more. 'Over there in France, under fire, with German planes dropping bombs all over the shop? I tell you, Carrie, I'm used to your father being in danger – he always is, whatever he's doing – but this is the worst he's ever been in since the last war finished. They're *all* going to be in danger over there. Your dad – our Joe . . .'

'And my Benny,' Dot said in a quivering voice. 'He's stuck over there too. Oh, *Mum*.'

Effie put her arm round her daughter and cuddled her. She couldn't think of a word to say. She'd never been one for platitudes, had always believed in speaking her mind, and she couldn't do anything different now – especially when she was as sick with fear for both Olly and Joe as Dot was for Benny.

She took one more look at the boats moving down the river. 'Look at them – pleasure-boats. Built for a day's outing up the river. What chance do they have? What chance do our boys have, if they've got to rely on little boats like that to get 'em home?' She whispered almost to herself, 'It'll be a miracle if they come home safe. A blooming miracle.'

'And they reckons a few liddle pleasure-boats like the *Countess* will be enough to take 'em off?' Hetty Endacott said. She and Jethro had barely talked of anything else since watching Robby take the *Countess* down the river at dawn. It seemed that everything was in chaos, as much at home as in Europe. The new emergency powers gave the Government the right to do whatever it wished. They could take your house, your boat, your husband and your son. In the cities, they were taking every bit of metal they could find – park railings, bandstands, even disused tramlines – to build new ships and aircraft. 'Folk are even being asked to give up their spare saucepans!' she exclaimed. 'How many saucepans do it take to build a destroyer, I ask you! And how *long* do it take? How many years do they think this war's going to last, for heaven's sake?'

Her husband shook his head. 'Don't sound to me as if it's going to last any time at all, my bird. Seems to me they'm desperate. I dunno what they can do, with all our boys trapped over there and only a few liddle boats like the *Countess* to get 'em home again.'

The music programme they'd been trying to listen to on the wireless had finished and someone was giving a talk. Jethro switched off and they sat in the small kitchen, trying to understand what was happening. The thought was in both their minds, but it was Hetty who gave voice to it. 'Our Jan's one of them soldiers waiting for a boat to come and pick un up. Oh my dear soul, whatever chance do he have?'

'As much chance as any of the others. Us got to look at it that way, Het. He've got as much chance as the next man – and don't forget, maid, our Robby's on his way over. He'll keep a special watch out for Jan, you can be sure of that.'

'But Robby's in danger just as much as Jan.' Her eyes filled with hot, stinging tears. 'Oh Jethro, what's happening to the world? Why do us have to give up our boys to all this terrible fighting? I wanted to see 'em grow up safe and peaceful, living good lives here in Devon, bringing up their own families the way they should. That's what life should be, not all this going off to foreign countries, killing other men and getting theirselves killed when they'm still young men. Didn't us have enough of this in the last war? Didn't us lose enough young chaps then? Your brother George, my Cousin Davey, all those other boys us grew up with, that should have had years of good life in front of 'em. Wasn't it enough that us lost them? Why do us have to go through it all over again?'

Jethro shook his head. 'I can't say, Hetty. Tidden for us to understand these things. Maybe us didn't finish the job proper last time. Maybe us let the Germans have too much too soon. But here us be now, and us got to do the best us can for our King and country. 'Tain't nothing else us can do, is there?'

She had to admit that this was true. 'It isn't that I begrudge the King whatever he need,' she said slowly, 'but I do begrudge Hitler. All this fighting – 'tis all his doing. None of it would have happened if it hadn't been for him. And now 'twill take a miracle to save all they poor soldiers, and our Jan amongst 'em.'

Jethro put his hand on her shoulder. 'Bear up, maid. The churches will be packed full everywhere come Sunday, the whole country'll be praying together, and 'twill be a strange thing if the Lord don't hear that and do something about it. If 'tis a miracle that's needed, 'tis a miracle He'll work for us. You mark my words.'

'I hope so,' she said, looking up at the photographs on the mantelpiece. 'My dear soul, I do hope so.'

Chapter Eight

The Admiral rang at last just as they were sitting down to dinner. Charles had sent word to the office that he wasn't coming in – the two old ladies and the indignant bride would have to wait – and then rung the Admiral, to tell him that he intended to take *Wagtail* to France. He'd expected another argument but the old man must have heard the determination in his voice, and simply said he'd be glad to have him along. He was standing by, ready to leave at a moment's notice.

Nobody had wanted to stray too far from the telephone, and in the end they had agreed on a rota for staying in the house. By the time they started their dinner, everyone was on edge and at the first ring, they stopped what they were doing and sat up straight. Paddy, just helping herself to new potatoes, was like a statue, the spoon held over the bowl, while Olivia was arrested in the act of passing round fillets of fish. Toby scattered peas all over the table, and Olivia looked frightened and uncertain. Sheila took in a quick breath and looked at her husband.

'I'll go.' He got up swiftly and went out into the hall. They heard him lift the receiver and speak into the mouthpiece. 'Yes? Stainbank here – Charles, yes. Oh hello, Admiral.' There was a pause while they all looked at each other. He spoke again in a different, graver tone. 'I see. Yes. Yes, of course. Yes, just as we said. I will. Yes, I'll make sure of that. We'll see you there, then. Yes, I'll tell them. Goodbye, sir – goodbye.' He replaced the receiver and then, after a moment's silence, came back into the dining room.

They all stared at him. For what seemed an age, nobody spoke.

Then Paddy said sharply, 'Is that it? Have they sent for us? For heaven's sake, Charles, don't stand there like a dummy – *tell* us. It was the Admiral, wasn't it?'

Charles looked at her. His voice was very quiet. 'Yes. The Navy's contacted him.' He sat down suddenly, the colour ebbing from his face, and stared around the table. 'They need every little boat they can get, just to take the men off the beaches and ferry them on to the ships.' He passed a shaking hand over his face. 'If we don't get them off, the Germans will cut them down like grass.'

'And Alex is there,' Sheila whispered, putting her hand on his arm. 'My poor brother.'

There was another short silence. The room was filled with sudden tension as everyone glanced at each other and then away. Then Charles said in a quiet voice, 'And I'm going too. In *Wagtail*.' He lifted his eyes and looked steadily into his father's face. 'I'm sorry, Dad, I know she's your boat and you refused me permission, but I can't, I *cannot*, stay safe at home and let old men and boys fight this war for me. The Admiral's over seventy and Peter Murphy's only seventeen. I can't sit back and watch them go into danger and stay at home myself, just because I've had TB. I'm fit and well now, and as good a sailor as any of them, and *Wagtail*'s well able to cross the Channel. If the Admiralty won't requisition her, I will.' He turned his head towards his wife. 'There's nothing I want to do less than leave Sheila and the children,' he said quietly, 'but there's nothing I want to do more than try to save Alex and the others. And that's what I am going to do.'

The silence this time was longer. Olivia covered her face with her hands. Hubert's thin, pale face flushed and he opened his mouth to speak, then closed it again. Paddy gave a cry, jumped up and ran round the table to kiss her eldest brother.

'Hooray!' Toby exclaimed, and jumped up as well to come and pump Charles's hand. 'Well said, bro. And I'll come too, of course.'

'*You* will?' Hubert said, trying but failing to mask his astonishment. 'But I thought—'

'You thought I was a slacker and a coward,' Toby said dryly. 'It's OK, Dad, I know. But all I'm scared of is *killing* people. I'm not afraid to go to Dunkirk with Charles, and I'll do my best to bring back as many British Tommies or whatever they may be, and hope that Alex is amongst them. I'm with my big brother in this – I'm not staying here while old men and boys go off and do a job I can do.'

'I think we'd better discuss this after dinner,' Hubert began, but Charles shook his head.

'There's nothing to discuss, Pa. I'm going, and I'll be pleased to take Toby with me. The Admiral said the Navy wants three to a boat, but I expect we'll be able to pick up someone else once we get to Dover for our orders.' He squeezed his wife's hand. 'Sheila's with me on this – we talked about it last night. She won't stand in my way, will you, darling?'

Sheila's eyes were filled with tears, but she looked directly at her father-in-law and said, 'Charles has to do this, Pa. Please make it easy for him.' Gently, she disengaged her hand and leaned across to her mother-in-law. 'The children and I will be staying here if you don't mind, until – until it's all over. I'll go over to Chichester and see my parents every day. If anyone can bring Alex back, it'll be Charles.'

Hubert looked at them and shrugged. 'Then it seems that there's no more to be said. I can see you're not going to take a scrap of notice of anything I say, so I may as well save my breath.' He pursed his lips. 'It's a sad day when you realise you're old and of no further use!'

'Not so sad as being young and of no further use,' Charles said, and gave his father a twisted grin. 'Anyway, there's plenty for you to do, Dad. Two Wills to rewrite and a breach-of-promise case, for a start! And I wish you the best of luck with all of them.'

The tension was broken, and the family, half-smiling and half in tears, bent to their plates once more. But nobody could eat much, and they were all relieved when the meal was over and they could leave the dining room. Paddy, who had not spoken since her own outburst, hung behind, and Toby paused beside her.

'I haven't forgotten what we talked about,' she said in a whisper. 'I'm coming too, Toby. I'm not being left out of this.'

He gave her his familiar grin and squeezed her arm. 'All right, little sis. I haven't forgotten either. But leave it just for now, OK? It's not the moment for any more bombshells – we'll tell Charles later. But don't be surprised if you find you've got a fight on your hands.'

'I shan't be surprised at all,' she said. 'And don't *you* be surprised when I win.'

Nobody could stop Paddy helping with the preparations. With her mother and Sheila, she raided the larder, taking out all the tins and jars that had been carefully stored away and packing them into boxes ready to be carried down the garden to the jetty. There wasn't all that much, since you weren't supposed to hoard, but everyone had a few things put by for emergencies, and this was an emergency if ever there was one.

The most important thing to take, Charles had decreed, was water. If the men had been waiting on the beaches for several days, water was likely to be difficult to come by. They gathered every can and bottle they could find and filled them from the tap, then turned their attention to food.

'There's quite a lot of flour,' Paddy said, bringing out a bag. 'We could make bread.'

'That's a good idea. You've got some fresh yeast, haven't you, Mother? If we start the bread now, it can be baked by the time they leave.' Sheila had recovered from her tears and was determinedly practical. 'I'll do that, and then I'll make a cake while the dough's proving. I saw some dried fruit just now – and there's that butter and the eggs from the farm that we were going to take home with us.'

'We could hardboil any that we don't use,' Paddy suggested. 'We – I mean, *they* – won't have time to do proper cooking.' She turned away quickly, relieved to see the door open and Toby come in. 'Oh good, there you are. There's another box ready here.'

'My goodness, it's like packing up a giant picnic! I hope you've put in plenty of sausage rolls.' He struck a pose in the doorway. 'What do you think of the modern knight in shining armour? I wanted to wear my cricket whites but Charles wouldn't let me.' He was clad from head to foot in dark blue, a thick guernsey over flannel trousers and a sailing cap covering his thatch of blond hair. 'I told him, we're not cat-burglars, we want the poor soldiers to see us but he's afraid we'll look dirty and let the British down.' He moved over to Sheila, who had already mixed the yeast with warm water and was now beating butter, eggs and sugar together in a bowl. 'Mm, that looks good – can I scrape it out when you've finished?'

Sheila slapped his hand. 'For heaven's sake, Toby, stop treating all this as a joke.' She laid down her wooden spoon and faced him. 'Don't you realise how *serious* it is? Men are being killed. Men like my brother, Alex, who haven't even had a chance to live their lives yet. And you – you think it's *funny*. A chance to dress up! You won't go and fight yourself because you think you're destined to be a great actor, so you leave it to other people to do the dirty work, but let me tell you this – if Hitler invades, there won't be any acting for you, my lad. You'll be a *slave*, like all those poor Jews and Poles. And serve you right!'

Her face working and wet with tears, she snatched up her spoon and began beating again. Toby stared at her, then shrugged uncomfortably and said, 'I'm sorry, Shee. I didn't mean to upset you. Only I can't see any point in behaving as if it's the end of the world—'

'It will be the end of the world for those poor men, if we don't get them home,' she retorted, beating as though the eggs and butter themselves were the enemy. 'It is the end of the world for the ones who are being killed now, this very minute. It's the end of their world.'

'I know. I didn't mean that. I just meant there's no point in making ourselves any more miserable than we have to. I know it's serious, and I'll do my best to help the poor blighters, but we can help them even better if we can make the odd joke. Keep cheerful at all times, isn't that the Boy Scout motto? A whistle and a smile. That's all I'm doing, Shee.'

She went on beating for a few moments in silence. Then, her voice still shaky, she said, 'All right, Toby. You do it your way if you have to, but keep out of *my* way while you're making your jokes, will you? I don't seem able to see the funny side of this.'

He moved away, rolling his eyes at Paddy. She frowned at him and indicated the pile of boxes growing at her feet. With a sigh, he bent and lifted them into his arms.

'I'm taking them down the garden by wheelbarrow – good wheeze, don't you think? I knew that strange contraption would come in handy sometime.'

'It comes in handy all the time, only you wouldn't know about that,' Sheila said tightly. 'It's called work.'

Toby raised his eyebrows and turned down the corners of his

mouth. Paddy scowled and followed him outside with one of the boxes.

'Leave her alone, Toby. She's terribly upset.'

'Well, so am I,' he said, loading his burden into the wheelbarrow. 'It's not as if I didn't know what work was! Acting's hard work too, just as much as gardening or drawing up people's Wills.'

'I don't mean that. She's upset about Charles as well as Alex. She's terrified he's going to be killed, going over to France.'

'So might *I* be killed,' he said. 'Obviously that doesn't matter to her at all.'

'It does, of course it does. She's frightened about both of you. But your jokes just upset her. Not everybody appreciates your sense of humour, Toby.'

'You're telling me,' he said mournfully. 'Did I tell you, I wrote this hilarious sketch to go in that revue I was in last summer and the producer wouldn't even look at it. I told him it would bring the house down but he wouldn't take any notice, just said that I—'

'Toby! I'll get cross with you myself in a minute.' She gave him a push. 'Take those things down to the jetty.'

He set off down the garden, whistling as he went. Paddy watched him for a moment, then hurried back through the kitchen. Her mother was standing at the larder, looking worried.

'Do you think they'll have enough jam? I've put in three each of strawberry and blackcurrant, but I've got all those pots of plum as well, that we made last year. Men do like jam and it will be so nice with fresh bread.' She turned to her daughter. 'You don't really think they'll be gone for long, do you? I mean, it doesn't take all that time to pop across to France, and if they've just got to pick up a few men and bring them home, they could be back in a day or two. I should think six pots ought to be plenty.'

Paddy looked at her. She had grown up knowing that her mother must be protected from bad news; ever since Paddy's own birth, Olivia had been frail and their doctor, who was also Sheila's father, had told Hubert that her heart was weak and that she mustn't be given any shocks. Olivia had replied that Paddy's birth in itself had been a shock and Paddy, being Paddy, had continued to shock her all through her childhood.

'I thought I'd had a little girl,' she said sometimes, watching in despair as Paddy flew across the lawn after a cricket ball or came down from a tree, her clothes torn and streaked with green. 'She might just as well have been a boy and be done with it.'

But although Paddy was a tomboy, there was a gentler side to her, and because she felt dimly that it was partly her fault her mother wasn't strong, she always treated her with a tenderness that wasn't so apparent at other times. Now, she moved across and put her hand on Olivia's arm.

'I'm sure six pots will be enough. Even Toby couldn't eat that many in a couple of days.' Privately, she wondered if they'd even have time to make jam sandwiches, but she dared not frighten her mother too much. She took out a saucepan to start boiling eggs. If this was a picnic, she thought, it would be the biggest picnic in the world. But, like Sheila, she couldn't help wondering just what little boats like *Wagtail* could do to save the thousands of men trapped on the beaches. How could such little ships, willing as they were, make any difference to such huge numbers?

Ours is not to reason why, she thought, packing jars and tins into yet another box. *Ours is but to do or die.* And for the first time, she was struck by the true meaning of the quotation.

Alex might die. Charles and Toby might die. And so might she herself.

Impulsive as she was, Paddy had a streak of patience in her too, and although it was a torment for her to remain silent, she waited until after dinner before commencing battle.

'I'm coming too.' Down on the jetty, with *Wagtail* bobbing gently beside them, she faced her two brothers. 'I can handle *Wagtail* as well as either of you, you know I can. And the Admiral said the Navy wanted three to each boat.'

'Don't be an idiot,' Charles said sharply. 'Of course you can't come. It's going to be dangerous. The Germans will be bombing and shelling the beaches, they'll do all they can to prevent us getting the men away. We can't take you into that.'

'I want to help save Alex.'

'And what help will you be if we have to think about looking after you?' Charles demanded. 'Anyway, the Navy won't let you go. The Admiral says we've got to sign on – we'll be virtually in the Navy ourselves for a month. What do you think they're going to say when a seventeen-year-old girl tries to sign on? They'll throw you overboard!'

'They won't have to know. I'll tell them my name's Patrick. I'll cut off all my hair.' She pulled the golden curls back tightly from her face. 'Look! I could pass for a boy, couldn't I?'

Charles shook his head in exasperation. Toby chuckled.

'Not for a minute, little sister. You're growing up, didn't you know that?'

Paddy glowered at him. 'They won't notice that. I'll wear one of your thick jumpers and a sailing cap. They will think I'm a boy.' She turned swiftly and laid her hands on Charles's arm. 'Please, Charles. You've got to let me come. You know how I feel about Alex.'

He turned away, embarrassed. Toby raised his eyebrows and said, 'Yes, go on, Charles. You know how she feels about Alex.'

'Don't be ridiculous,' Charles snapped. 'And don't encourage her, Toby. You're just a kid, Paddy – you don't know what you're talking about. It's puppy-love, that's all.'

'It's not puppy-love! And I do know what I'm talking about. I'm not a kid – I'm seventeen. Old enough to get married. Old enough to have babies.' She watched scornfully as her brother coloured. 'You're the one who's being ridiculous. Do you really think I don't know where babies come from – what being *in love* means?'

'Paddy, this has got nothing to do with the BEF—'

'Yes, it has, it has! Because it's Alex out there – *Alex*. You're going, aren't you. Toby's going. I'm as good a sailor as either of you, you know that. So why can't I come too?'

'I've told you – because you're a girl.'

'And that's the most stupid reason I've ever heard.'

'Look,' Charles said, sitting on the decking beside her and taking her hand, 'I know you think a lot of Alex, and I know you want him to get back safely. So do we all. But you heard what the Admiral said. There are hundreds of thousands of men over there. That's odds of hundreds of thousands to one that we'll even see him. We'll just be rescuing whoever we can. And how many d'you think we'll be able to carry in little *Wagtail*? Ten? Twenty? However many times we go back and forth to the beaches, we're only going to be able to take off a tiny fraction of all those men. I want Alex to be rescued just as much as you do, but I don't think for a minute that we'll be the ones to rescue him.'

Paddy was silent for a moment. Then she said stubbornly, 'But you might – and I want to be there. And anyway,' she added, raising her voice as Charles began to speak again, 'even if you don't save Alex himself, you'll be saving other men. I can still help.'

'You can't. I've told you, over and over again, you *can't* go. The Navy just won't let you. Women don't go to war, Paddy, and that's all there is to it.' He stood up.

'But I'm not going to war!' she cried, tears streaming down her face. 'I'm going to save people, not kill them! I'm not going to fight.'

'It doesn't make any difference.' He looked down at her, his face creased with both exasperation and regret, then turned to his brother. 'Come on, Toby. We've got to be off at dawn and we've still got our own things to get ready.' He laid his hand on Paddy's shoulder. 'I know how you feel, Pads. But you must see, it just isn't possible. You're needed here, to look after Mum and help Sheila with the children. That's your part in all of this.'

He tilted his head at her, half-encouraging, half-pleading. She stared back mutinously and he sighed and moved away. Toby got up slowly and followed his brother, then turned and gave his sister a wink.

'Chin up, sis,' he said in a whisper. 'People have run away to sea before now, you know. There's a tradition of it.'

Paddy raised her tear-streaked face and looked at him. He grinned and laid one finger along the side of his nose. 'Sometimes, they've even stowed away.'

Chapter Nine

Robby slept for little more than an hour before he was back in the wheelhouse. Although he was pretty sure that, once past Selsey Bill, the passage through the night along the south coast would be more straightforward, he was very aware that the *Countess Wear* was under his command and he was responsible for her. Responsible, too, for the lives of her crew.

As he unwrapped himself from his blanket, he saw that the darkness was now complete and he sighed with relief that they hadn't had any dangerously close encounters with other shipping. He came up to stand beside Jimmy, straining his eyes into the blackness.

'All quiet so far?' he enquired, and Jimmy nodded.

'There's quite a bit of other shipping about,' he said in a low tone. 'Listen.'

Robby listened and identified the deep note of engines, thrumming over the surface of the water. As he stared into the darkness he could see occasional swift flashes of light to indicate where they were, but none were close enough to worry him. Somewhere nearby, he knew, must be the *Berry Pomeroy* and the *Mew* and the other little ships that had joined them along the way. Now and then, he could hear voices from the other boats, carrying across the rippling water, and the soft plash of waves against the hull. A seabird cried somewhere, a wild and lonely sound, and high above was a mass of stars, sprinkling the sky with millions of points of light.

'I reckon it's safe to ease in closer to the shore now,' he said to Jimmy Bell. 'We'll keep watches for the rest of the night. Two hours' sleep each and two hours on deck. There's a long way to go before we've finished this job.'

'I reckon Danny could do with a bit of extra kip, if you don't mind me saying so, Skip,' Jimmy remarked. 'That dousing he got is bound to have took it out of him, and he ain't so used to being at sea as me and you.'

Danny started to protest, but Robby agreed with Jimmy. 'There'll be plenty of chances to show how tough you are later on. Get your head down now, while you can. Me and Jimmy will take the middle watches and you can do the six to eight – that's if you can get up that early!' He grinned, remembering how reluctant Danny had been to get out of bed when they were both at school. Danny made a face at him but ducked down below, where they had made a nest of blankets, without further argument. When Robby looked down a minute or two later he was already fast asleep.

They continued on their way, their passage broken only by regular plottings on the yellowing charts to mark their progress, frequent checks on the oil pressure and temperature of their own engines, and a constant supply of ship's cocoa brewed up on the Primus stove. Jimmy rolled himself up for a couple of hours' sleep and Robby stayed at the wheel alone, listening to the noises of the night and thinking.

Ever since he could remember, Robby had liked to spend the last few moments of the evening going through the experiences of his day and sorting them into some sort of order. Sometimes it had been a happy thing to do, sometimes not – he could remember more than once at *St Vincent*, soaking his thin pillow with silent tears as he relived the humiliations dealt out to him. But it had always helped and, once achieved, he could turn over and fall asleep with the sensation of something finished.

Tonight was very different. Tonight, for the first time in his life, he was in sole charge of a ship – albeit a small one – and on an important mission. Men's lives depended upon him – Danny's and Jimmy's to begin with, but beyond them a long procession of men he didn't know, never would know, but who were converging now on this place called Dunkirk, driven there by the enemy and depending on him, and others like him, to rescue them. If he failed, they would either be killed or taken prisoner, and the responsibility – and the guilt – for that would rest on his shoulders.

In his mind, Robby knew that the responsibility wasn't his alone. He was only an able seaman, acting under orders. But he'd been given this task because he was supposed to have learned to use his initiative, because he was a seaman and understood boats, because he was thought to be capable of doing it.

He reviewed the day that had just passed. The familiar trip down the river, just lit by a soft, pearly dawn. The red cliffs of Berry Head and Torbay which he knew so well. The passage across Lyme Bay and past Portland Bill. The fouling of the propellers. The magic of the sunset off the Isle of Wight.

The stars were so large and bright now that he felt he could pluck them from the sky. The sea was like dark, smooth glass, a black mirror reflecting the bowl of the sky above so that the *Countess Wear* seemed to be travelling through an immense sphere of glittering diamonds. He glanced behind and saw their wake, the foam a brilliant, luminous green lit by iridescent flashes. The beauty of it, seen so close when he was accustomed to being so much more distant on board ship, caught at his throat, yet he knew that the beauty itself was a danger, for surely the brightness could be seen from the air by any roaming German plane or from the seas by any warship.

On either side of him lay two very different shores – to port, the beaches of England, where people still lived free, and thirty or forty miles away to starboard, the coast of France where war was at this very moment tearing the heart out of towns, cities, villages and countryside. Where the enemy was marching ruthlessly through the land, killing and destroying all that stood in its path; where the British Army had been driven into a corner and could fight no more than a rearguard action while it waited for rescue.

I don't understand it, he thought. I don't understand how the world could come to this. All I can do is follow orders and hope they're the right ones.

As the English Channel began to narrow, he felt uneasily that he could hear the distant rumble of gunfire and explosions. Perhaps it was his imagination; or perhaps he was hearing something that really was there, but could only be heard because you knew it was happening . . .

You're thinking rubbish, he told himself sharply, and shone his torch carefully on the chart again.

By four, the sky ahead was beginning to lighten and he knew he was sailing into the dawn. Danny came up to stand beside him, stretching and rubbing his eyes, and they stood quietly together, watching as the red glow of the sun lifted itself gradually above the horizon. The darkness that had surrounded them turned to grey, and then colours began to be visible – the dark blue of Danny's jersey, the polished brown of the deck, the brave red of the ensign fluttering above. Robby looked about him and gave an exclamation of astonishment. 'Look at all they boats, Dan!'

The *Countess Wear*, which had set out on this voyage in the company of just two other craft – the *Berry Pomeroy* and the *Mew* – was now part of a huge flotilla. As well as the *Lady Cable*, which had also been with them most of the way, there were others which had joined in as they passed the various ports and harbours of the south coast – Portsmouth and Chichester, Newhaven, Rye and all the other little inlets where both working- and pleasure-craft were kept. Yet even though Rob had known they must be there, he had never dreamed there would be so many.

'Look at them all,' he said again. 'Ferry boats, motor cruisers, a couple of paddle-steamers there, see? – and two lifeboats, and— My God, Dan.' He stared at the motley fleet, forging its way determinedly through the waves. 'It makes you feel proud, don't it? It makes you feel real proud to be part of it all.'

The little ships were close enough for some of their names to be read, and Danny recited them aloud like a piece of poetry. 'The *Ferry King* and the *Inspiration*. The *Lady Anita*. The *Sun*. The *Amulree*. The *Caleta*. All they little motor cruisers don't look hardly big enough to have left their mothers. And that one, towing another boat – she don't have no name, just a number – *X209*. What's that?' He glanced enquiringly at Robby.

'That's a dockyard lighter – I've seen it in Portsmouth Harbour. Works out of Clarence Yard, the victualling station on the Gosport side.' Robby shook his head in wonder. ''Tis a big job, this, Dan – the biggest you'll ever have to do, I reckon. The biggest the old *Countess* will ever do, anyway.'

The sun was well up now, flooding the scene with apricot light and flinging a glittering pathway of burnished gold directly at the *Countess*'s bows. The Sussex Downs made a green whaleback on their port side, and Robby could see the white cliffs of Beachy Head jutting into the sea with the lighthouse nestling below. It was only forty miles to Dover.

And then the real voyage would begin.

Moonset and *Wagtail* crept out of Chichester Harbour soon after dawn, having rendezvoused at Stocker's Lake, where the two channels met, and proceeded together past Black Point and Eastoke Point, and so out into the Channel, heading for the southern point of Selsey Bill. The Admiral was at *Moonset*'s wheel, with George in charge of the engine and the young Sea Scout perched in the bow, dressed in his smart navy uniform of dark blue sweater, blue trousers and navy and white scarf. He was a tall, slender boy with thick black hair and dark brown eyes, and he gave a shy grin and a wave when the two boats met.

'Just you and young Toby, is it?' the Admiral called. 'I dare say we can pick up a volunteer when we get to Dover or Ramsgate. Or they may put a Naval chappie on board to see you over.'

'A volunteer will do.' Now that they were on their way, Charles was feeling calm and confident. The previous day's waiting had been an agony, and the night, with Sheila in his arms, sharply painful. At times during the dark, small hours he would have given anything not to have to go; but every time the thought entered his head he thrust it savagely away. This was his chance to take part, his chance to make a contribution to the war effort.

I don't even want a choice, Charles had thought, watching the hours go by as Sheila slept at last. I may never get another opportunity like this. In any case, it's a job that's got to be done, and I'm just one of those in the right place to do it.

The Channel was full of shipping – sleek grey destroyers, transport ships and ferries, tugs and lifeboats, all workmanlike ships, but there was also a fleet of other boats, large and small – cruisers and motor yachts like *Moonset* and *Wagtail*, trawlers, pleasure-steamers and holiday craft, all heading east. There were small fishing boats, dinghies, some of them towing even smaller craft. There were even one or two rowing-boats.

Charles and Toby looked at them in awe, and Toby said, 'They're going too. They're going where we're going.' And for the first time, his voice was truly sober, as if only now the reality was beginning to dawn on him.

In better times, the brothers and their father had done a lot of sailing around Chichester and Langstone Harbours, and in the Solent or out into the Channel, and now Charles's experience came to his aid as he calculated his course over the rocky shelf which stretched into the Channel for six miles off Selsey Bill. It was here that Drake had hoped to strand the Spanish Armada, but there was a narrow passage close inshore which could be negotiated if you knew how to find it, and which would save both time and fuel. Charles saw the Admiral make the same decision and head towards the shore, while craft that didn't have local knowledge veered south of the Owers buoy which marked the tip of the ledge.

'Might as well catch a few mackerel for our supper,' Toby said, trolling his lines over the stern. 'Save the stores for later.'

Charles nodded. His eyes were on the Admiral, standing at his wheel. George was beside him and young Peter in the bow.

'It's still hard to believe we're going to war,' he marvelled. 'I mean, look at *Moonset* – an old man, a gardener and a Sea Scout. It's crazy.'

'And look at us,' Toby said. 'An out-of-work actor and a bloke with lungs that only work at half-power –'

'– and a seventeen-year-old girl who won't take no for an answer,' said a quiet voice behind them, and Charles turned so sharply that *Wagtail* heeled and almost threw them over.

'*Paddy!* What the hell are *you* doing here? And what in God's name have you done to yourself?'

'Cut off my hair.' She pulled off the old blue sailing cap and ran her fingers over the shorn blonde crop. It was no more than an inch long, roughly cut so that it curled all over her head, like an aureole. 'I said I would, and I did.'

'Ma will go mad,' he said, staring at it. Paddy shrugged.

'It'll grow again. Anyway, nobody will know I'm a girl now.' Her figure was hidden under an old fisherman's jumper of Toby's. 'So I'm coming, all right?'

'No, it's *not* all right!' Charles exploded. He heard a smothered laugh behind him and turned on his brother furiously. 'You knew about this, didn't you! What in God's name do you think you're playing at? You irresponsible fools – both of you! You were told you couldn't come, Paddy, you were told over and over again.' He glowered at her. 'This is why you didn't come to the jetty to see us off, isn't it? We thought you were sulking.' He didn't tell her how hurt and upset he'd been by this. But he'd rather have been upset than do what he knew he must do now. He began to turn the wheel so that *Wagtail* veered round.

'What are you doing?' Paddy cried. 'Don't turn round, Charles.'

'I've got to. I have to take you back.' He was so angry he barely knew what he was saying. 'You know what this means, don't you? We'll lose hours and hours! We'll have to wait for the tide to get back in and then out again, and then there's all the explanations – Mother and Sheila upset all over again – they must be going mad wondering where you are as it is – and after all that it'll probably be too late. We'll miss the convoy across the Channel – we'll miss our chance to go at all – and that means God knows how many poor bloody soldiers left there because there's one boat less to take them off. That's what it means. That's what you've done.' He gave them both a withering glare. 'The pair of you! Stupid fools – stupid, selfish fools!'

Paddy stared at him, her face white and her eyes filled with tears. 'No, Charles, please! It doesn't have to mean that. You don't have to take me back. Mummy will know where I am by now. I left a note. And I *can* help – you know I can. I can handle the boat, and cook, and – and do First Aid. Please, *please* don't take me back.'

'You're only seventeen, and you're a girl,' he began, but she interrupted, her voice as furious as his.

'That's got nothing to do with it! I'm as good as a boy. Look at the Admiral – he's got Peter with him who's no older than me, and he hasn't done anything like as much sailing. Forget I'm a girl, Charles, forget I'm your sister. In another year I'll be able to join the Wrens – I've already registered – and I'll be in the war myself then, and nobody will be able to do anything about it. Less than a year. So why send me back now, when there are lives to be saved and we can save them?'

There was a brief silence. *Wagtail*, going in no particular direction, wallowed a little. Toby said quietly, 'She's right, you know, Charles. And this is an emergency – the biggest there's ever been. I really don't think we can turn back now.'

'The Navy won't let you go,' Charles said, turning the wheel a little to stop the rocking. 'You realise that, don't you? When we reach Ramsgate, they'll find out you're here and put you ashore.'

'Not if you don't tell them,' she said steadily, looking him in the eye. 'I can snug down in the forepeak again, same as I did coming out. *You* didn't know I was there, so there's no reason why they should. In any case, we're not an official boat – we weren't requisitioned. They might say *Wagtail*'s too small and send us back anyway, if you draw too much attention to her.' She waited a moment and then added beseechingly, 'Please, Charles.'

Charles stared ahead, tapping the wheel with his fingertips. He thought of turning back. If he did that, he would lose for ever his chance of doing something worthwhile in this war. He would have to go meekly home, and by that time it would be too late – too late to set out again, to join this makeshift fleet, this brave rescue. I'll never get another chance, he thought, never. And how will I ever face Sheila and her parents if Alex doesn't come back?

At last he sighed and turned the boat to face east again. 'All right. You win. We'll go on, and we'll see what happens when we reach Ramsgate. But I'm not telling any lies for you, Paddy. If I'm asked—'

'You'll do whatever's right. I know.' She wriggled her eyebrows in an attempt to be comical. '*My client, right or wrong.* The thing is, who *is* your client, Charles? The Navy – or the Army? The captain of a big ship, or the poor soldiers waiting on the beach?' She ducked down suddenly. 'The Admiral's looking this way – he's wondering why you've slowed down. I'll go back below and do something useful, shall I? I expect you're hungry, after all. I'll make a wad with that nice fresh bread Mummy and Sheila baked.'

She slid out of sight and Charles set course again after *Moonset*. He gave Toby a withering look.

'And you can take that grin off your face too. I meant what I said, Toby. Where we're going is no place for a girl. If anything happens to Paddy, I'll never forgive myself – or you. And neither will anyone else in the family. You've been a bloody fool.'

'I know,' Toby said. 'But she's right – she *is* as good in a boat as any man. And I couldn't see any way of stopping her anyway. I'll look after her. It's all right, Charles – you don't need to worry.'

'*You'll* look after her!' Charles exclaimed. 'When we're under fire, being bombed and trying to avoid mines and God knows what else – *you'll* look after her! You, who have never looked after anyone but yourself in your whole thoughtless, self-centred life!' He turned away, staring grimly ahead, his knuckles white on the wheel, furious with his brother and sister, furious with himself.

If I had any sense, he told himself ruefully, I'd do what I said in the first place, and go back. But I'd be breaking my promise to Sheila. And I'd be breaking my promise to myself – to do whatever I can towards the war effort.

'She'll never get past the Navy at Ramsgate, anyway,' he said. 'They'll find her there and chuck her off, and put a sailor on board.' And that, he added silently, will solve the whole problem, because she'll never be able to blame me.

He waved reassuringly at the white-haired figure in the boat ahead, and concentrated on keeping *Wagtail* on course.

Chapter Ten

Sheila had been the one to discover Paddy's absence.

Paddy was the only person missing from the party that went down to the jetty in the fresh, dew-soaked morning to see Charles and Toby off in *Wagtail*. Sheila herself had thumped on her door twice as she hurried downstairs to cook as good a breakfast as she could for the two men – cornflakes, then a few eggs and rashers, kept back from the stores that had been loaded aboard, some toast made from yesterday's bread, strong tea, and home-made jam. There would be no eggs and bacon for the family now for a while, she thought, but that didn't matter. The main thing was that Charles shouldn't go to sea on an empty stomach. She wished desperately that he needn't go to sea at all.

'Don't look so worried,' he'd said, squeezing her hand as she put the plate in front of him. 'I'll be fine. Think of all that fresh air! Just what the doctor ordered.'

'He didn't order you to go into danger.'

He looked at her soberly. 'Darling, you know how I've felt, sitting here in safety, making out Wills and breach-of-promise cases when other men are risking their lives. This is my chance to do something. I'm *needed*. Don't you understand what that means?'

'*I* need you,' she said. 'Wendy and the twins need you. What will we do if anything happens to you? You might not come back, Charles. I can't bear to think of it!' She bent her head on to her hands and the tears trickled between her fingers. Olivia, sitting opposite, began to cry too.

Charles laid down his knife and fork and patted her shoulder helplessly. Hubert, who was nibbling some toast, said, 'There are plenty of other women who feel the same as you, Sheila my dear, but their men have got to go. Charles has a choice, and I think you ought to be proud of his decision.' He patted his wife's hand. 'I know his mother and I are. Proud of *both* our sons,' he added with a glance at Toby.

'I am proud of him,' she wept. 'I just don't want to lose him. I don't want to be proud of a dead husband.'

'You won't be,' Toby said. 'I mean, he's not going to be dead. Look, you know what the Admiral said – this thing's only going to take a few days. The Germans aren't at the coast. As soon as they get there, we'll be coming home again. The Navy's not going to risk any more men than it can help. It's just a matter of ferrying them off the shore, that's all. A weekend jaunt.'

Charles looked at him, not sure whether Toby really believed his words or was just trying to reassure the women. Trying to change the subject, he said, 'Where's Paddy? Has anyone called her?'

'I did,' Sheila said, reaching for her handkerchief. 'I knocked twice. She just growled at me.'

'I dare say she's sulking,' Toby said cheerfully, 'because we won't take her with us. I'll eat her toast then, shall I?'

Sheila stared at him with loathing. 'Oh, you're so heartless! You could be going off now and never see your sister again, and all you can think about is eating her toast!' A commotion from upstairs announced that the twins were awake and she jumped up and threw down her napkin. 'Don't go yet, Charles. Let me get the boys up first. I want to come and see you off.'

'I'm sorry, darling, we need to use the tide. Give them a piece of toast each and bring them down to the jetty.' He glanced at his watch. 'We haven't got much time—'

Suddenly, the kitchen was full of bustle. The washing-up was left for Betty when she arrived as usual at nine, and the family gathered itself together. Sheila hurried back with a twin under each arm, still in her pyjamas, and Wendy trailing behind in an old pair of shorts and one of Toby's jumpers. Olivia began to panic about whether *Wagtail* was sufficiently stocked, and Hubert did his best to reassure her. 'They've got more food on that boat than we've got in the house, my dear. There simply isn't room for any more.'

'Where's Paddy?' Charles asked. 'She can't still be asleep, surely.'

'I'll go and knock on her door again,' Toby said, but came down a few minutes later shrugging and shaking his head. 'She's in a real sulk, won't come out at any price.'

Sheila tightened her lips angrily and Olivia made to go herself, but Toby stopped her. 'It won't do any good, Ma. And we don't have time for arguments.'

Charles hesitated, deeply unhappy about leaving without making things up with his young sister. He glanced at the clock, bit his lips, looked at the stairs and then decided that Toby was right. There was no time for argument, and Paddy might yet relent and follow them down to the jetty. He picked up one of the twins. 'All right, then. Let's go.'

They trooped off down the garden to the jetty, where *Wagtail* lay peacefully rocking on her mooring. The tide was just on the turn, about to start its fast run out of the harbour, so the quicker they got away, the better. Charles, who was carrying Jonathan, put the little boy down and gave him a quick hug. 'There you are. Be a good boy now, while Daddy's away.'

He turned to Nicholas and Wendy, and his daughter gazed at him with large, questioning eyes. 'Where are you going, Daddy? Is it the war?'

Charles looked at her, feeling helpless. He had never lied to his daughter. 'Yes, it is, sweetheart,' he said at last. 'But you don't need to worry. Uncle Toby will be with me, and we won't be gone long. I expect we'll be back by Saturday – soon after that, anyway.' He crouched down to look into her eyes. 'Will you help Mummy to take care of the twins? And Grandma and Grandpa? Will you do that for me?'

'Of course,' she said disdainfully. 'I always do. And you'd better look after Uncle Toby. He's not much use at looking after himself.'

Anxious though they were, nobody could help laughing at this, while Toby's face took on an expression of such comic astonishment that they laughed all over again. But Sheila's laughter turned to tears almost at once, and Charles took her in his arms.

'Don't cry, sweetheart. I'll be careful, I promise. And I'll be back soon.'

'Bring Alex with you,' she whispered, holding him tightly. 'Bring him back safe, too.'

'I will. I promise I will. Alex will be all right.' He turned to his parents and then said, 'We'd better go now. All aboard, Toby.'

The two men jumped on board. Charles took the wheel and started the engine, while Toby went to coil in the painter as Sheila untied it from the bollard. At the last moment, Charles hesitated, his eyes on the garden path. But no slim figure came into sight, and there was nobody at Paddy's bedroom window. With a deep sigh, he put the engine into reverse and backed the little cruiser away from the jetty.

The family stood in a tight group, watching as *Wagtail* moved out into the tide and slid away from them. Sheila, holding Nicky on her hip, gave a small, convulsive sob and put her free hand to her mouth. Olivia drew in a deep, shaking breath and Hubert moved between the two women and put an arm around each of their shoulders.

'They'll come back safe, my dears,' he said quietly. 'I'm sure they'll come back safe. And Jeremy will be with them too. There's nothing he doesn't know about the sea.'

'It's not the sea we're worried about,' Sheila retorted, and then shook her head at herself. 'I'm sorry, Dad. I didn't mean to snap at you.' She sighed. 'You're right, it's no worse than most women are having to suffer these days, is it? We've got away lightly so far. And it isn't as if they're going to fight.'

She glanced anxiously at her mother-in-law. So far, Olivia had borne up well, with only a few brief lapses into panic. Now, although obviously upset, her tall, slender figure stood straight and firm, and her eyes were dry. She was watching *Wagtail* as the boat moved into the distance, growing smaller until it passed Wickor Point and disappeared from sight. Then she braced her shoulders and turned away.

'Well, that's that. We'd better go back. These children haven't had any breakfast yet, and I promised to bake some scones for the WI tea. I noticed a few sultanas in the back of the cupboard last night – they might as well be used up. I'm glad you're staying here, Sheila. Paddy can help you with the children.'

Sheila looked at her. Her mother-in-law's face was as serene as if she had just waved her sons off for a day's fishing. She glanced at Hubert and he shook his head very slightly.

'I must admit I'd rather be here while Charles is away. I'll need to run back home for some clothes and the children's toys and things, though.'

'Of course. You go whenever you please, dear. There are plenty of us here to keep them amused. It will be lovely to have you all round us for a few days.' Her voice was determinedly light and Sheila felt a wave of admiration for her. Uncertain as her health was, and with both her sons gone on some bizarre and dangerous mission, she could still talk about scones, sultanas and having the family here just as if everything were normal. I suppose that's the only way to cope with it, she thought, and felt a spurt of shame at her own behaviour. Clinging to Charles like that, weeping and begging him not to go! Time you pulled yourself together, my girl, she told herself, and developed a bit of courage of your own.

They reached the house and went in through the kitchen. Betty was there already, washing up the breakfast things, but there was still no sign of Paddy. Olivia tutted.

'You go and fetch her, Sheila, while I get these tots something to eat. Wendy will help me, won't you, poppet? What do you think the boys will like – cornflakes or Puffed Wheat? Or there's Weeta-bix . . .'

Sheila left the kitchen and climbed the stairs, feeling irritation wash back. Honestly, Paddy was the end! A sulk was all very well, but she had no right to let her brothers go off without even wishing them luck. The trouble with that young lady was, she was thoroughly spoiled. It was time someone took her in hand and told her so, and Sheila was in the mood to do it. It was a pity she couldn't join one of the women's services right now – they'd soon set her right. There was no room for sulks or spoiled brats in the Wrens or the ATS or the WAAFs.

She knocked sharply on Paddy's door. There was no reply so she opened it, then felt her heart grow cold.

Paddy's room was empty, the bed neatly made. An envelope lay on the smooth, white pillow.

'She must have slipped out while we were having breakfast,' Sheila said for the fourth time as they sat round the kitchen table a quarter of an hour later. The children were eating bowls of cereal – a different kind each – and Betty had made a fresh pot of tea and put a cup in front of each of them.

Olivia held the note in shaking hands. Her face was white and all her tight control was slipping. 'The silly girl. The silly, *naughty* girl. How could she do this? She doesn't realise what it means – she doesn't understand the dangers. Hubert, we must stop them somehow. We must get her back.' Her voice was trembling, thick with tears.

Hubert gently took the note from her fingers and read it aloud, as if the words might have changed since his wife had read them a few minutes earlier. '*I've got to go. I'm as good a sailor as Charles and Toby, and I want to help save Alex. I love him. I love all of you too, and I promise to be careful and not do anything silly. I'll be back soon. Your loving daughter, Paddy.*' He laid the note down. 'I think she knows what it means, my dear, as much as any of us do. And you know how determined she is.'

'Determined to have her own way! Ever since she was a baby . . .' Olivia broke down for a moment, then pulled herself together and went on in a high, angry voice. 'Not do anything silly! Isn't this the silliest, most wilful thing she's ever done? Sillier than running away from school – sillier than getting herself expelled for slipping out after bedtime? Sillier than – than – oh, Hubert! Both my boys and now my girl, my baby! I can't bear it!' She turned into his arms, weeping against his thin chest, while the three grandchildren watched open-mouthed, their spoons clutched in their hands.

'Why's Grandma crying?' Jonathan asked in a fearful voice. 'Is someone dead?'

Betty came swiftly round the table. 'Now, there's no need for a little boy like you to be asking questions like that.' She sat down beside him and took the spoon from his fist. 'Finish up your cornflakes now, there's a good boy, and you can go and play in the garden for a bit, while Betty does the dishes. Then we'll go and pick some peas, shall we? You like doing that. And if you're very good, we might dig up some more new potatoes.'

'Can I dig up potatoes as well?' Nicky asked instantly, thrusting his spoon into the milk-sodden Weetabix.

'Of course you can. We'll all go. Now, madam,' Betty transferred her attention to Olivia, 'why don't you go and have a lie-down and I'll bring you a nice fresh pot of tea and a bit of toast? You're tired out, that's what's wrong with you. You'll feel better once you've had a rest.'

'I don't think I will,' Olivia said, allowing herself to be helped to her feet. 'And I'd really rather keep busy. The scones . . .' She put her hand on her forehead and swayed a little. Sheila jumped up and took her other arm. 'Well, perhaps just for a few minutes. Just half an hour. Then I'll come down and make the scones. It's all right, Sheila, Betty will help me. You stay here with the children.'

The two women left the kitchen and Sheila sat down again and looked at Hubert. In a taut, bitter voice, she said, 'The selfish little hussy! She should have known how upset her mother would be. She knows Olivia mustn't have shocks, and the past few days have been bad enough without this. Didn't she think? Didn't she think at *all*?'

'I'm afraid Paddy doesn't do a lot of thinking,' Hubert said wryly. 'Perhaps it's our fault – perhaps we have spoiled her. Our only girl, and coming so late. Life has always been easy for her, you see, and she can't believe that it will ever be anything else. And she's really very fond of Alex.'

'Yes, well, that's something that won't go right for her,' Sheila said grimly. 'He's fond of her too, but he's far too old for her. If she thinks that this stupid, hare-brained escapade will make my brother fall in love with her, she's in for a shock.'

Hubert sighed and nodded. He picked up a bib that was lying on the table and wiped Jonathan's chin. 'There you are, Jonny. You can get down now, all of you, and go out into the garden. Betty will come and see to you soon.' He watched them scamper out through the open door into the sunshine, and then looked back at Sheila. 'Let's hope that's the only shock she gets,' he said in a quiet voice. 'Let's hope it's the only shock for all of us.'

Getting Paddy back was more difficult than it seemed. To catch her, they would need a boat that could either outstrip or waylay *Wagtail*, by now already well out into Bracklesham Bay. Hubert racked his brains and remembered an old friend from law school who lived in Selsey and kept a boat there. He found the telephone number and rang him, only to be answered by the friend's wife who told him that the boat had been requisitioned by the Admiralty and gone on some unspecified mission – to Dover, she thought. Her husband was taking the boat there himself but expected to be home by the first possible train; she would get him to telephone Hubert when he arrived. Hubert thanked her and rang off. He turned to Sheila and lifted his shoulders.

'It will be the same story everywhere, I'm afraid. All the craft over thirty feet have been called up in the same way. We'll just have to wait until she puts in at Dover.'

'Charles will send her back,' Sheila said. 'He won't let her stay on board.'

'Of course he won't. Neither will the Navy. She'll be back here with her tail between her legs before we can say Jack Robinson.'

Sheila bit the side of her thumb. 'It's all Toby's fault!' she burst out. 'He must have connived with this ridiculous plan. He went up to her room after breakfast, remember? He came down saying she wouldn't come out at any price – well, of course she wouldn't! She wasn't even in it! And he *knew* – he knew perfectly well. He probably suggested it to her, the idiot! I'm sorry, Father, I know he's your son, but really—'

'Oh, don't apologise,' Hubert said ruefully. 'You're quite right – he is irresponsible. I'm afraid we seem to have made as poor a job of Toby as we have of Paddy.'

'I didn't mean that. I don't know what I meant. It's not as if they weren't nice people, both of them – Paddy's a lovely girl, and Toby could charm the birds off the trees – it's just that neither of them seems to understand real life. They seem to think it's all a game, and it's not.' She started to cry. 'It's not a game at all. Oh, I'm sorry – crying isn't going to help anyone.'

'It'll probably help you,' he said, and put his arms around her. His spare, bony body felt oddly comforting against hers. 'And I don't think they really do look on this as a game. Toby's always at his most flippant when the situation is serious, and Paddy is a very intelligent young woman. She understands the implications very well, I think. Her only trouble is that she's so intense. Try not to be too angry with her, my dear.'

Sheila sniffed and felt for her handkerchief. She blew her nose and wiped her eyes, then gave him a small, shaky smile. 'All right, I'll try. But when I see Mother getting so upset . . .'

'Olivia's stronger than she seems. She's been through one war already, remember. I didn't go myself as I was already too old to be conscripted, but her younger brothers did – both of them. She knows what it's like to see your loved ones go away to face danger.'

Sheila stared at him. 'Both of them? But I thought she only had one brother – Charles's Uncle Percy.'

'No, there were two. The other one was called Edward. He lied about his age to join the Army – he was only sixteen when he went. He was killed at the Somme, on the first day. To Olivia, he was her baby, and she never really got over her grief. She never speaks of him. Charles was only eight years old then, of course, and he was never told the truth. I think he still believes his uncle died of some childhood illness.'

'He's never even mentioned him to me,' Sheila said. 'And now Paddy's done almost the same thing – gone off to war when she's too young. And a girl, too. It's even worse for Mother than I thought.'

'As I said, she's stronger than she seems. And we can help her. Having you and the children here will make an enormous difference.' They heard Betty's footsteps on the stairs and he patted Sheila's back and put her away from him. 'Now, what is there to do? Did I hear you say something about new potatoes, Betty? Perhaps I could dig them up, with the twins to help me.' He paused and looked at Betty's face. 'What is it?'

The housekeeper's normally rosy face was pale. She came quickly into the room. 'It's the newspapers, sir. They've just come. Look! And the gardener's boy said it was on the News on the wireless too, only I never heard it this morning.'

'Neither did we.' Hubert took the sheaf of newspapers she held out to him. Her own *Daily Express* was on top, the headlines blazing across the front page, and he stared at them, while Sheila moved to read them over his shoulder. 'Great heavens above . . . So the news is out.'

'I suppose they couldn't keep it quiet much longer.' Sheila took the newspaper from him and read the report.

Through an inferno of bombs and shells the BEF is crossing the
Channel from Dunkirk – in history's strangest armada.
TENS OF THOUSANDS SAFELY HOME ALREADY
SHIPS OF ALL SIZES DARE THE GERMAN GUNS

Under the guns of the British Fleet, under the wings of the Royal Air
Force, a large proportion of the BEF who for three days have been
fighting their way back to the Flanders coast, have now been brought
safely to England from Dunkirk.

'There's a picture, look,' she said excitedly. 'It shows the coast of France and the sea full of ships. Oh, Pa!' She turned towards Hubert. 'It says there are even more soldiers over there, waiting on the beaches to come home. They're asking for all small boats that can make the crossing, to go at once. I know I should be proud of Charles and I am, I really am, but oh Pa, I'm so *frightened* for him. This report says they're being attacked all the time, and *Wagtail*'s such a little boat. What chance can they possibly have?'

'The same chance as everyone else,' he said gravely. 'Big ships can be bombed as well as small ones, my dear. It's a bad situation but it's an heroic one as well. Think of the fine job my two boys are doing.'

'And Paddy?' she said quietly. 'Pa, whatever will they do about her?'

Betty moved across the table and put her hand on Sheila's arm. 'Mrs Stainbank's told me about Mr Charles and Toby and young Paddy. You must be fair put about, but they'll be all right. God will take care of them.' Her lips trembled a little and Sheila saw tears in her eyes.

'Oh Betty,' Sheila said, getting up swiftly to grip the house-keeper's hand. 'What have we been thinking of? Your brother's over there, too, isn't he – over in France, in the BEF?'

'Yes, he is. But he'll come home safe, I'm sure he will.' Betty wiped her eyes with the corner of her pinafore and then lifted her chin. 'Why, he might be back in England already, and so might your brother as well, for all we know.' And then, suddenly, she covered her face with the flowery material and sobbed.

We've been so selfish, Sheila thought. As if Alex Rowley were the only local man over in France. There were other villagers as well, and one of them was Betty's own brother.

There was probably not a family in the land who didn't have some relative, friend or neighbour involved in this incredible affair.

Chapter Eleven

B y early Friday morning the *Countess Wear* had made Dover, sweeping across the calm blue water of East Wear Bay and under Abbot's Cliff. Shakespeare Cliff had loomed ahead, rising in a sharp, white escarpment before dropping down to the harbour. Beyond that, the famous white cliffs rose in a stalwart barricade; somewhere deep inside, although Robby and his crew were not aware of it, Admiral Ramsay was masterminding this unprecedented evacuation. They were calling it 'Dynamo'.

The sea was like glass. Outside the harbour was a throng of boats, jostling each other so closely that you could barely see the water between them. Their crews were mostly on deck, swapping what few facts they had, giving their opinions (of which they had many) and waiting for fresh provisioning and for orders as they prepared to embark on their journey across the Channel.

However, the ships that were preparing to go to Dunkirk were not the only ones to be seen that Sunday morning. There were others coming back.

'My stars above,' Danny whispered, standing beside Rob in the wheelhouse and staring at the steady flow of vessels. 'Look at that . . .'

A destroyer passed them, its decks packed with soldiers, its side scarred and battered. There was a jagged hole high up in its bow, another in its stern, and it was listing heavily to starboard. A paddle-steamer followed, similarly laden, and then a smaller ship, no more than fifty feet long, the men lying like sardines in every space they could find. It passed close enough for those on the *Countess Wear* to see their faces, grey with weariness, pain, hunger and thirst, many of them wounded and roughly bandaged; and they stared in dismay, only just beginning to realise what this operation must be like for those waiting to be rescued.

Robby felt his heart sink. These were the lucky ones, but how many had been unlucky? How many had been killed, or were too badly injured to move? How many would have to be left behind when the Germans finally succeeded in driving the British from the shores? And what about his brother Jan?

'Bloody hell,' Jimmy Bell said quietly. 'And they've been doing this now for – what? Three days, four? It must be a flaming nightmare over there.'

'Did that bloke say we'd got to go on to Ramsgate?' Danny asked. 'Why can't we go straight over from here? Why send us all the way up the coast?' He moved restlessly about the deck. 'I want to get on with it.'

Robby, feeling the same impatience, had gone back to the charts. 'The thing is, Dan, they made three routes across the Channel. The one from Dover – Z – went straight to Calais, but Calais is finished now, and anyone who goes that way gets shelled. We've got to take the longer route.'

A sudden roar of aircraft overhead made them all duck and they stared upwards at a flight of Hurricanes and Spitfires making for the French coast. A cheer went up from the fleet of boats and the planes waggled their wings.

'That'll sort 'em out,' Jimmy said with satisfaction, watching them disappear against the blue sky, but Rob felt a twinge of anxiety. On a clear day like this, you could see Calais from the cliffs of Dover, and the thought that the Germans were already occupying the port, only twenty miles away, was not a comfortable one. He looked at the chart again. 'Dunkirk's about twenty-five miles west-nor'-west up the coast – see? Now, in between us and them there's shallows and mudbanks and minefields and God knows what in the way, and a lot of ships too.' The other two men were leaning over his shoulder, following his pointing finger. 'See, these longer routes, X and Y, go through the Downs – that's not hills, it's this big area off Dover – and then turn west off Ramsgate by the North Goodwin lightship. Then Y keeps going right out to West Hinder before turning south for the North Channel and back down to Dunkirk.'

'Which one will we be taking?' Jimmy asked.

'Don't know yet. We'll be going over in convoy anyway. I suppose it'll be played by ear in a way – take whichever course seems best at the time.' He folded the charts, remembering that he was in charge of this little ship and its men, and responsible for their welfare. 'And I reckon the best course for us right now would be to get ourselves some grub.'

A destroyer surged by, and Robby recognised two large transport ships and two hospital carriers, already on their way to France. They were going the long way round, using the route called Y. He felt his sense of urgency deepen. This was it. This was what they had come for. Their passage along the Channel from Dartmouth seemed all at once to have been nothing more than child's play. Now, they were at war.

'*Naiad Errant,*' Danny said, reading the names painted on the bows. '*White Heather. Westerly. Llanthony* – I reckon she must be Welsh, don't you? And look at that little thing, can't be more than thirty foot long. *Jockette Two*, she's called – funny sort o' name – got a gun on her wheelhouse roof and all, just like a real grown-up ship.'

A Naval cutter drew alongside and the Lieutenant at the helm called out to them through a loudhailer. '*Countess Wear*! Are you fit to make passage now, or do you need supplies?'

'We've taken on fresh supplies, sir,' Robby called back. 'We're fit to go.' He felt a heavy lump in his chest. 'Which route shall we use?'

'The outside one – Y. Calais has gone – the Germans are shelling anything that passes. Same with Boulogne. All troops are being told to make for Dunkirk.' The voice was as brisk and unemotional as if the officer were giving them a bus timetable. He went on, 'There's a convoy going from the Downs at one-thirty this afternoon. You should be able to rendezvous by then. Once you arrive, go into the harbour and take men off the docks. There'll be Naval ships there to direct you, but you'll have to use your own initiative as well.' There was a brief pause. Then the Lieutenant said curtly, 'Good luck,' and the cutter moved away.

Robby looked at the other two. 'Well – this is it.'

'I'm ready,' Jimmy Bell said, his face set in determined lines.

'Me too,' said Danny, though his face was pale under his mop of thick black hair. 'How long will it take us to get there, d'you think?'

'About five or six hours, I should say.' A sudden deep rumble sounded across the glassy water and Robby asked, 'Did you hear that?'

'It sounds like thunder,' Danny said uneasily, but Jimmy shook his head.

'That's not thunder. That's shellfire. Listen – there it is again.' He turned and stared out across the Channel. 'Look.'

Far out in the Channel they could see puffs of smoke. They were too low on the surface to be able to see more than a few miles, and each man knew that the puffs, small as they looked, must be dramatically large. 'That's ships,' Robby said, his throat suddenly dry. 'That's Calais . . .' He swallowed. 'We need to get over there as fast as we can.'

'We can't go without the convoy,' Jimmy said. 'The Channel's littered with minefields. We've got to be escorted through them – no sense getting ourselves blowed up as well.'

'I know.' Robby looked again at the crowded seas. He felt a desperate need to be on his way, ploughing across the Channel with the rest of them. The *Countess* was ready. The crew was ready. A surge of impatience welled up within him, and he had to call on all his training to subdue it. Jimmy was right – it would be suicide to try to make the crossing alone. There were mines, other shipping, German aircraft and all the ordinary hazards of sandbanks and shallows to contend with. Using your own initiative was one thing – going against express orders was something quite different.

And yet . . . somewhere over there was his own brother, Jan, who had never wanted to be a soldier, who had wanted only a quiet, peaceful life in a small Devonshire village. Fighting for his life at this very moment, perhaps; hiding in woodlands or ditches; lying wounded or even dead by some French roadside . . .

'Let's make for this rendezvous,' he said abruptly. 'Maybe we can't go on our own, but we can be first in the queue. I want to get over there as soon as possible. I want to get on with this job.'

Charles and Toby were in the cockpit of *Wagtail*, drinking tea. Like the crew of the *Countess Wear*, who were an hour or two ahead of them, they had taken turn and turn about to sleep; but with the dawn all three of them were awake and Paddy had brewed up on the little stove that Hubert had had fitted in the galley. She sat on the steps just below the two men and looked up at the mother-of-pearl sky.

'I can't see why you won't let me come on deck.'

'Don't be more of a nuisance than you have to be, Paddy,' Charles said. 'You know perfectly well that if you're seen you'll be sent back. Not that I care – you're going back anyway, the minute we can put you ashore.'

'I'm getting tired of this argument,' Paddy said. 'Nobody will know I'm a girl now that I've cut off my hair. I can say I'm a Sea Scout, like Peter Murphy.'

'Don't you think the Admiral will recognise you? Or Peter? Of course they will! And the Admiral will say exactly the same as I've been saying – you've got to go home. You may as well make up your mind to it, Paddy.'

Paddy set her lips mutinously and glanced at Toby, who crinkled his eyes at her.

'Big brother's right, Pads. If the Admiral sees you, that'll be the end of it. You won't go against him.'

Paddy knew this was true. They were all fond of the Admiral, who was like a kind of surrogate grandfather to them all, always ready to race his dinghy against theirs or play the part of an explorer or a pirate in their games amongst the little creeks and bays of the big harbour, but she was aware that in his Naval life he had been a man of consequence, accustomed to being obeyed.

She swirled the tea in her mug, thinking about Alex. He had always been a special person in her life. The Stainbanks and the Rowleys had been friends for many years, the children growing up together, and Charles and Sheila had been childhood sweethearts. Alex was thirteen years older than Paddy but he'd promised, one day when she was a very small girl, to wait until she was old enough to marry him; she remembered the day he'd made her a ring of grass and slipped it on her finger, saying that now they were engaged. She'd kept the grass ring in a tiny box in her drawer until it had crumbled to dust.

Her feelings for him hadn't crumbled, though, and although she knew in her heart that it had been only a game, she longed to believe that he meant it. After all, he hadn't married anyone else and although (to her jealousy) he'd squired a succession of girls, there still seemed to be no one particular in his life. And there had always been a special bond between them, something more than mere friendship, something that on Paddy's side at least was what she believed to be love.

She'd thrilled with both fear and pride when he was called up and went away in his new Army uniform, and followed the news assiduously, trying to imagine where he was and what he was doing. Every night, when she went to bed, she sent up fervent prayers for his safety. Now, all she could think of was that he was in real danger, and that she had the opportunity to rescue him.

Nobody was going to prevent her from doing that. Nobody . . .

She crept up the steps and glanced cautiously around, surprised to see how many ships there were now in the flotilla. Like everyone else, she was impressed by the variety of craft. *Moonset* and *Wagtail* were amongst the smallest, but at every moment it seemed that new boats were joining them. It was like a vast regatta.

She took another look at *Moonset*. The Admiral was out of sight and Peter Murphy was at the wheel, concentrating on keeping his course straight. Paddy had known Peter all her life – he was only a few months older than she and had lived in Emsworth before his family moved to Bosham. They'd both attended the village school until Paddy was sent away to board, and they'd spent their childhood messing about in sailing dinghies or rowing-boats, swimming and picnicking, or roaming the creeks looking for birds' nests. There had been a group of them, eight or ten children allowed to run wild, like ragamuffins in their old shorts and shirts and plimsolls. The days had always been sunny and the summers seemed to have lasted for ever, and she thought wistfully of how lovely it had all been – so different from now, with the beaches forbidden areas and the shadow of invasion hanging over everyone's lives.

That's what we're fighting for, she thought, so that children can have long, happy summers and run free, and learn to be strong and independent. That's what this war is about – freedom and independence for everyone, not just a few.

Moonset was only a short distance away. She gazed at Peter's straight, slim figure and wished he would turn his head and see her. She knew that Peter wouldn't give her away; he was her friend. It would be comforting to know that she had a friend somewhere near.

As she watched, he glanced down at the hatchway leading to *Moonset*'s cabin and she saw the Admiral begin to emerge. Hastily, she ducked out of sight. Charles and Toby were right. If the Admiral saw her, she would be sent home at the first opportunity and she wouldn't dare to defy him.

She reached up for the other two empty mugs. Charles was bent over the chart again while Toby took a turn at steering. 'How far now to Dover?' she asked.

'Fifteen miles. We could do with some breakfast. We may not have time once we get there.'

'Cue for the cook,' Paddy said sardonically. 'You see, you do need me!' She slid through to the galley and got out the bacon and some of the home-made bread. It might be a good idea to cook all the bacon now, while she had the chance, so that it could be shoved between slices of bread later. There was cheese too, and the jam. Paddy had sailed enough to know that so long as you always had the ingredients to make a sandwich you could survive. She got out the frying pan and lit the stove.

What was Alex eating now? Was he hiding in ditches, being hunted through woods, or shot at? She had a sudden vision of him lying wounded and alone on some French roadside, with a convoy of German tanks approaching. Tears came to her eyes and the frying-pan seemed to melt and waver on the stove. She laid down her knife.

'Mmm, that smells good.' Toby dropped down to join her. He started to slice bread and then glanced sideways at her. 'Here, what's the matter? You don't want to take any notice of Charles, you know. He's just an old stick-in-the-mud. He doesn't really think you're a nuisance.'

'He does,' she sniffed, brushing her arm across her face. 'And I expect he's right. But it's not that, Toby. I keep thinking about Alex. What's he doing now? He might be hurt and starving. He might even be – be dead.' She turned suddenly and leaned against him, tears flooding into his jersey. 'I can't bear to think about it, but I can't stop myself. If anything happens to him . . .'

'Hey, now come on,' Toby said soothingly. He held her firmly and stroked the back of her head with his free hand. 'Don't get yourself into a state. Nothing's going to happen to Alex. He'll come home, right as rain, wondering what all the fuss is about, you see if he doesn't. Why, I bet he's on the beach at this very moment, doing a spot of sunbathing and looking at his watch, wondering where we've got to. He'll be all right.'

'You don't know that,' she said miserably, wishing it could be true.

'I know Alex. He always falls on his feet.' Toby gave her a hug. 'Come on, now, let's rescue this bacon before it sets fire to the boat.'

'Oh!' She gave a shriek of dismay and snatched the frying-pan from the stove. The fat was beginning to smoke alarmingly and the bacon was cooked almost to a crisp. Carefully, she lifted the slices out and put them between slabs of bread. The aroma filled the cabin.

'What's going on down there?' Charles called anxiously, and Toby moved over to the companionway. 'I can smell burning.'

'Everything's under control. Paddy's doing the bacon just as you like it. She's right, you know, we really won't be able to manage without her.'

'I don't know that we're going to be able to manage at all,' Charles said, sounding deflated. 'The Admiral's having a spot of bother. He's putting in to Folkestone.'

'Why, what's the matter?' Toby sprang up the steps and on to the deck, while Paddy hovered apprehensively below.

'Engine trouble. You can just hear it.' *Moonset* was some distance away but the unhappy note of her engine could clearly be heard across the smooth water. 'It may not be all that much, but he needs to have a look at it.'

'Oh, lor'.' Toby stood silent while they both gazed at the limping boat. 'But that doesn't mean we have to stop as well, does it? We can go on.'

'Don't be silly!' Charles said sharply. 'Of course we can't go on, not without the Admiral. We haven't even been properly requisitioned.'

'Well, does that matter? You don't have to have a ticket to go and rescue soldiers, do you? Didn't he say they need all the help they can get? That's why we're here, Charles. Look,' Toby seized his arm, 'we can just tag along with the others. Get a tow across, like he said. No one's going to ask questions, they'll be only too glad to have us along. If we can get a tow across, we'll have enough fuel to do the work while we're there, and then we can get another tow back. If we stay with the Admiral, we'll be in an official party – it'll mean a lot of red tape and all that fuss about signing on. This way, we can just slip over, do the job and then slip back again – no questions asked.' He paused. 'And no problems about having Paddy with us.'

There was a short silence. Then Paddy, at the foot of the steps, cried, 'Yes! Yes, that's it! Nobody will know – the Admiral's the only one who would recognise me. No one else is going to see me close to, not until we're there, anyway – and then it'll be too late. Please, Charles – say yes!'

He stared from one to the other, torn with doubt. 'It's not a matter of people knowing. It's the danger. If anything happened to you—'

'Look,' she said, 'Hitler's nearly at the French coast. The whole country's waiting to be invaded. Don't you think I'll be in danger if that happens? Even if we're not invaded, we'll be bombed. Everyone says so.' She came halfway up the steps to catch at his arm. *What's the point of keeping me safe today, just for me to be raped and killed tomorrow?*'

Charles looked at her and then away again. He gripped the wheel in both hands, concentrating on their course. Then, his whole face furrowed with the effort of his thinking, he drew in a deep, unhappy breath and met her eyes again.

'All right,' he said in a flat voice. 'You win. You're coming with us. But on one condition.'

'Yes!' she cried, her eyes aflame. 'Anything! All my jam for the rest of the war, if you like. Anything!'

'Worse than that,' he said gravely, 'and I really mean this, Paddy. You've got to do exactly as I say. The minute I say it. No questions, no argument, understand? We may not be signed on, but we'll treat this like a Naval ship, with proper Naval discipline, and that means obeying orders even before they're given.'

'Aye, aye, sir!' she exclaimed, saluting, and Charles sighed, not at all sure that he'd done the right thing. Then he turned his attention back to the Admiral. *Moonset* had changed course now and was heading towards the pier at Folkestone. Charles signalled that he intended to continue to Dover, and received an affirmative.

'You see?' Toby said. 'He doesn't need us to hold his hand.'

'I never thought he did,' Charles replied, and set his own course for the last few miles to Dover. 'I thought *we* were the ones who needed our hands held.' He looked at his brother. 'If any harm comes to that girl . . .'

'You'll blame me. Don't worry, I'm used to it!' Toby gave him his usual flippant grin and Charles closed his eyes.

'No,' he said. 'I won't blame you, Toby. I'll blame myself. I'll blame myself for the rest of my life.'

By dawn, Olly was in the Royal Harbour of Ramsgate.

The *Surrey Queen* had finally left her berth just before dark on Thursday evening, with a pilot aboard to take them to Greenwich; another had joined them at midnight and taken them the rest of the way. The crew, with the extra hands who had joined them, dossed down to sleep wherever they could find a space, and even Olly agreed at last that he ought to get some rest. There was a big job ahead of them, and you never knew when you'd get another chance to get your head down.

By now, they all knew that they were heading for the port of Dunkirk, where they would be principally required to fight fires both on the docks and on other ships while the soldiers of the BEF were taken off by the ever-growing convoy. To his relief, Olly had found that he wouldn't be required to take the *Surrey Queen* across the Channel himself. Like the *Massey Shaw*, it was now under the command of a young Naval Sublieutenant, who had arrived on board with a steel helmet and a chart of the minefields that would have to be negotiated between the Goodwin Sands and Dunkirk. Olly had stared at him in dismay.

'Minefields? Blimey, you lot don't half know how to spring surprises! This ship's got a steel hull – we'll be a giant flaming magnet.'

'Never mind that. The minefields have been swept clear – this job's been going on all week.' The Subby ducked under the canvas dodger and contemplated the men clustered on the broad deck. 'You're all volunteers, right? You're ready to sign on for a month under Naval orders? You'll get the proper pay, of course. But it's going to be dangerous. If you want to change your minds, now's your chance.'

The men glanced at each other. Then Chalky White said, 'We're used to danger. Wouldn't seem like real work without it, would it, mates?'

The others joined in a chorus of agreement. Most of them were experienced firefighters and the others, like Stan Miller, were tough dock workers who understood rivercraft and could handle the firefighting equipment as well. Some, like Olly, had sons, nephews or friends over in France and all were desperately keen to play their part in this incredible rescue operation. Nobody had any intention of backing out.

The journey down the river and round the coast had been made in company with several hundred other boats, most of them towed by sturdy Thames tugs. Many of them had been with the two fireboats from the start, collected first in Teddington by the boatbuilder Douglas Tough and coming downriver to pass through London.

Olly still felt doubtful about some of the smaller craft. Not so much the ketches and motor yachts, forty or fifty feet long and well able to cross the Channel even in heavy seas, and certainly not the tough, aggressive lifeboats which were built for the worst conditions imaginable – but how could little bits of things like these motor launches, for instance, hope to do any good?

He shaded his eyes and peered at a small, open boat, barely half the length of many of the others and with a beam of less than seven feet. The *Lady Isabelle*, she was called, floating calmly in a cluster of similar craft behind the tug that had brought them all this way and would probably take them on to Dunkirk. He'd seen her quite often when he'd taken Effie and the girls to Staines to visit Effie's mother – moored up river with half a dozen cane chairs in the cockpit, her awning up and her mahogany deck and hull polished so bright you could see your face in them. Fast enough in calm water, he thought, but what if the weather turns rough out in the Channel?

'Finished the brightwork, Skip,' Chalky White announced, appearing beside him with a tin of mutton fat and a handful of cotton waste. 'Not that we can call it that any more,' he added mournfully.

Olly looked at the brasswork which he and his crew had taken such pride in keeping so highly polished and immaculate. Like all the other boats requisitioned, they had been told to camouflage their vessels – and this meant covering hulls and metalwork with grey paint. Unfortunately, by the time the hull had been finished, the chandler's stores that Chalky and the others had gone to had run out of grey paint, and mutton fat was the only substitute they could find. It meant that everything was going to be slippery with grease until they could manage to get some paint – if ever they did, and if they had time to apply it – but at least they'd complied with the

Admiralty requirements. God knows what else we're going to have to do before this lot finishes, Olly thought.

'We smell like a bloody butcher's shop,' Jack Hodge grumbled. 'And what's going to happen if we get too close to a fire? We'll go up like a flipping pan of chips. Bloody home-made war this is.'

'That's as may be,' Olly said sharply. 'Ours is not to reason why. Some of us have got sons over there and we're only too pleased to be able to do summat about getting 'em back again. It doesn't matter about the brightwork – paint and mutton fat'll come off soon enough, once we're back in civvy street again, but for the time being we're paid-up members of the Armed Forces, and that means we obey orders.' Even if they did come from a pink-cheeked youngster who hardly looked old enough to use a razor, he added to himself, but he knew that the boy had probably been in action already. It didn't do to go by appearances these days.

Both the inner and outer harbours at Ramsgate were crowded with small craft. Olly looked at the little town, its shops and pubs and cafés clustered along the front, at the Clock House standing at the head of the Inner Basin, at the railings which ran along the promenade, high up on the white cliffs. It had been one of his and Effie's favourite places in peacetime. They'd come here every year for their week's holiday, ever since Joe had been a baby. The nippers had built sandcastles on the long stretch of sands, and Olly had joined in, his trousers rolled up and a knotted handkerchief on his head, digging a moat all round and a canal for the sea to run up as the tide came in. He'd paddled too, and when it was really hot he'd even stripped down to the bathing suit that Effie had made him, with no sleeves, when they'd first got married. They'd both thought it very daring, but nowadays you saw men of all ages in nothing but what they called 'trunks', no more than underpants, and no one took a bit of notice.

He remembered teaching the kiddies to swim from those sands. Olly was a good swimmer and he'd taken each one out in turn, riding his broad back like merchildren riding a whale, and then brought them back into the shallows where he would stand with his hands under their stomachs as they flailed their arms and legs and spluttered. Carrie had surprised them all by picking it up in no time and Joe hadn't been bad, but Dot had never managed to get the hang of it. She preferred to paddle or stay with her mum on the beach, lying on an old blanket.

It was here that Olly and Effie wanted to come and live when he left the Fire Service. They'd got their eye on a café on the front that they thought they might take over. During the past few years, they'd got to know Marge and Eric, who ran it, and it was pretty well understood between them all that when they retired, Olly and Effie would take their place. That time would only have been two or three years off now, Olly thought, but who knew what would happen before they could realise their dream? Would he and Effie ever live in Ramsgate, running their café and strolling across the road of an evening to look at the harbour or walk along the beach?

'What's that place, then?' Chalky White had put away his greasy tin and cotton waste and stood beside him, looking up at the Clock House. It was a big, grey building, dominating the harbour, with a turret in the centre where the clock showed the time to those at sea and on land. 'It looks official.'

'So it is,' Olly said. 'I dunno who first built it, but the Navy had it and then Trinity House. And summat called the Solar Transit Observatory.'

'What the hell's that when it's at home?' Chalky grumbled. 'Why can't they give things sensible names that ordinary people can understand?'

'Because it wouldn't sound so good, that's why. It'd be summat like "A Place to Watch the Sun Going Over". I mean, it'd just sound stupid, but that's what it means. Anyway, I went inside once and they've got the Meridian Line in there.'

'The what?'

'The Meridian Line. It's a big circle drawn round the Earth, and it goes through the North Pole and the South Pole and everywhere in the world on the same longitude. It goes through Greenwich as well, and that's why things are measured from there and why we has Greenwich Mean Time.'

Chalky stared at him and scratched his head. 'Who drew this circle then? I mean, he must have gone thousands of miles to do that. And why's it come through Ramsgate?'

'I told you,' Olly said. 'Because it's *on* the Meridian Line. And when they built this Clock House they thought it'd be a good idea to put a metal strip in the floor to show where it is. They uses it to work out navigation at sea. And they never actually *drew* one all round the world – it's an imaginary line.' He chuckled. 'Reminds me of that old joke I used to tell the kids – about the Equator being a menagerie lion running round the Earth. It was years before they got the point.'

The look on Chalky's face told him that it would probably be years before he got the point too, so Olly sighed and said, 'Anyway, we're not here to stand chewing the fat all day. We got a job to do. Didn't that young Subby say we were going to get more stores?'

Chalky nodded, glad to be on familiar ground again. 'They're bringing on umpteen cans of fuel and fresh water, and some grub. Look over there – the amount they're taking on board that scow is enough to feed a bleeding army.'

'Well, that's what they're goin' to be doing, ain't it,' Olly said soberly, and moved forward as a Naval pinnace came alongside. 'Our turn now, by the looks of it. Take hold of that painter, Chalky, and get fastened astern.'

Their own Sublieutenant Denison hopped over from the pinnace and began to organise the transfer of stores. Olly, Chalky and the others had no further time to marvel at the amount they were taking on board. Mostly, it was water and fuel – huge, forty-gallon drums of diesel which were lashed to the deck. Food would be required mostly for the crew, since they were going mainly to fight fires and wouldn't be picking up soldiers until the last minute – if there were any left to be picked up. Olly wished briefly that Effie were here. She'd have had the small galley working in no time, and been able to produce a steady stream of bacon sandwiches and mugs of cocoa to keep the firefighters going.

'This is what we've got to do,' Sublieutenant Denison said, appearing beside him with the chart. He flattened out a sheet of typewritten instructions and read them aloud: '*Proceed at your utmost speed direct to the beaches eastward of Dunkirk. From the Nore, proceed by Cant, Four Fathoms, Horse Gore and South Channels, or by any other route with which you are familiar . . .*'

He paused and looked at Olly, who shook his head. 'I've never been as far as this, let alone out to sea. I've never even crossed the Channel in a steamer.'

'Not to worry.' Denison seemed to have expected this, and went on reading: '. . . *with which you are familiar, to pass close round North Foreland and thence to North Goodwin Light Vessel.*'

'Blimey,' Olly said, 'does that mean we got to cross the Goodwin Sands?' Everybody, whether they were a sailor or not, knew how dangerous the Goodwin Sands could be.

The Sublieutenant shook his head. 'It's all right. There'll be plenty of other ships around anyway.' He glanced at the crowded harbour. 'A lot of these little chaps will be towed across – all we need do is follow them. And make for the black smoke.'

'The black smoke?' Olly was still staring at the chart, trying to make out the mass of lines that denoted sandbanks, prohibited anchorages, dykes and other mysteries he'd never needed to understand while fighting fires in the London docks. 'What black smoke's that, then?'

'Dunkirk,' Denison said tersely, and went on with his reading. '*From North Goodwin Light Vessel proceed direct to Dunkirk Roads and close to the beaches to the eastward. Approximate course and distance from the North Goodwin Light Vessel: South 53, East 37 Miles.* There are some notes about tides as well – they set about north-east and south-west during the time of ebb and flood at Dover. High water at Dover is about 5.30 a.m. and 6 p.m. BST. The tide flows at about one to one and a half knots.' He folded the sheet of paper and gave Olly an intent look, and Olly realised suddenly that the young Naval officer might be only in his twenties, but he spoke with the authority of a much older man – or a man with a good deal of experience. 'D'you have any questions, Mr Mears?'

'I dare say I'll think of a few as we go along,' Olly said. 'You're coming with us, aren't you?'

'That's right. I'm in command.' A trace of embarrassment crossed the Naval officer's face. 'I know you've been skipper of the *Surrey Queen* for years now, but while this operation is on, you've got to think of her as a Naval vessel.'

'It's all right, mate. We're in the Navy now – you're the skipper, and we're under your orders.' Olly grinned suddenly. 'S'pose I didn't oughter call you "mate", come to that! Oughter show a bit of respect and call you "sir", didn't I?'

The young man looked at him again as if he half-suspected that Olly was making fun of him, and then smiled. 'Just as an example, perhaps,' he said, and held out his hand. 'We'll get along all right,

Mr Mears. We've got an important job to do and the sooner we can get on and do it, the better.' He glanced along the boat. 'They've finished putting the stores aboard. I think we'll be making a move pretty soon. We're getting a skiff too, for going ashore if we need to. Are all your crew ready?'

'They're ready,' Olly said, and moved off along the deck, checking that everything was in order. He stood for a moment, thinking of the other important jobs they'd done – the fires they'd fought alongside the docksides, the warehouses they'd saved, the boats that had been in flames on the river until the *Surrey Queen* had come along, to save lives even if they couldn't save the craft themselves.

He'd known what he was doing then. He knew about fighting fires, knew where to direct the big hoses, knew how to keep his distance while being close enough to be effective. But he'd never had to go to sea to do it.

He glanced out past the harbour, across the glittering blue sea to where France lay like a dark ridge along the horizon, and he remembered what the Subby had said. *Make for the black smoke*. That was Dunkirk. He screwed up his eyes and stared at the dark smudge that hung over the distant coastline.

Blimey, he thought, is that it? The black smoke? I thought it was a cloud.

Is *that* the fire we're expected to put out?

Chapter Twelve

A t last they were on their way. Robby had brought *Countess Wear* through the Downs and joined the throng of ships milling about here haphazardly. It soon became clear, however, that the Navy had matters well in hand and gradually order was brought out of the apparent chaos. Within an hour or so, as the afternoon sun shone down, the convoys began their crossing.

There was barely time to register all the different ships there, but Robby's trained eye noticed a good fourteen tugs, each towing a dozen ships' lifeboats. Once more Danny stationed himself on the bow and recited their names: 'The *Racia*, the *Sun* – no, two *Suns*, one's number eight, one's number fifteen, the *Ocean Cock*, the *Tanga*, the *Foremost*, the *Fairplay* . . . My stars, Rob, look at what *they're* towing! *Sailing* boats!' He came back to the wheelhouse. 'There's hundreds going over,' he said in an awed voice. 'I reckon there's five miles of boats, all stretched out in a line.'

Robby, bringing *Countess Wear* up behind one of the clusters of towed boats, felt suddenly lonely for his companions of the passage from Dartmouth. *Berry Pomeroy* and *Mew* were still awaiting further orders, and some of the others that had accompanied them had been kept behind too, one or two even being sent back as unfit for the dangers of the voyage. He wondered how their skippers and crews felt about it – relieved or disappointed? How many of them knew what it was like to be at sea under fire, especially in a ship that hadn't been built for Naval action and was too small anyway?

Come to that, how many of the crews who *were* going had had that experience? And it wasn't as if they had a routine pattern to follow – this operation was like nothing that had ever been attempted before. He tried to imagine what it would be like, the Dunkirk harbour crowded with ships jostling for available berths, the town seething both with soldiers and its own citizens. German bombers overhead, the German army pressing ever closer, the noise of battle as the rearguard tried to keep them at bay while the evacuation took place. He knew that thousands of men had been saved already. How many more could be brought out of such conditions? How many would be killed or left behind to be taken prisoner?

He glanced around the convoy, still amazed by the variety of the other ships. What were those, flying the Dutch flag? And look at all the pleasure-steamers, some worked by big paddles on each side like mill-wheels. That one there, the *Whippingham*, was an Isle of Wight ferry – he'd seen it in Portsmouth Harbour beside the jetty of the railway station. And that one, that tubby little vessel with a yellow stub of a funnel amidships, surely that was a Gosport ferry, never away from its pontoon for more than ten minutes at a time as it made the short crossing to Portsmouth. He'd nipped across himself a few times on Saturday-afternoon shore leave from *St Vincent* – on that very boat, he wouldn't be surprised.

Close by, he noticed two long, narrow ships with streaks of red paint still showing in odd patches under the hastily applied battleship grey. They had big hosepipe monitors on their decks, and no wheelhouse protection for the helmsman, just a canvas dodger. They must be fireboats, come down from the Thames probably. He read the names painted on their prows – *Massey Shaw* and *Surrey Queen* – and at the wheel of the *Surrey Queen* he saw a big, grey-haired man standing as if he'd been built there, solid as a rock. As Robby gazed at him, the man glanced round and saw him. He lifted a hand, and Robby returned his salute, feeling oddly comforted. It was almost as if his dad had suddenly turned up and given him an encouraging nod.

Olly, too, felt a curious kinship with the young Able Seaman in the wheelhouse of the little pleasure-steamer. He's even younger than my Joe, he thought, but then I reckon a lot of the blokes fighting this war are no more than bits of boys. That's what happens in wartime, all the youngest and the best are sent off first. A wave of sadness swept over him. That was what went wrong in the last lot, what they called the Great War – the flower of British youth, sent off to be cut down in massacres like the Somme. And we've never got over it, he thought, never put them back. We haven't had *time* to put them back. Twenty years on, and we're doing it again, sending another lot to be done away with – and what'll happen if we lose them as well?

He too was amazed by the variety of ships, large and small, which had joined the convoy – most spectacularly of all, the fleet of Thames sailing barges, some under tow, some making their own way with massive brown sails.

'Just cast your peepers over them,' Olly said to Jack Hodge, who was standing beside him. 'Fair brings a lump to your throat, don't it. Forty or fifty years old, some of 'em, sailing along like queens. It's a real sight, innit.'

'Ah, it is. Be a crying shame when they does away with the Thames barges. Why, we've knowed some of them for years. There's the *Tollesbury*, look – the Sandwich Box we always used to call her because she was built at Sandwich and looks like a box.'

'That's right. My old dad told me she was called after a little fishing village in Essex where they used to load her up with grain and stuff from horse-drawn wagons. I always had it in mind to go there one day, see what it's like.' Olly gave a wave to her skipper, Lemon Webb, an old friend of his, and grinned as Lem saluted him as if they really were in the Royal Navy.

'Blimey, look!' Jack grabbed his arm. 'As I live and breathe – there's the old *Ethel Maud*. Sixty years if she's a day. Remember how she used to come up the river looking like a blinking floating haystack, all piled up with straw and hay for dray horses?'

'And go back with the manure,' Olly finished with a chuckle. 'I suppose they put it on the fields to fertilise the next crop, so in a manner of speaking the horses was feeding theirselves. Talk about waste not, want not.' He fell silent, awed as he always was by the sight of the great brown sails billowing majestically in the breeze. 'You reckon they're going to use them boats under sail when they gets to the Channel?'

'Don't see why not,' Jack shrugged. 'They sails 'em over in peacetime, and they got engines too, don't forget. Anyway, I don't reckon they got much choice, do you? They wants every boat they can get for this lot.'

'Well, they got a good shallow draft,' Olly said thoughtfully. 'They'll be able to get in close to the beach, and you could get a fair number of men on board. And they don't need much of a crew, only one or two blokes, and even then one of 'em's usually a boy.' He gazed at them with pride and respect. 'Used to be one of me and the missus's favourite days out, going to watch them race. They can get up a real speed in a stiff breeze, and turn on a sixpence.'

He gave the young fellow in the *Countess Wear* another wave and turned his attention to his course again. That's what this job was all about. Getting across the Channel and bringing those other young blokes back. That's why they were here – all these ships, big and little, forging across the blue-grey waters of the Channel, to snatch their boys from the jaws of the enemy. 'Blowed if we'll let you have them, Hitler,' he muttered to himself. 'Blowed if we'll let you have our boys . . .'

Crossing the Channel would have been like a Sunday-afternoon jaunt, had it not been for the shipping all around and the aircraft overhead.

In front of the convoy were the minesweepers. Their task was the difficult and dangerous one of not only detecting the mines but of removing, or sweeping them, from the path of the convoy to allow it safe passage; until they had done so, nobody could proceed. And although they'd swept the channel every day, you could never be sure, Robby thought, that they'd found all of them. There might always be another, lurking just below the surface . . .

'My stars,' Danny said, swivelling his head like an owl to look at the mass of ships. 'I don't even know what half of these things be. Them, over there,' he pointed at a dozen or so long, narrow boats, each with what looked like a garden shed perched in the stern, 'what are they? They look like canal barges.'

'Oh, they're skoots,' Jimmy said authoritatively. 'Dutch coasters. They've got some name nobody can get their tongues round, but that's what it sounds like more or less – skoots. Peacetime, they work along the coast and families live on 'em, just like they do on canal barges. That thing you say looks like a garden shed – you're right, it does an' all – that's where they lives. We got about forty of them signed up in the Navy, mostly lying up in the Port of London.' He craned his neck. 'And see them little 'uns there? They're cockle bawleys, they are. Built to be beached, so their crews can go cockling at low tide. I like a plate of cockles,' he added reflectively. 'Used to go collecting them off the beach when I was a nipper. Take 'em home in a bucket of water and then boil 'em up – smashing.'

'He's like a blooming walking encyclopaedia,' Rob said to Danny. 'Knows every ship on the water. Any questions, just come to Uncle Jim.'

'So will you know everything when you're my age and have been in the Andrew upwards of twenty years,' Jimmy said. 'Dunno what they're at, putting a nipper like you, still wet behind the ears, in charge of a ship.' He grinned to show that he was only joking, and jerked his head at Danny. 'Come on, we oughter be down below with the engines in case Skipper here wants to give us some orders.'

Left alone in the wheelhouse, Robby stood watching the scene around him. He had never seen such a vast crowd of ships before, nor such a motley one. The skoots, steaming in their own tight convoy, the paddle-steamers and destroyers clearing the way, the trawlers and the stately Thames barges with their brown sails using every scrap of breeze, and the holiday boats like his own, little river and coastal craft with their gaily painted hulls and funnels hastily camouflaged with grey. He thought of the trip down the River Dart from Totnes, no different from all those he and Danny had made so many times with passengers enjoying their day out, and wondered if the *Countess* would ever make those trips again. If she were bombed on this perilous trip, if the BEF couldn't, after all, be rescued, if the German invasion really did come, if the war was lost . . .

He thrust the thoughts away. There was no place for such doubts now, and no time for thinking. He needed all his concentration for keeping the *Countess* on her course and clear of any of the other small ships forging with such determination across the Channel.

His head was filled with noise – the thrumming of engines all about, the surge of the waves, the roar of aircraft overhead where the sky was busy with RAF and Fleet Air Arm planes, crossing from the English shores to perform a task similar to that of the minesweepers – sweeping the sky clear of Luftwaffe attack. The German Stukas could appear literally out of the blue, diving from the eye of the sun to bomb the port of Dunkirk, its docks and harbour, the men who were waiting there, and the ships coming to rescue them. Worse still, the airfields they were using were closer than those in England – many of them the very ones that the RAF themselves had been using until they were driven away. The Luftwaffe, like the German Army, had all the advantages. They held all the cards.

Danny came up from the engine-room and went into the bow. Robby watched him standing there, his black hair blowing back in the wind, looking out for the floating debris that was always a hazard at sea, and felt proud and glad to have his old friend with him. Danny might not have had the training or the sea-going experience that Rob had had, but he had already proved his worth with that courageous dive into the sea off Portland to clear the propeller. Even for a strong swimmer, that was a daunting job, but Danny had done it with a shrug and a grin, and then gone straight back to his duties afterwards. Robby knew that he would stand firm, rising to any challenge, and with that thought came a wave of confidence. With men like him and Jimmy, and Rob himself, in every one of these ships, the rescue was assured. They *won't* beat us, he thought savagely. They won't beat us because we're British and we're fighting for freedom. And, as if Jethro were beside him and speaking in his ear, he knew what his father would have said and echoed his words. *We're fighting with God on our side . . .*

'Seaweed!' Danny shouted suddenly, and Rob snapped to attention. 'A girt big mass of it, right ahead.'

Robby groaned. 'I hope to God we don't foul it. You can't go overboard in this sea, not with all these ships about.'

'Looks like some of the others have caught some,' Jimmy said, watching as two or three boats began to founder, their engines spluttering and choking. They held their breath as the *Countess* moved steadily onwards. So far, so good . . . but how could any ship get through this without winding some of the slimy, waving fronds around the propeller? Robby gripped the wheel tightly, unaware that he was praying aloud, cursing as a faint stutter in the note of the engine brought his heart leaping into his throat. If this whole operation was going to be fouled up by *seaweed* . . . And then, as suddenly as they had entered the mass, they were clear of it again and Rob heaved a sigh of relief. It was a miracle they hadn't picked it up, but perhaps this was a day for miracles. God was with them, and would stay with them.

'What we need,' Jimmy said, 'isn't ruddy minesweepers, it's

seaweed-sweepers. As if we didn't have enough to look out for, what with E-boats sneaking about under the water, and Stukas overhead – bloody hell, here they come again!' He ducked suddenly as an aeroplane screamed low over their heads. 'Where the hell did *that* come from? Look at the bugger! He's dive-bombing!'

The three men watched in dismay as the Stuka flew low over the convoy, dropping bombs as it went. To their relief, they all fell into the water, but the shock of their explosions rocked the boat and showered them with spray. A smattering of shrapnel clattered on to the deck.

'Tin hat, Dan!' Robby said sharply. 'Keep it on all the time. There's not much daylight left – they'll be trying to get as many kills as they can before dark.' He handed over the wheel to Jimmy and stretched his arms, glancing up at the sky. Even though he had been in action on larger vessels, he felt peculiarly vulnerable on this little riverboat and Danny, who had never seen action at all nor even been so far out to sea, was looking pale and tense.

A destroyer came up from behind them, passing on their starboard side. Rob gave it a glance and then let out a low whistle. 'Look at that – it's the *Wenlock*! My ship – the one I was on when I was detailed to take on the *Countess*.' He signalled to the ship and someone on deck waved back, although he knew they were too far away to recognise him. 'Well, I'm blowed, fancy seeing her here. Must've come straight up from Guz.'

'She'll be going into Dunkirk Harbour,' Jimmy said, watching as the grey ship drew ahead, almost disappearing in her own bow wave. 'Served on her meself, once. Over twenty years old, she is – launched during the last war. Bit of an old rust-bucket now, if you ask me.'

'Go on, she's not that bad,' Rob said loyally. 'She can still do the job. Look at her now – putting on a fair turn of speed, she is.' He grinned, feeling comforted by the presence of his own ship with his own mates aboard. With *Wenlock* at their side, the miracle seemed more possible. He thought of the familiar messdeck, his own hammock, the pin-ups inside his locker door. One was a picture of Betty Grable, the other of his sweetheart Molly. He wondered suddenly what Molly was doing now.

There was no time to think of home, however. The seaway was too busy with its crowd of boats, only the large ones with any wireless communication, and the sky was dark with the shadows of aircraft. He looked up and saw Stukas coming low and fast for another dive-bomb attack – caught the flash of bright flame as Bren and Lewis guns on some of the ships fired at them – felt his heart leap as one of the planes burst into a sudden ball of flame and hurtled into the sea. No chance of any survivors, and thank God it hadn't fallen on a ship – but again there was no time to think, for RAF planes were coming in too and a full-scale battle was going on over his head. The Spitfires were like gnats dancing in a sunbeam as they darted towards the enemy, fired and then jinked into the sun, invisible in its brilliant glow. Another German plane went down, its pilot baling out in a white puff of parachute, and one of the fleet diverted to pick him up. Then a Spitfire went as well, spiralling into the sea nose first, and Robby felt a moment of horror. He watched as the sea boiled and bubbled around the sudden whirlpool, and a few fragments floated to the surface. One of our boys was in that, he thought, and he never had a chance. And he felt a fierce anger towards the German pilot who had shot him down.

The aircraft disappeared as quickly as they had come. But now the sky was darkening for a different reason.

'What is it?' Danny asked anxiously. 'A storm blowing up?'

Jimmy shook his head. 'That's smoke, that is.' He paused, gazing ahead with sombre eyes. 'That's Dunkirk – and it's burning.'

'Blimey,' Olly said, staring in the same direction. 'That's a fire and a half.'

'Are we expected to put *that* out?' Chalky White and Jack Hodge were beside him. 'It looks as if half the bloody town's in flames.'

'I reckon it is, too.' He thought of Joe, somewhere in that inferno. 'Well, all we can deal with is the fires on the docks and hope the poor sods can get through the streets. I don't suppose the local brigade's up to much at the moment.' He turned to Sublieutenant Denison. 'What are we supposed to do when we gets there?'

The young man shrugged. 'We do whatever we can. It's not the kind of job you can organise in advance. But there'll be plenty of Naval ships there. We'll get our orders when we arrive.' He glanced at his watch. 'Should be about sunset.'

'We'll be working in the dark,' Chalky said.

Olly gave him a withering look. 'So what? We works in the dark often enough in London. Anyway, there'll be plenty of flames to light the place up, if that smoke's anything to go by.' He thumped his fist on the stanchion. 'I just wish we could push this old girl along faster.'

The sense of urgency that had gripped them when they began the trip was reaching an almost unbearable pitch. The convoy seemed to be growing, with more and more ships joining the rear so that a steady stream of vessels stretched back behind them, the last ones out of sight. A cloud of gulls wheeled above them, following the ships in the hope of scraps, and the mutton-fat smeared on the *Surrey Queen*'s brightwork drew them like a magnet. The men swore at them and chased them off, but they merely screeched with indignation and came back immediately, cocking their heads insolently as they scraped at the grey fat and covered the deck with their droppings.

Ahead, the destroyers and the minesweepers were forging a path as if cutting their way through jungle; above, Stukas and Messerschmitts patrolled the skies, harried by the Spitfires and Hurricanes of the RAF. And, coming in the opposite direction and making for home, was a stream of other vessels, each one low in the water, packed to the gunwhales with soldiers so that their decks were a mass of khaki. The ships' bows cut through the water like knives, as if determined to make the voyage as fast as possible, and a ragged cheer went up from the fleet going over to take their place.

'The sooner they get them off at Dover, the sooner they can go back again,' Denison said, watching soberly.

'But is there room for all these boats?' Olly asked. 'I mean, I dunno how big Dunkirk is, but—'

'There's miles of beach. So long as the men can get there, there's room. It's getting the vessels close enough in that's the problem. You've got a shallow draft, haven't you?'

'Bit under four foot.' It felt like it, too, Olly thought as the deck shifted beneath his feet. The sea had been calm but the turbulence created by so many ships going at full speed tossed it into broken surf, and white-topped bow waves that crashed against each other and flung salt spray into the air. The *Surrey Queen*, built long and shallow for riverwork, lurched and rolled; half its crew, unused to going to sea, were suffering from sea-sickness. The rest, with no job to do, sat on the broad deck or paced up and down, rolling with the motion, smoking cigarettes or drinking the constant supply of tea being brewed up down in the galley. A few were managing to play cards in the cabin but most were watching the other shipping and keeping an anxious eye on the skies. There was an air of barely suppressed impatience. Everyone wanted to get to Dunkirk; everyone wanted to get on with the job they had come to do.

Olly looked around at the convoy and thought about the thousands of soldiers still waiting for them in Dunkirk. He glanced at the young Naval officer beside him. Denison had told him he'd already been over to Dunkirk once, in a destroyer. They'd loaded up with men from the quayside and brought them back, and then the young officer, together with some of the others, had been detailed to take command of the little ships.

'What d'you reckon?' he asked. 'How much time have we got, eh? How many d'you think this lot's going to be able to get off?'

Denison shrugged. 'I don't know. Mr Churchill thinks about thirty thousand. That's less than a tenth of the number there. But it all depends on the conditions when we get there – what the weather does, what it's like in the town, how many troops are able to get to the beaches at all. And what the Germans do as well, of course,' he added, as three more Stukas flew over and swooped on the ships at the head of the convoy, spattering them with bombs and raking them with machine-gun fire. The two men held their breath, waiting for the massive explosion that would mean a ship had been hit.

'There she goes,' Olly said, his mouth turning dry as a huge spout of water erupted. 'Oh my Gawd . . .'

The explosion was several hundred yards behind them, too far for the *Surrey Queen* to reach, but in any case there was no fire nor, it seemed, likely to be any survivors. The casualty was one of the smaller vessels, a battered trawler that had joined the convoy soon after the *Queen*, and as the water settled around the remains of the hull, all that could be seen were a few scraps of wreckage floating on the surface. The little ship must have received a direct hit and gone down straight away. Short of a miracle, nobody could have lived through it.

The crew of the *Queen* had, to a man, flung themselves flat on the deck. Now they scrambled up and went to the stern, staring at the tumult behind them. The *Queen*'s bow lifted, and Olly yelled furiously at them. 'Get back amidships, you stupid fools. You'll have us all in the drink as well! Blimey, we don't need Germans to sink us when we got you lot.' They scurried back again, and he shook his head and rolled his eyes at the officer. 'Anyone'd think they were a lot of ruddy landlubbers.'

'It's a bit of a shock, seeing your first ship sunk,' the Sub-lieutenant said quietly. 'I don't suppose many of them have been under fire before.'

'Maybe not.' Olly thought back to his own Great War days. He'd been in the Navy himself, and had known what it was like to be in a battle at sea, but he'd never been attacked from the air. 'And never expected to be again, neither.' He turned his eyes ahead, watching the ships that were leading the pack into war. 'But we can't fool ourselves, can we? We're going to see more of that before we've finished this job. A helluva lot more.' He looked at the young man again. 'What's it really like over there?'

Denison hesitated. 'I don't know that I can describe it. It's changing all the time anyway. But think of all these ships,' he waved his arm at the flotilla, 'trying to get in and out of the harbour all at once, think of almost every building in the town on fire, think of dozens of planes flying over, doing their best to bomb and shoot you out of the water – and then think of the quays and beaches black with men, like ants coming out of their nest, all wanting to get aboard the next boat. And imagine a blanket of thick black smoke hanging over everything, and the noise of it all, engines, flames, aircraft, bombs, guns, men screaming and shouting – and then double it, no, multiply it by ten, a hundred, a thousand – and you might begin to have some idea what it's like at Dunkirk.' He paused. 'Not that it gives you any real idea.'

Olly and the others stared at him.

'It sounds a bloody nightmare,' Jack Hodges said huskily.

'Yes,' Denison agreed simply. 'That's just about what it is.'

Olly thought of Joe, one of the 'ants' on the beaches; and then of Effie and the girls, waiting at home. He had hardly known himself why he had kissed Effie goodbye as if he might not be coming back. It was as if he'd had a premonition, he thought with a little shudder.

Then he shrugged. It was no more dangerous than any other 'shout', when you looked at it straight. Firemen on land and on the river got killed, even in peacetime. You always knew that when you left home to go to work, it might be for the last time.

It was just that this job was going to be like all the 'shouts' there'd ever been, all rolled into one.

Wagtail had joined a tow just outside Dover. As Toby had prophesied, everyone else was too busy to ask questions and, with the rest of the milling throng of little ships, they were directed to a cluster being gathered together by a Naval tug and peremptorily ordered to pass over their painter. Toby, standing at the bow, did as he was told and watched while they were fastened to the motor yacht ahead. Then he ran back to the stern and took the rope passed to him by the ship behind them. When the tug finally took the strain, there were more than a dozen boats following behind, like ducklings bobbing along behind their mother.

'There you are, you see,' he said cheerfully, squatting at the top of the companionway. 'No problem at all.'

Charles didn't answer. Even under tow, you had to be careful to keep the boat on course and avoid bumping into the one in front, and he was still deeply unhappy about having his sister aboard. What Ma and Pa are going to say when we get home, he thought, I can't imagine . . . And Sheila, too. She'll be furious with me. I'm as bad as Toby. I should never have let her come.

Yet if he hadn't, it would have meant turning back – putting into Folkestone or Newhaven, both almost as busy as Dover with ships returning from France packed with troops. None of them would have welcomed a small boat trying to get in. And if he'd turned back earlier, taken her all the way home, he would have lost the chance to do something worthwhile. His *only* chance to do something worthwhile.

And then there was Alex. How could he possibly go home and face Sheila and her parents, without having even tried to save Alex?

They were now well out into the Channel. Even before arriving at Dover, they had seen the steady stream of RAF aircraft going over – the Defiants and the Ansons, the Hurricanes and the Spitfires, the Hudsons and the Swordfish. Now they began to see their engagements with the enemy and they stared upwards in awe and dismay as the battle raged above.

'Those are Junkers,' Toby said, shading his eyes. 'And – oh, hell's *teeth*!' He ducked down as six planes detached themselves from the formation and screamed low over the head of the convoy, dropping a

145

stream of bombs as they flashed past. Immediately there was a rash of explosions, erupting in the water, and a burst of flame and thick black smoke as a ship was hit. Paddy, coming up the steps behind him, cried out but her voice was drowned by the noise that shattered the air and, even as the last bomb exploded, the Junker that had dropped it was itself shot down by the Hudson that came up from one side. The German plane dived nose first into the sea, followed by a second and then a third, and then two more Hudsons appeared, flying almost at sea-level, to send three more dive-bombers spinning out of control, in flames and disintegrating as they spiralled into the water.

Above the Junkers they could see a dense cloud of Messerschmitts. They came lower, closing in for attack, but were almost as quickly scattered by a flock of Spitfires, only to circle high above and then return, each vying to come out of the sun. For nearly half an hour they fought, first one plane and then another shot down, until it seemed as if the sea might boil over with their turbulence.

'Look at them!' Paddy shouted, pushing herself up beside Toby to see better. She stood up, waving both arms above her head, and yelled at the British planes. 'Shoot! Shoot them down! Yes – yes – *yes* – oh, well *done*!' as another German plane fell in a ball of flame into the sea not 100 yards away. The waves bubbled and hissed, and a cloud of steam and fine, vaporised spray rose like a waterspout. She turned her head upwards and cried out again. 'Look! The pilot! He's coming down in a parachute!'

'Get below, Paddy!' Charles shouted. 'For God's sake, get below!'

'He's coming towards us!' She scrambled on to the deck and leaned over the side of the cockpit. 'He's going to fall in the sea! We must help him, Charles!'

'Paddy, get *below*.' He reached out for her but she dodged his hand. Toby too was on his feet, leaning perilously over the side. '*Both* of you!' His words were lost in the scream of another aircraft, flashing past so close that they could feel its slipstream. The parachute had fallen to the sea and draped itself over the waves in a billowing coverlet of white silk. 'Paddy, move back, before you get hurt.'

'We've got to help him. He'll drown.'

'We can't. He's too far away.' They watched as the airman struggled to free himself from the tangled lines of the parachute.

146

Charles looked helplessly at the boats in front of and behind him. They were all lashed together; it was impossible for any of them to release itself from the rest. He felt his body turn cold at the horror of the airman's situation, yet he knew there was nothing he could do. Then, to his relief, a small fishing boat detached itself from the crowd and bustled across to the mass of floating silk. Hands reached down and dragged the German aboard, and the boat returned to its position.

'He couldn't have been under tow,' Charles said, half to himself, and then with another furious glower at his sister, 'For God's sake, Paddy, get below. I thought we agreed that you'd obey orders.'

'*I* thought we agreed I'd be allowed to be useful,' she retorted. 'I can't do much to help if I'm stuck below all the time. You've got to accept it, Charles. I'm here, and you've got to treat me just the same as if I were a man.'

'I don't know what use you thought you were going to be up here on deck being bombed.'

'I wasn't being bombed.'

'We could have been bombed at any minute. We still could be.' Another flight of Stukas screeched overhead. 'Paddy, *please*.'

'Go on, kid,' Toby said. He was white-faced and trembling, but clearly making an attempt to regain his normal impudence. 'Sorry to have to say it, but Big Brother's right. You'll be more use at Dunkirk if you're still alive when we get there. And I could do with a cuppa,' he added with a rather shaky grin. 'Nothing like a cup of tea when you've been through a bombing raid.'

Paddy hesitated, then dropped below. 'But only to make the tea,' she called over her shoulder. 'I'm not going to be kept down here like a child. I'm part of this now, and you'd better make up your mind to it.'

She disappeared and the two brothers looked at each other. The aircraft had gone as quickly as they had come, and even the scattered wreckage of the planes that had been shot down was being left behind as the convoy forged steadily onwards. Toby drew in a deep breath and wiped his forehead.

'That was pretty nasty.'

'It's all going to be pretty nasty,' Charles said grimly, as shaken as Toby. Neither of them had ever experienced anything like this, and he knew that it was just a forerunner of what they were to undergo. 'But you can't say we weren't warned.'

'I know.' Toby was silent for a moment, then he said, 'I'm not sorry we came, though. Are you?'

'No,' Charles said, watching the long line of ships ahead and turning to look at the equally long line behind. 'I want to go on. I want to go on more than ever.'

Chapter Thirteen

Friday, 31 May

It was seven-thirty when the convoy finally arrived, and a full-blown air-raid was in progress. The entrance to the outer harbour was thronged with ships, and a thick pall of smoke, shot through with flame, draped a heavy blanket of premature darkness over the whole town. The aircraft roamed invisibly somewhere overhead, dropping their bombs at random, some to fall harmlessly into the sea, some to cause further destruction to the shattered town, some to score direct hits on the vessels that crowded around the bastions and piers.

'Gawd,' Olly said, peering into the swirl of black acrid smoke. 'It's a bloody shambles. We'll never be able to put this lot out.'

Denison shook his head. 'You'd better concentrate on ships on fire. The town will have to look after itself.' He ducked as a bomb exploded in the water not far away and showered them all with water. 'I don't think it matters which ones you choose – just work wherever you can.'

The men began to set up the pumps. Their sister fireboat, *Massey Shaw*, had arrived a little ahead of them and Olly waved his arms at her skipper. She too was under the command of a Naval officer, and he was signalling to Denison, crossing his hands in a negative gesture and pointing away from the crowded harbour. After a moment or two, the Sublieutenant turned back to Olly.

'Belay that. We're to forget the fires and go up the beach, concentrate on getting men off. Take as many as we can load aboard and get 'em back to Dover. That's what the *Massey Shaw*'s doing.'

'Forget the fires?' It was like telling Olly to commit sacrilege, yet he could see that whatever they did would be a mere fleabite in this inferno. The ships' crews would have their own firefighting equipment, and if they couldn't douse the flames they would have to abandon ship.

'The troops have first priority,' Denison said curtly. 'That's what we're here for. Turn east, past the Mole and up the coast. The beaches are full of men and they're being bombed and strafed as they wait. We've got to get them away.'

The two fireboats moved away from the harbour. Accustomed as they were to moving about a crowded river, with fires raging all around them, this was something beyond their experience. They knew the dangers of burning debris, thrown through the air by the force of an explosion somewhere within a building – a warehouse stocked with cans of paint, boilers filled with oil, huge crates of sugar; they were used to the searing heat of flames that reared forty, fifty, sixty feet into the sky; they had suffered the choking, stinging, blinding effects of smoke; every one of them had been burned at some time, and occasionally they'd seen their mates killed before their eyes. They knew, understood and accepted all the perils of fighting fire.

But at Dunkirk, there was something more. There was the implacable shadow of hatred that hung like the pall of black, filthy smoke over your head. And there was the urgent need to get through this crowd of ships, to find a space on the beach where the men who waited there could come aboard.

Because if we don't, Olly thought as he steered the *Surrey Queen* towards the crowded beaches, we're all going under the jackboot.

'My God Almighty,' Jack Hodges said. 'Look at that.'

Through the dusk, they could see the dark shapes of the destroyers anchored a mile or so offshore. Between them and the beaches, the sea was thick with smaller craft, bustling from beach to ship and back again. Taking no notice of the new arrivals, and even less of the bombs that rained on them from above, they jostled their way through the shallow water of the broad sands to where the men stood waiting.

It was the waiting men who had brought Jack Hodges's exclamation to his lips.

'Look at 'em,' he said again. 'Just *look* at 'em . . .'

They all looked. Even Denison, who had been across before,

shook his head in disbelief. 'I never saw the beaches last time,' he said. 'We were going into harbour, berthing up and letting them walk aboard. There's thousands of them. *Thousands*.'

The beaches from Dunkirk itself to Bray Dunes, Panne and Nieuport were long, sandy and shallow. They stretched out into the water, drying out at low tide to form miles of firm sand, a peacetime paradise. Olly could imagine them like Ramsgate, crowded with mothers and fathers in deckchairs, kiddies paddling, building sandcastles, playing with big rubber balls, picnicking on old blankets. Fathers like himself, teaching his children to swim with an old rubber tyre, boys diving like porpoises and standing on their hands in the water so that their legs waved above the surface. People enjoying themselves, people having fun, people living life as it should be lived with their wives and husbands and children. It all seemed like a dream.

Now, the dream had turned into a nightmare.

The wide, shallow sands were crowded not with fathers with their trousers rolled up and ice-cream cornets in their hands but with soldiers who had fought their way through France and been driven back by the enemy.

The sands were black with them. In long lines, like immense queues, they stretched out into the shallow water – up to their ankles; up to their knees; up to their waists, their shoulders, their necks. There was no pushing, no queue-jumping; they simply stood there, staring into the gathering dusk, waiting patiently for someone to come and take them away from their nightmare. And as they stood there, the German planes made their last sortie of the day, flying low between the pall of smoke and the surface of the sea, strafing them as they stood helpless beneath, so that they fell in their dozens, stumbling and buckling with their wounds, killed as they stood or drowning where they fell. And the little ships that had come to save them were hit as well, jerking and jinking in the water, their sides and decks holed and their crews struck, some of them killed and their craft sunk, some able to carry on. And so they, together with the ships that remained miraculously undamaged through the storm of machine-gun bullets, *did* carry on – pulling in close to the men, dragging them aboard, packing them in every space that could be found and then turning to forge their way back through the crowded waters to the destroyers and personnel carriers and ferries that waited to take the soldiers home to England.

For a few moments, the crew of the *Surrey Queen* stared. Then Sublieutenant Denison barked out a sharp order and they leaped into action. While Olly turned the nose of the fireboat shorewards, the men who had been standing by the monitor ready to reel out the giant hoses made all fast again. The pumps which would have sucked water from the sea were closed down, all firefighting equipment stowed away. The decks were cleared and as the boat drew closer to the waiting crowds the crew ranged themselves around the sides, ready to help the soldiers aboard. When they were as close as Olly dared go, they ran out the anchor. They were still about fifty yards off the shore.

'Get the skiff in the water,' Denison ordered. 'We can't risk going aground, we'll never get her off again. We'll have to ferry them out.'

Micky Martin and Ted Fletcher, two of the firefighters, had already been detailed for this task; they dropped the skiff over and hopped down into it. It took only a few minutes to row to the nearest queue of men, and Olly watched anxiously as the soldiers made a rush for it, clawing and grabbing at the sides in their desperation to get aboard. Micky and Ted bawled at them and even beat the clutching hands with their oars in an attempt to prevent what was sure to happen, but as Olly and the others watched, the skiff tipped perilously, filled and sank, leaving Micky and Ted floundering in the waves with the men they had gone to rescue. There was a howl of dismay from the crew of the fireboat, and the Sublieutenant hammered his fists on the wheel.

'That's our boat gone, dammit! The *idiots*.' He thought for a moment. 'We'll have to find another way to get them over. Can your men swim?'

'I dunno. I hope so.' Olly peered into the increasing darkness. 'The question is, will they be able to find us? Look, mate, we can't work in the dark. It's bloody impossible.'

'We can't leave them here either.' The young officer's voice was grim. 'And night-time's the only respite we get from these damned planes. Ah – looks as if they've made it. Good.'

Micky and Ted were at the bow, reaching up to be dragged back on board. Denison watched them. 'Some of the soldiers might be able to do that too. If they can swim . . .' Some were already trying, and Olly ordered the anchor up and tried to nose the boat a little closer inshore. He felt sand beneath the bow and stopped the engines again. 'Drop anchor! We can't risk going closer – we'll settle lower when we gets more men aboard.' He stared down, trying to see how many had managed to swim out. 'If we can just get 'em up from here . . .'

It was not so easy. Although her draft was only three feet, the sides of the fireboat stood at least as high again out of the water. Swimming men had no chance of reaching up to the deck and would have to be hauled aboard by men who were leaning dangerously far out towards them. And they were heavy – weighed down by sodden uniforms, packs and rifles. Nor did they have much strength by now to help themselves.

'This won't do,' Denison muttered, and peeled off his jacket. 'They're going to drown at this rate. Look, there are broken-down vehicles all over the beach – if we can get a line to one of them, the men can hold on to it and pull themselves along.' He raised his voice and shouted to Chalky and Jack Hodge, who were the nearest. 'Get me a hawser!'

'I'll send one of the boys—' Olly began, but the young officer shook his head.

'I'll go.' Chalky handed him the end of a coil of rope and before Olly could say another word he had gone, over the side, dragging the rope behind him. All that could be seen of him now was his head, bobbing amongst the debris that floated everywhere. The rope uncoiled as he went, and they watched in silence as his figure disappeared into the twilight.

'Blimey,' Olly said. 'That young chap's got a bit of spunk. I just hope he gets there all right – and back, too.'

It was almost dark. As Denison had said, the attack from the air had lessened, but it hadn't completely stopped. A few planes were still coming over, taking advantage of the last few rays of sunlight and dropping their last bombs in a desultory fashion, almost as if they hardly mattered any more. They fell into the sea, sending waterspouts high into the air and illuminating the area with brilliant flashes of searing white light, shot with scarlet flame. Some fell on the boats and their cargoes of exhausted soldiers, and the men on *Surrey Queen* watched in horror as a skoot nearby exploded in a vast shower of burning debris. One fell close to the beach, directly ahead of the fireboat, and for a brief second they saw the figure of Sublieutenant Denison, silhouetted against the glare as he waded through the shallows. A huge fountain of sand and water spewed into the air and then darkness returned. He's gone, Olly thought. The poor bloke's been blown to bits.

More debris rained down on the deck of the *Surrey Queen* and Olly staggered as something hit him hard on the shoulder.

It was a man's leg. It was still encased in the dark blue fabric of a Naval uniform.

'They're not allowing any more ships into the harbour,' Robby said. 'It's blocked with wrecks and God knows what. We've got to go along the East Mole.' The Moles were long piers that ran out for almost 1500 yards from the coast to form the outer harbour. 'We should be able to berth and take on men from the pier itself.' He turned the *Countess* away from the crowded harbour entrance.

The port was still suffering an air-raid. German aircraft were coming over in waves, and bombs were falling on buildings and wrecked ships already blasted almost to extinction. But by now the crew of the *Countess Wear* were learning to ignore the cacophony. Either the bombs would hit you, or they wouldn't. So far, they hadn't. The constant noise had become an irritant, something you had to live with, like blowflies in summer. If a bomb had your name on it, there was no avoiding it; and if it didn't, there was no point in worrying.

Jimmy was down below, keeping watch on the engines and waiting for orders, and Danny, standing beside Rob in the wheelhouse, let out a low whistle. 'My stars above . . . What in God's name has been going on here?'

Through the narrow gap between the ends of the two Moles, they could see the wide, wedge-shaped area that led to the inner harbour. As the third biggest port of France, Dunkirk was normally accessible to large ships, with seven broad dock basins and five miles of quays biting deep into the town, while the outer harbour gave shelter to many more. As an evacuation point, it should have been ideal.

But now all that had changed. For weeks now, the docks had been bombed incessantly. Warehouses and oil tanks were on fire and there was no longer any attempt to put the fires out; they simply died or spread further. The fires were a constant threat, now advancing, now retreating as they greedily devoured all that was in their path and lit the scene with the red glow of hell. The docks themselves were smashed; gigantic slabs of concrete and huge splinters of metal lay tumbled together. The gates were broken, leaving the basins open to the water that flooded in at high tide while great spars of wood stuck jagged fingers into the air; and the normal dockside machinery – cranes, trucks, lorries – lay broken and burned out on the shattered quays.

Even before the evacuation began, the bridge at the entrance to the inner basin had been demolished by bombs. Ships already inside were trapped and became sitting targets. The oil tanks on the east side, close to the entrance, were set alight, sending a dense and oily plume of smoke to blot out the sun and searing quays with heat. And as the evacuation progressed and the attacks continued, the inner harbour gradually filled with burning and sunken wrecks.

The outer harbour too was by this time a scene of devastation. The Moles weren't, as Robby had expected, solid concrete piers against which a ship could tie up and throw down a gangway for men to cross. Instead, the sloping face of the west pier made it impossible to lie alongside while the east, instead of being of solid concrete, was no more than a rickety structure of wooden piles, topped by a plank walk only five feet wide. It had never been built for ships, yet it was clear that ships had tied up there and troops been embarked. Now, the whole area was cluttered with wrecks: trawlers, naval pinnaces, motor launches, cutters – they lay beneath the water, some of them piled on top of others, or dragged helplessly at the pilings to which they were still moored. Some were on fire, some burned out, some simply full of water, their masts and funnels protruding above the surface. They looked lost and hopeless; a ships' graveyard – the saddest sight Robby had ever seen.

Small ships like the *Countess* were still coming alongside the outer line of the Mole. Robby edged his little holiday-steamer round, feeling for all the world as if he were bringing her into Totnes – and yet nothing could have been more different. Briefly, he had a vision of Totnes under fire like this, with enemy planes screaming overhead and bombs falling all about, with the town ablaze, its steep main street blocked with the debris of ruined buildings, its famous archway crumbled to a heap of rubble. That's what we're trying to prevent, he thought with a sudden savage twist of his heart. That's why our Jan joined the Army and that's why I'm here to bring him and all the others home again . . .

Danny sprang towards the bow, ready to moor the *Countess* to one of the piles. There were no proper bollards, for the Mole had never been intended for anything other than emergency moorings, but every few yards there was a pile which protruded further than the others, and Danny wrapped the painter quickly round one of these. The deck was several feet below the level of the walkway, where already a line of soldiers was waiting to come aboard. He looked up and shouted at them.

'All aboard, then! Who's for a trip round the harbour? All the sights, only a shilling a head – you'll have to jump for it though, we forgot to bring the ladder.'

The man at the head of the queue landed with a heavy thud. A dozen more dropped beside him and the *Countess* rocked. Robby glanced up in alarm.

'Hey – don't all come at once. You'll capsize us. Get over to the starboard side and some of you go astern. Spread out a bit . . .' He watched, holding the wheel steady as the soldiers streamed into the boat. Some were wounded and their mates helped them down, but he could see that even they were too exhausted to manage. They fell to the deck and staggered as they got up, reeling about the boat and tumbling in heaps of khaki wherever they could find a space. Their faces were filthy, their uniforms clogged with mud and oil. Their eyes were sore and heavy, rimmed with red. Some of them still carried their packs, others had lost or jettisoned them, though they had all kept their rifles in a firm grasp. They groaned with pain or relief as they fell, and soon the deck was crammed with bodies, pressed as close as sardines, and the *Countess* was low in the water.

'That's it,' Robby said at last. He called to Danny. 'We can't take any more.' But his words were lost in the blast of a particularly close explosion. The underwater shock thrust the *Countess* into the air, clean out of the water, and a soldier who was at that moment jumping down to her deck found himself bounced upwards instead. He came down between the ship and the Mole, and Danny shouted with dismay, but the man had disappeared under the black, oily water. The mooring rope too had come away, and as the *Countess* smashed down into the water again she lurched away from the piles and Robby wrenched desperately at the wheel to try to regain control. For a few minutes the boat wallowed, thudding against the piles and bouncing away, swamped by the spray and the sudden, vicious waves sent up by the explosion. The decks streamed with water and the men who were lying on them yelled and clung to whatever they could find – the steel stanchions, the wiring, even to each other.

Robby knew that it would be a miracle if none of them was swept overboard, but he could do nothing about it. His only concern was to get the fragile wooden boat away from the pier before she was smashed to matchwood, and he roared orders to Jimmy in the engine-room below. 'Full ahead, Jim – now astern – ahead again . . . *Half* speed. Hold her there. *Hold* her.' He was talking to himself as much as to Jimmy, desperate to save his vessel. He felt the ship judder and scrape beneath them as they passed over something below the water – a wreck? If they were holed now . . .

Another plane flew over and he was aware of the rattle of machine-gun fire. The searing heat of a bullet grazed past his cheek, but there was no time to concern himself with that. 'Come on, *Countess*,' he urged, unaware that he was praying aloud. 'Come on. You can do it, you can do it . . .' His voice rose to a shout, a yell of fury that he should be caught like this, on his first trip, with a load of soldiers aboard depending on him to get them home. 'And I *will*,' he bawled, his words unheard in the clamour. 'I will do it! I'll get you back – I will – I will – *I will!*'

The wheel was free in his hands. Whatever they had scraped on was left behind. They were away from the Mole, out in less violent seas. The aircraft had snarled into the distance and the raid was, for the time being, over. The fires still raged in the town and in the harbour, the smoke was still as thick and as choking, but compared with the turmoil of a few moments ago, all seemed to be peace. And the *Countess Wear* was answering to his touch as well as ever. She was not holed or damaged. Her cargo of men, the men they had come to save, were still aboard, and they were on their way home.

Robby sighed in profound relief. The first part of his task was done. Now he must ferry his first load to one of the waiting ships, before coming back for more.

Wagtail was kept on the tow until the little flock of ducklings was just off the sands at Bray Dunes.

Like the other ships, they had arrived in the thick of the air-raid. The air was filled with the roar of Junkers and the clatter of machine-gun fire, with the scream of low-flying Stukas and the shattering thunder of bombs that hurtled from their bellies. Charles and Toby stood in the cockpit, shaken by the violence and the fury of the raid, and sickened by what they saw as a small motor boat not far ahead of them was hit and blew into a million pieces, the debris briefly lit by a ball of yellow flame before it sizzled into the water. Paddy, who had come up the companionway, drew in a deep, shuddering breath.

'Those poor men. Oh, Charles.'

He turned on her. 'For the last time, Paddy – for God's sake, get below!'

'What's the point? We're here now, and you've got to let me help. Anyway, if we're hit . . .' she glanced at the floating scraps of wood that were all that was left of the motor boat '. . . I'm not going to be any safer down below than I am here.'

Toby, who had been staring at the spot where the boat had been, said, 'There's someone in the water.'

Charles whipped round and Paddy took the opportunity to climb the last few steps to the deck. 'Where?'

'There.' He pointed. Another wave of aircraft came over and they ducked as a plane swooped low above their heads. They heard the spatter of bullets, saw a row of small splashes in the water, heard a splintering sound as *Wagtail* herself was hit. Then it was gone, and they lifted their heads cautiously and looked again. 'See him?' Toby said, but his voice was doubtful now. 'Over there. But I think – I think—'

'He's dead,' Charles said harshly. 'You can see he is.' The body was floating face downwards, the jacket ballooning around it and a patch of dark red spreading over the water. Paddy cried out in horror.

'We can't just leave him there!'

'We can't do anything else. He's dead, Paddy. And he's not the only dead man we're going to see. What did you think this was going to be, a pleasant little jaunt over to France, pick up a few bottles of wine and some cheese, perhaps? There are going to be people dying all around us, and we can't pick them up. We've got to keep room for the living. They're the ones who matter now.'

'But dead people matter too.'

'Of course they do. But we *can't take them home with us*. We need all the space we've got – and that's little enough.' Another plane screamed overhead. 'Remember what I told you, Paddy. You obey orders. Even if you don't like them. *Especially* if you don't like them. And we don't pick up dead bodies.'

She stared at him. Her eyes were full of tears and he reproached himself again for letting her come. I'd never have allowed it if I hadn't been so desperate to prove myself, he thought. She shouldn't be here. She shouldn't be seeing these things.

A fleet of ships passed on their way back to England. They were led by a destroyer, but amongst them was the now familiar motley crowd of smaller boats. Paddy watched them, fighting her tears. She knew her brother was right, but the thought of leaving men floating in the water, wounded and perhaps not even quite dead, was something she hadn't anticipated. Suppose it was Alex, she thought. Suppose he was shot and blown up and thrown into the water and just abandoned. Suppose we were the ones to abandon him. I couldn't bear it. I just couldn't bear it . . .

A tiny motor yacht barely twenty-five feet long passed by and she craned her neck, wondering if Alex might be one of the soldiers on it, already on their way home. Thousands had already been brought back – he could be one of them. If he were, Paddy would put all her heart and soul and every ounce of her strength into saving the others, but she knew none of them could be quite as important as Alex.

'That's *Trilby*,' Toby said suddenly, pointing at the little yacht. 'I'd recognise that high prow anywhere. You know, Charles – she belongs to one of the Admiral's friends – chap who lives in Rye. She was in and out of Bosham all last summer.'

'So it is.' Charles shaded his eyes to look. 'She's pretty loaded, too. I wonder if that's him—'

The Stuka came at them so suddenly that they didn't even hear it. Nor did they hear the explosion of the bomb it dropped. They saw only the flames and the smoke as the *Trilby* disintegrated before their eyes, and they felt the shock of it as the blast sent water banging against their own craft. *Wagtail* lifted into the air, seemed to twist a little and then fell back into the sea. For a few moments they were certain that they would capsize. They felt the crash as she struck one of the other boats in the chain, and then they were rocking violently but still more or less upright. The other boat was miraculously undamaged, its crew as shocked as Paddy and her brothers. They stared at each other, stunned and shaking. Once again, the aircraft had disappeared.

Charles felt sick. In that last moment, he had recognised the man at the wheel of the little motor yacht. It was the Admiral's friend, an old shipmate who must have been well into his sixties. And the younger man with him – that had been his son. The Admiral had brought them both over to Emsworth a time or two the previous summer, and Charles had met them once when he and Sheila had been there for the weekend. He'd liked them both and hoped to meet them again.

Now, there was nothing left either of them or their boat. There was not even any debris floating on the surface of the sea.

He drew in a deep breath, feeling almost as if he too had been blown apart and needed to drag himself together again. The fleet was well within sight of the coast now and he could see the low line of the sand dunes with their fringe of tussocky grass. The aircraft had gone, but he knew they would be back. Meanwhile, there was work to be done.

'We're nearly there,' he said in a quiet voice. 'Look. They're unlashing us. We'll have to start going in to the beaches.'

They looked at the dunes and saw the derelict vehicles, the lorries burned out and destroyed. They saw the town, burning in the west. They saw the dense black smoke hanging like the shadow of death over the desolate coast.

They saw the men, waiting in vast crowds on the broad, sandy beaches. Waiting in long lines that stretched far out into the shallow water. Waiting for rescue.

Or for death.

Chapter Fourteen

I t was not Denison's leg that had struck Olly on the shoulder. For a few moments he had kept it there beside him, not knowing what else to do with it. It seemed wrong, somehow, to throw it over the side – disrespectful to the man who had accompanied them across the Channel and taken the burden of responsibility from Olly's shoulders. Yet it was no use to them nor to anyone else, and it wasn't the sort of thing you wanted lying in your boat ... After a moment or two of indecision, Olly picked it up, surprised by how heavy it was, and threw it into the sea, still feeling uncomfortable about it. I just hope it hasn't hit some other poor sod on the head, he thought in sudden anxiety.

''Ere he is,' Stan Miller said suddenly. 'Blimey, 'e's got a string of blokes with 'im an' all. Come on, Skip, time to repel boarders.'

Repelling boarders was the last thing they were going to do. Olly watched from his position at the wheel, holding the fireboat steady as Denison appeared out of the gloom, holding on to the hawser as he waded back to the ship. Behind him was a long trail of soldiers, moving slowly and wearily through the oily water, their faces black with filth, only their eyes and teeth showing any white. As Denison leaned away, they passed him by, clinging to the rope as the crew of the fireboat heaved them aboard. Even those who could not swim were able to walk out by holding on to the rope; almost out of their depth, they lifted their chins and let the rope take their weight. But even that couldn't help them all; as more and more grabbed the line, so it began to sag beneath their weight and Olly heard a shout of fear as one man began to go under.

Denison snapped out an order and began to wade back towards the beach. 'Let it go! Wait a bit – you'll all go down if you put too much weight on it. Come on, chaps, we're nearly there.' He stationed himself a few yards from the boat and began to shepherd the soldiers towards the rope, letting only half a dozen take hold at a time.

The task was made difficult by their weight, but there were many willing hands to help them, and some were able to swim further along the sides of the ship and be dragged aboard without the help of the rope. Blimey, Olly thought, however many are there? Bloody hundreds – thousands. And how many can we take? Fifty, sixty? But it was no use thinking like that. Fifty men dragged aboard the *Surrey Queen* were another fifty on their way home. That was the only way you could look at it.

'Cripes,' Chalky White panted as he dragged a burly Sergeant on to the deck and landed him like a huge fish. 'You oughter gone on a diet, mate.'

The Sergeant didn't see the joke. 'I ain't 'ad a bite to eat for days,' he growled. 'I ain't 'ad nothing to drink, neither. Nor's any of me mates. We bin waiting 'ere for you lot for the best part of a week an' there ain't a drop of water fit to drink in the whole place.'

'Sorry, mate,' Chalky muttered, and helped him to his feet. 'You go down below, and one of the blokes'll give you a wad and a cuppa.' He turned to hoist another man on board. 'Up you come, mate. Up you come.'

The men poured over the side. Some were in pretty good shape but they were all dirty, soaking wet, hungry, thirsty and deadly tired. Others were wounded or injured as well.

'Mind me arm, for Gawd's sake, it's broke –'

'Look out for old Lofty, his knee's smashed to bits. Me and Fred've bin holding him up between us –'

'Aah! Me *ribs* –'

'Me belly –'

'Me shoulder, it's bin put right out, see – aaah!'

'I can't help it, mate,' Jack Hodge panted as the Tommy he was hauling over the coaming screamed in agony. 'I can't bleeding help it! It's do or die . . . Someone'll be along in a mo, give you a sup of water and a fag.' He turned to another man with blood caked on his

162

cheek from a huge gash over an empty eye-socket. 'Blimey O'Riley, what happened to *you*?'

He didn't expect an answer. The soldier just rolled his good eye and stumbled away along the deck before collapsing amongst his fellows. The rest of the crew were dragging in more men, pulling them over the side without ceremony. There was no time to be gentle, no time to take care of injuries. They could be dealt with back in England. The vital thing now was to stay alive, to fill the boat and get them back home. That was what they were here for. That was all that mattered.

'How many d'you think we got?' Olly was keeping the fireboat more or less stationary. He peered down into the gathering darkness towards the place where he had last seen Denison. 'Reckon we're just about full now.'

There was a shout of dismay as the Sublieutenant clambered back aboard. Soaked in oil and blood as well as water, he scrambled up beside Olly and wiped the filth from his face. 'I've been back to the lorry and unlashed the rope. Go astern carefully – there's men all around, still trying to get aboard. We'll take these out to one of the ships and then come back.' He raised his voice and bawled at the desperate soldiers, 'Get out of the way, for God's sake! We can't take any more! We'll be back for you, and there are other boats coming anyway. Good luck!' He sank down for a minute, shuddering with cold and fatigue, and Jack Hodge appeared beside him with a steaming mug.

'Get that down yer, sir.' He addressed Olly. 'They've just about drunk us dry, Skip. Seems the Jerries bombed the town's water supply days ago – there ain't a drop in the place. Reckon we can get some more from the ship?'

'There are water containers coming over,' Denison said, gulping down scalding hot tea. 'They're bringing it in two-gallon jerry cans.' He gave a short, bitter laugh. '*Jerry* cans! They're taking it ashore to give to the men on the beaches, but we should be able to get some as well.' He glanced at the heaps of weary bodies packed on the deck. 'Poor sods,' he said compassionately. 'Most of them aren't even regulars. They've had hardly any training – and they get thrown into this.' He handed the mug back to Jack Hodge and scrambled to his feet. 'I'd better go and see what I can do for them.'

Olly had managed to bring the fireboat round to head out towards one of the ships. Other small boats were doing the same, like flocks of chicks heading for the mother hen. It was almost dark now and none were showing lights. We'll be lucky not to go crashing into each other, he thought. It's a shambles, that's what it is – a bloody shambles.

And yet – what else could anyone do? How else could these men be rescued and brought home?

'We'll get rid of this lot and then heave to for a couple of hours,' Denison said in his ear. 'There are a few boats warping together – we'll join on with them, get a bite to eat and a bit of sleep. The Luftwaffe should leave us alone for a while.'

'Be a good chance to go on getting them off the beach then sir,' Olly said. 'If only it wasn't so dark . . .'

He handed over the wheel and went to inspect his ship. Soldiers were packed everywhere – on the decks, in the cramped little cabin and galley, even in the engine-room. They sat propped against the bulwarks, leaning against each other in their weariness, their fingers clamped round mugs of tea. Lucky they've got their own tin mugs in their packs, Olly thought, because we weren't expecting a tea-party . . . And then he thought of the stores that had been loaded aboard back in London – it seemed 100 years ago – and his amazement at the amount that they'd been given. They knew even then we'd be loading up with soldiers, he thought. They knew the poor buggers would be starving hungry and half dead with thirst.

It was dark and gloomy down below, and the soldiers were too exhausted to talk. They slumped in silence, some of them groaning with pain. None were seriously injured, for it would have been impossible to get a badly injured man aboard the *Queen*, but for a man who had spent days or even weeks on the retreat, then hours or even days on the beaches being dive-bombed and strafed before standing for God knew how long in salt water waiting for rescue, an injury such as a broken arm or dislocated shoulder would be agony. Olly tried to imagine the nightmare they had been through, but even though he had actually seen it with his own eyes, he still could not visualise the true extent of the horror. Maybe nobody ever could, he thought, turning to go back on deck. Not unless you'd been through it yourself.

All the time, as he picked his way amongst the bodies, he was looking for one man. One face that was amongst the dearest in all the world to him – his son, Joe. But Joe wasn't there, and he knew that the chances of him coming aboard the *Surrey Queen* were slim indeed.

About the same chance as finding a snowball in hell, he thought, climbing up the short companionway.

Wagtail had no trouble in getting close enough to the soldiers. Her main problem was in preventing them from sinking her.

'I'll turn stern on to the beach,' Charles said, keeping the engines throttled right down as he made the final approach. 'They can climb in more easily there.' But the minute the little craft eased amongst the waiting crowd they dashed to get aboard, almost turning her over in their desperation.

'No!' Paddy shrieked, pushing them away as the boat tipped dangerously. 'Go back to the stern. You'll have us over!' Tears streamed down her face as she watched the frantic rush. I can't believe I'm pushing them away, she thought in anguish. I came all this way to save them and now I'm pushing them away. Oh, these poor men, these poor, *poor* men . . .

The queue had organised itself now and the soldiers had moved away from the sides and were climbing in over the stern. Paddy left her post and pushed her way through to the cockpit. *Wagtail* was rocking violently and thick, viscous water was slopping over the deck but she was concerned only with the men who were coming aboard, and how best to help them. Water, that must be their first need, and she scurried down to the galley, thankful that Charles had insisted on filling so many cans from the tap. For a moment she hesitated, wondering whether to make tea, and then decided that plain water was the priority. Tea could come later.

'Thanks, mate.' The private she handed the first can to grabbed and swigged it as if he hadn't seen fluid for days. Perhaps he hadn't. She tried to remember how long you could survive without liquid. Three days? A week? Food was not nearly so important. Feeling cruel, she took the can away and handed it to the next man. 'I'm sorry – you've got to share it round.' She saw his eyes flicker at the sound of her voice, then go dull. His eyelids lowered and to her alarm he slumped against the man next to him.

'Oh!' Paddy said in dismay, but the next man was already reaching out for the water-can. 'It's all right, chum,' he said, his voice dry and cracked. 'He's just dead beat. We all are.' He tipped the water down his throat. 'Bloody hell, I never thought God's ale could taste so good. Got any more?'

'We've got to share it round,' Paddy said helplessly, and the man nodded. Like all the rest, he was filthy and unshaven, his uniform streaming with water and caked with dark, clotted stains. He had a long gash down one cheek, scabbed over as if it had happened hours or even days before and the blood never staunched, and he held one arm awkwardly across his chest. Paddy reached out and he flinched away.

'It's all right. I'm not going to touch it. Is – is it broken?'

'Got a bullet through it,' he said tersely. 'It's all right, it's only what they calls a flesh wound – no bones broken. Gives me gyp a bit, that's all.'

'It must need cleaning and bandaging.'

'It can wait. It's waited a week already.' The man jerked his head. 'You go on and see to these other blokes, chum. Water to *drink*, that's what they need. Can't waste it on bloody washing.'

Paddy moved away, reluctant but knowing he was right. With luck, he would be back in England within a few hours and would be attended to then. She stepped over some of the bodies to fetch more water-cans.

'There's hardly any left!' Appalled, she stared up at her brother. 'I thought we brought heaps.'

'We've handed it all out.' He looked grim. 'All this bread – and *cakes*! Who thought of making *cakes*, for God's sake? It's water we need most and we've run out already.' He glanced round at the crowded boat. 'There must be over twenty aboard – we'd better get them away to one of the ships.' He shouted to Toby to get back to the engines.

'Twenty!' It seemed so few out of all the thousands on the beach, yet Paddy knew that *Wagtail* couldn't take any more and stay afloat. She looked at the soldiers. They had all had at least a gulp of water – not enough, but surely there would be more on the ship. Charles was right, the next essential was to get them away from the beach. The vibration of the engines beneath her feet told her that Toby was working below. For the moment, there was nothing more for her to do.

She sat down on the deck beside one of the soldiers. He was in private's uniform, his face grimy and unshaven, his eyes red with exhaustion. He turned his head slowly and looked at her.

'They didn't tell us it was going to be like this,' he said in a slurred voice.

'I don't think they knew,' Paddy said helplessly. Perhaps they couldn't, even if they did know. Perhaps nobody could ever describe what a battle – or a retreat – was going to be like. Especially one like this, with this strange armada of little ships, dragged from every port and harbour and inlet along the south and south-east coast. She looked more closely at the private and realised that he was not much more than a boy. 'What's your name?'

'Bill. Billy, me mum calls me.' He closed his eyes as if in pain. 'Wonder if I'll ever see her again.'

'Of course you will. We're taking you home now. You'll be back in Dover in a few hours, and then – where do you live?'

'Pompey. Portsmouth to you.'

'Portsmouth? Why, I live near there myself! I live in Emsworth!' She felt a sudden irrational kinship with the boy. 'Whereabouts?'

'Fratton. Dad works in the dockyard.' His voice sounded less weary, as if finding someone who knew his home town had put a tremor of new life into him. 'Got a brother in the Army too – dunno where he is now. I last saw him back at Arras.'

Paddy was silent for a moment. *Wagtail* was now leaving the beach and making her way towards the destroyers and passenger ferries anchored offshore. 'I hope he'll be all right,' she said.

'I don't suppose he is.' The voice was weary again. 'He was holed up in a shed when I saw him. Then the Jerries came and we had to get out. Every man for himself. I tried to find him but the shed was blown apart. I dunno if he got out or not.'

Again, she could find nothing to say. She touched his arm and he looked at her in surprise. Paddy remembered that she was supposed to be a boy herself, and drew back quickly.

'Here,' he said, as if remembering something, 'what day is it today?'

'Today?' She wasn't quite sure herself. It seemed weeks since they had left Chichester Harbour with *Moonset*. With a shock, she remembered that it had been only that morning. 'It's Friday – Friday the thirty-first of May.'

His lips twisted again. 'It's my birthday, then. And never even got a card!'

'Your *birthday*?' It dawned on her that soldiers must be having birthdays all the time, forgotten and ignored in the heat of battle or the drudgery of everyday camp life. 'How old are you?'

'Nineteen,' he said, and Paddy stared at the face, young beneath the grime and the stubble yet old in experience.

'*Nineteen?* You're not much older than me.'

He looked at her. 'So why ain't you been called up, then? Why ain't you volunteered?'

She looked speechlessly at him. 'Because – because . . .'

He turned his head away as if uninterested, and she saw his eyelids droop. Poor boy, she thought, he's worn out – they all are. She longed to put her arm around him and draw his head down on her shoulder, but knew that this was impossible. If he realised she was a girl . . . but then, if he had realised she was a girl he wouldn't have asked why she hadn't volunteered.

I suppose it wouldn't really matter if he did know now, she thought. It wouldn't matter if anyone knew. I'm here – they're not going to send me back now.

And yet – they still might. The ship where they were taking *Wagtail* now would be heading back towards Dover. Someone might yet decide that she should go with it.

She must still keep up the pretence.

The *Countess Wear* made two more trips to the Mole before calling it a night. By then she had taken off nearly 200 men. On their final trip to the nearest destroyer they were told to raft up to some of the other ships and get some rest.

'Some of them are going to carry on,' Robby told the others. 'The planes aren't attacking at night, so it's a good chance to get the boys off, even though it's dark. But orders are, we've got to get some food inside us and then a few hours' kip ready for the morning.'

'There's still blokes on the Mole,' Jimmy objected. 'What are we supposed to do, leave 'em there? We could fetch 'em off first, give 'em a bit of a fry-up and then shove 'em on board one of the ships come daylight. What d'you think, Skipper?'

'I think it's a good idea. They'd be better off with us than waiting on that ramshackle old pier.' Robby set course for the Mole again.

The darkness was lit by the flames still raging through the port, and a glow of dull orange lay over the sea. As they drew nearer to the Mole they could see the line of men still waiting there. Practised at the manoeuvre now, Robby turned the *Countess* and Danny leaned from the bow to throw the painter round the nearest pile. The men let out a ragged cheer and started to jump down to the deck almost before the boat was properly alongside.

'Hang on a minute!' Robby shouted. 'Let him get her tied up!' But the men were desperate. They had been waiting a long time. The fires of the port, coming closer all the time, were throwing out an almost intolerable heat. They were starved and thirsty, almost dropping with fatigue; they were wounded, injured and frightened – and they kept on coming.

Danny, trying to pull the painter tight, leaned out a little further. The boat rocked as the men scrambled aboard. It smashed against the pier and then bounced away again and Danny, still clinging to the rope, gave a yell and disappeared. There was a moment of confusion as the nearest men made a grab for him, and then a shout of dismay went up. Robby, who had been watching the stern, whipped round and Jimmy rushed forward, thrusting the soldiers aside in his panic.

'*Man overboard!* Danny's gone! Get her away from the pier, Rob – get her away, for God's sake!'

'Get back to the engines then!' Robby bawled, his words lost in the clamour, but Jimmy didn't need to be told. He was back, climbing over men who were in his way, and descending the steps with one headlong leap. Robby felt the idling engine spring into life and the boat backed away from the Mole. The half-dozen men not already aboard jumped for it and landed on the deck amongst their fellows. But for once, Robby was not concerned with them. His only thought was for Danny, somewhere down there in those black, oily waters. Danny, his childhood friend, who had come with him on this perilous voyage. Danny, who was such a good swimmer, who couldn't – *mustn't* – be allowed to drown.

Chapter Fifteen

Saturday, 1 June

'Get him up!' The soldiers were hanging on to the pier, reaching down through the wooden struts to where Danny was clinging to the piles in the black, swirling water. Rob watched anxiously, trying to keep the *Countess* away from the Mole while Jimmy kept the engines ticking over down below. If Danny tried to climb up just as the *Countess* swayed closer . . . He remembered the man who had slipped between the boat and the pier as they took on their first load. He had never surfaced.

'He's gone.' It was too dark to see what was happening in the water, and Rob's heart sank. Danny surely couldn't survive down there. The Mole was built well out from the shore, in deep water which eddied and sucked at the wooden piles. It was cluttered with debris from damaged ships – splintered planks of wood, doors, lifebelts, anything that could float – and thick with oil. If you didn't drown, you'd choke to death, Robby thought, and strained his eyes to try to catch a glimpse of his friend.

The soldiers continued to drop on to the deck. Like all the others who had come aboard, they were exhausted and lay where they fell, a heap of khaki-clad figures too worn out to move any further. Robby looked down anxiously. They had to move or no one else would be able to come aboard. Then a sergeant who had come down first started to push between them, bawling and kicking to get them to move. 'Come on, you lazy lot. Shift your bloody arses. You're laying right in the road – get up there, move over, let the dog see the rabbit . . .' He must be just as exhausted himself, Robby thought, but he wasn't letting up, and after a moment or two the men stirred themselves and crawled along the deck to make room for the rest to come aboard.

The *Countess* was packed with men. The queue waiting on the Mole seemed as long as ever, stretching away towards the blazing harbour. Another ship was trying to nose its way to the piles behind the *Countess Wear*. With a heavy heart, Rob signalled to Jimmy to go slow ahead, and turned her bow away from the pier.

No point in keeping them aboard all night, he thought. We might as well take them out to the mother ship and get rid of them. Then we can come back again and get some more. I can't rest, not now we've lost Dan.

He set course for the personnel ships and destroyers waiting like shadows a mile offshore. His heart was like a stone and his throat ached, but there was no time now to grieve for his lost friend. That would have to wait until later.

By then, there would probably be even more grief to bear.

Taking men to the ships that would ferry them back across the Channel was not the easiest task for a little boat like *Wagtail*.

The grey side of the destroyer rose like a vast metal cliff above the little motor cruiser. She swayed and shifted in the tide, and Paddy stared up anxiously, half-afraid that if nobody saw the little boat it would be crushed and no one would ever know it had been there. But the crew were keeping a lookout all the time for new arrivals, and there were rope ladders and nets for the men to climb – if they had the strength to do so.

'Up you go,' she said to the boy she'd been talking to on the short trip over. 'You'll be home in no time now.' She looked around for the man with the injured arm. 'Can you manage?'

'Bleedin' have to, won't I.' He scrambled awkwardly up the swinging rope ladder.

Most of the men were out of the boat now. Paddy heard Charles shout something and pushed her way back towards him. 'We need more water,' he said. 'Take the wheel while I go aboard and ask for some.'

'I can do that,' Paddy said, turning, but he grabbed her arm.

'Of course you can't! They'll see you're a girl.'

'None of the others have.'

'They didn't have time and they don't care anyway.' He jerked her back towards him and spoke more roughly than she had ever heard him. 'You agreed to obey orders – obey this one. Take the wheel.'

Dazed, Paddy did as she was told. She watched her brother climb the ladder and disappear. Toby poked his head up from the engine-room. 'What's going on?'

'Charles has gone aboard the destroyer to ask for water.' She held the boat steady, aware that every moment there were more little ships arriving to decant their cargo. A cockle-boat – a ship's lifeboat – a small fishing vessel. A motor cruiser, only a little larger than *Wagtail* herself . . . She glanced at it and then stared and stiffened.

'*Moonset!*'

Toby's head appeared again. 'What was that?'

'It's *Moonset* – she's just arrived with some soldiers.' Paddy craned her neck, peering through the darkness. 'I can see the Admiral! And Peter Murphy, and George – they're all there. Oh Toby, it's them, it really is! They're coming alongside us now – the soldiers are going to come over our deck.' Still gripping the wheel with one hand, she jumped up and down, waving excitedly. 'Admiral! Peter! Admiral! It's us – *Wagtail*! It's us!'

The other boat was now rafted alongside them and men were crossing the deck to scramble up the sides of the destroyer. The Sea Scout, Peter Murphy, came with them, supporting a man who could barely walk. There was another soldier on the other side, his head swathed in blood-soaked bandages. Peter stared at her in astonishment.

'*Paddy!*'

'Oh Peter,' she said, feeling tears pour down her cheeks. 'It's so good to see you.'

He continued across the deck, with the injured soldier leaning heavily on his arm. 'I've got to get this man on to the ship.'

'I know.' She moved to the other side and offered to help. The bandaged man put one hand on the ladder and started to climb. Between them Peter and Paddy got the lame one on to the bottom rung and he tried to haul himself up, but his leg hung uselessly and his efforts were feeble and obviously causing pain. 'Peter, let me go up ahead and pull – you can push from below.' She scrambled past and turned to grip the injured man's wrist. 'Can you hold my wrist as well? Hold tight.' His fingers were hard and rough around her slender arm, and she could feel the burning pain as they slipped on her skin. She tried to climb higher up the ladder, but his weight was too great. 'Peter, *push*!'

'I *am* pushing,' the Scout called back. 'I can't shift him!'

Paddy looked down at the man's face. He was filthy, as they all were, his lips stretched back in a grimace, his teeth shining against the oil-blackened face. His eyes glimmered white in the surging darkness and then disappeared as the lids came down over them. 'I think he's fainted,' she cried, and felt the man's grip slacken. '*Peter, he's going to fall!*'

She tightened her own grip but the bulky figure was too heavy and as he fell away from the ladder her fingers lost their grasp. Paddy screamed and twisted round in a desperate attempt to retain her hold on the ladder. She heard Peter shout below her, and then there was a commotion on *Wagtail*'s deck and a loud splash. Sobbing with shock and terror, she looked down.

The soldier had fallen into the water between *Wagtail* and the destroyer's sheer side. The other men, still waiting to climb the ladder, were leaning over the side of the smaller boat and trying to pull him out by the khaki overcoat ballooning around his body. Peter Murphy was in the sea too, struggling to hold the man's head above the water. Toby had come up from the engine-room and was trying to stave the boat away from the ship with a boat-hook. The weight of the soldiers leaning over the side was causing *Wagtail* to list dangerously.

'For God's sake!' the Admiral himself was booming from the deck of *Moonset*. He shouted up at Paddy. 'You, man! Stay where you are! Don't come down. The rest of you, get back from the side, you'll have the whole lot over. Two of you get that man aboard and for God's sake get the boy back as well.' His voice snapped out orders. 'Then bring the soldier back aboard. We'll have to get some seamen off the ship to get him up. All these chaps are too exhausted,' he added in a lower voice, and stepped across the decks to *Wagtail*. 'My God! *Toby Stainbank!*'

'That's me, sir.' Toby tried to grin but his lips wouldn't quite obey him.

'How long have you been here?' The Admiral was staring at him in disbelief. Toby shrugged and shook his head.

'I've no idea. It seems like all our lives. They're getting young

Peter aboard now by the look of it, thank goodness.' He nodded towards the coaming and the Admiral turned. The injured soldier had been dragged aboard and the young Sea Scout pulled in after him. He moved over to look at him.

'Thank God. Are you all right, boy?'

Peter lay on the deck, breathing raggedly and choking up filthy water. His dark hair was plastered to his skull but he looked unhurt and not too badly shocked. He managed a grin and the Admiral laid his hand on the boy's shoulder. 'Good lad. Get your breath back and then go back to *Moonset*.' He turned back towards Toby. 'Where's Charles?'

Paddy had clambered back down the ladder. She dropped to her knees beside the boy and pushed back his streaming hair. 'Are you really all right, Peter? I thought you were going to drown.'

'*Paddy?*' The Admiral turned back in amazement. 'Is that you? What in God's name are you doing here? What the *hell* was Charles thinking of, to let you come on a trip like this?'

'I'm helping.' She stood up and faced him. 'Charles didn't know anything about it until it was too late. I stowed away.'

'*Stowed away?*' The old man's eyes bulged. 'You silly young fool, this isn't a children's story! You'll have to go back at once. You can leave on this ship – I'll explain to her captain.' He turned and laid his hand on the bottom rung of the rope-ladder, then saw that Charles was about to drop into the boat. 'Oh, there you are. Look, this child's got to go back at once. It's madness having her here.'

'I'm not going back! And it's more important to get this soldier aboard. He's hurt – he needs help.' She was already helping Peter and the other two men to lift the wounded soldier into the stretcher that had been lowered. Two seamen had come down after Charles, ready to lift him aboard. The others watched as he swayed slowly and hazardously up towards the deck. Charles and Toby sighed with relief. The Admiral gave a sharp nod and turned back to Paddy.

'I'm not going,' she repeated steadily. 'And there isn't time to argue. There's too much to do. Anyway, it's just as dangerous to send me back – ships are being bombed and torpedoed all the time. I could be killed before I got a hundred yards.'

'You're a wilful, disobedient minx,' the Admiral began furiously, but the destroyer was preparing to move and there were shouts from above to get clear. Toby disappeared into the engine-room and

Charles took the wheel. Peter Murphy glanced at the Admiral and the old man hesitated, then shrugged.

'Very well. But I'll have more to say later!' He followed the Scout back to *Moonset* and Peter unlashed the rope that had tied them together. Most of the boats that had been crowding around the destroyer were already well clear, setting off back to the beaches, and *Moonset* and *Wagtail* turned to follow them.

'I'm not going to be sent back,' Paddy said, standing beside Charles in the wheelhouse. 'I'm not, Charles.'

He sighed. 'Paddy, you'll be put aboard the next ship. Never mind that it might get torpedoed – it's still more dangerous here. The Admiral won't let you stay, and that's all there is to it.'

The destroyer was moving fast now, cutting through the water on its way past the treacherous sandbanks offshore to the open Channel. They could see her bulk against the pattern of stars. Paddy said, 'I'm glad I'm here. I'm glad I was able to help some of those men. I know they won't remember me, but that doesn't matter.' She paused and her voice sounded a little shaky as she went on, 'I know we probably won't even see Alex. But for every twenty men *we* take, he gets a better chance of somebody picking *him* up. Someone will bring him home, Charles, even if it's not me. And I can help some of these others. So I'm staying. I am *not* going back – whatever anyone says.'

'Rob!'

In all the racket that was still going on, Robby should never have heard the voice. All the same, it penetrated some part of his brain, in the same way as a baby's cry can be heard by its mother when inaudible to everyone else. 'Hang on a minute, don't go without me!'

Disbelievingly Robby turned his head and stared back towards the Mole. The sky was dark now, but still lit by the glow of fires, and the pier stood out like a dense black shadow. And there, silhouetted against the raddled light, stood a gesticulating figure.

'*Danny!*' They were only a few yards off the Mole and he brought the *Countess* round again, turning her almost on a sixpence. Danny jumped, just missing two soldiers as he landed on the deck, and fumbled his way to the wheelhouse. There, his legs gave out and he slumped to the deck. Robby signalled to Jimmy to put the engines full ahead and steered the *Countess* away from the long arm of the Mole. Then he looked down at his friend.

'What happened? Are you all right? How did you get out?'

Danny rolled over. 'My stars, I feel bloody awful.' He clawed his way over the sprawled bodies of the soldiers and draped himself over the side, vomiting into the water. When he had finished, he hung there, clearly too weak to move. One of the soldiers roused himself sufficiently to drag him back to the deck, and he lay still.

Don't die now, Rob thought, staring down at him in terror. For God's sake don't give up now.

Danny stirred. Slowly, he sat up and then pulled himself to his feet. He stumbled over to the wheelhouse and scrambled inside.

'That were a close shave,' he said hoarsely.

'What happened?' Rob asked again. 'How did you get back on to the pier?'

'Climbed up the other side. No ships there, see. Bugger of a hard climb it were, an' all.' His body was shaking. 'Rob, there be men's bodies down there. The sea – 'tis all full of bits of men, just floating about. Arms and legs and – and—' his voice choked and he turned away, retching, 'and a head. I saw this head, it were all torn and bloody, there were bits hanging off,' he retched again, 'and its eyes – they *looked* at me. I thought for a moment it were going to say something.' He swayed and Robby put out a hand and steadied him as he gave a violent shudder. 'I didn't think I were going to get back,' he said. 'I'll dream about that head, Rob.'

'Not just yet you won't.' Robby felt his training like a steel rod through him, harsh and callous as it had seemed at the time, yet coming to his rescue when he needed it. 'We've got too much to do. Go below, Dan, and get Jimmy to give you something to drink and some dry clobber, and then come back up on deck. The *Countess* might be a holiday-steamer but she's carrying no passengers on this trip – except the ones we came to fetch, and they got their tickets in France.'

Danny gave him a startled look and then turned to do as he was told, lurching down the companionway into the engine-room. That too was packed with soldiers, and Robby doubted if Jimmy had either time, room or facilities to serve drinks, but Danny needed to have something to take his mind off his ordeal. In a few minutes, they would be by the mother-ship and they could embark the soldiers and go back for more.

The idea of rafting up and resting had been forgotten. Robby, like everyone else that night, was driven by the urgent task of retrieving as many men as he could from the seething beaches of Dunkirk.

The *Surrey Queen* was on her way back to Ramsgate. She had taken four loads of men to the troopship and now she was taking back a load of her own. There were a hundred or more soldiers on board, crammed in every available space – in the cabin, the galley, the forepeak, by the hoses, even in the engine-room, and standing shoulder to shoulder on the deck. A couple of the crew were down below brewing tea and cocoa, and others were going round with cigarettes. Jack Hodges and Chalky White, who had done a St John's Ambulance course, were doing their best to patch up some of the men who were wounded.

Denison stood behind the canvas dodger with Olly. He had spent most of the time during the embarkation in the water, hauling men along the line he had rigged up to the derelict vehicle on the sands, and was still soaked. There was nothing to be done about that, however, and he took the wheel and navigated the fireboat carefully through the throng of vessels and out into the open Channel.

'Strewth,' Olly said, glancing back. 'We're lit up like a blooming Christmas tree!'

Denison turned his head. The *Surrey Queen*'s wake was a glittering stream of phosphorescence. Each tiny drop of spray was lit with a pale, greenish glow, laying a pathway of brilliant light, a dozen feet wide and fifty yards long, directly to the *Queen*'s stern. Nor was it only the *Surrey Queen* which was thus illuminated; every ship, large and small, had its own sparkling causeway, and even the floating scraps of destroyed boats and aircraft were dazzlingly outlined.

'Bloody hell,' Olly said. 'If the Jerries see that . . .'

The Jerries had already seen it. Even as the words left his lips, he heard the first low snarl of approaching bombers. With a groan, he listened as the air gradually filled with their roar and the bombs began to fall. They hit the sea with a dull *crump*, sending glittering spray flying up from the surface, and the shock-waves hurtled through the water like missiles, setting the boats rocking violently. A trawler not far away went up with a shower of splintering wood. Another lurched and staggered as a bomb fell close beside it. A tug, towing a flock of assorted small vessels on their way to Dunkirk, was hit and sank at once; the boats, released abruptly from their bonds, veered wildly in all directions. One of them circled round and Olly realised it was trying to pick up survivors.

He heard the rattle of ack-ack guns as the destroyer leading the flotilla began to fire at the aircraft. A ball of flame erupted high above and began to spin downwards, hitting the sea like a volcano. Some of its debris fell in gobbets of fire on to the deck of one of the paddle-steamers, and a blaze started.

'If we could only get at the pumps!' Olly exclaimed, pacing the narrow space behind the dodger, but Denison shook his head.

'We'll pick up survivors if we can, but our job is to get these men to Ramsgate. We're a rescue ship now, Mears, not a fireboat. The sooner we can get them back to England, the sooner we can come back for more.'

The bombers had departed as soon as they had arrived. The fleet had barely faltered in its unwavering movement towards England; they had passed some of the sandbanks and were in deeper waters. Denison looked doubtfully at the compass. It had never been properly swung and to him it seemed that they were heading too far east, but presumably the leading ships were better equipped and more certain of their direction. He shuddered with sudden cold, aware of the uncomfortable dampness of his clothes and the grime that had seeped through to his skin.

'I'll need about six baths to get this lot off,' he muttered to Olly, grimacing with distaste.

'D'you reckon we'll do a quick turn-around?' Olly asked. 'I mean, the crew's more or less flaked out. Will they get time for a bit of kip?'

'I should think so. It'll take a while to disembark the men and we'll need to take on more water and fuel. I'll ask for a gun as well – it can be mounted on the foredeck, by the monitor. And a couple of hands to man it.'

'A gun! Well, I can't say it won't give me a bit of pleasure to shoot down one or two of those bloody Stukas.' Olly cocked his head. 'And if I'm not very much mistaken, here they come again . . .' His last words were lost in the roar, and once again they felt the judder of the shock-waves as bombs dropped into the sea and on the vessels unlucky enough to be in their path. One fell barely a length behind the *Queen* and Olly felt her stern lift so high that the propellers came clear of the water. She jinked violently to one side and then smacked down again, and Denison swore as he struggled to keep control of the wheel. Olly, thrown backwards by the impact, dragged himself upright and fell against the compass, knocking it out of its bearings. It wasn't much bloody good anyway, he thought grimly as he grasped the wheel to help Denison calm the ship as a rider might calm a panicking horse. Together, they got the *Queen* under control again and looked behind.

It might never have happened. The phosphorescent wake was following as blandly and innocently as if the *Queen* had never diverted an inch from her path. Perhaps she hadn't, Olly thought, dazed. Perhaps she'd just jumped out of the water and come down again in the same spot. It was as though he'd imagined the entire thing.

I'm dreaming, he thought with a wry grimace. I'll wake up in a minute, in bed beside my Effie, and find out that it was all a bad dream.

He knew, though, that he wouldn't. This was no dream. This was real. There was no knowing when – or if – he would ever sleep in his own bed again.

Chapter Sixteen

Sunday, 2 June

As Jethro had foretold, the church at Stoke Gabriel was packed with people who had come to pray for the safe evacuation of their Army. They listened to the vicar as he gave his sermon, and came out to stand in sober little groups about the churchyard, discussing the situation in low voices. Many of the women were in tears and the men's voices were husky, but their initial despair had been replaced by hope and determination. The little ships would bring the Tommies home. Why, two of their very own were going – the *Countess Wear* and the *Berry Pomeroy*, that they'd seen every day plying up and down the River Dart – and Robby Endacott, a boy they'd known all their lives, was in charge of one of them. It gave them a proprietorial interest and a confidence that all would be well.

Nevertheless, the same thought lay dark and unspoken in all their minds. Half a million men – and only a few passenger-steamers and ferries, not even built for going to sea, to bring them off the beaches . . .

Molly Lovering was in church too. She came over to Hetty, tears sliding down her plump, rosy cheeks, and Hetty folded her in her arms. 'Oh, Mrs Endacott! Is Robby going to be all right? Is he going to come back?'

'Of course he is, my bird. You don't need to fret about he. Doesn't his dad always say he's the sort who'd fall down a cesspit and come up smelling of roses? Our Robby's always been able to look after hisself. Look at it this way, the Navy must think a lot of him to have given him this job. A ship of his own! Think of that.'

Molly smiled rather shakily. 'I know, but the news is so bad, I can't help feeling frightened for him. They Germans – they're not going to let the soldiers get away easy, are they? They'll be bombing and all sorts.' She bit her lip. 'I'm sorry, you must be worried to death about your Jan as well. Oh, 'tis awful.'

'I know, Molly, but us mustn't give way to it. That'd be letting Hitler win, see. Us must just be brave and wait, and do whatever we can for the war effort. Now, my flower, why don't you come along and have your dinner with us today? You'm not wanted at the farm, are you?'

'No. Thank you, Mrs Endacott, I'd like to do that. So long as I'm not taking your rations.' Molly dried her tears on a scrap of lace that Hetty guessed was her Sunday handkerchief. 'I'll just go and tell Mother. She won't mind.'

'Poor little maid,' Hetty said, watching her. 'Never had to face nothing like this before. It's hard on the young ones.'

'Hard on us too,' Jethro said, putting his hand on her shoulder. 'I know you were awake half the night, Het. Tossing and turning hour after hour, you were.'

'And how would you know that, if you weren't doing the same? I hope I didn't keep you awake, Jethro.'

'No,' he admitted. 'I couldn't sleep neither. It's a bad job, this, but look at it this way, it have brought the country together. All over England, there's folk like us going to church and praying for our boys. I reckon He's up there listening to us, Het, and I reckon He'll answer our prayers.'

'I hope so, Jethro. I hope so.' Hetty reached out a hand to Molly, who had come back. 'Now, you come along of we, maid. I've got a nice rabbit pie for our dinner, and there's some early potatoes and peas and some fresh spring greens to go with it. And rhubarb and junket for afters.' She tucked Molly's hand into her arm and the three of them turned and walked out of the churchyard and made their way along the narrow lanes. 'Robby'd be pleased to know you was coming home with us. It's a pity we didn't think to ask Susie over as well, but with her living over to Dittisham, 'tisn't so easy.'

They paused for a moment to look at the war memorial, put up after the Great War, with the brass plate listing the names of those who had died: local names, of boys and young men they had known themselves, whose families still lived in the village. Collings, Narracott, Scadding, Luscombe . . . Eighteen of them altogether.

'Eighteen,' Hetty said, shaking her head. 'From a little place like Stoke! It's so cruel.'

'I know, maid.' Jethro put his hand on her shoulder. 'Ill-spared and sorely missed still. But us have said our prayers and us can't do more than that. 'Tis up to us to keep things right and proper at home for when our boys come back. 'Tis what they'm fighting for, after all.'

She nodded. 'I know. But it makes me feel ashamed to think how often I've walked past this cross and never stopped to look at they names and think for a minute about those boys. Us knew them all, Jethro. Us went to school with them and messed about down on the shore and rowed about on the river with them. And this memorial – 'tis supposed to remind us, yet us walks past it time after time without ever giving it a thought.'

''Tis human nature,' he said gently. 'We don't really forget, not deep inside, and I reckon they knows it, too.'

They stood for a moment, remembering, and then walked on. The two women picked a few late primroses and some of the bluebells that clustered so thickly on the high banks and laid some at the foot of the cross, taking the rest home. Hetty liked to have a few flowers about the house and grew ox-eye daisies, lupins and antirrhinums in the garden for bringing indoors. When they arrived at the cottage, she found the vases that her mother had left her, and the glass bowl she and Jethro had been given for a wedding present, and arranged the flowers in them with a few sprays of leaves. 'There,' she said, standing back to admire them. 'Make a lot of difference to a place, a few flowers do. I hope you'll always have a few about when you and Robby are wed, Molly.'

Molly blushed. 'I don't know that we're getting wed, Mrs Endacott. I mean, Robby hasn't asked me. He might not want to get wed.'

'Not want to get wed! Why, don't be foolish – of course he'll want to get wed. All men want a home to come back to, with a nice little wife and a few children running about, and our Robby couldn't do better than you. He'll be asking you soon, don't you fret.'

'I don't know,' Molly said, a little miserably. She sat at the table, her fingers playing with the fringe of the green chenille cloth, and then looked up. 'Sometimes, I can't help wondering if he doesn't have other girls as well as me. You know what they say about sailors – a wife in every port.'

'Not my Robby,' Hetty said firmly. 'I dare say he might've had one or two little romances while he was at Gosport or in Devonport – he'm a man when all's said and done – but there'll have been nothing serious. Just a liddle bit of wild oats, that's all that will have been. You surely don't doubt what he thinks about you, Moll.'

'Well, not really.' Molly thought of the half-hour she and Robby had spent in the dell beside the river, and felt her cheeks grow warm. 'It's just that everything's so strange these days. Nobody knows what's happening, and I have this awful feeling that . . .' Her face crumpled suddenly and she broke into a sob. 'Oh, Mrs Endacott, suppose he don't come home! Suppose he don't ever come home!' Once started, the tears couldn't be stopped. 'I was thinking about him all night,' she sobbed, 'and saying my prayers and everything, but I can't find enough words. That's why I went to church this morning. I thought they might have the words there, but they don't. There aren't enough words to ask God to save all they poor men trapped over there. I just want to pray for Robby, but it seems so selfish. There's Jan, and my cousin Ned, and all they others, and you can't pray for one and not all the rest. But I don't know how to make God listen!'

Jethro had come in while she was weeping. He moved across the kitchen and laid his hand on her shoulder. He had taken off his black jacket and tie but was still in his best, stiff-collared shirt, with his trousers held up by the braces that Hetty had given him for Christmas. He waited for a moment and then said, 'You don't want to worry yourself about God, maid. He knows the words, even if you don't, and He be listening up there. Never doubt that.'

Molly stopped crying and looked up at him. Her eyes were red and swollen, and her body was still shaken by dragging sobs, but there was a note of hope in her voice as she said, 'Do you really believe that, Mr Endacott? Do you really believe it's true that God listens?'

'I know it's true,' he said firmly. 'I know it, because I know God. And so do you, really, if you'll only open your heart and let Him in. Now, Mother,' he went on without changing his tone, 'I think this maid could do with a cup of tea, and I know I could. And when I've changed out of these things, I'll bring in those tatties I dug up yesterday, and the two of you can get the dinner ready while I has a sit-down outside and smokes a pipe. There may be a war on, but 'tis Sunday dinner-time and I don't see no reason to change our ways for Hitler.'

Molly bit back fresh tears and smiled at him, feeling a grateful warmth spread over her body. She and Robby had laughed sometimes at Jethro Endacott's certainty but there was no denying the comfort she was finding in it now. Perhaps I'll come to it too, some day, she thought. And I do believe – I just don't feel I *know*, like Mr Endacott seems to.

He went upstairs to change and Hetty bustled about the kitchen, putting on the kettle and riddling the fire in the range to make the oven hot. The rabbit pie was already made and had been put in the larder to keep cool until Hetty was ready to cook it, and the sticks of rhubarb were in the saucepan, chopped into small pieces.

Molly closed her eyes and let the peace and warmth of the kitchen flow into her heart. Once again, she found herself praying, and this time the words came naturally – not the long, clever words she had thought were necessary, but simple, easy words that came straight from her heart.

Bring Robby back to us, she begged. *Please bring Robby back to us. And Danny too, and Jan and all the other men that we love here at home, whoever they are. Bring them back safe, please.*

That was all she wanted. There was nothing else to say.

'I know I've never bin much of a churchgoer,' Effie said to her daughters as they ate toast and margarine for their breakfast that morning, 'but I reckon we oughter go along to St Paul's and say a few prayers for your dad and our Joe, and all them other poor souls over in France.'

Dot nodded. Her face was pale and her eyes rimmed with red. 'I've been thinking about Benny all night. It's three weeks since I heard from him. I thought at first they were just having trouble getting the post through, but now – well, I dunno what to think.' She turned woebegone eyes from her mother to her sister and whispered, 'I keep thinking he might be dead.'

Effie touched her arm. 'I know, love. But we mustn't think like that. We got to keep hoping for the best. And you'd have heard if anything'd happened to him. Same as we'd have heard about our Joe.'

'No news is good news,' Carrie chimed in. 'That's what they say. You just got to keep looking on the bright side. They lets people know quick enough when anything happens.'

'But they wouldn't let *me* know, would they? It'd be his mum they'd send the telegram to.'

'Benny's mum'd send word round quick enough, you don't need to worry about that,' Effie told her. 'And you went round there on Friday, didn't you? She hadn't heard nothing then?'

'No, but—'

'Carrie's right, we just got to keep hoping,' Effie said briskly, hiding her own fears. 'Now, what about this church service? You two coming with me? Because we oughter be getting ready if we're going.'

They cleared away the breakfast things and put on their best clothes. Dot brushed her long dark hair into loose waves, like Vera Lynn's, and put on a blue frock that she'd made last summer, with white polka dots and short, puffed sleeves. She tied a strip of the same material round her favourite straw hat, and looked at herself in the mirror.

'You are lucky, being able to wear puffed sleeves,' Carrie grumbled, leaning past her to put on her lipstick. 'They make me look like a builder.'

'Go on, you're not that big.' Dot looked at her sister's reflection. Carrie was wearing a green and white striped blouse and dark green skirt, with a broad-brimmed hat perched on top of her smooth brown hair. 'I think you look really smart.'

'Well, you got to make an effort for church. Especially St Paul's.' They turned as Effie came down the stairs in the navy-blue suit, the one she always wore, and adjusted her white pillbox. 'Mum, you look as smart as the Queen of England.'

'Go on with you. I haven't got her furs, for a start.' Effie checked her white handbag to make sure she had sixpence for the collection, and opened the front door. 'Still, I don't reckon we'll let the side down. Come on, you two, stop admiring yourselves. We'll have to put our best feet forward if we wants a decent seat.'

They marched off through the streets, passing the Mansion House and coming through the churchyard. The Cathedral rose from the clutter of mean, narrow streets like a monument to beauty, the dome floating like a serene white globe against the blue sky. They paused for a moment, gazing up at it, then hurried to join the crowds flocking through the doors.

'Blimey, we oughter come an hour ago,' Effie muttered as they crammed themselves into the back of the huge, crowded nave and were almost blown out of their seats by the swelling notes of the organ rising into the enormous dome. 'There must be hundreds here.'

The prayers came easily to her lips, familiar from the days when she had been sent regularly to Sunday School and church as a young girl. She'd done the same with Dot and Carrie, and with Joe too, when they'd been little. She thought it gave kiddies a good grounding in what was right and wrong. And she was glad she'd done it now. There was a definite comfort in being here, with all these people, all praying and singing and hoping for the same thing.

They finished with a hymn that everyone knew and loved, the one which was most appropriate of all on this day: 'Eternal Father, Strong to Save'. As the entire congregation, led by the choir, almost lifted the roof with their singing, Effie felt the tears come to her eyes and stream down her cheeks.

> *'Oh hear us, when we cry to Thee,*
> *For those in peril on the sea.'*

Her Olly was in peril on the sea, and Joe and Benny were in peril over in France. And so were thousands and thousands of other men – husbands, sons, brothers, friends. Could a few hymns and prayers do anything to save them?

When the service was over and the congregation poured out through the great doors and filled the streets again, the three of them turned their steps once again towards Blackfriars Bridge. The two fireboats had gone, but there was still a flock of boats coming steadily down the river. Effie and her daughters leaned on the parapet and watched.

'D'you reckon they're going too?' Dot asked at last. 'D'you reckon all them little boats are really going to France, to fetch Joe and Benny and the others home again?' She paused for a moment and then added, 'I don't know if all that praying and singing and stuff will do any good. I mean, they can't all come back, can they? Some of them are going to get killed.'

Effie was silent for a long moment. Then she put her arm around her daughter's shoulders and said, 'It's war, innit. Of course some of them are going to get killed. We got to face that, Dottie, love. But that don't stop us hoping – and praying. You pray for the ones you love, and you pray for all the others, and when you stop praying you just got to leave it to God.' She turned and looked down at the crowded river. 'You can't do nothing more than that. Just hope and pray, and leave it to God.'

In Emsworth too the churches had been filled, and afterwards the High Street and St Peter's Square were filled with people discussing the news, their faces grave and anxious.

'There've been any amount of ships going from Pompey,' someone said. 'Isle of Wight ferries, some of 'em – just the job for carrying troops.'

'Half of 'em were in service already,' someone else added. 'Turned into personnel carriers and minesweepers, things like that. Trust our Government not to be ready – we could have been building new ships all through the thirties. Given a lot of people jobs too, that would, instead of having that Depression.'

'How many d'you reckon they'll bring back, then? Mr Churchill reckons about twenty or thirty thousand, I heard, but there's a lot more than that over there. Nearly half a million, isn't it? That's a lot of young chaps to lose all at once – worse than the Somme, that'd be.'

'Don't you talk like that! That was before he knew about all them little ships going over. I bet we'll get back thousands more than that. Hundreds of thousands.'

Sheila, who had been to the Roman Catholic church, glanced sideways at her mother-in-law's face. She knew that, like her, Olivia was desperately worried about Charles, Toby and Paddy. At the same time, Sheila's own heart was also aching for her brother Alex. I know I'm being selfish, she thought miserably, but I don't want to lose him.

Even though they were non-identical twins, Sheila and Alex had always been very close. They had been separated, of course, when Alex was sent away to school, but had never lost that closeness, and it was Alex whom Charles had chosen to be his best man. When Alex had completed his medical training, he had come home to join his father's practice in Chichester, and the two families, already friends, had met often. Today, Sheila's parents were coming over to Curlews to lunch, and she wondered how they had reacted to the news of the BEF's predicament.

They arrived about half an hour after the family had got back to Curlews. 'We went to Mass,' Anne Rowley said, kissing Olivia's cheek. 'The church was absolutely full. Oh Sheila.' She embraced her daughter. 'You must be *so* worried about Charles.'

'And Alex, Mother. I'm worried about all of them.' They held each other for a moment or two, then Sheila went to her father. He was looking old, she thought. He'd retired a year ago but had to return to work as soon as Alex had enlisted. Now this fresh fear was bearing down on him, bringing a stoop to his shoulders and a frailty to his thin face. She studied him anxiously, hoping that he wasn't ill.

'You're not doing too much, Dad, are you?'

He shrugged. 'I'm doing what I have to do, just as everyone else is. The practice isn't too busy at present, thank goodness, but who knows what we'll have to deal with if they bomb us. Or invade.'

'Do you really think they will?' Fear clawed at her heart and she turned instinctively to reach for her children. Wendy was, as usual, deep in a story and the twins were clamouring round their grandmother, who never failed to bring them some small present. Today it was a small knitted toy each – a purple giraffe for Jonathan and a green elephant for Nicky. She smiled apologetically at her daughter.

'The wool was left over from a Fair Isle pullover I knitted for Alex just before war broke out. He only wore it once – I don't think he liked it much.'

'I'm not surprised,' Sheila said. 'He must have looked like a caterpillar.'

The others laughed, but their laughter was dangerously close to tears. There was a moment of silence and then John Rowley said, 'Let's talk about something else. It does no good to worry about it.'

Gradually, the conversation turned to other matters – the cut in the butter ration, the price of bread, the appeal for park railings and old bandstands for building ships. Hubert asked if John Rowley had listened to the new series of plays about 'The Saint' on the wireless and they went on to discuss other detective stories, of which they were both avid readers. Dr Rowley favoured Dorothy Sayers and her Lord Peter Wimsey, while Hubert preferred Agatha Christie, but both agreed that there had never been anyone to touch Conan Doyle.

'Holmes is the finest detective ever created,' Dr Rowley declared, 'though he doesn't give Watson enough credit, to my mind. Treats the man like a buffoon. He's a practising doctor, for heaven's sake!'

'That's Doyle's joke, though, isn't it,' Hubert said. 'He was a doctor himself, after all. I think if you read the stories really carefully you'll find that Holmes knew very well that he couldn't get along without him.'

And I can't get along without Charles, Sheila thought, holding Nicky close against her. She glanced at her mother and her mother-in-law, knowing that they were feeling the same. You had to pretend to be cheerful, if only for the sake of the children, but nothing could take the cold fear from your heart. Nothing could really help you to forget what was happening now, this very minute, over there in France.

PART TWO

Chapter Seventeen

When the order to retreat came, it found Sheila's brother Alex Rowley in a dilemma.

Until then, Alex's war had been surprisingly comfortable. Working as a doctor in his father's practice in Chichester, he had been one of the first to be called up into the Royal Army Medical Corps, given the rank of Captain and then drafted to the 7th Battalion of the Duke of Cornwall's Light Infantry.

'Cornwall?' he queried. 'But I live in Sussex. Shouldn't I be—?'

'Doesn't matter where you live, Rowley. You go wherever you're needed. The Cornwall's is an excellent regiment with a fine record. Served with distinction in the Great War and will no doubt honour themselves just as much in this one. Now, you'll go to Aldershot first for basic weapon-training and then to Oxney Park for Company training, and possibly on to Basingstoke. The rest of the battalion is currently in Kent so unless they've moved on by the time you finish, that's where you'll join them. Is all that clear? Any questions?'

'No, sir.' Alex left the office with his head reeling. Weapon-training? Company training? But I'm a *doctor*, he thought. I'm not going to fight.

All soldiers, however, had to learn to fight, or at least to defend themselves, and Alex found his boyhood rabbit-shooting expeditions on the South Downs useful when it came to the first part of his training. He quickly learned to handle his revolver, was indoctrinated into Army hierarchy, ranks and discipline, and realised that it was essential. You couldn't be a civilian doctor in the Army; you had to be a soldier as well, or you would simply be lost.

Most of the orderlies were also bandsmen and musicians, not expected to fight unless it became inevitable, but to perform essential nursing tasks. After his basic training, it was Alex's job to set up his travelling field hospital. The orderlies, some of them experienced soldiers, some as raw as himself, slowly became a team and Alex felt his confidence growing. He was almost looking forward to going to war.

The battalion left England in October, 1939 and by November, Alex was on the border of France and Belgium, billeted with the local doctor and working in a casualty clearing station some miles from the main camp.

'You'll notice quite a lot of difference in your patients from those you're accustomed to,' Major Breakspear had told him when Alex first arrived. 'For a start, they're not generally ill. They're fit young men with injuries such as gunshot wounds, shell splinters, burns and that kind of thing, some of them even self-inflicted. Men who want to get out of the Army tend to go for their feet, in the main – blow off a toe or two, that sort of thing – so look out for that. They've been patched up by the First Aid crew by the time we get 'em. We get a few shell-shock cases too, especially after an engagement with the enemy.' He paused. 'They used to punish 'em for that in the Great War but we're a bit more civilised now, thank God.'

The 7th Cornwalls were positioned near the Belgian border. When Alex had first arrived, the Germans were well to the east, but now they seemed to be advancing a little nearer each day. The battalion had been involved in a number of skirmishes and there were rumours that the German artillery, especially the great Panzer tanks, might prove too much for the BEF.

The Major was inclined to treat this phlegmatically. 'You'll always get these minor setbacks. Can't win every battle. The main thing is to win the *war*.'

Alex found himself enjoying the Army more than he had expected; he was surprised and pleased by the feeling of 'family' he found within the battalion. That was one of the good things about the Army, the Major told him.

'It's not like the Navy, y'see. A sailor can be drafted to half a dozen different ships in as many years, but once a soldier's in a regiment, he stays there – unless he's promoted out of it, of course. We had one Colonel who refused promotion three times because it meant he'd have to move on. Had to take it in the end, of course, but he was nearly in tears the day he said goodbye to us.' He leaned forward, knocking his pipe on the camp table. 'You see, if the men know each other and care about each other, they'll work together all the better in a tight corner. In the Navy, it all depends on discipline – the whole ship can go down if one fool refuses to obey an order. But soldiers have to fight on their own initiative. Got to obey orders, of course – no question about that – but when you're in the thick of a battle there might not be any orders given. Got to do your duty first of all, then look out for your mates. You all depend on each other, d'you see. That's where the regimental feeling comes in.'

Not that there were many battles to be in the thick of, just then. Now and then, a flurry of casualties came through as the battalion fought off another enemy attack, but in between bursts of activity Alex found himself with time on his hands. He enjoyed exploring the Ardennes, with its steep, thickly wooded valleys and, as he spoke good French, making friends with the local people. He was given a special welcome by the village doctor, with whom he was billeted.

'You must join us for *le déjeuner*,' Jean Pasteur told him when he first arrived. 'My wife has relatives in England – her aunt married an Englishman from London. She is very old now, of course, but there are cousins. They came to stay with us once, a few years ago, and we were to visit them one day, but with things as they are now . . .' He shook his head.

Madame Pasteur welcomed him, and he sat down to a hearty French meal of thick pea soup, calves' livers and apple tart. Sitting opposite him at the table was the Pasteurs' daughter, Ginette, and every time he looked up he caught her eyes on him, a brief glimmer of dark brown before they slid shyly away. She was about twenty-one or two, he guessed, of medium height and as slim as a boy. Her soft brown hair was worn loose and fell in gentle waves to her shoulders; her mouth was full and although her smile was shy, it was also warm.

'Are people here anxious about the war?' he asked the doctor. 'You must feel it is very close.'

'Oh, we shall be all right here. The Ardennes is impossible country for military action – the forest is too dense, and the terrain bad for tanks. The Germans will never come this far, even if they get through Belgium. Besides, they're too busy with the occupation of Poland. And then I suspect they will turn their attention to Norway and Denmark. They intend to take over the whole of Scandinavia, you know. Of course, they will be defeated and then perhaps Hitler will see the error of his ways.'

Alex nodded. He had never taken much interest in politics and accepted the doctor's opinion, although it did seem odd that they should be setting up a casualty clearing station if no casualties were expected. Afterwards, he walked in the garden with Ginette and she said, 'Do you think my father is right, that the Germans won't come here? I am afraid that they are more powerful than he thinks. This Hitler – he has taken over so many countries. Why should he stop at France?'

'Because the other countries were too small to resist him, I suppose, and France is much bigger,' Alex said, hoping he was right. 'And you have us on your side now. Besides, your father knows the country around here. He's right, it's difficult for an army to move in such rugged terrain.' He stopped and looked down at the French girl. She was so slender, so fragile, as if she would break if held too tightly, and although there was nothing childlike about her he felt a sudden desire to protect her. As he gazed down, she lifted her face and met his eyes. There was a moment of stillness and then she smiled and took his hand, leading him on along the path. In a few moments they were back at the house and Alex thanked his hosts and went upstairs to the bedroom they had given him, his heart and mind in turmoil.

After that, he took his evening meal at the doctor's house as often as he could escape the mess dinner at the camp. The doctor was a *chasseur* and often brought home game – a brace of rabbits with which Madame and Ginette made tasty stew, or half a dozen pigeons. There was always cheese, and a bottle of red wine to wash it down, and afterwards they would sit and talk as Madame sewed, or play cards together. He went to church with them too, sitting beside Ginette in the narrow pew and kneeling beside her to receive the Body of Christ.

As the weeks passed, Alex began to feel more and more a part of the family. He also knew that he was falling in love with Ginette – had probably fallen in love with her on that very first evening – and he was almost sure that she had fallen in love with him. It was a wrench to leave her to go back to England for a few days' leave at

Christmas, and several times he almost told his sister Sheila about her. But nothing had been said; it had been all sweet, shy glances and a touching of hands, and he was afraid that to bring something so fragile, so ethereal, into ordinary conversation might shatter it. At home in Chichester and Emsworth, it seemed as insubstantial as a dream.

When he returned to the village, however, and walked back into the doctor's house, he felt as if he had come home; and one look into Ginette's dark brown eyes told him that it was no dream.

'I've missed you, Alex,' she said simply, and held out her arms.

'Ginette . . .' he whispered, and put both his arms around her, feeling the softness of hers as she wound them around his neck; her slender, pliant body pressed against his, the small breasts firmer than he had expected. She smelled of lily of the valley and summer roses. He kissed her again, his senses swinging about him, sky, trees and grass wheeling in a circle on the edge of his consciousness, and then he caught her tightly against him, no longer afraid that she would break. His hands found the shape of her body, the narrowness of her waist, the curve of her breast, and the little hollow at the base of her throat.

At last he lifted his lips from hers. 'Ginette . . . Ginette, I love you. I've loved you since that first evening – the moment I saw you – every time I looked across the table. I've wanted to kiss you for so long . . .'

Still the battalion stayed where it was. January and February were bitterly cold. The ground was covered in snow which froze to a thick blanket of ice and lasted for weeks. The Germans had advanced very little; the war seemed to be concentrated in other areas. As spring came at last, Alex began to think that they would soon be moved.

'The 2nd Cornwalls are having some trouble near the Maginot Line,' Major Breakspear told a group of officers one day in March. 'It's bad country there – heavily wooded, and very hilly, and the platoons are spaced too far apart to support each other. There's a vast area of no-man's-land, crawling with German patrols. Our chaps have been setting ambushes for them, but it's impossible.' He sighed. 'Unfortunately, there was a raid a couple of nights ago and a whole platoon was lost. Fourteen men, and two Royal West Kent signallers.'

Alex stared at him, feeling suddenly cold. He had almost forgotten they were at war. For months now the various battalions deployed along the Belgian border and into the Maginot Line had been doing nothing much but guard their positions and carry out the hard but mundane toil of digging trenches, erecting pillboxes and setting out long stretches of barbed wire, that had been so much a part of warfare twenty years earlier. Apart from a few injuries resulting from this activity, and an occasional influx from further out, where men had stumbled upon a mine, he hadn't had much to do and most of his thoughts had been taken up with his growing love for Ginette. This news brought home to him the sickening reality. They were at war. Men were being killed, only a few miles away. The snow and ice of the bitter winter, which had made movement almost impossible, was thawing fast and the brief respite was over.

A few days later the Major told him that the 2nd Cornwalls were moving back to Wattrelos, the village where they had been billeted a few months earlier. Here, close to the Belgian border, they went back to their tasks of digging trenches and wiring. And then more news began to come through, from another area entirely.

'The situation in Norway is bad,' Alex said gravely to Ginette as they took their usual evening walk in the big, wooded garden. It was early April; the snow had gone and the sheltered banks were yellow and purple with primroses and violets, just as they must be at home. 'The Germans have gone in, as your father predicted they would. It means that we'll have to defend them.'

'But you won't be going?' She looked at him in sudden fear. 'They won't take you away, Alex?'

'I hope not, but who knows what will happen? We're committed to fighting Hitler. We'll have to go where the threat is greatest. But I don't think we'll leave France undefended.' They had both stopped and he held her hands in his. 'Would – would it matter very much to you if I went away, Ginette?'

'Of course it would!' Her hands were like tiny birds, the fingers fluttering in his palms. 'I would be distraught.'

'Would you really?' He hesitated, then said, 'It would break my heart to leave you now.'

The garden was very quiet. A branch rustled overhead and a bird trilled a brief snatch of song. A red squirrel scampered down the trunk of a tree, saw them and scurried back up again. Alex released one of his hands and lifted it to touch Ginette's cheek with his fingertips. She turned her face so that her lips met his palm, and he felt her butterfly kiss.

'Oh Alex,' she murmured. 'I don't want you to go away.'

Her words brought reality rushing in and he stepped back a little so that he could look down into her face. 'I'll have to, though,' he said sadly. 'Not yet, perhaps, but one day. Oh Ginette, how am I going to be able to leave you? In danger, too. If the Germans come . . .'

'But they won't come here. You heard what Papa said. The terrain is too difficult.'

Alex shook his head. 'Perhaps not through the Ardennes, but they'll try to come into France. You may not be able to stop them.'

'We are the French,' she said proudly. 'And besides, we have you British on our side. We can stand up to Herr Hitler and his thugs.'

'I hope so,' Alex said. 'I certainly hope so.'

The news continued to be bad. After only a fortnight, the British withdrew from Norway. It was more than a defeat – it was an admission that Hitler was too strong. And with that admission came the first real fears for the rest of Europe.

The day came when Alex went to the Pasteurs' house with the worst news yet.

'The Panzer battalions are advancing and the Ardennes forests aren't enough to keep them out. Those tanks are more powerful than anyone realised – they can travel over almost any terrain. You're in danger here. And I think the regiment will be moved very soon.' He stared at them helplessly. 'I won't be here to help you. None of us will.'

Madame Pasteur gave a small cry and raised one hand to her mouth, biting the back of it. The doctor crossed the room swiftly and put his arm round her while Ginette moved quickly to Alex's side. He gripped her hand and turned to the doctor and his wife. 'I think you should go away.'

'But where could we go?' The doctor gestured helplessly. 'Are you saying that France will fall? That we will give in to the Boches?'

'No, of course not. But there'll be fighting. Everyone will be caught up in it. One side or another – it hardly matters which – will come into the village. They'll take over your homes, use them as battle stations. They may be destroyed. If that happens, you'll have to leave anyway, and it'll be so much more dangerous then.' He glanced down into Ginette's white face. 'I want you to be safe,' he said. 'I want all of you to be safe, so that after the war I can come back and marry Ginette.'

There was a long silence. Ginette's hand was so tightly gripped in his that he was afraid he would snap her fingers, but when he tried to loosen his own she would not let him. Her nails dug into the heel of his thumb. He glanced swiftly at her for reassurance and saw by her face that she had already accepted his unconventional proposal. Together, they faced her parents.

'I'm sorry,' he said at last. 'I know I should have asked your permission first, but I had not intended to speak so soon.'

The doctor waved one hand. '*C'est rien*. My wife and I – we have seen how things are between you. We've talked about what we would say if you came to us. These are strange and difficult times, and such things must be dealt with in a different way.' He sighed and moved across to the window, staring out at the forest where, perhaps even now, the Germans were gathering beneath the trees. 'I will not say that we wouldn't rather our daughter married one of her own countrymen, but you are a good Roman Catholic, and that is more important. My wife's aunt, after all, married an Englishman and she never regretted it. And we have grown fond of you. We would trust you with her.' He turned back to face them. 'If Ginette wishes to accept your proposal and marry you after all this is over, then of course she has our blessing. I can only hope that we all live to see the day.'

Alex found that he had been holding his breath. He let it out slowly and turned to Madame Pasteur. She nodded, smiled and held out her arms, and Ginette jumped up and ran to them, then turned to her father. Alex followed, kissing Madame's upturned cheeks and then shaking his future father-in-law by the hand.

'There is only one thing,' Ginette said in a high, excited voice. She came to Alex's side again and twined her fingers about his. 'I don't want to wait until after the end of the war. I want to marry Alex now. I want to be his wife *before* he has to go away.'

Her parents stared at her in consternation. 'Now? My child, you can't be serious. A wedding? There is so much to do, so much to arrange. People to invite . . . It can't be done all in a moment.'

'Yes, it can! Papa has just said that things have to be done differently now. We don't need a big wedding, with lots of invitations and guests. All we need is ourselves and the priest.' Her face was alight. 'It can be done in a few days. We don't need smart invitations to tell our friends – you know how news travels in the village. Please, Papa – Maman – please say yes. Then, whatever happens to us, even if we have to leave here, I shall be Alex's wife. I shall be a married woman.'

'You may be a widow before the war is over,' her father pointed out. 'Have you thought of that?'

'Better a widow,' Ginette said in a low voice, 'than a spinster for the rest of my life.'

There was a brief silence. Monsieur Pasteur glanced at his wife and Alex held his breath. At last the doctor spoke again.

'Very well. We will arrange it as soon as possible.' There was a glint of humour in his eyes as he looked at Alex. 'I assume you have no objection? This is what you want as well?'

'Yes – oh yes,' Alex said hurriedly. He felt dazed, as if he'd been trundling along on a slow train which had suddenly turned into the record-breaking Royal Scot. Then the warmth of Ginette's excitement touched his heart and he drew in a deep, ragged breath of joy. 'It's everything I want, *monsieur*,' he said simply. 'Ginette is everything I want. I'll treasure her as my wife.'

'We are trusting you to take care of her, however difficult the times may become,' the doctor said gravely, and Alex nodded.

'I will. I'll take every care that I can. But she's still your daughter, and I am in the British Army. I may have to leave her in your care until it's possible to take her to England. And I have to speak to my commanding officer as well.'

'Of course. And now – a little brandy, I think, to celebrate. It is not every day that one's only daughter becomes engaged to be married.' The doctor moved towards the big cupboard where he kept his dwindling stock of drinks. He took out the bottle and four glasses, and Alex and Ginette squeezed each other's hands.

I'm going to be married, Alex thought in wonder. In a few days, I'll be a married man – a husband. He thought of his own family, who knew nothing even of Ginette, and wished he could let them know. But letters had been difficult lately, and there was no telephone line to England now – no way of sending any communication.

Never mind. He would let them know as soon as he could. And he would get Ginette to England at the first opportunity. His father and mother would look after her – she would be safer in Chichester than in France, if the Germans really did break through. And Sheila and Charles would welcome her as well. She would have two families, as well as her own half-English relatives, to call her own as soon as he put his ring on her finger.

'A ring!' he exclaimed, almost choking on his brandy. 'Where am I going to find a wedding-ring?'

Ginette laughed and lifted his left hand. On the little finger, he wore the signet ring that his father had given him for his twenty-first birthday. She slid it from his hand and fitted it on to her own.

'There!' she said, raising her hand so that the gold glowed in the lamplight. 'There is our wedding-ring, Alex. I'll give it back to you in a moment, but when the *père* asks for the ring, this is the one you shall give him. It's the one that will remind me most of you when we are apart.'

The doctor and his wife smiled, but Alex knew that their pleasure was touched by fear. No one knew how long this war would last or what might happen to them all before it was over. Ginette might, as her father had pointed out, very easily be a widow in as short a time as she had become a wife. All you could do was take what joy life gave to you, and hope that it wasn't snatched away again before you had time to relish it.

He turned and looked down into the small, glowing face, and knew that if love could win the war, the enemy would have no chance.

'*Married?*' Major Breakspear echoed. He lowered the glass of whisky he had been drinking and stared at Alex. 'Is this a joke?'

'No, sir.' It didn't come easily to Alex, at thirty years old, to have to ask permission to marry from a man he hadn't even known a few months earlier, but he knew very well now that he was under Army discipline. 'I'm absolutely serious. Ginette – Mademoiselle Pasteur – and I want to be married as soon as possible, and her parents are in favour as well. I've got to know them well during the past few months, and we know that if the battalion's moved soon we may not see each other for a long time. And anything could happen before that,' he added sombrely.

The Major frowned and stared at the table in front of him, tapping it with his fingers. They were in his own tent, part-office, part-living accommodation, and the evening meal had been over for half an hour. I ought to have seen this coming, he thought. The boy's scarcely ever in the mess during off-duty times. I knew he was seeing a lot of the doctor and his family. I should have realised it was the daughter who was the attraction. But – marriage? In these circumstances?

'You know the situation is extremely grave,' he said at last. 'The Germans are bombing the life out of Holland and they're going into Belgium. I'm not at all sure either the Dutch or the Belgians are going to be able to hold out against them – the Dutch are on the brink of surrender now. If we lose them, we'll be in considerable danger ourselves. We may have to leave the Ardennes – and we may have to leave very quickly. You won't be able to protect your wife if that happens.' He looked up at Alex. 'Do you realise how difficult that would be for you? From the Army's point of view, what a *distraction* it would be?'

'It will be just as difficult, and just as much a distraction, even if we aren't married, sir. And if we are, she'll be a British citizen, entitled to British protection. If the worst comes to the worst, she could go to Paris, to the British Embassy there; she could go to England, to my family. She'll be safe there.'

'There is that,' the Major allowed. He thought about it again. The young man was right – the thing had happened, and there was no going back. Marriage would, as he said, entitle Mademoiselle Pasteur to a degree of extra protection – provided the French held out against Hitler. And surely they would. Prime Minister Reynaud seemed determined to hang on, despite his heavy losses at Tirlemont. If he could just hold the Meuse . . .

And if he couldn't, and the Germans took Sedan? If Holland did indeed surrender? And the Belgians too? Major Breakspear rubbed his hand across his face. The situation would be of the utmost gravity. The BEF might even be forced to withdraw.

A wife caught in the thick of such peril was the last thing a young Army officer, ill-trained and a civilian at heart, needed at such a time. And yet, as young Rowley had pointed out, she would be no less of a distraction without a ring on her finger. And with that, and her marriage certificate, she would be entitled to Army protection.

He came to a decision.

'I'll talk to the Colonel about it,' he said, lifting his eyes to Alex's apprehensive face. 'But I think you may take it that you can visit the church with your fiancée. And I hope you will invite me to the wedding.'

Alex Rowley and Ginette Pasteur were married a few days later by the village priest. Major Breakspear and the Colonel were both present, together with some of the Pasteurs' closest friends. They went back to the doctor's home for a quiet meal and a glass of champagne, carefully put away when war broke out, to save for better times. Then the guests departed and Alex took his bride up to her bedroom, the bedroom he saw for the first time that night, to begin their married life.

In less than a week, it was disrupted.

'The Germans have broken through!' he told the Pasteurs, rushing in late for supper. 'They're heading this way. Our men have been doing their best to hold them, but they've suffered terrible losses – casualties are pouring in – I have to go back at once. You must get away quickly, as they're killing everyone who stands in their path. Go now! Take just the most essential things, but for God's sake, go!'

They stared at him, their eyes wide with fear. Ginette clutched at his jacket, then turned and ran back to her parents. She buried her face against her father's chest, then threw her arms around her mother. All three were talking at once, too fast for Alex to catch more than a word or two. Ginette waved her hands in the air, as if urging them away, but they shook their heads. She glanced swiftly at Alex, as if to ask his help, but he could not respond. There was a sudden silence and then Madame Pasteur began to cry.

'What is it? What were you saying?' Alex demanded as the doctor took his wife in his arms, murmuring words of comfort. 'Tell me, Ginette!'

'They won't go,' she said hopelessly. 'They won't leave the village. Papa says he must stay, he's the doctor and the people will need him, and Maman won't go without him. Oh Alex, what do you suppose the Germans will do?'

'I don't know. We don't know what's happening. There are rumours that the Allies are retreating from Belgium. There've been terrible French losses at Sedan. They say the Dutch are on the point of surrender – they may already have done so.' He gave her a hunted look. 'I don't know what to believe. One report says that all is well and we're beating back the enemy, and the next says that we are about to retreat. Someone said today that we may even be ordered to leave France.'

'*Leave France?*' she whispered. 'All of you?'

'It may be just a rumour,' he said miserably, and then caught her in his arms. 'Ginette, my darling, I have to go back. I told you, there are casualties. Their wounds are terrible – I'm needed there. Try to make your parents see sense. It's not safe for any of you here.'

'But where can we go?'

'I don't know,' he said again. 'The roads are crowded with refugees from other villages. They're making their way south. Go with them – go to Paris if you can, and ask for help there. And write to me as soon as you can. I'll come back for you, I promise I will. I'll come back for you the first moment I can.'

'No!' she screamed, winding her arms about his neck, digging her nails into his skin. 'No, you can't leave me – I won't let you! I'm your wife, I want to go with you. Take me to England with you. Please!'

'Sweetheart, I *can't*. You're needed here, to help your parents.' He unwound her arms and held her by the wrists, gazing down into her face. 'If only I could take you with me, but we're a fighting battalion. There's no place for wives. And your parents need you.'

She dropped her arms by her side and he slowly loosened his hold on her wrists. They stood gazing at each other for a long moment, then she slipped her arms about his neck again and lifted herself on tiptoe, raising her face to his.

'One kiss,' she said in a husky voice. 'One kiss, *mon chéri*, and then you must go. But – don't let this be goodbye. Come back again before you leave the village. Come to me again tomorrow, or the day after. I'll still be here.'

'I hope you won't,' he whispered, though it broke his heart to say it. 'I hope by then you and your mother and father will be far away, somewhere safer than this – for a while, anyway. But I will come, my darling. I'll come once more, before we go.'

He laid his lips on hers and they clung together, each endeavouring to put into the kiss all the love that was in their heart. At last it ended, as softly and sweetly as the first kiss of all, and she laid her head against his breast for a few seconds before stepping back.

'*Au revoir*,' she said quietly. '*Au revoir, mon chéri*. Come back to me soon. My heart will always be yours.'

Alex touched her cheek with his fingertips. He went to his parents-in-law; he gave Madame a kiss and shook Monsieur's hand. Then he took just a few steps and was through the door and gone.

Ginette stood for several minutes without moving, staring at the door as if willing it to open again and re-admit him. But it remained closed and, moving stiffly, she went to the table, pulled out a chair and sat down. She folded her arms on the table, buried her face against them, and began silently to cry.

Her mother and father went to her, one on each side, and laid their arms across her shoulders. They did not speak. They simply stood there, immobile; as if posed by a photographer for a bizarre studio portrait; as if waiting for the Germans to come.

Chapter Eighteen

A ll Jan Endacott knew was that they were withdrawing from their position.

He didn't even know where they were, save that it was somewhere in France, close to the Belgian border. The 7th Cornwalls, fighting to hold back the enemy advance, had been outflanked when the Germans broke through on their eastern flank. The battle that had ensued was the fiercest and bloodiest Jan had experienced so far, and he was surprised to find himself still alive at the end of it. By then, they had lost almost all their ammunition and transport and it was a dishevelled, ragged troop that shambled back to relative safety, only to be told to move on again and make for Armentières.

Some of the tougher soldiers raised a faint cheer at that and began to sing about the famous Mademoiselle, but their chorus was only half-hearted and soon faded into silence. The Germans were on all sides, sniping at them from woods and fields as they tramped along, and shelling them on roads that they had thought were a safe distance from the front line, and they all knew there was nothing funny about their situation.

'Front line!' Sam Trotter said with a bitter laugh as he and Jan emerged from yet another ditch, not even bothering by now to brush away the dead leaves and muck clinging to their uniforms. 'There ain't no bloody front line no more, chum. We might as well give up now, if you ask me. It's only a matter of time anyway.'

Jan trudged beside him, thinking about his parents and how they'd begged him not to go. 'You'll have to kill people,' his mother had said, tears in her eyes as she clung to him. 'You've never been one for killing, not even hens or rabbits. Don't rush off straight away, son. Wait and see what happens – it might all come to nothing yet.'

But Jan had had to go. He hadn't wanted to join the Navy, like his younger brother Robby, but he'd enjoyed being a Boy Scout, and the Territorial Army had been a natural progression. He liked the weekly training and the fortnight once a year under canvas, pretending to be soldiers and getting paid for it. He'd known, of course, that if war ever broke out he would be committed to the Regular Army, but he hadn't ever thought it would happen. When it did, it was as if he was caught up in a machine and he couldn't get free even if he wanted to.

Now, he didn't know whether he was marching towards death or prison camp. Either way, it seemed that his companion was right – there was no other route out of this mess. All they could do was go where they were directed, and take whatever came.

For a little while, it seemed as if the enemy had disappeared. The sniping and shelling stopped and they were able to pause and take stock. A number of men had been killed and left where they fell; others had been wounded and their friends were doing their best to help them along. Some, with injured limbs hastily bandaged, were supported by their friends, the rest were carried on rough stretchers. One man, his eye smashed and his head streaming with blood, was raving with pain; another died as they stood there. All these men would normally have been sent back to the casualty clearing station or a field hospital, but the Captain said that they would be withdrawing as well. 'We'll just have to do the best we can for the poor chaps.'

Most of the group were cooks, clerks and mechanics like Jan, who might have been trained to fight but had never seriously expected to do so. The officers in charge were young and inexperienced, and seemed totally bemused. It was obvious that nobody knew what to do next.

'What a bloody shambles,' Sam muttered. 'Look at 'em – supposed to be officers and don't know their arse from their ear'ole. Still wet behind the ears – be crying for their mummies next.'

The sound of a motorcycle engine made them all dive for the ditches again, dragging the wounded with them. The man with the damaged head screamed and fought, but was pulled roughly down;

the others endured as stoically as they could. Then there was a collective sigh of relief and they all scrambled out again.

'It's one of ours! A flipping despatch rider – now perhaps we'll get some decent orders.' Sam gripped Jan's elbow as they gathered round the motorcyclist. He pushed back his goggles and stared at them.

'Where the hell are you lot going?'

'Armentières, mate. We're going to see Ma'mselle,' one of the privates said, and the others raised a feeble laugh. The motorcyclist shook his head.

'Forget it, chums. You're making for Dunkirk. The Jerries have got us surrounded. We're being evacuated – they're sending all the ships the Navy can muster. It's every man for himself – and that's an order.' He thrust his foot down hard on the kickstart, but Jan stepped forward and laid his hand on the handlebars.

'Hang on a minute. Where's Dunkirk? What do us have to do when us gets there?'

The despatch rider looked at him and then pulled his goggles down again over his eyes. 'You'll find out, mate. And it's on the coast, about twenty-five miles north of Calais. Just make for the black smoke – you'll see it soon enough. Now get your hands off my bike. I've got to round up all the troops I can find and then get there myself, and I ain't got time to stand round chewing the fat with you lot.' He thrust aside Jan, who had leaped forward to prevent him, twisted the handgrip and roared away up the road. Jan picked himself up from the road and the soldiers looked at each other in consternation.

'Us oughter've told him there's Jerries back there,' Jan said.

Sam shrugged. 'Well, you tried, didn't you? Silly fool never give us a chance. Anyway, they've probably moved on by now.' They heard the distant sound of a shell exploding and looked at each other again. 'It might not have been him,' Sam said uneasily. 'And there ain't anything we can do about it now. Where's this place he says we've got to go to?'

'Dunkirk,' one of the young officers said. He drew a tattered sheet of paper from his pocket. 'This is a map they put in the *Daily Telegraph* a couple of weeks ago – my uncle sent it to me. He was in the Great War, thought it might come in handy.' He spread it out against the back of one of the men. 'Look, this is where we are, roughly, and there's Dunkirk. If we keep on in this direction, we ought to be able to find it. There are bound to be signposts.'

They set off again, straggling along the road and hardly bothering to march now. Sam and Jan took one of the wounded between them, winding his arms about their necks and supporting him so that his injured legs were kept as much as possible off the ground. They looked at each other over his drooping head. Every man for himself, the despatch rider had said, but you couldn't leave your mate lying helpless in the road with the enemy on its way.

'Maps out of the newspaper!' Sam said in disgust. 'Signposts!'

Jan said nothing. He tried to remember how he had come to be here, tried to make some kind of sense of the past few months since he had left Devon. He was beginning to wonder if he had ever really lived that life at all; if Devon, his family and his sweetheart Susie really existed. Perhaps he had only imagined them. Perhaps this endless trudge, this miserable fear, this squalid hiding in ditches, was all he had really ever known.

Like his younger brother Robby, Jan had spent his boyhood roaming the fields and woods along the banks of the Dart and learning the ways of the river. He hadn't shone brightly at school but by the time he was fourteen there was little he didn't know about the countryside and, being a handy sort of boy, he'd got himself apprenticed easily enough to the local blacksmith. He'd spent his days contentedly shoeing horses and working with wrought iron, and had been making a pair of decorative gates for one of the big houses when war had been declared; he had hoped to get more jobs like that, maybe even make a bit of a name for himself. One day soon, he'd thought, he and Susie might get wed. Now, it all seemed like another world. A dream. And *this* world had turned into a nightmare.

Tired, wet, dirty and hungry, he trudged along the road with his mates. All that mattered now was putting one foot in front of the other. All that mattered, in this nightmare world, was getting to this place called Dunkirk.

In another group of the 7th Cornwalls, separated from Jan Endacott's after the battle that had finally driven them back, Joe Mears was driving a lorry. He had been driving it for days now, moving in convoy with a string of other vehicles – lorries, tanks, field guns and armoured cars. Packed in the back of the lorries were infantrymen and artillery. Nobody knew where they were going or why. They knew only that they were at war and must follow orders.

They drove mostly at night, each following a faint, glimmering patch of light beneath the lorry in front. Joe had painted his own rear axle white and fixed a lamp above it so that the man behind could follow him. It was all the light they had. The noise of their engines, drowned as it was by distant gunfire and shelling was less important.

By day, the convoy sheltered in whatever cover they could find – woods, barns, villages. Along the road and lanes they could see long lines of people – refugees, fleeing from the German invaders. They seemed to have no idea where they were going, except that they wanted to get away. Joe, lying in a wood on a bank above the road, watched them in horror. Old women, hobbling along carrying a basket in each hand as if they'd just been shopping, younger women pushing prams heaped high with possessions, old men with bicycles and wheelbarrows, all festooned with an assortment of bags and cases. Children, stumbling and crying with fatigue. None of them knowing what lay before them.

Behind them, the Germans were coming ever closer, with their Panzer tanks, half-tracks, lorries, and a massive force of artillery – some guns still hauled by horses. Overhead, German aircraft buzzed and zoomed, so that travel in daylight became a mission of suicide. And rest for the troops was intermittent and short; while making their way back towards the coast, they must hold back the German advance for as long as possible. Every day they must stop and turn on the enemy that followed and harassed them, holding them off just long enough to get some sleep.

As yet another dawn lightened the darkness, Joe found himself in a small hamlet of grey stone houses and narrow alleyways. The lorries were driven into clearings in the surrounding woods and the men stumbled wearily into the village, hoping to find water and provisions.

The place was deserted. Its people had fled, were almost certainly some of the refugees he had watched pass by the day before. The cottages, little more than hovels, had mostly been emptied. There were a few sticks of furniture, a pan or two dropped in the haste to get away, an old mattress pushed into a corner. It had been a poor enough place to live, Joe thought as he stood in someone's kitchen and stared around him but, meagre as it was, it had been their home and they couldn't have wanted to leave it.

There was no food left behind. The men scraped together what remained of their rations and the Lieutenant ordered Joe to take his lorry and get provisions from the nearest town.

'As far as I can make out, we're just about here,' he said, unfolding the tattered map that had been their guide. 'There ought to be some shops about five miles away. Maybe ten. Get whatever you can. Pay whatever you must.'

Joe started his lorry again and set out. He'd been hoping for some sleep, but he could see that the unit wouldn't go far on the paltry amount of stores they had left. An army marches on its stomach, wasn't that what they said? You couldn't march many miles if your stomach was empty.

The Lieutenant was right. The nearest town was about seven miles away and when Joe drove cautiously through the streets he was relieved to find that life appeared to be going on here more or less normally. True, there weren't many people about and those that were watched him with suspicion, but the shopkeepers supplied him with a few provisions – enough to keep them going for a day or two, he reckoned – and before long he was back on the road, heading for the deserted village.

Deserted was the right word. Once again, there was nobody about. Joe stared around him, wondering if he'd missed the route and come to the wrong place. But no – there was the little church on the square, and there was the well and the pump where they'd drawn water. He found the clearing, too, where they'd hidden their vehicles. But there were no vehicles there now. The unit had gone.

Joe searched through several of the houses in the hope of finding someone, but they were as empty as they had been when the unit first arrived. At last he dropped into an old wooden chair with a broken back and closed his eyes. The only reason he could think of for their sudden disappearance was the imminent arrival of the enemy. He could leave again and try to find his unit, although he had no idea which direction to take, or he could stay here and, if it came to it, fight. He had a lorry full of provisions, food and water that his mates needed; it was his duty to try to find them, yet if there were Germans about and he took his lorry out on the road now, in broad daylight, he would be an easy target. And he was tired; tired to his bones.

A movement in the corner of the hovel caught his eye and he felt a prickle of apprehension. Slowly, he turned his head. A small dog was crouching there, watching him; a rough-haired terrier, white with a brown patch over one eye, its thin body trembling and fear in its dark brown eyes. For a moment they stared at each other, and then Joe held out his hand.

'Come on, boy. Come on. I won't hurt you.' He dredged up a word or two of the smattering of French he had learned. '*Ici. Viens ici.* Come on, feller.'

The dog crept forward on its belly and Joe reached a little further until it could sniff his fingers. Cautiously, he rubbed his hand over its head and the dog whimpered and crept closer until it was lying at his feet. Its body was warm under his hand, but its bones were too close to its skin.

Why, he thought, it's no more than a pup. Poor little blighter.

'Come on,' he said, getting to his feet. 'We'll get some grub out of the lorry and then we'll kip down for the night. We'll look for the others in the morning.'

The dog gobbled down a slab of tinned meat and then fell like a stone into a dead sleep. Joe, eating almost as much, clambered into the back of the lorry and lay down amongst his few stores with the dog beside him, feeling a kind of comfort in the warmth of its thin body.

He did not go to sleep immediately. His mind was too busy. From wondering where the rest of the unit had gone and what he should do to find them, his thoughts turned to his home and family, his father Olly and mother Effie, his sisters and his girl Connie, working at the hairdresser's. And from there, they wandered into a confused recollection of the months that had passed since he saw them last . . .

Joe had joined up the minute war was declared, setting off in high spirits, determined to save his country. He knew more about boats than he did about guns, and Olly had been bemused by his decision, asking why he hadn't gone into the Navy. But Joe had shrugged and laughed and said he saw enough of boats in his civilian life and here was a chance to do something different, a chance to take a few pot-shots at some Germans. He could have added that the Army recruiting office was the one he passed every day on his way to Tough's Boatyard and he'd just happened to make his decision as he was walking by, so turned right and went through the door without thinking any more about it.

Training, first at Maidstone Barracks and then at Axminster, had come as a shock. Joe considered himself hardy enough, and he'd been out on the *Surrey Queen* on plenty of shouts and learned to fight fires, but the Army wanted more of you than that. You had to run and jump and climb with a heavy uniform dragging you down, a ton weight on your back and a rifle slung over your shoulders. You had to learn to obey orders instantly, no questions asked, no arguments. You had to spend nights in wet ditches without complaint and cook your rations over a small fire without giving away your position. Most of all, you had to learn to kill.

'Forget he's a 'uman being,' the Sergeant bawled at the recruits when they hesitated. 'He's the enemy, and if you don't kill him first, he'll kill you. He's a bag of straw, that's all – like these strung up over here. So run at him and given him all you got with your bayonet, all right? And I want to hear you all yell – yell at the tops of your bloody voices while you're doing it, see?' He waited while they made their first run, pointing their bayonets and shouting, then bawled at them again in disgust. 'You sound more like a ruddy Sunday School choir on its annual bleedin' outing! *Yell*, I said – not sing bloody nursery rhymes!'

They had barely finished their training when they were sent to France. Joe just had time to dash home for a forty-eight-hour leave, to say goodbye to his mother and the family and to Connie, and then he was on the train for Dover, ready to go on board ship and be transported to France.

When he came home again at Christmas he'd felt like a different man. Home was different too – the rooms smaller and more cramped. Not that he was used to a palace, that was certain, but he'd been living in big huts or tents with a crowd of other men. He'd had to watch his tongue – his mother didn't like bad language in the home – and he'd been restless, unable to fit back comfortably into the family circle, aware of what was going on in France, unwilling to go back to it yet impatient to do so. By then, he'd seen people killed – some of them his friends – and he'd killed others. He'd run at the enemy with his bayonet outstretched, just as he'd been trained to do, yelling as the Sergeant had taught him, and felt the point drive into a human body – not a bag of straw at all but a human being, flesh and blood and muscle and bone. He'd seen the man's face change, watched the mouth open in a scream, seen him vomit dark gouts of blood. He'd withdrawn his bayonet and stared as the body fell in front of him, thrashing in its final agony, limbs twisting and writhing. I did that, he thought. I killed him.

Almost too swiftly to be recognised, a vision of his mother's face flashed through his mind. That poor bugger's got a mum somewhere, he thought. And a dad and maybe sisters and a girl as well. And someone's got to tell them what I've done. Someone's got to tell them I killed him.

He had been thankful to go back to his unit after Christmas and take ship for France once more. While the war was on, this was where he had to be, and once his leave was over he wanted nothing more than to get back at the enemy and kill, kill, kill until they were all gone and life could return to normal again.

Only we won't be normal, he thought as he lay beside the puppy and felt the bones sticking through its warm, pulsing skin. None of us'll ever be normal again. We'll have changed for ever.

Chapter Nineteen

The casualty clearing station was evacuating. They could do no more, the senior surgeon told Alex as they hastily packed up stretchers, camp beds, bandages and equipment. Most of the BEF were on their way to the coast by now anyway and there would be few coming here. The Germans were either killing them or taking them prisoner. And if the clearing station hung about much longer, that would be their fate too.

The wounded who had not already been sent on were loaded into the field ambulances, and the orderlies and stretcher-bearers climbed into the lorries that stood waiting. The camp had been dismantled, and there was a mood of urgency. A motorcycle despatch rider had come roaring into the field with the news that the Germans were in the next village, and if they didn't get away at once, they would be trapped.

'The next village?' Alex stared at them. 'But – which way are they going?' His heart sank as he realised that the Pasteurs' home lay directly in their path, and he turned swiftly to the Major. 'Sir – my wife! I'll have to go to her.'

'My God!' The Major stared at him in dismay. 'Your wife – I'd forgotten for the moment. Are they still there? Didn't you warn them they must leave?'

'I tried to persuade them,' Alex said. 'Her father's the village doctor though, and he refused to leave his patients. But if the Germans are coming here . . .'

'Yes, of course. You must go. She's a British citizen and is entitled to our protection. Her parents must leave as well. It's not safe for anyone round here now – the whole village will be on the move. Look, Rowley, take one of the trucks but for God's sake hurry, man. There's no time to lose.' A Subaltern rushed up with a question and he turned away. Alex raced over to the line of trucks waiting to go, and threw himself into the driver's seat. He heard a yell as he gunned the engine into life, but ignored it. The Major could explain or not, as he chose. Alex had room for nothing in his mind now but Ginette.

I should have *made* them leave before, he thought as he took a corner on two wheels. I should have stayed there until they promised to go. But he knew he couldn't have done any such thing. The Pasteurs were older and wiser than he, they knew their country and they were part of the village community. They would never have left just because he, a foreigner, said so.

He drove along the narrow lane, his heart thundering in his chest. Suppose he was too late. Suppose the Germans got there first. Suppose they were coming from two or even three directions, converging on the village. Suppose . . .

Oh Ginette, Ginette, he thought in anguish. I can't leave you now. I can't.

The last turning brought him into the village, directly opposite the high wall of the doctor's garden. The gate was closed and all looked just as normal. The village street was empty. It usually was at this time of day, with everyone enjoying their lengthy lunch-hour, but to Alex the quietness was sinister. Perhaps the Germans had been here already; perhaps the people had fled. Perhaps some of them were lying dead in their own homes.

He brought the truck to a screeching halt outside the house and tumbled out, pushing at the tall iron gate. To his relief, it gave under his touch and he thrust his way through, trying to restrain himself and go cautiously, but too anxious to take much care. If a German were here now, he thought, he could pick me off in no time, and what use would I be to Ginette then? But if a German were here now, he would have Ginette in his power and Alex knew that caution would be the last thing on his mind.

He drew his revolver, thankful that his brief training had included the use of firearms and that he'd spent quite a lot of time in his boyhood taking pot-shots at rabbits. At least he knew how to use the thing . . . As he stumbled up the path, he saw the front door begin to swing open. He stopped, already bringing the weapon up to take aim, and then felt his shoulders sag with thankfulness as he saw Ginette standing at the top of the steps.

'Alex! What are you doing here? I thought—'

'The Germans are coming,' he said breathlessly, pushing her into the hall. He slammed the door shut with one foot and took her in his arms. 'They're only a few miles away. Your parents – they must leave at once. There's no time for argument – everyone has to go. They're burning the houses, Ginette, and they don't care whether anyone's in them or not.'

'Oh no!' Her pupils widened and the colour drained from her face. 'Alex, it's not true!'

'It *is* true.' He heard a sound at the back of the house and looked up to see Madame Pasteur coming from the kitchen, her face a mask of fear. 'Madame, you must leave at once, you and your husband. There's terrible danger if you stay.' He met her eyes and saw that she understood. 'Get away from here, get away as fast as you can.'

The doctor appeared behind her. 'What's this you're saying Alex? The Germans, coming here? But the Army – our soldiers and yours, the Belgians—'

'The Belgians have surrendered. We're in retreat – we've been told to make for the coast. There'll be ships there to take us away. *Please*,' he begged them, 'collect as much as you can carry and leave as soon as possible. I'll help you, but I can't stay long. We're packing up the whole station. I've got to be back in half an hour.'

'You'll take Ginette with you,' the doctor interrupted in a firm voice, and both women turned to him in astonishment. 'You must. She's your wife. You can take her with you to England.'

'But Papa . . . ' Ginette turned from Alex to her father, and then back to Alex. 'Papa, I can't leave you!' Her face was torn with anguish. '*Maman* – I don't know what to do!'

'Go with your husband,' her mother told her. 'That's where your place is now. And you'll be safer in England. Go with him now, quickly, before they come.'

'But I can't!' Her voice rose in a wail. 'I can't leave you and Papa. Where will you go? How will I know what happens to you? How will you manage without me?'

A furious knocking on the door made them all jump. Alex caught Ginette against him and she buried her face in his battledress jacket, while the doctor went to open the door. The local Mayor stood outside, his face white and working.

'Jean, have you heard? The Germans are coming here – everyone is leaving. I'm sending Pierre round with the cart, he'll take what belongings you can pack quickly. Hurry, for God's sake – we haven't much time.' He rushed away before they could reply, and the doctor closed the door again and turned to face them.

'You heard what Georges said. There's not a moment to lose.' He laid his hand on his daughter's shoulder. 'Go with Alex, my dear. You'll be safer with him and with the British Army. Your mother and I will be all right. We'll go to your aunt in Marseilles – we'll be safe there, I'm sure. It will all be over before the Germans get that far. But we'll be much happier if we know you're in England.'

Ginette looked at him and then turned again to Alex. He looked down into her frightened eyes and spoke gravely. 'You must choose, sweetheart. I won't force you to come, but your father's right. You will be safer in England.'

'But that means leaving them to be in danger without me!'

'We won't be in any less danger *with* you,' her father pointed out. 'And your safety will be a constant worry for us. You're a beautiful young woman and the German soldiers . . .' He lifted his hands and shrugged his shoulders.

Madame Pasteur took her daughter in her arms. 'Go, my little sweet,' she whispered. 'Go with God. We'll see each other again before long, I know.'

'I must take some things with me. A few clothes – my photographs.' Tears streaming down her face, the girl tore herself away and ran up the stairs. Alex looked at her parents.

'You must pack too. You heard the Mayor – there really isn't any time to lose. Is there anything I can do?'

Madame stared at him, suddenly bewildered. 'Pack? But what shall we take? Must we leave everything behind? My piano,' she turned to her husband, 'your books and instruments? *C'est impossible!*'

'Pack whatever is most important to you,' Alex said, glancing anxiously up the staircase. 'But hurry, for God's sake.'

They vanished, and a few moments later Ginette came running down the stairs. She was wearing her best blue coat and a hat she kept for Sundays, and carrying a small leather suitcase. 'I've got my best clothes – the dress I was married in – and my photographs of Maman and Papa and Noisette – she was my kitten, she died last year – and my Bible. I can't get any more in. Will it do?'

She handed him the case and he stared at it, bemused. Her best clothes – her wedding-dress, a photograph of a cat who was now dead. 'You're dressed as if you're going to a party,' he said.

'Well, I'm not going to let those *Boches* see me looking like a dowd,' she flashed, and turned as her mother appeared at the kitchen door with a box full of pots and pans. 'Maman, let me help you with that. Whatever are you taking?'

'My cooking things, of course. A woman must have her own pots and pans. And my Limoges china that your grandmother left me.' She stood back as Alex pushed Ginette out of the way and lugged the heavy box out of the front door. 'I hope there's room in Pierre's cart.'

'I hope he has a strong horse,' Alex said, and saw with relief that the doctor was carrying only his own bag of instruments and medicines, and an overcoat over his arm. 'I think you ought to take some extra clothes as well. But not your best things,' he added, with another glance at Ginette's hat with the lacy veil that hung over her eyes. 'They may get spoiled.'

'They'll get spoiled if we leave them here,' Madame retorted, and hurried up the stairs. The sound of hooves and a rattling of wheels outside announced the arrival of Pierre and his cart. He jumped down and came in, a burly man with shaggy black hair, and carried the luggage out unaided, wedging it into a corner of the cart. The two women reappeared with another bulging suitcase. They stood at the door for a moment, half-bewildered, unable to believe that all this had happened so quickly, that they were about to abandon their home.

Madame burst into tears.

The doctor patted her arm. 'I know, my dear. I know.' He took the key from his pocket and locked the door, then turned to his daughter. 'Go with God, *ma chérie*. We'll be together again soon, I know. Write to us at your aunt's – we'll get a train and be there by evening. Everything will be all right.'

She clung to them both, weeping, until Alex took her by the arm and led her to the truck. He lifted her into the passenger seat and scrambled into his own.

All along the village street, they could see people hurrying out of their homes. They carried bags and cases; some of them pushed carts or babies' prams. Some were trying to balance cages of squawking hens or hutches of crouching rabbits on their other luggage; children clutched squirming cats, dogs ran alongside. One man was driving half a dozen cows who were more concerned with grazing in the gardens than escaping from Germans. There was even an old man, huddled in a nest of blankets, in a large wheelbarrow.

They closed their doors behind them and set off along the road, a dazed and frightened motley of old and young, and the doctor and his wife joined them, Madame riding in Pierre's cart, the doctor walking beside it. Alex and Ginette watched in sick dismay.

'I don't know how they'll manage without me,' Ginette said in a shaking voice. 'I feel so guilty, letting them go alone.'

'There are plenty of people to look after them,' Alex said gently. 'And your father's a doctor, after all. If anyone can manage, he will.' He touched her cheek. 'He's right, you know. You'd be in much greater danger if you stayed. For their sakes, you must come with me.'

She said nothing for a moment. Then she lifted her face and he was relieved to see the strength and spirit return to her eyes. 'Very well, then,' she said, raising her chin defiantly, 'let's go. Let's go to England now, if we must, and plan how we can come back and defeat these cowardly *Boches*. They may have driven us back this time, but it won't last. It's a small matter only – we'll win eventually. This is not the end of the war, not by a very long way!'

Alex smiled at her and started the engine. He turned the truck in the road and drove back to the clearing station. He was feeling extraordinarily and, he thought, unreasonably happy. As if, with Ginette at his side, he could accomplish anything.

When they reached the field where the clearing station had been, it was empty. Only a few patches of yellowing grass showed where the tents had been. The entire section had gone.

Alex caught up with them a few miles further on, but it was enough to prove to him, if proof were needed, just how serious the situation was. Nobody was waiting for anybody; if you lagged, you were left behind. It was as simple and as brutal as that, and Alex's heart chilled at the thought.

'We're useless mouths, you see,' Major Breakspear said, hopping into the truck to ride with them. 'That's what they call us. Nothing personal, mind – but in times like these it's the fighting men who've got to be fed and looked after. The rest of us are better out of the way.'

'But you look after the wounded,' Ginette said, turning to look at him.

He regarded her for a moment and Alex realised that to him she presented yet another logistical problem. Her marriage certificate made her a British citizen and entitled her to all the help the Army could give, but the situation made the presence of a woman a serious disadvantage. Another useless mouth, he thought bitterly, yet if he'd been asked to do anything differently he would have refused. To have left Ginette now, in the path of the Germans, would have been unthinkable.

'We have all the wounded we can cope with already,' the Major said. 'Our duty now is to get them to safety. Naturally, if any more come to us we'll do what we can for them, but the men following will have their own doctors and nursing orderlies. All that's different is that we can't provide field facilities any more.'

There were refugees on this road too – the now familiar straggling crowd of villagers trudging along, already weary and beginning to cast off the few possessions they had brought with them. The children were exhausted and crying, and a miasma of hopelessness seemed to hang over them like a cloud. They looked round fearfully as the convoy approached, then as they realised the vehicles were British their faces lit with hope and they ran into the road, holding out their hands and imploring for help. The first few vehicles stopped, but there was no room for passengers amongst the wounded and the medical equipment, and as the truck passed them Alex saw the hope dying from their eyes and despair take its place. He felt as if a black cloak of shame had settled over his whole body, and turned away, unable to face their reproach.

'We can't help everybody,' Major Breakspear said, more as if he were reassuring himself than Alex. 'We do our best, but it's an impossible task. Our duty is to get as many soldiers home as possible, and make them fit to fight again.'

'Yes,' Ginette said with sudden bitterness. 'What do a few babies and old men and women matter when there are soldiers to think about?'

There was a moment's silence. Alex glanced sideways at his wife and saw the pain tightening her face. He knew she was thinking of her parents and the villagers she had known and loved all her life, trailing away from their own homes. The Major folded his lips but when he spoke his voice was calm, as if he too understood.

'Of course they matter, my dear. They're what we're fighting this war for – for people to live their own lives in peace and liberty. If there were no soldiers, or if we had never come to France at all, do you think things would be any better today? Do you think Hitler wouldn't be marching over your country just the same?'

Ginette hesitated, then shrugged. 'No. He would be here. But you are in retreat! You're leaving us.'

'Only so that we can come back,' he said firmly. 'And make no mistake about it, Mrs Rowley – we *will* come back. And when we do, we'll send *him* into retreat.'

She looked at him in sudden surprise. 'Mrs Rowley! Do you know, you are the first person to call me that!' Her smile broke out for the first time since Alex had seen her appear at the front door over an hour earlier.

She turned back to Alex and smiled at him – a shy, self-conscious smile that touched his heart. With all that had happened, he thought, she can still be pleased to be called by her married name. By *my* name.

She put her hand on his arm and he took his from the wheel and covered her slender fingers for a moment. They drove in silence for a while, concentrating on the warmth that was flowing between them. And then they heard the roar of aircraft overhead and the three of them cried out and ducked.

A flight of German aeroplanes was casting shadows over the convoy, and the rattle of machine-guns began to crackle on the air.

Chapter Twenty

Every man for himself. That's what the motorcyclist had said. Jan had never really believed that it would come to this. The whole troop of them, the unit he had trained with and come to France with, were closer than brothers now; yet in this their most desperate moment they were separated. Order and discipline had gone by the board – they were to get back to the coast as best they could, each man thinking of his own safety. And it wasn't selfishness, the Lieutenant had told them as they stood dispiritedly round him in the road. It was their duty. They were fighting machines, owned by the King, and it was their duty to get back to England in order to fight again.

'Well, it might be every man for hisself,' Sam Trotter said, 'but that don't mean to say we can't stick together while we can. Way I see it, it's our duty to look out for each other too.

Some of the others nodded at this, but the officer shook his head. 'We're a moving target, staying in a large group. We've got to split up. It gives us all a better chance.'

'How about small groups?' Jan asked. 'Three or four. That won't do no harm. Sam and me – us don't want to leave old Bert here. Us can help un along, same as us've been doing.'

The officer looked doubtful, but balked at telling them to leave Bert behind. He shrugged and moved away and gradually the troop split up into knots of three or four, as Jan had suggested, and melted into the trees. Jan and Sam looked at each other and then hooked Bert's arms around their necks again.

'Bloody fine mess this is,' Sam grunted as they moved slowly along the grass verge. A line of poplars stretched ahead, narrowing to a point on the long, straight road. 'I reckon the others is well out of it.' The man with the smashed eye had lapsed into total delirium the day before and died during the night. Jan felt ashamed of his own feeling of relief when the ravings had finally dwindled to an anguished muttering and then stopped altogether. He tried to tell himself that it was the relief you felt when you put a sick animal out of its misery, but he knew that it was partly thankfulness at not having to listen to it any more. At last he could get to sleep . . . Was this what war did to you? he wondered. Made you so callous that all you cared about was getting some sleep, and if it meant someone had to die to give you the peace and quiet you craved, so be it?

'You two better leave me and go on by yourselves,' Bert said suddenly in a rasping voice. 'You heard what Lefty said. Every bloke for hisself. I ain't never going to make it like this.'

'Don't be daft,' Sam said roughly. 'How can we leave you here? The first Jerry that comes along'll finish you off.'

'He'll finish us all off if you stops with me.' Bert paused for a fit of coughing and Jan saw specks of blood spatter the ground. 'Look, pals, you can see the state I'm in. Whass the use of me going on? I'm a goner anyway.' His face contorted with pain and his eyes slid from one to the other. 'You can finish me off yourselves if you like. Best thing all round.'

Jan felt horror crawl over his skin. 'That'd be murder!'

'It'd be a kindness. You wouldn't let a dog suffer like this. Go on, mate – one shot'd do it. I wouldn't know nothing about it.' Bert's weak voice grew pleading. 'What good am I going to be to the King if I do get back? I'm going to lose this leg anyway. First thing a doc's going to do is saw it off, even if I ain't got gangrene to start with. I'm not going to be no fighting machine no more. You'll only hold yourselves up and that'll be two more good men lost. Come on, now. One shot. That's all it needs.'

Jan and Sam looked at each other. In Sam's eyes, Jan recognised his own feelings. Bert's words made sense, or would have done had he been no more than a machine, or even a dog – but he was a human being. More than that, he was their mate. Their brother.

'Us needs all our bullets for Germans,' he said, and saw Sam nod. 'Look, there's a cottage up ahead. Maybe us can get shelter there for a few hours.'

They made their way to the cottage, set back from the road at the edge of a small copse. Jan knocked on the door, then pushed it open.

225

They peered inside, then went through the doorway and looked around.

'Hullo?' Jan called and then, remembering where he was, '*Bonjour?*' That was the limit of his French and he reverted to English. 'Hullo? Anyone at home?'

'Maybe they're hiding,' Sam said, and called in his turn: 'It's all right – we're English. *Anglais.* We won't hurt you, we just want shelter for the night and maybe a bite to eat, if you can spare it.'

They waited, but there was still no answer. Bert groaned and they lowered him carefully on to a settle.

The room they were standing in was evidently the main room of the house, kitchen and living room combined. There was an open fireplace used for cooking, and one or two battered pans on the floor close by. The dresser held a few cups and plates, but there were also wide spaces on its shelves, as if most of the crockery had been taken away. A bread crock stood open and empty, and the larder too was bare except for a few forgotten scraps. Two or three carrots had rolled into a dark corner and the rough wooden table was littered with bits and pieces of useless bric-à-brac.

Jan opened a door in the corner and went up the narrow stairs. The room above was the same size as the kitchen and held an iron bedstead and a rickety chest of drawers. Along one part of the floor was a bare patch, as if a mattress or pallet had lain there. A few garments lay scattered about: a torn shirt, a man's beret, a woman's shawl. Jan bent to pick up a roughly-carved toy aeroplane and felt a lump come into his throat.

He went downstairs again. 'Looks like they made a run for it. Took their bedding with them – everything they could carry. Had a kiddy too, I reckon.' He held up the wooden aeroplane, and Sam nodded.

'That means the Jerries have been here already – driving people out of their own homes. They're doing it to block the roads, stop us getting away.' His face darkened. '*Bloody* war. *Bloody* Germans . . . Well, there ain't much we can do about it now. At least we can doss down here for the night, give poor old Bert here a bit o' rest. Don't suppose you found any grub anywhere?'

Jan shook his head. 'Only those carrots. Might be something growing in the garden.' He went to the door again and looked out. 'There's a bit of a vegetable patch. And a well – at least us'll be able to draw some water. Maybe catch a rabbit, make some stew.' He thought wryly of his mother, anxious because he'd never liked killing animals. You wouldn't worry now, Mother, he thought. I'd kill a cow, if one happened to walk by – though not till I'd milked her first!

'Let's get some water, then. That'd be a start.' Sam showed his empty water-bottle. Jan still had a few inches left in his, but Bert's was almost all gone. They couldn't survive long without more fresh water. They made Bert as comfortable as possible on the settle, and went outside to the well. Jan lifted the lid and they stared down into the depths.

For a few minutes, neither of them could speak.

'Oh God,' Sam said at last, and Jan echoed him. 'Oh God. Oh, my bloody, fucking God . . .'

Every man for himself.

Joe Mears woke to find the puppy pressed close against his chest, its breath warm on his face. He opened his eyes and stared about him, puzzled for a moment. Since joining the Army he'd got used to waking in strange places, but he was also used to being in a tent or a hut with a lot of other men, all breathing and snoring and muttering. Now, he was alone except for this small dog, bony but warm, snuggled against him in the back of his lorry.

'Well,' Joe said, staring into the brown eyes, 'what d'you reckon we oughter do now, eh?' The dog blinked and Joe grinned a little. 'Don't understand English, do you, but I don't suppose you knows a lot of French either, so you might as well start learning now. What we going to call you, eh? Look a bit like a pirate, you do, with that patch over your eye, so I reckon we'll call you that. That's what you got to answer to from now on, see? Pirate.'

The dog wagged its tail and went to the back of the lorry, looking down. It had obviously never jumped so far before and Joe hopped down himself and then lifted the wriggling body in his hands and set it on the ground. It ran off for a few yards, then squatted.

'Ain't even old enough to lift your leg,' Joe said. 'What happened to your ma, eh? And the people what owned you?' Cautiously, his rifle in his hands, he peered out from the shelter of the trees at the nearest houses. The village looked as deserted as before, with only a few stray cats squabbling over some scraps in the road. Pirate saw them and gave an experimental growl, and Joe grabbed him.

'No, you don't. You're too young to chase cats. You stop with me and we'll find summat to eat and then think what to do next. I dunno where the rest of the blokes have gone. Shoving off like that.' He carried the puppy back to the lorry and dumped it in the back while he found some paté and a loaf of bread. 'S'pose we'll just have to try and follow them. We're in France now, from what the captain was saying, so I reckon they must've been making for Calais. Maybe we'll get reinforcements there. Anyhow, we're going to be needing some more fuel before we're very much older, so we better get moving.' He glanced around a little anxiously. After the harassment of the past few days, with the Germans constantly on their tails, everything seemed uncannily quiet; not so much peaceful as ominous. Anybody could be lurking in those trees, he thought uneasily and, with Pirate in his arms, climbed rather hastily into the cab.

He had gone only a few miles when he caught up with half a dozen other soldiers, tramping in the same direction. At the sound of his approach, they dived for the nearest ditch, but when he stopped and called out they emerged and he looked down at them. There was a sergeant and five privates, and he recognised the cap badges of the 18th Hampshires.

'Blimey, you look in a bit of a state. What's bin going on?'

'There's a war on, ain't you heard?' The sergeant took off his cap and rubbed his face with it. The men looked weary and dishevelled, their uniforms dirty and their chins rough with stubble. 'We've bin told to make for Dunkirk. Every man for himself. That where you're going too?'

'I dunno where I'm going,' Joe said. 'Lost my lot yesterday. I was hoping to catch up with 'em. Dunkirk? Where's that?'

The sergeant shrugged. 'On the coast somewhere. Make for the black smoke, that's what they said. We're going to be evacuated – sent back to Blighty.'

'What, all of us? There's bloody thousands . . .' Joe stared at them and rubbed his own chin. In his haste to get away from the deserted village, he hadn't shaved either. 'Well, you'd better climb aboard, mates. I dunno how far this Dunkirk is, but it's a bloody sight further than a Sunday-afternoon stroll down the park.' He looked at the sergeant. 'You come up front with me, the others can get in the back. There's some grub there too if you want it. Mind my dog,' he added as the man climbed in beside him. 'I only just got him – don't want him squashed to death.'

'What the hell you got a bleeding dog for? Ain't we got enough to worry about without setting up a bleeding pet-shop?'

'Got left behind in the village.' Joe let out the clutch and the lorry moved on. 'Come up to me like I was the last man on earth and licked me hand. Couldn't leave him behind for the Germans to play football with, could I?'

The sergeant gave Pirate a suspicious look and the puppy climbed on to his lap and reached up to snuffle his chin. The man creased his mouth and said, 'All right. You can stop there. Got a dog of me own at home.' He looked at Joe. 'How come you're on your tod?'

Joe explained and as they rolled along the road they exchanged experiences. The sergeant's platoon had been doing much the same as Joe's unit, fighting a rearguard action on their way back to Calais, when the order had come through to make for Dunkirk. By that time, they had lost over half their men. They'd managed to load the wounded into a couple of lorries and sent them on ahead while they did their best to defend the roads, but the flood of refugees had blocked the way and the lorries had been forced to take to the back lanes in an attempt to get round. They had disappeared and nobody knew where they were now.

'I dare say they'll have got through,' Joe said uncertainly.

The sergeant lifted his shoulders. 'Maybe.'

They drove in silence for a while. The roads were still empty, as if the refugees had found a better way. The sergeant sat with his rifle on his lap, somewhat impeded by the curled-up body of the puppy, keeping a sharp lookout to both sides. In the back, the men had eaten as much as they could and were watching the road behind. Some had fallen asleep.

Another village came into sight and Joe pulled off the road and stopped behind a barn. 'Better have a look before we go in. There might be Jerries.'

'I'll send someone in.' The sergeant leaned into the back and detailed a couple of the men to reconnoitre. 'The rest of you get out and hide in amongst them trees. We're a sitting target here. I'll take a look at that barn. Got a flashlight?'

Joe left Pirate still asleep in the cab and they circled round the big wooden building, their rifles at the ready. There were no sounds from within. The big main doors had a small man-sized entry set within them and, slowly and quietly, they pushed it open and peered into the darkness.

There was nothing there.

Joe stepped inside and switched on his torch, shining it into all the corners. The barn was completely empty. He didn't really know what it ought to have in it at this time of year anyway – it was May, so presumably too early for harvest – so perhaps it should be empty. Nevertheless, there was something uncanny about this cavernous depth without so much as a farm implement, a beast or a bale of hay to be seen. Surely farmers used their barns for *something* when they weren't full of hay?

'I don't like it,' the sergeant said. 'It don't seem right, somehow.'

'Just what I was thinking.' Joe flashed his light round again. 'You'd think there'd be summat here.'

'Well, there ain't. Still, I reckon we could kip down here for a while – drive the lorry in through them big doors, out of sight. The blokes are pretty well done in – bin walking most of the night. We're better off dossing down by day and moving on when it's dark.

Joe thought for a minute. He'd had a reasonable night's sleep himself so he didn't need rest, and he was still worried about his own unit. They'd gone on without him, but also without food. They'd be needing the provisions he'd got in the lorry. 'I think I oughter go on, see if I can find my mates,' he said. 'I'll come back in a few hours, pick you up again.'

The sergeant nodded. 'OK. I'll get the blokes in. Reckon we'll be safe enough here. Want to leave the tyke?'

They went back to the lorry where the puppy was still curled up asleep on the front seat. Joe shook his head. 'I'll keep him with me.' The two men looked at each other, aware that Joe might not be able to keep his promise to come back. He said, 'I'll leave you some grub, in case I'm gone a while.'

He drove the lorry into the barn so that they could unload some of the provisions he had bought. Joe wondered if the town was still carrying on as normal, or whether the invaders had reached them too and driven them from their homes. There was no going back for him, however. It was his job to go on, to find his unit if he could.

And if he couldn't? If what the sergeant had said was true, it was every man for himself. If he couldn't find his own unit, and he couldn't get back to this one, he'd just have to make for the place the sergeant had told him about.

Dunkirk.

The road was eerily quiet. Joe drove along between the poplar trees, glancing nervously to right and left across the wide, flat fields. He wasn't at all sure that this had been a good idea; the lorry could be seen for miles and anyone with half an eye would know it was British. But it was either that or stay skulking in the barn until nightfall, and if he did that he would never find the unit. And they needed the food he'd got in the back.

'I dunno, Pirate,' he said to the sleeping puppy. 'I dunno what I oughter done. I mean, it's all very well saying every man for himself, but I dunno that my blokes got that order, do I? And I can't leave 'em to starve. Seems to me I got no choice. I gotta go on till I catches up with 'em. But I don't like this quiet. It don't seem natural, not if the Jerries are really pushing us –'

His rambling monologue was interrupted sharply by an explosion somewhere behind him. The road seemed to buckle and rise into the air ahead of him and the lorry rocked. Almost simultaneously, he heard the scream of aircraft overhead and the rapid crackle of gunfire tore at his ears. The heat of a bullet skimmed along the side of his arm and he flinched sharply. The lorry swerved violently from one side of the road to the other as Joe fought to keep control, the wheel twisting under his hands. The puppy, yelping with terror, was trying desperately to scramble on to his lap, its claws scrabbling at his thighs. Overhead, the swift black shadow of an aircraft, like a huge menacing bat, swooped so low that he ducked in his seat; another trace of bullets ripped into the tarpaulin cover of the lorry and he heard a bang as one of the tyres was hit. The lorry lurched and swerved again, jerking and bucking like an uncontrollable horse, then tipped on to its nose in the ditch and fetched up against one of the poplar trees. The engine spluttered, coughed and died. The planes had gone.

Silence crept back, broken only by the whimpering of the puppy.

'Bloody hell!' Joe found himself crunched up against the door. Pirate was whimpering frantically down by his feet and there was a strong smell of petrol. 'Here – we better get out of this. Come on, chum.' He found the door handle and thanked God when it worked. All the same, opening the door, when the lorry was on its side and you had to lift the heavy panel bodily away from you, wasn't easy. He managed it after a moment or two and scrambled out, clutching the wriggling puppy against his chest, then dropped down to the ground.

'Cripes!' The drop was greater than he had expected, straight into the ditch, and although there was soft mud at the bottom he felt his ankle twist and slipped sideways to land half in the mud, half against the bank. He swore, slithered for a moment and then managed to steady himself. The world rocked a little around him and then settled. He leaned against the side of the ditch, panting.

The first thing was to get away from the lorry in case it was about to catch fire or blow up. He could hear aircraft again – coming back to see if there was anyone left alive, he guessed – and he kept his head below the grasses that grew along the edge of the road. He wouldn't put it past the Jerries to fire a few more rounds into the vehicle and strafe along the ditch, so the further he got from it, the better. He gave an anxious thought to his rifle, still leaning against the front seat. Go back for that later, when the coast was clear. Get some grub too, if the lorry wasn't a burned-out wreck by then.

The puppy had squirmed free of his arms but was too frightened to run away. It crouched in the mud at his feet, whimpering. The plane came over again and Joe ducked lower, looking up through the fringe of grasses to see the black crosses painted on the underside of its wing. An ME 110. For a brief moment of horror, he could see the pilot, staring down, and then a sputter of fire made him duck even lower. The man couldn't have seen him, not down here in the ditch camouflaged by his tin hat and mud-covered khaki uniform and with grass over his head, but for a split second he could have sworn their eyes met. Then the plane was gone, the sound of its engine snarling into the distance, and there was quiet once more.

Joe waited for a few minutes and then climbed cautiously out of the ditch. He stood for a moment or two, peering carefully up and down the road, across the fields and into the sky. There was nothing about, but he could see a column of smoke rising into the air a few miles back the way he had come. He stared at it and remembered the barn.

'The bastards,' he whispered.

Pirate was trying ineffectually to climb out of the ditch, crying piteously, and Joe looked down at him. For a moment, in a surge of helpless rage, he felt like smashing his boot against the little dog's face, crushing him into the mud in a mess of blood and bones; but no sooner had the thought entered his mind than he thrust it away and bent to pull the animal into his arms. Pirate licked his face and he bent his head and rested his cheek against the warm, hard little head, feeling tears hot in his eyes. What a mess, he thought. What a fucking mess.

There was no point in going back. The area was so flat that he could still see the barn, the only building for miles around. He could see the flames that enveloped it and the smoke that rose above; there was no chance that any of the other men had survived. And, quiet as it had seemed, the road was obviously under surveillance. It was up to him now to get out of sight and save himself. He still had to try to find his own unit and, failing that, to go to this place called Dunkirk.

The first thing was to get his rifle back. Joe's training had been brief and hurried, but it had been hammered into him that a soldier must never be parted from his rifle. He went back to the lorry, relieved that it showed no signs of catching fire, and walked all round it. With some difficulty, he clambered back into the cab and retrieved his pack, rifle and bandoleer of ammunition. Then he got into the back, gathered up as much food as he could carry and dropped back to the road, where Pirate was waiting with noisy anxiety.

'Shut up, you daft bugger,' Joe said, rubbing the dog's head. 'Now look, if you want to stop along of me, you got to walk. I know you're only a little chap but you've had a good breakfast and a kip, and I got some more of that paté stuff you like. We'll get down the road a bit, away from the lorry, and then have a bite to eat, but there's not going to be no fun and games, we ain't got time.'

Together, they trudged on along the road, Joe feeling uncomfortably exposed and listening for the approach of aircraft. In the distance, he could hear gunfire and explosions; plumes of smoke rose on the horizon. The Jerries were busy enough now, he thought bitterly. Must have been having a lay-in when it was so quiet earlier. He wondered if other battalions were managing to hold them off, if the sounds were those of combat or of the ravaging of villages such

233

as he had seen earlier on the retreat from Belgium. That 'every man for himself' order: could the BEF really be in full retreat? And if they were, how the hell would they ever get back to England? There were bloody thousands of them.

After about an hour's walking the pair came to a crossroads. There was a small wood on a knoll nearby and Joe made for its shelter, thinking that he would be relatively safe in stopping there for some food and a rest. He climbed up the bank and settled down amongst the trees, with Pirate huddled against him. They shared a tin of corned beef, being rather more careful now that the rations were limited, and Joe leaned back against a trunk and closed his eyes. Just a few minutes' kip, he thought. That's all I need.

He woke with a jump about an hour later, suddenly aware of the sound of feet tramping down the road. Instantly, he clamped his hand round Pirate's muzzle, and slid down to lie flat on the ground. Cautiously, he parted the undergrowth and looked down at the road.

Below him, coming along the other road, was a party of about twenty men. They were in British Amy uniform, but they were shambling rather than marching and his skin tingled as he saw that their hands were bound roughly behind them. Beside them were a dozen Germans, marching with fixed bayonets and using them to prod any man they apparently thought was lagging. The Germans looked as triumphant as the British looked downcast. But for Joe, the worst moment came when he recognised their shoulder flashes and realised that the faces of the soldiers were familiar.

They were Cornwalls. They were from his own unit.

Appalled, he reached for his rifle. It was loaded and he was taking a sight before he realised that all he could do was make matters worse. He might kill one German – maybe two if he was lucky – but the rest would be firing back at once, chasing up the hill into the little wood. He would be routed in no time, and all he would achieve would be to be taken prisoner along with the rest – if he wasn't killed. Worse still, the Germans might take it out on the others – even kill some or all of them.

He lowered the gun. They were too far ahead anyway, now. Joe's rifle skills were recently acquired and not very great; he'd passed his tests during training, but only just. I wasn't cut out to be a soldier, he thought miserably, watching his friends hobble away down the road. I oughter joined the Navy – at least I knows a bit about boats. I ain't never going to be a hero.

The road was empty again. He lay on the ground, feeling a dark cloud of guilt settle over him. He ought to have done something. He ought to have tried, at least. He ought to have killed at least one German before thinking of saving his own bloody skin.

Pirate pressed close against him, whining softly, and licked his wet cheeks. Joe put his arm around the dog and then buried his face in its warm body. He remembered the dog he'd had when he was a nipper – a terrier, not so very different from this one. Chum, they'd called it, and it had been his chum too, sleeping on his bed at night, following him everywhere. He'd just about broken his heart when the coalman's cart had run over it one day.

'Well, mate,' he said at last, 'it's just you and me now, I reckon. We'll stick together now, won't we. And I reckon we'd best do what those other poor sods were doing – lay up by day and get along best as we can by night.'

He sat up and looked around at the horizon. The sky, the pale tender blue of early summer, was spread over with dirty streaks of smoke from fires. And in the direction from which he had come, he could see something else. A long queue of people, some pushing handcarts, some carrying bags and suitcases, some more fortunate ones with a horse and cart or a laden donkey. As they came closer he saw that there were soldiers amongst them too – British, French and Belgian, all of them moving with the same hopeless, defeated gait.

Blimey, he thought. It's true then. The Jerries are beating us all back. We've had it. And they're all heading in the same direction. They're all going to Dunkirk.

Chapter Twenty-One

They were there in the well, the three bodies – the farmer, his wife and their young son, tangled together just as they'd been thrown in. It looked as if they'd been shot first, but neither Sam nor Jan wanted to examine them any further. They slammed back the lid and stared at each other, and then Jan stumbled off to a nearby bush and was violently sick. There was almost nothing in his stomach to bring up, but he heaved and retched just the same until at last he stopped. Shaking and covered with cold sweat, he made his way unsteadily back to where Sam was still standing.

'Bloody hell,' he whispered.

Sam nodded. His face had turned a pale greenish colour. 'The bastards. The fucking bastards.'

'Why?' Jan asked huskily. 'Why did they do that? A farmer – what harm could he do them? And that poor woman – and that kid, he only looked about seven. What's it all about, Sam?'

'Buggered if I know. But I'll tell you this –' Sam looked him in the eye '– we're right to be fighting this blasted war. Scum like that got to be stopped before they ruin the whole world. And that means we got to get back to England, so we can stop 'em doing this sort of thing to *our* families. So we can start again.' His face was grim, and for the first time Jan felt a real determination grip his mind. He still didn't fully understand what the war was about, but he was as certain as he'd ever been of anything that Sam was right. The Germans could not be allowed to get into England and treat his people as these poor devils had been treated. The evil that Hitler was spreading all over Europe had to be stopped.

'Let's go back inside and see to Bert,' he said. 'Us can't stop here, not without water. He can have what's left of ours and then we'll—'

He stopped suddenly as a shot rang out from inside the house. They looked at each other, fearfully at first and then with dawning knowledge. As one man, they turned and ran back indoors.

Bert lay sprawled on the floor where he had been thrown backwards by the recoil of his rifle when he had shot himself in the mouth. His eyes, still wide open, stared at them with an expression of surprise. There was very little left of the back of his head.

This time, Sam was sick as well.

Make for Dunkirk. Make for the black smoke. Follow the signposts. Never mind that they didn't have any names on them that you could recognise, follow them all the same. And never stop listening, never stop looking from side to side, never forget for one instant that there might be German snipers behind that wall, in those bushes, taking a sight through those smashed windows. More than anything else, never give in. You had to get there. You had to get back to England, because if you didn't – you and the thousands of other soldiers limping and trudging and marching along these country roads – the Germans would get into England and the whole of Britain would be finished. And that meant the whole of Europe. Crushed, under the iron heel.

The two men tramped on side by side, not speaking. There was nothing to say. They had both seen sights they had never thought to see, even in wartime. Trained to obey orders, they followed the last one they had been given, their minds too dulled to question any more. Dunkirk. The signposts. The black smoke . . .

Now and then, German planes flew over, but they didn't attack. They seemed to be taking an interest, swooping low as if to stare at or perhaps just frighten the two soldiers. 'Spotter planes,' Sam said in a dry voice, and Jan nodded. The water had been finished and his throat was burning. If only they could have got a drink from that well – but his mind shied away from the memory like a panicky horse.

It was growing dark when they caught up with a group of soldiers sitting by the roadside. They had heard the sound of their voices when they were about 100 yards away, and crept forward, afraid that they might be Germans. At last they drew near enough to hear the words, and Sam gave a laugh of relief.

'It's all right, mate. They're ours.' He strode forward more boldly and hailed them but the soldiers were equally nervous and leaped to their feet, their rifles ready to fire. Sam and Jan stopped and put up their hands.

'Blimey, don't shoot, mates. We're Tommies, same as you. Here, you can't spare a cup o' water, can you? We're parched.'

A corporal stepped forward and examined them closely. Sam gave him a grin and a wink, and Jan tried to do the same, but to his dismay the world suddenly began to wheel about him, the whole scene rocking in front of his eyes, then jerking back to where it had started from, only to rock again. He felt sick, sweaty and icy cold and, as the corporal's face seemed to pass him for the third time, his knees buckled and he crumpled to the ground.

When he came to, he was lying on the grassy bank and someone was holding a water-bottle to his lips. He sipped and then seized the bottle in both hands and sucked desperately. The owner protested and tried to take it back, but Jan wasn't open to reason at that point and gripped it fiercely. It was almost empty when the other man finally got it away from him.

'Well, ta very much, mate. I just 'opes you knows where we can get some more of that.' His words were indignant, but his eyes were friendly and Jan gave him a feeble grin.

'Sorry. Haven't had a sup all day. Found a well, but . . .' He turned his face away and closed his eyes again.

''Twasn't fit to drink,' Sam said from somewhere nearby. 'Jerry'd bin there first, see – chucked a lot of rubbish down.'

'So which mob you with, then?' the corporal asked, and when they told him he shook his head. 'Ain't seen none of them. You better tag along with us.'

Jan struggled to sit up. 'We were told to get ourselves to Dunkirk. Make for the black smoke.'

'Thass right. Thass what we're doing. We dunno which way it is really, but this is the road everyone else is going along so we reckoned it must be right. We got a couple of lorries hid away in the trees over there. Reckon we can squeeze you aboard as well.'

Jan felt a great surge of relief. With transport, they could surely get to Dunkirk in a couple of days. He wanted nothing more now than to be back in England, with English grass under his feet and English voices all around. He knew that any respite would be brief, but just to be out of this for a few days, even a few hours, would be enough to set him back on his feet, enough to help him forget the sight of that French family – if it was possible to forget. He didn't think he would ever be able to get the sight out of his mind – the woman's open eyes, staring at him from her ruined face, the boy's hand reaching up as if begging for help, the man crushed beneath them both, half under the surface of the dark red water . . .

And Bert too, sprawled across the kitchen floor, his rifle on the floor where it had fallen from his lifeless hands. Before they left, Jan and Sam had dragged the body outside and scraped a shallow grave in the trampled vegetable patch. It hadn't seemed right just to leave him there. Jan had left Bert's green dog-tag – the one that always stayed with the body – strung round his neck, but he'd got the brown one safe, along with a few bits and pieces they'd taken from his pockets – a couple of letters, his watch, a photograph of a young woman with a bright, smiling face and an older couple, the man looking very much like Bert. When he got back to England he'd find out where they lived and write to them, send them Bert's things, maybe even go to see them.

The soldiers were on their feet now, making their way back through the trees to where the lorries had been parked. The spotter planes seemed to have gone and everyone was cheering up as they scrambled back aboard. Sam climbed up into the first lorry and Jan found room in the second. The corporal got into the front seat with the driver and the two lorries pulled out of the trees and back to the road. They trundled off and Jan leaned back and closed his eyes.

'So where were you when all this started?' one of the other men asked, and Jan recounted his experiences as well as he could, still not mentioning the family down the well. He didn't think he'd ever be able to tell anyone about that. The others nodded.

'Bin much the same for us,' the first man said. 'Five days we bin going – no, I tell a lie, six it must be now. Tell you the truth, I dunno what today is. Tuesday? Friday? Middle of next week? Not that it matters. I ain't got no appointments.' He gave a short, dry laugh. 'Except with a ship to get me back to Blighty.'

'Started off with twenty vehicles, we did,' another man chipped in. 'Lorries like this, and motorbikes. I had a Triumph, smashing bike, brand new it was. We were over the other side of Ypres when we come up against the Jerries. Well, what with their tanks and machine-guns, and the flaming dive-bombing, we didn't stand a chance so we was told to get out of it. We didn't really know where to go but we pulled back and then some despatch rider come up and said we were to make for the coast. Dunkirk. Said there'd be ships there to get us off.'

'Easy as that!' the first man said sardonically. 'Just like going on a Sunday-school outing. Course, the Jerries knew where we was all the time. They'd come along every now and then and cut a few of us down with their bloody machine-guns and a bomb or two, just for the hell of it. We've lost men and vehicles every day. Now we're down to two trucks, and we've had to siphon fuel out of the others just to keep these on the road.' He chewed his lips and then added, 'What I'd like to know is, where are our boys? The RAF have got airfields in France, so why ain't they seeing these buggers off?'

Some of the others growled their agreement. It was as if they'd been abandoned, left to make their own way back with no grub, no water except what they could find, and no one to tell them what they were supposed to be doing.

Jan closed his eyes again, trying to shut out the babble of noise. A wave of exhaustion had swept over him and he wanted nothing more than to sleep. It didn't matter that the lorry was bouncing along on a virtually unmade road, that he was squashed uncomfortably against the man next to him, that he was still hungry and thirsty. He just wanted to sleep, knowing that he would be in a different place when he woke, knowing that for just a little while at least he didn't have to do anything for himself. This was the purest luxury he could imagine.

The voices faded. He could still hear them, but the sense of what they were saying passed him by. His mind drifted away from them, back to Devon, and for a moment he was standing again on the banks of the Dart, watching the blue river wend its way between the green fields. He was in the forge, hammering out a new horseshoe on the anvil while Squire's favourite mare Bess waited patiently just outside. He was, very sharply for an instant, watching the *Countess* make her way down to Dartmouth, with his brother Robby at the helm in his Naval uniform . . .

He woke with a jerk. The air was filled with an unbearable roar and the lorry had skidded to a halt. The men were shouting and piling out of the vehicle, making for the ditches at the side of the road. One of them grabbed Jan's arm and dragged him roughly over the tailboard. Still half-asleep, Jan tumbled into the ditch. Cold, stagnant water splashed on his face and into his mouth, and he spluttered and came to full consciousness, staring about him.

The sky was blotted out by the shadows of three great planes and the air was filled with the fierce rattle of machine-guns. The rough road on which they had been travelling suddenly melted and blew up in a great ball of flame, streaked black with smoke and oil, and scattered with chunks of tarmac and stone. The first lorry went with it, scraps of twisted metal and parts of bodies flying past. An arm, still clad in its sleeve, hit Jan a glancing blow on the shoulder. He flinched away in horror, looking up as he did so, and threw his own arm across his face to blot out the sight of the plane screeching overhead, so low that it was almost touching the road. Machine-gun bullets spattered the road. He felt himself yelling but could hear nothing above the roar of the aircraft and the rapid clatter of the guns. Someone kicked him and he turned, cursing, and saw the man who had dragged him here. They both swore together and then clung to each other, almost like lovers, in the dank, muddy water.

It was over in minutes. The planes were gone. There was a moment or two of silence, and then Jan became aware of a crackling sound and a pervading smell of burning oil, cloth, scorched flesh. The other man moved, trying to push him off and, cautiously, he raised his head and peered over the edge of the ditch.

The other lorry was a blazing wreck. It lay on its side, half in and half out of a crater, and a pall of dust and smoke hung over it, swirling in the vicious orange flames. Bodies lay scattered all around; some could almost have been asleep, others were battered and torn. The arm that had hit him had been flung a few yards further before coming to rest against a bush. Another was lodged in the branches of a tree. There were other parts that were not so easily identifiable, flung like litter amongst the other debris.

A few men were on their feet, tottering aimlessly and shocked amongst the carnage. The corporal was already trying to gather them together. Jan crawled out of the ditch, turned to help the other soldier drag himself out, and staggered over to the corporal. On the way, he saw a body which had lost both legs, the buttocks obscenely exposed in the road, the torso almost untouched, the face not even dirty.

It was Sam.

Joe Mears had tagged along with a small group of soldiers. There was a sergeant with them, but he seemed to have given up any idea of issuing orders or organising them into a disciplined unit, so they trudged together with the refugees, giving a hand here and there. Joe carried a small girl for about a mile, with Pirate scurrying valiantly at his heels, and then they came to another crossroads and met a group of refugees coming from the opposite direction. Some of the women were crying and the children looked tired and dirty.

'What's going on, then?' Joe set the little girl back on her feet. 'Ain't that the way to Dunkirk?'

The sergeant detached himself from the knot of soldiers. 'I can speak the lingo a bit. I'll find out what's up.' He went over to them and began a laboured conversation with the civilians. After a while, they shrugged and started to move away, and the sergeant came back.

'They're all going that way.' He pointed south. 'They reckon the Jerries aren't bothering with that part – yet. They think they'll be safer there.' He glanced at the soldiers, leaning on their rifles. 'They've come from Dunkirk.'

The men stared at him. '*From* Dunkirk? But that's where we're supposed to be making for.'

'I know,' the sergeant said grimly. 'Seems the Jerries have been at it already. Bombing it – setting the place afire. They've druv all the people out and it's a ghost town now, but it's still where we got to make for. That's where the ships are coming to get us away.'

'And what bloody hope is there of that?' one of the men demanded. 'The bastards won't even let our ships near.'

'Well, you tell me what else we're going to do, then!' the sergeant exploded. 'Look, we got our orders – make for Dunkirk. There ain't nowhere else to bleeding make for, is there! There won't be no ships nowhere else. We don't have no flaming choice. And at least we know we're on the right road.' He glared at the men and seemed to remember that he was, by reason of his rank, in charge. 'And while we're at it, we might as well smarten up a bit. There won't be no civilians under our feet now so we can march properly. Show these bloody Jerries we're still soldiers and not a bunch of deadbeats. Get fell in!'

It was quite a comfort, Joe thought, to be marching again, to feel part of a formed body, bound by the Army discipline that, even after so short a time, had become part of him. He felt his back straighten and his head lift. Pirate whimpered at his heels and he lifted the little dog into his arms. 'Poor little blighter,' he said. 'You've walked a hell of a long way and you ain't had nothing to eat for hours.' There were still a few tins of corned beef in his pack, along with some paté, and he guessed that some of the others had provisions as well. They'd probably stop soon for a bite and a rest.

They trudged on. The sergeant soon lost his spurt of energy and the marching degenerated once more into an untidy shamble. Joe's mind drifted back to the rest of his own platoon, presumably on their way to some POW camp, and to the men he had left in the barn. He wondered if any of them had survived that blast. And this new lot that he'd fallen in with now – how many men had they lost since they started to pull back? One or two of them had talked a bit as they tramped along, but most were too weary and disheartened to speak. He wondered what chance they had of actually reaching Dunkirk in the first place, let alone getting away.

Every now and then they could hear the distant sound of aircraft, the boom of an explosion, the rattle of gunfire. The Germans seemed to have forgotten this particular road, or perhaps they had it in mind to come back later. Like all the others, Joe kept a constant eye open for shelter – a ditch, a clump of trees, a bit of broken wall. He wondered wryly whether they would ever again be in a position to stand and fight, and what had happened to the 'planned withdrawal'.

Dusk was falling when they stopped at last in a small wood by a stream. They fell on their knees, slurping water into their open mouths, and Joe unpacked his provisions. The other men, wiping their wet faces, eyed them and the sergeant said, 'Hand that over here.'

'What d'you mean?'

'You heard. That grub's got to be shared round.'

Joe hesitated. There was enough here for each man to have about half of what he really needed. 'What do we do when it's all gone?'

'What we bin doing for the last three days,' the sergeant said. 'Go without. And that bloody dog don't get nothing, neither.'

'Oh yes, he does!' Joe said. 'He's my dog and he's stuck to me all this while. I ain't going to let him starve now.'

'You feeds him from your own rations, then.' The sergeant gathered up the tins and dealt them round to the group of men. They wrenched them open with the keys that were glued to the tops of the cans and tore at the slabs of meat, wolfing them down. Joe realised that they really were starving. He'd thought *he* was hungry, but he'd had something to eat only a few hours ago. If the sergeant was to be believed, these men hadn't had anything for three days. Chastened, he gave Pirate a few scraps from his own share and silently apologised to the dog that he couldn't have more.

'Anyone know how far it is to this Dunkirk?' he asked, but nobody answered him. With food and water inside them, they had all slumped back on the ground and closed their eyes. Only one remained awake, keeping lookout with his rifle on his knees, and when Joe looked at him he gave a curt shrug, as much as to say that he didn't know and didn't care. In a way, Joe thought, it was true. It was as if they had given up hope of ever getting away. As if they expected to go on shambling along the badly-made French roads for ever, or until the Germans found them and killed them, as they had already killed so many. Dunkirk was just a word, a myth. Like Heaven, it wasn't a place you ever really expected to reach.

Hell, now – that was different. Hell was here and now, in the past and in the future. Hell was being strafed and bombed and seeing your mates blown to bits. Hell was an endless trudge to nowhere, while you waited for more guns and more bombs to come and finish you off.

Hell was all too real.

Chapter Twenty-Two

Alex and Ginette had had a taste of hell too.

That first attack by the Stukas had brought the convoy to an abrupt standstill. Ahead of them, the leading lorry had been hit by a bomb and was in flames. Those inside another had jumped out and scuttled for shelter at the side of the road; only one had made it. One of the ambulances had been strafed and the men inside were riddled with bullets; none was still alive. Most of the other vehicles had been hit, and in several of them there were men injured, bleeding, dying.

It was all over in a matter of seconds. The aircraft were gone, and the air was filled with the sounds of crackling flames and groaning, weeping, screaming men.

Alex's truck had escaped. He and the Major immediately leaped out and ran to the injured. Other men were jumping out of their vehicles to join them. Some were wounded, but none of them badly, and they were all more concerned with helping than with receiving help.

Ginette was at Alex's side when he reached the first ambulance. With two or three of the orderlies, he lifted out the injured driver and laid him on the road. Then he turned and saw her. 'Get back! Return to the truck!'

'*Mais non!* I can help – I am a doctor's daughter.' Careless of her best blue suit and the little hat that was still on her head, the young woman knelt on the road beside the injured man. 'I used to help my father.' Her hands moved gently over the man's body. 'I don't think he's been hit anywhere else. It's his head.' Blood was running from a gash in his forehead. She spoke to him in English. 'Can you hear me, *m'sieur*? Can you speak?'

The driver opened his eyes and stared at her. 'Blimey,' he said in a weak voice, 'I've died and gorn to heaven. Are you a flipping angel?'

Ginette smiled. 'Not at all. And you haven't died. You've been hit by a bullet, but it's only a graze, I think. It hasn't entered you.' She glanced round and snapped her fingers. 'Will someone bring me some bandages, please? And some water to bathe this wound.'

Alex knelt beside her. 'Ginette, go back to the truck,' he repeated. 'I can deal with this.'

'I asked for bandages,' she interrupted him. 'This man needs his wound attended to at once.'

'Ginette . . .'

She looked up and met his eyes. 'Alex, please. I can do this. I helped my father often in his surgery. This is a small flesh wound, nothing more. There are others that need your attention. Now, please – ask someone to bring me the bandages.'

He got up and left her. She was right, he thought, there were others who needed a doctor's attention, but there were still more who needed an undertaker.

'What are we supposed to do with the bodies?' he asked, coming upon Major Breakspear kneeling by a wounded sergeant. 'Do we leave them here, at the side of the road, to be gnawed by animals?' He thought of the cemeteries they had seen in Flanders, miles and miles of white crosses. 'How did they manage to bury all their dead in the Great War, while they were in the midst of battle?'

'We can bury them ourselves if we have time.' The Major glanced around. 'Anywhere will do – a ditch, one of the trenches left over from the Great War. I've seen plenty of them used that way. But the Germans will see to it if we have to leave them.' He saw Alex's expression and smiled grimly. 'It's part of the Geneva Convention, Rowley. We treat the fallen with respect, whoever they may be.' He gave the sergeant a nod and stood up. 'You'll do for now. The best we can do for our dead, Rowley, is to remove their brown dog-tags so that we know who they are, leave the green one so that the Germans can notify our people where they lie, and take any personal possessions we can carry to send to their next-of-kin. The Germans will do the rest. It's the living we must think of now.'

Alex hoped he was right. With the other doctors and orderlies he moved about amongst the wounded, doing what he could. For some, nothing could be done except to try to ease their pain. He found a box of morphine that had broken open, the phials scattered on the road, and gathered up those that were undamaged. There were syringes and bandages lying around, as well as slings and splints, and he detailed a young orderly to put them all together in one of the ambulances. At least we're all medical staff here, he thought. No matter how many of us are injured, those who are able can still help the others. He wondered how other convoys were faring, without the facilities of a field hospital to support them.

Working as quickly as possible, keeping a lookout all the time for returning Stukas or German soldiers, they patched up the injured as best they could and assembled them into the vehicles that were still fit for service. Each ambulance and lorry was loaded with wounded men, with orderlies and doctors to look after them on the journey. Vehicles which had been too badly damaged to drive were completely disabled. When all was done, Alex and the Major looked at the bodies still lying at the side of the road.

'Do we really just have to leave them there?' Alex asked, still doubtful that the Germans would care for dead men.

'Well, we can't take them with us.' The Major had set someone to collect their dog-tags and personal belongings and put them all into a sack; their rifles and bandoleers were loaded into one of the trucks. 'In some parts of France, the countryside is dotted with little graveyards from the Great War – places where the men were buried more or less where they fell and crosses put up. They were reburied later by the War Graves Commission. I suppose we could do something like that.' He glanced at the convoy waiting to leave. 'We can't keep these men hanging about though. They need proper attention.'

'Leave me and a few men behind,' Alex said. 'We'll bury them and catch up with you. The ground's soft here – it won't take too long.'

The Major thought about it, then nodded. 'What about your wife?'

Ginette had come to stand beside Alex. She said, 'I will stay too. I can make crosses from sticks. At least then someone will know there are Christian men buried here.'

'It's a foul job,' the Major said, glancing round at the torn bodies. 'But I agree, we can't leave them. Be as quick as you can. I want the convoy together and you're needed.' He paused and then said to Alex, 'A word with you, Rowley.'

They moved away and he glanced over his shoulder towards Ginette and spoke in a low voice. 'You've got to get your wife into some different clothing, Rowley. That blue coat and hat she's wearing – they're ridiculous. Hasn't she got anything more suitable?'

What's suitable for retreating with the British Army? Alex wondered, but he shook his head. 'I don't think she has, sir. She came away in a hurry, you see, and I don't think she realised—'

'A uniform,' the Major interrupted. 'She'll have to be put into uniform. And cut off that hair. If we get ambushed . . .'

'But we don't have any spare uniforms.'

Major Breakspear turned his head, and Alex followed his glance. He saw the bodies lying at the side of the road and felt the colour drain from his face. 'You mean we should . . . ?'

'Well, they're not going to need them again, are they!' the Major said harshly. 'You should be able to find something that fits.' He gave Alex a straight, direct look. 'I know it's not pleasant, but this isn't a suggestion, Rowley; it's an order.'

Alex returned to Ginette. She said, 'Is he telling you to take me home again? To leave me to make my own way back?'

'No! Of course he's not.' He paused, uncertain how to put the Major's order into words. 'He's worried about your clothes,' he said at last, aware of the absurdity of his words.

'My *clothes*?' She looked down at her already ruined costume, and then said, 'Ah. I see. They are not suitable, is that it? I should have known this for myself. So what does he say I should do? Take the uniform from a dead man? From one of these boys?'

Alex nodded unhappily. 'I'm afraid he does.'

Ginette stared at him for a moment, then shrugged. The streak of practicality he had seen in her before, when she had gone from man to man, tending wounds that were surely more horrible than anything she could have seen in the village, surfaced again and she lifted one shoulder. 'Then that is what I must do. I don't think the soldier will mind, do you, if I take his uniform back to England for him? Only, we must know who he is, so that I can give it to his mother when I have finished borrowing it.'

'You'll have his dog-tag,' Alex said, with a feeling of huge relief. 'The brown one – see, they have these two, a brown and a green.

Green goes to ground – stays with the man and is buried with him, so that he can be identified later. The brown one goes home.'

'And if anything happens to me,' Ginette said, still with that French practicality, 'you will know.'

'Nothing will happen to you,' Alex said, and touched her hand. 'Nothing will happen to you while I am here to prevent it.'

The vehicles moved off. Together they found a young private whose uniform was not too badly damaged, and Alex and one of the orderlies quickly stripped him. While Ginette slipped behind a bush to change, he and the rest of the orderlies set to work with their burials. It was a grisly task, made worse by the fact that they had known and worked with these men, had played cards and sung songs with them, seen photographs of their wives and children. Still shaken by the attack and its aftermath, they did their best to close their minds to what they were doing, and shovelled the remains into a wide, shallow pit.

'We ought to say something,' one of the men said. 'I mean, it's like a funeral really, isn't it?'

Alex nodded and they stood for a moment at the side of the grave, their caps held to their chests, and recited the Lord's Prayer. Then they piled earth and mud over the pitiful heap and watched while Ginette, looking small and unfamiliar with the bulky uniform belted tightly around her slim body, stepped forward and placed her crosses at both ends. In silence, they climbed into the truck and left the scene of the attack.

Once again, the road was quiet. There were just two vehicles still smouldering, three others that were no more than blackened, broken metal, stabbing grotesque fingers at the sky, and a wide, shallow grave marked by rough wooden crosses made with sticks, to show that they had ever been there.

They caught up with the convoy just as it was approaching a small town. It had been more or less abandoned, the Major told Alex, but there were a few stubborn French who refused to leave, and another unit which had arrived an hour or two ahead of them. This was composed solely of vehicles and intended for transporting soldiers to the battlefields. Now, they were transporting them away.

'We've already taken the remains of three regiments to Dunkirk,' their CO said when he came over to compare notes later. They had settled themselves into a school by then, turning it into an overnight hospital and barracks. 'That's where the rescue's going to be, apparently, but there wasn't a ship in sight when we came away. God knows what's going to happen to them. They're sitting ducks where they are.'

'But hasn't Dunkirk been bombed already?' the Major asked. 'We've been told to make for the black smoke – I assumed the place was on fire.'

'It is, but a lot of the smoke is from the oil tanks. We set them on fire ourselves, to create a smokescreen so that the Luftwaffe can't see where to aim. That won't help the ships on their way here, though, nor the men on the beaches. And that's another thing – the beaches along that coast go out flat and shallow for hundreds of yards. How are they going to get ships in close enough to get the men off?'

The Major shrugged. He was a professional soldier and trained not to question orders. He had all he could cope with, just looking after the wounded men in his care. 'Our job's simply to get there,' he said. 'I dare say London have got some plan up their sleeves.'

The CO looked as if he doubted this, but he was a trained man as well and wasn't about to start damaging morale by casting doubts on a situation that already looked black enough. He frowned at the map that lay on the school desk in front of them.

'Do you need our transport?' he asked. 'Or d'you have enough of your own? Our orders are to go east and pick up any troops coming through from that direction – Belgium and the Ardennes.'

Alex could see that the Major was tempted. Their own transport was much depleted and wounded men took up more room than fit ones. But he shook his head. 'No. Their need's probably greater than ours. What about your chaps – do they need any medical attention?'

Alex went back to the room he had been allocated to share with Ginette. It was highly irregular, but she couldn't be left to sleep alone and indeed he didn't think she would have accepted such a thing. They had brought a couple of camp beds into what must have been the headmaster's study, and she was sitting on one now, wearing the nightdress she had worn on their wedding night.

'Do you realise,' she said as he came in and leaned wearily against the door, 'we have not yet had a proper honeymoon?'

'I don't think we can count this as one,' he said, coming across to kiss her. 'Oh my darling, I'm so sorry about all this.'

'Why? It's not your fault. I'm just glad we're together.' She rested her cheek on his shoulder and added, 'But I do worry about my parents. If they've been attacked too . . .'

'I'm sure they won't have been. It's the troops the Germans are after. They'll be safe, going south.' He hoped fervently that this was true. 'I'm glad we're together as well, Ginette, but I wish that you were safe too. You should have gone with them. It's too dangerous for you here.'

She shrugged. 'It's no use to talk like that. I am here now. Tell me what it will be like in England, instead.'

Alex lay down on his camp bed. 'In England now there'll be bluebells out in all the woods and along the hedgerows. There'll be apple blossom on the trees and birds singing as they build their nests. The swallows will have arrived, and the cuckoo, and the fields will be full of lambs.' He smiled at her. 'Not so very different from France, really.'

'It will be very different,' she said. 'It will be England. And we shall have a good life there together, when all this is over.' She lay down on her own bed, close beside him, and laid her arm across his chest.

Alex reached up and took her hand. He brought it down to his cheek and kissed her palm.

'Yes,' he said. 'We'll have a good life there together, when all this is over.'

Chapter Twenty-Three

The next day, the vehicles began to run out of fuel.

They didn't all run out at once, of course. First one lorry faltered to a stop, then another. A field ambulance packed with wounded men drifted to the side of the road and refused to move again. Another, coasting carefully down even the most gradual slope to eke out every last drop, came to a halt beside a small wood.

As each one failed, the men and provisions it carried were transferred to another, the increasing weight making fuel consumption even higher. Then the abandoned vehicle was set alight. 'I know it goes against the grain to destroy good equipment,' Major Breakspear said, watching the first one burn. 'But there's no sense in leaving it behind for the enemy.'

'We're not going to have any transport left soon,' Alex said. 'All the vehicles must be pretty low. What are we going to do when we can't drive any further?'

'It may not happen. We may be able to get some fuel from a garage.' They both knew, though, that this was unlikely. Every village they passed through now was deserted, its shops and houses stripped of everything useful. Small local garages, which never had large stocks of fuel anyway, would have none left. And the main form of transport – the horse and cart – had been taken by the fleeing villagers, to carry their own possessions.

'It's the wounded men I'm worried about,' Alex said to Ginette. All those who could walk were now going on foot, to save weight in the lorries and ambulances. Once the vehicles had all gone, the men who couldn't walk would have to be carried by stretcher. 'It's going to be a hell of a job to get them as far as Dunkirk. And we don't have much time. The Major says there are several battalions holding a perimeter around the evacuation area, but they're being pushed back all the time. We don't want to get caught up in that, not with so many wounded already.'

'We can fight too,' Ginette said. As well as the uniform, she had been given the dead soldier's rifle and bandoleer. 'I can shoot. My father is a *chasseur*, remember – he often took me hunting in the forest.'

Alex glanced at his wife, marvelling once again at this slim, delicate-looking woman who seemed to be as tough as a rod of steel. Even though the body they had found had looked lean enough, the uniform was still too big for her and she had had to roll up the sleeves and trousers, and gather the thick khaki serge tightly round her waist with the broad belt. Boots had been a problem but, padded out with several pairs of socks she could walk in them, although at first she had kept tripping over the toes. Now, she was marching along as if she were out on a hike, swinging her arms and looking fiercely determined, her shorn hair curling round her head.

'I don't know what the Sergeant's going to say about your haircut,' he said with a sudden grin. 'It looks as if it's been cut with a knife and fork!'

'It's the latest style from Paris,' she said haughtily. '*Très chic*. Shall we sing?'

'Sing?'

'Yes, sing. Don't soldiers always sing when they are on the march? What's that song I heard some of the men singing in your camp – "Mademoiselle from Armentières"? Teach me the words of that song.'

'I don't think so,' Alex said hastily. 'I don't think you'd appreciate them. What about one of your own songs? When I was at school we used to sing "Frère Jacques".' And I bet the men know some different words to that too, he thought, hoping they'd remember he had his wife with him.

Ginette gave him a mischievous glance. 'I don't think you should concern yourself with rude words,' she said. 'Not when we are in this situation.'

Alex turned his head to meet her eyes and burst out laughing. Ginette was right – with the enemy on their heels, wounded men on their hands, the last of their vehicles about to peter out by the roadside and air attacks likely at any moment, it did seem rather absurd to worry about the words of Army songs.

'Better for them to cheer themselves up,' she said, and lifted her voice.

> *'Mademoiselle from Armentières, parlez-vous.*
> *Cut up your drawers with garden shears, parlez-vous . . .'*

'Ginette, for heaven's sake!' But the nearest men, after a startled glance, had already taken up the chant and it spread quickly along the line of trudging soldiers.

> *'The Innkeeper had a daughter fair, parlez-vous.*
> *The Innkeeper had a daughter fair, parlez-vous.*
> *The Innkeeper had a daughter fair,*
> *With lily-white tits and golden hair,*
> *Inky-pinky, parlez-vous.'*

'You see?' Ginette said in a tone of satisfaction. 'They feel better already.'

By noon, all the vehicles had run out of fuel and been destroyed. The group of soldiers, some of them on stretchers, gathered by the roadside to discuss what should be done next.

'I think we'd better stop anyway,' Major Breakspear said, glancing at the sky. There had been aircraft in the distance all morning and the sounds of explosions and firing from the perimeter. 'We've been lucky not to have been attacked again, but one of those beggars is going to spot us soon. We'd better rest up until evening and then go on in the dark.'

They were close to another small village. Alex and another Captain were detailed to go and reconnoitre. Ginette stood up. 'I'll come too.'

'No, you'd better stay here,' Alex began, but she flashed her eyes at him.

'I can be of use! Do you have another French person here?'

'You're in a man's uniform.'

'I think they will know I am a woman. Or perhaps not, if it is better so.' She was already striding out along the rough, potholed road. Alex sighed and looked at the Major.

'I'm sorry, sir. She hasn't had Army training.'

'I can see *that*, Rowley. But perhaps she's right – there's no doubt she speaks better French than any of the rest of us. I just hope the Germans haven't got here first. Take a couple of others with you.'

Together with a corporal and a private, Alex and Ginette set off, keeping to the edge of the road. The country here was open and flat, with little cover, and they kept a wary eye out on all sides. As they entered the village itself, Alex pulled Ginette back against a wall.

'Keep out of sight. We don't know who may be about.' He edged along the wall, his revolver ready in his hand. The corporal followed, with Ginette third and the private bringing up the rear.

The village was very quiet. The houses were built facing away from the road, with small windows high in their blank walls and tall wooden gates leading into their hidden courtyards. There was a *lavoir* in one corner, its water running clear.

'We could wash!' Ginette whispered, but Alex shook his head.

'Not until we know it's safe. I don't like this quiet – it looks as though the villagers have gone. And we need water for drinking more than we need to wash.' He crept further, with Ginette and the two soldiers close behind. There was still no sign of life.

Two chickens ran out from a half-open gateway. Alex jumped and quickly brought up his revolver, then lowered it again sheepishly. The chickens stopped and began to peck at the weeds growing against the wall.

'They'd do for our dinner,' the corporal muttered. 'Anyone know how to wring a chicken's neck without making it squawk?'

The chickens lifted their heads, regarding the intruders with bright eyes, then squatted down in the dust and began to shake their wings energetically. The private aimed a kick at one of them as he passed.

'Don't do that!' Ginette exclaimed, and the corporal turned and scowled at her. She bit her lip and put her hand over her mouth. 'I'm sorry.'

The narrow street curled round and opened out suddenly into a wide, deserted square. Alex stopped abruptly and then, without a word, pushed Ginette back into a gateway. The two soldiers slid back round the corner and pressed themselves against the wall, rifles at their shoulders. Very cautiously, the corporal inched his head round the wall and took in the scene again.

The square was completely empty. Except for a large German tank, right in the middle.

'That's it, then,' Major Breakspear said when they made their way back to the convoy. 'Nothing to be had there, not even water. And we can't afford to linger here either. Pity. How many of them d'you think there were?'

Alex shrugged. 'Hard to tell. There was nobody about – perhaps they were resting up in the houses. But we didn't see any other vehicles, either, so unless there were others hidden in the streets, I imagine they must be an advance party.'

The Major nodded. 'I'd be surprised if they'd got many troops this far yet.' He glanced at the still smouldering lorries. 'I'm surprised they haven't seen this smoke and come to investigate, too. We'd better be on our way.' He looked towards the village, then back the way they had come. 'Damned nuisance. We'll have to go across country. At least it's flat.'

Flat it certainly was, but it was also criss-crossed by narrow dykes and wire fences to keep the cattle from straying from the small square paddocks where they grazed. Progress was painfully slow as the fit members of the party carried their wounded fellows on stretchers, or supported them with weary arms. Now and then they found a track leading to a wooden bridge, but many of these had been demolished, probably by earlier battalions determined to halt the enemy's advance. The water in the dykes was shallow, but when one of the privates stepped in to help a stretcher across he found his boots sinking nearly a foot deep in soft mud. After that, they fixed their bayonets and stabbed them into the water to gauge the depth before scrambling across.

'You don't have to lift me,' Ginette said. 'I can walk through just as well.'

'Go on, light as a feather, you are,' the Regimental Sergeant-Major said, depositing her on firm ground. Alex bit his lip, aware that his own level of strength was far below that of these trained soldiers. I should be carrying her, he thought. But he was already bowed under the weight of his own pack, stuffed with medical supplies as well as the usual accoutrements, and the Sergeant-Major was a big, burly man and had swung Ginette off her feet before Alex had had a chance.

'It's all right, sir,' he said to Alex. 'I won't take advantage.'

The whole area reminded Alex of the Cambridgeshire Fens – a wide, flat, greenish-grey area of tussocky grass and narrow channels. Like them it was probably below sea-level and liable to flooding. It was also very exposed. He glanced at the cloudless sky, wondering why they hadn't been attacked again.

'What's that?' Ginette was beside him, trudging through the tough grass. She had thrown away her suitcase and was carrying a soldier's haversack on her back. In it, he knew, she had crammed both her wedding-dress and the photograph of her cat. Her boots and trousers were thick with mud, her jacket smeared with the blood of the dead soldier, her soft brown hair cropped short and ragged round her head. 'That black smudge – is it rain coming?'

Alex followed her pointing finger. The smudge lay low on the horizon. It shifted as he watched, spreading higher, and grew into a puffball of thick, dirty grey.

'It's smoke,' he said quietly.

'Smoke! But isn't that where we're going?'

'Yes. We were told to make for the black smoke.' He realised that Ginette had probably not been aware of this. 'Did you think that the harbour was going to be safe? Operating normally?'

'Yes,' she said in a small voice. 'I thought there would be ships there. I thought once we were there, we would be safe.'

Alex's heart sank. I shouldn't have let her come with us, he thought again. I ought to have made her go with her parents. I ought to have sent her south, away from the German advance . . .

'My darling,' he said, taking her hand, 'nowhere is safe now. Even England may not be safe, if the Germans drive us back. They'll invade, just as they've invaded Holland and Belgium and your own country. All we can do is fight them, the best way we can.'

She looked at him. Her brown eyes were very bright and there were angry red spots on her cheeks. 'Then that is what we shall do,' she said, lifting her chin. 'We'll fight them. We'll fight them to the very end.'

Joe Mears was still with the troop he had tagged along with. They had rested for a few hours in the wood and then set off again under cover of darkness. By the time dawn lighted the sky they had reached the fen country. They stopped and stared at the dreary landscape of wide, flat fields with their chequerboard pattern of dykes and fences.

'Blimey,' the sergeant said. 'We go over that lot, we'll be seen for miles.'

'That's the way we got to go, though,' Joe said. He was holding Pirate in his arms and at the sound of his voice the puppy licked his chin. 'See the smoke? That's Dunkirk.'

'And what's the flaming use of going there, then? Bleeding place is on fire.'

They stood in a dispirited row, staring at the smudge on the horizon. The road was built up above the fields, visible for miles around, with no sign of any other road joining or crossing it. There were ditches running on either side. To make for the smoke, they would have to cross the wide, flat expanse before them, exposed to the view of any Germans in the vicinity and with nowhere to shelter from air attack.

The sergeant spoke at last. He was a regular soldier, a man of about forty, heavily built but greying. His voice was weary, as if he'd had enough. 'Well, the order was every man for himself. I reckon this is where we goes our own separate ways.'

'How can we?' Joe looked round at the others. 'We've all got to go the same way. Over there – across that lot. There *ain't* no other way.'

'We don't all have to go together, though.' The sergeant looked as if he'd like to put Joe on a charge for insubordination, if only he had the energy and there was a glasshouse handy for Joe to be sent to. 'This is what we do. We all hunker down here in this ditch and we goes off one at a time, see? Give each other quarter of an hour.' He glanced at the little group and thought for a moment. 'That's three hours in all. The ones waiting can get a bit of kip.'

'In the ditch?' Joe glanced at the channel at his feet. It was filled with brown, sludgy water. He hefted Pirate a little higher against his shoulder. 'No, thanks. I'll go on by meself – see if I can find a better way. I don't reckon much to hanging about here for another three hours.'

The sergeant glared at him. 'You disobeying my order?'

'You said the order was every man for himself,' Joe pointed out. 'And I'm not even in your mob to start with.' He turned away from the ditch and heaved his haversack on to his back. 'I reckon you were pleased enough to see me last night when I had some grub, but now me room's better than me company, so I'll say cheerio.' He took a step along the road, then turned back. 'And good luck, mates,' he added awkwardly. 'See you back in Blighty.'

He trudged off along the road. Two of the others followed him; the rest dropped down into the ditch with the sergeant. Joe glanced to one side and saw two figures making their way across the first dyke.

The three men walked along in silence for a while. Presently, one of the others said, 'Don't reckon much to our chances, do you?'

Joe shrugged. 'As good as anyone else's, I'd say. I'm Joe Mears,' he added. 'Seventh Cornwalls.'

'Sid Hopson. And this is Dave Fawley. West Kents.'

'Nice dog,' Sid said. He was a thin, dark-haired man with half-closed eyes who didn't have the air of a regular soldier. Probably called up, like me, Joe thought, putting him down as a bus conductor in civilian life. Fawley was different – a corporal, big and raw-boned, with ginger hair and a red complexion, and a confident swagger. He marched slightly ahead of the other two, as if he were in charge.

Joe stroked Pirate's head. 'Picked him up back on the road. Just started to follow me, poor little perisher. Not much more than a pup.'

'What you going to do with him, then?'

'Take him home with me, of course. Can't leave him here, can I?'

'Don't see why not,' Fawley said without looking round. 'Plenty of dogs scavenging about. Soon learn to look after himself.'

'*I'm* looking after him,' Joe said. 'Give him to my girl when I gets back to Blighty. Always wanted a dog, she has. Well, she can have this one.'

'They'll never let you take him.' Fawley still didn't even turn his head. 'Dogs carry rabies, don't you know that?'

'Go on, Pirate ain't got rabies.' Joe was silent for a moment. 'What *is* rabies, anyway?'

'Mad dog disease. First, you get scared of water—'

'Well, he definitely ain't got it, then. Nor've I.' Joe stopped and unscrewed his water-bottle, dismayed to see that it was half-empty. They had all filled their bottles before leaving the stream but there had been no running water since then and Pirate was the only one prepared to drink the murky ditchwater.

'Pirate?' Sid said. 'Is that his name?'

'Well, it's what I bin calling him. I reckon he knows it now. You got a dog at home, Sid?'

'Nah.' Sid shook his head. 'Missus don't like dogs. Cats is what she likes. We used to have three of the perishing things but when the war broke out the Government said we had to have pets put to sleep, so she took the two oldest down the pets' place. She wouldn't take the little 'un, though. Not Ginger. Said we'd got to have something to keep the mice down.'

They fell silent and Joe's mind went to his girlfriend Connie. He'd written to her regularly and looked forward to getting her letters, but there hadn't been any post since before the withdrawal had begun. He wondered what she was thinking, what the Government was telling people at home, whether she even knew about the Army being on the run. He felt a sudden longing to be with her again, sitting on the settee in her mum's front room, having a kiss and a cuddle. Last time he'd been there, at Christmas, they'd talked a bit about getting engaged. He wished they'd done something about it now. He wished they could have got married.

There were his parents too, and his sisters. They probably thought he was having a quiet time in some French billet, drinking wine in a café and eating snails and frogs' legs. They couldn't have any idea that he was separated from his battalion and tramping through France with a puppy in his arms. He thought of his dad, working on the fireboat, and his mum in the café serving up bangers and mash, the windows all steamed up and the air full of cigarette smoke and the smell of fried onions.

I'd give anything to be there, he thought. Anything.

The puppy squirmed in his arms and licked his chin again. He looked down into the brown eyes.

'You're going to like it in Blighty,' he said. 'Connie'll treat you like a king. So will our mum. And I expect Dad'll take you on the fireboat with him sometimes. And I'll take you to the park, too. Hyde Park, now, that's nice for dogs. Run about on the grass, under the trees . . .' His words were drowned by the sudden roar of aircraft and he groaned. 'Oh no, here they come again! Bloody hell!'

The aircraft thundered overhead. There were four or five of them

– Stukas, Joe thought as he flung himself and Pirate into the ditch at the side of the road. He heard the harsh rattle of machine-gun fire and felt the searing heat of a bullet pass close to his shoulder. Mud and water erupted only inches from his face, almost choking him, and Pirate squealed with terror and wriggled frantically out of his arms. Joe yelled and tried to grab him back, but the puppy had gone.

'Pirate? Pirate, come back!' The aircraft had vanished, roaring away into the distance and Joe scrambled to his feet, climbing out of the ditch and brushing wet leaves, sticks and gobbets of mud from his face and clothing. His mouth and nose were clogged with filth and he retched and spat. 'Pirate,' he choked, blinking through the veil of murky water running down his face. 'Pirate, come back. Where are you?'

'Never mind the bleeding dog,' someone rasped from the ditch. 'Give me a hand with this poor bugger.'

Joe turned, rubbing the rest of the mud from his face. Fawley was on his knees in the turbid water, trying to lift out the limp, sagging body of the third soldier. Joe dropped quickly into the slime and put his hands under Sid's shoulders, lifting him clear. He was a dead weight, his straight, dark hair streaming with water and thin sludge, and blood oozing from a ragged gash in his temple. His face was so white that Joe was sure for a moment that he was dead, but then he groaned and turned his head weakly to one side. Carefully, they lifted him out and laid him down at the side of the road.

'Strewth,' Joe said. 'Poor bloody sod. A bullet must've scraped him.'

Fawley didn't answer. He was already rummaging in his pack for First Aid gear and, while Joe washed the wound with a few drops of precious water from his own bottle, he unwrapped plasters and a bandage. He examined the gash and said, 'It don't look too bad. The bullet just scraped him, like you said. It's pretty deep, though – he'll be a bit groggy.' He supported Sid into a sitting position. 'Here, mate, have a drop of water.'

Sid's head lolled but his eyelids fluttered open and he managed to drink a little from the bottle the corporal held to his lips. Then he moaned faintly, as if the effort were too much, closed his eyes and slumped back against Fawley's arm. The two men looked at each other over his head.

'He ain't going to be able to walk,' Joe said in concern. He looked around. The sky was clear and there was no sign of aircraft, but they could appear literally out of the blue. 'We got no cover here at all. What are we going to do?'

'What can we do? Just carry on, same as we been doing. Only this time we got to drag Sid along with us.' Fawley bent and spoke in Sid's ear. 'Come on, mate, can't go to sleep here. We got to make for Dunkirk, remember? The ships to take us home? Well, it ain't no use waiting here, there's no buses. We got to use Shanks' pony. Up on your feet, now, come on.'

Sid moaned again but they hauled him to his feet and he stood unsteadily between them, swaying on shaking legs. Joe shook his head but Fawley was determined. He hooked Sid's arm around his neck and gestured to Joe to do the same. With the wounded man hanging between them, his feet scraping on the ground, they began to lurch along the road.

'That dog of mine's gone,' Joe said presently. 'Scarpered, he has, poor little bleeder. Frightened out of his wits, he was. Don't suppose I'll see him again.'

'Plenty more dogs about,' Fawley said. 'You shoulda seen some of the dogs I saw, week or so ago. Hunting dogs, they were, kept in a big compound. Copped a bomb one night when the Huns came over. Never seen nothing like it. Bits of bodies all over the shop. I saw one of 'em, big chap he was, jaws like a steel trap, just laying there with his belly ripped out. At least your tyke's loose. He can fend for hisself.'

'Suppose so.' Joe was depressed, all the same, about losing Pirate. They'd been through so much together and he'd set his heart on taking the pup home to Connie. He thought of the big brown eyes that had gazed up so trustfully into his and felt a lump in his throat. Blimey, he thought, I'm getting soft.

Sid moaned and they paused for a rest, setting him down carefully on the grass verge. Joe looked at him with some anxiety. His face had a greenish tinge and he was breathing quickly. They gave him some more water.

'What d'you reckon?' Joe said in a low voice. 'Is he going to make it?'

Fawley shrugged. 'Dunno. We can't leave him here, I know that. Got to do the best we can.' He hauled Sid to his feet again. 'How d'you feel, mate? Ready to go on?'

Sid muttered something unintelligible and they hooked his arms around their necks again and staggered on. I don't know how long we can manage this, Joe thought. That gash on his head had looked proper nasty and God knew what sort of germs had got into it from that ditch. Suppose it went septic? Neither he nor Fawley would have anything in their packs to deal with a problem like that. And how long could they support him, anyway? He might be only a skinny little chap, but he was still heavy.

'Get down!' Fawley said, stopping suddenly. 'There's some people ahead.'

They slid down into the ditch, hardly noticing the muddy water now. Joe raised his head and peered cautiously between some tussocks of grass. A group of about a dozen people were making their way slowly across the fields to their right. He stared at them hard and then breathed a sigh of relief.

'They're ours, mate! They're Tommies. On their way to Dunkirk, I reckon.' He jumped out of the ditch and waved his arms. 'Hey! You! Tommies – over here!'

'Get down, you bloody fool!' Fawley grabbed his ankle and jerked him back. 'One trigger-happy idiot, and you'll be shot. Wait till they get closer.' He lifted his head and stared hard. 'I think you're right, all the same.'

They waited a few minutes. The little group had stopped and were obviously uncertain what to do. Their position was totally exposed and they had no cover. They could either turn and go back, or continue on, hoping that Joe didn't turn out to be one of the enemy. After a minute or two, Fawley stood up carefully and raised both arms into the air.

'It's OK, mates. We're English. West Kents.'

'And Seventh Cornwalls,' Joe reminded him.

'And Seventh Cornwalls,' Fawley called. The group, which had started to move again, stopped and turned to each other. Then one of them shouted back.

'Cornwalls? So are we!'

'Cornwalls?' Joe echoed, and leaped out of the ditch. As they hurried over, he could see their shoulder badges and knew that they had spoken the truth. He knew their faces, too. He felt a huge surge of relief.

'Blimey,' he panted as the newcomers splashed through the last ditch and clambered up to the road. 'Am I glad to see you! You're from the casualty station, ain't you? You're the doc?'

'That's right,' Alex said, coming forward. 'I'm Captain Rowley, and this is Major Breakspear. Have you got someone injured?'

Chapter Twenty-Four

Sam wasn't the only man killed in the first lorry. They all were – blown to bits, some of them not even recognisable, scattered over the road, the ditches, hanging on the wire fences. Jan and the other men from the second lorry, shaken and sick, staggered about trying to find dog-tags, picking up a few scattered belongings, gathering what remains they could into a respectful heap. He laid what was left of Sam a little way apart and muttered a short, private prayer over him. They hadn't known each other long, but what they'd been through together had made them mates.

'Right,' the corporal said at last. 'Make sure there's no weapons left laying about, and we'll get on our way. Good thing we've still got one lorry.'

'Not that it'll take us far,' the driver remarked gloomily. 'I reckon we're just about out of petrol. Five miles, maybe ten – that's all.'

'Five miles is better than nothing.' The corporal got into the seat beside him while the others climbed up into the back. The driver started the engine and they moved slowly off, leaving the other vehicle still smouldering and the pitiful heap of human remains lying beside the road.

Jan couldn't speak. He'd had no idea, when he left his little Devon village, what war could mean. He knew about the Great War, of course he did. Men from his own village – from his own family – had gone and never come back, but nobody ever talked about it much. Those who had come home just wanted to get on with their normal, peacetime lives and forget about the trenches. Perhaps they ought to have talked about it, he thought. Perhaps if they'd told us what it was like, this lot would never have happened.

Yet he didn't know whether he himself would be able to talk

about what he'd experienced, once he got home. Would he sit down one evening and tell his mum and dad all he'd been through? Would he tell Susie about the family in the well, about Bert shooting himself in the mouth, about Sam? Some things you just couldn't talk about. Some things you'd just got to forget, or they'd drive you mad.

The lorry trundled on. The men were silent, most of them taking the chance of a bit of shut-eye. Jan stared out through the canvas flaps at the back. He hated this bleak, flat countryside with its criss-crossing dykes and wire fences, and felt a fierce longing for the rolling hills and good red earth of Devon, the blue river snaking down to the sea and the brown and purple uplands of Dartmoor in the distance. What am I doing here? he wondered dismally. Why couldn't I stop at home, shoeing horses and making wrought-iron gates and marrying my Susie?

Why did there have to be a war?

The lorry's engine coughed, spluttered and then died. The driver pulled it into the side of the road and the men groaned and clambered out. They stood round in a dejected circle.

'Well, that's it.' The driver kicked one of the tyres. 'No more fuel.'

The corporal took charge. 'We knew it was going to happen. We've got a few more miles along the way, so now we just got to put our best foot forward and walk. *March*,' he added firmly.

'We can't leave it like this, though,' the driver objected. 'When Jerry comes along, all he'll have to do is put in some fuel and he's got a good lorry to use for Hitler. We've got to wreck it.'

He took a can with a trickle of petrol in it from the back of the truck and sprinkled it over the inside, then set fire to the canvas hood and stepped well back. The flames licked along the sides, caught at the driver's seat and spread around the cab. In a few moments the fuel tank had ignited and the lorry was ablaze.

The driver turned away without speaking, and the corporal snapped out an order to form up. Jan found himself at the back of the little group. They marched off along the road, disheartened, hungry and thirsty. They had used up almost all their food and were in desperate need of water. Evening was drawing in; it was the best time to be on the move, but they were too tired. Their marching turned to trudging and then to shambling.

'I dunno that I can keep going much longer,' the man next to Jan said. His voice was slurred and he had already stumbled several times. 'I'm going to fall asleep on me feet in a minute.'

Jan glanced at him. His eyes were half-closed and even as he spoke, he slumped forward. Jan reached out an arm and caught him.

'Put your arm round my neck, boy. That's it. And t'other one round Ginger's. Now you can doze off if you like, see, and we'll keep you going.'

The three in front did the same. It was hard going, but turn and turn about it gave everyone a brief rest. In the end, however, they were all too exhausted to keep going and, although the corporal made one or two half-hearted attempts to get them to smarten up, eventually he was forced to call a halt.

'We'd better rest up for a couple of hours. Not for too long, though – don't want to miss the boat.'

'You reckon there'll be a boat?' one of the soldiers asked. He sat down on the grass verge with his head resting on his hands, elbows on his knees and his feet hanging over the edge of the ditch. 'You know what that bloke said about black smoke. If the bloody place is on fire, they'll never get a ship in the harbour.'

'*One* ship?' one of the others scoffed. 'They'll need bloody hundreds to get all the troops away. We ain't got a cat's chance in hell.'

'Tell me what else we can do, then!' the corporal snapped. 'Turn round and walk back till we find some Huns to give ourselves up to? You can if you like – *I'm* not going to spend the rest of the war in a POW camp. Live to fight another day, that's me. Anyone who doesn't agree might as well start walking now. I daresay Jerry'll welcome you with open arms.'

Jan took out his water-bottle and stared at it. There had been nothing inside it since early morning, but he tipped it over his mouth all the same. One small drop found its way to his lips. He screwed the top on again and put it back into his pack with a heavy sigh.

'I'll walk on if you like,' he offered. 'See if I can find any water. There must be some somewhere.'

'You got to rest . . .' But the corporal was just as weary as the others and he nodded. 'All right, then. It's every man for himself, anyway.'

'I'll be back,' Jan said, wondering if the corporal thought he was taking the chance to go on alone. As if anyone'd want to, he thought, trudging on along the darkening road. All on your own in a strange country which seemed to be deserted, apart from the occasional distant glimpse of refugees or maybe other soldiers, picking their way across the bleak landscape, and always with the dread of one of those sudden Junkers attacks; or maybe coming across a troop of German soldiers, full of good grub and driving those great Panzer tanks bristling with guns . . . No, he didn't want to be on his own. For two pins, he'd turn round right now and go back to the others, say he couldn't find any water, say he needed to rest as well.

But somehow, almost as if they belonged to someone else, his feet kept going. His body felt so tired that it could have been floating. When he peered into the darkness, it swirled about before his eyes like a dense black fog. There was a bitter taste of bile in his mouth and his lips and tongue throbbed. A high-pitched noise was ringing in his ears. Planes, he thought. It's more planes coming to bomb us. But he didn't care any more. It didn't seem worth bothering about.

After a while, he stumbled over a stone and fell. It didn't seem worth getting up, either. He lay on his front, arms stretched out in front of him, and fell asleep.

The others came upon him an hour later, as they lurched along the road, just rested enough to stagger on for a few more miles. They almost tripped over him, felt him over in the dark, decided he was still alive and hauled him to his feet to be supported between two others, in the same way as he had been supporting them. Hardly knowing what he was doing or where he was, and half-dreaming of the Devon countryside, Jan reeled along until, after a while, he began to wake up again and was able to support himself.

Resting every hour or so, helping each other along, they managed a few more miles and, as dawn began to seep over the sombre fields, they could see that the black smoke of Dunkirk was closer. They stopped for a moment and stared at it.

'Bloody hell,' Ginger Barnett said. 'Every building in the place must be on fire.'

'Well, we knew that, Barnett.' But the corporal's voice was uneasy, even a little awed, and everyone there could understand why.

The town was surrounded by wide canals and some of the

268

buildings on the outskirts were still more or less untouched. Others, further in, were shattered and broken; even at this distance, the men could see church towers like jagged teeth and large buildings with their damaged roofs making a broken silhouette against the sky. The smoke they had been using as a landmark for all this time hung like a heavy grey blanket over the whole area, shot with crimson and yellow flames. The sky was already busy with aircraft and, even as they watched, something exploded and a huge flame shot through the dense black shroud.

'Bloody hell,' Ginger said again. 'Have we got to get through that lot?'

'Well, there ain't no other way to the harbour.' The corporal straightened up and gave them all a fierce look. 'We ain't giving in now, are we? We ain't come all this way just to lay down in the road and beg Jerry to take us home. I'm going back to Blighty.' He set off along the straight, flat road, and the others looked at each other and shrugged.

'He'm right,' Jan said. ''Tis no use standing here like target practice. Us better go along of he.'

The thought of getting near to Dunkirk and possible rescue – unlikely though it looked – spurred them on. They were further encouraged by the discovery of a *lavoir* in a huddle of deserted cottages, where the water was relatively clear and they were able to drink deeply and even sluice their faces. Jan dunked his head into the cool running water and ran his fingers through his hair. He was just taking another drink when the sound of gunfire nearby brought them all to their feet.

'Germans!'

'It might not be,' the corporal muttered. 'Get under cover and hold your fire till we know for sure.' He eased around the corner of the nearest cottage, his rifle cocked. Jan and the others watched him, their eyes darting from side to side. There was nobody in sight.

The corporal disappeared round the corner. After a moment, Ginger followed him and the others began to file very slowly behind, each waiting a minute or two before edging out. Jan was last. Left alone, he waited nervously. The seconds ticked by. Still no sound. A minute had passed. A minute and a half. He started to move.

The explosion knocked him back ten feet. It blew part of the corner of the house off and left him on his back, miraculously clear of the shattered stones of the wall, choking in a cloud of grit and dust. Completely winded, he lay for a moment unable to move, then rolled over, grabbed his rifle and began to crawl for the shelter of the *lavoir*. He slid down into the running water, ducked his face in to clear the grit, and then peered over the stone edge.

As the dust slowly settled, he saw a small group of German soldiers come round the battered building. Rifles held ready to fire, they edged as cautiously as Ginger and the others had done a few moments before. They were looking this way and that, obviously not sure whether there were more British in the area. Jan froze, certain that they would come over to the little stone shelter of the *lavoir*, but before they could do so someone snapped out an order from behind them and they went back, shrugging and calling out. They're telling their captain there's no one here, he thought, and felt his body sag with relief. A few moments later, he heard a vehicle start up and then disappear into the distance.

Nevertheless, it was another half-hour before he dared come out and then he crept very slowly, his uniform soggy and heavy with water. At least I ought to be clean now, he thought wryly, as he moved stealthily along the village road. It took a lot of courage to look round the damaged corner but he knew he had to do it. He had heard no sign from the others, but there might be someone wounded, unable to call for help. He couldn't leave without finding out.

The explosion must have been caused by a grenade. As well as taking off the corner of the house, it had blown a small crater in the road and rubble lay all about. The buildings had obviously been used as battle stations; their windows were smashed, their doors wrecked and splintered. One had been burned out. Items of luggage and furniture, pushed into the road or dropped by the inhabitants as they fled, were littered along the pavements. There was nobody about.

Jan stared at it, his heart almost breaking. There was something about it that reminded him of home – of his own little village on the banks of the Dart. For a moment, he was transported back there, but instead of the village street he knew so well, with its thatched cottages and tidy, colourful gardens, he saw it like this one – smashed, destroyed and abandoned. A lump rose in his throat and he felt hot, angry tears in his eyes.

'The bastards! The bloody insane *bastards*!'

He had never known it was possible to feel such rage. If a German had appeared at that moment, he would have throttled him with his own two hands, with the hands that didn't even like wringing the necks of chickens. He would have throttled Hitler himself and taken pleasure in doing it. The rage tightened his chest, reddened his cheeks, burned his whole body. He scarcely knew what to do with it. He picked up a rock and threw it viciously against a wall.

Then, deflated, he turned away. It did no good, he knew. There were no Germans here, and none of his mates. They'd been taken away – wounded or not – as prisoners of war. He was left alone.

I'll carry on all the same, he vowed, setting his face once more in the direction of Dunkirk. I'll get there, and I'll get on a ship and I'll get home. And then I'll do whatever the Army wants me to. I'll fight to the death to stop this happening to Stoke Gabriel and Dittisham and all the other villages I know.

The rage he felt now would carry him right through the war.

The Germans must have been an isolated patrol who had managed to get through the line still held by the rearguard of the retreating British, and Jan saw no more signs of them as he walked wearily along the road leading to Dunkirk. He did, however, see a good many more soldiers and refugees – the former heading towards the port, the latter heading away. There were crowds of men making for the black smoke now – a growing mass of unshaven, khaki-clad men who not long ago would have marched with their heads held high in proud confidence. Now, they were shaken and defeated, wanting only to get away; and yet there was still a spark of defiance, lit by the same rage that had fuelled Jan's resolve. They had lost a battle but they hadn't lost the war. They weren't beaten. They would be back, and next time the Germans wouldn't have it all their own way.

As dusk fell, Jan joined up with a group of other soldiers. They had found a deserted cottage with a well, thankfully uncontaminated, and here they were able to replenish their empty water-bottles and grub up a few early vegetables from the garden. They lay on the floor, almost too weary to sleep, and by dawn they were on their way again. Now that they were getting close to Dunkirk, they marched with more purpose, doggedly determined to get there for whatever ships could still enter the harbour. How this would be achieved in a port that was so clearly under fire and bombardment, they didn't know, but there was nothing else for them to do, no other order to follow. If Dunkirk failed them, they would stand on the beaches and fight to the last drop of blood. But Dunkirk would not fail them. Dunkirk *could* not fail them.

The sounds of gunfire and shelling were louder and closer now. They came from both behind them and ahead, as if they were surrounded by fighting. The air was throbbing with the noise of aircraft, hidden by the pall of smoke, and every few minutes the ground shook with the thuds and crumps of explosions not far away.

The area within the perimeter, still being held around the Dunkirk area to enable as many men as possible to escape, was shrinking as the rearguard was pushed nearer and nearer to the coast. Jan had been aware of it somewhere behind him all the time, but now he began to wonder if the Germans would catch up with them before they even reached the port. Surely there were enough of them here to put up a good fight . . .

But the BEF was in disarray. The men were split up from their own battalions. For days now, they had had little sleep, food or water. They still had their rifles, but were almost out of ammunition. Most of their vehicles had been destroyed; the few still on the road were crammed with injured men, and many of the soldiers on their feet were helping others. They were in no condition to make a stand.

Jan found himself at the head of the throng. None of the others were from the 7th Cornwalls but it was enough to be with fellow Britons. They talked a little amongst themselves, but for the most part they marched in silence, too numbed by their experiences and their condition to swap stories, tell jokes or sing.

A few straggling houses came into sight, and then a few more. The smoke was not much more than a mile away now, drifting over them like clouds to obscure the blue sky. The clear, honest warmth of the sun was dulled by its surly heat.

'Where's this place we're coming to?' Jan asked. 'Looks like a town.'

The man next to him shrugged but a sergeant said, 'I saw a sign back there. It's called Furnes.'

'We're getting near the sea then,' a corporal walking just behind

Jan called out. 'I've seen a map. It's only about half a mile now. We can follow the canal into Dunkirk.'

Half a mile! The thought put heart into them all and their pace quickened. Soon, just as the corporal had said, they came to a stretch of water and realised that they were at the junction of two broad canals. The bridge was still intact and they crossed and turned west towards Dunkirk, with the morning sun on their backs.

'They're still bombing it,' Jan said, suddenly realising where the aircraft were heading. 'You can tell by the sound.' A massive explosion shook the earth. 'And that one – that's out at sea. They're bombing the ships as well!' A wave of panic shuddered through him. 'What chance do us have? What's the point of going to Dunkirk at all, just to be blown to bits?' His feet stopped moving and the men behind him shoved into each other.

'What the hell—?'

'Bloody idiot's stopped – get a move on, can't you? We got a boat to catch!'

'But we're not going to catch it!' Jan was trembling, almost in tears. 'Can't you hear? They're blowing the whole flaming place to bits, they're bombing the ships and the harbour and everything. We're never going to get out of here, never! It's crazy, they're just sending us all over France because they don't know what else to do with us. They *know* we're all going to be killed – we've just got to keep on walking till it's all over. I wish it was all over now, I wish I'd been killed when t'others were, in the village. I wish – I wish . . .' He broke down, crumpling in a heap, sobbing with desperation and fear and exhaustion.

'Get him up! *Get him up!*' The sergeant's voice was harsh and Jan felt the toe of his boot in his side. 'I don't want no panic! Get him on his feet – *now*.' A couple of privates heaved Jan upright and held him between them. The sergeant pushed his face close to Jan's. His cheeks were red with sunburn and rough with the stubble of several days; his eyes were slits of fury. 'Now you listen to me, my son,' he snarled. 'I could have you chucked in the canal for that little tantrum. I'm in two minds about doing it anyway. But I'll give you the choice, see? You can either walk to Dunkirk with the rest of us, and take whatever's coming to you, or you can swim. The canal goes all the way and I'll personally make sure you swim every last bloody yard of it. And you needn't think you're going to wear the King's uniform while you're doing it. You ain't *fit* to wear the King's uniform. Now, what's it to be?'

His speech had given Jan time to pull himself together. He dragged a deep breath down into his lungs and said, 'I'll walk. Sorry, Sarge, I just—'

'I don't bloody want to know what *you just*,' the sergeant growled. 'But if you does it again, in the canal you go, and no backchat. Now, let's get on. We got a job to do, and if we got to get back to Blighty before we can get on with it, then that's what we'll do. I dunno if you perishers realise it, but we're in the British Army and we got a war to fight.'

The muttering rabble that had formed behind the two men started to move again. They were approaching the beach now, and the aerial bombardment had increased. The ground had become sandy and swollen into dunes, freckled with tough, tussocky grass. The men came over the crest of the slope and stopped again.

'Bloody hell,' the sergeant said in a low voice.

Chapter Twenty-Five

A lex cleaned Sid's head as well as he could and put a clean bandage round it. 'It's not too bad – didn't penetrate the skull. He's groggy now, but he'll be all right.'

'Missus always did say I had a thick head,' Sid said faintly. He was sitting at the side of the road. His colour had returned and he gave Joe a faint grin. 'Thanks for that, mate. If it'd bin left to Dave Fawley, I'd still be in the flaming ditch.'

'Been trying to get rid of you for years,' Fawley said and gripped his shoulder. 'Have to think of something else now.'

The little group stood considering what to do next. The Cornwalls had had enough of scrambling across dykes and wire fences, and were thankful to find a road that appeared to be going in the right direction. Yet when they looked at the huge blanket of smoke hovering over Dunkirk, they wondered how this could possibly be correct. The town was obviously under constant attack. Great formations of aircraft were passing over all the time, apparently too concerned with bombarding the harbour to bother about the straggling army making its way along the roads and across the country, and puffballs of smoke could be seen as more bombs were dropped.

'There can't be anyone left alive,' Ginette whispered. 'The whole place must be destroyed.'

'There must be someone, or they wouldn't still be bombing it,' Alex pointed out. 'Not that that's exactly a comforting thought. But where else can we go? That's where the ships are supposed to be coming – there's no point in going anywhere else.'

'If we stay around here, we'll either be killed or taken prisoner,' the Major added. 'I know the likelihood is pretty high that that's what'll happen if we go on, but do we want to try, or do we just want to be sitting ducks for the next Panzer that comes along? Anyway, we've got our orders. Make for Dunkirk. And, when the worst comes to the worst, it's every man for himself.'

They set off along the road. Sid was able to walk now, albeit rather unsteadily and supported by Dave Fawley. There were other men also being supported by their mates, as well as the half-dozen stretcher cases. Two badly wounded men had died as they crossed the fields; they had been buried in shallow graves, with their rifles (bolts and ammunition removed) dug in to mark the place. Two of the others appeared to be deteriorating, and Alex and the Major were keeping a careful eye on them. Water and rations were desperately low.

'I don't want a drink,' Ginette said when they paused for a few minutes and Alex offered her his bottle. 'Give it to that poor man with the broken legs. He needs it more – they all do.'

'I know they do. But it's not going to do them any good if we don't keep our own strength up. If we get dehydrated, we won't be able to look after them.' He offered her the bottle again. 'Drink some, Ginette.'

She took the bottle and let a mouthful run past her lips, then handed it back. Alex was right. No one was having enough fluids. Water just had to be shared around so that they could all survive until they next had a chance to fill their bottles.

More and more people were joining the throng straggling towards Dunkirk. There were small groups, whole platoons, and men who had been travelling alone by night and hiding in woods or old barns by day. Now, despite the attack concentrated so fiercely on the port, they still felt a desperate need to get there whatever the dangers. Everyone seemed determined to keep going, with only the shortest pauses for rest. In any case, there was little cover in this wide, flat area. Even at night, the German bombers need only fly over and drop bombs at random to score quite a lot of hits.

'God knows what we're going to find when we get there,' Major Breakspear said to Alex. 'I've been to Dunkirk before and know that there's an excellent harbour there, with a good many basins, but it's reachable only through a narrow passage between two long piers. This bombing must have destroyed a lot of that. I don't see how they can get the ships in and out.'

'Perhaps they're going to use the beaches,' Alex said doubtfully. 'I've never sailed in that area – my home's in Chichester and we used to potter about the Solent mostly – but I've done a couple of Channel crossings and looked at the charts. Isn't the area north of Calais very level and sandy?'

'It is. But the tide goes out a long way, so it's shallow. They'll never get the ships in close enough.' The older man thought for a minute. 'I suppose they could use their lifeboats to ferry men over, but it'd be a long job. They won't be able to get many away at a time.'

Alex glanced round at the long line of soldiers trailing along the road. This is just a part of the entire BEF, he thought – and a pretty small part. There must have been men making for Dunkirk for days now, and then there's the rearguard, trying to hold off the Germans as long as possible before they follow us. Thousands of men. Perhaps hundreds of thousands. It's an impossible undertaking.

Once again, he regretted allowing Ginette to come with him. She should have gone south with her parents. France was a huge country – surely the Germans would never be able to take it over completely. They couldn't have enough men to occupy such an enormous area as well as fight a war that was developing so many fronts. The far south was bound to remain safe. She would have been far better off to have gone there.

However, she was with him now and he must look after her. His main desire was to get her home to Chichester where she could stay with his parents. As a doctor's daughter, she would fit into the household easily – she could even help his father in the practice. And Alex himself could go wherever he was sent next, knowing that she'd be there waiting for him whenever he was able to return.

Thinking of his parents led him on to thinking about his sister, Sheila. He wondered if she had heard about this retreat yet and was anxious about him. Would he ever see her again? And Charles, and the children – Wendy and the twins? He wondered how much they had grown by now and if they'd remember their Uncle Alex when – *if* – he ever got back.

Alex's face softened when he thought of Paddy. He'd always been especially fond of her, with her bright, sparkling spirit and her tomboyish ways. He thought of the way they had joked about getting married as soon as she was old enough, remembering the little grass ring he had made her once, with a daisy on it, and slipped on to her finger as an 'engagement' ring. Yes, it would be good to see Paddy again.

'What are you smiling at?' Ginette asked him, and he turned to her.

'I was just thinking about the family at home. You're going to love them, Ginette, and they're going to love you.' He felt a sudden pang of terror at what unknown dangers they must face before Ginette and his family could meet, followed swiftly by a renewed determination to get her to England. To get all these men to England too, he added to himself, looking at the walking wounded and the stretcher cases they had managed to bring this far. We've almost reached Dunkirk. We're not going to let them beat us now.

However badly Dunkirk was damaged, however difficult it was to get the Army away from French shores, he felt suddenly convinced that it would be done. The sense of determination that had surged through him then must be echoed throughout all the doggedly marching men now making for the black smoke. And it must also be surging through those in England whose job it was to run this war, to send thousands of men to battle – and, when necessary, to bring them back.

There was no handy school building, nor even a cottage for the 7th Cornwalls to shelter in that night. They walked on for as long as possible as darkness fell and then found a small clump of trees in which to shelter. Alex, the Major and Ginette went round tending to the wounded men as best they could. The wounds needed bathing and clean dressings applied, but apart from dabbing on some disinfectant there was little that could be done. They handed them over to the orderlies, and sat down at the roots of a tree to share out what little food they had left, then tried to make themselves comfortable on the rough, hard ground.

Alex spread his greatcoat out for Ginette to lie on, then wrapped it round her. 'You'll get cold without it.'

'And so will you,' she whispered, and held out her arms.

He touched her cheek gently with one finger. 'I'm sorry about this, Ginette. I'd no idea it would be this bad. You should have gone with your parents.'

He heard her sigh a little. 'I think about them all the time, *chéri*. I feel as if I'm being torn in half. They wanted me to go to England, and I wanted to be with you – but now I'm not sure. I don't know what I should have done.' Her sigh had a faint sob in it. 'If only I knew they were safe . . .'

'I'm sure they are. The Germans are concentrating on this part of France now. They won't be going south. If your parents can get to Marseilles . . .'

'We have family and good friends there,' she said. 'They'll be looked after.'

They were silent for a few minutes. Then Alex bent and kissed her cheek.

'Go to sleep now, my darling. We all need our rest. We don't know what tomorrow is going to bring.'

'Tomorrow,' she said wistfully. 'This time tomorrow, we may be back in England.'

'Yes,' Alex said quietly, 'we may.'

They were on the move again before dawn. The rest had helped them all, although water was now desperately low and the rations were almost gone. With a few minutes' rest every hour or so, they trudged on.

Joe was now one of the stretcher-bearers. Sid could manage with Dave Fawley's help, but a sergeant who had been shot in the thigh yet still managed to keep walking for some time had finally collapsed. They heaved his burly body on to the last spare stretcher and Joe took the front while one of the nursing orderlies took the back.

'I tell you what,' the orderly said, 'I'd rather be playing the trumpet than lugging old Biffy round France. You wonder sometimes how you come to be doing things, don't you? I mean, what could I've done different, so that I needn't have ended up here?'

Joe couldn't follow this piece of philosophy. 'I dunno what you mean, mate.'

'Well, I mean if I hadn't sat in our back kitchen when I was a kid and told my dad I wanted a go on his trumpet, and if he hadn't let me and said I hadn't got a bad blow for a nipper, and if I hadn't joined the Army as a bandsman, well, I wouldn't have been here today lugging old Biffy through France, now would I?'

Joe untangled these words and then said, 'No, but you'd probably have joined up anyway when war broke out and then you might be laying dead in a ditch by now. I reckon you was meant to come to France. I reckon we all were. Like bombs having your name on them – it's all worked out and we can't get out of it, whatever we do.'

'My mum says that. She says whatever will be, will be.' The orderly thought for a moment, then added, 'Mind you, she didn't say that when my dad tripped over the cat and smashed half her best tea service!'

They walked on in silence for a while and then the Major called a halt. None of them could march for long; almost all the fit men were either supporting a walking wounded or taking turns in carrying a stretcher. Ginette had been moving from one sick man to another, administering sips of water, wiping sweaty brows or simply placing her hand on theirs for a few moments. They all knew that she was Captain Rowley's wife, and several of them had begun to call her an angel. She laughed and said, 'A funny sort of angel, looking like this!'

'You're looking lovely, darlin',' one of the corporals, wounded in his face, croaked. 'Bloody sight better in that uniform than us ugly buggers.'

Ginette smiled and smoothed his hair out of the way of his injury. 'You're all very handsome. Nearly as handsome as the French, in fact!'

The Major called for attention and the little band gathered round him. The crowd of retreating soldiers had formed themselves into groups, either in their own units which had managed to stay together, or as clusters of lone soldiers. They moved on or stopped according to their own condition, and most of them passed on by. One or two, who hadn't yet found a unit to join, stopped on the fringe and listened.

'We're getting near Dunkirk,' Breakspear said. 'We've all heard and seen the increased aerial activity. It's obvious that the closer we get, the more dangerous the situation is going to be. However, we have no choice – it's our duty to do our best to return to England. Remember that, all of you. *Not* returning – unless you have no choice but to be taken prisoner – will be counted as an act of desertion.' He paused and looked around at the motley crew – filthy, bedraggled, their uniforms torn and muddy, many of them wearing bloodsoaked bandages or leaning on makeshift crutches – and said, 'A smart soldier is an efficient soldier. If we can't dress smartly we can at least march smartly. From now on, we act as if we are proud to be Cornwalls. Atten-*tion*!'

The order was barked out so sharply that most of them did indeed leap to attention; even those who couldn't do so tried to straighten their shoulders and lift their chins. The Major gave them another look and nodded.

'That's better. Now, form up and let's go forward together. Show whoever's there in Dunkirk – friend or foe – what the Seventh Cornwalls are made of. *By* the left, *qui*-ick – *march*!'

Once again they set off. Joe had been relieved of stretcher duty for a time and marched as well as he could, but like everyone else he was almost unbearably weary. His stomach rumbled with hunger, his legs felt weak and his mouth was burning with thirst.

'I hope to God they've got a few ice-cream carts on this beach when we get there,' he said to his neighbour. The march was once more dwindling to a stumbling walk. 'Wonder if they'll have thought to bring water and a bite to eat. I don't suppose they got any idea what we're going through here. Think we're camped out in nice cosy tents, boiling up tea and playing cards.'

'I tell you what,' the other man said. 'What I've been worrying about is an invasion. I mean, with all of us stuck here, who's to stop the Jerries just crossing the Channel and marching in? They've got Belgium now, and Calais, and all them ports down that way. I dunno why they'd even bother about us now – bomb a few ships, and we're high and dry while they go and take our homes and our wives and every bloody thing.'

Joe stared at him. 'Do you really think that?'

'I dunno what to think,' the other man said morosely. 'I just think it's all a flaming bloody mess. I don't think they know what they're doing, none of 'em. They starts these things and they just grow and grow. Spread all over the world like bloody weeds, they do, and nobody can stop them. And it's us poor buggers who have to go and do the dirty work – fighting and killing and getting killed, when we don't even know what it's all about, not properly. I mean, where's the sense in it all, eh? Tell me that.'

Joe couldn't tell him. 'I never even thought about that,' he said in dismay. 'I never thought what might be happening at home. They could be getting bombed this very minute.' He thought of Mum and Dad and the girls in London, right by the docks – surely one of the main targets for the Germans. And suppose this bloke was right and the Germans were invading! They might be there already, marching into *his* home, holding *his* mother and sisters at bayonet-point. And Connie, too . . . it didn't bear thinking about.

'We got to get back,' he said, quickening his pace. 'Bloody hell – I'll swim if I have to.'

The Major called another brief halt. They sat at the roadside, taking a sip of water. There wasn't much left. Joe looked at the ditch and wondered what kind of germs lurked there. He rested his head on his arms.

I've never felt so fed up in all my life, he thought. There's never been nothing as bad as this. I didn't know anything *could* be as bad as this. Stuck here in France, with all the English Channel between me and home, not knowing what's going on there, not knowing if I'll ever see any of them again . . .

Something wet touched his hands. He ignored it. It pushed hard against him, and he heard a small whimper. For a moment, he seemed to freeze solid, and then, slowly, he lifted his head and stared.

A wet, black nose. Two trusting brown eyes. A small white head with a brown patch over one eye.

'*Pirate!*' he exclaimed, and swept the little body into his arms. The pup was even thinner than he remembered, but just as warm, just as wriggly, just as excited. 'Pirate, where the hell did *you* come from?'

'Oh, is he yours?' A private passing by in another unit had stopped and was looking down at him. 'He tagged on with our lot about four miles back. We knew he was looking for someone – he kept running off and sniffing at different blokes and then coming back. Looks like it was you.'

'Yes,' Joe said. 'Yes, it was me.' He buried his face against the warm, panting body and felt a wave of hope buoy him up. 'I reckon I ought to've called you Lucky,' he said to the dog. 'You're my lucky mascot, you are. And you're coming the rest of the way with me – all the way back to England. OK?'

The puppy gave a small, contented whimper and settled into his arms. Joe stroked his head.

'You're going to be my Connie's birthday present,' he whispered. 'I'll take you back to England and give you to her meself.'

Chapter Twenty-Six

'**B**loody hell,' the sergeant said again, and Jan silently echoed his words, unable to find any of his own or a voice in which to speak them. All the way along the roads and across the unfamiliar French countryside, he had never been sure what they would find when they eventually reached Dunkirk. He couldn't picture the scene awaiting them, couldn't imagine what it would be like to see the ships trying to enter a harbour that was being incessantly bombed, that was on fire and shrouded in dense, choking smoke. As time had gone on, he had veered from being determined to get back home no matter what the obstacles might be, to despair at ever seeing England again. Deep down, he'd thought he was going to die, as he'd seen Bert and Sam and so many others die. He had only kept going because there was nothing else to do while he waited.

Now he stared at the little ships crowding the sea, as near as they could get to the beach, and caught his breath.

The beach extended on either side, ten miles of broad, pale sand that in better times would have been crowded with French families on holiday. But these were not better times, and the men who crowded the beaches of Bray Dunes and La Panne were not on their holidays.

The sands were black with them. Men in stained, muddy khaki, swarming about with no apparent purpose. Men sitting in attitudes of weary hopelessness. Men lying where they had dropped, too exhausted to pick themselves up. Wounded men, tended by their friends or just abandoned. Dead men, half-buried in the shifting sands, stiffened into grotesque postures. And even, most bizarrely of all, a few men kicking a ball about amongst the dunes.

Thousands and thousands of men.

The tide was half-out, leaving a wide expanse of rippling wet sand. There were men there too – long queues of them, grouped at the edge of the tideline and stretching out into the shallow water. They stood up to their ankles, their knees, their waists, as if setting out together on a long cross-Channel walk. But they weren't walking. They were just standing – standing in the water, waiting for the rescue they had been promised.

Jan dragged his eyes away from the thick, shifting mass of men, and looked out to sea. He blinked, rubbed his eyes, stared and blinked again.

'Why, there must be all the boats in England out there,' he said. 'Look at them – fishing boats, sailing dinghies, posh motor boats, tugs – why, there's even one or two holiday-steamers, just like the ones what go up and down the river where I live. Where've they all come from? Who sent 'em?'

'I reckon somebody's bin thinking about us after all,' the sergeant said slowly. 'They must've knowed we'd need to get off the beaches and they sent all these little tubs to get in close.'

Above them, above the heavy blanket of smoke that dimmed the sun and turned the bright day into twilight, the German bombers snarled and thundered and let their bombs fall, sometimes into an empty patch of sea, sometimes on to a ship or a huddle of men; both sea and beach were spattered with explosions that flung great sprays of sand and water into the air, reddened with blood and torn, wretched scraps of human remains. There were wrecks, too, wrecks of small boats that had come all the way across the Channel only to be smashed to pieces; and wrecks of bigger ships, foundered on the sands offshore, lying with the sea washing in through the gaping holes in their hulls. And on the beach there were wrecked vehicles, burned or bogged down in sand. Someone had even built a pier of broken-down lorries, jutting out into the water for the men to scramble along to reach the rowing boats, dinghies and ships' lifeboats that were ploughing through the wreckage to reach them.

'I thought it'd be destroyers and frigates, things like that, coming to get us,' Jan said. 'Naval ships. But these are the sort of boats we see down on the Dart – the sort folks use for a spot of fishing, or chaps with a bit of money have built for their holidays.' He shook his head. 'Why, they'm barely big enough to leave harbour, some of 'em. How've they got across the Channel? There must be mines and all sorts – and who's in charge of 'em?' The more he thought about it, the more astounding it seemed. 'It's a miracle,' he said wonderingly. 'A bloody miracle.'

'It'll be a miracle of we manages to get aboard one of 'em,' another man said gloomily. 'There's thousands queued up here. And look at the state of 'em! Look at the state of *us*!'

Jan turned and regarded the group behind him. His moment of panic was over, but he knew that they, like himself, were near their limits. Their heads ached, their stomachs ached, their mouths and throats were burning, their limbs weak. A lot of them had diarrhoea or kept pausing to vomit, and often the vomit contained blood. Yet they had still kept putting one foot in front of another, trudging along the road towards the black smoke. They had still kept going.

They had kept going because there was nothing else to do and, now that they were here at last, the sight of the throng of little ships and the huge crowd of men on the beach, stretching as far as the eye could see in this thick, acrid haze, was both inspiring and daunting. Who would have believed that all these tiny craft could have come all this way, through such dangers, to rescue them – and who could dare to hope that with so many thousands of men on the beaches, such little boats could ever succeed?

'Well, us don't have a choice, do us?' he said at last. 'Here us be and here us got to stop, until one or t'other of them comes for us.' He turned and plodded heavily through the sand, weary of the men he had been with, weary of the dizziness that kept overtaking him, weary of the whole blooming war. He felt too weary even to panic any more, so that when a Stuka thundered below the cloud and along the length of the beach, dropping bombs as it went, he simply watched dully as sand blew outwards and upwards in a series of explosions. He knew that there must have been men killed. Knew too that it could as easily be himself next time – but what was the point of caring? If it had your name on it . . .

'Here, mate. Have a drink of water. You look all in.'

Jan turned his head disbelievingly towards the man standing over him. He was dressed in seaman's gear – dark blue trousers and jumper, with a navy-blue tin helmet on his head and sea boots – and he was carrying what looked like a tin water-container. As Jan stared at him, he unscrewed the cap and held it out. 'Come on, mate. Drink up. I bet you haven't had a proper drink for days.'

'No.' Still unbelieving, Jan took the container and tipped it towards his mouth. Cool, fresh liquid ran between his lips and down his dry throat and he gulped it down, desperate in case it might be suddenly taken away. But the man just stood there watching, with a grin on his face as if it gave him real pleasure to see Jan so thankful.

'There,' he said when Jan took the container away from his lips at last. 'Bet that feels better. All you blokes are like this, had nothing much to eat or drink. It's just as bad in the town, too – water supplies been blown up, see.' He made to take back the container. 'Want any more? Only there's a lot more blokes need it too.'

'Just another mouthful.' Jan was reluctant to let the water go. He drank again and then handed it back. 'How did you know to bring water?'

'Stood to reason, didn't it? There ain't no NAAFI canteens over here now. The ships coming over to pick up you blokes, they're all loaded up with grub and water. Someone'll be along with a plate of fairy cakes in a mo, I shouldn't wonder!' He grinned and moved on, offering his container to the next exhausted arrival, and Jan lay back in the sand, feeling the thump in his head diminish a little. Hunger still gnawed at him, but that wasn't as bad as thirst. You could be hungry and still live for weeks – but without liquid, you had only a few days.

For the first time, he began to feel a flicker of hope. The Authorities at home did, after all, know what was happening. They knew there were thousands of men all coming to the same place, they knew they would need small boats to get them offshore; they knew the men would need food and water. Someone had thought of it all; someone back home had got things organised.

As Jan lay there in the sand he sent up a little prayer of gratitude to whoever it was who had seen what would be needed and had done something about it.

If ever I meet that man, he thought dreamily, I'll be proud to shake him by the hand.

The 7th Cornwalls were a small, raggle-taggle band by the time they reached the beach.

Pirate was not the only dog accompanying them now. All the dogs of Dunkirk, it seemed, had been driven out of the town by the noise and the stench of bombing, the constant shelling from the German guns at Gravelines, and the flames and smoke of burning oil and buildings. They had followed the soldiers to the beaches and stayed there, running about on the sands in a yapping frenzy of panic or attaching themselves to men in the hope that they would be looked after. Some of them were adopted by men who just needed something warm and living to comfort them; some died of their own wounds and lay, lost and forgotten, on the sand.

Joe had buttoned Pirate into his jacket for the last mile or so, so that he could continue to carry a stretcher, and when they came over the dunes and stopped at the top of the beach the little dog poked his head out and whimpered to be put down. Slowly, staring at the scene before him much as Jan had done an hour or two earlier, Joe unfastened the buttons and set him on the sand.

'Blimey,' he said in a low, wondering tone.

Alex and Ginette stood beside him. Ginette made a soft sound in her throat and felt for Alex's hand. He gripped her fingers firmly and drew her against his side. A tear slid down her cheeks.

'*Chéri*, it's terrible.'

'Terrible?' Alex said. 'It's wonderful. Look at all the little ships, Ginette – little ships come all the way from England to fetch us and take us home. Think of what it means. People from all along the south coast, maybe even further than that, have lent their own boats, boats they love and cherish, to come here through all this danger just to carry us back. They may never see them again. These boats – these little cruisers and motor yachts and fishing boats – they're part of their lives. They're almost as important as their homes and families. Yet they've sent them out – maybe they've even brought them themselves – because we need them. It's the most wonderful thing I've ever seen.'

'Yes,' Joe said slowly. 'You're right, Captain Rowley. It's bloody wonderful – excuse my French,' he added to Ginette, and then caught himself up again. 'I mean – I didn't mean – well, anyway, it *is* a wonder. A miracle.'

'A miracle,' Alex repeated. He stared at the long lines of soldiers, moving slowly but steadily towards the little boats working so busily in the shallow waters. The clouds hung heavy and low, and the sea was red with blood and scattered with a macabre flotsam of broken bodies. He saw a small boat, filled with soldiers, suddenly disappear in a shower of water and splintered wood, and felt sickened. And yet, this was war. Men would be killed. It couldn't be avoided.

As long as more men got away than were left dead on this grim, sandy shore. As long as enough got back to England, to defend it from the invaders and fight another day.

'A miracle . . .' he said quietly.

The voice penetrated Jan Endacott's consciousness as he lay half-dozing against a sand dune. *A miracle*. But it was not simply the phrase that caught at his attention, dragging him out of the daze into which he had fallen. It was the voice. It was a voice he knew.

He turned his head and saw that yet another group of soldiers had arrived on the beach; a motley collection of tramps if ever he'd seen one, he thought. About a dozen or so, all told: a Major, a Captain and a few nursing orderlies with some wounded men, several of them on stretchers. He looked at their faces, grimed with mud and thick with stubble, and then at their shoulder flashes.

'My stars!' he exclaimed weakly. 'You'm Cornwalls!'

The men turned quickly. They stared down at him and then Joe came over and dropped on his knees beside him.

'Why, if it ain't Jan Endacott! You remember me, don't you? Joe Mears, from good old Blighty? We done our training together.'

'Course I remember.' Jan struggled to sit up. 'I lost track of you when us had to go our separate ways. My stars, Joe, 'tis good to see you again.' His head spun and he slumped back again. Joe quickly slipped an arm behind his shoulders and glanced round, and Alex came over.

'I know this man – I've treated him at some time.' His brows came together and then his face cleared. 'You're a Devon man – Endacott, isn't that the name? You had a sprained ankle.'

Jan grinned faintly. ''Tis better now, thanks, sir. Glad to see you'm well. And the Major, and t'others.' He glanced at Ginette's slim figure in the overlarge battledress, her face dirty like the others but innocent of any stubble. 'I remember most of 'em, anyway. Not that young feller.'

Alex smiled. 'That's my wife,' he said. 'Her father was the doctor in the village where we were billeted.' He felt Jan's forehead. 'How are you feeling? Have you been wounded?'

Jan shook his head. 'No sir, I'm all right. Just a bit mazed with all the noise and not having much to eat or drink.' The dizziness overtook him again and he put his hand to his head. 'Someone gave me some water just now. I drank it and then I remembered . . .' He swayed where he sat, and Alex lowered him gently to the sand again. 'I remembered the well,' he whispered.

'The well? You got water from a well? That should be all right. Most of the wells are pretty deep, and as long as the water's not been fouled . . .' Alex stopped as Jan turned his head aside and vomited. 'You'd better just rest,' he said gently. 'Don't think about it. Don't think about anything. We'll look after you, Endacott. We'll get you back to England.'

He straightened up and stared at the scene before him: the dunes, black with men sitting, lying, wandering about, queuing in the sea with the incoming tide reaching up their bodies; the sea, massed with wreckage and bodies, yet still with small boats ploughing determinedly back and forth, hauling men on board and ferrying them out to the destroyers and personnel ships that waited to take them back to England. Thousands of men. Tens of thousands of men.

How long will we have to wait here? he wondered. How long before we even reach the edge of the water, before we can join the queue? How long before we get these starved and wounded men back to England?

It seemed hopeless. And yet, as he looked again at the little ships that had come to rescue them, he knew that hope could not die. Not while there was this fortitude of spirit to keep it alive.

'We'll all get back to England,' he said.

PART THREE

Chapter Twenty-Seven

Monday, 3 June

The first thing Effie did, the morning after the service in St Paul's, was to send Carrie round to the electrical shop with the accumulator from the wireless.

'We got to be able to hear the News. It's daft, letting it run down like that. Leave it on the step with a note for Mr Huggins – he'll find it when he opens up.'

Nobody liked lugging the heavy glass tank full of acid round to the shop, but it had to be done if you wanted to hear the wireless. Carrie did as she was told and then came round to the café with a copy of the *Daily Sketch* under her arm. Dot was with her.

'Look at this, Mum. Look at this picture on the front page.' She spread it on a vacant table and they stared at the photograph of a ship packed with men in tin helmets. 'And look at the headline – it says four-fifths of the BEF have been saved. There's more inside.' She turned to page 3 and began to read aloud. '*Three hundred thousand Germans, with artillery and bombers, are hammering day and night at the heroic Allied defenders of Dunkirk as the remainder of the BEF and French units embark*. Oh Mum!' Her face was white as she took in the numbers. 'That's nearly as many of them as there are of our boys.'

'Yes, but it does say more than four-fifths of ours are safe,' Effie reminded her, though her heart was shaking. 'And look, they reckon they'll get another hundred thousand off in the next forty-eight hours.' She read on a little further. '*The RAF yesterday destroyed 35 enemy planes over Dunkirk and probably another six*.' She skipped the next bit, which reported that eight of the Allied planes were missing and that a thousand Nazi planes were engaged in the Channel section. *A thousand!* Whatever must it be like? 'And see this bit, about food and water being dropped by parachute – that's good, isn't it? And there's a hundred of our warships and twice that many transport ships bringing them back.' She folded the newspaper and went back to the stove, deep in thought. There had been no attempt by the reporter to raise people's hopes that all their men would come back safe, but surely amongst all those thousands Joe and Benny would have a chance. And Olly too, in his fireboat.

'They're coming to Ramsgate, Mum, a lot of them,' Dot said. 'They're hungry and thirsty and some of them are wounded. The authorities are asking for volunteers to help, even if it's just to hand out cups of tea.'

Effie had started frying sausages and mashed potato for the breakfasts of the men who worked in the market. She put down the tin frying-slice and looked at her daughters.

'Ramsgate?'

'Yes,' Dot said. 'And I'm going down to help. I might even see my Benny. Even if I don't, at least I'll be doing something. I can't just stop here doing nothing, Mum.'

'No, love, of course you can't.' Effie thought for a moment, then lifted the sausages from the pan and dumped them on a plate with the fried mash. She started to untie her pinafore. 'I'll come too.'

'*You* will?' Carrie stared at her. 'But what about the caff? You can't close it.'

'You can stop and look after it. Get that girl Betty over, the one that comes in if anyone's poorly. She's always asking for a job here. I know she's only ninepence in the shilling, but she can wash up and do the fries.' Effie was working briskly as she talked, checking the supplies, putting up the plates that had already been ordered, refilling the big brown teapot. 'Me and Dot will go to Ramsgate and see what we can do. We'll go to Eric and Marge's – they're right on the front, they're bound to be doing tea and stuff, and they'll be glad of a hand. There's your dad and our Joe, as well as Benny,' she added sharply as Carrie opened her mouth to say something. 'I want to be there for them, and we can't all go.'

Carrie closed her mouth again and nodded. She had heard her mother tossing and turning during the night, heard her tiptoe downstairs for a drink of water, and had seen the tired, red-rimmed eyes this morning. She had heard all this because Dot, sleeping in the double bed the sisters shared, had tossed and turned as well, and Carrie had heard muffled sobbing and put her arm round Dot to try to comfort her. Of course she was worried sick about her father and brother too, but she knew that somebody had to look after the café. Good thing I had that row with Bert Hollins, she thought, or I wouldn't have been working here now.

'You go, then, both of you,' she said. 'I'll see to things here. And if you sees Dad or our Joe, you give 'em an earful from me, leaving me to do all the work while you jaunts off to the seaside!'

Effie smiled a little waveringly and gave her daughter a kiss. 'We'll go straight off. Now look, if that gent with the bowler hat comes in, you give him an extra sausage, all right? Because if it hadn't been for him, we wouldn't have had any idea what was going on and we wouldn't have gone down to Blackfriars and seen your dad on the *Surrey Queen*. And don't forget to call in for that accumulator. Newspapers are all very well, but it's the *Nine o'Clock News* on the wireless we wants. And we'll be back – well, when we're back, I suppose.' She looked at Dot, standing by the doorway. 'We'd better go home and pack up our nighties. Goodness knows how long this job's going to take.'

They left the café and picked their way through the market stalls and the litter of discarded boxes, cabbage leaves and so on that would be gathered up later by scavenging children and taken home, or sold to the rag-and-bone man for a few halfpennies. Almost everything could be used again, Effie thought. They'd learned to do it through the Depression of the 1930s and were doing it even more now. Saucepans, old jumpers, bits of string and paper bags – nothing was thrown away when it could come in handy another time. Everything could be put towards the war effort.

At home, she and Dot quickly stuffed the few things they'd need into a couple of shopping bags. Their nightdresses, a scrap of soap, a tin of Gibbs' toothpaste and their toothbrushes, two clean pairs of knickers, since they might be away a few days, and a clean vest.

'I'm not taking a vest,' Dot said. 'It's been so warm these past few days.'

'Not take a vest! Of course you'll take a vest, my girl. You know what they say – ne'er cast a clout till May be out.' Effie reached out for the thick woollen garment Dot had put back in the drawer, and rolled it up ready to go into the shopping-bag.

Dot took it out again. 'It's June now, Ma. Anyway, it makes me look all lumpy. I'm not wearing it, not in the summer.'

'You don't know how cold it'll be at Ramsgate, with all them sea-breezes,' Effie said, but her heart wasn't in the argument and she let Dot put the vest back into the drawer. 'Well, I think that's all, don't you? We'd better get ourselves over to the station, see if there's a train.'

To get to Ramsgate, they had to catch a train at Victoria station. They went on the bus along the Embankment, climbing to the top deck so that they could look out at the river.

'There's still a few boats coming down,' Effie said. 'I can't hardly credit it. What's going on over there, that they needs all them little tubs? And how are they going to get across the Channel? It'll take days.'

'They're being towed over by the bigger ships,' Dot said. 'I suppose they can go quite quick. And I don't suppose the Germans are letting them all get away with it, do you? They'll be trying to stop them as much as they can . . .' Her voice faded as she realised the meaning of her own words, and she stared at her mother, suddenly white-faced.

Effie put out her hand quickly. 'Dot, don't think about it. It don't do no good. We just got to wait and see – and do whatever we can to help. That's the best thing.'

'I know, Mum. But looking at them boats – it just seems to bring it all home, somehow. And I can't help thinking about what's happened over there. I mean, it's in all the papers and on the wireless and everywhere. And our Joe's somewhere in it all, and my Benny – and now our dad.' She turned to her mother, tears suddenly streaming down her face. 'Mum, what will we do if none of them comes back?'

Effie thought of her husband, her son, both somewhere on the beaches of Dunkirk, under fire, bombed, hungry and exhausted, perhaps wounded. The images flashed across her mind and she felt a wave of panic. Then she took a deep breath and set her jaw.

'Now, you just stop thinking like that, my girl,' she commanded sternly. 'I've told you already, *it don't do no good*. Of course they'll come back. What did we go to church for yesterday, if it wasn't to ask God to send 'em back?' She thought guiltily of all the other people who had been in St Paul's praying for their own men. 'And even if they don't,' she added a little less firmly, 'there ain't nothing we can do but help the ones who do. It's a *war*, Dot. You don't remember the last one, but I do. We just got to do whatever we can. It don't do no good to give way. Now, you mop up them tears, there's a good girl.'

Dot felt in her sleeve for a hanky and did as she was told. They had reached Westminster Bridge and were now within sight of Big Ben and the Houses of Parliament. Mr Churchill was probably in there now, taking over as Prime Minister from Mr Chamberlain, who had promised 'peace in our time'. Fat lot he knew about it! Effie thought contemptuously. Making up to Hitler, believing in all his promises. Well, Mr Churchill had said all along that this was what it would come to, and now he was in charge maybe he'd be able to do something about the wickedness of the man.

That's if it wasn't too late. If we could just get our boys back home, fit and able and ready to fight again . . .

'That's what all these little ships are doing,' she said suddenly, and Dot looked at her. 'What I said. Doing whatever they can. It might not be much – they might only be able to bring back a few men each. But it's something. And it all adds up, don't it. If everyone does a little bit, it adds up to a lot.'

The bus trundled slowly up towards Parliament Square. Passengers came and went. The conductor swung up the stairs, calling out for fares and cracking jokes. Dot said, 'I've heard they're going to take on women as conductresses. I might go in for that, if I can't get into one of the Services.'

'Well, it'd be better than factory work.' They were getting near to Victoria station now and Effie began to collect up her bags. 'Come on, love. Let's hope there's a train going to Ramsgate soon.'

'I've just thought,' Dot said, following her down the stairs. 'I wonder if they're even sending trains there at the moment. I mean, with it being a seaside resort, they might not think it's worth bothering with.'

'Oh, I expect they will. After all—' Effie stepped off the bus on to the pavement and then stopped dead. She turned to her daughter and said, 'My giddy aunt and all her brothers, Dot. Look at that.'

The station concourse was swarming with soldiers. Clad in dirty, often bloodstained uniforms, their faces still grimy, many of them bandaged or propped on makeshift crutches, they crowded around trolleys and tables that had been set up and laid with cups of tea and huge piles of food. Women were serving them as fast as they could, passing them mugs, which the soldiers downed in one gulp, and sandwiches and buns which they crammed into their mouths before moving on. And as Effie and Dot struggled against the tide to get into the station, they saw that the platforms were lined with trains crowded with yet more soldiers – some getting off, others getting on, in a scene of complete chaos.

'They're the blokes who've come back,' Dot said. 'Mum, our Joe might be here! And Benny too! They might be back already!'

Effie grabbed her arm. The girl looked as if she might go diving into the crowd at any minute, looking for her sweetheart and her brother. 'You come here, our Dot. So they might be, and if they are we got nothing else to worry about, have we? But I still want to go to Ramsgate. There's your father too, don't forget, and they won't be bringing him back by train. He'll have to bring the *Surrey Queen* up the Thames himself, but it's Ramsgate he'll be going to first, and I mean to be there when he arrives.'

'They'll never let us on a train,' Dot said, staring at the confusion. 'Look, the ticket offices are all shut, they're not letting anyone on. The trains are just for the troops.'

'If they're bringing men from Ramsgate and all them places, they got to take the trains back, haven't they?' Effie pointed out. She set off towards the platforms, dragging Dot with her. 'Come on! There's some of them WVS women going down there with a trolley – we'll tag along with them. Nobody'll say nothing.'

Dot looked doubtful, but Effie was already marching along the platform, wearing the look she wore when someone complained about the food in the café or said the tea was like dishwater. Not many of the costermongers in the market were willing to do battle with Effie when she looked like that, and it seemed to be working now too. The man by the end of the platform stood back as she bore down on him, and within a few minutes they were standing beside an empty train. The WVS ladies were setting up their trolley alongside some others and looked at Effie and Dot enquiringly.

'Are you the extra helpers Mrs Dawson said she'd send along?'

'Sorry, we're not,' Effie said. 'We're going to Ramsgate. D'you know if that's where this train's going?'

'Well, I know it's just *come* from there,' the woman said

doubtfully. 'I suppose it must be going back for more troops. Ethel,' she called, raising her voice, 'do you know anything about volunteers going to Ramsgate? Only there's two ladies here saying that's where they're being sent.'

The other woman was busy with a large tea-urn and shook her head. 'Nobody's said anything to me about it. But this train's going back there in a few minutes, so you'd better hop aboard. They're all going back empty, as fast as they can unload at this end.'

'The men are being sent all over the place from here,' the first woman told Effie. 'All over London to other stations and then all over the country. Going to camps and barracks, you see. There's been thousands through.' Someone called her name and she turned away. 'Anyway, that's your train and it sounds as if it's getting up steam so you'd better jump on quick.'

'Come on, Dot,' Effie said, making for a door. 'Get a move on, we don't want to be left behind.'

'But what about tickets?' Dot gave up and followed her mother. The train was now making the urgent, huffing noises that meant it was about to move off. They leaped into the carriage and fell into seats opposite each other, breathing heavily. The engine gave a huge shudder and then a long, despairing sigh and seemed to thrust itself into motion like a horse throwing its shoulders into the shafts.

'There,' Effie said in a tone of satisfaction. 'That was all right, wasn't it!' She peered out of the window at the crowd of weary, shuffling soldiers. 'Oh Dot, those poor boys. Those poor, poor boys . . .'

The trains were not only going to London; they were running all along the south coast as well, filled with soldiers on their way to barracks, camp or even home on a short leave until their regiments could be re-formed. They stopped frequently along the way and at every stop there were members of the Women's Voluntary Service or the Women's Institute, with trolleys and tea-urns. The men crowded to the carriage windows, grinning and waving as the women handed them mugs of tea and buns, and the whole thing took on a strangely festive air.

At Chichester, Olivia, Anne Rowley and Sheila were amongst those waiting on the platforms. When the first train pulled in, nobody knew quite what to expect. They stared, aghast, as the engine drew to a halt and the faces appeared at the windows.

'Oh, those poor boys,' Olivia breathed, echoing Effie Mears's words.

Her air of fragility had left her in the last few days. It was as if the emergency had given her new strength; as if she had mentally rolled up her sleeves. As soon as it was known that the troops would be coming through, she had set about organising a reception committee. The men must be given a proper welcome, a hero's welcome, because heroes were what they were.

She and Anne Rowley had both joined the WVS as soon as it was formed a few years before the war. People were beginning to worry about Hitler even then. Nobody had wanted to believe that there would be another war, but it was better to be prepared and the purpose of the WVS was to be prepared for any emergency. Now was their chance to prove their worth.

'They look exhausted,' Sheila said in a low voice. She looked at the faces, pale beneath the dirt and the dry, scabbed blood, and saw that even the red-rimmed eyes could still twinkle and the cracked lips smile. They came off the train, queuing for the tea and buns, grateful for the small comforts. Someone had brought a box full of packets of cigarettes and was handing these out as well, and the soldiers lit them at once, closing their gritty eyes in bliss as they drew the smoke deep into their lungs.

'Thanks, love. You dunno how good this is,' one of the Tommies said to Sheila. He had lost his battledress jacket and his vest hung on him in shreds. She could see deep grazes on his shoulders. 'I was three days on them beaches,' he went on, gulping down the scalding tea as if it were stone cold. 'Thought I was a goner, and that's the honest truth. And for a whole day of that, d'you know what I done? I just stood in the water, stood there until them little boats come and took us off. I tell you what, I wasn't never much of a one for boats but I bless the day that feller in that little cockleshell come and fetched—'

'Here, move along for Christ's sake,' a voice behind him interrupted. 'We ain't here on our holidays, you know. Someone else wants a cuppa besides you.'

The man shrugged, winked at Sheila and moved on. The next soldier took his place and, almost automatically, she handed him a mug of tea and a bun. He grinned his thanks, and she saw the weariness behind the smile. 'Was it true, what he said?' she asked. 'Three days on the beach – a whole day just standing in water?'

'If that's all he had,' the soldier said tersely, 'he was one of the lucky ones. So am I. There's plenty of blokes never made it – got bombed or shot. It's chaos over there, missus. Nothing but chaos.' He moved on, shuffling in his weariness, and Sheila felt her heart grow cold.

Chaos. And Charles and Alex were there . . .

'Come on, Sheila,' Anne said sharply. 'I know what you're thinking but you've got to put it aside for the time being and concentrate on these men. There's nothing we can do about Charles and Alex and the others. It's these poor chaps we have to think about now.'

Sheila bit her lip and turned back to the teacups. Her mother was right, she knew. There was nothing they could do about the men who were still in France; their task now was to help those who had returned. And as she set herself back to the work, handing over mugs of tea, buns and sandwiches, taking her turn at cutting bread and spreading it with margarine and jam, filling the urn with more water, she found herself almost able to put her husband to the back of her mind, almost able to forget that he was somewhere off the beaches of Dunkirk, perhaps being bombed and shot at, perhaps already dead.

Almost. Not completely.

The trains were reaching even as far as Plymouth. Molly Lovering and Susie Lashbrook, going to Totnes for market day, saw the crowd flocking towards the railway station and followed them. They stood on the platform staring at the packed carriages.

'They'm Frenchies,' said a woman standing nearby, her voice indignant. 'What be they doing here, then? Given in and left us in the lurch, like they Belgians?'

'I suppose they want to get away from the Germans too,' Susie said doubtfully, looking at the unfamiliar uniforms. 'I don't know why they'm coming to Devon, though.'

'Anyway, 'tis not their fault what's happened,' Molly reminded them, and went on bitterly, 'I don't suppose they has any more say in it than our boys. Just has to do as they'm told, like Jan, and didn't even want to be soldiers, most of 'em. That's the trouble with war.

They say we'm a free country here but we're not, not really. Come a bit of trouble and we all has to do as we'm bid, even if it means killing folk we've never met.'

The woman who had spoken first turned on her. 'Here, what be you doing, talking like that? 'Tis unpatriotic, that's what that is.' She glared at the two girls. 'What be you, Fifth Column or summat? Spies?'

The words caused heads to turn all along the platform. Molly flushed scarlet and took a step forward.

'Say that again! I'm no spy, Martha Biddle, no more than you are! I've got a sweetheart gone over to Dunkirk on one of they little ships – Robby Endacott. You known him yourself since he were a babby; he's skippering the *Countess Wear*. It's men like him and Danny Bray who are risking their lives in this war, saving soldiers, and women like me and Susie here and all of us others, that have had to send our men away when us would rather have 'em at home. So don't you call me a spy, Martha Biddle, nor a Fifth Columnist neither! And let's give these poor men here a proper Devon welcome – French or not. They looks as if they needs it.'

The other woman reddened, but when those who had been attracted by the commotion voiced their agreement, she bridled and turned away. Molly and Susie ignored her and stepped forward to the nearest tea-trolley.

'Here, we can help for a bit.' They carried mugs of tea to the men crowding the windows of the train and held them up. The faces split into grins of gratitude and eager hands reached out. Strange voices called words of thanks in a language the girls didn't understand.

'*Merci, mesdemoiselles, mille remerciements.*' They gulped the tea down and made comical faces. '*Du thé anglais!*' they said, and laughed.

'What are they saying?' Susie asked a shade indignantly. 'Don't they like it?'

'I don't think they drink tea in France,' Molly said with a grin. 'They drink coffee, don't they? Anyway, they seem glad enough to have a hot drink, whatever 'tis.' She took back the empty mugs. 'I'll get these washed.'

There was no more time to talk and the shopping they had come to do in the market was forgotten as they dashed to and fro, filling mugs with tea and taking it to the men. The train's stop was no more than fifteen minutes and then it pulled out again on its way to Plymouth. The women who had been so busy paused for a few minutes and looked at each other.

'Are any more coming?' one of the organisers asked, and another shrugged. 'We don't know. I should think so – we'd better be ready for the next lot.' She looked at Molly and Susie. 'You girls have been very helpful. Have you got time to stay, or are you busy?'

Molly glanced at Susie. 'Well, we're supposed to be going to the market – we're both in service, see. But I'm sure Mrs Halford wouldn't mind me stopping a bit longer. What about you, Susie?'

'I don't know.' Susie bit her lip. 'I've got to get back to Greenway. Mr Turner brought me in his trap. I'm to meet him at twelve – I think I'd better go.' She looked at Molly. 'If you see Jan – tell him I was here looking out for him, will you? Tell him I had to go.'

Molly nodded. She knew exactly how Susie felt, could feel the same fear in the pit of her stomach. Jan, Robby, Dan – they were all caught up in the same danger and none of the women would be happy until they were all safe home. She put her hand on Susie's arm and squeezed it gently. 'I will, Sue. And if I do see him, I'll let you know straight away. I'll ring up Greenway from the telephone box. And we'll come back here whenever we can get away, shall us? I wants to be here when Robby gets off that train.'

Susie nodded. 'And I wants to be here when Jan gets off.' She turned and hurried away. When Molly turned back, she saw Martha Biddle looking at her. Their eyes met and the girl felt a pang of shame for the way she had spoken.

'I'm sorry I fired up like that, Mrs Biddle. I was a bit upset, like.'

'I know.' The older woman hesitated, then said, 'I'm sorry too, Molly. I never meant to call you a spy – it just slipped out. We're all upset, that's the truth of it, seeing these poor boys coming back in such a state, and thinking about all the others that are still over there. Your Robby's doing a good job and there's no call for us to quarrel.'

'We'm all in it together,' Molly said soberly. 'We've got to pull together too.' She lifted her head. 'I can hear another train coming. Let's see if the ladies wants us to start pouring tea.'

Chapter Twenty-Eight

Monday, 3 June

Ramsgate was jampacked with soldiers.

In long, stumbling lines, they came off the flotillas of ships that arrived in endless succession at the eastern wall of the harbour. Shaken, bewildered, seasick, many of them bloodstained and bandaged, they leaned upon each other, yet so relieved were they to be back on English soil that they could almost all summon up a grin of sorts. Some, unhurt and in better condition, managed a cheery wave and thumbs-up; but even they were exhausted, wet and dirty from their long wait on the beaches and in the sea. Their legs staggered and buckled beneath them, and as soon as they could the men collapsed on to the benches along the front, on to the harbour wall or just on to the pavements. They looked as if they would never move again.

All along the front were stalls, serving tea, coffee and cocoa and manned by the WVS, ARP and other volunteers from all over the town. Effie and Dot were in the café, slaving harder than they had believed possible at making sandwiches and pots of tea to send out to the men who thronged the streets. They had been welcomed with open arms by Marge and Eric, both exhausted by the last few days' efforts, and by the other organisations who had been setting up canteens, dressing stations and impromptu hospitals. Even the 'Merrie England' funfair had been pressed into service to deal with more serious injuries, and the lift from the beach to the upper promenade creaked up and down constantly, carrying the wounded to the clifftop hotels that had been commandeered.

'What are all those kiddies doing?' Effie asked, looking out of the café window at children and young girls, all making their way to the dock gates. 'They're carrying bags of something or other.'

'That's postcards,' Marge told her. 'They're asking every soldier who they'd like a postcard sent to, to say they're safe. Then they're taking them straight up to the post office. Those families will know their boys are back by tomorrow morning.'

Effie stared at her, then looked out of the window again. 'My Joe could have sent one! If he's back already – oh, if only he is!' She turned to Dot. 'But we won't know – we're here! Oh Dot!'

'It's all right, Mum. Carrie's at home – she'll let us know.'

'How? Marge and Eric aren't on the phone, are you, Marge?'

'Well, then she'll write, won't she. Come on, Mum, let's get on with these sandwiches. There's men out there starving.' Dot thrust a loaf into her mother's arms. 'You slice and I'll put on the margarine and fish paste.'

Effie did as she was told. For a moment, a wild hope had seized her heart that her son might be out there at this very moment, writing a postcard to send home, telling her he was safely back in England. And so he might be, she thought, glancing out of the window at the mass of khaki uniforms. He might even be on his way home in one of those trains. He might be sitting in our back room at this very minute, taking off his boots and asking our Carrie to make him a cuppa.

Or he might be still in France, waiting on the beaches. Queuing up to his neck in cold water, waiting for someone to come and bring him to safety.

Eric, who had been out with the ARP, came back in and caught the tail end of the conversation. He came over to Effie and said, 'I didn't have time to tell you when you first got here, Eff, but there's a fireboat in the harbour. Not the *Surrey Queen* – I looked. It's called the something-or-other *Shaw*. D'you know it?'

'The *Massey Shaw*? Yes, of course I know it!' Effie made to put down the loaf, then picked it up again, holding it against her chest and slicing frantically. 'They work together, the two of 'em. They came down the river together. How long's it been there? Has it been to Dunkirk? Are you sure the *Queen*'s not there as well?'

'I didn't see her, but there's ships coming and going all the time. Mostly the big ones – destroyers and minesweepers, and passenger ferries, things like that. All the little boats that went over, they must still be there. Why don't you go down and have a look?'

Effie hesitated, the last quarter of the loaf still pressed against her bosom. She bit her lower lip and looked at Dot and Marge. 'There's such a lot to do here.'

'Tell you what,' Eric said. 'I'm going back down the harbour, soon as you got these sandwiches made. I'll look out for the *Queen* and if she's not there I'll see if I can have a word with the skipper of the – what did you call it?'

'*Massey Shaw*,' Effie said. 'Oh Eric, would you? And come and tell me as soon as you can, if there's any news? And if the *Queen* is there—'

'I'll be back like a shot,' he promised her. He stood watching as she sliced the last of the loaf and picked up another. He was a thin, scrawny man, as brown as a nut from long years spent living on the seafront, but his eyes were tired. He and Marge had told Effie that they'd been working all the hours God sent and a few He'd been keeping back for emergencies, first of all helping to stock up the small ships and boats before they went to France and now feeding the exhausted soldiers, as well as the boatmen who had brought them back. Just now, Eric had been out to one of the villages to collect more bread – every bakery for miles around had been working overtime, producing loaves for sandwiches, while the farms had been sending all the milk, eggs and bacon they could spare, and women in both towns and villages had been making cakes. It was a wonder, Eric thought, where all the ingredients were coming from, but the Government was playing its part too, sending extra flour, fat and even some dried fruit. It seemed as if the entire area was hard at work making sure the returning troops had a fitting welcome.

The railway station was busy too. The lines had been closed to all but troop trains, which were leaving as soon as they were full. Effie and Dot, arriving on an almost empty train, hadn't even had to pay their fare. The guard had noticed them and asked what they were doing, and when they'd told him they were going to help, and that Effie's husband was on one of the ships that had gone to Dunkirk and she had a son who was a soldier in France, he'd shaken both their hands. 'They're doing a grand job, all of 'em,' he'd said, brushing the back of one of his hands across his whiskers and blinking rapidly. 'I tell you, it fair makes you weep, it does, to see them lads coming back. Fair makes you weep.'

Dot finished another pile of sandwiches and packed them into the cardboard box Eric had brought back with him. 'There you are, that's another one full. There's one here too – can you carry them both?' She put one into Eric's outstretched arms and plonked the other one on top. 'We'll have some more ready when you come back.'

'Flipping production line, this is,' he grinned, and hurried out through the door she was holding open. Dot let it go and turned back to her work, but before it could close someone else had thrust it open and was filling the doorway. She turned, thinking it was Eric, and gave a shriek of surprise.

'*Dad!*'

'What's that? What did you say?' Effie had taken the opportunity to slip out to the lavatory outside the back door. She came running back into the café '*Olly!* Oh, *Olly!*' She blundered through the tables and chairs towards him. 'Oh, it *is* good to see you! Thank God you're all right!' She fell into his arms and hugged him. 'I've been so worried about you.'

'It's all right, love. You don't need to worry about me. I'm right as ninepence.' He put his big arms around her and held her tightly. 'You oughter know it'd take more than a few Jerries to get the better of me and the *Surrey Queen*. Anyway, what're you doing here? I thought you'd be back home, working at the caff. Given you the sack, have they?'

'Don't be so daft.' She pulled herself out of his hold. 'Me and Dot come down to give Marge and Eric a hand. And I wanted to be here in case you come back. And our Joe, too,' she added quietly. 'I don't suppose you've seen nothing of him?'

Olly shook his head. He sat down heavily at one of the tables and Effie took a proper look at him. His big face was rough with stubble and his grey moustache was straggly and stained. His eyes were red with fatigue and he looked as if he hadn't had a wash for days. His clothes were dirty and stiff-looking, as if they'd been soaked over and over again in saltwater and allowed to dry on him, and there were dark stains that looked as if they might be blood or oil, or both.

'There ain't a chance of seeing anyone you know,' Olly said as Dot put a mug of tea in front of him. He picked it up and sucked it

307

into his mouth. 'That's good. I'm not saying he ain't all right, mind,' he added hastily. 'I'm just saying there's so many of the poor perishers over there, waiting to be took off the beaches, that you just got to get 'em aboard as quick as you can and you don't even look at their faces. Our Joe could've bin aboard the *Queen* all the way across the Channel, and I wouldn't have knowed. Though of course, *he'd* have knowed,' he added, thinking about it. 'He'd have knowed he was on the *Queen* and got through the crowd to find me.'

'I was hoping you'd have brought him back yourself,' Effie said despondently. 'But I know that was daft. There's so many of them, like you say.'

'Someone'll bring him back,' Olly told her. 'There's any amount of boats working to get 'em off the beaches and on to the ships. You wouldn't credit it, Eff – little tubs that you wouldn't think would ever go to sea, no more than rowing-boats, some of 'em, gone all the way over to France, chugging backwards and forwards, doing the best they can even if they can only take four or five men at a time. It's a wonderful sight, it is really.' His face sobered as he thought of it. 'Mind you, I dunno that wonderful is the word for it, exactly. There ain't nothing *pretty* about it – but it gives you a good feeling to see it. It makes you feel as if there's some hope. If we can do this – get all these little boats together, send 'em all that way, and bring thousands and thousands of our boys home, then maybe we can win this bloody war, whatever Hitler does.' He drank the rest of the tea. 'Well, I just come in to see Marge and Eric and get a bit of a wash and a kip, if you don't mind, Marge, and then I'm off again. They're stocking the *Queen* up again, see, so we got a couple of hours to get our breath back.'

Effie stared at him. 'You're going *back*?'

'That's right, love. The job ain't over yet, not by a long chalk.' He got up and moved towards the back of the café, but Effie laid a hand on his arm to stop him.

'But ain't you done your bit, Olly? You been over there for days – you're worn out. You're not a young man any more. Ain't there no one else could take the *Queen*? Some Naval chap?' Her grip tightened. 'I don't want you going back there again, Olly, honest I don't.'

He shook his head, his expression sombre. 'I got to, Eff. It ain't just our Joe – it's all them other blokes as well. Boys no more than eighteen or nineteen, some of 'em. They've been walking for weeks, just to get to Dunkirk – nothing much to eat, hardly anything to drink, being shot at by Jerry planes as often as not, gunned down on the road. Now there's thousands of them on the beach, just standing there waiting to be brought home. They got nowhere else to go. I *got* to go back, Eff. I mean, suppose I was the last boat there and our Joe was on the beach with no one else to help him . . . I got to go.'

'There's my Benny too,' Dot said in a small voice. She had been listening with horror to her father's words, trying to imagine what he had seen. 'And the Jackson boys from round the corner, they're over there too. Any amount of people we know have got someone over there.'

'Someone's got to do it,' Olly said heavily. 'And it's me knows the *Queen* best. That Naval officer we got on board, he's a good bloke, but he don't know the *Queen* like I do. We all got to do the best we can, Eff.'

She nodded slowly. 'All right, love. I can see you're right. I just wish it didn't have to be you, that's all.' She turned away and picked up a fresh loaf. 'You go and have a wash while I do you a fry-up. Then you can doss down for a bit. Will someone come and tell you when the boat's ready? Do they know where you are?'

'Jack Hodge'll come over. The rest of them are kipping down on board but I wanted to come round here, see if we could get a message to you. Saved me the trouble, finding you here!' He gave her a quick kiss and went through the door to the kitchen where Marge was frying bacon for sandwiches. 'I'll have two eggs with that, Marge, sunny side up, half a pound of tomatoes, four mushrooms and some black pudding, and make it snappy!'

'As the man said when he ordered a crocodile steak,' Marge retorted, and gave him a push. 'You go and have a wash in the sink, Olly, you're not fit to sit at a decent table. And it'll be bacon and eggs and a few slices of fried bread. Might be able to rustle up some baked beans to go with it but that's all.'

'Whatever it is,' he said as he stripped off his filthy shirt and stood in his vest at the sink, 'it'll be like manna from Heaven after what we been living on the last few days. In fact, I ain't really sure when it was I last had anything to eat at all. We ain't been thinking much about grub.'

By the time he had scrubbed his chest and arms, washed the

grime from his face and dunked his head under the tap to sluice the dirt of smoke and dust from his hair, the fry-up was ready and Marge had found an old shirt for him to wear. 'It's not Eric's, you'd never get into his, it was left here by one of the holiday people last year. He never bothered to write for it so I put it into a cupboard. Can't do nothing about trousers.'

'It's all right. I reckon I'll have to go to the doctor to get these took off!' He sat down at one of the tables and tucked into the heaped plate that Marge set in front of him.

Effie and Dot were still working away at their sandwiches and Eric had been back in for another two boxes full. Outside, the harbour was still busy with ships coming in loaded with troops, and the quays and promenades were thick with khaki-clad soldiers. The scene was one of apparent confusion, but it was a scene of joy as well, for each returning soldier was a man saved from the Germans, and even those who were injured knew that they would soon be in a clean, comfortable bed and looked after. A sense of relief hung like a shimmering cloud over the whole town.

'I'll tell you what,' Marge said as Olly finished his fry-up. 'Olly can go upstairs and lay down on our bed for an hour or two. Why don't you go with him, Effie love? You were up early, I know, and then you've had a long journey to get here. Me and Dot'll keep things going, then we can have a rest when you get up.'

Olly hesitated. 'You'll let me know the minute I'm wanted back on the *Queen*, won't you?'

'Of course I will. They know where to come, don't they? Well, we're easy enough to find. Now, off you go, and you too, Eff. You've hardly sat down since you got here. And no hanky-panky, mind, you're supposed to be going to sleep!'

Effie gave a squawk of laughter and as she turned to go upstairs Olly slapped her bottom. 'Hanky-panky, indeed – at our age!' she scoffed.

'You mind your tongue, girl,' her husband warned her. 'I ain't too old yet – but Marge is right, I'm too bloody tired! I need all my energy for tonight.' They reached the bedroom. It was a tiny room, almost filled by the double bed, a large, old-fashioned wardrobe and a bow-fronted dressing-table. Olly put his arms round his wife. 'I'm glad you're here, Eff,' he said quietly. 'It's done me a power of good to see your face. I tell you what, I was sorry I went off like that, without telling you what was up. Only I didn't really know myself then, see. But I oughter said a proper goodbye.'

'It doesn't matter,' she said. 'Me and the girls went down to Blackfriars to see what was going on. We saw you and the *Queen*, and we saw all them other little boats going down the Thames. Then we found out what was going on and me and Dot decided to come down here. Carrie stayed behind in case Joe came home, and to help keep the caff going.'

He nodded. 'Well, it's good to see you. Now let's lay down and get a bit of shut-eye. This business ain't over yet, Eff. Not by a long chalk.'

They took off their shoes and lay down together under the green satin eiderdown on top of Marge and Eric's bed. Olly stretched out his arm and Effie lay close against him within its curve. She felt the warmth of his big body and heard the snore as he fell asleep. I used to grumble at him about his snoring, she thought. I'll never moan about that again.

She laid her arm across his chest, desperately tired yet not wanting to go to sleep. She knew very well that he was going back into terrible danger and she wanted to stay awake, treasuring every moment he was here. He had been lucky to come out of it once; it stood to reason he'd have to be very lucky indeed to get out of it a second time.

She fitted her body against his, as she had done for the past twenty-five years, and fell asleep.

Sunset was just touching the sky with the first few feathery plumes of pink when Jack Hodge came to the café door to tell Olly that the *Surrey Queen* had been loaded up again and was almost ready to sail. Marge shouted up the stairs and Olly and Effie came stumbling down. Marge handed them both a mug of tea as they appeared and gave Jack one as well.

'I'm coming to see you off,' Effie told her husband, and Dot nodded and said she was coming too. 'Then we'll come straight back here, and Marge and Eric can get a bit of rest.'

Outside, there was a strangely hushed air over the town. The sun was going down now, a huge red ball sinking into the sea, and everything was touched with apricot, with the soldiers' uniforms a muted reddish-brown. The stalls along the front were still as busy, serving coffee, tea and mugs of cocoa. The boats in the harbour rocked gently at their moorings as men worked aboard them, bringing on more food and water for the troops and checking the engines; many of the smaller craft had not yet been fitted out for the summer and were struggling. A passenger-steamer was tied up to the quay of the outer harbour and men were coming ashore, moving slowly and supporting each other. Some were carrying stretchers. It all seemed to be happening at a slightly slower pace than usual, as if they were all underwater.

'You wouldn't think there could be so many men,' Effie said softly. 'However many are there over in France?'

'I think it was about half a million,' Olly said. 'I heard that Mr Churchill reckoned we could only manage to bring back about twenty thousand, but it's my belief we've brought a lot more than that. We had over sixty on the *Queen* alone, and we'd already taken half a dozen loads to the ships.'

Effie tilted her head. 'What's that noise? A sort of dull booming – a bit like thunder. It sounded like an explosion somewhere.'

Olly glanced at her. 'It's guns, Eff. German guns, on the coast of France.' He hesitated. The explosion was probably a ship being bombed, but there was no point in telling Effie. She'd find out soon enough from someone else.

She looked at him in horror. 'Guns! Are you going to be passing them?'

'No, love. We go a different way now.' He didn't tell her, either, that the Jerries were shelling along the beaches as well, from Mardyck in the south and the fringe of Nieuport to the north. There was no sense in making things worse.

They came to the jetty where the *Surrey Queen* was moored and stopped for a moment. Olly turned to say goodbye to Effie, but she was staring at the deck in disbelief.

'Whatever's that?' Before he could reply, she answered her own question. 'It's a gun! You never told me you were going to have a *gun* on deck.'

'I didn't know.' He stared at the Lewis gun mounted on the deck. 'I suppose it's in case of air attack. We got quite a bit on the way over.'

Effie put both hands to her mouth and stared at him. She made a sudden involuntary choking noise. 'Olly, I can't bear—'

'Yes, you can!' he said with a sudden harsh note in his voice. 'You *can* bear it, Eff, because it's our Joe I'm thinking of, and Dot's Benny, and all the other boys that are still over there on those beaches, being shot at and bombed and shelled while we stands here argufying. I've told you, someone's got to go and fetch 'em home, and there's no one knows the *Queen* like I do, so it stands to reason it's got to be me. Just think about it, Eff – suppose I stopped at home and our Joe never come back, what would we think for the rest of our days, eh? Wouldn't we always wonder whether he was on that beach and there wasn't nobody left to pick him up, and if only me and the *Surrey Queen* had been there, we might've been the ones to find him?' He took her arms, forcing her to look at him. 'Wouldn't we always think about that and wish we'd done different? Well, I *don't* want to think that, Eff, and I don't think you do either. So give me a kiss, there's a good girl, and let me have a smile to remember. And don't you worry – I'll be back before you've had time to say Jack Robinson.' He held her tightly for a moment, kissed her hard and then turned to his daughter. 'Cheerio, Dot,' he said gruffly. 'You look after your ma now, all right? See you again soon.'

'Cheerio, Dad,' she whispered. 'Look out for Benny, won't you?'

'Cheerio, Olly,' Effie said tremulously, and lifted her eyes to his. She gave him a wavering smile, knowing that it wouldn't take much to turn to tears, and bit the inside of her lip hard. 'You just take care of yourself, see? I can't run Marge's caff on me own, when this lot's over.'

He grinned and waved as he climbed on to the fireboat's deck. The rest of the crew, some replaced now by more Naval ratings, were waiting and as soon as he was in his place behind the dodger they cast off. The *Surrey Queen* moved slowly away from the quay and out into the Channel.

'Well, that's that,' Effie said, taking a deep breath as she gave a last wave and then turned back towards the town. 'Let's go and see how many sandwiches we can make before suppertime, shall we?'

Chapter Twenty-Nine

Monday, 3 June to Tuesday, 4 June

Olly hadn't told Effie everything about what he had seen and experienced during the past few days.

He hadn't told her about the arms and legs he had seen floating in a sea that seemed to be almost all blood. He hadn't told her about the men who had panicked and run amok on the beach, throwing themselves into the sea, pushing their fellow soldiers over in the water in their desperate attempts to climb on to a boat. He hadn't told her about the officer who had turned on his own men, firing at them because they were risking the lives of so many more. He hadn't told her about the ships that had been blown up before his very eyes, the survivors swimming frantically and screaming for help, nor about the ships that had collided, one slicing the other completely in half before turning over, weighed down by its unbalanced load of soldiers. Some of them were lucky, picked up by empty boats on their way to the beach; others had drowned.

Olly hadn't told Effie because it was bad enough to have these images burned into his own mind. He didn't want her to see what he had seen, even if only in her imagination. He didn't even know how to describe it. He knew he would never, ever, be able to forget it.

And he knew that, as long as there were men over there to be saved – his own son probably among them – he would have to do his best to save them. He, the *Surrey Queen*, and all those other little ships that were plying back and forth. Until the final order was given that no more men could be taken, they would all be there, snatching British soldiers from under the noses of their enemies.

The crossing was almost as dangerous as the actual rescue from the beaches. All the time there were the threats of stray mines, German E-boats, air attacks and shelling from the coast of France itself. Nobody knew how many ships, large and small, had been lost, and the Lewis gun on the *Surrey Queen*'s deck was only one of many that had been fitted on to those that had returned to Ramsgate, Dover and the other ports where rescued troops were being taken in. They were to be manned by Naval ratings, and Sublieutenant Denison told Olly that several German planes had been brought down already.

'I don't think we've got much time now,' he said as they set out into the Channel. 'The Germans must be close to the perimeter. Our rearguard won't be able to hold out for much longer, and we want to get them off as well. I wouldn't be surprised if this is the last night.'

'Nobody thought it'd last this long,' Olly agreed, and looked round at the armada of ships, just visible in the gathering dusk, forging across the choppy sea. 'But nobody thought all these little boats would do so well, did they? I tell you what, people'll be talking about this for the next fifty years. The next *hundred*.'

The armada sailing now was a strange one, a medley of ships large and small, most of them battered and pock-marked with shells and bullets, their sides scraped and splintered from their brushes with piers or other vessels. Amongst them were three large ships so decrepit that Olly could not take his eyes off them.

'What the policeman are those old crocks?'

Sublieutenant Denison glanced at them. 'Blockships, I should think. They're for blocking the harbour. Once we've finished with it, we'll sink them inside and render it useless. Don't want to leave it in working order for the Jerries.'

'Blimey.' Olly stared at the three old vessels, tottering along behind the long string of ships. 'They don't look as if they'll even make it over there.'

Denison grinned. 'There were three others that didn't. One of them barely got out of Portsmouth Harbour before she had to be towed back. Another couldn't keep up, poor old soul, and the third got into all kinds of trouble but was supposed to be going anyway. I don't know what happened to her then – perhaps she made it after all. Anyway, that's all they have to do – get to Dunkirk. After that, it's a very honourable end.'

As well as the fleet crossing to France, there were other ships returning to England, all loaded with troops; some of these vessels were badly damaged. The *Royal Daffodil*, one of the first ships to reach Dunkirk, went by listing heavily. They could see that she was badly holed and that her list had been deliberately created by moving everything possible to port, so that the damage was kept clear of the water. Soon afterwards, they saw the *Ben-My-Chree*, a personnel ship, evidently damaged by a collision, and two trawlers which had been peppered with gunfire. It seemed that every ship was carrying damage of some sort, and Olly knew it was unlikely that the *Surrey Queen* would escape unscathed.

It was dark by the time they drew near to Dunkirk. A fog had hindered the last part of the crossing, but the town and beaches were lit by the raddled, flickering glow of fire. Orders were being passed from ship to ship and Denison said, 'We're to go to the harbour again. They're taking off the rearguard and the French.'

'The French?' Olly could hardly believe his ears. 'Blimey, ain't they got their own ships? The Jerries haven't taken over all the French ports, have they, only Calais and Boulogne. Why don't they go to some of their own places?'

'It's not for us to question orders,' Denison said sharply, and Olly remembered that he was still under Naval discipline. He fell silent and turned the bows towards the dull crimson glow over Dunkirk. It was a wonder there was anything left there to burn, he thought, and remembered that when they had first heard they were coming to Dunkirk – it seemed like years ago now – they'd thought they were coming to fight fires.

Nobody could have fought the sort of fires that had raged through that town. It must have been like the Great Fire of London, which had torn through the old streets close to the very area where Olly lived now. I hope the poor buggers who lived there got out in time, he thought. And I hope our blokes who've been fighting in the rearguard have managed to get through to the docks so that we can take them home again.

They were picking their way through the approaches, littered with both wrecks and moving craft, and more dangerous than ever. As they came near the harbour, they could see that it was a confused jumble of small craft. The boats – many of them French – were in total chaos: destroyers sounding their sirens, which seemed some-how shriller than the British ones; fishing boats and other vessels trying to enter the harbour while others were coming out astern; some managing to evade each other, some colliding; and small craft dodging between them all the while, as they veered manically to and fro. The East Pier itself, to which the *Surrey Queen* had been directed, was swarming with French troops, all shouting at each other even though it was impossible to hear their words.

'Bloody hell,' Olly said angrily. 'We're not going to be able to get anywhere near the pier at this rate. There's all our destroyers and transports too – what are they going to do if this lot don't sort theirselves out?' He peered ahead. 'Blimey O'Riley, look at all those flaming wrecks!'

The charts given to each skipper at the beginning of Operation Dynamo had showed a number of old wrecks around the entrance to the outer harbour and its approaches. Now, there were at least a dozen new ones lying in the water – a huge mass of jagged metal waiting to rip the bottoms out of any ship unlucky enough to pass over them. Some had been bombed, some had struck mines, some had collided with the pier or with other ships, but the end result was the same: a hulk on the seabed, some deep enough to be safe but others lying in shallow water, their masts or funnels or shattered bows rearing above the surface, a threat to all those who tried to enter. Still there was the *Clan Macalister*, which had been sunk by bombing several days earlier, settled on the seabed with most of her deck above water and providing a useful decoy for German planes to waste their bombs on ever since.

'I dunno why they bother with blockships,' Olly muttered, trying to steer his way between them. 'The place is just about unusable as it is.'

'*Look out!*' Denison yelled, and Olly saw a corvette, just clearing the harbour entrance. In the crimson half-darkness it was almost impossible to make out shapes clearly, but he realised in that second what the Sublieutenant had seen – a French trawler, moving rapidly towards the corvette. The two ships crashed almost as soon as Denison had shouted and Olly, appalled, bellowed an order to reverse the engines. The *Surrey Queen* almost stood on her bow, water churning all around her, missing the collision by inches, and the crew rushed to their stations as the corvette's port bow opened up to the waterline and the sea gushed in.

'She's cut her degaussing lines,' Denison said grimly. 'Stupid Frogs!'

'They're taking men on board,' Olly said, peering through the flickering gloom. 'They've swung together, see, and the soldiers are crossing to the trawler easy as winking. We'd better get out of the way in case the corvette sinks. Don't suppose you know which one it is?'

'Yes, I do,' the Sublieutenant said, staring intently. 'It's the *Kingfisher* – I've been on board her – know the captain. Well, she won't be much good for anything now. She'll have to turn back to Dover and hope to God she doesn't hit a mine on the way.'

The two ships were clearing the entrance now and Olly was able to steer the *Surrey Queen* to the West Pier. But even as he approached, he knew that this was going to be useless. The fireboat was low in the water, its deck far below the lofty pier, and the men queued up along it looked down at the deck and shook their heads. He stared up at them in exasperation, gesturing to them to jump, but they backed away and it was obvious that they weren't going to risk it.

'Bloody hell,' he said in disgust. 'What do they teach these Frenchies? Look, you got to get down here if you wants to be took to England,' he bawled at them. 'We can't lift the bloody boat up to you!'

Just then, Chalky White and Jack Hodge came staggering along the deck with a ladder which was part of the ship's normal firefighting equipment. They reared it into the air and propped it against the pier. To everyone's relief, it reached to the walkway and the men began to climb down; within ten minutes, the ship was crammed with French soldiers, as dirty, unshaven and exhausted as the British had been.

'That's it,' Olly said, glancing anxiously at the waterline. 'We must have getting on for a hundred on board now. Can't take no more.' He began to reverse away from the pier. 'There's another bus coming along behind.'

One of the French officers ducked into the shelter of the dodger. 'Are you the captain of this vessel?'

'That's right, mate.' Olly was accustomed to the accent of the

French onion-sellers who came to the East End markets, and this man was speaking good English. 'Go and find yourself somewhere to doss down for a bit. It'll take us a while to get you off to a ship.'

The man shook his head. 'I wish my own accommodation.'

Olly stared at him. 'Your own what?'

'Accommodation. My own private quarters.' He lifted his chin and gave Olly an arrogant stare. 'I am an officer. I do not sleep with my men.'

'On this ship,' Olly said, 'you sleep where I say.' He turned his attention to the delicate task of steering through the wrecks. The officer stayed where he was.

'I wish my own private—'

'Oh, for Christ's sake!' Olly poked his head out from behind the dodger and yelled to the first man he saw. 'Stan! Come here a minute, will you?' The ex-sailor, who had been taking round cans of water, straightened up and stepped over the recumbent bodies. 'This *officer*,' Olly said meaningfully, 'wants his own private room. Think we can oblige?'

Stan Miller looked at him for a moment. Then he turned to the Frenchman, who was breathing heavily through his nose with impatience, and spoke with the exaggerated courtesy of a hotel lackey. 'Oh, I think we can arrange that, sir. With private facilities and all, if that's what you want. Come with me.'

The two disappeared down the companionway and Olly chuckled. Denison, standing beside him, gave him an enquiring glance. 'Where on earth is he going to put him? The cabin's full to bursting point – there's not an inch of space anywhere and certainly nowhere private.'

'Oh, there is,' Olly said, and cursed as he narrowly avoided the jagged superstructure of yet another wreck. 'There is – and like Stan says, it's got all mod cons and somewhere to sit down as well. I'm sure the *hofficer* will be comfortable there, though he might get disturbed a few times on the way home!'

Denison burst out laughing. 'The *heads*! Well, it serves him right.' They were out into deep water now, clear of the danger of sunken ships. 'That was a good night's work,' he said more quietly as the *Queen* settled down to a steady speed. 'You've done a good job, Mears. I think this might be the last trip we make.'

Olly said nothing. He knew that he would be as glad as anyone to get home again, with their perilous rescue behind him. Yet even though the *Surrey Queen* had snatched hundreds of men from the beaches and the harbour of Dunkirk, even though she had saved so many soldiers and taken them home to live and fight another day, he knew that he had not achieved the one thing that had been most important to him.

He had not brought back his own son.

The men on the *Countess Wear* had lost all sense of time.

It was four days now since they had first arrived at Dunkirk. During that time, they had worked almost incessantly, going backwards and forwards between the piers and the ships, loading and unloading their human cargo until they had almost stopped seeing them as men and looked on them as no more than boatloads. Yet every now and then, they would be reminded of who the men really were, and why they were here. When a boy no older than seventeen stumbled on board and collapsed in a heap, weeping for his mother; when a much older man, with stubble darkening his face, took the youngster in his arms and cradled him like a baby; when a jagged lump of shrapnel came out of a sudden burst of shellfire and sliced into them both, killing them where they lay; when half a dozen soldiers nearby raised their rifles and fired viciously at the Stukas that shrieked and swooped overhead, and scored a direct hit on the pilot, sending the plane spinning into the sea not fifty feet away, swamping them all with its spray.

They remembered too when a dozen dogs scrambled aboard from the pier, wet and terrified. Nobody owned them – they had simply followed the troops, desperate for human comfort, and nobody had the heart to throw them back into the sea, so they huddled in a corner, shivering and rolling their eyes and whimpering loudly whenever a shell or a bomb exploded. When the *Countess* warped together with a couple of skoots the Dutchmen took them aboard. They would find themselves in England eventually, Robby thought, and hoped they would be given a home. He doubted it, though; the Government had already said that most domestic animals should be put down, so it seemed hardly likely that strays from Dunkirk would fare any better.

Danny had recovered from his latest ducking and was working as strongly as ever. I don't know how we're all keeping going, Robby thought. They had had a few rests, rafted up against other ships, even shared a meal with some of the other crews, but they were always back at work after a few hours. You couldn't sleep easy, knowing there were desperate men on the shore, or standing up to their necks in the sea, helpless against German shelling or air attacks. You couldn't lie in your bunk listening to the sounds outside, the drum of the engines, the shriek of planes, the cries of those who were injured and drowning, without having to get out and get back to the job again. There'd be time to sleep when everyone was back in England. And, as Jimmy remarked once, if you got killed yourself before then, it wouldn't matter if you were tired anyway. There were probably plenty of beds in heaven. Nice soft ones, too, with an angel to bring you a cuppa in the mornings.

After working off the piers for some time, the *Countess Wear* had been sent to the beaches to make way for some of the larger ships. There, they anchored as close in as possible and acted as a go-between, ferrying men from very small craft that could carry only a few at a time, to the destroyers and personnel ships that lay further out.

'How many d'you reckon we've taken off now?' Danny asked as they crammed the last man aboard and pulled away from the beach. 'I reckon it must be nigh on a thousand.'

Robby nodded. 'Wouldn't be surprised. We've been loading a couple of hundred a time but I don't know how many trips we've made.' He spoke absently, watching the other ships with one part of his tired mind while with another he made swift calculations. Two hundred at a time – at least five trips – Danny was right, they must have shifted at least a thousand men. A thousand! he marvelled. Who could have thought that the little *Countess Wear*, built to take happy folk on holiday trips on the river, would . . . He let out an exclamation. 'Well, I'll be buggered!'

'What?' Danny, who had been about to go below, pushed his way back through the crowd of soldiers and came up beside him. 'What be the matter?'

'Nothing. Nothing's the matter.' Robby shook his head and gave an amazed little chuckle. 'It's *Wenlock*, that's all. See? We saw her going into the harbour when we first got here. My stars, I'm glad to see she's all right.'

He set course for the familiar shape, wondering what tales his old shipmates had to tell. 'This lot'll keep us talking for months down in the seamen's mess,' he said to Danny. 'Mind you, us don't want to tempt fate. Us got to get back first. Many a slip 'twixt cup and lip, that's what my mum always says, and—'

'*Look out!*'

A Stuka screeched overhead, dropping bombs in a long, deadly line. They spattered into the sea, sending fountains of water spraying upwards, and one of them exploded close to a trawler coming towards them fifty yards away. The trawler lifted clear of the water, seemed to hover for a moment and then fell back and turned over. At the same time, two other ships disappeared completely in a bubbling cauldron of flaming oil which spread rapidly across the sea. Robby jerked the wheel to avoid it, then twisted it back again as he saw men swimming desperately in the burning water, raising their arms and screaming for help.

'We've got to pick them up.' It was a miracle they'd survived the blast, he thought. The trawler had been coming away from the shore – it must have been full of soldiers. They had been thrown clear into the water when the boat turned over, and a good many of them had survived. Already exhausted and now almost certainly badly burned, they would drown if not picked up quickly.

Other boats were turning towards the scene. Robby saw two small cabin cruisers making for the survivors and breathed a sigh of relief. Smaller and closer to the water, they would be able to lift the men more easily and bring them to the *Countess*. He stood off a little and watched as the choking survivors were hauled out of the water. But before they could reach him, another plane shrieked out of nowhere. Bombs fell in a straight line of death and Robby, watching in horror, saw one go straight down the funnel of the waiting destroyer. There was the tiniest of pauses and then an explosion that seemed to rock the entire beach, sending huge broken waves in every direction, and the ship disappeared in a vast, searing ball of flame.

'*Christ Almighty* . . .'

Robby stood transfixed, his hand locked on the wheel. *Wenlock* – his ship, filled with his own shipmates, men he had trained and worked and sailed with, men he had been to war with – destroyed just like that. His oppos, blown to smithereens before his horrified eyes. Knocker and Lofty, Spud, Titch, Spearmint and Jimmy the One, the First Lieutenant, who had given him his orders to come to

Dunkirk – all gone. For he knew that nobody could have survived that explosion, happening deep inside the ship. There was not even any wreckage, other than a cap or two, a few scattered possessions, a snaking length of rope. They were all gone.

The Stuka, its job done, had disappeared. Robby felt sick. He turned to Danny and gestured to him to take the wheel.

Danny shook his head. 'I know what you'm thinking, Rob, but 'twon't do. You got to keep going, boy. Won't do no good to give in now. And anyway, I got me own work to do. There's all they poor perishers off the trawler to take aboard.'

The two motor cruisers, knocked off-course by the waves set up by the explosion, had turned and together, as if in tandem, they chugged across the spreading oilslick towards the *Countess Wear*. Rob, sickened but holding the wheel steady, watched as Dan and Jimmy went forward to help the shivering soldiers aboard. He glanced at the crews of the little boats. An old man, with bushy white hair and the unmistakable bearing of a Naval officer and a dark-haired boy. A man of about thirty and a youngster with thick, roughly cropped fair hair. And then, coming aboard, men whose tunic shoulders sported badges he recognised.

The 7th Cornwalls. Jan's regiment!

His heart leaped. These were men who knew his brother, who had served and fought with him, who had waited on the beach with him. Had he been in the trawler with them as well?

And if he had, was he one of the survivors? Or had he gone down with the ships?

Chapter Thirty

Monday, 3 June

The 7th Cornwalls had been on the beach for three days before they even had a chance of getting on to a boat.

'I don't reckon we're ever going to get away,' Dave Fawley said, staring at the huge throng of men crowded thickly on the sands. 'I mean, look at us all. It don't matter how many those little boats takes off, there's twice as many arriving all the time. We ain't got a chance.'

'We'll have no talk like that,' Major Breakspear said sharply. 'We've as much chance as the next man. And if we don't get off, we'll make a stand right here on the beach until we're ordered otherwise. We're British soldiers, and don't forget it.'

Dave shrugged but said no more. He sat with his back against a dune, cushioned by a stiff tussock of grass, and gazed morosely at the scene, too depressed and weary to appreciate the wonder that Alex had experienced at the sight of the little boats working so busily and bravely between the shore and the ships. Like the thousands of other men massed on the beaches, he had walked for days with the burden of defeat like a heavy load on his shoulders. A regular soldier, Dave had never learned to face defeat; all his training had been directed to winning, to killing before he could be killed, coming out on top. The order to withdraw had been a blow to both his training and his self-esteem, and had settled like a blanket of misery around his shoulders. To arrive on this long, bleak beach and find himself surrounded by thousands of equally defeated men, with – as far as he could see – almost no chance of being rescued, was a bitter disappointment.

I'd have been better off standing up to the Jerries, he thought gloomily. I'd have been killed, but at least I could've taken a few with me. We're like sitting ducks here – and there's not a bloody thing we can do about it.

Joe Mears and Jan Endacott were sitting together in a hollow scooped out in front of one of the dunes. They'd been friends during their training period but had got separated during the fighting. There was little to say, yet both found some comfort in being with men with whom they had shared those early, bewildering days when they had been introduced to the Army and the harsh, fearsome reality of war, coming so soon after.

Pirate was lying close to Joe. He was surviving on scraps of food given to him out of Joe's own rations. Bully beef and cold baked beans had been brought round by the sailors who had come ashore from the little ships, carrying cartons of food and cans of water. Water for the dog had been a problem until Jan suggested scooping a small dip in the sand and lining it with the edge of Joe's tarpaulin cape. The man holding out the can had hesitated – the water was meant for soldiers, not dogs – but Joe had 'accidentally' jogged his arm and some of the liquid had spilled into the makeshift bowl. Pirate had slurped it up thirstily, his tongue hanging out for more, and Joe fondled his ears.

'You reckon they'll let you take that little feller back?' Jan asked, lying back after his own drink from the can. The water was never enough, but it soothed their burning throats and helped the bully beef down. The bread was dry after its journey across the Channel, and as hard to swallow as ship's biscuits, but they were all so hungry that they barely noticed it. They chewed thankfully and thought about what they would eat when they got home.

'A good old fry-up,' Joe said longingly. 'My old ma runs a caff in the East End. I'm going straight round there when I gets back and she'll give me the whole works – eggs, bacon, black pudding, fried bread, the lot. Twice. And a pot of tea for six, all to meself.'

'Our eggs are straight off the farm,' Jan said. 'And we killed our own pig, back-along. There's still some bacon and ham from him, I reckon. Herbert, his name was,' he added reflectively.

Joe stared at him. '*Herbert*? You mean you give him a name and then you *ate* him?'

'Well, he was one of the family,' Jan said with a touch of indignation. 'Of course we give him a name.'

Alex, Ginette and the Major were patrolling their stretch of beach, doing their best for the injured. They had used up all their own medical supplies, but more had been brought ashore along with the water and food, and they were able to bandage a few wounds and splint some of the broken limbs. Apart from that, there wasn't much that could be done.

'They need to be back home in a hospital,' Alex said to Major Breakspear as they surveyed the long lines of men lying and sitting on the crowded beach. 'But God knows how many are going to live long enough to reach one. Even supposing we can get them on board a ship, a lot of them are too far gone to make it across the Channel.'

'It's the fit and able we've got to get back home first,' the Major said. 'Seems harsh, I know, but they're the ones who are going to be ready to fight again. Once we're off the scene, the Germans will move in and take the rest prisoner. They'll put the wounded into hospital.'

'Are you sure?' Ginette asked, her voice threaded with doubt and distress. 'Won't they just kill them where they lie?' She turned to Alex. 'They're murderers, everyone knows that! I wouldn't trust them an inch.'

The Major shook his head. 'They'll follow the Geneva Convention. Prisoners of war have to be looked after, just as bodies have to be given proper burial. Nobody likes being taken prisoner, and of course we'll take back as many as we can, but those that are left will be all right. Once the withdrawal is complete—'

'And should they be bombing and shooting at us as we withdraw?' Ginette demanded. 'Should they be harrying us when we are no more threat to them? Is *that* in your Geneva Convention?'

The men were silent. There was no answer to the questions that the beleaguered soldiers were asking. Where was the RAF, who were supposed to be holding back the Luftwaffe? Where were the French? Why had the Belgians surrendered and left them so exposed? Why were they here in the first place? What was this war all about?

The sergeant strode up and down the lines, haranguing all that he heard voicing such doubts. 'We're here to defend our country, ain't we? That's why we came, and that's what we're going to do. This ain't a defeat – it's a *withdrawal*. It's our job to get back alive.

326

It's our *duty*.' He stopped and laid the toe of his boot along the ribs of one of the most vociferous of the grumblers. 'You! You don't want the Germans overrunning our country, do you? Raping your wife and daughter – your *mother*? Then stay alive, you lazy, whining sod. Gawd knows you ain't much use to the Army, but you're bloody in it now and you'll *stay* in it, all the way back to Blighty. And no more whingeing, understand? Or you'll feel the toe of my foot again and it won't be tickling your tummy.'

The days and nights dragged on. For some of the time, they were left in peace but every few hours they would hear the scream of the dive-bombers and burrow into the sand, trying hopelessly to evade the bombs and gunfire that spattered the beach. Most of the attacks, however, were directed at the ships lying offshore and the smaller vessels plying back and forth. Those soldiers on the beach who still had ammunition, fired at the aircraft and even scored a few hits, but the rest could only sit and watch helplessly as their rescuers were blown out of the water.

'Look at that!' Jan exclaimed in dismay. 'That little scrap of a boat, blown to smithereens, and them poor buggers in it been waiting days. It ain't fair!'

'I've give up expecting things to be fair,' Joe said sourly. 'I don't reckon nothing's fair in this life. You're either lucky or you ain't, and their luck all ran out at the same time.' He stared sombrely across the sands, crawling with men, filthy with blood and excreta, at a sea that was red with blood, glittering with oil and littered with a drifting flotsam of corpses. I'll never be able to tell nobody about this, he thought. Not Mum, not Connie, not even Dad. I'll never be able to talk about it at all.

By now, the evacuation was taking place mostly at night. It seemed as if the crowd would never diminish, but as the third day drew to its close, the 7th Cornwalls found themselves, to their surprise, at the edge of the water. Supporting those of the wounded who could stand, they moved into the lapping waves. Alex and Ginette stood at the edge, torn with doubt as they looked back at the stretcher cases, still lying on the beach.

'We can't leave them,' Ginette said.

'We have to.' Alex's voice was filled with misery. 'You heard what the Major told us. The Germans are only a mile or two away. The evacuation's almost at an end – this is going to be the last night. If we stay here, we'll all be taken prisoner, and what use will we be to Britain then?'

Major Breakspear was behind them. He said, 'The boats with the shallowest draft are coming in closer for the stretcher cases. We're able to walk out to deeper water. We're not leaving behind any more than we absolutely have to, Ginette. And there are orderlies with them. Alex is right – it's our duty to accept the rescue.'

They waded out into the sea in a long, weary line. Ginette, already hot and uncomfortable in the thick khaki serge, felt it grow sodden and heavy around her legs. She stared at the darkening sky, reddened by the fires, and at the oily, cluttered sea, and felt a tide of disgust and fear rise within her, tasting bitter in her mouth. I would never have believed it could come to this, she thought. Standing here in the cold sea, surrounded by such terrible sights, waiting – hoping, praying – for some little boat to take me away from France. How did it come about? How did all this happen?

And where were her mother and father now, and all the friends and neighbours, the people she had grown up with? She wondered if she would ever see them again, and sent up a heartfelt prayer for their safety.

The water had reached her thighs. She took a deep breath and felt through the gloom for Alex's hand. He gripped hers tightly and drew her close. 'Are you all right, my love? It won't be long now.'

'How can you tell?' she whispered. 'There have been men waiting in the water for days. We've seen them.'

'Because I think the Major's right. This will be the last night.' He looked over his shoulder at the beaches. There were fewer men left now; most of the evacuation was taking place from the piers and they could see the dim silhouettes of the ships, clustering round the harbour approaches. 'Almost all our men have gone. They're taking the French now.' He squeezed her hand. 'We'll be in England by dawn.'

'Oh Alex, if only you're right.' A wave lapped round her waist and she gave a cry of terror. '*How much deeper is it going to get?*'

He turned his head in sudden fear. 'Ginette? What is it? Are you afraid of the water?'

'I can't swim!' she cried, reaching out with both arms. 'Oh Alex, I didn't know it would be like this. This horrible uniform – it's weighing me down. I can't stand! I'm *falling*!'

'Lean on me! Take off the tunic!' He ripped at the buttons, wrenching the sodden jacket from her shoulders. 'And the trousers – it doesn't matter what you've got on underneath!' Together, they struggled in the water and he lifted her into his arms while he tried to pull off the unwieldy garments. The Major, realising what was happening, waded over to help and they dragged the heavy serge away from her. Clad only in her underclothes, Ginette hung in his arms, shivering and crying. 'I'll carry you,' he said. 'It's all right, darling. I'll keep you safe.' He was half-sobbing himself, afraid as he had never been before at the sight of his wife's fear, at the realisation that they were almost out of his depth and certainly beyond hers. The water buoyed her up, but her terror had almost overcome her and she sobbed and clung to him, almost knocking him off-balance. Desperate now, he stopped and tried to regain his stability; and then, as he stood there with his feet planted wide apart in the soft, muddy sand that shifted so treacherously beneath them, he saw a small boat heading through the dusk towards them. A motor cruiser. A boat that he was almost sure he recognised.

'It's *Wagtail*!' he gasped disbelievingly. 'It can't be! It's *Wagtail*!' And then his feet slid from under him. He staggered and fell and, with Ginette still in his arms, he sank into the oily water and the soft, shifting sand.

Chapter Thirty-One

It seemed to Paddy that she had spent her entire life aboard a small motor cruiser, lifting exhausted and often wounded men from the sea and ferrying them out to a destroyer. It seemed that she had never known anything other than the fiery darkness of a smoky sky, the roar of enemy aircraft, the rattle of gunfire and the crashing explosions as ships were blown apart by bombs. It seemed as if Emsworth, the Curlews and the sheltered, peaceful life she had known until now were nothing but a dream.

'All right, Pads?' Toby asked her as they watched yet another load of men clamber thankfully into the holiday-steamer now taking their passengers out to the destroyers, and *Wagtail* turned back yet again towards the shore.

She brushed her hair out of her eyes. It felt sticky and thick with dirt, and she was glad she'd cut it short. She put her hand on her brother's shoulder and leaned against him for a moment.

'I think so. How long is this going to go on, Toby?'

'I don't know. I don't really care, either.' There was a new, grim note in his voice and she looked at him in surprise. 'You know, coming here and seeing all this – well, it's made me feel differently. I can see what a fool I've been, messing about with my life, pretending to be an actor, letting other people do the dirty work. I can see why Dad and Charles and the Admiral think so little of me. They think I'm a slacker – and so I am. I can't think of one useful thing I've done in my whole life. Not one!' He kicked savagely at the coaming. 'I'm a waster, Paddy. A complete waster.'

'No! You're not a waster – you're a good actor. One day you'll be a fine actor.' She caught at his arm. 'Toby, you mustn't think like that. We're all different – we can all do different things! Of *course* you're useful. You give people pleasure – isn't that important?'

'Not as important as fighting for your country,' he said. 'Not as important as saving lives.' He turned away, staring through the gathering darkness at the soldiers waiting in long, patient lines in the water, some of them almost up to their necks. 'When all this is over and we're back home, I'm going to volunteer. I'd still rather save lives than kill people, so I'll try to get into the Medical Corps like Alex, as an orderly or a stretcher-bearer, or something. But if I can't do that, I'll go wherever I'm sent and do whatever I'm told. I don't want to be a hero, Paddy – I just want to do my bit. I've left it long enough.'

'I shall, too,' she said, looking towards the shore. 'Mummy and Daddy don't like the idea of me volunteering, but I've had to register and if this war goes on – and it *is* going on, isn't it, Toby – I'll have to go away. I don't care what I do – I can't just go tamely home and do nothing, not after this.'

She went back to stand beside Charles at the wheel and Toby returned to the engines. Beside them, *Moonset* was moving at the same speed; the two little ships had been working together ever since they had found each other. There was a sense of something coming slowly to an end. The aircraft attack on the beaches had lessened; the few planes coming over now were concentrating on the harbour. Although the sands were now darkened, they knew that there were fewer men there. They had either been taken off or were making their way back to the piers. Perhaps this was to be, as someone had told them, the last night. Perhaps in a few hours they would be joining the long convoy home again.

And we still haven't found Alex, she thought sorrowfully. It was crazy ever thinking we might see him, in all these thousands of people, but I never stopped hoping. Even now, I can't stop hoping – not until the last chance has gone.

'Paddy,' Charles shouted in her ear, and she felt her body stiffen at the note in his voice. 'Paddy, can you see those men standing in the water?'

She leaned forwards, straining her eyes. The long queue looked no different from any other. She said, 'Yes, but—'

'I don't know for sure,' he said, and she could feel his excitement trembling through the air between them, 'but one of them could be Alex.'

'*Alex?*'

Paddy scrambled out of the cockpit and along to the bow. She leaned dangerously over the edge, peering into the darkness. 'Alex? Alex? *Alex!*'

'*Wagtail!*' The voice came back to her, roughened by weariness and thirst, incredulous, yet unmistakable and she gave a yelp of joy. '*Wagtail*, is that you? Who's sailing her?'

'Us!' she shouted. 'Me and Charles and Toby! We've come to get you!' Her voice broke then and tears streamed down her cheeks. The boat was nosing gently towards the line of men and she could see him now, quite clearly, filthy and soaking wet, standing at the head of it and holding a slight, pale figure in his arms. 'Oh Alex, we thought we were never going to see you again!'

'Get back, Paddy,' Charles called. 'I want to turn so that they can come in over the stern.' She knew the drill by now, but in the excitement of seeing Alex at last, she had forgotten everything. Gulping back the tears, she hurried to the cockpit and leaned over the stern, holding out her arms. Toby was below, keeping the engine ticking over, and Charles turned his head. 'Alex,' he said, in a tone of deep thankfulness. 'My God, it's good to see you.'

Alex held up his arms. The figure draped across them moved slightly and Paddy leaned forward, slipping her own arms beneath the slim body. Toby came up from the engine-room and moved quickly to help her, and together they brought Ginette aboard and laid her in the bottom of the cockpit. She stirred, rolled over and retched.

'It's a girl!' Paddy gasped, and knelt beside the shaking body. 'Toby – Charles – it's a *girl*!'

There was no time to say more. Relieved of his burden, Alex hauled himself aboard and knelt down beside her. He gathered Ginette into his arms, stared intently into her face, then gently laid her down again and turned on Paddy. 'What the hell are you doing here?'

'Well, thank you!' Paddy exclaimed indignantly. 'That's a fine welcome, I must say, after I risk my life to come and save yours! And who's this?'

'Never mind that!' He jumped up again. The rest of the men were

332

coming aboard now – Joe with Pirate once more buttoned close against his chest, Dave Fawley and Sid – whom he had refused to leave – the Sergeant, Jan, Major Breakspear and a dozen others. They crammed themselves into the boat, squeezing into every space, until Charles called out that they were full. Beside them, *Moonset* was equally loaded, and a few yards on either side there were other boats all working quickly in a valiant attempt to clear the last men from the beaches. The word had spread that this was to be the last night of the evacuation and a sense of urgency had gripped them all; a sense of determination that no one was to be left behind. It was a sense that was bordering on panic.

'Get back to the ship, quickly,' the Admiral called across. He had been working tirelessly for days now, taking only short periods of rest, and even in the gloom Charles could see how haggard he looked. 'Get these men back, and we can fetch another load. After that . . .' He faltered and put out his hand, and made an involuntary and helpless movement.

'Admiral! Admiral, are you all right?'

'Of course I'm all right!' the old man retorted testily, recovering himself. 'Just slipped a bit, that's all. Did I hear someone say you'd got Alex?'

'Yes! Yes, it's him!' Charles heard the thrill of jubilation in his own voice. He had never really believed that they would be the ones to take Alex home, but neither had he been able to let go of the hope. 'He's staying on board *Wagtail* now,' he added firmly. 'We'll take him all the way back.'

The two boats had arrived at the steamer and hands were reaching down for their warps. As the men began to climb aboard, Jan gave a shout of amazement.

'It's the *Countess*!'

'The who?' Joe was behind him, waiting to climb the rope-ladder. 'Don't tell me we've got *another* bloody woman here!'

'No – it's the *Countess Wear*! I know her – she works on the River Dart.' Jan was hanging on to the ladder. He turned to look down at Joe and the ladder twisted suddenly, throwing him off. With a yell, he toppled backwards, struck the coaming of *Moonset* and slid into the black, oily water between the three tossing hulls.

'My God!' Joe was back on *Wagtail*'s deck, reaching down, but someone else was quicker. Danny, who had been helping the men aboard *Countess Wear*, had seen what had happened and dived after him. He disappeared from sight and, at the same moment, young Peter Murphy the Sea Scout leaned over from *Moonset* and pushed the boat clear of the steamer.

Robby appeared on the *Countess Wear*'s deck, gripping the rail and peering down. 'What's going on? What's happening?'

'It's Jan, my mate.' Joe lifted his head towards him. 'He was just saying he knows this boat, then he fell off the ladder and disappeared.' He searched the surface of the water with his eyes. 'Oh, why can't I bloody swim!'

'Jan? Did you say Jan?'

'That's right. Jan Endacott, comes from Devon.' Joe's voice was impatient. 'What the hell does that matter? He's under the bloody water now, that's the important thing, and some young chap's gone in after him and I can't bloody see either of them! Oh, Christ Almighty – *Jan!*'

Robby came down the ladder like a spider. 'He's my brother,' he said breathlessly. 'And Dan that's gone in after him is my best friend. There they are!' he exclaimed, pointing as two heads broke the surface. 'Oh, thank God.'

'I've got to pull away a bit,' Charles shouted at them. 'We'll hit the steamer – we could crush them both. They need a bit of room.'

'But we'll be too far away . . .'

'They can board *Moonset*. She's closer, and there's more room on her – she's unloaded her men.'

Danny was holding Jan's head above the water. He turned and began to swim the short distance between the high sides of the *Countess Wear* and *Moonset*. Peter, who was still thrusting hard against the side of the bigger boat, let go as Danny got Jan to the stern, and moved along the deck to help him. The Admiral, standing at the wheel, held the boat steady, and the soldier and the young Sea Scout began to struggle with the heavy body.

Robby slid over the side and made for the other boat but it was clear that, even with his help, getting Jan into the boat was going to be too difficult. They were all tired, almost all their strength gone, and for a moment it looked as if both Robby and his brother were going under.

'They're not going to manage it,' Paddy said, standing beside Charles. 'Oh, Charles, they're not going to get him up.'

'I'll go too. Get down to the engine-room, Paddy.' Toby was over the side. Paddy gave a cry, but did as she was told, put the engine into neutral, then dashed up again to see what was happening. She and Charles watched anxiously as Toby swam the few strokes to the other boat, set his shoulder under the helpless body, and began to heave. The sea was choppy now, tossing the little boats unsteadily from wave to wave, and as fast as they managed to lift Jan clear of the water, they were flung back again. The task seemed impossible.

'Put the engine into slow ahead,' Charles ordered. 'We'll try to get a bit closer. They may be able to board us more easily, as we're sitting lower in the water.'

She slid down the ladder and the note of the engine changed. Very carefully, Charles eased the boat closer to *Moonset*. They came alongside and the Admiral looked over.

'Good man. Raft up.'

'Chuck the warps over to the other boat,' Charles called to Alex. 'If we get the two boats together, they'll be a bit steadier. Blast this choppiness!' He manoeuvred *Wagtail* close alongside *Moonset*, watching to make sure that the men in the water were clear of the propeller, and nodded as Alex and Peter Murphy between them fastened the two boats together. 'We'll be able to get them aboard now.' He called out to Peter Murphy. 'Hop over here – you can do more to help from our stern, now.'

Peter jumped across to *Wagtail* and scrambled to the stern. He leaned over and grabbed Jan's arm, hauling as the two men in the water heaved from below. Paddy knelt beside him, dragging on one of Jan's sleeves and, slowly, the half-drowned man began to slide out of the water. Coughing and retching, he began to move for himself, pushing with both hands on the transom as Toby and Dan thrust from below. Suddenly, as the balance of his weight shifted at last, he toppled over into the cockpit, where he lay beside Ginette, vomiting oily water. Robby and Joe knelt beside him, almost beside themselves with thankfulness.

'Well done!' Charles cried, and Toby, still in the water, stuck one thumb into the air, showing his teeth in a grin. He gave Danny a push. 'You get up next.'

Danny was easier to haul aboard. He fell into the boat beside Jan, then scrambled to his feet. 'Us'd better get back aboard the *Countess*, Rob.'

'I know. I want to take Jan with me, though. Can we get him up the ladder?'

'Course we can.' Joe was up too, helping lift Jan as Toby too came over the stern. The sick man stood more steadily on his feet now, but even in the glowing darkness they could see the dark smudge of blood on one temple. Together, they manhandled him up the short rope-ladder and over the side on to the deck of the *Countess Wear*. Jimmy, who had been keeping the boat steady with the help of some of the more able soldiers, came up to give Rob a clap on the shoulder, then returned to the engine-room. Robby leaned over and called down to the two boats below.

'Send up the rest of the men. We'd better get away – I can hear planes coming.'

'Oh, not again!' Paddy exclaimed, and turned to scan the crimson sky. She could see nothing against the sullen cloud of smoke, but as she stared she began to hear the low, menacing throb of engines and knew that Robby was right. The German planes, which had left them alone for the past few hours, were on their way again. She felt a wave of fury shiver through her body and swore loudly.

'My God, Paddy, where did you learn such words?' Toby was beside her, breathing rather raggedly. 'Ma would have a fit if she heard you talking like that.'

'Ma's not here,' Paddy retorted, and went forward to release the forrard-warp as Peter Murphy jumped back aboard *Moonset*. The two boats, empty now of soldiers, moved away from the steamer and began to head back to the beach. The sound of aircraft was closer now, and they were all gripped with a sudden sense of urgency. This was the last night of the evacuation, and there were men still there. They had to get off as many as possible.

The rumble of engines became a roar as the planes swooped low overhead. Once again, in a sickeningly familiar pattern, bombs fell in a line of explosions between them and the ships further out. A huge, brilliant ball of orange lit the horizon as something blew up – a destroyer or a personnel carrier – maybe one of the hospital ships whose red crosses of immunity had been so steadfastly ignored. Hundreds of men, Paddy thought with a feeling of shock that had been so often repeated that it had now turned to a numb, weary misery. Men who had thought they were on their way to safety, killed on the last lap of their terrible journey. It wasn't fair.

Another plane came, even closer, dropping its stick of bombs by the beach. A Dutch skoot not far away disappeared in a shower of wreckage. A crater on the beach was lit briefly by a painful flash of yellow. A bomb whistled close over *Wagtail*, so close that she thought they must be hit. And when the explosion sounded in her ears, filling her head with searing white light that screamed and echoed like a million banshees in her skull; when the little ship rocked and lifted beneath her, seeming to hover in the air before slamming down on the water again with a judder that shook every plank, every last rib, she was certain that they had been hit.

There was a moment of silence. The sea itself seemed shocked by the violence of the impact. Then *Wagtail* began to toss again and Paddy, crouched in the bottom of the cockpit beside Ginette, found herself up to her waist in swirling water. Quickly, she grabbed the other girl's arm and pulled her up. 'Come on. You'll drown. We've got to bale out.'

'Are we holed?' Charles shouted. 'Toby, are you below? What's the damage?'

Toby's head appeared at the top of the steps. 'It's OK. No damage that I can see. It's just water we've taken on board. Crikey, it was close, though, wasn't it. I thought for a minute—' He stopped suddenly, his eyes fixed in a stare of horror. 'Oh, my God! *Moonset* – the Admiral!'

'What?' Charles turned his head and Paddy, who had already begun to bale water from the cockpit with a bucket, paused and followed Toby's appalled gaze. 'Oh, no!'

Moonset's stern had been ripped away. The bow and midship floated on the water, rapidly filling, and they could the Admiral himself, still clinging to the wheel, and Peter Murphy on the bow, already turning back towards him.

'*Charles!*' Paddy screamed. '*We've got to do something!*'

He was already turning *Wagtail*'s nose towards the wrecked boat, but Toby was quicker. Once again, he was over the side and swimming through the littered water. As he reached *Moonset*, Peter was holding the Admiral in his arms. The remainder of the boat was almost full of water and heeling dangerously, and Toby scrambled to help him. Together, they dragged the old man away from the wheel. As they entered the water and struck out again for *Wagtail*, the Admiral supported between them, the broken boat disappeared.

'Oh Charles,' Paddy cried in a heartbroken voice.

'They've got the Admiral,' Alex said from beside her. 'That's all that matters.'

'But George was on board too! He must have been down below – he must have been killed. Alex, it's horrible!'

'Oh, my God.' He stared soberly at the swimming men, then snatched the bucket from her and went on baling. 'There's nothing we can do for him now. Our job is to keep this boat afloat – we've got to get some of this water out.'

They watched anxiously as the two men swam slowly and awkwardly back towards *Wagtail*, their journey made all the more difficult by the clutter of wreckage tossed back and forth by the choppy waves. As they did so, another plane flew over, dropping its burden along the beach, and a cockle bawley not far away exploded. Once again, wreckage showered into the air. Charles gave a yell and *Wagtail* veered wildly.

'*Go away!*' Paddy shrieked, leaping up and punching her fists at the sky. 'Go away, you horrible, horrible Germans. Go away, go away, *go away!*'

'They've been hit,' Alex said tensely. 'Oh, dear Lord, they've been hit.'

Paddy gasped. Both hands now at her mouth, she gazed at the patch of oily water where Toby, Peter and the Admiral had been swimming. She gave a sob.

'There's one of them!' Charles exclaimed as a head broke surface. 'It's Peter. And there's the Admiral . . .' His voice faded as they all realised at once that the Admiral must be dead, his body torn and twisted as he rolled over in the water. Peter tried to support him, but failed and the body fell away. He swam helplessly about, and then turned and came towards *Wagtail*. Wet and dirty as his face was, they could all see his tears, and as Paddy reached out to him she could barely see for the flood in her own eyes.

'Where's Toby?' Charles cried as Peter was hauled aboard.

'I don't know.' The young Sea Scout collapsed against the coaming. 'We were trying to hold the Admiral up, and then we were hit. Something knocked the old man out of my hand, and I think Toby was hit as well. He shouted out to me to save the Admiral and then he – he just disappeared. I couldn't find either of them. I lost them both.' He broke down with great, shuddering sobs, and Paddy

338

crouched beside him, her arms around his slender body, stroking his head and comforting him.

'It wasn't your fault. It's those horrible Germans. It wasn't your fault at all. Oh Peter – poor, poor Peter. You did your best – you're a hero.' She held him close and he turned into her arms.

There was a moment of silence as they all looked at the patch of water. There was wreckage; there were bodies of men now long dead; there were parts of bodies that had been floating there during almost the whole of the exercise, washed in and out by the tides. But of Toby and the Admiral there was no sign.

'They were all heroes,' Ginette said, coming to stand beside Alex, and she looked around at the little group in the boat. 'You are *all* heroes. Every one of you.' Her eyes moved to Charles and then sharpened. 'But what's the matter with you? You're hurt!'

Paddy gave an exclamation and jumped up. Charles's left arm was resting awkwardly on the wheel. She made to touch it and he flinched away.

'It's all right. Something hit me – a bit of shrapnel or metal, I think. It's not serious.'

'Let's have a look.' Alex pulled aside the heavy, wet wool of the guernsey Charles had been wearing now for several days. There was a jagged rip in the shoulder, already thick with congealing blood. 'You're right, it's a flesh wound but it's a nasty one – looks deep, may have chipped the bone. I need to put a pad on it.' He glanced around. 'I don't suppose for a minute you've got any bandages.'

'Used them all up, I'm afraid.' Charles shrugged his good shoulder. 'Look, we're on our way back now. I can get it seen to in a few hours.'

Paddy tore off her own jumper and pulled off her shirt. 'Use this.' She handed the garment, not much cleaner than Charles's, to Alex and he folded it into a thick wad and slid it inside the guernsey. Charles wrinkled his lips but said nothing, and Alex pulled the guernsey back over the pad.

'Is he going to be all right?' Ginette asked. 'He's lost quite a lot of blood.'

Charles looked at her. His eyes were hollow with fatigue, grief and now pain. He still did not know who she was, or how she came to be here, but none of that mattered now. He knew that the evacuation of

Dunkirk was almost over; yet there were still men on the beach. There was still work to do.

'Come on,' he said, setting *Wagtail*'s nose once more towards the shore. 'Let's get another load. Alex – Paddy – one of you look after the engine, will you? I want to get this job done.'

Chapter Thirty-Two

Tuesday, 4 June

The evacuation was over. The little ships, once more in convoy behind the large destroyers and personnel carriers, strung themselves out in lines five miles long. Almost all of them were loaded with as many soldiers as could be crammed aboard. Every one was crewed by men who were at the limits of their exhaustion.

Jan and Joe were both aboard the *Countess Wear*. Robby, his fatigue temporarily forgotten in his relief and gratitude at having found his brother after all, was at the wheel, with Jimmy in the engine-room and Danny in the tiny galley making mugs of tea. The soldiers, who had not had a hot drink for days, gulped it down as if it were nectar.

'Blimey, that's the best thing that's happened to me since we started to back off,' one croaked, handing back the mug. 'Ain't got a fag as well, have you? You're a pal.' He lay back on the deck, soaking wet, filthy dirty, haggard and unshaven, and blew a cloud of smoke blissfully around his head. 'I didn't think we was ever going to get off that ruddy beach.' He gave Danny a rueful look. 'Sorry about the stink, mate. There wasn't no lavvies on the beach, and standing in the water all that time . . . I reckon it'll take half me skin away when I finally takes off these trousers.'

Many of the men were injured, either from bombs or bullets, or from being struck by wreckage. Some had been roughly bandaged but a good many of them had simply scabbed over with congealed blood and even minor wounds were turning septic. Some were only half-conscious, the effort of standing in the water for so many hours, starving and thirsty, having taken a severe toll. Some were slipping into delirium. Some seemed unlikely to live to see the shores of England.

On *Wagtail*, the atmosphere was sombre. They had taken another two loads off the beach, and when the order to discontinue had finally come they had packed aboard as many soldiers as they could. Charles, at the wheel, was hemmed in by standing bodies; there were men on the bows, crammed into the cabin and even in the engine-room. In the forepeak, where Paddy had hidden just a few days – days which seemed like years – ago, there were soldiers cheek by jowl. Paddy herself, together with Ginette, was passing out the last of the stores they had brought with them – jars of jam, which the men scooped out with dirty fingers, and cake which was torn apart and stuffed into starving mouths; even the last of the bread that had been baked so long ago, stale and hard but dampened by sea-water, was swallowed in sodden lumps. I just hope they're not poisoning themselves, Paddy thought anxiously, but she couldn't refuse the men whatever food there was. There had been little for them on the beach, and for the past few days of their journey back through France.

She still had no idea how Ginette came to be with them. Alex had been too busy attending to the wounded to say anything, and explanations must wait. As the long night faded into dawn, it was important only to get safely back across the Channel and bring the men home. Nothing else, for the time being, mattered.

When she thought of anything at all, it was of the Admiral and her brother Toby, left behind in the water. The Admiral, who had been part of their lives as long as any of them could remember – a sometimes crusty old man, yet always ready to take part in the adventures beside or on the water, teaching them to sail, to tie knots, to fish, to camp on the stony beaches of Bosham and Emsworth. And Toby – dear, flippant, light-hearted Toby, who had wanted so much to make his mark as an actor, who had never been taken seriously by anyone in the family, who had been held in contempt as a lightweight and even a coward – yet had died a hero, trying to save the old man who had scorned him. Had the Admiral realised it was Toby who had been with him at the last? she wondered. Had he known it was Toby's arms which held him in the water, and Toby who died at the same moment?

Her throat ached and tears blurred her eyes. She shook them away angrily. This was no time for weeping – there would be time and enough for that, more than enough, once she got home. The years ahead would not be sufficient for all the grieving she would do for her brother, nor for the old man she had loved, nor for all of the soldiers and sailors, unknown to her, who had died during these terror-filled days and nights. The memory would go with her to her grave, never to be fully spoken of. The enormity was too great.

'Paddy.'

She turned her head. Peter Murphy was standing beside her, his dark eyes deep with concern. 'Are you all right?'

She sniffed and wiped her nose on her sleeve. 'Mm. Just thinking.' She gave him a small smile. 'Better not to think. Oh, Peter.' She reached out suddenly and gripped his shoulder. 'I'm so glad you're here!'

He hesitated for a moment, then pulled her into his arms and held her close. She felt his narrow body, hard against hers, and rested there for a moment. Then she moved herself away and gave him a wobbly grin.

'Work to do. It's nearly morning – we'll be getting orders for breakfast soon. Will you help me take round these last few bits of fruitcake?' She gave a small laugh, almost a sob. 'Someone told me it was a crazy thing to bring, but it's been the best of all – at least it doesn't go stale!'

The tears she had tried so hard to keep back began to flow again. They streamed down her cheeks and she caught her breath in another great sob. And yet, she discovered, it was possible to go on working even as you wept. It was possible to think of other people even as you grieved. It was possible to keep going even though your body was crying out for rest.

It was possible to go on living, even after you had lost so much.

As dawn cast a soft, pearly light over the Channel, the convoy came out at last from beneath the blanket of smoke and fire. For the first time since they had arrived in Dunkirk, the men aboard the little ships sniffed cool, fresh air and felt a finger of hope touch their weary hearts. They struggled to lift their heads for their first glimpse of home soil, and when the white cliffs of Dover came into view, a wavering cheer went up from each boat.

'We're nearly home,' Charles said quietly. During the past few hours, as they came slowly across the shallows and troughs of the sandbanks he had handed the wheel to Paddy, but now he took it back again. 'It's almost over.'

'It *is* over for Toby and the Admiral,' she said, and the tears threatened again. Fiercely, she rubbed the heels of her hands against her burning eyes. 'Oh Charles, it's so unfair.'

He was silent for a moment, then shook his head and said, 'It's no more unfair for them than for any of all those others who died. War isn't fair, Paddy. Life isn't fair. And d'you know something? It seems to me that until we realise that, we're not much use to anyone. It's only when we can stop yelling and shouting about things being fair that we can really start giving our all.'

'*We've* given our all,' she said, and he smiled and took one hand from the wheel to put his arm round her shoulders and give her a hug.

'I know. But I think we've learned things too. Don't you?'

Paddy nodded, but before she could speak, Alex came to her side. He had Ginette with him wrapped in a blanket, and he took her hand and held it out towards Paddy and Charles, saying, 'There hasn't been time to tell you before, but I want you to meet Ginette.' He paused. 'My wife. We got married a few weeks ago.'

There was a long silence. Charles glanced quickly at Paddy's face. She had gone white, and he tightened his arm around her shoulders as she swayed towards him. He said, '*Married?*'

'Yes. I was billeted with her family. We fell in love and – it seemed better not to wait. It was difficult to let you know. Then, when the withdrawal began, my Major agreed she should come with me.' He paused, and added, 'We didn't know then what it would be like.'

He was still holding out Ginette's hand and Charles took it, hoping that his hesitation hadn't been noticed. He glanced quickly at Paddy again, then said, 'I'm sorry. It's a strange way to meet a new sister-in-law. But I'm very glad to meet you. I'm Charles – Alex's sister is my wife. And this is *my* sister.'

'Paddy,' Ginette said, smiling at the younger girl. 'I know. I am so happy to meet you, Paddy. Alex has told me so much about you.'

'Has he?' Paddy had recovered herself and took the outstretched hand. She felt its coolness in her palm, and turned it over to look at the ring on Ginette's finger. 'It's Alex's signet ring,' she said stupidly.

'I know. There wasn't time to buy another ring, so this is our wedding-ring. And I don't want another one now.' Ginette lifted her hand and laid her lips on the ring. 'Paddy, I hope you will welcome me into your family. I shall need a friend when I am in England and Alex goes away again.'

There was a short silence. Paddy stared at the ring, her eyes misting again. She thought of her immature love for Alex, of their teasing promises to marry when she was grown up, of the grass ring with the daisy in it which he had made for her and which she had kept until it had crumbled away. As her childish love would also have crumbled away, if she had not deliberately kept it alive.

She glanced up and, over Ginette's shoulder, caught Peter Murphy's dark eyes fixed upon her face. She thought of the terror she had felt when he had been in the sea, possibly lost in the explosion, and sent him a small smile.

'Of course I'll be your friend, Ginette,' she said, and kissed the French girl's cheek. 'We're almost sisters. Of course we'll be friends.'

The convoy continued up through the Dover Roads and along the coast of east Kent. By now, they could see Ramsgate, with the harbour laid out in front of the town and the promenade railings all along the cliff top. The top road was black with people, as black as the sands of Dunkirk had been, and as the armada came within earshot, those on the ships could hear the cheering of those who were waiting for them. They began to wave and call out, and laughed and wept with joy as they saw the Union Jacks waving from the promenade. The skippers of all the little ships loosened their painters and chains and brought their craft in to raft up alongside each other, and one by one they began to unload the precious cargo they had risked so much to bring home. The soldiers came ashore, their tired faces split with grins, waving their hands and sticking their thumbs in the air as they found places to rest – places where, for the first time in weeks, they could be safe, where they could be met by smiling faces and given comfort, help and attention.

Charles, Paddy, Alex, Ginette and Peter Murphy stepped across the deck of the *Countess Wear*, with which they had shared their last adventure, and found Jan and Rob, together with Danny and Jimmy

345

and Joe, with Pirate – who had just eaten the best meal of his young life – fast asleep on his knee. They sat on the bare wooden benches, sticky with blood and oil, and sea water, and looked at each other.

'I wanted to say thank you.' Joe said at last. 'But it don't seem enough. There don't seem to be nothing I can say that would be enough. There was times when I thought I'd never see England again – yet here I am. And it's thanks to people like you, bringing all them little ships over to fetch us home. I tell you what, if anyone had told me that would happen, I wouldn't never have believed it. I wouldn't straight.'

'Nor would any of us,' Alex said quietly. 'But it did happen. It was a miracle, and it happened to us all. We'll never be able to forget this. Never.'

'Never,' the others echoed, and it was as if they were proposing a toast. 'We'll never forget.'

Chapter Thirty-Three

The sun was climbing high towards noon as the two fireships, *Massey Shaw* and *Surrey Queen*, made their way slowly up the River Thames towards their home berths. At each fire station they passed, a crowd of firefighters stood on the quays and the banks and cheered. Warehouses, churches, houses and jetties were festooned with Union Jacks, and on one quay there was even a band playing. It was almost as if the war itself were over.

It wasn't just the fireboats that were coming back. Many of the 'little ships', as everyone was now calling them, were returning to their riverbank homes, to be lovingly cleaned of the oil and blood and other detritus of their journey, to be repaired and patched up and put back in their little boathouses or moored against familiar jetties. But there were others which were not coming back. Some were being retained by the Navy for patrol duties – for mine-spotting or sweeping, as anti-aircraft vessels, and for numerous other unspecified tasks. And there were many, from large passenger-steamers like the *Gracie Fields*, launched only two or three years before the war, to small family motor cruisers like *Moonset*, that had been lost; blown from the water by mines or bombs, riddled with so many bullets or shells that they had sunk, or rammed accidentally by other ships.

Nearly 340,000 men had been saved by the Royal Navy and the small boats requisitioned to help them – far, far beyond Winston Churchill's estimate of 20,000 – but many others had been lost; some of them on the beaches of France, some in the ships, big and little, which had come to save them. Sailors, soldiers, airmen and

347

civilians uncounted; but mourned as the Admiral, Toby Stainbank and George Barlow would be mourned in the villages of Bosham and Emsworth, and as others like them would be mourned in towns and villages up and down the land.

Joe Mears was on the bridge of the *Surrey Queen* with his father. He had found the fireboat lying against the harbour as he came off the *Countess Wear* on the previous afternoon, and his heart had leaped as he realised that amongst the men scrubbing the deck was his own father, Olly. He had called to him at once, and Olly had straightened his back and turned disbelieving eyes towards him.

'Joe? Our Joe?'

'That's me!' Joe jumped from the harbour wall and landed on the *Surrey Queen*'s deck. He grabbed his father's hand in both of his and shook it hard. 'Blimey, Dad, it's good to see you! Don't tell me you took this old crate over to Dunkirk yourself!'

'Here, don't you go casting nasturtiums at the *Queen*. She done a good job.' Olly rubbed his free hand across his eyes, brushing away the sudden, unexpected moisture. 'Our Joe . . . I thought you were a goner, I did really. All them trips to the beaches and never a sight. I didn't know what I was going to tell your ma.'

'Go on, you don't get rid of me that easy.' Joe's weariness had temporarily vanished. 'You should've known I'd turn up again, like a bad penny. You was just looking in the wrong place, that's all.' He looked at the boat he knew so well, noticing the stained decks, the dull, greasy brightwork, the Lewis gun still mounted on the deck. 'Proper old warship!'

'She done all right,' Olly admitted. 'Reckon we brought back a thousand blokes, all told. But it was you I wanted to bring back.'

'Well, now you have,' Joe said. 'See – here I am on board the *Surrey Queen*. Anyway, talking of Ma, I'd better let her know I'm here. Someone told me there's people sending postcards . . .'

'No need for that,' Olly said, his grin almost splitting his face. 'She's here in Ramsgate, waiting for you! Come down with Dot, she did, and they've been working like slaves in the caff with Marge and Eric, getting up sandwiches and pots of tea and God knows what. I tell you, there ain't a loaf of bread to be got anywhere in Ramsgate – it's all going for you blokes. Like a bloody great tea-party, it is!'

Together, they left the *Surrey Queen* and strode along the crowded harbour front to the café. The stalls and canteens were still

348

serving out tea, sandwiches and buns to the last of the troops to disembark, and the fleet of buses which had worked day and night to transport them to the railway stations were still trundling up the hill. To all appearances, the town seemed little different from how it had been for the past nine days – yet there was a sense of relief in the air, a sense of a job well done. The soldiers were cheered as they stumbled wearily along the pavements, their hands shaken and their backs patted so that, rather than as a defeated army, they were treated as heroes. And so too were those who had sailed in the little ships to fetch them: the little ships, many of which had never been to sea before, crewed and skippered by both sailors and civilians, which had between them brought back over eighty thousand of the men from the beaches near Dunkirk.

In the little café, Effie and Dot were still making sandwiches with the last few loaves of bread, while Marge was in the kitchen baking buns with the last of her flour. Everyone in Ramsgate and the surrounding villages had contributed from their own stores – butter, margarine, flour and sugar brought from the backs of cupboards where they had been carefully stowed, eggs fresh from hens kept in farmyards and back gardens, jams and pickles made last autumn and stacked in larders. Now, it was almost gone. There would be just enough to feed the last of the troops.

'It's going to be as bare as Old Mother Hubbard's cupboard here once this is over,' Effie said, slicing and spreading. 'I dunno what you're going to live on, Marge.'

'I dare say the Government will send us in a bit more.' Effie opened the oven door and pushed in another tray of buns. 'It's a good job we've got an extra big stove. Mind you, I think every woman in Ramsgate's been baking these past few days. All pulling together, like the men going over with the boats.'

Effie nodded, her face saddened. She knew that Olly was safe, for he'd nipped up to the café the minute the *Surrey Queen* had docked yesterday, but there'd still been no word of Joe. Olly had sat at one of the tables, his head in his hands, desperately upset that he'd not brought his son back, and although Effie had done her best to console him, pointing out that amongst the thousands and thousands of men on the beaches, it would have been a miracle if he *had* seen Joe, in her heart she'd been just as bitterly disappointed. She sat beside him for a few minutes, patting his shoulders, and then he straightened up and gave her a rueful look.

'Sorry, love. Acting like a flipping girl, I am. It's true – anyone could have brought our Joe back. He'll turn up, right as ninepence. He's probably at home with our Carrie now, feet up on the table, eating us out of house and home and spinning yarns same as always. Just because I didn't find him meself, don't mean he didn't get back all right.'

'That's right, love,' Effie said shakily. 'It'll take more than a few Germans to stop our Joe coming home for his supper.'

There had been one bit of good news, however. Dot, popping out to one of the stalls with a tray of buns, had run right into her own sweetheart Benny, who was sauntering along the prom, she said, for all the world as if he was out for a Sunday-afternoon stroll. She had dropped the buns there and then and flung herself into his arms, knocking him into another soldier who had staggered and fallen into the man behind him until, for a moment or two, it had seemed that the whole lot would go down like ninepins. Luckily, they'd all managed to stay upright, with a lot of catcalling and whistling for Dot and Benny, and some of the soldiers had gathered up the buns which were easy enough to wipe off, and Dot had brought Benny into the café as if she were bearing a golden trophy. It had cheered them all up and given Effie renewed hope that her Joe might come waltzing in, just the same.

She was thinking of this as she cut through a pile of Marmite sandwiches, and chuckling to herself at the memory of Dot's face, when the door opened and two big men walked through. She glanced up, smiled with pleasure at seeing Olly, and then felt her mouth drop open and her heart turn over at the sight of the man behind him. For a second or two she stood absolutely still, the breadknife held aloft like Britannia's trident, and then she gave a scream, dropped the weapon and rushed forward.

'Joe! Oh, you're back, you're safe – oh thank God, thank God. Come here and let me give you a kiss. Oh my boy, let me have a look at you.' She held him away, looking him up and down. 'Are you all right? You're not hurt, are you? When did you get back? Have you had anything to eat? You must be starving – sit down here, and have a sandwich. *Dot!*' she called through to the kitchen. 'Your brother's here. Bring him a cup of tea. Oh Olly! It's our *Joe*!'

'I know it is, love,' Olly said, grinning widely. 'Come aboard the *Queen*, he did, casual as you like. Come over last night – one of the last to get off the beach. Who says the Mearses ain't a lucky family? Been walking through France for days, then got stuck on the end of the queues – but he's here now, and that's all that matters.' He clapped his son on the shoulder as Dot came hurtling out of the kitchen and threw her arms around her brother. 'We'd better let our Carrie know, quick as we can. She stopped behind in London, see,' he told his son. 'We thought you might go straight there.'

'So I would, too, if I hadn't spotted the old *Queen* laying by the wall. I was detailed to go off on one of the buses. Given a week's leave while they gets things sorted out. I suppose all the camps must be full by now.'

'They've got trains going all along the south of England,' Olly said. 'Only the troops can use 'em. You and Dot'd better come home on the *Queen*,' he said to Effie. 'We've been told we can have a bit of a rest now but we got to go home tomorrow. London can't manage without us any longer.'

'No more can I,' Effie said, hugging his arm against her. She set a huge plate of sandwiches and buns in front of her son, and Dot added a large mug of tea. 'There you are. Wrap yourself round that. I bet you've not seen grub like that since you went to France.'

'Well, not since we started to withdraw, anyway,' Joe said, attacking the sandwiches with gusto. 'And I reckon I'll come on the *Queen* too, Dad. No point in taking up space on a train when I can go in me own luxury liner!'

Marge and Eric had come out of the kitchen and stood smiling, as glad to see Joe as his own family had been. They'd known him ever since he was a little boy, here on holidays with his parents, and had been as anxious as Effie about both him and Olly. Now, although they knew the war was by no means over and there would be many more dangers to face before it was finished, they could share the relief that this part, at least, had been a success.

'You go and have a lay-down on our bed,' Marge said to him as he wolfed down sandwiches and buns. 'Your dad can go back to the ship, and fetch you when they're ready to sail. But just for now, we'd like you to stop here.'

'That's right,' Eric agreed. He laid one hand on Joe's shoulder and the other on Olly's. 'It ain't often we has the house full of heroes.'

The *Countess Wear* was kept by the Navy too. Holiday trips had stopped for the duration of the war, and if she had returned to Devon it would have been to be laid up in one of the creeks – a bad thing for a wooden ship. Robby, Jan, Jimmy and Dan took her round to Folkestone and left her there in the charge of the harbourmaster until she was called for, and then boarded one of the trains going along the south coast to Plymouth.

The journey was long and slow, with frequent stops for the crowds of soldiers to be fêted and fed. As they chugged through the countryside, men and women in the fields stopped and waved their hats, and children sat on bridges to cheer. They stopped in towns, where the platforms were lined with trestle tables loaded with yet more sandwiches and buns, urns of tea and great jugs of orange squash. They stopped at wayside halts where local farmers' wives came running, with their aprons filled with crusty, new-baked cottage loaves spread with yellow butter. They stopped in villages where the stations had been draped in flags and bunting, and the local innkeeper handed out tankards of ale.

The soldiers in their carriage quickly realised that the three men had been in one of the little ships that had brought them home from Dunkirk. Weary as they were, sleeping most of the way and waking only at the stops, they made their gratitude clear. Robby, who had never even thought of being thanked, was embarrassed, and Danny retreated into bashful silence, but Jimmy took it all as his due and would have entertained them for hours with his stories had they not fallen asleep.

'Where will you be going, Rob?' Danny asked after a bit. 'I mean, now that *Wenlock*'s gone, you haven't got no ship, have you?'

Robby sighed. There had been so little time to think about what had happened to his ship and shipmates that their fate had been pushed to the back of his mind. He was reluctant to bring it out now and look at it again, knowing that the shock and horror was waiting and afraid that it would overwhelm him.

'I'll have to go and report at Devonport,' he answered, concentrating on the future rather than the past. 'They'll decide where to send me next.' Grief rose in his throat and he swallowed it down angrily, determined not to be caught out here, on this train filled with soldiers. 'What about you, Dan? Will you go back to the boatyard?'

'Shouldn't think there'll be any work there for a while,' Danny said. 'No, I reckon I'll volunteer. I'd be called up soon anyway. Try and get in the Navy with you. Hey – be good if we were on the same ship, wouldn't it!'

At last they were on the home stretch. The train had reached Exeter, where it stopped for a mysteriously long time, and then set off on the seaward route, down the banks of the Exe and then along the seafront at Dawlish, in and out of the red sandstone tunnels and past the mudflats with their flocks of wading birds. Danny, who had never been this far on the train before, stared out in fascination and even Jimmy forgot to be blasé as he admired the scene. But Robby stared at it without seeing. His mind was still full of the memories of Dunkirk – the darkness even during daytime, the shadows cast by the smoke, lit by streaks of brilliant flame; the acrid smell of burning oil; the corpses floating in the reddened, oil-streaked sea; the sudden vicious air attacks, the shelling and explosions, the screams of men as they were tossed into the water, wounded and dying; the long, long queues of soldiers waiting as the tide ebbed and flowed about them, waiting for hour upon hour as the little ships came and went, every one of them overloaded and yet still able to take so pitifully few.

And *Wenlock*. His ship, blown apart at almost the very last minute, one of the final casualties of Dunkirk.

I should have been aboard her too, he thought. They're dead, and I'm alive. I should have been there . . .

At Totnes station, Rob, Danny and Jan got off the train. Jimmy was going on to Plymouth where, like Robby a few days later, he would report to Devonport for further orders. He had quarters there and his wife would be waiting for him. They all shook hands and wished him luck, wondering if they would ever meet again, and the last they saw of him, as the train pulled out again and he leaned out of the window, was his square, crinkly face beaming and his blue eyes as bright as on the first day Robby had seen him.

'He was a good oppo,' Rob said as they heaved their kitbags on to their shoulders and set off along the platform. He looked at the familiar town with its tall red church-tower and shook his head. 'It seems like years since I came up from Guz to take the *Countess* down to Dartmouth. But it's not even a fortnight ago. I wonder what happened to the *Berry Pomeroy*. We never saw her again once we left Ramsgate, did we? And George Ellery – I hope he's all right.'

'He didn't go over,' Danny reminded him. 'Took the boat down there and then come home, didn't un? Been sitting at home all this time, snug as a bug in a rug.'

They walked out of the station. Robby's head was still filled with noise – the thrum of engines, the scream of aircraft, the bursts of firing and cries of the men. His steps seemed automatic, as if his feet put themselves one in front of the other without his volition. I'm never going to get it out of my head, he thought. I'm never going to be able to hear anything again without hearing that ship blowing to bits and my oppos yelling for help. It's going to be there with me, always . . .

'Robby!'

The voice stopped him in his tracks. He turned his head slowly, disbelievingly, and there she was, running towards him, her arms held out, her hair flying behind her. He dropped his kitbag and took a step towards her, then another. And then she was in his arms, her soft body pressed close to his, her lips warm and moist on his face. 'Oh, Robby!'

'Molly,' he said slowly, and leaned his head on her shoulder. 'Oh, my dear soul, it's you . . .'

Chapter Thirty-Four

Tuesday, 18 June

The ancient church at Bosham was filled with those who had come both to mourn the Admiral and to give thanks for his life. In the front pews were the few family members – a cousin or two, a nephew, two nieces, all of whom had come down to visit him from time to time. But the real mourners were in the pews behind them – the Rowleys and the Stainbanks. And for them, this was the second memorial service in as many days, for Toby's memorial had been only yesterday.

Dunkirk was over, but not forgotten. It would never be forgotten – the massive rescue of so many men, snatched from under the Germans' noses by the armada of valiant ships. Winston Churchill, speaking in the House of Commons, had paid tribute to the whole operation as 'a miracle of deliverance', and had put new energy into the country with a rousing speech of defiance. *'We shall fight on the beaches, we shall fight on the landing grounds, we shall fight in the fields and in the streets, we shall fight in the hills; and we shall never surrender.'*

The country was still haunted by the spectre of imminent invasion. Britain seemed to stand alone, a tiny island kept safe only by the seas that buffeted its shores. The British and Canadian troops still in France had been evacuated from Cherbourg, although not as dramatically as the BEF had been brought home from Dunkirk. The Norwegian campaign was over, the Germans were in Paris, and Mussolini had brought Italy into the war, beginning with a bombing raid on Malta. South African bombers had struck at Italian bases in East Africa and Libya, and so both Africa and the Mediterranean had been brought into the ever-increasing conflict. The European war was fast becoming a second world war.

Yet the country was strangely uplifted, filled with the fervent, patriotic defiance that had been instilled in them by their Prime Minister. Dunkirk – a 'massive military defeat', was nevertheless a triumph. And it was the little ships that had caught at everyone's imagination. The little ships, flocking from river, from backwater, from harbour and bay until they were all gathered together to cross the Channel in a bold stroke that must have taken the enemy's breath away.

Already, Dunkirk was taking a place in history that had been given to only a few. Soon, Sheila thought as she stood beside her husband in the old Saxon church, it would become a legend.

Charles's arm was in a sling. The wound he had received during those last minutes had been treated now and would soon heal, although he would always carry a scar. He touched the place gently with his fingers, feeling grateful that he had at least one mark to show for his war service, although that gratitude was swiftly overtaken by guilt, as he thought of his brother and the Admiral.

'If I hadn't insisted on going,' he had said to Sheila the night before, 'Toby would still be alive now. He wouldn't have gone without me – the Admiral wouldn't take him. And maybe even the Admiral would be alive too. And poor old George.'

'You can't know that,' Sheila said. Charles had told her what he could about his experiences at Dunkirk, but like everyone else who had been there, he found it almost impossible to describe the scenes he had witnessed, the horror and the drama of it all; the grinding hard work, the exhaustion that you somehow ignored, the pain and the misery and the sheer hell . . . 'You can't know what would have happened if you hadn't been there. You can't know that any of them would have come back alive.' She paused for a moment, looking at him as he sat on the bed, wretched and miserable as he grieved for his brother and his godfather. 'And they knew what they were going into, just as you did,' she went on quietly. 'The Admiral had been to war before. He probably wanted to die in action. And Toby – Toby must have known in the end that he could be a hero too.'

'And it's better to be a dead hero than a live coward?' Charles said wryly. 'Is that what you're saying?'

Sheila sat down beside him and slipped one arm around his

shoulders, taking his hand in hers. 'Darling Charles, I don't know which is better. I really don't. All I know is that we've been caught up in this dreadful war and it's going to get worse. Whether we're invaded or not, a lot more people are going to be killed. And there's nothing we can do about it. All we can do is what we believe in. The Admiral believed in going to Dunkirk. So did Toby, and Paddy and all the others. So did you. And not all of you came back.' Her tears fell on to their linked hands. 'But we'll never forget them. Never.'

Now, in the ancient Saxon church, she stood between her husband and her brother and remembered those words. Around her, the stone columns rose to the roof, and the muted singing of the choir was lifted to the beams. Turning her head sideways, she could see her new sister-in-law, Ginette, who had already made herself a part of the family, and then Paddy, with her hair now growing into a soft, short bob. Since coming home, she seemed to have acquired a more adult quality, an aura of quiet competence and understanding that came from having been through great experiences. The passion that had driven her to Dunkirk was still there, would always be there, deep in her spirit – but now it was controlled. Calmly, quietly but with determination, she had carried out her vow to volunteer for war service and applied to join the WRNS, and now she was waiting to be called.

Beside her was Peter Murphy, the Sea Scout who had known her all his life. He too had volunteered and would soon be in the Royal Navy. There was a deep friendship between them, a closeness that might one day become something more, or might simply remain friendship. Sheila hoped they would both live long enough to find out.

Olivia and Hubert were on Charles's other side. Both had been aged by the loss of their son and their oldest friend. Sadly, they did their best to sing the hymns, kneeling to pray for the two men they had loved so much, wondering – as everyone must be wondering – what more this war would bring? They had already lived through one long world war; now, it seemed that they must endure another. Why was it happening? Why did it go on?

The hymn came to an end and Sheila knelt with them. She could not understand, any more than the rest of them. She could only grasp at the fact that Hitler must be stopped, that his evil could not be allowed to march across the world. Whatever happens, she thought, however terrible the things that are yet to come, we must always hold on to that. We *can't* let this happen to our world.

Suddenly, without any warning, she was shaken by sobs. Her tears fell fast and hot on to her folded hands and slid down her wrists and her arms, losing themselves in the black sleeves of her blouse. She felt Charles's hand on hers, gripping it warmly, strongly, and she bowed her head deeper and prayed as she had never prayed before; for the souls of the Admiral, of her flippant, teasing brother-in-law, of all those who had already died at sea, on land and in the air. And for those who had returned as well; those who had come back from Dunkirk to fight another day.

Especially, she prayed in gratitude for the men who had crossed the Channel to save them, in that incredible fleet of little ships.

The Little Ships of Dunkirk.